Stories Of
The Heart
(Tragedy to Triumph)

By
Rayola Kelley

Hidden Manna Publications
P.O. Box 3572
Oldtown, ID. 83822

Stories of the Heart (Tragedy to Triumph)
Copyright © 2018 by Rayola Kelley

ISBN: 978-0-9864066-3-8

Except where otherwise indicated, all Scripture quotations are taken from the King James Version.

Dedication

I want to
dedicate this
book
to the women
who have striven
for excellence
in their Christian
life regardless
of the challenges.

Special Acknowledgment

*I want to thank
Wanda Hiebert
and Jeannette Haley
for their friendship and
proof reading of this
book.*

Contents

Introduction

You are about to meet twelve women who have been creatively fabricated, but their lives and challenges represent many women who have had to face the same issues of the heart. You will follow them into emotional whirlwinds that twist them into the vortex of diverse storms that threaten to ruin every aspect of their lives.

As you meet each of these women, you'll envision nuances of women you personally know or perhaps you will even see someone you are very familiar with in their stories. As you journey with them through their different struggles, you might discover a hint of your own life story. More than likely you might find yourself relating to their disheartening history and the subsequent tide of inner conflict that could be raging in your own soul.

Perhaps you'll find yourself relating to the roller coaster ride of raw emotions that present a challenge for any person's resolve. There may be times that you will find yourself crying with them over their brokenness, angry at the injustice of their plight, and laughing at their adventures. Some of these women may stand out more than others, but there is one thing that is certain, once you walk with them into the depths of brokenness, loss, and despair, you will never forget their story or the solution that is brought out in Biblical teachings.

In spite of the opposition that confronts each woman in this book, this is a message of hope. In their times of darkness the Light of heaven permeates the upheaval of their lives, presenting the remedy. As a result, each individual story paints a clear picture regarding the source of the problem in comparison to the solution and the manner of healing it brought to their souls.

And ye shall seek me,
and find me,
when ye shall search
for me with
all your heart.
(Jeremiah 29:13)

The Seeking Heart

Susan Ellison didn't know which way to turn. She thought she had her life all figured out, but what stood before her was challenging not only her thinking, but her resolve to stay the course she had cleverly laid out for herself. The truth is she had written off all involvement with men for the present, but now she found herself in a tricky situation that demanded she reconsider her resolution.

Initially she had been realistic in admitting to herself that there was no way she could avoid the matters of her heart when it came to its deepest and most secret desires. Susan, however, had tucked such desires away in a nice little room and locked them away so no one could open that door. Now a man by the name of Samuel Carlson was knocking on her locked door. Granted, he was not making romantic overtures towards her, but she felt an unexpected attraction towards him; therefore, she was bracing herself.

Even though Sam did not meet her idea of a prince charming riding a white horse, there was something about him that was kind, lovable, reliable, and trustworthy. He was average in height, and although his physique did not fit into a category of being trim and lean, his way of facing the challenges of life made him appear strong, causing him to emerge beyond his average stature to heights of excellence. His dark hair reminded her of the prince charming she had imagined in her childhood, but there was an added bonus; it was also curly and he wore a neatly trimmed mustache. There was also sweetness about him that softened his round face and sparkling brown eyes, highlighting the fact that he was a nice looking man.

As if talking to Sam, she couldn't help but verbally vent the struggle that was taking place, "Sam, why did you come into my world at this time! There are so many matters left undone in my life, I'm not ready for you. I'm not ready for THIS!"

Thoughts of him always caused her much confusion. On the one hand, she was relieved that he was not making any serious advancement towards her, while on the other hand she secretly wanted him to. She struggled over how she would respond if he did make any overtures. She wasn't sure if she wanted to push him away, or submit to her intense feelings. The latter clearly frightened her.

Before Sam came along, she had eloquently debated the matter of such a relationship in the court of her reasoning. She felt her logical presentation proved time and time again why she wanted to put any romantic involvement off until a future time. Secretly, she knew that such postponement was simply her way of avoiding what really ailed her. The truth was she was afraid of any real involvement with a man at an intimate level. She was afraid of the vulnerability, the possible rejection, and the utter disappointment of discovering that the ideas of successful marriages were a fantasy at best.

The other aspect was that as a plain woman of twenty-three, she could not fathom why Sam would be interested in her at any level, unless there was some secret agenda on his part. She was aware that there was an attractive person hiding beneath various layers of fear and uncertainty, but she had painstakingly avoided bringing any real attention to herself from the opposite sex. She wore loose-fitting clothes to hide her petite figure and avoided highlighting any of her facial features with makeup. Her long brown hair was always combed but it was left straight and stringy.

Susan had many reasons for not wanting to venture the way of romance and marriage. She always felt the two went together; therefore, if she was to agree to romance, it would be in lieu of marriage. In her mind without marriage as a goal, romance was nothing but a dangling branch that had no safety net underneath it to ensure the wellbeing and safety of the parties involved. To her way of thinking, the cultural iconic practice known as "American dating" was like doing a dangerous high wire act. She knew that there were many on both sides of the aisle who wouldn't agree with what would surely be considered a "silly" notion on her part.

The other facet of Sam that was causing a dichotomy for her was his faith. She had somewhat believed there was a God but had long ago been turned off to pursuing any real belief in Him. She had personal reasons for her attitude, one of which included "religious hypocrites." In the past she had tried religion, seeking answers for many questions, but the religious hypocrites shunned her because she didn't look the part nor did she speak the language. She walked away from it all with only more questions and skepticism.

When it came to Sam, he had a different type of religion. There was something alive about what he believed, probably because he actually lived it. He acted as if he spoke face to face with God and actually had a deep relationship with Him. This had been foreign to her. Secretly, she sensed her heart wanted the same type of relationship with God, but again the all-to-familiar fear would rise up and convince her that this "God" would most likely overlook her or reject her altogether.

She remembered when Sam first approached her at her job as a dental assistant about God. After prepping him for an examination, there was a small window of waiting in which Sam must have sensed she had some vulnerable spots. He had briefly entered in with her and invited her to church. His caring and understanding ways immediately caused her to put her wall down and consider his invitation. She realized that he probably saw her as a possible convert for his faith. Admittedly, she appeared as a poor, lost waif, but she was a "waif" that harbored much speculation about the unseen world that she didn't understand--a world that appeared to be illusive to her.

It was obvious all these factors about Sam were causing confusion to her. Since he piqued her interest, out of curiosity she accepted his invitation and timidly attended his church. She sensed there was something different in his church but for some reason it eluded her. The desire to solve the mystery of it kept her coming back each Sunday. However, she found herself becoming restless in her soul, leaving her with a type of desperation she couldn't explain. She heard the preacher's words but for some reason they weren't penetrating her understanding. Even though she could see on a physical level, she couldn't perceive or grasp the simple message that was being presented on a spiritual level.

Susan once again resorted to the courtroom of her reasoning. She had to admit that just because she found herself being attracted to Sam, that there was no indication on his part that he had like attraction towards her. She chided herself that she was making nothing into something, but she still felt the wise thing she needed to do was prepare herself just in case.

Now, she must once again present her case in the courts of her mind as to why she avoided any real romantic involvement. It started with her parents' relationship. Most of her life she watched her parents play games with each other. Her mother manipulated emotionally and her father would placate her mother to keep her off his back. The end result was her mother was spoiled and unhappy and her father, who was outwardly optimistic, was often emotionally divorced from what was going on in the family and was self-serving in his pursuits. Susan knew such games lacked integrity and allowed couples like her parents to avoid facing "the elephant" in the room. Since nothing was really confronted and resolved in their relationship, matters escalated into greater tension and frustration between them.

She had longed to see honesty, respect, and purity established in her parents' relationship, but for that to happen drastic changes would have to take place in them personally. They would have to first change their attitudes toward one another, but sadly they justified their attitudes at the expense of the other. There needed to be boundaries that would ensure respect for each other, but neither one wanted to battle it out with the other to forge such boundaries. Her mother was frustrated because there were no boundaries, yet if her father made any advancement to exert such disciplines, she would be furious with him. If Susan's mother tried to establish some type of boundary for her husband, Susan's father saw it as an affront against his manhood and leadership, causing his frustration and anger to raise its head in defiance.

When Susan was in high school, she witnessed the same games that existed between her parents taking place in a different arena. She watched the so-called "dating game" from the sidelines. Young men flaunted the women on their arms as if they were prized trophies, and women held onto their young men's arms as if they were a claimed prize. It seemed as if they were trying to secure some type of purpose or identity in a relationship that reeked with immaturity and uncertainty.

In her mind she wasn't willing to be someone's trophy, nor was she interested in claiming anyone for herself. She didn't want to need someone to bring her identity and purpose. She clearly witnessed the devastating results of such a practice in her parents' relationship with disturbing results.

It was obvious that her mother had looked to her relationships as wife and mother to secure her purpose, only to find herself miserably disappointed. In fact, Susan found that her mother was trying to live through her. At times her mother tried to push her towards relationships with the young men who had shown some type of interest in her. It was as though her mother wanted to recapture and experience her youth through Susan because she had clearly cut short her youth when she married at age seventeen.

Her father was a hard worker, but he also sought for avenues in which he could pursue his personal goals outside of his family. He often looked to activities that proved to be empty which prompted him to seek after other causes. It was obvious that neither of her parents were content or satisfied in their relationship with each other.

It was also apparent that this type of relationship in the dating arena not only left individuals disappointed, but it made them vulnerable to emotional wounding. She couldn't count the times that she watched her classmates reel over a broken relationship. To her their reactions not only showed immaturity, but silliness, especially when they threatened to end their life over it.

The other aspect of the dating game was the fallout that happened when a girl found herself pregnant. If she chose the narrow path of having the child, she would often quit school and forever fade into the everyday masses. If she had any dreams they would have to be put on hold or let go of altogether.

Susan was not sure of her dreams, but she didn't want to lose sight of her possibilities before she first tested the waters. She wanted to experience different aspects of life.

As she was presenting her case in the court of personal logic, she could sense a "rattling" taking place in a room located in the recesses of her mind. She had spent many years ignoring the "rattle" and convinced herself that what was secured in the far room didn't affect her attitude and way of thinking about the matter of men and intimacy.

However, as she was considering the evidence before her, the rattling and shaking became louder. Her reasoning began to chide her that if she didn't face what was in the room, nothing would be resolved for her, preventing her from ever moving forward. However, she wanted to avoid the room because she really didn't know what benefit she would receive by opening the door to it.

That room held a dirty secret that sometimes haunted her. The torment of it was usually sparked by a small flame of memory. Memory would awaken guilt that in turn rose up and condemned her, while shame made her feel dirty and unworthy. Confusion would then ride on the backs of both guilt and shame as she struggled with the injustice of it. Even though she was a victim, guilt made her feel that she was responsible in some way and shame caused her to perceive that it was justifiable--that in some sick way she had asked for it.

Intellectually, she knew all the accusations were a lie, yet confusion caused her to second guess her feelings in regard to what happened. And, what happened is that she was molested from the time she was five years old until she was ten by a relative.

"Molestation" what a profane, cruel word, and yet it could not begin to describe the devastation it leaves in its wake. This relative had first conditioned her to trust him and his so-called "innocent" advancements towards her. Each time he touched her it became more personal, assuring her that his actions were a sign of his love, thereby, they were acceptable. As his touching became more inappropriate, confusion took center stage in Susan. However, as his seduction gripped her

13

immature reality in greater measure, he indoctrinated her to believe that she desired it as much as him, producing guilt. The nail of shame was added because she knew it was wrong, but she was too ashamed to tell someone, which resulted in feeling helpless to do anything about it.

In the night, when she struggled with the horrific affront on her innocence, anger would rise out of her cocoon of confusion. As she silently screamed into the darkness she felt that her cries were falling on deaf ears. In fact, she felt she was in a glass cage that had a mirror facing outward. She could look out and see what was going on, but when others looked her way, they would only see their reflection. She felt totally invisible, alone in her suffering, and hopeless in her ordeal.

Once again, she was feeling the darkness of that terrible time engulf her as night began to settle in her room. It was Sunday and she had attended church that very morning, but her experiences there made her more aware of the inconsistencies in her life. She had been sitting at the desk in the bedroom of her small apartment looking at the Bible she had read at services, but she felt no comfort and assurance. The inner darkness she felt once again consumed her and made her feel like a frightened little girl all over again. At such times she did what she always did, she sought the false safety of the blankets on her bed. She slid underneath them and proceeded to tuck herself in as if her blankets were a sleeping bag, a cocoon of safety.

As she lay under her bedding, struggling with the ugliness in the locked room of her mind, she began to remember a time many years ago when she had cried out to what appeared to be a "great open space of the sky" for help. She had heard there was a loving God out there in that never ending space who always heard the cries of others. However, when she cried into the darkness, nothing happened. In her fragile immature mind she wrestled with the mocking reality of her situation. If there is a God, why did He allow such innocence to be trashed by the perverted bullies of the world? Why did He not help someone like her? Her only conclusion was that if He exists, He must not love or even like her. It was then that she decided she wouldn't love God and that she wouldn't like Him either.

It was also at that time of great hopelessness that she closed herself off to everyone. Even though she had convinced herself that she was being noble and wise about her present attitudes towards both men and God, they actually served as a protective armor to prevent any further feelings of betrayal and rejection. This protective armor may have kept people out, but it also had become her personal, emotional prison.

After five years of abuse from the relative, his wife caught him in the act of exploiting her. There was much upheaval that ended in the relative's wife divorcing him, and him losing all rights from seeing his own children. It was clear that the matter was quietly taken care of because the molestation stopped, but for Susan there was no emotional resolution because it was "swept under the rug" to never be spoken of again.

To her family, the situation was over, but for her the whole, terrible incident was always there to make an ugly entrance into her consciousness, ready to produce confusion about feelings of love, pervert what could be pure in a relationship between a man and a woman, and cause mistrust in her towards men in general.

She recognized that she had not dealt with her ugly past; rather, she had simply closed it off. But, because of its haunting influence and existence, it had clearly defined her present attitudes and lifestyle. The prison was preventing her from experiencing life, as well as bringing a cloud of darkness upon her idea of her person and her womanhood.

It was clear that the door to the room had been opened by the key of her reasoning. Memories were now screeching through the corridors of her mind, setting her emotions on edge. Feelings of guilt, shame, and fear that had been hidden in the locked room were once again being unleashed and were now running amuck. It seemed that on the heels of her emotional upheaval insanity was consuming what little sanity she had managed to salvage.

Susan didn't know what to do or where to turn. However, a light began to flicker around the edges of her mind. As she focused on the light, it became more defined as she heard the reassuring words of encouragement that the pastor of the church had spoken that very morning, "God will hear cries sincerely directed towards Him." While she tried to focus on such a thought, another voice slammed against her resolve.

It was an accusing voice. Granted, it sounded reasonable and true to her logic. The voice sarcastically reminded her that God didn't hear her before and that He wouldn't hear her now, for His ears were deaf. Then the voice became heightened in its declaration by affirming that they were deaf ears because God didn't exist, He was an idol, an emotional crutch, a figment of people's imagination.

The statement that God didn't exist sounded foreign to her very being. She suddenly realized that Sam had demonstrated through his life that there was a God, that He existed, and that anyone, including her could have the same type of relationship with Him as he did. It became obvious that her seeking heart was yearning for the reality of

God. She had to believe that everything that was said about Him was true. She didn't know what it meant to have such confidence, but she could not ignore the desperation that was growing in her inner soul.

From the depth of her being she cried out to God. She didn't know what to say except what was on her heart. "O God if you're there, silence the incessant noises bombarding my mind, and bring peace to my tormented soul. Help me in my confusion. I don't understand why things happen, but I know that I'm broken over it, lost because of it, and fearful that there is no way out of this abyss. They say You're love. I desire true love, but it's foreign…confusing…and seems unobtainable. Show me Your love, help me to understand it in the right way." She paused to see if there were any further words waiting in the wings to be presented. When only silence met her, she concluded with this simple benediction, "I guess this is where I say, 'Amen.'"

Upon saying, "Amen", the floodgates of her emotions broke and emerged into a river of tears. She found the very depths of her sorrow breaking forth in what seemed like great billows of water washing over her with healing. She cried over her lost innocence, she mourned over her broken life, she grieved over what appeared would never be, and she raged in helpless frustration against the destructive seeds that had taken root in her soul and were now manifesting themselves in her life and attitude. As the tears flowed, she felt walls collapsing, dams bursting, and the last defense of her resolve being swept away by an incredible peace.

She had no idea how long the ordeal lasted, but she knew something supernaturally had happened to her. She was full of peace but she also felt totally spent out and sensed that she had been emptied in some way. She was not sure how to feel about it, but she cherished the peaceful calmness she felt in her soul. She wanted to rest in it, and like a cloud she felt herself drifting off into a restful sleep.

***

Susan bathed in the rest that now filled her inner being, but something unexplainable was changing the environment. She found herself becoming somewhat agitated, as she realized that her rest was being interrupted. At the time she could not say if she was awake or still asleep, but she found herself sitting in a small, square waiting room. She had no idea what she was waiting for, but she knew that her name was to be called. At the time it seemed all quite strange to her because she was the only one sitting in the room.

Finally a door opened, and her name was called by a person who walked through the door. She was surprised by the person's appearance. Rather than being a female receptionist, it was a man. Instead of the man being young, he had the appearance of being old. His face reflected wisdom, but showed kindness and compassion. His hair and beard were white and long.

Susan stood to greet the man. He introduced himself as Joshua Wiseman. Wiseman seemed as if he could see into the very recesses of her soul. Even though she felt exposed, she didn't feel nervous under his inquisitive gaze.

"Susan, do you know why you're here?" he inquired.

Susan shook her head no. Her admission was quite clear and she was forthcoming in her response. "I don't understand where I am, and to be honest with you I think the whole matter is somewhat strange."

A smile moved across Wiseman's lips. She could tell that he was holding back a chuckle, but his eyes were revealing that the concealed joy and laugher were resonating through his being.

"You made a request to the throne of God. The request had to do with understanding what genuine love is. I'm here to answer your question. In fact, you'll be taken on a special journey that will enable you to discover such love for yourself."

Susan was caught off-guard. To think that the events presently taking place were for the sole purpose of answering her prayer was a bit overwhelming. She felt awe surge through her being, excitement lifting her up, and praise taking hold of her tongue. She had never experienced such glorious ecstasy, nor could she explain the liberty of inspiration that danced and twirled on the surface of her tongue. It was both extraordinary and exciting

However, her logic immediately began shouting at her. It was telling her she needed to protest such a notion, run away from the surreal experience, or even laugh at it, but something, unknown and far greater than her logic and strength, was causing her to quietly stand in the presence of this man.

Even though Susan was standing still outwardly, much was going on inwardly. It seemed as if the surreal uncertainly from within was being brought into order by what appeared to be a border collie. This dog was rounding up all of her emotions into a neat circle bringing order to her inner being.

As Susan looked into the eyes of Wiseman, she sensed he knew exactly what was going on within her. Without speaking there seemed to be a complete understanding formulating between them. She smiled at him, ready to submit, ready to take the journey.

17

Wiseman held out his hand to her. She timidly took his hand, as firmness and strength took hold of her, bringing complete calmness to her soul. He led her through a door into a long corridor. She could see there were various doors lining the hallway. Each door was a different color and had some type of sign on it. Besides the presence of many doors, what stood out to her was the color of the passageway.

The hallway was gray. There were no real shadows, and it was clear that it was void of vibrant colors. She could not put her finger on it, but something was missing. She looked up at Wiseman for an explanation.

Wiseman seemed to read her thoughts. "What's missing, Susan, is contrast. This hallway represents those gray areas of life that leave us without any clarity of understanding, causing much confusion. Everyone will walk through this hallway at different times in their life. However, the hallway reminds us that we'll be brought to doors of decision. What doors we choose will depend on personal preference. Behind each door there are lessons to learn, but there are also traps, detours, and possible consequences. It's for this reason that I'm assigning you two companions."

Susan couldn't hide her disappointment. "I thought you would be the one to take this journey with me."

"I'll be with you Susan and available to bring instruction to you along the way, but I'm assigning two companions that will lead you through this hallway so that you'll be prepared to understand when I do bring any instruction. Keep in mind there must always be preparation before any wise instruction will be properly received."

He motioned with his hand to something standing behind her. Suddenly she felt sandwiched between two distinct presences. The presence on her right was smaller and possessed subdued features but displayed much authority, while the one on her left was a bit taller with sharper features, and seemed to possess a type of sensitivity that spoke of insight.

"Let me introduce you to your two companions. They will lead you to certain doors for your benefit, and you must follow them. The one on the right is 'Discretion,' while the one on the left is called 'Discernment.' Heed my instruction concerning these two companions. Discretion is on your right because you must first seek his guidance as to what you must be aware of in each room. It's only after you've sought the understanding of Discretion that you can obtain insight from Discernment as to what you must avoid to prevent yourself from falling into any trap. Discretion will bring restraint to you so you are not set up in compromising ways and Discernment will reveal the way in which you are to walk through a matter to ensure personal victory."

Wiseman paused to allow what was being said to sink into Susan's understanding. Susan was surmising that her journey to discover true love wasn't always going to be a pleasant experience.

"Very good Susan!" Wiseman's words brought her back to the present. "You've just learned your first lesson about love. To discover what comprises true love may not always prove to be pleasant. This is why you need your two companions. It is easy to take a wrong detour in your journey and end up with a wrong understanding."

Susan nodded her head in agreement. She would submit to Wiseman's instruction and hopefully take heed to her two companions.

"It's getting late and it's time for you to begin your journey." Wiseman interjected into Susan's thought process. He stepped aside and waved his hand towards the hallway.

Discretion tugged gently on her shirtsleeve and Discernment raised his hand and pointed it forward. Susan began to move onward with her two companions. As they began walking down the corridor, it appeared as if it was becoming narrower and longer.

Discretion spoke for the first time. "It seems that there are endless possibilities when it comes to love Susan, but the way to true love is narrow."

It was then that Discernment took his clue, "And, few will find it."

They stopped in front of the first door. Discretion placed himself between Susan and the door and looked intently at her. "This is our first door, but I must warn you, we'll pick up another companion in this room. His name is, 'Rudiment', 'Rudy' for short. This companion will bring another take on love. I can point you in the right direction, but Discernment will bring the necessary contrast between what I show you and what Rudy will be offering you. Take heed Susan, the choice will be yours, along with the fruits and consequences of your decision."

The name on the ornate brown door was "Expectation". The stylish manner in which it was painted on the door reminded her of tole painting. The lettering formed a rainbow in shape and color, which gave it a playful and welcoming invitation. When Susan saw the name on the door, Discretion gave her a warning. "You must consider where expectation begins, how it operates, and where it will lead you. It has a way of being playful when it comes to attractions, especially wrong attractions."

"And, it can prove to offer very attractive traps," Discernment warned.

Susan never thought about the origins of expectation, but she began to recognize that for her most of her expectations had all ended in a ruinous heap of disappointment. She then realized that she had expectations about life and about love, but she had never really thought about if they were truly realistic and obtainable.

Discernment opened the door, and true to Discretion's words, Rudiment was there to greet her. He was attractive to look at. He appeared to have class and he greeted her in such a pleasant way. "Welcome to my world, Susan. You'll find that all of your desires can be fulfilled in this room."

At this time Discernment gave her a quiet look as if to tell her to take note as to what had been emphasized. She noticed the word "desires" stood out to her, but what desires, and where did they originate from? Beside how would Rudy know what she desired?

Rudy enthusiastically asked her to follow him. She could tell he was excited about taking her into his world. When she entered the main room she was shocked to see a long table with a variety of attractive desserts. It was a banquet room and it appeared as if the best had been prepared.

Susan stood dumbfounded before the table. "Who is this banquet for?"

As Rudy waved his hand towards the great feast, he declared, "It has been prepared for you Susan. You can have it all. You can taste whatever you want; touch whatever your fancy desires."

Susan looked at all the desserts, and noted that each one had a different name assigned to it. She looked at Discretion. He nodded towards a cake that read, "Marriage and Family." Even though Susan had strong opinions about such matters the cake looked a bit heavy. She desired something lighter.

She then looked to Discernment, he pointed towards another cake that was entitled "Companionship," but it looked a bit plain and Susan admitted she desired something with a bit more finesse to it. She once again looked to Discretion, he nodded towards another dessert. It was called "Intimacy," but she couldn't tell what it was made of. When it came to love, she desired something that she knew was a sure thing. In her mind it was a way of avoiding being hurt.

It was after the third strike that Rudy directed her attention to the most exquisite cake of all. Its design spoke of a masterpiece and its beauty almost caused the other desserts to pale in comparison. There was a seduction to it that she sensed could literally consume a person. It was as if it was too good to be true. It was at that moment she felt Discernment ever so lightly tap her shoulder. Warning alarms went off in her soul and she sensed the dessert was overrated and most likely hiding something that would prove to be destructive. It was then that she looked at the sign attached to it. It read "Sexual Ecstasy."

She quickly backed away from that dessert and turned to see another one. Although beautiful and even playful, it appeared unstable. When she read its title she knew why it appeared unstable. It was called "Games of Love." She thought to herself it should be renamed, "Manipulation."

Susan knew that she had just dodged a couple of unpleasant bullets which caused a bit of apprehension in her. However, she was beginning to feel hungry. It was clear that she wanted to partake of what this table offered, especially since it was prepared for her. She had to find a dessert or desserts that appeared harmless enough that would prove to be acceptable to the eye and satisfying to her desires. However, she had to keep in mind that whatever she ate, it was clear that it would be her choice.

As she considered the desserts, she found there were a few that caught her eye. They were located in the middle of the great table. She hurriedly rushed past the many other desserts in order to examine the ones that had caught her attention. As she considered the first one she came to, it appeared to be a bit too mushy for her. Its title was "Emotions." However, the next one seemed to fit all of her ideas. It was fluffy in appearance but displayed ingredients that could bring satisfaction. It was called, "Happiness."

With great expectation as to the satisfaction the dessert would bring her, she almost inhaled it. It brought such ecstasy to her taste buds, but once she swallowed it, it left her almost sick. Instead of meeting her expectations, it left her disappointed and weak.

She looked at the next dessert that read "Romance." It still had the appearance of being light, but it was not fluffy. It appeared to have the sweetness of colorful fruits integrated in it. She had always desired romance. In her mind it was associated with love and feeling special. Instead of inhaling it as she did the previous dessert, she simply took a big bite of it. Its taste tantalized her taste buds with excitement, but as soon as she swallowed it the excitement wore off leaving her feeling empty.

The final dessert that had caught her attention was entitled, "Adoration." She had always desired to be adored. She wanted to be the center of someone's attention. It was clear that the other two preceding desserts were void of any lasting substance. The appearance of "Adoration" made it appear light, but there seem to be more firmness in its structure. She had learned a valuable lesson from the other desserts. This time she took a small bite of "Adoration". The taste gave her feelings of exhilaration, but she found she could not swallow it. She began to choke on it and tears welled up in her eyes in protest. It was at that time she turned to Discretion, he motion her to spit it out. As she was struggling with her calamity, Discernment pointed to an exit. She agreed and Discretion and Discernment took each arm and whisked her through the exit.

She was still choking and coughing when she came face to face with Wiseman. When she looked into his face something was a bit different. It looked to her as if his hair and beard were not quite as white or long. He silently watched her until her choking and coughing ceased.

"It doesn't appear as if your experience in the particular room of expectations served you well, Susan," commented Wiseman.

While nodding her head towards the exit, and still trying to catch the full capacity of her breathing, Susan confessed her confusion about her experiences in between breaths, "I don't understand what just happened in there?"

Wiseman's look brought a sobriety to Susan's soul. "Susan," he explained, "Rudiment, points to the foundation of the world. The world is set up to influence people who are ignorant with worldly philosophies, by indoctrinating them in their naive state to adopt self-serving desires. And, because of inexperience the world will also condition them as far as pursuits, which will always prove to be idolatrous, unrealistic, and repulsive. Like the brown door, it reminds us that expectations tied into the world, are of an earthly nature and are bound to the present age. They promise a false security and fleeting happiness. These expectations may offer pleasure, but such pleasure will prove temporary, for there is no life in any of it."

Susan realized her heart's desires set her up to prefer that which had no real substance.

Wiseman continued his instruction, "Discretion and Discernment tried to point you to what must be present for true love to take root and grow, but the world perverts that which is pure, making it unattractive to fleshly senses. What must be present for love to take root are healthy relationships and for them to grow there must be intimacy. Your desires had more to do with the idea of love and what it could do for you personally rather than experiencing the reality of love. Such ideas are based on the influences and philosophies of the world. Since the world is temporary and cannot provide that which is lasting and significant, it will leave you empty, disappointed, and leave a sharp, acrid taste and odor."

Susan realized that her desires were selfish, and the pride of her selfishness made her overlook what was important in order to chase after that which would feed her arrogant desires. After all, she felt she had a right to taste such desires. It became clear to her that she was no different, in fact, probably worse than the people she had been unmercifully judging, such as her parents. She had to acknowledge there were more dynamics involved in healthy relationships. They just didn't happen. In fact, such relationships had to be forged by hard work and real commitment on the part of both parties. Genuine commitment ensures faithfulness will be present when all the fluff of the world ceases, enabling those committed to endure the daily drudgery and demands that will follow.

"It's time for Discretion and Discernment to escort you to your next door."

Susan was about to object but Wiseman was already walking away from her. After her last experience, she preferred to skip the other doors, but it was obvious that her journey was not over. Wiseman's word was final and she could do nothing but comply.

Discretion and Discernment once again stood beside her. All three begin to advance down the hallway. It amazed Susan that they were passing many doors. Discretion must have sensed her silent question about bypassing the other doors. After all, she thought she would get to choose the doors.

"Susan, these doors are connected with certain desires. Your wisdom to restrain yourself from partaking of many of the desserts in the former room spared you of being tempted to even consider many of these other doors. There would be no point of attraction or seduction that would catch your eye. If we led you to such doors, you would be offended by them, and consider it a waste of your time. . However, you are obligated to enter the doors we lead you too because of your previous choices. Remember choices will always lead you to other doors."

"We're here." Discernment interjected.

The three of them stood before a beautiful purple door. However, its sign was stenciled with the words, "Virtual Reality."

Susan could not imagine why they stopped at that door. She was not into computers, video games, iPads, or blackberries. She also thought it quite odd that the door gave the appearance of royalty, but the sign was stenciled, clearly a contradiction.

Discretion once again interrupted her thought process, "It's very wise of you to note there're inconsistencies between the door and its

23

sign. You'll also be greeted by someone named 'Whimsical,' who will serve as a guide for this next room'"

"I don't understand why my preferences brought me to this door?" Susan inquired.

"You will in due time." Discretion quickly replied.

When they opened the room, Susan was surprised. There was no visible evidence of technical devices. Rather, there appeared to be separate little cubicles that were partitioned by dark curtains. Unlike the first room that was festive, this one seemed subdued. Rudiment had been at the door prepared to greet her, but Whimsical was nowhere in sight.

Just as Susan was making a mental note of Whimsical's absence, she entered from one of the cubicles in a grand manner. It was as if she was in some type of performance mode. It was all quite strange to Susan, but she figured she best note Whimsical's mannerisms.

"Forgive me; I was preparing a place for you, Susan. Welcome to Virtual Reality! I understand you don't have much time. Follow me to your room."

Susan found herself a bit confused over Whimsical's knowledge that she didn't have much time. She wasn't aware of any time limitation, but she had to admit she was anxious to get through this whole scene.

When they entered the room Susan was greeted by what appeared to be a big screen that seemed to consume the cubicle. There were various buttons located in front of the screen, along with a comfortable chair to sit in.

"Have a seat in front of the screen," Whimsical instructed Susan, "and I'll explain to you how this works."

Susan complied.

"First of all you hit the button that is labeled "Theme." Once the theme is chosen, you can push any of the buttons in front of you as a means to define or bring about the theme according to your perspective of it. By pushing any of the buttons, you can create your own reality concerning the theme, ultimately, experiencing any reality you prefer."

Susan looked at Whimsical. "Why would I want to create my own reality about something?"

Whimsical was a bit taken aback by Susan's question; however, Susan felt that Discretion had a smile on his face and Discernment had a twinkle in his eye.

"Do you really like your reality Susan?"

Susan's answer revealed what she thought about any conjured up environment, "Like most people there are things I would like to change about it, but it is what it is."

"But, this gives you an opportunity to see life from your preferred perspective." Whimsical said in a whiny voice. "Consider all the technology that people are caught up with that tantalizes their senses and imagination. It has given people various opportunities to live in whatever reality they desire, and once they put their mind to it there is nothing that can restrain them from what they have imagined to do."

Susan felt her eyes narrow as she asked her next question, "And, are they happier or better off for it?"

In an irritating voice, Whimsical retorted, "Just give it a try!" Her voice then softened, "It's harmless because you can direct everything from the chair."

Susan could not help herself. "I feel like the wizard in the story of the 'Wizard of Oz.' If, I remember right, he pushed buttons and pulled levers to produce certain effects, especially the one about having the power to change a matter. If I understood the story correctly, each person had the means to change their plight by changing their attitudes."

"Is there not something that you would like to direct in your life?" Whimsical almost pleaded, "What about love? You could put for your main theme, 'love' and then use the button to establish how you want love to be established or realized in your life."

Susan looked skeptically at Whimsical. "In other words, I'm like an arm-chair quarterback who plays the game of real life from the sidelines, while avoiding the actual experience of it."

By this time Whimsical was becoming frustrated. "Everyone that comes in here is excited about directing their reality! I don't understand why you're questioning such an opportunity!"

Due to past experiences, Susan already had the answer for her, "Because after I push the buttons, I'm still left with my present reality. To me it is an exercise in futility."

"I'm expecting other people!" Whimsical impatiently interjected. "I'll leave you alone to consider the buttons and decide whether you want to discover your virtual reality. After all, you have the power within you to change what is happening in your life.

"For instance, if you have dreams about such things as love, push this button that is marked "Dreams," and you'll find out how to make them come true. Do you have goals in a certain area? You can push this button labeled "Goals" and discover how you can bring them about. Do you have secret wishes? Push this button and they'll be realized. Remember, you have the power within to make such things happen. Now I'll leave you alone!"

Whimsical left the cubical in a huff.

Susan sat silently for a moment and then looked to Discretion. "Why am I here," she asked in a weary tone.

Discretion instructed her to choose the theme of "love" and push one button. Once she pushed the button of her particular choice to direct her reality, she simply needed to hold it down until she was past all the options presented to her. It would be like fast forwarding the program. He explained that the answer to her pursuit for virtual reality would be found at the end of the exercise.

She hit the button, "Theme" and typed in the word "love." She then chose the button, "Wishes." Like everyone else she had secret wishes to experience love and had a fantasy about how it would play out in the end. She held it down until it came to the end of the sequence of questions and options. The words blinking on the screen summarized where such fanciful wishes brings one, "Wishful Thinking." She realized at that point that all virtual reality would take a person on a high flying ride of exciting possibilities, only to bring him or her to a disappointing end.

The next button she hit was, "Dreams." People love to ride high on the waves of dreams, expecting a certain ending, but at the end of "Dreams" was the word "Unrealistic."

She chose "Notions" next, and at the end of it was "Castle in the Sky Nonsense". She couldn't help but hit the button "Happiness" which was summarized in one word "Fantasy." Her final choice was "Affections" which ended with the words "Fickle Sentiment."

Susan sat quietly in front of the blinking screen. It was just as she suspected, all unrealistic notions about love would automatically lead a person on a journey of hopeful expectations seeking treasured promises waiting at the end of each rainbow, only to end with the individual being shot down by reality, resulting in disillusionment. It was all an exercise in vanity, leading to one dead end after another, but she couldn't figure out why she had been exposed to the silly exercise. Discernment motioned for them to leave. As they were preparing to exit the cubical through the door they had entered, Whimsical noticed them leaving and called after them, "Did you try the program, Susan?"

Susan stopped and looked at Whimsical. "Yes I did, and it's just what I thought it was, a joke, an April fool's trick on the mind."

They exited the room leaving Whimsical red-faced and sputtering about how foolish and silly she was for not taking the opportunity of benefitting from the endless opportunities and avenues virtual reality offered. However, Susan left the room feeling very irritated. Once again she came face to face with Wiseman.

As before she noticed Wiseman had changed from their last encounter. He was taking on a more youthful appearance, but His eyes held the wisdom of the ages and His smile, unspeakable joy.

"Susan, I gathered that your last room proved a waste of time."

Susan could not help but express her frustration, "I've no idea why you sent me into that room. It didn't test me in any way, nor did it benefit me. I thought it all to be lame and silly!"

Wiseman still had a smile on his face when he answered her "Susan, you're right in your conclusions about trying to create your own virtual reality. It is a waste of time, but the natural tendency of people is to waste their time by trying to change or adjust the reality they are bored with or proves to be unpleasant. The truth is the only way you can change present reality through virtual reality is through self-delusion of the mind. The only way the tone of any environment can change is not through personal efforts, but by a willingness to accept present reality for what it is and choose what attitude and approach you are going to adopt towards it.

"As the name, 'Whimsical' implied you can't trust those things which don't embrace reality. In fact, Whimsical had to sell you on the idea. Like the last room you experienced, all such ideas are all founded on a lie. The desire for a different reality can make a grand entrance through various sources of media such as books, music, theater, TV, sports, and movies and so forth, but none of it is real. In fact, the idea of controlling your reality falls into the categories of witchcraft and the New Age. It can condition people to believe that they can control their own reality which will be comprised of nothing more than wishful thinking, unrealistic desires, worldly pursuits, castle-in-the-sky notions, and sentimental gibberish. Such pursuits will lead you to a dead-end and leave you disappointed and devastated.

"However, the personal test for you Susan that goes with this room is not obvious. People have two ways in which reality affects them. They can go into self-delusion and think it is possible to wish, claim, or dream any unpleasant reality away, or they can become skeptical about everything. You Susan, are a skeptic.

"You were wise to see through the vanity of such exercise, but you failed to see that you've gone to the other extreme. In relationship to the first extreme of self-delusion, people will overlook what is true and real because it does not live up to their unrealistic notions. As for your type of extreme, you'll refuse to recognize what is possible and, therefore, rejecting any hope of it as being true. In essence, you'll quickly reject what is possible or could be real.

"The truth is fantasy finds its origins in what is real, but perverts it because it is not realistic or within people's power to bring it about a certain way. As a result of encountering counterfeits, people go to the other extreme and become skeptical and unreceptive towards ever experiencing real love. Every person, including you, can know real love, but as you've already acknowledged, it can't be directed or orchestrated. However, it is also on the shirttails of reality that skepticism makes an entrance. It is a product of hopelessness and resentment because a person cannot control past, present, or future realities when it comes to love, relationships, and life in general.

"There is a certain conceit to your handling of this matter, Susan. For example, you know there are different ways in which women handle the offense of molestation."

The word "molestation" caught her attention. How could Wiseman know about her past, and yet she suspected he knew everything about her? She looked as him with a questionable look, but he continued on his discourse.

"Some buy the lie that since they have been defiled and are considered to be trash that they allowed themselves to be either used up by men, or they go in the other direction by figuring out how to manipulate men for revenge. You have wisely avoided going down either of those self-destructive paths, but you have also perceived yourself for being the wiser for it. You think you are clever to hold every person arms-length, but what are the fruits of your clever conceit?"

By this time Susan felt completely undone. Wiseman was right on target, exposing the real motive behind her skepticism. It was her way of controlling her environment, but any future life was clearly passing her by. She could stand back and judge others for their foolishness, but she was proving to be a fool in her own right.

Wiseman's words continued to hit the mark, "Susan you need to come to center as to the fact that the gifts of life do not comprise one big joke. You are wise to recognize reality, but due to your skeptical attitude you lack discernment to be able to know, trust, and receive what is true and real for yourself. Such an inability produces isolation and makes for a lonely existence."

Susan knew that Wiseman was right at every point. She looked down at the floor. "I guess I failed the test."

"Susan, look at me." Susan looked into the tender eyes of Wiseman, "You didn't fail the test Susan; rather, you were given an

Rayola Kelley

opportunity to see your pride and attitude. You must never let your unrequited dreams and the whimsical, perverted, unfulfilled realities of others trip you up in either way. If you desire what is true, then you must wisely learn where to seek for it."

Meekly Susan asked, "Where do I look for the truth when it comes to true love," she paused, "when it comes to hope for a different life, a different way?"

Wiseman softly answered her question, "Susan, you must seek the truth for yourself, but if you truly desire truth, the minute you encounter it, you'll recognize it."

Wiseman walked away, leaving Susan with her two companions.

"Are you ready to continue on," Discretion asked Susan?

Susan slowly nodded her head yes. The experience was leaving her weary and feeling completely unraveled. All along she thought she had it all figured out. She was now catching glimpses into her own soul, and even though she had been the victim of other sins, she had found her own soul to be darkened by personal decisions, pride, and fleshly, selfish pursuits. She was hoping the journey was over, but she knew that there was more. She felt anxious about the unknown aspect of what was ahead, but she also knew that she was destined to find her answer at the end of the long hallway.

Discernment touched her arm and the three of them continued down the corridor.

Susan could not help but think that the hallway was becoming narrower, and the more she tried to see the end of it, the more it seemed to take on the impression of infinity. The very idea of infinity caused the small flame of hope she possessed to take a backseat to growing anxiety.

Discretion warned her, "Susan, be careful how you evaluate a matter. Just because it looks a certain way to you does not make it so. Our perceptions are often tied up with our feelings and notions. In such a frame of mind, you can't trust what you perceive."

Susan took a deep breath and released it slowly as a means to regain her concentration.

They stopped in front of a beautiful ornate black door. Engraved in it was the word, "Imagination." It was painted in velvet. She made moves towards the door, but felt Discernment touch her arm as if to warn her. As she stopped and stepped back to consider the door, she noticed how beautifully "Imagination" was engraved and painted on the door; however, it seemed that the word itself began to change before her eyes. She remembered how imagination played a big part in the last room. As she realized the danger of undisciplined, carnal imaginations ruling a person's reality, the word on the door began to take on eerie forms, and some of the letters became slanted and uneven. The end of each letter contorted into jagged barbs, taking on a grotesque form that set all the alarms off in her soul. The eerie distortion of the word made the door formidable.

Susan backed away from it and looked at Discretion, "I'm not going through this door, even if it means that my search for true love will end here!"

Discretion smiled, "No one can make you go through that door, Susan. In fact, you have been wise to sense Discernment's warning. You must always be sensitive to any spiritual warning."

"I don't know why you have brought me to this door," Susan questioned, "if you knew that I would avoid the temptation to enter in."

"Susan, you must remember that you were willing to enter into it. It was only after Discernment touched you that you stopped, stepped back and examined the door. If he hadn't warned you, you might have very well entered it without even thinking about it and exposed yourself to great perversion. You must always beware and be sober about what you're exposing yourself to.

"Everyone has a choice to enter any door that has not first been sealed by God." Discretion continued his discourse. "Imagination was given as a tool to open up people's curiosity to explore the possibilities of what God has in store for them. God's best will prove to exceed individuals' imagination. However, the world perverts the imagination and that's when it becomes a door that leads to a frightening reality that always promotes a culture of death. Sadly, it's not only a popular door with most people seeking some type of reality that feeds the lust of their flesh, but it is preferred. It is natural for people to go from emotional fantasy to wicked imagination."

Discernment added, "Many people innocently enter this door regardless of inner warnings or concerns, but they enter into an arena that is precarious. On the other side of this door are such temptations as drugs and pornography. Like the sign, the reality past this door is clearly distorted, perverted, and frightening. It is best described by Genesis 6:5, 'and that every imagination of the thoughts of his heart was only evil continually.'"

"Susan, the pride of the heart serves as a platform in which the imaginative thoughts are born," Discretion explained. "From the conception of these thoughts, desires take flight on the wings of unrealistic expectations. As expectations grow these desires formulate a frightening reality where experiencing such expectations become the pursued goal as deluded individuals convince themselves that it's their right, and their privilege to partake of such darkness. It's in this arena that people trespass into that which is evil. They partake of forbidden fruit, often robbing innocence of its purity, and leaving victims in its wake. Susan, you were such a victim of wicked imaginations."

Susan knew what Discretion was saying. Her molestation found its origins in the prideful, wicked heart of her deluded relative. He didn't care that he robbed her of her innocence and purity for he convinced himself that he had a right to partake of her innocent fruit and defile her with his warped perspective of so-called "love." In a sense, he believed she was here just for him to explore and exploit according to his vain, wicked imaginations.

Discretion continued his exhortation, "God created a garden for man in which to fellowship with Him, but because man rebelled in that garden, he's now in a fallen condition where sin, haughtiness, wicked arrogance, and perversion defines his life, his reality, and his pursuits. This condition has produced a barren spiritual wilderness in the world that is void of life and hope. However, out of love God reached out to man to once again bring him into a Garden of Fellowship with Him so that he may experience His life, His sweetness, and His hope."

Upon the completion of Discretion's exhortation, Discernment signaled the end of any further instruction when he stated, "It's time to go."

They started down the hallway, but it seemed to become narrower and longer. In fact, it became so confining that they were forced to walk single file. It felt as if they were slowly ascending as the air became thinner. Darkness began to enfold them. Susan was thankful that Discretion was in front of her preparing the way and Discernment behind her, guarding the way. She found comfort that she was boxed in and could do nothing but trudge ahead in spite of becoming weary. Susan struggled with each step, but the further she proceeded up the narrow passageway, the more she thought it foolish to quit or turn around. However, she was about to say something when a light began to penetrate the darkness.

As the light penetrated her surroundings, she realized that she was no longer in a hallway but on a small pathway. She also discovered that she was alone.

Discretion was not in front of her and Discernment was nowhere to be found. Confusion and fear begin to grip her. She knew darkness was behind her, but an unknown light was in front of her. Discretion was not there to explain it to her and Discernment was not present to warn or direct her about possible traps.

She struggled in her mind. Logic chided her for taking on such a venture, and imagination screamed at her that she was foolish, while reason was eerily quiet. She stood still and as she quieted her emotions by reminding herself that this journey was an answer to her prayer. It was at this point of remembrance that reason once again made an appearance. She was reminded that her two companions must have done their part and led her out of the narrow way to the light, and now she needed to trust that the light signaled the end of her journey. Besides, she told herself, she had come too far to turn back.

Susan began to ascend the path leading to the light. As she followed the path, it led her to a bend. As she came around the bend she saw something that made her knees weak and almost caused her to collapse. The light was highlighting a cross. She could make out a figure on that cross. She didn't know who was on that cross but she feared that when she came into the light, she would see herself on it. Her journey had given her a keen awareness that she deserved to be judged as much as the next person, and that she belonged on the brutal instrument of judgment. In fact, she felt even more undone in her soul by the sight of it, and the light was now penetrating her innermost being, revealing the darkness that she knew had engulfed it.

Before the revelation of her own darkness, she had always compared herself to her violator. She had consoled herself that she was an angel compared to him. But, because of what the journey exposed about her inner person, she was now aware that she was no angel, and that she also had violated something precious, pure, and holy. Guilt came down on her conscience like a judge's gavel. She could scarcely walk, afraid to face the inevitable about her sinful ways, arrogant judgments, and deviant character.

As Susan came to the front of the cross, her eyes were glued on her feet. Each step she took proved to be heavier than the last. Her feet stopped in front of the cross, but she did not dare face it, as she stood with downcast eyes. Finally, she slowly turned to face the cross, but shame kept her eyes glued to the ground. However, she knew she had to look up; she had to face the reality of the cross: that someone was hanging from it. In her mind, she would look up to see her face. Even though she could not understand how this would answer her prayer about love, she knew that she had to take courage and face the terrible judgment that the cross represented.

Her eyes began to make their way up the blood-stained tree. She noticed the nail pierced feet, the ravaged body that clearly was not hers but that of a man, His arms were extended along the horizontal part of the cross, and His hands were nailed against it. At last her eyes looked upon the face of the one who hung there.

Susan's knees buckled, as she fell upon them. Even though bloody and beaten, the face was the face of Joshua Wiseman. She could still see behind the blood and bruises, the precious face of wisdom that had instructed her, the kind look of gentleness that had encouraged her, and a glimmer of the twinkle of joyous wonder in his eyes that had made her heart light. It was also then that she realized the real identity of Joshua Wiseman. He was none other than Jesus Christ, the Son of the Living God.

Then the glorious words that the pastor had recently quoted from John 3:16 came to her mind, "For God so loved the world, that he gave his only begotten son, that whosoever believeth in him should not perish, but have everlasting life."

Susan realized that she was looking at love personified. Love has been lifted up on a cross by God for the world to see. Although brutality was associated with it, it simply expressed how far genuine love would go, how sacrificial it was, and how devoted and enduring it would prove to be. It was then that she recognized that Jesus had been lifted up on the cross in her place. She alone had to come to this place because He had died for her, to address her wretched state of sin, despair, and death. He did it because He *LOVED* her. He did it because He *PREFERRED* her. There was nothing selfish about His love for He clearly honored her over His own well-being. Out of love He gave it all on her behalf, secured all the treasures and promises of heaven for her, and opened the way for her to know and experience the fullness of His love. He had indeed answered her prayer.

It was then that Susan knew genuine love could not be found anywhere but in God. The pastor's words and sermons began to make sense. God's love could not be experienced outside of the work of the cross, and no other man could offer it or give it except by or through the man Christ Jesus. Christ Jesus: what a name, what a man! Deity wrapped in humanity, formed with the disposition of a servant, but fashioned as a man and ordained to be the Lamb of God who would take away the sins of the world--who would take away her sin.

Tears filled her eyes, and overflowed down her cheeks as she asked for forgiveness. She reached up to receive His mercy, experience His gentleness, and embrace His love. She felt His grace flow downward as love lifted her heavenward in the light of salvation.

The revelation of His love began to enfold her like the gentle arms of a loving father. She felt acceptance, and for the first time she truly knew she had been forgiven, while the decayed remains of her life fell to the wayside. She felt revived in her spirit and warmth in her soul for now the light of His love and life were present. She felt like a new creation as the old was being consumed by the judgment of the cross and a new life was taking root. She was elated, for now she was becoming identified with the work of heavenly redemption, established in high places with her newfound love.

Susan felt as if she was floating. She was being bathed in joy and peace. She was now ready to face life because she knew she was no longer alone. She no longer had to guess about or imagine what true love was, for she had been found by the Shepherd of love, embraced by the Savior of love, established in a spiritual household by the Lord of love, accepted by the Father of love, and betrothed to the Lover of her soul.

She felt her body floating downward. The next thing she knew is that she was in her bed. The journey was over and her prayer had been answered. Her life would never be the same, for the Morningstar had risen in her soul. Now she would sleep until the rising of the sun, knowing that all was truly well with her soul.

***

It was Sunday and Susan was excited about going to church. It seemed as if she had been in a whirlwind for the last few days. It had been a week since her spiritual odyssey had occurred, and it was clear that she was becoming a new creation. The first thing she needed to do was make some changes in her appearance. She had her hair done at the beauty salon and went to high end consignment shops and discount stores for new clothes. The Lord was gracious enough to fit her with an attractive wardrobe.

She not only had a different hairdo and nice clothes, but her countenance was different and she had a spring in her walk. Her transformation was receiving much attention from those at work. Some silently considered her a type of wonderment, while others made comments of encouragement, and a few asked her what happened to bring about such drastic changes. Although new in her faith, she shared that the Son of God, the Living Christ was the one who was making all the difference in her life. Admittedly, she was enjoying the new person she was discovering and seeing in the mirror each morning.

That Sunday morning would be special because she clearly had something important to share with the congregation, beginning with Sam. She now possessed the good news of salvation. She knew that

34

like the angels in heaven, Sam would rejoice over her being found by the Great Shepherd and being placed in His flock. Since Sam worked with the young people, she knew where to locate him. Sure enough he was right where she knew he would be.

Since Susan was running a bit late, she quickly walked up to him. "Hi Sam!"

His back was to her when she had approached him. And, when he turned around to return her greeting, the look on his face spoke volumes. He had expected to see Susan, but the person who stood before him didn't exactly look like Susan. It was her voice, but everything about her was new, strange, and different. When he went to speak, he stumbled over his simple greeting of hello.

Susan had no idea that her many changes would affect him in such a way. He was practically speechless. She smiled at him. "Sam, I just wanted to thank you for being faithful to the Lord, and I want you to be the first to know, I've received Jesus as my Precious Lord and most gracious Savior. If it wasn't for your willingness to be his vessel in example and in sharing your testimony, I would have never encountered Jesus' love and healing."

It was obvious that Sam was in a bit of shocked. Susan could see that he was still trying to process everything in order to respond, but the service was about to begin.

"If you want to, we can talk later Sam. Right now the worship service has begun and I don't want to miss any of it!"

Sam slowly nodded his head in agreement.

Susan proceeded to the sanctuary. Now that she had freely experienced and received genuine and lasting love, she knew she had the freedom to give it to others. She didn't know what the Lord had in mind for her where Sam was concerned, but the one thing she did know is that she had not only found satisfying and sufficient love in the right place, but in doing so, she had discovered the true lover of her soul.

And be not conformed
to this world; but be ye
transformed by the
renewing of your mind,
that ye may prove what
is that good, and acceptable,
and perfect, will of God.
(Roman 12:2)

Transformation

Chloe Merriweather walked slowly into the timeworn gym. It was like visiting an old friend she had known for two decades. It was something she had long planned to do, but until now, she had never managed to make her way back to the small community where she had spent her adolescent years. When she left, she didn't feel that she had been able to give the community and the gym, along with a few friends, a proper farewell. Due to recent invitations to a couple of special events, she could now check that particular activity off of her to-do list.

The gym's exit lights seemed to welcome her into the dimly lit atmosphere. As her feet moved across the wood floor the sound of her steps echo off the walls. As each echo receded, it was overlapped by those that followed suit. In Chloe's senses the echoes began to take on the sights, smells, and sounds of days gone by, days when she sat on the bleachers and cheered for her school's basketball team in the midst of screeching tennis shoes skidding on the floor, stifling heat and the odor of sweat wafting up to the ceiling. The environment was charged with electrifying excitement. There were also those days when bad weather drove the students into the gym's confines to continue outdoor activities and exercise, sometimes producing groans, laughter, and exhilaration. In the small community, many days for most of the citizens of the blue-collar sawmill town centered around the subculture and social life of the school's activities.

It had been ten years since Chloe had seen the gym. The last time she experienced its many sights and sounds was at her high school graduation. It seemed that after her name was read as being part of the graduation class of 2003, she was whisked off to enter through a door into another world that offered her immense opportunity. However, the opportunity would only be available for a short time. She realized if she was going to discover her destiny, she had to quickly walk through the door before it closed. She indeed embarked on a new adventure, but she had to leave the old behind without looking back.

The timeworn gym implied nothing had changed, but yet everything had changed. Granted, the gym was still the same old gym, but Chloe was not the same person who had left behind the small school, the people, and the community in pursuit of the opportunities that quickly began to temper her life in a new way.

As Chloe stopped in the middle of the circle outlined on the gym floor, she could see that the lights of the scoreboard had not been turned off. That scoreboard marked more than victories or defeats for the local team, it also marked some specific events for her. Memories, some sweet, some bittersweet, and some sad began to parade before her. Her years in this school resonated with reminiscences that brought a smile to her face, but then, there were those events that became mileposts in her life. They marked grave challenges that would later determine the path that she was now traveling.

For Chloe, it was natural to go backward in time to the first day she entered the halls of the school. She was nine years old, and it was the fourth grade. Her widowed grandfather had moved her to the community to be close to his sister. Even though the two siblings had been estranged off and on during their lives, her grandfather felt that Chloe needed a woman's influence.

Chloe had lost her mother when she was eight. Her father, Bud Merriweather, was true to his last name. He "budded" the most when he was carrying out his devious schemes, was always merry as long as he could separate people from their money, and proved to be a fair-weather husband and father. For most of Chloe's first years of life he was in and out of trouble and jail. It was obvious he was irresponsible and incapable of being a parent. After her mother's funeral he had his last brush with the law and the gavel finally came down pronouncing a long jail sentence.

How well she remembered that sad day when her mother's lifeless body was laid in an inadequate coffin and placed in a potter's grave. There were very few people who attended her mother's funeral. Her father hadn't even bothered to inform her mother's estranged father and aunt of her death. In Chloe's mind, it seemed so unfair and cruel. Her mother at one time had promises of prominence and wealth, but it was all squandered and lost on a dead-end relationship.

After her father was incarcerated, she had nowhere to go but to become a ward of the state. It was then that her estranged grandfather was informed of her predicament by the state, and although they had never met, he came to her rescue and took full responsibility for her welfare.

However, Chloe was a hellion and difficult for her grandfather to handle. Due to her father's unhealthy influence on her life, combined with the fact that her mother spent most of her time working before her untimely death due to cancer, Chloe learned early how to take care of herself, while becoming streetwise. To those who knew her she proved to be a contradiction. Due to her mother insistence, her speech was impeccable but she could quickly adjust her manner of speech as well as her appearance in order to fit into the environment. It was clear to everyone that saw her that she not only was a tomboy, but one you did not want as an enemy.

Chloe wore coveralls that were marked by the rubble that littered the streets where she spent most of her free time, and her mannerisms made her appear as if she was a tough scrapper. Most of the time her dirty face wore a scowl to hide her insecurity and her tongue was sharp to push back any aggressor with street language. She wore her greasy, brown shoulder-length hair under an old dingy gray beret, but behind her tough exterior was a caring person who was fiercely loyal to those she cared about. She was a sensitive person who often expressed her softer side when she sat at a piano.

The lady next door, who kept her eye on Chloe for the first eight years of her life, was the one who discovered her musical talents at a very young age. Chloe could hear a piece of music and actually repeat it on the old piano. The woman saw her musical ability as a way to corral the wild little heathen into some constructive activity. Like some experience in books, Chloe discovered that she could emotionally travel places in music that aroused her imagination. She found she could play all types of compositions that offered an array of emotional experiences that at times inspired a type of beauty and expression that changed the mood of her soul.

For example, Chloe could travel to great depths and heights with masterpieces written by such composers as Mozart, Bach, Beethoven, Chopin, and Handel. Likewise, she also liked to move with the beat of the ever-changing songs of the present, as well as bop with the harmonies of the 50's, declare her rage against what was considered the establishment with the songs of the 60's and 70's, cry with melancholy country songs, and swing with jazz. She had to agree with the person who said that there is nothing that expresses the prevailing mood of a culture or a generation like the music it adopts. It was indeed the only way she could express herself without letting down her guard.

However, Chloe had guarded her talent. She felt it was her secret and if people knew about it, they would somehow abuse and ruin it for her. It was also her place of escape where she directed the cadence of life without interference or interruption from the chaotic outside world that was constantly buffeting her with sorrow, disappointments, changes, and uncertainties.

Chloe had quietly let out a sigh of relief when her grandfather, Leon Cain, came to pick her up on that spring day from the CPS worker. She found that her mother's description of him was correct and found herself immediately being drawn to his quiet, mild-mannered ways. Chloe became a bit dismayed when her grandfather brought her to the small community a month later. He had purchased a second hand store in the town he had grown up in with his sister, Eloise. The store had a small apartment in the back that became their home. It was a bit crowded, but Chloe found some consolation in an old piano that she would play when her grandfather was not around.

However, the most challenging aspect of her new change came in the form of her spinster great-aunt, Eloise Cain. The Cain family was the hub of the town. The family owned a sawmill that had provided employment for many in the community and surrounding areas. Her grandfather had started out working in the business and later served as the manager, while his sister learned the business end.

Chloe's mother came later. She was born when her parents were in their late 20s. Due to complications at the time of her birth, Chloe's mother was the only child, and became a special gift to her parents. Even though the sawmill provided Leon with the means to support his family, Chloe's grandfather walked away from the business in despair after his daughter left with the infamous Bud Merriweather. He decided to pursue another position away from tormenting memories, letting every aspect of the family operation fall to Eloise.

Chloe remembered her mother occasionally mentioning her strict aunt, who had no patience for foolish incompetence. Even though her mother's description of her aunt didn't put her in the best light, the tone of her mother's voice always rang with unusual sentiment.

When Chloe first met her great-aunt who had invited her for dinner at her mansion, she stared at the stern looking woman of medium height and weight with grey hair that nicely framed her round face. She stood motionless as her aunt's steely blue eyes looked her up and down as if she was a commodity at a store. Her expression implied she didn't approve of what she was seeing.

Her aunt's informal greeting and attitude towards Chloe's grandfather made her relationship with him appear impersonal and cold, causing the grand matriarch to appear indifferent to the young impressionable Chloe.

The décor of her aunt's home also complied with the first impression Chloe had of her. It made Chloe feel as if she was in a time warp, while the environment it produced reminded her of a lifeless tomb. Eloise Cain appeared to be isolated from the outside world, surrounded by another time. No doubt she was a loner. Granted, she was a grand businessperson who effectively ran the sawmill operations with the same precision as the saws that cut wood at the mill. She also employed a woman who cleaned the house and prepared the meals and a butler who did other chores besides driving her to her destinations, but it was quite obvious that she was frugal and ran a tight ship. It seemed that in her isolated world, she was somewhat suspicious of people's intentions.

In spite of her air of aloofness, she was a powerful influence when it came to the actual community, carrying on a family legacy that many depended on for stability and security. Her opinion was sought after and respected, and her word usually became final.

Chloe already made up her mind before she met this legend that she wasn't going to take any insolence from her. When Eloise Cain looked Chloe up and down, Chloe scowled at her. When her aunt saw her scowl, the eyebrow over her right eye arched in disapproval while her other eyebrow tilted downward giving the impression that she was sizing her up for battle.

Chloe wondered how her aunt managed to pull such a feat with her eyes. Since it made her aunt appear intimidating, she noted that she would figure it out so she could take on the same pose for future use.

It was obvious that Eloise Cain would not tolerate what she considered insolence from Chloe. Both females had strong personalities, and it was clear that the battle lines were being drawn. Chloe sized up the situation and braced herself for the first blow. No doubt the older Cain would have the advantage of years and experience, but Chloe had youth, wit, and a strong resolve to learn quickly the art of survival. She had survived the streets and no doubt she would survive any affront Eloise Cain could throw at her. Clearly, neither one would accept disrespect from the other, nor would they wave the white flag of surrender.

As suspected, the first punch was clearly thrown by the elder Cain, "My heavens girl, where ever did you find your attire, from the dumpsters on the street?"

"In fact, that is where I dug up my attire!" Chloe retorted, and to make the apparent irritation sink deeper into her aunt, she added, "Don't ya think it gives me a certain distinction?"

Eloise looked at her great niece as if she were a cat looking at her prey, "Yes it would be quite a distinction, one of meritorious recognition I must say... that is if you considered your attire in light of pigs wallowing in a pigpen!"

Chloe had to admit her great aunt was brash in her response. It was clear she was a worthy opponent, and she must not underestimate her. Secretly, she welcomed such a challenge. It had been awhile since Chloe had sparred with someone at such a level.

Chloe had learned there were different levels of fighting. The most ignoble response was the physical contact of brute force and violence. Physical strength and endurance was often the determining factor in such conflicts. The second type of fight came from anger and rage, seeking restitution or revenge. Often self-control proved to come out on top in such a fight. Finally, there was the third type of battle: that of wit. It was in this arena that Chloe had discovered that cleverness would often prove to be the determining factor in most combats.

Wit was made up of the ability to seize the moment and look for the small window of opportunity to act decisively. It also had an uncanny ability to defuse a matter with a bit of humor, reducing casualties. As a result, such wit could outsmart those with strength, sidestep rage and anger, and show tremendous skill as the sharpness of intellectual prowess of conflicting parties clashed like two swords in a duel.

Chloe also knew that both of them were testing each other to see which spots were vulnerable. She knew that it would be a wise move on her part to hold back some of her skills, rather than lay all of them on the table at once. In a way she had to become unpredictable. The element of surprise was a clever way of keeping the opponent off balance. Meanwhile, she wasn't about to give her opponent any ground. She stood there staring with complete resolution at her aunt as if to maintain her ground of independence. Even though she knew her aunt had a legitimate point about her dress, she couldn't show any weakness or surrender even in the slightest way. Her aunt would have to fight for every inch of territory if she was to make any inroads into Chloe's kingdom. Such advancement would only come by her aunt gaining her respect and trust.

Eloise looked at her brother, "My guests are waiting. You know the rules, Leon, before anyone sits at my table for dinner, hands must be clean and heads must be free from creepy crawling creatures and animal residues."

Chloe knew that her aunt was indirectly making reference either to the unseen creatures that could have found a nesting place in her somewhat unkempt brown hair or to her dirty beret. She had to admit she had hit a vulnerable spot. Chloe had to refrain herself from responding in hurt and anger; therefore, she managed to highlight her firm tone, through the small slit of clench teeth and lips with her most refined language. "I washed my hair and have cleaned my hands, but as for my hat, I'll take it off, but it will remain close to me. I'll never let it out of my sight," and she added, "It's the only gift my father ever gave me."

For a moment, Chloe watched compassion take center stage in her aunt's eyes. It quickly took a bow, and then exited. It was at that time that she realized her aunt also had a human, compassionate side to her. Granted, it appeared she had a hard exterior, but Chloe suspected that it guarded her vulnerable side. Chloe began to wonder if she was not looking into the face of an older version of herself. It was true her aunt had been exposed to the finer things of life and was refined in her speech and mannerisms, but she was also very human. Chloe wondered what the mirror of this woman's life could reveal about her own character.

In a more subdued tone her aunt conceded some territory, "Fine, you may hang your hat on your chair, until you are finished eating."

Chloe was thankful to see her aunt's tender side. She had learned on the streets that those who have a tender side are most apt to be fair and honest in the battles they fight. She could now trust that even though her aunt might prove to be a tough opponent due to her immovable opinions and ways, she would not intentionally be a cruel one.

When they walked into the dining room, Chloe was completely taken back by the size of the table and all the food that graced it. She was also a bit surprised to see four other people already seated at the table. There were two women, an older woman and possibly her daughter and two boys that probably were the sons of the daughter. Chloe surmised that age wise she fit between the two boys. The older one appeared to be close to a couple of years older than her and the other one a couple of years younger. She would later discover that her guess almost hit the bullseye.

The older woman stood up to greet her grandfather. Chloe sensed that they had a history together. They grasped arms and gave each other a warm greeting. The woman looked at Chloe with kindness emanating from her face, and there was softness in her eyes. She declared, "And, who is this young lady?"

Her grandfather then made the introductions. "Marybeth, this is my granddaughter Chloe and Chloe this is a dear friend of Eloise and me, Marybeth Williams." He pointed towards the other lady and the two boys, "And, this is her lovely daughter Sarah Reinhardt and her two sons, J.R. and Freddie.

Marybeth warmly greeted Chloe with a hug, surprising her. In a reserve response, Chloe brought her arms half way up and lightly hug the woman. Taking a step back and looking at Chloe's features, she made the comparison that Chloe was well aware of, "Chloe, you look like your mother!" Nodding at her daughter and then looking at Chloe, Marybeth added, "my daughter, Sarah and your mother were the best of friends since they were in grade school together. Your mother was like a second daughter to me."

Getting up from the table, Sarah nodded in agreement. "You do look like your mother, Chloe, and it's so good to finally meet you." Sarah reached her hand out to Chloe to shake it. Chloe also reservedly took her hand to acknowledge her friendly overture.

Chloe realized that she was being introduced to the former world of her mother. Through the years, the young street wise girl managed to glean bits and pieces about her mother's past. Chloe had concluded there was a time her mother must have been young and beautiful, full of dreams and hope, but due to her involvement with Bud Merriweather, she had become estranged from her family and her former life, causing great loneliness in her.

As the pieces were coming together in Chloe's mind, it was obvious that it was the typical story that surrounds the passions of first love. Being naïve and quite protected, Laura Cain was too inexperienced to realize that Chloe's father was not a knight in shining armor; rather, he was a two-bit con. Laura had shunned all warnings from her parents, raged against her aunt's interference to expose her beau's questionable character, brushed off concerns from her friends, and in total defiance slammed the door on her old life, by eloping with Bud Merriweather.

Chloe was quite aware that after her mother's marriage to her father, her mother's existence became sorely difficult. A picture did emerge for Chloe after watching her father move in and out of her life. At different times it became clearer after hearing her parents argue over his irresponsible ways. At times her mother would say things, revealing that she felt that she had brought the travesty on herself. Due to her tender age, Chloe couldn't completely understand her mother's plight, but there were times when she was given glimpses into it. Her mother confessed once that it was her wretched pride that had blinded her to the great hardship that stood before her as she struggled to stand and prove that all the voices of her past were wrong about Chloe's father. However, the reality of her situation constantly dealt harsh blows against her resolve, as guilt became her prison bars and shame her companion, while mocking condemnation stood guard at the prison door of her soul.

The only bright hope and connection to her former life came in Chloe's birth. Chloe was named after her grandmother, a grandmother Chloe only briefly encountered a few times in her life when her mother had secretly met with her at a designated location. She remembered how her grandmother smelled of lavender, and that she always had a special little gift for her name-sake. She was also aware that her grandmother would slip some money into her mother's hand. Although reluctant to accept it, Laura would have to swallow what little dignity she had left and accept it for the sake of her daughter.

It seemed that right after the few meetings she had with her mother, Laura Cain Merriweather's misery always escalated. Chloe would hear her sobs in the night. One night Chloe quietly made her way to her mother's bedroom. She lightly touched her on the arm to comfort her. Her mother took her small hand and assured her she was alright. However, even at her young age she could sense the grave loneliness, regret, and hopelessness that were tormenting her mother.

Laura Merriweather aged before her daughter's eyes. As a result of living a harsh existence, Chloe recognized that her mother tasted the bitter dregs of life. At times her mother would give Chloe glimpses into her own attitude towards life. Through these glimpses Chloe was able to conclude that her mother felt she was living a wasted life of despair that was constantly being sacrificed upon the altar of ridiculousness. In Chloe's mind she knew that this despairing status culminated in her mother dying before her time.

Chloe brushed back the tears. She couldn't remember her mother's laugh for it had long ago given way to sorrow. She couldn't remember her smile, for her face had also long ago succumbed to stress. Most of her memories of her mother were painful. Perhaps her grave represented the real tragedy. With only a very few to mourn her, Laura Merriweather, a woman of such high hopes and dreams was laid to rest in a box coffin and put in a pauper's grave with a small plaque for a headstone. A life snuffed out by misery, consumed by loneliness, wasted away by vanity, and now silenced by an indifferent grave.

As memories began to form a mosaic in Chloe's mind, connecting a fuzzy past with the strange present, she noted that the two boys sitting at the table remained quiet as they listened to the exchange.

She also noticed they were trying to size her up as well. She was directed to the chair beside her grandfather who was placed at the end of the table, positioning her next to the younger boy, Freddie, and across from Marybeth. The great matriarch of the family, Eloise sat at the head of the table as if she was royalty, ready to orchestrate the events.

Chloe realized she was hungry and could not wait to dig into the delicious looking food to quiet the hunger pains of her stomach. However, before any food was served the royal matriarch of the home signaled that they were to hold hands, and then she asked her brother Leon to say the blessing for dinner.

The last thing Chloe wanted to do was hold Freddie's hand. With an almost disdainful look on her face, she simply took the ends of his fingers while grasping her grandfather's hand. She sensed that Freddie was not wild about touching her hand either. Admittedly, it was all quite foolish to her since she never sat at a table with either parent to eat a meal, let alone saying a blessing. Prayers had always been absent from her home.

As Chloe heard her grandfather say the blessing, she was struck that it seemed natural to him. It came across as being so simple and sincere that it actually touched some unknown cord in her being. She was not into religion, but the prayer, although alien to her reasoning, became calming to her soul. On the street, religion was viewed as being for the weak or as a great avenue where there were numerous opportunities to scam those trying to do good deeds, or who represented charitable organizations. After all, on the street if it could not be used in the game of survival, it would be mocked and considered worthless.

After the prayer, savory pot roast, mashed potatoes, green beans, and homemade rolls were passed around. Chloe took advantage of the amount of food that paraded before her and piled it high on her plate. With her left arm propping her on the table while holding up her knife, she used the fork in her right hand as a pitchfork, swooping food up and tossing each big bite into her mouth. Her taste buds were being awakened by tantalizing flavors that she had only dreamed of in the past, but thought them to be a figment of her imagination. She became totally focused in consuming the food before her and was not aware that she had become the center of attention.

Chloe realized the only noticeable noise in the room was her ravenously consuming the food. As she looked up at her grandfather, she realized he appeared nervous and embarrassed. She then looked around the table to see an array of looks. Marybeth had an amused look on her face, while Sarah was trying to hide a smile behind her hand, J.R.'s face showed a bit of shock, and Freddie's mouth was opened, displaying complete astonishment. However, the one look that was really telling was that of Eloise. She had a horrified look on her face, which had turned white as a sheet. Chloe did not know if her great aunt had suddenly taken ill or if the food was proving to be disagreeable.

Looking at Freddie she chose him as the target to break the silence, "Hey kid, what ya looking at?... Don't you think you better close your mouth before ya catch a fly?"

It was then that Eloise collected her senses, and in a crisp voice broke the blanket of silence over the rest of the table. "First of all Freddie's proper name is not "kid," and in my home each person will be properly addressed by his or her name. Secondly, he's not sure what to do?"

"What do you mean?" Chloe curtly asked.

It was clear that Eloise had an answer ready. "First of all, he doesn't know whether to duck or put up a shield to repel the flying objects of food that are bombarding him from your direction. He's also probably trying to figure out if he's sitting by a horse that chews loudly, a pig that is rooting out its food in a trough, or a predator that's ravenously tearing its prey apart while gulping its food without properly chewing it... And, as for me I've lost my appetite altogether!"

Chloe realized that her eating habits reflected her lack of proper upbringing. Her mother, who was raised to be a lady, didn't have the time or opportunity to teach her daughter any real manners. Granted, her mother often corrected her speech, but not her table manners. The woman who somewhat watched over her during her mother's absence could not corral her enough to teach her much of anything except the piano. The street had been her teacher. Perhaps it had instilled in her the instinct of a predator that must survive at any cost. At that moment she felt exposed and embarrassed.

Chloe fought to hold back a mixture of tears and anger. She almost felt like a wounded animal, cornered by the harsh reality that there was no way that she was going to save face. She did the first thing that came to her mind. She would flee the scene, but before she made an exit she would get in the last word, "I wouldn't want to be responsible for ruining your dinner! I'm out of here!" She grabbed at the beret hanging off the back of her chair and stamped out of the dining room through the front door of the house.

When she stepped onto the veranda, she suddenly felt alone and unsure. Where would she go, except return back to an empty apartment? What would she do, insist on continuing in her unrefined state and remain an outcast in her new existence or choose to accept the ways of the "brave" new world that stood before her. She knew she was at some type of crossroad. It would be her choice and her destiny.

Chloe also knew the despair and secret cries of her own heart. She wanted a normal life, a place that she could call home, a place where she belonged. It was clear to her that she didn't want to return to the mean, cruel streets of the past, but she was not sure if she was ready to face what seemed like the senseless pettiness of do's and don'ts of the present world to finally secure a home for herself.

***

Standing in the gym, Chloe shook her head as she remembered the dining room scene. She had to admit she must have appeared utterly crass to the onlookers at the table. Memories of how lonely she felt on the veranda that day, once again became fresh to her, vividly reminding her of other scenes, events, and decisions that clearly shaped her life from that point. On that day, hurt and bewildered, she had wandered over to a bench and sat down to consider her options. She suddenly felt the soft touch of a hand.

Looking up she saw the understanding face of Marybeth. "Are you okay, Chloe?"

Chloe had a great urge to strike out with some wisecrack, but thought differently when she considered the kind, sincere look on the woman's face. It was then that she went against all of her survival training on the streets and decided to be honest about what she was feeling. In a despairing voice she made an honest confession, "I'll never fit in this world, but I don't know where to go."

Marybeth sat down beside Chloe and put her arm around her shoulders, "Chloe you may not fit in this world right now, but it's your world because you belong here. This is where your family is. This is where your roots are."

"I don't have roots here," Chloe responded in a whiny voice.

"Yes you do because of your mother. This was her family, her home, and at one time her life. The people who knew and loved her are here. You are clearly an extension of her. In fact, for a couple of individuals here, you represent a second chance, which is so very important for them to bring resolution and healing to an open wound."

Chloe guessed who Marybeth was referring to, "Oh sure! I'm probably a burden that my grandfather is stuck with, and a disgrace to the queen in the house," she said as she nodded her head towards the mansion she had just left. "And-d-d will probably prove to be a spectacle to the people of this-s-s …fine community!" She waved her hands toward the quiet street.

Marybeth let out a small chuckle, "No doubt you'll add some spice wherever you go, but to your grandfather you have brought hope back into his life, and as for Eloise, I've no doubt that you will bring…" Marybeth hesitated. Chloe could see she was trying to nail down the appropriate words. "You'll bring purpose to her life."

"How do I bring hope to grandpa and possibly bring some type of purpose to the queen bee who has everything?" Chloe inquired in frustration while looking down at her feet.

Chloe could tell that Marybeth was still somewhat amused, but her hazel eyes quickly flashed a bit of sorrow and her voice became sober. "When your mother left, your grandfather withdrew into a small world of depression that was wrought with the 'what ifs,' followed by guilt as to what he could have done differently, which ended in condemnation. The sorrow became so great for your grandfather that your grandmother spared him from knowing the sordid details of your mother's life. That is why he was not present when your grandmother secretly met with your mother."

Closing her eyes and remembering another time, Marybeth continued to run the reel that comprised the past. It was as if she had located an old, dusty chest that had been locked away in an attic, and was gently extracting each memory to once again resurrect it to confirm its importance. "As for your Aunt Eloise, she had great hopes for your mother. She saw her as continuing the legacy of the Cain family. When your mother ran off with your father, Eloise seemed to emotionally close herself off to avoid ever becoming hurt and vulnerable again."

Marybeth smiled as if she had just captured a tiny, but delightful morsel that she needed to share, then she looked at Chloe once again, "You know when Eloise was sharing with me about you and your grandfather coming here to live, there was a spark of life in her eyes and a hopeful tone to her voice."

In greater frustration, Chloe responded, "I'll never be what the queen wants me to be."

Marybeth was quick with a response, "Chloe, you must always maintain your personal spice. Granted, it'll be challenged, but you must be true to who you are. It is the only way you're going to discover who you are intended to be.

49

"Each of us has a destiny, but there are very few who discover it. You have what it takes to find your destiny. You're very intelligent and you've a type of cleverness when directed in the right way will eventually turn into wisdom."

Marybeth's eyes then narrowed a bit and seemed to penetrate into Chloe's soul as Chloe looked into her kind face, "And, you know as well as I do if you placated your great aunt that it would be the demise of a healthy relationship for the two of you. Your aunt can fare quite well when it comes to challenges."

Chloe could not help but point out what was obvious to her, "But, I'll never be refined. Those... table manners, ...whatever... seem stupid and a waste of time. A person could starve to death just trying to figure out how to eat something around here. To me if it's meant to be eaten, then what's the big diff in how it's done?"

Marybeth broke out in laughter. "Oh, Chloe, how right you are! You do have such a way of cutting through the particulars of a matter. But, in defense of "good manners," they're never out of style. It takes clever people to grasp what we call "protocol." Protocol separates the civilized world from the uncivilized by bringing a certain order and respect to our conduct that will not cause offense to others. It may seem stupid and petty but it puts people on a certain playing field that will ensure mutual respect."

"Who's going to teach me this 'protocol' stuff?" Chloe asked. "I can't see the queen bee doing it because it' will most likely turn into the 'clash of the-e-e Titans.'" Shaking her head she added, "Sure enough it's bound to turn into a bloody war, leaving no witnesses behind."

"I will be glad to help you in that area," Marybeth quickly volunteered her service. "You can come to my house and I'll teach you what you need to know. But, Chloe promise me that you'll see this as a new experience. And, the experience before you is not intended to change who you are, but refine you in such a way that you will be more well-rounded as a person," she paused, "an individual who displays strength in character, excellent ways in conduct, and beauty in self-control."

Chloe knew that Marybeth was talking about things that were foreign to her, but amazingly at the same time she understood what she was saying, even at the ripe age of nine. After all, she had not just dropped into the ways of life; rather, she had been experiencing the different aspects of life for most of her short existence.

Slowing getting up from the bench, Chloe looked at Marybeth, "I'll accept the challenge."

"Good!" Marybeth responded. "Chloe, will you now come back into the house with me?"

"Na, Ms. Marybeth, I think I'll head back to the apartment just to have some time alone. Ya know what I mean."

"Yes I do Chloe."

As Chloe began to walk away, Marybeth called her name. Chloe turned around to face her again. "You know Chloe, you may look like your mother, but mentally and character wise, you're a lot like your Aunt Eloise."

Chloe sheepishly smiled, "Ya, I know, but I don't have to like it," and while letting out a long sigh, shaking her head and drawing her lips into a thin line, she added, "Noooo, not one bit." She turned away and started walking back to the apartment, leaving Marybeth in a state of laugher.

Admittedly, Chloe's decision to accept the challenge put her in another ballpark. She sensed something had changed in her that day. She couldn't explain it, but it caused her to look at things differently.

She first noticed it when it came to her relationship with her grandfather. Even though Chloe had never met her grandfather until the day he came to pick her up from the CPS office, she felt she knew him. Her mother had spoken about her father's kind, tender ways and admitted how much she regretted deeply hurting him. True to what she already knew about him, her grandfather didn't say anything about what transpired at the dinner table. However, Chloe noticed he looked wearier than before the dinner incident. It was clear that he didn't know how to handle the situation. Chloe remembered what Marybeth told her about him and her mother. Since he was informed about her death after the funeral, he didn't have an opportunity to make amends with her or say goodbye. Suddenly, she felt an overwhelming compassion for him. She even became more determined to learn all she could about manners so that he could be proud of her, as well as avoid being swallowed by the same type of regret that plagued her mother to the grave.

Although she occasionally visited her great aunt with her grandfather for tea, and not dinner, Chloe could even appreciate her from a distance. Granted, the battle lines were still in place and for the sake of others, there was a formal agreement that insured a surface peace between them. It was signed and occasionally delivered in an icy silence, but in spite of the chilly or uncertain standoffs, Chloe found herself feeling compassion towards her as well.

Meanwhile, Chloe became a good student in the art of protocol. There were still areas that Chloe was not quite ready to abandon, such as her dress, but Marybeth proved to be a patient and experienced teacher in spite of some of the limitations put on her. However, it became clear at different times that Chloe's old mannerisms had a way of making themselves known.

That became obvious on that infamous day where another important line was drawn. Spending time with Marybeth, Chloe had learned about her life, as well as her daughter's. They were both widows. Marybeth lost her husband to a massive stroke a couple of years prior, but Sarah was a recent war widow. All that was left for Sarah were memories, pictures, and some war medals that were neatly tucked away in her dresser. In spite of their losses, the two women were troopers. They tried to see the silver lining in each dark cloud and brought laughter to those things that were a product of what they referred to as "the lighter side of life." With Chloe, there was no shortage of material that could bring a chuckle, smile, and occasionally laughter to their environment. Chloe didn't feel that they were laughing at her; rather, they were teaching her to laugh at the situation, giving her the means in which to freely enjoy her different experiences.

Chloe's presence at Marybeth's home also brought her into contact with J.R. and Freddie. From watching other brothers interact with each other through her short life, she concluded that they were typical brothers. As the eldest, J.R. felt superior to his younger, irritating brother, while Freddie looked up to his older brother and wanted to play in the same league. However, J.R. spent a lot of time trying to ditch the younger nuisance to pursue more mature activities with his older friends. This set up the union between two unlikely individuals: Chloe and Freddie.

This unlikely pair began to hang around together. Amazingly, they became friends. They took on various roles from cowboys and Indians to soldiers and detectives. They used the woods and some of the abandoned buildings to act out each fantasy and character. Eventually, their most preferred role was that of detective.

They would make up a scenario and set out to solve the mystery. It required wit to identify a possible problem and ingenuity to collect the evidence that would solve the crime. Oftentimes the people in the community became their unwilling suspects and the latest gossip their leads. Tiptoeing quietly they snooped by listening at doors and windows for conversations that offered valid clues, hoping to solve the latest mystery that floated on the waves of suspicious whispers. Occasionally, they had some close calls and were almost caught in the process of acting out their undercover investigations. Still, it was all in good, clean fun.

However, on one infamous day, Chloe found herself in an awkward position. Her great-aunt actually invited her to dinner, along with the same people who had witnessed her first embarrassing fiasco. Perhaps Chloe could redeem herself this time and her aunt would lift the unspoken ban on her from the dinner table. Thanks to Marybeth and Sarah, she now possessed manners that did not cause offense to others. However, Marybeth went one step further and did the impossible. She actually conquered what Chloe felt amounted to Mount Everest, when she managed to talk Chloe into allowing her to do a total makeover on her, which included a new hairdo, a dress, and shoes.

The morning of the dinner and her debut, Chloe found that she could no longer withstand the persuasion of the two ladies and finally subjected herself to curlers, along with a dress rehearsal. The hair makeover was torturous with the shampoo, conditioning, and bits of brown hair falling on her shoulders and the floor with each snipping of the scissors followed by blow drying her hair and the application of the hot curling iron. She couldn't believe that women went to such great lengths to look good, and for what or who! She refrained from looking in the mirror because she felt the mirror would confirm her suspicions that she probably looked like a "dork." With great resolve, she fought the impulse to somehow undo her hair and flee the scene before the finished product could be unveiled.

She had never worn a dress according to her recollection and knew that she would have to be careful of how she sat. Marybeth had been wise enough to find a nice plain pattern for a dress, and was trying to bring it all together with her new fashionable hairstyle.

With her hair rearranged on her head, Chloe slipped into the blue dress with a white collar and then slipped into the new shoes. She felt strange, and when she looked at herself in the mirror, she was somewhat shocked. It seemed that the new hairdo and clothes were highlighting certain aspects of her appearance that had been formerly hidden under a sassy attitude and a dirty gray beret. She actually looked like a girl! She didn't know whether to be excited or depressed about the changes. Although it was strange, uncomfortable, and made her feel somewhat foolish, she actually took a liking to it.

As she stood admiring her first glance of her womanhood at the grand old age of ten, she heard Freddie calling her from outside the window. "Hey, Chloe, where are you?"

Chloe decided that she would see how Freddie would react to her new found identity. When Freddie saw her, instead of being in awe, he seemed a bit put out. "You can't play detective in that get up," he whined.

Chloe felt anger creep up from beneath the surface of a stressful cloud that had already created a blanket of frustration. She quickly shoved back her anger by reminding herself that Freddie was at a dumb age where boys were selfish; therefore, indifferent to anything that did not fit nicely into their plans.

Ignoring Freddie, she walked to the tree swing and with as much grace she could muster up, sat down on it while trying to keep her knees and legs together. She realized that the challenge before her was not simple. The short years of un-lady-like habits had brought her to an uncomfortable place, but she was bound to conquer the unknown wilderness that lay before her. Now at age ten, she could easily change mannerisms, but she knew that it would take resolve and patience to make them a natural response.

As she was thinking of the challenge before her, J.R.'s mocking voice broke through her thoughts. "What do we have here, a Miss Princess?"

Chloe turned and scowl at him. "What's it to ya, scum?"

"Wow, the Miss Princess knows how to talk trash. Maybe, you need to keep your mouth shut so you will not disturb your new image," J.R. quickly retorted.

"And I guess you've become an expert on royalty," Chloe responded in a huff.

Freddie was quietly witnessing the encounter between his older brother and Chloe. When he heard Chloe's last statement, he excitedly interjected, "We're of European royalty. In fact my full name is Fredrick Commodore Reinhardt. I was named after a relative that was not only of a royal family but he was an officer in the military."

"Wow, I'm impressed. What about J.R? Surely, J.R. stands for something royal." Chloe was clearly setting up the gullible Freddie to spill the beans.

"Shut up Freddie, it's none of her business as to what my name is," J.R. piped in.

However, Freddie was clearly ignoring his brother's admonition and fell into Chloe's trap. "J.R. was named not only after royalty but a great statesman."

"Shut up Freddie!" J.R.'s voice was beginning to rise in panic.

By this time Chloe was becoming quite interested in what the initials J.R. stood for. She wanted to know what he was hiding. After all, it could prove to be ammunition for her in any future confrontations with him. It was also clear that Freddie was on a roll and was not about to be prevented from revealing the truth.

"J.R. stands for Jerome Reginald Reinhardt." It was almost as if J.R.'s full name tumbled out of Freddie's mouth.

"Jerome, my my…what an interesting name. Should I officially call you Jerome?" Chloe asked with a smirk on her face.

Through clenched teeth, J.R. made his preference known, "My preferred name is J.R."

Chloe clearly discovered that J.R. was touchy about his full name and she couldn't blame him, but she couldn't help but send her digs deeper. In a snide way she sent the next jab, "You don't like Jerome, well how about Reginald?"

J.R.'s apparent frustration was clearly coming to the foreground, and in a louder tone, he made his feelings known. "My name is J.R.!"

Shooting another dig at him, Chloe went further in her attempt to unravel the haughty young man. "You must not like Reginald either, how about Reggie for short?"

"Enough is enough!" By this time J.R. was close to shouting. "You need to shut up about my name Chloe, or else!"

"Or else what Reggie? You don't scare me with your threats!" she shouted back.

As if to walk away from the shouting match, J.R. turned sideways and glared at her with intense penetration, "If you were not a dumb girl, I would show you 'the what else.'"

Chloe felt the old street wise tomboy in her rise up in great indignation. She would give this young man an opportunity to defend his honor and carry out his dare. "Well don't let me, being a girl, stop you at carrying out your 'what else!'"

That was the moment when Chloe took off out of the swing like a shot and tackled J.R. from the side. They both fell to the ground and begin to roll. Freddie later admitted they look like two cats fiercely rolling on the ground, trying to get the upper hand in subduing the other. J.R. was trying to fend off Chloe's fists by grabbing her arms, but she proved quick and efficient. She even managed to hit him in his left eye and cheek area with a quick jab from her right hand.

The encounter only stopped when two pairs of hands managed to separate the two and stand them upright, facing each other. Those hands belonged to Marybeth and Sarah.

"What's going on here," Sarah asked in a demanding tone!

"Nothin," came the reply from both Chloe and J.R at the same time.

"For something being nothing, you both look in sad shape," Sarah huffily countered.

Chloe could see some scratches on J.R. along with a welt on his left cheek, while his left eye was red and no doubt was about to take on a rainbow of colors.

In a light hearted way, Marybeth broke what seemed to be a stalemate, "Both of you need to come into the house and get cleaned up. We have a dinner to go to."

It was at that time Chloe remembered her attire and all the work that the two ladies went through to make her presentable for the dinner. She had no idea what she looked like and dreaded what the mirror would inevitably reveal. She felt her body go into a slump. Head down, shoulders drooping, she allowed Marybeth's hand to guide her to what seemed like the chambers of doom. All her attempts to become lady-like were undone in a few minutes by a stupid dare.

True to Chloe's suspicions, the mirror revealed that she was a sight to avoid. Her hair was in total disarray, her dress dirty and tattered in places and her nice shoes had telltale scuffle marks on them. All in all she looked like a girl who just came from a day on the streets, only she was wearing a dirty, tattered dress.

Chloe felt miserable. She was still that obnoxious street girl. It all appeared hopeless to her. The verdict was in: Womanhood would elude her and she would never fit into the family or the community. She felt doomed and conceded in her mind that the one thing she could be certain of was being banned from her great-aunt's table the rest of her life.

As Chloe was shaking her head in dismay, she caught a reflection in the mirror of Marybeth slightly grinning.

"I'm a funny sight, ain't I Marybeth?" Chloe stated in complete dismay.

"I'm not laughing at you; rather, I'm quite amused that you brought my grandson down in such a manner. You know young men like him need to be brought down a few notches once in a while to show them they are not as clever or strong as they think they are." In a more serious tone she added, "Chloe regardless of how lady-like you become, you will always be a fighter, and that is alright. However, you might reconsider the methods you use to express yourself in such situations. Now let's get you cleaned up and ready for dinner."

"It's no use. Everything is ruined," Chloe whined.

"I must admit, that the situation before us might prove to be a bit challenging, but it's not impossible." Marybeth answered with determination in her voice and on her face.

Sure enough, a whirlwind of activity ensued that caused Chloe to feel like she had been put through a washing machine and then hung out to dry in a gale. The results even surprised Chloe. Granted, between Marybeth and Sarah, they had to buy her a new dress and shine her shoes, but they managed to get her cleaned up, her hair washed and restyled in a way that even seemed more pleasing to Chloe. By the time dinner came, Chloe was ready to reveal her latest makeover to the world. Surely, the transformation would ensure her reinstatement to the dinner table of the grand matriarch of the Cain household.

Chloe could tell her grandfather was surprised and excited about his granddaughter's new appearance. He took her hand and the two walked happily to the front veranda of Eloise's home. As the group approached the front door, it was decided for the purpose of protocol who would escort whom to the table. Chloe's grandfather would escort Marybeth, Freddie, his mother, while Marybeth instructed J.R. to escort Chloe to the dinner table. Even though there were attempts to cover up J.R.'s black eye and bruised check, it was still noticeable. Chloe was sure that J.R. would balk at such an idea, but instead he nodded in agreement.

As they entered the door, Chloe's great-aunt was quite surprised to see her great-niece in her new attire. "I must say, you look like a young lady, Chloe. Well done."

"Thank you Aunt Eloise, but the well done must go to Marybeth and Sarah."

With a relieved look on her face, Eloise beckoned them towards the dining room. Chloe's grandfather not only gave his arm to Marybeth, but offered it to his sister, while Freddie offered his to his mother. Chloe and J.R. were the last to enter the dining room.

J.R. offered his arm to Chloe. In a quiet voice, he broke the wall of silence that had been present between them, "You look very nice Chloe."

Chloe had reached her hand out and taken his arm, but found herself taken back by his statement. She looked into his eyes and face to see if he meant it. Rather than seeing a smug, mocking look on his face, she actually could detect a certain humility and sincerity in him.

In spite of being a bit shocked, she was able to respond in a way that showed she, too, had been disciplined, "Whyyy...thank you...J.R," she quietly answered.

Letting out a sigh of relief and a smile on his face, J.R. responded, "Thanks for not calling me Jerome or Reginald."

With a glint of mischief in her eye, Chloe teasingly replied, "You're neither Jerome nor Reginald, but you could be a Reggie."

J. R. chuckled, "Tell you what. You can call me Reggie when we're alone. But, it'll be between the two of us. Deal!"

Chloe let out a small giggle, "That's a deal, Reggie."

The impatient voice of Eloise penetrated their conversation. "Dinner will be served when all parties are properly seated at the table."

J.R. and Chloe smile knowingly at each other. "Are you ready?" J.R. asked Chloe.

"I'm ready, Reggie." Chloe replied.

They walked arm in arm into the dining room and like a real gentleman, J.R. pulled out the chair for her. Chloe surmised that she would have to keep calling J.R. by his initials to avoid forgetting their agreement, but when special opportunities would arise, she would call him that special name when she was assured others were not within earshot. Clearly, she had earned the respect and right to do so and she was not about to concede it, but now she would have to earn the right to sit at her aunt's table. No doubt such a feat would prove to be a breeze compared to the battle that had claimed such casualties as her dress along with some of her newly acquired womanhood.

***

"Ahhh…, Reggie, that infamous battle seems to be many lifetimes ago," Chloe softly whispered to herself, smiling at the memory.

She did win the right to sit at her aunt's table that fateful night. Chloe could tell that her aunt was quite pleased with the transformation that had come over her great-niece. In a way she had gained the respect of two very important people in one day. It was obvious to her that respect had clearly changed the dynamics of her relationships with both J.R. and her aunt.

The scoreboard light once again caught her attention. Who would think that a simple scoreboard would play such a vital role in a person's life? It is not that she was an athlete whose victories or defeats had been attested to by the scoreboard; rather, it marked the place where some pivotal points of her life occurred. In a sense it revealed the score when it came to some of her relationships.

The first important point was meeting Vanessa Adams under the scoreboard. Chloe was 13 and she was finding that both she and Freddie were outgrowing their relationship. He had found other friends and interests which left her alone. It was clear that it was an awkward time for Chloe, and that she didn't fit into the girlish cliques of the school. She saw most of the girls her age as being silly, as well as taking themselves too seriously. They were trying to capture adulthood before they had successfully experienced and survived their adolescent years. In her mind, they incessantly bored her as to their so-called "maturity" with their silly plans, games, and airs to impress each other as well as the opposite sex.

One day while standing under the scoreboard watching the different activities in the gym, Vanessa came up to her and introduced herself. She was a new girl in town and had spotted Chloe standing alone. By all appearances Vanessa didn't fit in the cliques because she was slightly heavy and tall for her age. Chloe was a bit shocked at her friendly overture but quickly discovered that she was what Chloe considered a real person with some common sense. They immediately hit it off and from that point a friendship developed that enriched both of their lives. Even though Vanessa was a grade behind, they always arranged to meet each other at the scoreboard during their lunch hour or after school to discuss their personal challenges and plan their other activities. Vanessa proved to be a true friend. She was always there for Chloe and Chloe reciprocated by always being there for Vanessa except on one occasion.

That occasion had to do with the opposite gender. Within a year's time Vanessa had blossomed into a beautiful flower. She lost weight and even though she was taller than most in her class she managed to wrap it up in a type of graciousness that gave the appearance of royalty. Needless to say, as Vanessa neared her 13th year, the boys in the upper class begin to pay attention to her. They would try to gain Vanessa's attention whenever she and Chloe were trying to discuss the happenings in their life or their schedule, especially when they were under that infamous scoreboard and the boys were practicing basketball. The main crux of the problem was that Chloe could tell Vanessa liked the attention.

Chloe had guy friends like J.R. and Freddie, but not boyfriends. She thought the games and tension that existed between the genders of her classmates were close to being ridiculous. She perceived that much of their activities towards each other were for the most part silly and awkward. It was clear that they were inexperienced and were trying to come across as experienced in the art of romance and courting. She would have nothing to do with it, and for her friend to be caught up with such nonsense was the same as treason in Chloe's mind.

It was on a certain Friday after school that their relationship hit a crisis point. They had agreed to meet at the scoreboard to walk home together in order to figure out some plans for the weekend. When

Chloe arrived, it was obvious that Vanessa was definitely responding to one of the school's most popular upperclassmen's advancements. Chloe's temper and patience hit its peak and she fled the scene before she exploded and experienced a meltdown in front of Vanessa and some of her classmates.

She remembered walking down the main street with her emotions in turmoil. She was angry, hurt, disappointed, and felt abandoned. When she reached the corner of an intersection, she paused under a streetlamp, struggling to understand, and compose her emotions. Suddenly, the voice of her great-aunt cut through her thoughts.

Since she had gained the right to sit at the matriarch's dinner table, the two of them had managed to get beyond the icy standoff to develop a somewhat surface relationship that was pleasant enough for both of them. However, Chloe wasn't sure that it would advance past the shallow waters without them experiencing possible undercurrents and even some riptides that could disrupt their calm surface at any moment.

"Chloe, you look upset. Is there something wrong?" Eloise inquired.

Chloe looked at her aunt to determine if she was really concerned. Her steely blue eyes seemed to be a little softer than the first time she met her.

"There is nothing wrong, everything is peachy," Chloe curtly retorted.

"If everything is peachy, why are you looking as if you lost your best friend?"

Chloe held her head down. Tears were close to spilling and only silence would not betray her emotional turmoil. Eloise, ignoring her struggle to maintain her composure, pertly asked, "Chloe, I'm going to the ice cream parlor for some sherbet. Why don't you join me, and perhaps we can get to know one another better?"

Chloe felt too emotionally weak to resist her great-aunt's suggestion, so she nodded her head and begin to follow her into the ice cream parlor like a whipped puppy.

Once settled at a table, her aunt ordered sherbet, while Chloe decided to give in to her foul state of mind by ordering a sundae with all the trimmings. She waited for her aunt to make a comment about the calories, but she said nothing.

After a few minutes of silence, Eloise broke the silence, "Chloe, don't you think it would be better to talk about what is wrong than to emotionally burst at the seams or drown it in a sundae? You look like a volcano that is ready to blow its top."

Chloe had tried to hide her emotional chaos, but for her aunt to see it, it had to be quite obvious. She knew if she didn't talk about it, her emotions would seethe and eventually come out in some destructive way.

"The truth is, Aunt Eloise, my friendship with Vanessa is over with!"

"Did you have a fight?" Eloise asked in disbelief.

"No!"

"I don't understand? You and Vanessa have been inseparable for the last couple of years. What happened?"

As Chloe tried to formulate the words in her mind, she realized that she did not have a legitimate reason for the breakdown of her relationship with Vanessa. She was almost embarrassed to admit to her aunt why she was so upset with her "former" friend. However, as she looked at her aunt, she knew that the matriarch wasn't about to drop the subject. It was then that Chloe decided to confess everything.

Eloise quietly listened to Chloe explanation of how her prized relationship with Vanessa went awry.

As Chloe was relating Vanessa's latest infraction, she was seeing clearly that her attitude and response had been silly. She had no good reason to act in such a way, except that Vanessa's actions were causing her to feel awkward and out of place, hurting her feelings and making her feel abandoned.

After her explanation, Chloe quietly waited for her aunt to chide her for such silliness, but Eloise remained silent.

It was Chloe who broke the silence, "I know this sounds stupid, Aunt Eloise."

"Not stupid, just very human." Eloise replied, "Chloe, you've been bitten by the green- eyed monster of jealousy."

"Jealousy, no way! You can't tell me you agree with kids my age getting caught up with romance and dating. It's just plain dumb, and I thought Vanessa was smarter than that!"

"You're right Chloe, I don't agree with young people in that age bracket being focused on such activities. However, young people your age are experiencing changes in their bodies and emotions. Since, they don't have experience or wisdom backing them up, they often go with the emotional swings of these new changes. The truth is, it is a natural reaction."

In frustration, Chloe stated, "I don't have such feelings or emotions that would prompt me to run out and try to find some boyfriend."

Eloise smiled, "Chloe, young people have the same challenges, but it doesn't necessarily happen at the same age or time period. Girls are like buds on a flower in the gardens of the world, ready to be admired, and then picked before their beauty and strength fades with the seasons of life. Some bloom early spring and others late spring, while the boys are like saplings in the forest. They too shoot forth their leaves and fruits at various times in the seasons of growth and change. However, the transformations that take place in such tender buds are part of life. Nothing can stop the cycles of life. Vanessa is blooming right now. And, like all young ladies who are trying to come to terms with their worth and purpose in this world, she can easily be swayed by flattery and attention."

"That'll never happen to me!" Chloe firmly declared.

Eloise chuckled. "Chloe, it'll happen to you one day when you least expect it, and probably with the young man you would least suspect, but meanwhile you probably feel like a lone wallflower, a mere lifeless decoration that is being overlooked by your best friend and peer. You feel abandoned because you can't go where Vanessa is in order to share her experience and ensure a common ground. Without that common ground there is a feeling of separation on your part. Such feelings of separation translate into betrayal and hurt and usually turn into jealousy.

"In fact, there was an incident when your mother was jealous over Sarah being caught up with some guy; and, like you, your mother was ready to call off the friendship."

"What happened?" Chloe curiously inquired.

Her aunt looked into her eyes before responding, "Clearer heads eventually prevailed because the friendship had merit and the two of them realized it and managed to salvage it.

"Jealousy is a foul creature, Chloe. It torments, isolates, destroys, and will ultimately cause some type of embarrassment. We all have it but we must be honest about it when it raises its ugly head. You need to be honest about it so that you can put this matter in the right perspective."

"Regardless of when I bloom, I still can't imagine giving into such silly ways." Chloe retorted.

Eloise's knowing look was preparing Chloe for some bits of wisdom. "It's true that our decisions will determine to what extent we get caught up with the notions, ideas, and feelings in regard to the opposite sex. We can spur the notions and reject ideas, but feelings have a tendency of taking us captive in unlikely ways. Crushes and first love make up those initial feelings. They are often escalated by immature notions, cultural influences, and overactive hormones. If a person keeps grounded when such feelings unexpectedly erupt on the scene, the individual will eventually discover if there is any merit and depth to them."

Her aunt paused with a sigh before she continued, "I have the greatest confidence that you will keep grounded in such matters, Chloe, but don't deceive yourself that you'll be immune from such feelings. Such deception will make you more vulnerable to the power of persuasion such feelings can have on your emotions and affections. You must guard yourself and keep the matters of the young tender heart in perspective."

"Have you experienced such feelings, Aunt Eloise?" Chloe asked.

Eloise smiled as memories were coming to the forefront, "Yes, I have. The initial feelings are glorious, then they become confusing and tormenting because you don't know what to do with them, and if not reciprocated, you become miserable. Such feelings can prove to be bittersweet.

"You didn't give way to them, did you Aunt Eloise? After all, you arrr..."

"An old maid," chuckled her aunt. "My present state started out being a choice, but eventually it became a matter of convenience which turned into a state of comfort, and now It's a habit, a lifestyle.

"Everything is a matter of choice, Chloe that will graduate into some kind of habitual state. This state will often become well-guarded by convenience and comfort, including harnessing or ignoring feelings. You must honestly decide whether you allow feelings to dictate to you or whether you define how those feelings are going to influence you.

"I'm in my present state because of what I first considered to be honorable choices, many of them motivated by my sense of duty to continue the family legacy in this community; but others because of suspicion and fear. Sadly, I've come to realize that different experiences in life can pass one by when the individual settles for what becomes normal to them."

Surprised, Chloe responded, "Suspicion and fear—I don't understand, Aunt Eloise. You would not be the type to fear others."

Eloise smiled at her great-niece. "Fear comes in many forms. My greatest fear was being vulnerable to hurt and failure. Due to money and community position, my suspicion was that I couldn't trust possible beaus of being sincere in their intentions toward me. I didn't realize that my father had transposed his suspicion towards perspective beaus on me, and sadly I transposed them on your mother."

At the mention of her relationship with Chloe's mother, Chloe could tell that other memories were being awakened in her great-aunt. She knew if she was going to be given any insight into her mother's life by

63

her aunt she would have to remain quiet, while Eloise processed her feelings and became comfortable in talking about them.

A bit hesitant, her aunt managed to continue, "Chloe, I loved your mother very much. I saw her as the one who would continue the family legacy. On one end your grandfather protected her too much and on the other end I was pushing her to be someone she was not. Without knowing it both your grandfather and I made her weak instead of strong. We failed to prepare her for life. In essence, we failed to let her experience the different emotional bumps that come during adolescence. These bumps not only serve as small preludes to the gale winds that come in adulthood but they prepare immature individuals to face and stand in them. In the end, your mother felt smothered by your grandfather and resented me. I don't have to tell you the disastrous outcome. You became the recipient of the fallout.

Chloe realize that this conversation was a turning point between her and her aunt. For the first time Eloise was allowing her great-niece to see into her soul. No doubt there would be future scrimmages between them, but there would also be the common ground where their two souls could meet again in mutual respect and understanding.

Aunt Eloise continued to share her nuggets of wisdom. "You're a stronger individual than your mother, but you are human. You need to keep in mind that during this vulnerable time of life, beaus will come and go. Puppy love will fade with each new crush. New feelings will subside with reality, but a good friend only comes along once in a lifetime and can never be replaced.

"What I have been reminded of lately Chloe, is that we may lose our rank in our close friend's life, but we will never lose our emotional place of importance in their hearts."

Curious, Chloe inquired, "You were recently reminded?"

"Yes I was. It was during the time your mother left that another devastating separation occurred with a dear friend of mine. It was my hurt and anger that caused the separation, just like your unwarranted hurt and anger could cause a separation between you and Vanessa if you allow it. When I recently approached my friend to reestablish our relationship, that dear friend reminded me that a special place had been prepared just for me, and that no one could fill it but me.

"Chloe, you must remember that the attention of young people is fickle because emotions are like roaming waves on the ocean of life. They are struggling to be established in their lives, to find their place in this world. However, the places people make in their hearts for others, such as dear friends, will not change unless it is torn down by neglect, abuse, and rejection."

64

Chloe knew her aunt was right. "Why does life have to be so confusing and decisions so difficult? Why can't it be simple? Does it have to change in such a traumatic way?" Chloe asked in a despairing voice.

"Everything must experience a type of birth and growth. But, for both to take place, the infant stages of life must travel through a type of channel of death. It is like the butterfly. Before it reaches its potential to reflect beauty, fly, and reproduce, it must go through metamorphosis. No one can see the complete transformation because it is taking place within a cocoon. However, its initial stage of being a caterpillar must completely cease for it to reach it ultimate potential as a butterfly with its designated beauty and glory.

"People start out in an infant stage like a caterpillar, and the teenage years are like the cocoon. If teenagers are in a good family unit, they are somewhat protected while a type of metamorphosis takes place in their bodies. But, the greatest transformation occurs in the soul. How they handle the changes within, and the decisions they make about God, relationships, and life, will determine if good character will be forged in them. Character will determine the beauty that is formed in the soul, the heights to which they will reach, and how they will manifest the life that has been, and is, being developed in them.

"Chloe don't let the green-eyed monster or the experiences of testing the waters of new feelings and territory defile or destroy your friendship with Vanessa."

Once again the scoreboard lights brought Chloe back to the present. Chloe's aunt had been right about everything. The lights of the scoreboard reminded her that she indeed discovered that she was very human, possessing jealousy, as well as being subject to the unexpected.

The first memory that rose out of the ashes of the past was an unexpected event. She was sixteen, and it was under the scoreboard that she encountered the first leap of her heart towards the most unlikely guy. It was at a school dance. Chloe was never into such activities, but her friends encouraged her to attend. As she stood under the scoreboard like an inanimate wallflower, she secretly wished that some guy, any guy, would at least come up and ask her for one dance. J.R. had a date, but must have observed her plight and came to the rescue. What most people didn't know is that as a good friend, she had secretly taught J.R. all the waltzes and modern dances so he could take the most popular girl in school to the dances.

65

Once J.R. exposed Chloe's dancing abilities in that first dance to the rest of the guys, she spent the rest of the night floating across the floor in melodious grandeur. It was not until the second to the last dance that her heart fluttered in a temporary ecstasy across the arena of her soul, arousing her affections for the tall, nice-looking young man who graciously asked her for a dance. Just as her aunt had warned her, the feelings that were swirling around her soul were glorious, but confusing. She never would have suspected this young man as being someone whom she would have such feelings towards. He was one of the most popular guys in school. He could have any girl he wanted, and as a result she knew he would never see her in any romantic light; therefore, she had to take her feelings captive and secretly lock them away in a guarded room.

As for her friendship with Vanessa, she had taken the wise advice of her aunt, allowing reason and not jealousy to prevail. The friendship remained intact through some rough waters, but each challenge caused the friendship to become seasoned with experience and maturity.

As friends, they were there for each other. They went through various stages of growth, exploration, and even through deep valleys of crises. The memories of those deep valleys were vivid in Chloe's mind. The sights, sounds, and feelings surrounding those times seemed as fresh as if they happened yesterday.

The first deep valley involved Chloe. She was fifteen at the time. Like always she was standing under the scoreboard waiting for Vanessa so they could go for a coke. However, it was her aunt Eloise who found her under the panel. A school official had helped her aunt locate her. The minute she saw her aunt's face she knew something was terribly wrong.

"There you are Chloe," were the first words out of her aunt's mouth.

With almost a panic in her voice Chloe was quick to respond, "What's wrong, Aunt Eloise!"

"Come! Your grandfather has had a heart attack. We must get to the hospital!"

"How bad is it?" Chloe inquired as she matched her aunt's hurried stride through the gym door, down the hallway and out the main entrance doors of the school.

Eloise's tone was urgent and abrupt as she answered, "I'm not going to try to soften the truth for you Chloe. It doesn't look good."

It seemed like time stood still for a moment to only restart in slow motion. As Chloe struggled to process this latest event, the same question haunted her as she tried to break through the shock. First her grandmother, then her mother, and now, will it be her grandfather as well? Must she lose everyone she loves?

Everything became a blur for Chloe as she tried to wrestle with the rage that was rising up inside of her against what seemed to be unfair. In her short time on earth, sorrow had weaved much of the tapestry of her life. The last six years with her grandfather had brought stability and happiness to her life. But it was clear, that the thread of sorrow was being added once again to the mosaic of her life.

When she saw her grandfather attached to various machines and tubes, it was reminiscent of her mother's last days in the hospital. She had managed to tough it out through those long days of watching her mother slowly die, but she couldn't bear watching death steal her grandfather's life.

Chloe fled from her grandfather's bedside into the fresh fall air. What would she do, where would she go? The essence of her world lay in a hospital bed, fighting for his life, and in a strange way fighting for her life. She went to her one place of refuge, to the store, where she could become lost in her piano music--music that would express the despair of her soul.

She didn't know how long she played the haunting melodies that not only revealed the melancholy state of her soul, but the anger that was seething beneath the dark blanket of despair. When she was confronted with, "Why did this have to happen," she would distinctly pound each note and chord out on the keys, and when she came to the, "What if grandfather dies," great sorrow, as an unseen entity, took hold of her fingers, as if to direct harmonious movements across the piano. She could tell her feelings were being poured out through her fingers as the music was expressing the tragedy that confronted her.

Chloe had become lost in her music until she sensed a presence in the room. She quickly quit playing the piano and pulled her hands down into her lap. It was then that she turned around to see her great-aunt and Vanessa quietly observing her with a surprised look on their faces.

"I didn't know you played the piano, Chloe," commented her aunt. "Obviously, you have a natural ability to make that piano not only sing, but express your heart and soul."

"What are doing here?" Chloe asked in a despondent way, while turning back to face the keyboard of the piano.

Eloise had her hand on Vanessa's back. As if guiding Vanessa, they both moved slowly towards Chloe. "You have a lot of people who are concerned about you and are at this moment looking for you to make sure you are alright. Vanessa and I had a hunch you might be here."

Chloe retorted, "I would appreciate it if you leave me alone."

"We can't," her aunt replied.

Looking at her aunt, "What do you mean you can't?" Chloe angrily replied.

"Because right now you need us, and I need you." Eloise paused, seemingly to collect her own emotions. "I too love your grandfather. He has always been a dear brother to me, as well as a wonderful friend. Like you, I am afraid of losing him."

Chloe aunt's response snapped her out of her personal pity party. She could see a mixture of sadness and tears in her aunt's eyes. Chloe could restrain herself no longer. She rose from the piano bench and flew into her aunt's arms. Both of them quietly wept as they clung to each other, while Vanessa gently put her hand on Chloe's back to let her know she also was there to support her.

With her head buried in her aunt's shoulder, Chloe asked, "What can we do for grandpa, Aunt Eloise?"

"Pray, my dear." Eloise responded.

Chloe pulled back in exasperation. "Pray! I prayed for my mother to get well and she still died. Pray! You have to be kidding!"

Chloe's excited exclamation was interrupted when J.R. and Freddie came into the store to let Eloise know that they had not yet located Chloe. Both of them were relieved to see that she was in good hands and Chloe was relieved that her emotional state was being somewhat defused by the interruption.

Eloise motioned all of them to sit down on whatever furniture was available in the small space. She instructed J.R. to call his grandmother on his cell phone to inform them that Chloe had been found.

Eloise then directed her attention towards Chloe, "Chloe, your grandfather wanted me to give you something if anything should happen to him. He had been waiting to personally give it to you at the right time. To me this would be the right time."

The great matriarch located a small key in the little pouch that had been secured in her handbag. She took the key and went to the old desk that Chloe's grandfather used to do his bookkeeping. She pulled out a small mental box from the top drawer.

Chloe recognized the box. Her grandfather had kept personal things in it and always kept it under lock and key. If she showed any curiosity towards it, he reminded her that since it contained matters that were none of her business that she must not pay any mind to it.

As Eloise opened the box lid, she dug through the papers and odds and ends and located a size 10 envelope. She turned and faced Chloe. Slightly tapping the end of the envelope on the palm of her other hand, she began her explanation. "I have read the contents of this letter. In a way it has set me free and I believe it has the potential to give you direction and hope. Since these young people are your friends, I feel it is only right that you be allowed to share this moment with them. Perhaps they can assist you as you wade through any possible emotional reactions."

Eloise handed the envelope to Chloe. It was addressed to Leon Cain, but Chloe immediately recognized her mother's handwriting. Her hands shook as she took the four-page handwritten letter out of the envelope to read it. Tears blurred her eyes, making it impossible for her to read. She handed the letter back to her aunt and asked her to read it.

"Dear Dad,

There is so much to say and so little time to say it. When you receive this letter I will have moved on from this present world. I am so thankful I have already made peace with mother, but now I need to make amends with you and Aunt Eloise, so will you please pass this letter on to her.

First of all I want to ask both of you for forgiveness. I had no intention of hurting either of you. At that terrible time in my life I felt stifled and became lost in confusing feelings. I didn't know where to turn or run to, and Bud presented himself as my savior who would make sense out of my world. I was not running away from something as much as I was trying to run to something, to find myself outside of your stifling protection and Aunt Eloise's plans for me.

I have to admit that at that time I questioned both you and Aunt Eloise's intentions toward me, but hindsight has shown me, you both wanted the best for me. However, in both of your attempts to protect and guide me, you made me weak and vulnerable. I am not writing this to hurt either one of you for it was my choices that brought me to this place; rather, it is my way to prepare you both to receive my most precious treasure, Chloe.

Dad, you and Eloise are the only real responsible relatives that Chloe will have after my departure. In a way she represents a second chance for all of us. For me, she will become an extension of what could have been, and for you and Aunt Eloise, she could very well represent an opportunity to establish a real legacy where our family is concerned.

The legacy I am talking about is not a physical one, but a spiritual one. As I face death, I have been reminded of all those times you both insisted I attend church, Sunday school, and other church activities. Remember when I finally, at the age of ten, asked everyone at Aunt Eloise's dinner table about spiritual matters concerning the salvation of my soul? It was Aunt Eloise, who answered all my questions. In front of you and Mom and others, she led me to Christ.

I was so excited, but you know the rest of the story. I left Jesus behind and became lost in a world of seduction, lust, delusion, and despair. Sadly, it has taken me facing my own death to be reminded of the life I once experienced and enjoyed in Christ. I want you to know I have repented of my wayward ways and once again made peace with my Jesus, and now I am ready to go home.

However, I am concerned about Chloe. She is all I am leaving behind. She is my precious gift from God, the only good thing that came out of my relationship with Bud. And, now I entrust her to you and Aunt Eloise. I am thankful she will never be weak like me, but I know underneath she is angry at God and life and is not ready to listen to me about such matters. She puts on a tough front, but I know she is afraid, deeply hurt and feels disconnected and lost to what is real and lasting. This is why my dying wish is, that like myself, she is also offered the gift of heaven and the opportunity to discover the everlasting legacy of eternal life by both you and Aunt Eloise.

You need to know I have and always will love you both.

Affectionately,

Your prodigal daughter,

Laura

Silence enveloped the room as each person present wrestled with the emotions the letter had stirred up within them. The changes in her

70

great aunt and some of her insight about her mother now made sense to Chloe. Chloe's mother had made her peace with her aunt, bringing healing to Eloise's soul.

The letter also showed that in the end Laura Cain Merriweather had become a strong, courageous woman. Here was a young woman, who in the prime of her life bravely faced death. In a way she had discovered the secret of life in the face of death and resolved to pass the secret on to her daughter.

It was Chloe who finally broke the silence. "What did my mom mean by referring to herself as the prodigal daughter?"

By this time Aunt Eloise had seated herself in front of the desk in preparation to answer any questions or concerns, while Vanessa sat beside Chloe on the piano bench, J.R. sat in an old comfortable living room chair among the many other sale items in the room, while Freddie plopped himself on the arm of the chair.

"Chloe, there is a story about a prodigal son in the Bible. Like your mother, he left home to find his life. In fact, he took his inheritance and wasted everything on foolish activities. He totally lost his way and eventually he ended up scrambling for food in a pigpen. It was there that he came to his senses and realized that being a servant in his father's house was better than wrestling with pigs over food in their own pigpen. That is when he decided to go home."

Obviously engrossed in the story, Vanessa could not help but ask the question, "What happened to him when he came home?"

Eloise smiled at her eagerness to know, "His father saw him afar off, ran to meet him and embraced him. He welcomed him home by putting the best robe on him, a ring on his finger, and calling for a celebration. The older brother was not pleased and was very jealous that his younger brother was being treated like a returning hero especially since he wasted his inheritance. The father made this timeless declaration to his eldest son, 'For your brother was dead, and is alive again, and was lost, and is now found.'"

Chloe was disturbed by the fact that she somehow was lost and needed to be found. "Aunt Eloise, how is it that I am lost? I don't understand; I know where I am."

"Chloe, being lost in this way means to be spiritually lost. When a person is spiritually lost, it means he or she is lost to God. Even though God knows how to find the individual, the person doesn't know how to find Him. In fact, like you most people do not realize they are lost and need to be found."

"Why are people lost to God?" Chloe asked.

Eloise was ready with an answer. "It is because of something called sin. Sin is rebellion against God. Because of sin reigning in man, he's not interested in loving, obeying, or pleasing God who is his Creator. Like the prodigal son in the story, man has basically left God to go do his own thing, while squandering what God has provided for him. Like the father in the story, God is waiting for his wayward children to realize that the world is one big pigpen and ultimately will leave their soul barren."

Chloe impatiently wanted to cut to the chase, "Aunt Eloise, if God knows where we are, why doesn't He find us? It doesn't make sense!"

"There are a couple of reasons why God does not just find someone. The first reason is, everyone has their own free will. If a person sees no need to be found or doesn't want to be found, they'll avoid being found; therefore, rejecting God's overtures. Secondly, the prodigal son had to come home under his own volition, before he could properly receive from his father. God desires us to come home so He can give us the life He has for us, but we must want to. We must see our need to come home and seek forgiveness for our wayward ways before we can be restored."

Beating Chloe to the draw, Vanessa asked, "If someone wants to find their way home, what would it require?"

Eloise grinned at Vanessa, while glancing at Chloe, "You must be born again from above."

In a frustrated tone, Chloe chimed in. "Born again, that doesn't make any sense, Aunt Eloise!"

"It does if you consider it in light of the metamorphosis process of a butterfly. When you are born again, it means you receive a new life from heaven that will make you a new creation. As you take on the new, the old will cease to be. It is a spiritual life; in fact, it is the life of Jesus Christ."

"Who is this Jesus, Aunt Eloise," Chloe asked.

"He is God's only Son," Freddie piped in.

"That's right," Eloise added. "He is God's solution to the sin problem. Sin causes a vacuum in our soul that often torments and drives us. We know there is more, but no matter what we try to fill that vacuum with, our soul remains restless and dissatisfied.

"Out of love God sent Jesus to fill that vacuum with His Spirit and life. The Son of God became the bridge that actually closed the gap between man and God that was caused by sin. In order to become what we consider to be the bridge of reconciliation, Jesus had to become a ladder that was able to connect man to the bridge by being lifted on a cross. On that cross He paid a price for our salvation. He tasted death so we can taste everlasting life."

"Can't a person simply be good to make it to heaven?" Vanessa asked.

"Good question, Vanessa," Eloise replied. "Because we are born into a fallen state that is inclined towards sin and darkness, we are incapable of always doing right and being good. Granted, our ways might be decent, but they will not be counted as right or good by God. The Bible tells us our best is like filthy rags to our holy God. The only way we can be considered right is if God sees His Son in us and the only goodness we can possess will originate from the Spirit of God dwelling within us."

"Going to church doesn't make you a Christian either," J.R. added.

"You are right J.R." Eloise exclaimed. "It's a tendency of most people to think if they're affiliated to religion through family affiliation with a particular church and have regular church attendance, that they're on their way to heaven. For a person to be saved they must individually receive the gift of eternal life from the Father above."

It was clear that the words Chloe's aunt was speaking were hitting their mark. Although intellectually Chloe was trying to understand the overwhelming awe that was beginning to take hold of her, she was aware that her soul was soaking up the information and her spirit was being quickened in an unsettling, but exciting way.

Chloe had one more question for her aunt, "Why has it taken you so long to share this information with me? Granted, you and grandfather have invited me to the church, but because of my past, the concept of religion was a big-turn off, but this information is not about some religion or church, it is about.t.t..." Chloe struggled with finding the right description.

"It is about a relationship with the living God," her aunt said with an understanding smile. "And, the reason I didn't share it with you Chloe, is because I had rebelliously veered away from the Lord. Remember how I told you about the friend I became separated from?" Chloe shook her head. "Well, that friend was Jesus. I was angry at God because He didn't make things turn out the way I wanted them to turn out. This was especially true when it came to your mother. I felt the Lord had let go of your mother, but as her letter showed, He had not forsaken her--He was waiting for her to come home. But sadly, I let go of Him.

"In my anger and hurt, I erected a wall between God and myself and as a result became harder and more rigid in my religion and deeds. I lacked real heart towards God. Everything became empty, and I didn't like myself and felt like a hypocrite.

"I didn't realize that because of what happened between your mother and me that I perceived myself as a complete failure. I felt like I had failed God, your mother, and your grandparents, and it broke my heart. After reading your mother's letter a while ago, I began to allow God to heal me so that the wall could come down between Him and me, and I could receive His forgiveness. It was His forgiveness that revived my love for Him and restored the relationship I once had with Him, but I had to first repent like the prodigal son, turn from my miserable plight and come back to what I knew was true and right."

It was then that Chloe felt that her aunt looked right into her soul to impart her next statement, "There is no excuse for my silence, Chloe but the valley I have been in has been long, lonely, and dark, but now the light of His healing has brought me back to the place where I left Him when your mother left--the place He made just for me."

Chloe could see that her aunt had indeed revealed the deep places of her heart and soul, and, for Chloe there was only one remaining question. "Aunt Eloise, what must I do to receive God's gift of life?"

Vanessa excitedly piped in, "Yes, I also want to know how to have a relationship with God."

Looking around at the others, J.R. followed Vanessa, "You know I have received Christ, but I have taken my Christianity for granted. I have failed to really grow as a Christian. I think it would be good for me to rededicate my life."

"Don't leave me out," Freddie interrupted. "I have gone to church most of my life but I cannot remember ever personally asking Jesus into my life.

It was obvious to all in the room that Eloise Cain was thoroughly pleased by the response. "All you need to do is open your heart to Jesus, to receive God gift, and in prayer ask Him to forgive you and impart His life to you. I will lead you in prayer," she said with a smile.

All four bowed their heads and followed Eloise in prayer, "Lord Jesus, forgive me for my wrong ways, my selfish attitudes, and my prideful demands. I realize I need You to come into my life and save me from wasting my life and walking down a wrong path. I want to make You my Lord by dedicating all of my life to You for Your good pleasure and eternal purpose. Thank You for hearing my prayer and saving me today. In the name of Jesus, the name above all names, Amen."

Chloe didn't know how the other three felt, but a burden seemed to be lifted from her as joy and peace began to flood her soul. For the first time in her life she felt free from the sorrow that had plagued her, while the tormenting, restless emptiness of her inner being had been filled with a sweet presence she couldn't describe.

The joy that Chloe was feeling seemed to be also bubbling out of the others. There was excitement in the air. It appeared like everyone wanted to celebrate in some way, but there was no place in the store for such merriment.

Then Chloe remembered her grandfather was fighting for his life. "I don't understand everything that just happened, but I know if God can save me, He can heal grandpa."

Aunt Eloise smiled, "Let's pray for him right now."

Each one bowed their heads, and Eloise simply asked the Lord to heal her brother. After her prayer, Chloe looked at the others, "I know he's going to be alright because I have a peace about it."

The lights of the scoreboard brought Chloe back to present reality. That simple prayer of salvation had not only changed her life, but her direction. True to His word, God did heal her grandfather. In fact, she was there to celebrate his 75th birthday.

One of the first events that happened after her conversion is that her mother's coffin was exhumed, and her mother's remains were brought home to rest in the family cemetery. Her decayed empty shell of a body was laid to rest in a beautiful white coffin by Chloe's grandmother's grave. There was even a memorial service so that everyone who knew and loved Laura Cain Merriweather could properly say good bye. Chloe was surprised to see how many came to the memorial service. Instead of feeling alone and abandoned, she now had other people around her who would mourn the passing of a special life, as well as rejoice that in the end her mother secured a spiritual legacy that would never perish.

Chloe still remembered the sweetness of the time that followed her conversion. The four young people that had embarked on a more defined path that day not only grew in their friendship with each other but they grew in their Christian walk as they attended church and youth meetings together, that is until they graduated from high school.

J.R. was the first to try his wings. He ended up going to college and becoming a high school coach. He also married one of the most popular girls on campus. From what she heard, they appeared to be the perfect couple. They had a little boy, but their marriage began to go through troubled waters. Apparently, she was a Christian in name only and didn't have the same moral compass that he did. She proved to be unfaithful to him, and one night as she and her adulterous companion were on their way to their hideout, they were in a fatal car accident that snatched both of their lives, and most likely flung them into a Christless eternity.

Chloe shuddered to think about the emotional turmoil that J.R. must have experienced. Life had clearly thrown him a fastball that ended in great personal loss. At least he had his little boy, and according to Marybeth, he was an exceptional father. In fact, he was the coach at this school and doing well.

As for Chloe, her great-aunt Eloise had avoided repeating past failures as far as directing Chloe's life, but at the same time she would not let her hide or bury her musical talent. She made sure she had the best music teachers that would refine and bring out her musical ability. After high school Chloe was swept off to Europe where her musical gift flourished, opening incredible doors of opportunity for her. It was in France that she was entrusted to the teacher who would bring her musical ability to the heights of its potential, opening many doors for her to play concert piano for symphonies, as well as occasionally going on limited tours to perform personal concerts. However, she preferred to play the old hymns and her favorite place to play the piano was at country churches.

Even though Vanessa and Chloe went down different paths, they kept in touch. Vanessa fell in love with a soldier and married. While pregnant with their first child, her husband was killed in action. Chloe realized that within a ten year period, she witnessed a generation of men fighting and dying on foreign soil to maintain the fine line of peace and sanity in the world.

It was during that tragic time that Chloe stepped out of her hectic concert routine to support Vanessa. They both embarked together in the deep valley of loss and despair. Even though Chloe managed to be there for the birth of her godchild, Emily, she knew Vanessa needed further support. That is when she encouraged Vanessa to contact Sarah Reinhardt. Even though Sarah had recently remarried, she was more than willing to minister to Vanessa providing an avenue for them to become great friends.

It was during that same time that Freddie and Vanessa renewed their friendship. Freddie had become a detective for the local police station. As they enjoyed their friendship, it blossomed into romance. In fact, the second event she would be attending was their wedding. She was to be the maid of honor, while J.R. would serve as the best man.

Chloe had to admit that she felt a bit anxious about being home and seeing some of the old gang after a ten-year absence. As she was musing on these things, footsteps suddenly interrupted her thoughts.

Looking up, she recognized a familiar figure walking through the gym entrance.

As the man saw Chloe, he stopped. "Is that you, Chloe Merriweather?"

Chloe responded to the voice, "Yes it is Reggie."

***

In what seemed like one big leap, J.R. was in front of Chloe, embracing her. Chloe was a bit surprise at J.R.'s excitement to see her.

He stepped back to look at her while keeping his hands on her shoulders, "It's really you Chloe."

Chloe's eyes searched the face of her old friend. She could tell that much of J. R.'s youth and strength remained intact, but his eyes spoke of a depth that could only be produced by sorrow and suffering. "Yes it is! Didn't you expect me J.R.?"

"Of course, I knew you were coming home, but I didn't expect to meet you here."

Chloe smiled, "This gym," she said, looking towards the scoreboard, "especially under the scoreboard represents some important times to me. You might say I was remembering."

J. R. laughed. "Your memories would not include your first time of having dinner at Eloise's or our fight?"

Chloe chuckled, "Right on both counts, but I also was remembering the day Aunt Eloise explained the salvation message to the four of us and the commitments we each made to the Lord."

J. R.'s face became solemn. "That was quite a day. Even though I have occasionally strayed from the Lord, He has always been there to bring me back to Him and get me through the rough times."

In a hushed voice, Chloe delicately responded to his plight, "I heard about some of your rough times, J.R., and I'm so sorry."

J. R. acknowledged her condolence with a nod. Dropping his arms, his eyes took on a far-away look, "Chloe, when I married Rachel, my lusts were driving me. If I had been honest about the warning signs and listened to my heart, I would never have married her. It was not only a challenging and tormenting time, but it was a much-needed humbling time for me.

"I had allowed much of the world and my lusts to influence my thinking about what was important and as a result, swayed from the center of what brought meaning and value to my life. And, now I live with the fallout and failure of it."

"If you had not traveled that difficult route, you would not have your precious son," Chloe interjected.

The mention of his son brought a smile to J. R.'s lips, "You're right, Chloe. Kirk is a great little guy. In spite of everything that has happened in his short life, he has brought so much comfort, laughter, and joy to my life. I can hardly wait for you to meet him!"

"Marybeth talks so much about him in her letters," Chloe added, "I know she enjoys taking care of him and is glad you both live with her. It's because of her letters, I feel I already know him," Chloe replied. "But, I'm excited to officially meet him."

"Not to change the subject, but what memories do you have regarding that old scoreboard," J.R. inquired, and then added, "I was about to turn off its lights."

After all her reminiscing, Chloe was ready with an answer, "I met Vanessa under the scoreboard. I was asked for my first dance by you under that board, experienced my first crush under it, and heard about my grandfather's heart attack while waiting for Vanessa there."

"I remember asking you for that first dance, but who was the lucky stiff that actually caught your attention. Do I know him?" J.R. asked.

"Yes, you do, but it doesn't really matter," Chloe answered him with a smile, while quietly admitting to herself that she was flattered by J.R.'s statement and curiosity.

Practically pleading with her, J.R. persisted in trying to pry the guy's identity out of her. "Come on Chloe. You can tell me. We're still good friends and we are both past the teasing stage, and I promise not to tell anyone."

Chloe saw no need to open the door to that well-guarded room. She had almost forgotten that she had locked those feelings away, and she was surprised that it seemed so important to J.R. She looked into his curious, but kind brown eyes, "That was years ago J.R. Like old newspapers, it's old news that has become yellow with time and the print has faded. It has lost its usefulness and is now locked away in the room of insignificance."

Chloe could tell that the curiosity bug had definitely bit J.R. but she saw no need to share her secret. To break the gridlock that had ensued over her secret, she made a request. "I've spent more time here than I anticipated. Why don't you escort me to my car? Grandpa and Aunt Eloise are expecting me right now."

J.R. grinned and held out his arm. They linked arms and walked in silence to her car, both knowing that there would be other opportunities to talk.

The two events that warranted Chloe's return home collided, causing a whirlwind that snatched her up into an array of activities. There were various gatherings of family and friends that were highlighted by reminiscing and laughter, but there were also the private conversations that verified the strength of the older relationships. There were tender moments with her grandfather in the swing on the veranda, the late night conversations with Aunt Eloise, the times of giggling with Vanessa, and the lunches with Marybeth and Sarah. She met Kirk, got reacquainted with her old friend, Freddie, met Sarah's new husband, and enjoyed her goddaughter, Emily.

The night before Freddie and Vanessa's wedding found Chloe musing while gently swinging on the old veranda swing. After her grandfather's heart attack, Eloise insisted that he sell the business and both of them move in with her so she could keep an eye on her brother. Chloe never would have imagined on that first day she entered the door of the mansion that she would ever live in it and call it home.

But, it was home to her. It was where she belonged and had grown in the greatest legacy of all, her spiritual life. Eloise had become a giant to her in different ways. She mentored her spiritually and challenged her personally to always reach for what was excellent by giving her the best, and inspiring her to do what was honorable. Chloe knew her aunt had given her the best in a loving sacrificial way and she wanted to somehow reciprocate. As she meditated on her options, J.R.'s voice penetrated her thoughts.

"Beautiful night, isn't it Chloe?"

"What are you doing here, Reggie?" Chloe asked.

"I was taking a walk and noticed you out here. Sorry if I interrupted something important."

"Nothing that I can't later resume. I was just thinking," Chloe answered.

With the hint of a mischievous smile he stated, "I was thinking too."

Chloe sensed he was dangling some type of bait before her. She decided to humor him, "What were you thinking about?"

"Who was that guy at school that caught the attention of your heart?"

Surprised that J.R. wouldn't let go of her secret, she decided to find out whether it was important to him to know, or whether he was teasing her. As she studied his face, she sensed that for some unknown reason it seemed to be important to him. "Why do you want to know?"

"I have my reasons," he replied.

"How good is your memory" she asked.

"Why do you ask?" he inquired.

"Because, if you have a good memory, you might be able to uncover the mystery man."

By this time J.R. was showing signs of confusion. "I don't understand, Chloe?"

Chloe smiled. She had to admit she was enjoying this, perhaps a little too much. "It seems you remembered the dance we all attended, and you even felt sorry for me and asked me to dance."

"Yes I do, but I didn't feel sorry for you Chloe. I knew you were probably the best dancer in school, and I also knew if the rest of the guys knew how good you could make them look on the dance floor, that you would be dancing the rest of the night. And, I was right!"

"Yes you were right J.R. Well, the guy who danced with me the second to the last dance was the one who made my heart flutter for a short time until I locked the feelings away."

Chloe could tell that J.R. was confused as he struggled to remember that night. He was clearly sorting through his memories and finally located a particular fact, "I don't understand Chloe. If I remember right I was the one who danced the second to the last dance with you."

Chloe remained silent as the information sunk in. She watched as J. R.'s facial expressions changed from confusion to surprise, and then landed on the runway of reality.

"I'm the guy that caught your attention?"

Chloe nodded her head yes.

In a frustrated tone, J.R. replied, "But, you never said anything or let on that you had any other feelings for me other than being good friends."

Chloe in a quiet tone responded, "I have to admit I was surprised J.R. when I experienced those feelings. I was not expecting them and I must say I would have considered you an unlikely candidate because of the type of relationship we had with each other. Perhaps it was all the dancing that primed me and maybe it was the environment that unlocked my feelings and made them sensitive, or it could have been that for the first time I saw you as the man you are, tall, handsome, considerate, and gracious."

J.R. had been standing, but the latest revelation caused him to lower himself into a chair facing her. "Why didn't you tell me?"

"Come on J.R. You were the most popular guy in school. You could have had any girl you wanted. I could not imagine you being interested in me, other than being a good friend. Remember, I was a very late bloomer when it came to such matters. I also remembered what Aunt Eloise said about beaus coming and going, but a good friend is hard to find and keep. I decided our friendship was far more important than my feelings."

J.R. smiled, "We have been good friends, but I have to admit I had to put down jealousy when I was watching you dance with all those guys. I was a bit surprised as well when I found I was attracted to you in such a manner. That is why I asked you for that second dance."

It was Chloe's turn to be surprised. The latest information created an environment that caused everything to take on a surreal tone for her. "You were attracted to me? You have to be kidding, Reggie!"

J.R. smiled at Chloe, "The first time I saw you with your gray beret, I saw someone special that was hiding behind a big attitude. The day we had the fight, I really thought you were pretty in your dress, but I didn't know how to handle it so like a dummy I became sarcastic.

"You know, Chloe, I have secretly kept track of your career as much I could. I realized a while ago that I have missed our friendship, but because of my secret attractions towards you, I have also wondered what it would have been like if we had gotten together."

"It was a good thing we didn't get together," Chloe exclaimed.

In a surprised, but almost dismayed tone, J.R. asked, "Why would you say that? We were good friends, and there were aspects of our personalities that pointed to the fact that we could be a good pair."

Chloe was quick with her response, "For one reason you would not have Kirk, and secondly, we were not ready for such a relationship. At the time of our attractions, we were nothing but tender buds. When young people are tender, they don't have the character to always withstand the challenges of life. I had to first find out who I was and you had to find out who you were destined to be before there could be any real mention of, or pursuit of such a relationship."

Looking down, J.R. shook his head in agreement. "You're probably right, but now I feel it is too late to pursue such a relationship with you. You are experiencing a new exciting life. Youuu... are going places and why would you come back to what represented the old life? And besides," he paused, "I have blown it in such a way, I don't feel like I'm worthy of you."

Chloe gave a soft laugh, and J.R. once again looked into her face as if he was trying to read her expression. "That's funny," Chloe stated, "when I first came here, I thought I was unworthy and would never fit in this place, but then I encountered stages of transformation in my life that allowed me to become part of this community. But, I have learned that transformation is not about outward change but inward change. It points to a different perspective, redefined values, and a healthy grasp on reality.

"The reality of it is J.R., that thanks to Aunt Eloise's persistence that I walk through doors of opportunities, I have experienced what the world offers, only to discover that what is important is what I left behind: home, family, Christian service, and legacy. My mother ran away from here to find her life, but I am coming back to secure a greater purpose, a more excellent calling. In a way I have always known that my life is really here.

"Aunt Eloise and my grandfather have made sure that I have had the opportunity to really find out what was important to me. And, now instead of constantly receiving the benefits that are the fruits of others' sacrifice, I'm coming back to give, give my all to the Christian legacy my aunt has tried to maintain in this community."

"Does Eloise know you are coming back?" J.R. asked. Excitement radiated from his handsome features.

"No not yet. Chloe answered. "I'm sure she'll be pleased, but maybe not surprised. Perhaps she knew that I would discover the real treasures of life and come home. She has sacrificed much for me as well as others in this community, and it's my turn to reciprocate. I realized that what my aunt represents is someone who would be considered the greatest in the kingdom of God, for she is a true servant. She has learned to use all of her resources to influence and serve people in an honorable way for the glory of God. What she has done is not just about a legacy that she has sacrificed to try to maintain for herself, or even for me, but for the community. The running of the sawmill, the wisdom of her experience, and most of all the depth of her spiritual life in Christ. All of this is a legacy worth maintaining, a legacy of servitude. It's honorable and worth consideration and dedication." Chloe sighed before she continued, "I hope it's a legacy that I will do honor to."

The tone in J. R.'s response was one of surprise, but it also was laced with hope, "What about your music?"

"I am going to redirect my music. I love sharing my music with churches and the people I love most. Music is one of my passions but not my destiny. Granted, it touches heartstrings, but I want to do more than that. I want to do what my Aunt Eloise does in her everyday grind. She ensures honorable lifestyles, provides opportunities, shares her wisdom, influences positive policies in this community, and is available to share the saving message of God's grace with anyone who will listen."

J.R. leaned forward. Taking Chloe's hands in his, he looked into her eyes, "Perhaps this is not the time and I will probably sound a bit selfish at the moment, but does this mean there is hope for us?"

Chloe smiled at him, "There is not only hope, J.R. but if God wills it, it will be so. Remember our lives do not belong to us, they belong to God and we must consider all matters in light of His bidding."

"Chloe, forgive me for maybe being a bit presumptuous," J.R. stated firmly, "but I have sensed that it is what God wills."

With her hands still in his, Chloe gazed steadfastly into his eyes. Her winning smile and endearing words no doubt penetrated his heart as she said, "We will see Reggie, we will see." Chloe sensed that J.R. was right, but in the meantime, she had come home to begin a new journey, a journey of discovering her greater calling, climbing ever higher on the perpetual mountains of transformation, to finally fulfill her ordained destiny as a servant of the Most High God.

The LORD is nigh
unto them that are of a
broken heart; and saveth
such as be of a contrite spirit.
Many are the afflictions of the
righteous: but the LORD
delivereth him out of
them all.
(Psalm 34:18-19)

Broken

Hope Foster was examining the broken chain of her necklace. She gingerly put it in an envelope, which she tucked away into a small compartment of her purse for safekeeping. It all seemed so surreal, but the stinging reality caused tears to slowly escape from the corners of her eyes.

How she had valued that necklace! It had been given to her by her father on her thirteenth birthday. He had always fondly called her, "Princess." When he handed the necklace to her, he explained it would only fit a princess. It was a heart pendant, and she realized that it was partially there. It was apparent that there was another piece to it that someone else held or wore around his or her neck and when the two pieces were fitted together it made a complete heart.

She suspected her father secretly owned the other piece and that one day he would pull it out at some pinnacle time of her life to show and confirm his love for her. She already knew that he loved her, but he always had a way of being sensitive to where she was emotionally and mentally. Through the years he had given her many surprises, some that were incomplete, but later completed when he unveiled the real gift. His gifts always showed that he was there to encourage her in some way.

She remembered the time she unwrapped a small box to find a key inside. She was fifteen. Even though she had not taken driver's education, she was hoping it was to a car. It proved to be the key to a beautiful hope chest that he had secretly made to surprise her.

However, her father was not present to pull out a surprise that would somehow make life tolerable during the present situation. No doubt the event constituted a crisis, one of the worst that Hope had been exposed to in her short life of seventeen years, but he was in no position to come in and save the day with some sensitive gesture. In fact, he was far away.

Her father, Steven Foster was a staff sergeant in the Marine corp. He had been deployed to participate in some secret mission in the Middle East. When he left all seemed well on the home front, but it was a façade. He left behind a pressure cooker that erupted in Hope's face. She still could feel the heat of the vehement stream engulfing her heart, burning it with what felt like searing coals of cruelty that left a gaping hole in it. The wounding was so deep she felt it would never heal, that her heart would be forever festered and scarred by the day's happenings.

Usually she didn't know what started such affronts because she never knew what was going to open the floodgates of anger that often erupted on the scene of her life like streams of hot lava. As she considered her life, in most cases she didn't know whether to duck, run, hide, or brace herself. It seemed like when Hope was trying the hardest to avoid or curtail a violent outburst that is when it would always happen. However, this time she knew what caused the explosion, and she knew that she had actually triggered it.

The eruptions came from "Mother." That is what Hope was instructed to call the woman when she was old enough to understand. She had heard other girls called their mothers names that spoke of innocence, endearment, and simplicity, but it was clear that the term "mother" was the one title that had always defined Hope's relationship with this woman. She recognized that the term "mother" spoke of respect, but when it came to the woman she called "mother", it was to establish the fact that the woman did not appreciate being in that particular position and that they would both do the best they could with the unpleasant circumstances. There seemed to be indifference on Mother's part to treat her like a valued daughter, as well as meet her emotional needs, making it clear that a divorce had taken place when it came to any real affection between them. When it came to Hope being in the same room with her, the edginess to the woman's tone when she addressed Hope confirmed her attitude towards her, which was that of "bearable tolerance."

Hope could not count the many times she tried to adjust to the bombardment of criticism from the woman who ruled the house with an iron fist. However, if she managed to comply in a certain area, the rules would once again change in that situation. It was obvious that mother's standards changed according to the high tides of her feelings and emotions. She was like a wave on the ocean, tossing everyone around in her world like small, toy boats.

Perhaps that is why her father had made various sacrifices to juggle his different duty assignments. He served as both a boot camp instructor and a recruiting officer, and only accepted overseas assignments as long as he could take his family. Granted, he had studied electronics during such times and was now doing top secret work for his beloved Marine Corp, but Hope had suspected that he did everything he could to keep the family together as a means to protect her from "mother."

The relationship between Steven Foster and his wife was also precarious. He would refuse to fight with her which caused a thick blanket of tension between them. She would egg him on by attacking his manhood, declaring he was a lousy excuse of a man, an inept husband, and a weak father. No matter how verbally cruel she was, he never retaliated. He would often sleep on the couch. It was during those times that Hope would occasionally come in and sit with her father. He would hold her in his arms while she shared her deepest desires. They would speak of future vacations, her goals to attend college, and her future spouse. She always told him that she wanted to marry a man just like him.

Hope was aware that Mother was not happy in her marriage. In fact, she wasn't happy about anything. She complained about their housing, the base they were stationed at, the community they were located in, Hope's so-called "insolence," and her father's "ineptness" to make an acceptable life for them. Unlike Hope, she apparently had no awareness of her husband's sacrifice to provide for both of them.

Because of his preference to keep the family together as much as possible, Hope's father had risked being passed over for promotion. But, it was clear that there was no debate that Steven Foster was a Marine through and through, and was completely committed to the corp.

He had been in foster homes most of his life. He only alluded to his former life with sketchy information when he spoke of it to Hope. He always stated that the Marine Corp had been the best parent, provider, teacher, and protector he ever knew. The men and women he served with became brothers and sisters. He always told Hope that he was satisfied with his military life, but she was the one who made his life complete. Since her father was satisfied with his life in the Marines, she didn't delve too deeply into his past by asking probing questions.

However, there was something different about this latest duty station he was assigned to. She didn't know why, but her father had requested this particular assignment. It seemed as if he was more interested in making sure they were settled in the area than his duty assignment, which could entail secret missions.

She still remembered the day he took off for parts unknown, to do a top secret task for an uncertain period of time. When Mother was busy doing other things he had taken Hope aside and given her the name and phone number of a man. He told her if she needed help that she was to call the number. She had quickly tucked it away in the pocket of her favorite jacket for safekeeping.

Hope remembered clinging to him before he left. She could hardly bear to see him go. She brushed any tormenting notions away that he might not be coming back. Steven had leaned over to give his wife a kiss, but she quickly turned her cheek to him. He simply backed away from her and told her good-bye.

He had not even been gone 48 hours when Mother brought a so-called "friend" home for dinner. It was obvious that it was not a newly formed relationship. Hope looked at him with suspicion, but Mother gave her a certain look, warning her she better walk lightly or she could feel the stinging force of her hand. Within a week's time it was obvious that the two of them were becoming an inseparable item, spending most of their waking hours together. Even though Hope was naive, she knew that Mother was being unfaithful to her father.

Hope was used to her mother's indifference towards her, but she could not accept the blatant disregard that she was showing her father and their marriage. Hope began to feel resentment growing, which was beginning to turn into anger. Admittedly, she didn't know how much of the resentment and anger had already taken root through the years, but she could feel it seething beneath the surface. It both frightened and empowered her. Both she and her father had taken much abuse from this woman, but everyone has a limit as to what he or she will endure. Either Mother's friend had to go or else...

Hope had not yet finished the, "or else" part of her thinking when it happened: the confrontation.

Mother came in from being with her friend most of the day. She informed Hope that he would be coming to dinner.

Hope could not help but ask her, "What about father?"

"He has nothing to do with it," Mother quickly retorted.

"What would father think of your relationship with this man?" Hope continued her cross examination.

"He's just a friend," Mother stated in a threatening tone. "In fact, Hope you should begin to call him "uncle" since he'll be a big part of our lives from now on."

Even though Hope knew mother to be forthright and crude about her attitudes and feelings, she felt she was crossing into what she considered to be foolish audacity.

"Do you think I'm so stupid I don't know what's going on between the two of you?" Hope felt her voice ascending along with her temperature. "The word they use for your type of relationship with this new 'uncle' is 'adultery,' is it not?"

Mother flew at Hope in a fit of rage. She slapped the side of her face with the back of her hand, knocking Hope back a couple of feet.

"How dare you speak to me in such a despicable way," she screamed at Hope. "Who do you think you are? You are nothing but a great inconvenience to me. I've given you the best years of my life and this is how you repay me! Why you sniveling ingrate! You can call me whatever you want to."

Hope struggled to bring her emotions under control before responding loudly. All the time she was running a small part of the chain of her heart necklace through her fingers for comfort. But, she couldn't hold back her feelings nor let such an opportunity of expressing herself about this woman's "motherhood" pass without setting the record straight. "It's obvious to me all of these years that I was nothing but a grave inconvenience to you!"

Once her pent-up emotions started coming out Hope couldn't stop herself from expressing the rest of her feelings. "But, how can you claim that you have given me the best years of your life! I've received nothing from you but crumbs at best and abuse at worst. The truth is you've never been a real mother to me. You never have loved me like Dad and you don't care about me. You've simply put up with me!"

A sneer appeared on Mother's face. That is when she walked up to Hope and grabbed her necklace and ripped it off of her neck, and flung it across the room.

Hope was stunned at Mother's response. Then she vindictively went in for the kill.

"Where's your loving father now? He is out playing soldier, leaving you with me to do as I want with you! But, let me set the record straight. I've already filed for divorce from your pathetic father. I even put the papers in his duffle bag for him to find later. And, as for you, you worthless ingrate, I agreed to keep this from you until he returned from his war games, but I think it's time you know the truth. I AM NOT really your mother!"

This last statement hit Hope with such a great force that she almost buckled to the floor. However, in that instant a cascade of things began to make sense out of the senselessness that had plagued her relationship with this person.

It was obvious that the woman was enjoying the moment of truth as she continued her raving. "I met your father when he advertised for a babysitter for his infant daughter while he played army. I applied as a babysitter and received the position. And later, for personal reasons on both of our parts, it eventually seemed right to make it a permanent relationship. Your father needed someone to care for his brat, but as for me it was simply a financial arrangement. Before he married me I had to agree to be your mother." She almost spit out the word, "mother."

Hope didn't know if she should be relieved that this woman was not her mother or succumb to a greater sense of rejection she had always felt because of her attitude towards her. Even though the light was dawning in her mind, it was also becoming clouded by questions. She already knew the lousy substitute in front of her wouldn't answer her questions even if she did know all the answers.

"Since you are almost 18years-old, you are old enough to fend for yourself. Be thankful that this is military housing. If it wasn't, you would be leaving tonight, but instead I'm leaving, but not before I take every stick of furniture with me as a form of payment for putting up with you and your father all these years. I'll leave you both with your clothes."

She turned around and began to dial her friend on the phone. Her words were short and crisp. "I'm so out of this g-d forsaken place. Bring the truck and muscles." She clicked the phone off and busied herself with making her move.

True to her threat she took everything. In a stunned state, Hope helplessly watched the woman and her friend empty the house. If Hope was sitting on the couch or chair, she had to get up so they could move each piece of furniture out to the truck. She finally ended up in her bedroom sitting on the futon she used for a bed. However, they also came for it along with her sheets and the dresser her clothes were in. Her clothes were literally dumped on the floor as each drawer was quickly emptied. She ended up sitting in front of her closet doors, ready to make her last stand if necessary.

When the hateful woman came into her room and looked at the defiance on Hope's face as she sat in front of her closet door with her purse on her lap and the clothes from the dresser drawers lying in a heap on the floor, she shrugged her shoulders and conceded that there was nothing of value left to take. Hope knew she was included in her summation. It was then that the woman spun around, triumphantly walked towards the front door and slammed it on her way out. Hope didn't know if it signaled the last nail in the coffin of her relationship with her and her father or if it was "Mother's" way to seal her up in a lifeless tomb to rot away in utter despair, or both.

Hope remained in front of her closet for the longest time, trying to sort through the events and latest revelations. She realized that it took only three-and-a-half hours to strip the house of its possessions. Hope didn't put much value in things because they had moved so many times that stuff would be lost, marred, or destroyed. However, she had never felt so alone. She had encountered much rejection from the woman of the house, but her father had always been there to encourage her. Even when he was away due to military obligations, she knew that his absence was for only a short time, but in this particular situation the unknown began to take the forefront and torment her.

She had no money and nowhere to turn. And, even though the revelation that the woman was not her mother brought some understanding and relief, she couldn't help but wonder where her real mother was. Why was she not in her life? Did her biological mother reject her like the woman who had been living behind a false title? Questions bombarded her, but she was only met with silence.

Hope realized that she just couldn't sit there and wallow in self-pity. After all, she was sitting in an empty house alone. She had to collect her senses and count her loses and gather what resources were left behind.

She opened her closet doors. She was relieved to see her sleeping bag and the card table and chairs. At least she could unroll her sleeping bag on the floor to establish a sleeping place, and put up the card table and chairs to eat, read, or meditate.

She walked into the living room, where paper and other non-essential materials were strewn across the floor. Like her, each scrap had been clearly discarded and left behind as if to make a strong statement on behalf of the phony that had just vacated the residence. Since the appliances were very old, it was obvious that the woman didn't want to bother with them.

Hope examined the empty cardboards and drawers, then bravely opened the refrigerator door. There were only a couple of things left in the old fridge which included the Chinese leftovers from the night before. *Well*, she thought, *at least I have one meal, but after that I need to make some inquiries.* She knew she could seek help from the military and the Red Cross. Even though, she was almost 18, the CPS could still step in, but Hope remembered sketchy details of her father's life about his ordeal in foster homes, and she wanted to avoid becoming part of the system, even if it would be only for a couple of months.

Hope was never informed about financial matters, but she surmised that her father's checking account was probably empty. She knew enough that she needed funds not only for food, but other essentials to sustain some semblance of life in the hope of keeping the household running until her father's return.

She went into the bathroom. All that was left was her hairbrush, her toothbrush, and a small roll of toilet paper. The woman had even taken Hope's personal cosmetic bag, and there were no towels or rags with which to wash or bathe. The old washer and dryer were still in their cubbyhole, but the new hoses that were purchased for the washing machine had been confiscated.

The final room was her father's bedroom. The bed and dresser were gone. Like her clothes, his were dumped into a heap in the middle of the room. She peered into the closet. True to her word, the wicked opportunist had left his clothes, but to Hope's delight, she had counted his extra duffle bag as strictly being filled with his clothes. She was excited because she had helped her father pack the bag and knew that there were articles in it that she could use, such as a wash rag, towel, soap, a roll of toilet paper, and a compact set of eating tools that included a small pan, plate, and a couple of utensils.

She pulled the duffle bag out of the closet and meticulously unloaded each item. She put the useful articles from the bag in their proper place and went back into her father's bedroom to carefully fold his clothes that were on the floor, and put them neatly into his closet. She took the Chinese food and heated it on the stove in the small pan from the duffle bag. It was pretty tasty for being a leftover.

By this time darkness was beginning to fall causing the light to flee. She was thankful that it was summer, and that the nights weren't long, nor were they cold. She made sure the front door was properly locked as well as the windows, and she turned a night light on in the kitchen. She then went to her bedroom, sat on her sleeping bag, and rested her back against the wall.

Hope was emotionally drained, but she sensed that sleep would elude her. Even though she was still in a state of shock, she knew her life had unraveled right in front of her, and like her clothes, lay in a heap. Nothing made sense and everything was questionable. The "whys" came from every direction, filling up every compartment of her mind with doubts, fears, and uncertainties.

Although numb, she knew that her life had been violated. It had been ravaged, stripped, and broken. Before, she may have been a cracked vessel, trying to keep everything in, even though bits and pieces of her resolve were seeping through the cracks from years of emotional neglect and abuse from the substitute "mother." But, now she could sense that she was a totally broken vessel, discarded by indifference, cruelty, hatred, and vengeance. There was no semblance to her life, and everything seemed insane and untrustworthy, even her confidence in her father had been greatly shaken. Why had he not told her the truth? WHY? WHY? WHY had he not told her?

Her hands formed into a fist, and she began to squeeze them tighter and tighter until she felt her fingernails becoming embedded in her palms. It was then that she started to feel waves of frustration and revulsion flowing over her. She didn't know whether to scream, sit there until it consumed her, or wait until it passed over her, no doubt leaving her in a puddle of hopelessness.

Hope simply sat still, waiting for each wave to slam her up against the shoreline of despair. Tears stung her eyes, and she knew that she could no longer hold back the sorrow that had been dammed up by years of mistreatment and rejection.

She didn't know how long she sat there with tears silently running down her cheeks. She felt her teardrops dropping into what seemed to her to be an abyss of darkness and softly splashing on her blouse. At some point she finally dosed off. She wasn't aware that she had fallen asleep until the sun's rays alerted her that a new day was dawning in spite of the depressing darkness of the night that still enfolded her soul.

Life would go on, and so must she. She had to keep moving no matter what had occurred the night before. Even though her neck was stiff from sleeping in a sitting position, the real pain that plagued her was emotional. She managed to drag her body out of her uncomfortable "floor bed" to the bathroom. When she looked in the mirror, she could not believe the person looking back at her. Her eyes were red, and she had dark circles under them. There was a slight red spot on her cheek where she had been slapped. Her hair and clothes were in disarray.

She took the wash rag and tried to soothe her face with cool water. She brushed her teeth without the toothpaste. Hope did the spit bath routine and was thankful for clean underwear and tried to strengthen out her disheveled clothes. She combed her shoulder-length dark brown hair the best she could, remembering this was the day she was to wash it but she would have to settle for wrestling it into place with her hairbrush.

Hope decided that her first action of the day was to visit the command post and alert them as to what had happened. She wasn't sure what they could do, but she knew that the Marine Corp watched out for its own. She would then go to the Red Cross to see what options she could pursue. She put on her favorite jacket and headed out the door for her planned destinations.

When she visited with those at the command post, the Officer on duty was called in to hear her story. She stressed that she didn't want CPS to get involved at this stage. Her father's records were pulled so they could consider her situation in light of her father's orders. Notations were made in the log book for future reference. A picture was even taken of the welt on the side of her face to keep as part of her father's file. She could tell that the officer greatly sympathized with her and told her that the Corp would be in touch with her as far as financial or legal actions.

When she was leaving, the officer on duty took money out of his billfold, quickly pressed it into her hand, and whispered, "This will keep you going until further arrangements can be made."

Hope then visited with the Red Cross. Again she was met with sympathetic looks and words. The woman at the desk assured her that they would coordinate with the Marine Corp in order to help her. She then handed Hope her phone number and told her to call her if she needed any assistance before matters could be worked out.

The kindness of both the officer and the woman at the Red Cross served as a ray of sunshine penetrating the darkness that tormented Hope's soul. Because of the relocations through the years and her relationship with the imposter mother, she had made it a habit to keep to herself. She had convinced herself that her father was enough and that she didn't need anyone else. However, her father's absence revealed the immaturity of her thinking.

She did need others. She needed someone to care and to help her wade through the maze of her life. She needed direction as to what to do, advice as to how to go on, and assurance that not all was lost. She needed a lifeline.

As she slid her hands into the pockets of her favorite jacket, she felt the piece of paper her father had given her before he had left. She pulled the paper out and read the name, "Lance Barton." She reasoned that since her father had taken the time to give her his name and phone number, she might as well call him.

Lance Barton picked up the phone after a couple of rings with an inviting and cheery greeting. Hope introduced herself to him and told him the instruction her father had left her.

"Do you need help?" Lance asked her with the hint of concern in his voice.

She gingerly answered him, "I hate to admit it, but I do. I don't know you, but my father has never steered me wrong. He must have a lot of confidence in you to entrust me to you."

"Your father and I were best friends," the stranger replied. "We joined the Marines at the same time, and that's how we met. Even though we've failed to keep in touch at different times, we've never lost the comradeship that we established through boot camp and our first duty assignment together. I was glad to hear from him when he called me about a month ago and asked me if I would be willing to be available to assist you if you called me. Where are you?"

She told him she was standing outside of a café that he was well acquainted with.

"I'll be there in about fifteen minutes and we can talk."

Lance told her what kind of vehicle he drove and she told him what she was wearing. True to his word, he was there in fifteen minutes. When he got out of his vehicle, Hope was struck by the fact that he was not only tall and handsome, but he had a neat appearance of a Marine along with classy mannerism about him.

He walked up to her with a smile reached out his hand to her. She automatically responded and noted that he gave her a strong, firm handshake. Still holding her hand, he laid his other hand over hers and reassuringly patted it.

"The last time I saw you, you were barely out of diapers. And, my, you've turned out to be a beautiful young woman."

Hope was about to look behind her to see if he was talking to someone else. She knew how she looked and felt far from being beautiful. However, excitement leaped up in her for he had a history, not only with her father, but with her. Just maybe he could answer some of her questions.

"Have you eaten?" he asked.

"I'm not really hungry."

"Well, how about having some kind of drink with me while we talk."

Hope agreed and followed him into the small café. She ordered orange juice and he ordered coffee.

As the waitress walked away from their table to fill their small order, Lance looked at her. "Are you ready to tell me what happened?"

Hope looked at him to see if he was even really interested. The kindness and the intensity in his clear brown eyes told her that he was ready to listen.

"How much of the story do you want to hear", she asked.

"If I'm going to assist you, I probably need to hear all of it."

Hope slowly began to recount the scene that had taken place between her and her father's wife. Eventually all the sordid details came tumbling out, including what the woman had said to her about not being her mother.

As she looked him in the eyes she couldn't help but state the obvious, "You probably already knew she wasn't my mother."

"I never knew your real mother." Lance answered her questioning look. "Much of what transpired between your birth mother and your father happened before and after boot camp. While in boot camp, your dad did mention that he had a beautiful girlfriend and that one day he was going to marry her. We were later stationed together after we went through the training for our separate fields, and that is when I discovered that your father had you and was married to the woman you knew as mother. I met her once, but I must say she didn't leave me with a very good impression. She reminded me of an opportunist. Your father was vulnerable and she was the type that would take advantage of it."

She couldn't help but ask if he knew anything about her father's past and family. Hope could tell that he was weighing what he should say. "I need to know what you know, Mr. Barton. You have to tell me." Hope almost pleaded.

Lance took a breath. "I know your aunt."

Hope was shocked. "I have an aunt? All I know about Dad is that he grew up in foster homes. It was clear that he didn't want to talk about his past."

"Yes, you do have an aunt," Lance replied. "And, you are also right, your father did grow up in foster homes, but he had a sister. In fact, this is the community that both your father and I grew up in, but we attended different schools and met for the first time in boot camp.

"What I do know for a fact is that your father and aunt were split up after they were taken away from their mother. Your aunt was nine and your father seven at the time they were put in foster homes, but your aunt managed to keep track of him while they were growing up and they occasionally saw each other.

"However, something happened between your father and your aunt that caused a big rift in their relationship. But, it's not for me to say. Your father introduced your aunt to me after boot camp, and through the years our paths have occasionally crossed. When they have crossed, your aunt always asked me if I knew where you and your father were."

He stopped to let the information sink in. "Since I lost touch with your father around five years ago, I had no current information to give her. And, when your father contacted me, there was no real opportunity to tell him that your aunt was looking for both of you. I figured when he came back I would cross that bridge with him."

"My aunt is looking for us?"

"Yes, she is Hope, and I will be glad to introduce you to her. Perhaps she could be part of solving the problem that you are facing. I'll be glad to see you through this matter until your father returns, but there is something about family being involved that can bring certain comfort to an individual."

The idea of having an aunt was strange to Hope, and she felt anxiety about the notion of meeting her. Things were going too fast for her, but on the other hand, she wanted answers, and no doubt her aunt had them.

"I'm not very presentable, but I think I would like to meet my aunt."

Lance stood up from the table. "I'll have to look up her address and phone number in the phone book. I'll contact her and see if she is up to receiving a visitor or two."

He went to the phone booth just outside of the café and began to thumb through the pages of the phone book. He must have found the number because the next thing Hope knew he was talking on his cell phone.

He hung up and walked into the café. "Are you ready? We're going to your aunt's home."

Lance paid the tab and the next thing she became aware of was that she was seated in his pickup and on her way to meet her aunt.

"Does she know I am coming?" Hope inquired.

"No, she doesn't. I figured I would surprise her." Lance replied with a mischievous smile on his lips.

Anxiety started to take center stage in the pit of Hope's stomach, "Won't she be taken by surprise at my sudden appearance?" Hope asked. "I mean do you think this is fair to her?"

"I'm not worried about it. I know that it's something she has been hoping for. Don't worry, it'll work out fine."

Hope felt herself starting to sweat. It wasn't something she wanted to do in her present condition. She wasn't sure if she wanted to tell him she had changed her mind or jump out of the vehicle and run as fast as she could in the opposite direction. However, before she could make up her mind, the pickup stopped in front of a nice home. It was beautifully landscaped in the front, and looked inviting enough, but Hope had her suspicions as to how welcome she would be.

Lance came to the passenger side of the pickup and opened the door for her. He offered his hand to help her out of the vehicle. With a bit of trepidation, she took his hand. Once out of the pickup, he took her by the arm and led her up to the door.

He rang the doorbell. She could hear a dog barking in the background. The door opened. A man of medium build with somewhat graying hair and a receding hairline stood in the doorway. When he saw Lance, he grinned and the two men shook hands.

"It's great to see you Lance, how have you been doing?"

"Why mighty fine, Norman. It's great to see you!"

Serving as a welcoming gesture, he waved both of them into the house. As they entered into the living room from the small hallway, a woman came from the kitchen area. As Hope looked at her, she could see some slight similarities between her and her father. She could only assume that this was her aunt.

"Look Deidre, its Lance and he brought a guest with him."

Deidre walked up to Lance and gave him a sisterly hug. "It's so good to see you Lance. And, who's your guest?"

"Well Deidre and Norman, she is why I'm here. It'll be made clear to you as soon as I introduce her. This is Hope, your brother, Steven's daughter. And, Hope this is your aunt and uncle, Deidre and Norman Zeller."

Waves of emotion rolled over her aunt's face. In seconds Hope saw shock, joy, fear, excitement, insecurity, and sorrow. Her uncle remained silent but had a surprised look on his face that was highlighted by a pleasant smile. Hope even noticed two young people standing in the archway of the living room watching with great interest in all that was transpiring with their own looks of surprise.

Hope awkwardly smiled, "It's nice meeting you both," she spoke in a timid manner, "I hope this is not too much of a shock to either one of you. I have to admit I'm a bit loss for words." She paused, "To be honest with you I didn't know that either one of you existed until today. Forgive us if we're intruding into your activities. We can leave until there is a more convenient time."

Hope felt that her nervousness had caused her to divulge too much information all at once.

It was after Hope stopped speaking that Deidre shook herself out of the state of shock, rushed up to Hope and wrapped her arms around her. Hope sensed that her aunt was quietly weeping as she held her tight. Hope's uncle touched her arm as if to say, "Don't concern yourself. You're indeed welcome."

It seemed like Deidre held onto Hope for a long time and as a result Hope could not help but hold onto Deidre. When her aunt did step back with teary eyes, she took both of her hands and looked into

Hope's face. It was like she was taking in everything about her niece, making a mental picture, and marking an important milepost that would be forever engrained in her mind.

Then she looked back to see the two young people quietly standing behind her. "Children come and meet your cousin."

Hope couldn't believe it. That morning she started out with only a father, now she had an aunt, an uncle, and two cousins.

Both came forward with smiles on their faces. "Hope, these are your cousins, Keith and Stephanie. I might add she was named after your father."

Hope could tell that Keith was about her age and Stephanie was perhaps a couple of years younger. They both excitedly shook her hand, and acknowledged that it was great to finally meet their cousin. She could only reciprocate in a shy manner.

By this time Hope's mind was in a spin. She felt dizzy from the circumstances. As she was trying to wrap her mind around all the happenings, she heard a voice coming from a side hallway.

"Hey, what's all the excitement about?"

An older woman entered into the living room. Hope immediately noticed there was something so familiar about her that she felt drawn to her.

"You'll not believe it!" Deidre declared as she quickly moved towards the woman and taking her by the hand, whisked her in front of Hope. "Your prayers have been answered!"

The woman looked at Hope with a quizzical expression. Deidre went on to explain her statement, "Mom, this is Steven's daughter, your eldest and first granddaughter."

Both Hope and the older woman mirrored the same expression of astonishment, as they stood there stunned by the revelation. It was immediately made clear to Hope why she was so drawn to this woman. She could see some of her father in the woman's face and mannerisms.

Hope was again at a loss for words, but her grandmother declared her joy, "Hope, what an appropriate name! God has indeed allowed me to realize the answer to my many prayers by meeting you today!"

She joyfully caught Hope up in her arms and to reciprocate Hope found herself holding onto her grandmother as she joyfully danced around with her. In all the excitement, Hope realized that her depression had lifted and she was smiling with her grandmother at the incredible moment of discovery they were sharing together.

Hope didn't know how long it was before the excitement toned down to the level that reason could make an entrance. The room was lit with expectation. It seemed like questions filled it even though no one was really speaking.

Hope's grandmother took her by the arm and was ready to take her someplace so they could talk, but Deidre had other plans.

"Mom, I know you're anxious to get Hope to yourself, but dinner is ready. Keith and Stephanie set two more places at the table." Deidre looked at Hope and at Lance, "Hope and Lance, I hope you're both hungry because you'll be staying for a late brunch!"

"I never turn down food," Lance replied, "and as for Hope I know that she could probably use a good meal right now."

Everyone looked at Hope. Emulating concern her grandmother asked her, "When did you eat last Hope?"

Hope stumbled a bit as she thought about the last time she ate. "My last meal was last night."

Hope's grandmother looked alarmed and her aunt looked surprised.

"A lot has happened to Hope in the last 24 hours" Lance interjected, "But, she'll have to explain it to you after she has eaten some food."

Hope's grandmother held onto her one arm, while her aunt took the other arm and they escorted her into the dining room and set her down in the chair. The rest followed suit.

Keith was asked to say the blessing over the food. This was all quite strange for Hope since she was never exposed to religion, but she'll never forget her cousin's prayer, "Lord, we thank you for your many blessings. You've given us so much, and today you've put back together what was broken in the past, and have blessed us beyond measure by bringing Hope home to us. We just ask a blessing on this food, and please be with Uncle Steven wherever he is. Help him to know we are waiting for him to come home to us as well. In Jesus' precious name, Amen."

Tears came to Hope's eyes. She realized she was home. She had been given a lifeline in the form of a piece of paper in her father's handwriting. She didn't know what tomorrow would bring, but nothing could rob her of the precious moments she had experienced on this day. The questions would be asked and the answers would follow, but right now she just wanted to bask in the joy, excitement, and expectation that enfolded each of them at the dinner table like a sweet fountain of healing balm.

***

So much happened since the day Lance took Hope to the home of her aunt and uncle. From that point on everything changed. She shared her story with her newly found family. Her grandmother was appalled to hear what happened to her and even gently touched the red spot on Hope's face where she was struck, and her aunt was trying to be lady like in her wording concerning the actions of the woman, while Uncle Norman was conversing with Lance about what steps needed to be taken to protect Hope and any possible assets that might be left. Even though everyone had other questions, they were tabled until the situation with Hope was resolved.

Lance shared with Hope and the rest of the family how Steven gave him access to a secret checking and savings account that were both in Steven and Hope's name. As Lance revealed the amount in each account, Hope surmised that her father had been secretly putting away money in these two accounts for a long time. She wondered just how much money her father really left in the joint checking account he had with his now estranged wife.

Hope learned that due to illness, her grandmother had to put her furniture in storage and move in with her aunt Deidre. It was obvious that grandmother was on the mend. It was decided that very day that they would take grandmother's furniture out of storage and furnish Hope's house with it, and her grandmother would stay with her until her father came home. When her grandmother found out that Hope's bed had been nothing more than a futon, she insisted that while the men were getting her furniture out of storage, Hope along with the other two women of the household would go shopping for a bedroom set.

From that point all the activities created a whirlwind that picked Hope up and moved her through the happenings of the rest of the day. That night the house she had shared with her father and his wife had been changed into a real home, and she had a new bedroom set that gave confirmation that her new changes had begun. As her grandmother slept in her father's bedroom, she slept in her new bed amidst new beginnings. That night her sleep was peaceful.

Beginning the next day the picture of her newfound family's past began to emerge. Her grandmother and aunt both had a story, which supplied missing pieces of the mosaic that had been clearly shattered by sad circumstances. It was obvious that as lives became broken by different situations relationships were ultimately wrecked as well, causing incredible carnage.

Hope's grandmother was the first to lay out the pieces of her life. Cassie Regal (her maiden name, which she legally took back after a failed second marriage) had been a drug addict up until ten years ago. She lived from one fix to the next. She had tried to be a good wife to the father of her two children, but he was also lost in the world of drugs as well. She attempted to be a good mother to Deidre and Steven, but drugs were her god. Sadly, they were also the tools of an unseen enemy that held her captive, robbing her of life, devastating those around her, and destroying relationships. Even though she loved her children, they were sacrificed and became victims of an insane, frightening world that had no security or point of reality.

As a result, she lost everything from her family to her self-respect. Due to an overdose, the father of her only two children simply failed to wake up one day, forever lost in a culture of death, and now forever gone from the present world. Even though she lost her husband and loved her children, she could not free herself from the evil tentacles of her drug-induced world. Being the oldest, Deidre became a mother to Steven and a caregiver to her mother in an attempt to keep the family going.

Hope began to gain a better understanding of her father's gentle character. Even in his sweetness, Steven had tried to help his mother. Cassie shared how she always called Steven, "her man," because of the sweetness, forgiveness, and kindness he showed her in spite of her state. However, due to obvious neglect, eventually the CPS stepped in and took her children away from her, separating Deidre and Steven, and putting them in separate foster homes. Deidre fared well in the home she was placed in, but Steven was not so fortunate. He ended up being moved from one home to the next.

After years of living in a world that had peaks of ecstasy, deep pits of paranoia and depression, slippery trails of anxiety, and physical meltdowns, Cassie came to the end of herself. One day when she had come down from her latest high, she looked in a store window and didn't recognize the reflection of the person looking back. She could see she wasn't far from slipping into the dark abyss of death. She had lost everything, two marriages, two children, a healthy existence, and all self-respect. She would be leaving behind a mute legacy of unresolved issues, mountains of regret, and canyons of torment comprised of the "what ifs" of a matter. Guilt gripped her, shame seized her, and condemnation cruelly passed a rightful sentence on her of hopelessness and death.

It was then that Cassie Regal knew she needed to get help or she would die. In her muddled mind, she couldn't accept the idea that her life would leave no constructive impact, nor a legacy that would be passed down to the next generation. She couldn't die until she made amends with her children. She knew they would probably slam the door in her face, but she had to try to leave them with the knowledge that she did love them in spite of succumbing and drowning in her selfish, self-absorbed cesspool that had been created by a lifestyle of drugs.

Cassie explained to Hope that through a series of events she encountered caring people, living walking letters that introduced her to the Man. When Hope questioned her about the Man's identity, that is when her grandmother revealed the source of her change and joy, the Man was Christ Jesus, the Son of the living God.

When Hope's grandmother mentioned the name of Jesus, her face lit up and took on a shine that spoke of such love and ecstasy. It was clear that the Man, Jesus, was real to her. She explained that Jesus saved her, healed her, and restored her. And, although Aunt Deidre was skeptical at first when Cassie had reached out to her to make amends, Deidre couldn't help but see the change that had happened in her mother's life.

It was the change in her mother that caused Deidre to also consider the Man, Jesus. In a short time she, too, had an encounter with the Christ who forever changed her life, attitude, and estranged relationship with her mother. And according to her grandmother, Uncle Norman, Keith, and Stephanie were swept into the loving arms of God as well, bringing incredible healing and restoration to a family that had been terribly broken.

When it came to Aunt Deidre, Hope would discover the great pain in her heart that was still attached to the split that took place between her and Hope's father at the time of her birth. Apparently, her father sought out his big sister to help him with a newborn baby. Hope's mother was underage when she conceived her. Her parents wanted to charge Hope's father with statutory rape, but since he'd barely turned eighteen and had joined the Marines, they refrained, but forbade him from marrying or seeing her again.

The parents of Hope's mother wanted Hope to be adopted by a responsible family, but because Steven was the declared father on the birth certificate, he refused to give them legal permission and opted to raise the child himself. When he sought his sister out for support, she was expecting her first child and could not see how she could help him. She chided him for thinking he could raise a baby by himself. She encouraged him to adopt the child out, but he refused and walked out of the house. That was the last time Deidre saw her brother. She had tracked him down at different times through military channels and had written to him, asking his forgiveness, but never received any reply.

Since there was no answer from him, Deidre concluded that her brother would never forgive her for her rash advice, and admitted that she was so thankful that he had not taken her immature, selfish counsel of putting Hope up for adoption.

Deidre's mention of letters sparked Hope's memories. She recalled that her father's wife always went through the mail. As certain memories came to her, Hope shared with her aunt how she had caught the woman periodically discarding what appeared to be personal letters. She thought it to be odd, and the one time Hope questioned her about it, she simply told her it was from no one who was of any importance. After hearing her aunt's story, Hope suspected that the letters that were being discarded could have been from her aunt. After learning about what happened between her father and aunt, Hope surmised that the sorrow that often peeked out from behind her father's brown eyes whenever he was asked about his family was a result of his estranged relationship with his sister. Knowing his character, she could not imagine her father not responding to his sister's attempt for reconciliation.

The new knowledge about her parent's plight caused Hope to try to imagine what happened over 18 years ago. It seemed that her parents were in love, but due to her mother's age, the love was doomed from the start. Caught in the middle of it was Hope.

Hope began to appreciate her father's commitment to keep and raise her. It must have seen to Steven Foster, that he and his small baby daughter were being pitted against the greatest obstacles and best arguments the world could muster up. However, her father wouldn't allow himself to be separated from the baby that was representative of a love that he must have greatly valued.

Hope wondered what her biological mother thought about the whole scenario. It was apparent she had no say over the circumstances. She was caught up in some nightmarish whirlwind. Hope couldn't help but wonder what her mother's name was and what she looked like. She pondered if she had somehow encountered her in her life. Hope concluded that she knew one thing; she knew what questions to finally ask her father when he did come home.

Another person she learned the history of was Lance. Hope began to appreciate this gentle man's kindness. He seemed to take the position of protector of both her grandmother and her. He would come over almost every day and check on both of them, as well as always availed himself to take the two of them places or do errands for them. Because of his daily presence a strong bond quickly developed between the three of them. Within a few days of meeting Hope, he even copped a pet name for her, "Pumpkin."

She once asked him that since she perceived him to be a great catch, why he was not married. He would teasingly say that he was waiting for her to come to full maturity before considering such an avenue. One day she had caught him in a melancholy mood.

Hope approached him indirectly about his love life by asking him about his past. He started to tell her about his normal, but satisfying boyhood. He shared how his greatest moment was when he met Jesus, the Son of God and became a Christian at age 14. He graduated to sharing about the time he joined the Marines where he met her father and they immediately developed a bond because they were from the same community. It was after he shared bits and pieces about his friendship with Steven Foster, that he confessed that he had fallen in love with what he considered a very special woman.

Lance had thought this woman fit all of his highest hopes. Even though she did not confess the Christian faith, he had such expectations for the two of them because the relationship felt so right to him. The woman agreed to give his faith a chance. They went to church together, and she heard about what Jesus did on the cross for her, but after a couple of months of attending church, she concluded that she was alright without a Redeemer. Eventually, it became evident to him that even though his feelings went deep for her, their relationship would not work. Their breakup ripped out his heart and tore at his Christian resolve. He emotionally backed away from most relationships, including the one he had with the Lord. In his mind, he had failed both the Lord and the woman.

Hope felt confusion. How could he let such a thing as religion come between him and the woman he loved? Such conviction appeared almost fanatical to her, but she also was aware that her grandmother had the same intense conviction when it came to her beliefs. How could such conviction on one hand bring so much joy, but on the other hand bring such pain?

"I don't understand, Lance," Hope inquired, "how could you give up your true love for religion?"

"It's not because of religion that I gave up the woman I loved, but it's because of Christ," Lance replied. "I couldn't betray Him or His Word. As believers, we're not to become one with those who are spiritually unevenly yoked with us. I got myself into that situation because I was being disobedient to the Lord's instruction. I've no one to blame for the fallout but myself. I brought a reproach to Jesus, broke the woman's heart, and brought sorrow to myself."

Lance hung his head as he replayed the events in his mind. His voice seemed to become quieter and more simplified as he explained the believer's Scriptural responsibility towards such a matter. "Christians make a mistake when they think that they are an exception to God's instructions, instead of submitting to their protective rule. Occasionally, there may be certain circumstances that call for responses that seem contrary to His instruction, but such incidents are usually backed by scriptural and trustworthy confirmation."

Hope had not seen such conviction until she encountered Lance and her grandmother and her aunt and family. In her home, God was never mentioned unless His name was being used in an unbecoming expression. Religion was labeled a crutch for the weak, churches were mocked or criticized, and people who attended them were either called hypocrites or fanatics. She realized that such views came from her father's wife, but he had never said anything to refute them.

It dawned on Hope that she was not only curious about this Jesus, but she was impressed that those who followed Him held Him in such high regard. She did not understand the dynamics behind it, but she wanted to explore it for herself.

Hope's opportunity to explore the realm of Jesus came the third Sunday after her grandmother moved in with her. The first Sunday everyone was trying to emotionally land and bring order back into their worlds, while on the second Sunday her grandmother was feeling poorly due to a bout with a cold. However, when the third Sunday was coming full speed ahead, her grandmother informed her that she was going to church and that Hope was more than welcome to come with her. When Lance found out about it, he offered to take both of them to church. He admitted to Hope's grandmother that he was looking for another church to get away from some unpleasant memories. Even though Hope's grandmother had no idea what the memories entailed, Hope knew that he was making reference to his broken relationship with the woman. She could tell that even though it happened three years ago, he was still raw and uncertain because of it.

Sunday morning brought a bit of anxiety to Hope, but she was also secretly excited. She was quietly hoping that her expectation was not too high, but she really wanted to discover what her grandmother already possessed.

The first impression that struck Hope when she entered the foyer of the church was the friendliness of the people. Perhaps, it was her grandmother that generated such openness. It seemed she had many friends and fans. The minute the three of them entered the door, people began to surround her. There were hugs, kisses, and laughter.

Many told her how they had missed her the last few Sundays. In between all of the greetings, her grandmother managed to introduce Lance and her newly discovered granddaughter to the crowd.

Hope could tell some were quite surprised to hear that her grandmother had a son and another granddaughter. Hope deduced that the matter of her father had caused such a deep pain in her grandmother's heart that she wasn't willing to talk about it to even her Christian friends.

Even though Hope was being introduced to many people at once, she took note of four people. The first one was a man by the name of Lawrence Tyler. For his age, Tyler was a nice looking man. He was stately, and his silver hair highlighted a pleasant face and a moustache that clearly outlined a contagious smile. Hope noticed that he seemed somewhat smitten by her grandmother. Another person that stood out was Mildred Collins. She was friendly and could bring a smile to anyone's face. Her bubbly personality caused any foul moodiness to quickly lift. The other two people were sisters. Their last name was Kirkland. It was quietly whispered to Hope by Mildred that both were unmarried. These sisters seemed to be respected and well-liked by those of the church.

The first sister Hope took note of was Carla. She was the church secretary. She had dark brown hair and blue eyes that seemed to be smiling. She handled her medium built frame in a graceful way. As she quietly studied Carla it seemed that everything about her was refined and properly regimented. It was obvious to Hope that Carla was not trying to exhibit a veneer of perfection; rather, she had experienced a process in her life that had perfected her in many ways. Even though her eyes danced with joy, Hope sensed that the joy was also hiding some sorrow. It was obvious that Carla and her grandmother were good friends. As Hope considered the type of person Carla was, she quickly concluded that she might make a good match for Lance.

Carla's sister, Tiffany, was the more outgoing of the sisters. Unlike her sister, Tiffany did not appear to possess grace, but she made up for it by bringing a spontaneous element to her surroundings. She had blond hair, brown eyes, and was petite in structure. Hope secretly concluded that although she could appreciate Tiffany's ability to bring a spark of life to her environment, she still preferred the grace of Carla.

Her grandmother led Hope into the sanctuary and sat down in a pew. Hope watched how the four people who she took note of in the foyer also sat down in the pew with the three of them. However, Carla sat beside her grandmother and Hope sat between her grandmother and Lance. Tiffany sat on the other side of Lance, followed by Mildred and Lawrence at the end of the pew. Secretly, Hope wished she could rearrange everyone. She suddenly realized there was a matchmaker in her, just itching to put people together who she perceived would make perfect matches.

Hope had to remind herself that she was not there to play matchmaker. She was there to find out about this Jesus. She didn't know what to expect or whether she would come out with any understanding, but at least she met some very interesting people.

The pastor walked to the pulpit and welcomed everyone followed by a prayer. He asked for God to reveal Himself to the seeking hearts of people and to answer their silent prayers and questions. After the prayer, he encouraged each of them to prepare themselves for worship. Hope did not know what such preparation entailed, but she figured she would watch the others. She quickly learned that worship meant singing songs about God, and to God.

As she watched those around her, she began to see each one had their own way of approaching worship. Some closed their eyes, others lifted up their arms, and there were those who clasped their hands together and looked upward as if they were singing a prayer. Once Hope ended her observation, she had to admit she enjoyed the songs and actually forgot about herself and her matchmaking as she became caught up with a power that was lifting her above the matters of the world. She had to secretly admit that she was shocked, but pleasantly pleased that she was being touched by the unseen world that was somehow associated with this Man, Jesus.

Finally the pastor got up to give his message. Hope will never forget the theme of his message along with some of his words and examples. It was if it was branded on her soul, for it seemed that he was speaking directly to her. It was on "brokenness."

The pastor explained that due to sin, fierce rebellion against righteousness, and independence from God's authority resides in every person, and how people's lives become broken. He pointed out that there is brokenness because sin wounds the spirit, bruises the soul, tears the heart, torments the mind, and rips relationships apart. Sin ultimately divides and separates people into lonely worlds of despair and isolation. He went on to explain that sin often uses the unpleasant circumstances of our lives to set us up, and then at the right moment they become a hammer to break us into what seems like millions of pieces, but God provided a remedy that not only could bring healing to those areas that have been wounded, ripped, and torn, but would bring about complete restoration. God provided His Son. Jesus Christ, God by nature, He came in human form to not only address the devastation of sin, but to bring healing and restoration to people's lives and their relationships, especially their relationship with God.

The pastor went on to explain how sin breaks people's relationship with God with these words, "He can't look at sin for He is holy, He can't condone it for He is just, and He can't ignore it for He is love, and love will never rejoice in wickedness. Since sin has been passed down to everyone from the first man, Adam, all men have experienced separation from God. Whether it is loneliness in the soul, leanness in the spirit, disconnection in relationships with others, or feeling like a restless wave upon the ocean of humanity each environment reveals that those who experience such things aren't anchored by faith to the immovable Rock of Jesus. The truth is, there is no real hope, no real purpose, and no real direction outside of Jesus. If a person who has these symptoms is honest with him or herself, the person will realize that he or she has indeed become lost to God in some way."

The pastor's words became sharp as they penetrated Hope's very being, exposing the barrenness of her own spirit, the emptiness of her soul, and the brokenness of her heart. Tears welled up in her eyes as if a geyser had been untapped. She realized she was indeed broken by the sins of others and by her own sins. Life had set her up, and at the right time had become a hammer, landing hard, relentless blows to her resolve. Like her broken necklace, sin had ripped much from her that was precious, leaving her broken, vulnerable, and yes, even lost.

As Hope began to feel the unbearable depths of her spiritual barrenness, the pastor's voice broke through her despair as he was reminding the congregation that no person has to accept or remain in such a devastating state. He encouraged those who sensed this separation between God and themselves to take courage. He then made this statement, "You do not have to accept your plight. God offered His Son as a gift of love, and His Son offers the gift of life. To know or receive the fullness of God's love, all you have to do is humbly admit that you need to be forgiven of sin, saved or delivered from a lost state of despair and hopelessness, and cry out to Jesus to save you from the bleakness of this life and give you His everlasting life. If your heart is sincere, He will hear your cries and save you from the fate of your sin. If you desire this but need guidance, do not hesitate to come forward. I'll pray with you to receive God's gift of love and life."

Hope felt like she was being lifted up from the pew as she stood. She felt her grandmother take her arm and they both walked toward the front. She saw others making their way to the front. Many kneeled in total abasement. Hope and her grandmother kneeled as well. She felt another hand on her shoulder and looked up to see her aunt's face, full of joyous tears. With her arm around Hope's shoulder, her Aunt Deidre also kneeled down with both of them. Tears were freely flowing from all three of the women's eyes. She felt a presence in front of her and when she looked up she saw Carla's face.

Carla kneeled before her. "I know you expected the pastor, but he motioned some of us to help him minister to the many people who've come forward. I hope you don't mind, but I felt led to not only pray with you, but to be one of the first to welcome you into God's Kingdom and into a new heavenly family."

Hope could have not thought of a better person to guide her at this most important time of her life. With a smile she nodded her head in agreement and Carla led her through a simple, but humble prayer that asked Jesus to forgive her of all of her sins, and invite Him to come into her life and save, heal, and completely restore her into a living relationship with God, giving Him permission to be her Lord.

After Hope said "Amen," all four ladies, with tears of joy freely flowing down their cheeks, stood up and embraced in a moment of celebration. Hope felt clean, new, and revived. She didn't understand everything that happened to her, but she knew her life would never be the same.

As each lady walked back to their pews, Hope looked over to see that the pastor and Lawrence were praying with Lance. She could see that it was an emotional time for Lance. She knew that he was already a Christian, but knew that there had been brokenness in his life that needed attending to.

After the service, Hope officially met the pastor and his wife. As her grandmother's friends came together in the foyer, it was agreed that along with Lance, her aunt and family that they all should go out to lunch and celebrate that the Lord Jesus Christ had added one more precious soul to His living Church.

At the restaurant, even though Hope ordered her favorite dish of fish and chips, she noted two other details about the luncheon. Everyone was sitting in the right place. Lance was seated between Carla and her sister Tiffany, Lawrence by her grandmother, and Hope felt like she was the guest of honor, placed right in the middle of all of the activities. The second thing she noted was the excitement at the table. There was much conversation about the faithfulness and grace of God when it came to reaching heirs of salvation and healing broken hearts. There was also a giddiness that often erupted into laughter, as different people shared about some of their life experiences.

That day Hope walked away completely full. She wasn't only physically full of her favorite food, but for the first time she was aware that she was also spiritually full because of her salvation experience and glorious time with her new family.

It was hard to say goodbye to everyone, because Hope didn't want the day to end. However, when she and her grandmother arrived home, Hope's spiritual experiences continued on into the night. Hope and her grandmother talked about what it meant to be saved and what lay before her: a lifetime of learning what it means to be a disciple or follower of Jesus. Hope asked many questions, and her grandmother used the Bible to answer them.

The next day Hope's grandmother took her to a Bible Book Store to buy her a Bible. She guided her to a reliable study Bible and instructed her to choose whatever color she wanted as far as the cover. Hope chose a burgundy color. Her grandmother then had Hope's name engraved on it. She also brought a Bible cover to protect her new Bible, a concordance and Bible dictionary for her.

That night Hope's grandmother guided her through the books of the Old Testament and the books of the New Testament. She then showed her how to use her helps in the Bible as well as the concordance and dictionary. After making sure Hope understood how to use the different tools, her grandmother gave her a small daily devotional. Together they agreed to set up a specific time in which they would both pray and study the Bible together and talk about what they were learning or what concerns were upon their hearts.

It was clear that Hope's grandmother was ensuring that Hope would begin to cut her teeth on the Word of God. At first it seemed a bit overwhelming when she opened the Bible, but the more she began to learn about its truths and principles the more excited she became about her time with her grandmother. Her aunt, and cousin Stephanie sometimes joined them in their prayer and study time, which even brought a wider perspective to different approaches and Scriptural understanding.

The one person Hope and her grandmother prayed for every day was Steven Foster. The military had informed Hope that her father was alright, but the mission was proving to take longer because of diplomatic complications. Since it was sensitive the communication was sparse, but the military had also assured her that he was also informed that she was doing well.

Hope also had another prayer that she quietly prayed every night before she went to sleep. She asked the Lord to help her find her real mother. She also asked Him to give her mother a sincere, motherly love for her. Hope knew she never wanted to feel the sting of rejection again from another parent figure.

In her new life, Hope didn't have much time to dwell on such matters as her father. Cassie discovered that her granddaughter wanted to be a librarian. It so happened that Lawrence Tyler was on the board overseeing the community library, and Cassie Regal had no problem asking him if there was any way that her granddaughter could gain some experience in the field to see if that was truly where she belonged. Lawrence was quick to oblige Cassie, and Hope found herself having hands-on experience in Library Science.

Hope quickly became active in the church. She attended various activities that entailed evangelism, visiting the sick, and helping those who were in some type of distress. With the presence and encouragement of her cousins, Hope began to make friends with those in her age group. But, what made it more pleasant was that Carla was the one who often made sure the different activities ran smoothly. It was not unusual for their paths to cross.

Hope knew that since Carla officially led her to Christ that she would always have a special place in her heart. Every time she had something to do with the church secretary, she was reminded of her notion that Lance and Carla would make a great couple. What fanned the flame was that Stephanie confided in her that she also thought the two would make a great couple. They had even quietly discussed how they could get the two together without being obvious. A plan was agreed upon by both of them, but the major responsibility fell on Hope to bring about the events.

Hope approached her grandmother with the idea of having Carla and Lance over for dinner. She also thought it would be nice to invite Lawrence. Her grandmother agreed with the idea, but threw a wrench into the plans by adding Tiffany to the list. Granted, Tiffany was a nice enough person, but at this point Hope felt some jealousy and resentment towards her for unknowingly complicating her matchmaking plans. Hope was also aware that she couldn't let her grandmother know her real motive behind her plans. Even though they were still getting acquainted, Hope knew her grandmother well enough to know that if she found out what her granddaughter was up to, she would accuse her of meddling. In Hope's mind she knew what she was doing. It didn't matter from which angle she approached it; she couldn't have imagined a nicer and more compatible couple than Lance and Carla.

The date was set and the invitations went forth and were accepted. The trap was being set. Hope would place Lawrence by her grandmother and Lance between the two sisters and pray that the prospective bachelor would take notice of the right woman and it would be reciprocated.

The night arrived for the snare to be set. Hope felt a tinge of guilt about her plan, but she was convinced that if it worked, those involved would later thank her. However, Hope's plan failed to get off the runway. The men separated and talked to each other and the women were busy talking with her grandmother. When it was time to sit around the table, Lance took a seat between her and Tiffany. The conversation between the people at the table proved to be generic. If Lance was taking notice of anybody, it was Tiffany and not Carla. Hope was becoming miserable about the whole situation. It was obvious that her plans were not working. As she sat at the table, she felt her countenance fall. She was trying to be light and respectably engaged in the conversation, but she felt disheartened. Her attempt to be matchmaker was proving to be short-lived and a miserable failure.

As she was looking at Carla, something caught her eye. She rubbed her eyes to make sure they were not playing tricks on her, but there it was. About this time every eye began to focus on her.

"Hope, are you alright?" her grandmother asked.

Hope shook herself out of her suspended state. She stood up from her chair, and gave a quick reply "Excuse me for a second, I need to get something. I'll be right back."

She hurried to her bedroom and quickly located the object. She enfolded it in her hand and brought it out to the table. With every eye upon her, she sat down and stared at the floor as she struggled to collect her thoughts in order to put them into words.

Then she looked at Carla and in a measured tone said, "When I was 13, my dad gave me a very special gift. However, it seemed incomplete, and he didn't give me any explanation. I sensed that one day it would be completed and I would understand the significance of it. Perhaps, Carla, you could help me solve the problem."

Hope extended her arm across the table towards a curious Carla and opened her hand to uncover the treasure of the heart necklace.

Carla stared at the pendant in disbelief. Slowly taking the necklace out of Hope's hand to study it closer, it was obvious that Carla was trying to contain her emotions. In a restrained voice she asked the question. "What's your father's name?"

Hope was only vaguely aware of the others at the table. But, she sensed her grandmother was carefully watching the interchange between the two of them, while Tiffany's hands flew to her mouth to hide shock. The two men looked puzzled.

Hope looked Carla in the eyes. "His name is Steven Foster. He's a Marine."

Carla seemed to let out her breath. Her initial disbelief gave way to recognition as tears welled up in her eyes. Joy took center stage as the sweet softness of a mother's look began to mingle with the tears in her eyes.

Hope heard herself asking the question that had been tucked away in a special place in her heart for the past weeks. "Are you my mother?"

Carla stood up from her chair, still holding the necklace. She walked around the table to face Hope and looked her in the eyes. "What do you think?" Carla then took Hope's half of the necklace and fit it against the half of the heart pendant that was around her neck, revealing that they were a match.

Hope could no longer contain herself. Throwing her arms around her mother, Carla embraced her daughter as joyous tears freely flowed down both of their cheeks.

"Oh, Mom! I've been looking for you since I found out the truth," she cried. It was such joy and freedom for Hope to use that one special word, "Mom." That word had silently waited to be set free by the genuine love of a mother.

"And, I've been looking for you my daughter." Carla tearfully responded.

By this time, it was becoming clear to everyone that they were witnessing another miracle of God, the miracle of bringing hearts and lives together in a marvelous way. Hope felt her grandmother's arms enfolding the two of them as she laid her head on Carla's shoulder. Hope heard her grandmother say to Carla, "I've always been thankful for your friendship, but now I must thank you for one of the greatest gifts of all: my granddaughter, Hope."

Carla and Hope held each other for the longest time, until Tiffany tapped her sister on the shoulder. "Hey, you know she's my niece. Don't I get to officially hug her?"

Hope felt guilty for feeling poorly towards Tiffany. It wasn't her fault she was messing up her silly plans: plans of trying to actually pawn her mother off on Lance.

Carla stepped back and Tiffany moved to stand in front of Hope, "Hope, I've always wondered about you. I felt slighted as an aunt that I never had the opportunity to be part of your life. We can't make up for lost years, but we can make up for lost time by making the best of the present and the future. It's great to finally meet you."

Hope smiled at her, "Aunt Tiffany it's great to meet you, and I'm sure we will make up for lost time." Although Tiffany was shorter, Hope had to admit she had a firm way of hugging her.

After everyone left, grandmother retired for the evening as mother and daughter talked way into the night. Carla learned about Hope's plight with her father's wife. She could tell her mother was distressed and sad about what her daughter had experienced. Hope also learned that her parents were deeply in love, but due to Carla's age, she had to accept the circumstances of their situation. Carla described Steven Foster as being gentle, kind, and forgiving. Hope was beginning to realize that even though life had thrown many punches at her father, he had kept the same gentle and forgiving ways.

Steven and Carla had kept their relationship a secret, but the conception of Hope brought their secret love to the light. Carla's parents responded with indignation and rage. They wanted to make Steven pay; therefore, they were threatening to start legal proceedings against him. Since Hope's father had a possible rape charge hanging over his head, Steven and Carla both felt they could do nothing but comply with her parents' demands.

Carla admitted she had greatly resented her parents for what was forced upon her and Hope's father. She was tormented because her arms longed to hold her baby daughter and her heart's desire was to see her mature. It plagued her that not only was she deprived of the love of her life, but the odds of her having anything to do with Hope's life appeared slim.

Carla shared what was said between Steven and her the last time they saw each other. She had told Steven that the baby in her represented their hope for a future together. As those last precious memories were parading before her, Carla looked at Hope and said, "My parents wouldn't allow me to name you because they maintained you were not mine to claim. Even though they separated me from your father, I wouldn't allow them to strip him of being your father. I also knew that I had to provide some token to connect me with my baby. I had decided to look for some necklace for a daughter and possibly a watch for a son. I had actually picked out the necklace before I had you and had given the money to your Aunt Tiffany to pick it up once I found out you were a girl. She picked it up on the very day you were born and I sent your half to your father with a note that he was to give it to you when you were old enough to understand it. I explained how I would hold my daughter's heart, and she would hold mine until we were brought together, to reconnect and become a whole family. Praise God for the resolution. Now you sit before me, precious and beautiful. But you know what is amazing, Hope, I would have never dreamed that your father would actually establish a memorial of our love by naming you, our precious daughter, 'Hope.'"

Hope was overwhelmed by the idea that she was a living memorial of her parent's relationship and the necklace was a token of her mother's love for her. She also suspected that her father never ceased to love Carla, but circumstances would once again step in as a means to keep the two lovers apart.

Carla admitted that she knew that Steven had one sister, but other than that tidbit, he never shared anything about his family with her; therefore, there was no point of connection. Once she was no longer subject to her parents' authority, she tried to locate both of them through the military channels, but discovered Steven was married. She felt utter despair and went into depression. It took everything in her not to try and contact him, but she felt it would be unwise for her to interfere with his new life.

Eventually the despair caused her to go into deep depression. She felt like giving up, but it was during that time she discovered there was hope. She found a caring church and Christ found her. He took the torment away from her and gave her hope that perhaps one day she would see or meet her daughter. He even restored her relationship with her parents. She secured her present job as church secretary, allowing her the opportunity to move back in the area where she had known Steven, in the hope of somehow connecting with him or the daughter she didn't know.

Carla looked at her daughter, "Now my hope is realized. It's unbelievable that the one thread of hope to make peace with my past is sitting in front of me."

Carla once again took Hope in her arms. They both held each other as the silence of the night enfolded them. The only noise that softly whispered in their ears was the rhythmic beats of their hearts: they were now merging together in a sweet crescendo of joy.

***

Hope was excited. It was hard to believe that it was her 18th birthday. It marked a milepost that she wanted to record not only to memory but to the photograph albums. She already felt like she had Christmas and all her birthdays combined in the last few months. She had been in such a whirlwind. One woman had walked out of her life, leaving her devastated, but God opened a door and gave her a mother, grandparents, aunts, uncles, cousins, and friends. The only one missing from the picture was her father.

She didn't know what was happening with her father. So much had happened that Hope's mind was still spinning and her emotions felt like they had been on one gigantic roller coaster. The military told her he was alright and once again assured her that they had informed him that she was in good hands. Hope doubted that he knew any of the details. She wasn't sure what her father would think about everything that had occurred in the last few months, but she knew one thing; he was in for the shock of his life!

Hope heard the laughter of her family and friends in the back yard. They were happily getting the birthday celebration ready. Included in her ever-growing family were her mother's parents and older brother and his two children. Carla's parents actually cried when they met her and profusely apologized for their unreasonable ways. They confessed that they felt confused, betrayed, disappointed, and angry when Carla had confessed she was pregnant at the age of sixteen. They focused all their anger on Steven and set out to make him pay, resulting in a separation that had haunted them for over eighteen years. Hope found that she actually liked them and realized they were confronted with challenging and overwhelming circumstances.

There was also Lance and her aunt Tiffany. They were becoming an item, which meant Lance could one day become her uncle. Hope still felt embarrassed and silly about her failure as a matchmaker. It was clear that God knew better. She had decided to retire from that short-lived "profession."

She also thought about the church. The pastor and his wife had known about her mother's past, and when God brought her and Hope together, the first ones Carla shared the good news with was the pastor and his wife. They clearly rejoiced with her, but felt that she needed to share the good news with the congregation in a way that would disburse with any suspicion and possible gossip.

Hope will never forget that Sunday. The pastor told the congregation that Carla had something very special to share with them. He reminded the congregation that the real ministry of Christians is about reconciliation. He then reiterated, "It is always God's heart to unite in reconciliation, lives that have been broken and ripped asunder. As believers we must be like the angels of heaven, always ready to be the first to rejoice over such reconciliation."

Hope knew that for her mother to share some of the not so pleasant details of her life would require courage on her part, but both of them also knew the end of the story. God's hand had brought the desired and prized reconciliation the pastor made reference to.

Carla shared about the sins of her youthful past and that a baby girl had been produced, followed by heart-breaking consequences. She related how the child had been taken away from her and how for years she had searched to find that baby, and prayed that God would have mercy on her and somehow allow her to see or meet her.

Hope would cherish the final words of her mother forever in her heart, "I want you to know that out of mercy and grace God answered my prayers. Through unusual circumstances He brought the two of us together, right here in this church. When you meet my daughter some of you will realize what those unique circumstances involved." And, as Carla looked at Hope, she extended her hand towards her. "Everyone, I want you to meet my precious daughter, Hope Foster."

Hope rose out of the front pew, walked up the stairs leading to the podium and took her mother's hand. It was clear that some people were shocked, but many stood up in excitement, clapping, and rejoicing with them. After service both mother and daughter were thronged by many well-wishers. There were those who admitted they had been greatly blessed and inspired by Carla's testimony.

Hope smiled as she mentally relived these precious moments. The celebration outside interrupted her musings, bringing her back to the present. As she leaned over to pick up her glass from the end table and rejoin the celebration outside, she heard the front door open. Stopping in her tracks, she could feel herself holding her breath in anticipation. Before she could turn around she heard his voice and the words she had been waiting for, "Happy birthday, Princess, I'm home!"

Hope spun around and flew into her father's arms. Laughter erupted from both of them as he swung her around with joy. It was as if she were a little girl again, welcoming her daddy home. His strength seemed to never waver no matter her age or size.

He set her down on her feet and stepped back, while holding both of her hands, to look at her. "How have you been?" he asked. His voice was tinged with concern."

Hope knew her father would be completely overwhelmed by everything that happened in his absence; therefore, she decided early on what to share with him first. She was also aware that others were anxious about his return for various reasons; therefore, she wanted to address what she considered to be a possible obstacle up front to a pleasant homecoming. It was her way of preparing him as a means to steer him through choppy waters quickly so they both could hopefully ensure smooth sailing in the end. "Oh Dad, I have so much to tell you, but the first thing I want you to know is that I've become a Christian."

Hope's father seemed to be taken back by her statement. She couldn't read his face as to whether he approved or whether he was upset about it.

Suddenly, Steven Foster smiled, "Praise God!" He has taken care of you!"

At this point Hope was stunned. "What do you mean Dad?"

Oh Hope, I was so concerned for you when I found the divorce papers. I suspected awhile back that my wife was up to exiting our marriage, but I was hoping she would put it off until I got back. When I saw those papers, I knew you're in for it and there was nothing I could do to protect you. It tormented me, and I didn't know what to do. Out of desperation I went to the chaplain to see if I could get an emergency leave. He assured me that he would do what he could, but he also told me about Christ. He encouraged me to turn to Him and trust the matter to Him. That night in desperation, I did turn to Him, and found peace about the situation. Later the chaplain led me to Christ, and even though at times I felt anxious, I would commit you into His hands. Praise God, I did receive word within a couple of weeks that you were okay."

"Okay? I'm more than okay!" Hope declared as she excitedly jumped up and down.

They were both laughing. It was then that Steven looked around the room. "It looks like you are doing okay." He paused, "This is not our furniture!"

"You're right Dad. That woman took everything except our clothes. What about her, are you getting a divorce?"

A puzzled look came over her father's face. As almost an afterthought, he filled Hope in on the details, "She wanted money, but thanks to the savvy jag lawyers, she was threatened with child abuse and abandonment, meaning you, and she decided to accept whatever terms I stipulated. Our divorce will be finalized in a couple of months." Just as the last words rolled out of his mouth, the question that had been clearly on his mind seemed to burst forth, "Where did you get such nice furniture?"

"Well, Dad, this furniture belongs to the person who has also been taking care of me," she paused, "although my bedroom set belongs to me. It's hard to know what to tell you first, but it all started with the lifeline you left me: you know Lance's phone number."

"Lance gave you the furniture and has been taking care of you?" Steven asked with a puzzled look.

119

Just as she was about to explain, Hope heard her grandmother's voice from behind her.

"It's my furniture Steven." There was a slight pause to let Hope's father process who spoke the words as he looked in her direction. "Hello son," Cassie gently added as Steven's eyes riveted on her.

Hope watched her father's face. He was trying to grapple with what he heard and what he was now seeing. He was stunned, and even blinked his eyes to make sure that what he was seeing wasn't some mirage. He slowly let go of Hope's hands and stepped around her.

"Is it really you, Mom?"

"It's been awhile since you have seen me, but it's really me. Steven," Cassie tearfully stated.

Hope could tell that her father was almost in a state of shock. He was trying hard to connect to present reality. Cassie once again filled the space of uncertainty, "Son, I wouldn't blame you if you shunned me, but know I've always loved you and I just pray you'll forgive me for all the hurt and rejection I've brought into your life."

"It's really you, Mom?" Steven's words proved he was still trying to assure himself it wasn't some dream.

"Yes, it's really me, Steven. You have and always will be my man."

Hope's grandmother's final words proved to be the stimuli that stirred Steven out of his shocked state. With two large steps, he was embracing his mother.

Through tears of joy and sorrow Cassie continued to repeat what had been on her heart for so long, "Forgive me my son. Forgive me."

Steven took a step back and looked at her with such exuberance and tears welling up in his eyes and voice. "Mom, there's no need to forgive you, I know it was the drugs."

"Oh, Steven, it was my bad choices," Cassie said in a lightheartedly, "but, I'm so thankful that circumstances didn't harden your tender, compassionate heart. You've always been quick to understand and forgive, and that's why you'll always be my man."

It was either curiosity or perhaps the excitable exchange that was taking place in the front room, but the group outside started making their way inside. The first one to make an entrance was Stephanie.

When Steven saw her, he looked at Hope, "Who's this pretty young lady? Is she one of your new friends, Hope?"

Aunt Deidre stepped out from behind her daughter and with a trembling voice introduced her, "No Steven, she is my daughter, Stephanie, your name sake."

Hope wasn't sure what was going on in her father. Instead of him being stunned, he took on a quizzical expression.

"Like mother, Steven, I hope you can forgive me for my selfish, insensitive ways so many years ago."

A compassionate expression began to resonate from Steven's face, and more tears began to well up in his eyes. He walked up to Deidre with a smile on his face, "Sis, there is nothing to forgive. It's so great to see you, and meet your...uh,...my name sake."

Deidre flew into Steven's arms and buried her face into his chest as he fully embraced her. He took his right hand and tenderly brushed the side of Stephanie's face. Stephanie's response was to move closer to her mother and uncle, knowing that her uncle's arm was long enough to include her into the embrace. Steven kissed his weeping sister's head and brought Stephanie closed to his shoulder with the swoop of his arm.

It was then that Norman and Keith came into Steven's sight. Steven took his right hand and shook his brother-n-law's hand while still embracing the two Zeller women.

It was as he was shaking his hand that Norman introduced Keith, "This is Keith, our son and your nephew. He has wanted to meet you for some time."

Steven smiled at Keith, and used his left hand to firmly shake Keith's right hand. Keith steadfastly held onto his uncle's hand. When he let go of it, Steven used the same hand to reach around Keith's head, bringing it slightly forward as a means to give him a type of hug.

Hope could tell that this family reunion was long overdue. It was obvious that her father still held his mother and sister close to his heart. Now he had a nephew and niece to include into his family.

Hope kept positioning herself in order to watch her father's reaction. She didn't want to miss any of the scenes that now were playing out. There was still one person she wanted to see how her father would respond to once his eyes landed upon her.

Her father finally saw Lance, and about that time Hope's aunt and cousin parted like the Red Sea, allowing Steven to shake the hand of his friend and thank him for taking care of his daughter. It was then that he was introduced to Lawrence and Mildred. Tiffany had been silently standing by Lance's side waiting for her turn.

When it was Tiffany's turn to be introduced, Lance looked at Steven, "I probably don't have to introduce you to Tiffany."

Hope could tell her father was trying to search his memory.

"Lance, Steven and I have never formally met," Tiffany explained. "We know of each other indirectly." Tiffany then looked at Steven, "My sister is the one you know."

With a perplexed look, Steven posed the question that was clearly dancing around his mind "Your sister! Who's she?"

Tiffany looked past Steven and nodded her head toward someone standing behind him.

Hope's father turned to see who this past acquaintance was. When his eyes landed on Carla, it seemed as if all the air went out of him. Amazement rolled over his face; sorrow made a quick appearance, but quickly gave way to a contained joy.

"Carla!" Steven whispered.

"Hi Steven, welcome home," Carla said with a weak, uncertain smile.

Looking at Hope, and then back at Carla with a confused, questioning look he whispered, "Does Hope know?"

When he looked at Hope she took the heart necklace, which had been recently repaired, and waved it at her father; and, when Steven looked back at Carla, she smiled and likewise held the necklace up for him to see. Hope could tell that in his shocked state he was relieved that the truth had come out.

He noticed that Carla's parents along with her brother and family were standing to the side of her. She was aware that her grandparents had a bit of trepidation about facing the man they had threatened to destroy. Hope could tell her father was quickly considering his options as to what he would do. To reveal his character, Steven nodded his head at them and slightly smiled as he slowly walked towards Carla indicating that he wanted to put the past behind him. Relief broke on their faces as they smiled back at him. He walked up to Carla and took both of her hands and looked into her eyes. "Where've you been Carla Kirkland?"

With a sigh of relief and in a calm but lighthearted voice, Carla responded, "Why, Steven Foster, I have been waiting for you to come home."

Hope could tell by the glow on both of her parents' faces that they still loved each other deeply. She remembered what her grandmother said in one of their conversations, "True love never fades with time; rather, it becomes refined like expensive wine."

"There're a few other introductions to be made that can wait." Cassie asked as she looked at Steven, Is anyone hungry?" A chorus of voices answered, "Yes!" "Son, you must be hungry," Cassie added.

Steven nodded at his mother. I will escort the princess to the outdoor party. "Then looking at Carla he said, "And her mother to the table" It was clear that Hope's father was not about to let go of the love of his life.

With a smile, Carla took Steven's right arm. "Steven, I do not plan to ever let go of my family again."

Hope took her father's other arm as he began to lead the joyous procession to the backyard to begin the birthday celebration.

Hope felt like a vessel overflowing with joy unspeakable. She was learning that when God does something, He does it well. A family had been broken, but He used a bad situation and an unassuming lifeline of reconciliation to unite them. A couple had been separated, but the Lord had bound them together with a token of hope. Like a necklace of pearls, the Lord connected each pearl of forgiveness, promise, and love together with the string of circumstances. He then completed the necklace by knitting together the torn and broken hearts, to at last bring reconciliation to a shattered family and fulfill a couple's destiny by opening the door of hope and promise for them to become one, securing what had been put in motion years before, by finally bringing a family together.

For what is a man profited,
if he shall gain the whole world,
and lose his own soul?
or what shall a man give
in exchange for his soul?
(Matthew 16:26)

Shattered

Andrea Bigelow looked in the mirror with great scrutiny. She closely examined to see if everything was in place from her clothes and hair to her makeup. Most of the time Andrea, felt confident that after she had thoroughly examined the image in the mirror, everything would end up in its proper place. However, recently something was not right about the reflection that was peering back at her.

She could not explain it but it seemed that there was something that didn't fit into the perfect image. She wasn't sure about what she was seeing. Granted, she had seen small glimpses of it in the past, but she ignored them. However, lately it seemed that this irregularity was becoming more prominent in its appearance. It was as if she no longer could ignore it, for it was beginning to ever so slightly mock her.

Andrea knew that the reflection she was seeing reflected aspects of her soul. Something had been gnawing at her for some time. However, as she examined every aspect of her life, she was confident that whatever the struggle was, it could not originate with her goals or lifestyle. She was living the different aspects of the American Dream. She was working her way up the corporate ladder of an investment company. In her mind there was nothing to stop her from reaching the pinnacle of worldly success.

She had learned early in life how to play the game. It all had to do with presenting the right image. To be successful, you first had to exhibit an appearance of achievement. You had to fit in with the right crowd, which required wearing the right clothes, making sure you had the latest hairstyle, properly applied makeup, and your associates had to be successful people. You had to expose yourself to the proper environment in order to learn the ropes and be noticed by those who were in positions of power.

Andrea had decided early in her life that she was going to be a mover and a shaker. She was not content to accept crumbs. After all, that is what plagued her childhood years. She couldn't count how many times she experienced the leftovers of life. Her parents divorced when she was the ripe old age of eight. She and her brother emotionally wrestled with an event that was beyond their control, and the result was that it cast them into a vacuum of uncertainty and into a tormenting world of despair.

Her father began to pursue his own life. Only when duty required him to take note of his children did he regard them. It seemed that when he abandoned ship where his marriage was concerned, he also abandoned his children. They were part of his old life and he was now on to new and better things. It was clear he didn't want to be bothered by any aspects of his old life. He acted as if his children were points of inconvenience and unnecessary burdens.

Sadly, her mother also pursued a new life. Only she would parade her conquests in front of her children. Andrea lost count of the men that her mother brought home. Some, although married, were seeking new adventures. Others were simply opportunists looking for a one-night stand, and those who stayed for any period of time proved to be users. Even though Andrea was in her formative years of childhood, she knew the score. Her mother was also using men to fill the gnawing vacuum left in her life. Andrea knew there was something wrong about her mother's lifestyle, but it became the "norm" in their household. However, the end results were always the same: Andrea became the mother and counselor as her mother waded through each broken relationship, shattered emotions, and the despairing of her heart.

The one thing Andrea remembered was the loneliness. The three of them were living in a dark apartment. At night her mother would often leave her and her brother alone in her pursuit for happiness. She had asked the people in the next apartment to keep an eye on them, but her brother was only ten. In spite of the watchful eyes and ears next door, they both felt alone, and even though neither one would admit it, they were both afraid.

For the two young siblings the fear translated into frustration and anger which they often took out on each other. Since there were only two bedrooms, Andrea slept on the crouch in the front room. One night her brother locked the front door without her knowledge. When their mother came home late that night, she didn't have a key to let herself into the apartment. She tried to softly knock on the door in hopes of awaking Andrea, whose head was located right by the door. But, because of the deep sleep of depression, Andrea didn't hear her. It was not until the next morning that her mother's knock finally roused

Andrea out of her sleep. When she opened the door, her mother angrily slapped her across the face, sending her flying backwards.

Andrea had been half asleep, but when her mother slapped her she became fully awake. She was stunned at her mother's reaction. Apparently, her mother spent a very cold night trying to figure out how to keep warm. She would drive around a bit and then try knocking softly on the door to awaken her daughter. In spite of the cold, her mother was hot under the collar, and even though Andrea had not locked the door, she felt the force of her mother's frustration and anger towards the situation in the unexpected slap. That day her mother had to go to work without any sleep.

It was then that Andrea concluded that life was unfair. Right didn't always come out on top, while a façade was often preferred for truth, and regardless of age, innocence could easily be sacrificed on the altars of worldly selfishness. Her conclusion left her disillusioned, and the shattering of her innocence by the reality around her gave way to skepticism.

As skepticism took center stage, she began to see the value of playing the games of the world in spite of the sick reality and perverted perceptions they established. Since it seemed most people didn't care about the matters of right and wrong, all one had to do was figure out how to play the game. It was clear to Andrea that most of the world played such games. It was the way of the world, and regardless of what was sacrificed along the way, it was not only accepted but expected. It was the way to keep up the delusion without being haunted by any real standard of morality or tender conscience.

It was from this premise that Andrea developed a survivalist mindset. She decided she would survive no matter what. She would overcome every obstacle and come out on top. And, thanks to the examples around her, she devised the right games. That is when she quickly learned early on that it was all about image. The right appearance could hide ignorance and ineptness. The right pose could hide fear and uncertainty. The right air could give the look of self-confidence and control, and the right countenance could seduce, manipulate, and control people.

Andrea learned quickly that as long as she played the game correctly, which entailed "scratching the back" of the right people to ensure that her back would be "scratched" at the appropriate time, that she could position herself to be recognized in the arenas of the world. Granted, it required a personally shrewd compromise on her part, but in order to play such a game all she needed was the ability to properly recognize, feed, and pacify the pride of the person.

Feeding the pride was the means to cater to a person's particular delusion about him or herself as to his or her importance in the scheme of things. There also had to be a façade of conformity, a willingness to agree with the insane ideas of those who held the reins of control. She knew that it was an effective way to keep the monsters that resided in the confines of touchy, fragile egos at bay.

The group of people she initially tried this game out on were her boyfriends. She had watched the men in her mother's life use her, and Andrea wanted to first beat the men that came into her life at their own game. She would be the one that would seduce them for her own benefit.

Even though Andrea had felt in control of what she would offer up on the different altars of the world in order to advance her goals, she knew that she had clearly been conditioned by her childhood environment to know what offerings would be required to forge ahead. She learned early that the first offering was that of purity. In order to fit in the world, purity had to not only be sacrificed, but any moral or simple notions that were attached to it had to be shattered and left along-side in the trash heap of what used to be innocent hopes and dreams.

Her purity was first offered up when she was fourteen. Granted, she was not really emotionally or mentally there when it happened. She was dabbling in alcohol and drugs to not only fit in with the crowd, but to take the edge off of any naïve notions that would make her vulnerable. She wanted to partake of this prized experience that had been touted as being unique and satisfying.

The world's subtle presentation as to what constituted the path to popularity on many fronts, including high school, clearly required one to take the path of promiscuity. However, for Andrea her first experience in that particular arena fell short, shattering the expectation that the world had attached to it, deeming it nothing more than propaganda. Physically, she felt something happened, but it seemed that she lost something rather than gaining something of worth. Emotionally she was left disappointed and empty by the experience, but if she was to be accepted she had to keep up the false façade of the world.

It was then that she realized that the world's presentation of the sexual revolution was nothing more than a sick fantasy. Perhaps in the right context, there was something special to discover in the experience, but the world had reduced it to be nothing more than a tool to advance one's selfish pursuits of conquering or by giving the appearance of being conquered to gain a reputation of possessing some type of control. She knew if there was any significance to it, the world had also managed to diminish it to a base exercise that promised some great emotional peak, but ended up exploiting untried emotions, proving to be a disappointing dip in the road marked experiences. From that point on, every time Andrea resorted to taking the path of promiscuity where her emotions were easily exploited, she simply shut them off to avoid feelings of disappointment and emptiness.

Although, Andrea had become tough in her resolve, her conscience managed to rise up occasionally and bring some seething accusation against her methods. Granted, some men gladly accepted her different overtures as a game that benefitted both parties in some way, but there were a few that were clearly hurt by her shrewd, indifferent methods. However, in such games victims were to be occasionally expected and she couldn't let her conscience get the best of her. After all, today was a special day for her and she could not allow her past to depress her or her methods to prick any real sense of right or wrong that still might be left.

Today Andrea was going to receive the promotion she had been working towards. She had proven many times during the dipping and rising of the volatile stock market that she knew how to keep her wits about her, and even found ways to do some damage control. It was clear that she had the abilities and talents to take the assistant position that had just become available underneath her supervisor. But, in spite of her proving her abilities, being a woman often meant she had to prove herself ten times more than her counterpart. It was for this reason she often used the few advantages that womanhood allotted her. She cleverly wove a web of seduction for her boss. Although unethical, he seemed more than happy to play her game, allowing himself to be entangled into her ambitious plan.

Andrea felt confident that her plans were nicely coming together. However, when she walked into the main office area, Roma Dalton, the receptionist appeared to be frazzled. When it came to office business, Roma and Andrea watched each other's backside. It was a man's world and both women understood that it was wise to find good allies to serve as extra ears and eyes.

When Andrea met Roma's eyes, she could tell that not all was right in their office. Roma rolled her eyes and quickly glanced at the boss's office. Silently, she mouthed, "Big trouble."

Andrea walked up to the door of her supervisor's office with trepidation. She had worked on some accounts the night before. These accounts involved rich clients that were investing large sums of money in the market. Such accounts had to first be reviewed by the supervisor who had to sign off on them. She had placed them in her briefcase in order for her boss to review them first thing so she could proceed to present the different portfolios to her perspective clients for their final approval.

She knocked on the door and was let in by a tall man with brown hair, gentle brown eyes, and refined manner. Andrea assumed that he was around her age. Even though there was evidence that the present situation was proving to be disconcerting to him, his smile was welcoming and his voice was inviting as he beckoned her to enter through the door of the office.

"I'm sorry to disturb you. I'm Andrea Bigelow." Andrea's voice seemed a bit strained to her ears as she introduced herself. Her eyes quickly made a glancing sweep of the room and she noted that there was one other man in the office besides the one who had opened the door and her supervisor. She quickly noted that files dotted much of the landscape of the office. Andrea looked into the clear eyes of the one who appeared to be the doorkeeper, "I need someone to give final approval to a couple of my accounts so I can present it to my clients today."

It was then that the man who answered the door introduced himself. "My name is Kyle Davidson," and pointing to the other man, "and this is Boyd Gibson." Gibson nodded at her while Mr. Davidson explained their presence and intention to her. "We're here from the main office to clarify some transactions." Davidson then looked over to her boss and then back at Andrea. "We have no desire to impede the activities of this office."

Davidson looked at Andrea's supervisor. "Take Ms. Bigelow to the conference room where you can freely discuss the portfolios."

Andrea could tell her supervisor was in an uncomfortable spot. His usual controlled demeanor was unraveled and his expensive clothes seemed to take on an appearance of being slept in. His attractive face was marked with worry lines and his lips seemed pale and thinner than usual. Instead of walking with strides of self-confidence, his posture made him look like a beaten man. She could only surmise that the inquiries that were being made had to do with some of the land investments he had been tenaciously overseeing.

Andrea was aware that her supervisor along with his former assistant had worked hard on selling a plan to the main office that involved lucrative land deals in their area. Since the two men were the brainchild behind the plan, they guarded each deal. When her boss' assistant suddenly turned in his resignation and left the company, the usual rumors and speculations followed his departure. However, Andrea stayed away from the temptation to become part of the rumor mill. His exodus had been unexpected and strange, but Andrea saw it as an opportunity for her to secure his position. Even though she was trying to educate herself more about the workings of land investments on her personal time, she stayed away from seeking her boss's help. Andrea felt her best policy was to remain aloof from the office gossip and ignorant about any possible facts that might prove negative and possibly criminal.

Her boss led her into the conference room where he took the side chair at the large table. She took a chair on the opposite side of the table so she could look at him. Her boss wearily looked down at the table, while motioning with his hand for her to hand him the portfolios.

While taking the portfolios from her briefcase to hand them to him, Andrea broke the silence, "Aren't you going to tell me what is going on?"

Her supervisor looked up into her eyes, "Are you sure you want to know what's going on?"

Andrea was taken back a bit by his question. "Of course I want to know! Why would you ask such a question?"

"Because you seem to prefer to remain indifferent and aloof as to what is going on in this office lately."

Andrea realized that her boss had been struggling with the events that were now culminating in his office. He had clearly noted her indifference. It was obvious to him that she wanted to benefit from the situation, while avoiding getting her hands dirty. The truth is her boss needed someone to confide in, and because of their relationship she was the likely candidate who could prove to be that confidant. But it was clear to him that she was distancing herself from what was going on, and in so doing left him dangling alone above the fiery caldron of annihilation.

"Since you've asked Andrea, I'll let you know what is going on. It's the typical scenario of white-collar crime. The temptation to impress, compete, or be considered a successful winner by the world often requires one to reach beyond one's means in order to ride high on the waves of so-called 'success.' The temptation opens the door to pursue and live the decadent lifestyle afforded to a few, to taste forbidden pleasures even if it is for a few moments, and to ultimately beat the system at its own games."

Andrea could tell her boss was in deep reflection as he paused to replay the events that were now changing the landscape of his life. "It was so subtle at first, Andrea. Just take some funds here with the intention of paying them back as the means to soothe the conscience and hide your dirty little deeds. Once you rationalize it the first time, it becomes easier to justify it the next time. Before long you are in the grips of something that you can't explain, but it becomes addictive.

"Perhaps it's a sense of power that you feel when you're dealing with lots of money, or it could be the feeling that you are smart enough to figure out how to beat the system. You convince yourself you can keep ahead of the tsunami. There'll always be one more deal around the corner that will keep you afloat until you figure out how to fill the big hole you have dug with each excuse, each justification, and each lie you have told yourself. The biggest lie of all is that if you get caught it will prove to be worth it, regardless of the consequences."

Andrea felt shock waves come over her. Her relationship with her boss revealed his moral inconsistencies, but she had avoided considering that such deviations included embezzlement and fraud.

"Don't look so shocked Andrea! You know you're part of the scenario."

"Just what do you mean I was part of the scenario?" Andrea retorted in a defensive manner. "I didn't know what you were doing in your land deals."

It was clear that her boss was on edge by his next statement, "But, you enjoyed the fruits of it! Where do you think I got the money to lavish you with gifts and trips to beautiful places? Don't forget I also support a copious lifestyle when it comes to my wife and children. I made lots of money but not enough to support the two distinct lifestyles I have been living."

Shame made a quick appearance on Andrea's face. Her boss obviously saw its entrance and continued in his explanation.

"Andrea, we are both adults. I knew what you were doing. It was the first time I've been unfaithful to both the company and my wife, but I knew you were seducing me so you could climb to the top. I was a big boy and I was ripe for the picking. I convinced myself that by playing along with you that I would benefit greatly by what you were willing to give away. Even though I was married, I felt I deserved my other life with you. After all, I worked hard and my life with my wife wasn't that exciting, while you brought excitement, suspense, and a bit of danger to my existence."

"I didn't ask you to take such risks for me," Andrea interjected.

"Come on Andrea; don't get self-righteous on me now! You knew about my wife and family, and were willing to rob her and my children of my time and affections to climb to the top. Neither one of us considered their feelings for one minute! Whether we thought we could get away with it," he paused as he shook his head, "or actually deserved it or convinced ourselves that it didn't matter that we might leave them as carnage in the wake of our selfish pursuits, we clearly deprived them of what was rightfully theirs. It was not mine to give you what belonged to them and it was not yours to take it, but neither one of us cared enough to stop the deception and immoral conduct and do what was right."

He continued his exhortation, his eyes penetrating the steel wall that guarded her resolve, "Andrea, you're one smart cookie. You had to suspect that there was something wrong as far as the financial end, but you chose to play ignorant so you could enjoy it. Regardless of the ignorance you claim about the financial end of this mess, once again it wasn't my right to morally or legally take the money from others, and it wasn't yours to receive it without questioning where it was coming from. Whether it was being directed away from my family or the investors of this company, if you were being honest with yourself, you would have known the benefits were not yours to receive and would not have agreed with such practices."

Andrea began to feel sick at her stomach. She had ignored much so that she didn't have to face what her actions were costing others. She had managed to keep her boss' wife and children faceless and nameless, so she didn't have to face the hard reality that their lives could be shattered by her actions. She had silently questioned where her boss's money came from, but allowed her logic to push it aside by convincing herself she was worthy and deserving of his lavish attention regardless of the source.

Shame was wrapping its tentacles around Andrea's very being. Guilt was causing her neck and shoulders to feel the gravity of the matter as it began to weigh heavily in the room and on her conscience.

Due to the blanket of shame, Andrea could no longer look her boss in the eyes. However, in a quiet voice she asked him the question that was dangling in the air. "What's next?"

Andrea squirmed uncomfortably, and even though she was staring at the table, she still felt the penetrating eyes of her boss as he answered her question. "What's next? I'll have to face the consequences. I'll have to first face my wife and children. I dread that the most because I'll possibly lose my family. Rightfully so, for I don't deserve them.

"My wife has always been there for me, and now I'll have to confess that I've betrayed everything good and right in our marriage and I'm badly in need of her forgiveness. I must openly admit I was willing to sacrifice my family, along with my self-respect for something that was fleeting and temporary in the name of selfishness and ego. And, if my wife manages to forgive me and shows incredible grace by staying with me, she will heap even greater judgment on me, forcing me to face just how undeserving I am of her love and devotion." He paused as he let the truth settle like a heavy shroud in the room. "And, then I finally have to go to court where I will face the judge, hear my jail sentence read, and be required to repay those I betrayed. And, now that I've lost it all, it'll take the rest of my life to pay back even a pittance of it. The victims will never see all the money I've stolen from them."

Andrea could tell that her boss was becoming consumed by regret, but she couldn't help but ask the second question that hung in the air. "What's going to happen to the people in this office?"

His answer was quick, "I don't know, but I no longer have any authority to appoint you as my assistant. I don't know if the main office will send people to fill these positions, or which positions are up for grabs within this office. You could try your seductive methods with Kyle. He is the CEO's nephew and the good news is he' is not married. No doubt he has some pull with headquarters."

Andrea's boss' statement was a stinging rebuke that slammed against her already raw conscience. She knew she had it coming, but she still had not expected him to take such aim at her. As she found herself embroiled in the emotional upheaval that was taking place in her inner being, her boss's voice broke through the upheaval to bring her back to reality.

"Andrea, look at me." Andrea slowly lifted her eyes from the table to look at her boss. His eyes were intense, penetrating into the recesses of her soul.

"I've something to say to you. I've had to face myself the past few weeks. I had convinced myself that no matter what, that the so-called 'fun' I thought I was having in our relationship was worth the consequences. Right now the bitterness of it all clearly outweighs the 'fun' I supposedly had with you."

"The self-examination I've been forced to do lately has shown me that I don't like what I've seen about my personal character. I have to admit I've struggled not to direct all of my anger and resentment at you by blaming you for my predicament. I've realized that it has been my desire to taste your forbidden fruit, while playing the blame game by falsely accusing my wife of not making me happy. It allowed me to lower my guard with you in the first place, compromise whatever integrity I had, and fling that which was worthwhile, such as my self-respect, my family, and career, to the wind of chance. Granted, I was wrong, but so are you."

His words were like a sharp knife that began to shred the hard places of her heart as he continued his rebuke. "You're an opportunist and a seductress and you've tempted me with tasting your fruit by making it available. I realize if it wasn't you, it could have easily been another vixen that would entangle my pride in the same way, because my selfish attitude and misguided ambition set me up for the fall."

Andrea felt the seams of her resolve beginning to split, as his words continued to hit their mark, and she felt the hard encasement around her emotions crack. She struggled to keep herself together, while reinforcing her sagging defenses against the onslaught of his words.

"If you were not so willing to use aspects of your womanhood to entrap and manipulate me to obtain your goal, we both might not be sitting here today talking about this painful situation. What I want you to know is that even though I take full responsibility for my actions, I have to admit that I intensely dislike you. In fact, I loathe you because you were not there for me. I was good enough to use, which clearly showed me what I already suspected, you really didn't care for me. Our relationship was a matter of my fleshly based lust and your greed. I played the fool and ended up becoming one. I know that my attitude towards you will not keep you awake at night because in this game we expected casualties, didn't we?

"In spite of my intense dislike for you, I have a bit of last advice I want to give you." Andrea watched as his eyes narrowed and his voice became resolved. "It's not worth it! The road you are on will prove to be a dead end, and the methods you're using to arrive at whatever ambitious pinnacles you are striving for will leave the taste of bitterness in your mouth and emptiness in your soul. Remember, all pinnacles have limited margins at the top and always have a downside to them.

"My present trouble has reminded me of my past religious influences. I was taught about the high cost of playing in the devil's arena, and this world is the devil's arena. To play in his arena, you'll be required to sell your reputation and barter away your soul, along with any valuable relationships. In the end, it'll all prove to be useless chaff that will be easily picked up by the ever changing winds of this world and disbursed into a vacuum of nothingness."

Andrea felt her eyes widen from the fear that begin to grip her. She knew that in spite of his contemptible feelings towards her that he was trying to salvage what bit of self-respect he had not yet sold, and resurrect some chivalry in the end by warning her. He could have remained quiet about his ordeal, and allowed her to taste the bitter depths of the abyss that she was digging for herself with each moral compromise and unethical maneuver.

He then looked at the portfolios in front of him. Andrea knew that he had confidence in her abilities to develop a folio that was conducive to her clients' needs and goals. He signed on the perspective line and slid each one of them in front of her. He then stood up and walked back into his office to face his execution, leaving her alone in the conference room.

Andrea knew she was at some type of crossroads. Regardless of the fact that she was not part of the fraudulent land investments, she was part of bringing her supervisor down to a most despicable state. She had helped create the crises in his personal life and in the office, while managing to dodge the bullet. As she considered her options, fear fiercely renewed its grip. The question was not, if she wanted to change; rather, it came down to whether she could change. She had mentally and emotionally programmed herself in such a way that everything she did was either a natural reaction, in lieu of personal survival, or an expected maneuver to ensure her best interests were maintained at all times to guarantee the outcome.

As Andrea sat at the table, considering the uncertainty that seemed to loom in front of her, the same loneliness that plagued her as a child threatened to rise from unseen depths of darkness and claim her once again. As the tremors of fear and loneliness shook her inner being, she had to wonder if she had really missed the bullet after all.

***

Andrea now had to face the answer to her question, "Could she change?" Admittedly, she had quickly slid back to her old ways. At first she resented Kyle Davidson and his intrusion into the operation of the office. Within a few days of Davidson temporarily taking over the operations of the office, she became acutely aware that she was back at square "A". Rumor had it that she was being considered for the assistant supervisor along with Cory Jackson, but she was aware that her past participation could thwart her goals.

In Andrea's mind Cory was alright, but he was not as experienced as she. He had not developed that certain intuition that was necessary to read both clients and the trends of the market. Each client must be matched with the trends that would not only make them dividends but would bring them a certain sense of security. In the present environment it became obvious to Andrea she was in a race; therefore, her competitive juices were churning in her mind.

It also appeared to Andrea that since Kyle was the nephew of the CEO of the company that everything had been simply handed to him. Since Andrea had to work hard for all she had achieved, her logic was that it was all quite unfair. Instead of operating from reason, she allowed the feelings of injustice to drive her. She reasoned that the only way she could get what she deserved was to conquer Kyle Davidson, to seduce him into her world.

At first she thought of her seduction as a cat and mouse game. She would have to somehow win his confidence in order to isolate him from outside influences that might stop her from fulfilling her objective. In her mind it was a way to make the corporate office pay for what she considered to be the functions of the "good old boys club", and obtain the prize that rightfully belonged to her. She consoled herself that since Kyle was a grown man he could choose to resist her overtures.

To Andrea's amazement, her attempts to seduce Kyle never materialized. If she attempted to meet with him alone, he always had his secretary, Betty Jensen present to take notes for him. This practice not only put a lid on Andrea's plans, but it caused a great deal of frustration and simmering desperation in her. Somehow she had to get control of the situation to ensure the success of her ambitious plans.

The desperation caused Andrea to make subtle overtures to him. At the right times, she would give him a certain seductive look with her hazel eyes or flip her long brown hair a certain way to entice him. In the right circumstances she would ever so lightly touch his arm or hand as a way to get his attention or laugh in a certain tone. However, each attempt seemed to fall to the wayside. Kyle Davidson never broke his stride or seemed to take notice of her overtures, causing Andrea to wonder if she had lost her touch.

In spite of the frustration and the desperation Andrea felt about her plight, within a couple of weeks of Davidson taking over the office, she found herself secretly respecting him. He ran a tight ship. Everything was carried out in a professional manner including how he addressed the employees and how they were to address him. Formality was the mode of operation and the policies of conduct reflected the theme as well. It was obvious that each policy was put into place to discourage any unethical personal interaction between brokers and their supervisors.

Andrea wondered if Kyle knew about her affair with her boss. If he did, it might explain why he never allowed himself to be left alone with her, avoiding any subtle attempts for her to gain his interest. And, if he was turned off by her previous relationship with her supervisor, she had to conclude that she had no chance to win him over to her way of thinking.

One night as Andrea was mulling over her plight, she realized something that sent shock waves through her being and made her feel vulnerable. She actually was attracted to Kyle Davidson. She had no idea as to how it happened. Her work load at the office was doubled due to the departures of the supervisor and his assistant. Andrea had been on a dead run to keep up with the clients and their needs and questions as well as take on new clients. Since she could not initially carry out her plan to seduce Kyle, she had to at least impress him with her work ethics. Secretly, she was trying to make herself indispensable to the company. Granted, she was becoming tired and overwhelmed at times, but she figured she was young enough that she could handle the work load.

Andrea also realized that she had been so intent on ensnaring Kyle that she now found she was being ensnared by her own traps. Her attractions towards him were not only new to her, but unnerving. They made her feel exposed. She then decided she must pull in any attraction and subdue it. She needed a clear mind if she was going to figure out her next moves.

Although Andrea saw every new challenge as being invigorating, she felt that her resolve was not as strong as before. It seemed as if there were a few cracks in her armor. However, she surmised that once she got a working plan in place that the challenge before her would restore her back to her original intensity and pace. But, she had to first figure out how to penetrate Kyle's defenses.

It was becoming clear that there seemed to be a fortress surrounding Kyle. Andrea knew if she was going to conquer Kyle, she had to learn about him to uncover his weak areas. In order to do that she would have to gain the trust of the one person who knew him the most and watched out for his interests. That person was his secretary, Betty Jensen. It was obvious that she was Kyle's first line of defense. Betty was old enough to be Kyle's mother. She was a pleasant enough person, but there was an air about her that quietly served as a warning that one must not underestimate her. Even though she wore the handle of being a secretary to Kyle, Andrea sensed she was also his personal friend and advisor.

The first thing Andrea had to find was some type of means that afforded her the opportunity to build a relationship with Betty. She had noted that Betty took her lunch break at the same time in the break room. Even though Andrea ate her lunch at her desk or on the run, she had to adjust her mode of operation to carry out her plan.

The next day, Andrea put her plan into action. She followed Betty into the break room. Betty sat at the table at the far end of the room. Andrea casually made her way over to the table and asked her if she could sit with her.

Betty's penetrating blue eyes quickly sized Andrea up. After a few seconds Andrea must have met with her approval for she smiled and waved her hand towards the chair next to her, "Feel free to join me Andrea, I always like company when I have my lunch."

Andrea sat down in the chair and methodically took her apple, yogurt, knife, spoon, and water bottle out of her bag. Betty studied the articles in front of Andrea, "Is that all you eat?" she asked in a motherly tone.

"If I eat too much, I get indigestion," Andrea responded with a smile. "Do you always eat by yourself?" Andrea inquired.

Betty chuckled, "Yes. You're the first one to come to the lion's den and risk being eaten by me."

Andrea looked at her with a questioning look, while waiting for Betty to explain her statement.

"Don't you know I intimidate people?" Betty continued on with her discourse. "I'm the boss's snitch. My question to you Andrea is, are you not concerned about what others might say when they see you with me?"

Andrea was quite aware that she had been the subject of the other brokers' and office workers' gossip in the past.

"I assure you Betty, being the object of gossip in this office is nothing new for me. I've been the subject of much gossip in the past. Come to think of it, that's why I probably avoid the lunchroom because of the gossip taking place in it. I see gossip as petty, and coming from people who have too little to do and are probably small minded. There are far more interesting things to talk about than the personal lives of others."

Andrea realized she may have given a bit too much information away. Her confession about avoiding the place in the past might cause Betty to become suspicious as to her motives for her being there at this particular time. She was not used to slipping up in small ways. It was clear she had to note her discrepancy, as well as steady the shaking inside. She forced herself to concentrate on Betty's facial expressions, studying her to see if there was any indication that she was aware that Andrea had just given herself away, or whether she knew about her past activities. If the secretary recognized the slip, or knew about Andrea's indiscretions with her former boss, she never let on.

"Since other people's personal lives are off the table, what interesting subjects would you like to talk about Andrea?" Betty asked.

Andrea knew she had to be clever about what she asked to keep Betty from suspecting her real motives. "I would like to know about who established policies for the different offices? I have to admit I appreciate the discipline that Ky...uh... Mr. Davidson has brought to this place."

Once again Betty smiled, "That is an easy enough question. Each office establishes its own policies as far as conduct and certain procedures. The policies that Mr. Davidson has established here are based on his Christian convictions."

The first bit of insight Andrea received about Kyle stunned her, but she quickly recuperated to continue her inquiry. "I never suspected that Mr. Davidson was a religious man."

Betty's eyes narrowed and her smile diminished as her voice took on a firm tone. "Andrea, my description of Mr. Davidson was not in reference to him being a religious man; rather, what motivates his policies is that he is a devoted Christian."

Andrea didn't quite know what she stepped into, but she could tell that her inexperience in this particular area caused her to slip up again. "I'm sorry Betty; I didn't mean to downplay his convictions or policies. To me a religious man and a Christian are the same."

"You can be religious about anything," Betty stated in a decisive tone, "but Christianity isn't a religious ritual or a practice; rather, it's a way of living. It's not something you do, it's something you become."

Andrea could hear the conviction in Betty's voice. "Are you a Christian, Betty?" Andrea gently asked.

"Yes, I am Andrea. If it wasn't for my relationship with God that was firmly established through Jesus Christ, I wouldn't be here today. He saved me from complete ruin and has given me a new life."

Betty's words went deep into Andrea's soul and struck a chord of familiarity, producing curiosity. "I have to admit, Betty, I've never really been exposed to God. I would be interested to hear how He...uh...helped you, but I need to get back to work. Perhaps, we can talk again some time." Even though eating lunch with Betty fell into Andrea's plan, she felt that her motive was sincere about learning more about the Christian life. Such an unadulterated motive actually made her feel strange.

"But you've hardly touched any of your food, Andrea," Betty stated.

While packing the articles back into her lunch bag, Andrea latched on the closest and most honest excuse, "I just remembered that I promised to call one of my clients at this time of day."

"I'll be here tomorrow, at the same time and place." Betty assured her, "And, I'll be glad to tell you my story, and maybe you can tell me about your life."

Andrea was not interested in sharing any of her life, but Betty had certainly lit a fire in her soul, and stirred up her curiosity to know more about the Christian way.

The next day Andrea and Betty did meet for lunch. Betty willingly shared her story, but it unnerved Andrea. Except for receiving Christ and marrying a Christian man, she lived a similar life that Andrea was now living. Betty described herself as being like a woman in the Bible named, Rahab. She had prostituted herself as a means to not only survive the world but advance in it, but one day she encountered those who carried the message of God, the message of life and hope. Like Rahab, she had also heard about God in prior years, but it was in her later years that she discovered Him.

According to Betty, God had also greatly intervened on her part to save her and her family like He had for Rahab. The Lord had also tossed to her the red cord of redemption that was eventually used by the Spirit of God to lower her down into God's enfolding arms of love, mercy, compassion, and grace, saving her soul from complete ruin. And, like Rahab who married an Israelite by the name of Salmon to become part of the lineage of Jesus Christ, "The Messiah," Betty also married her Salmon, only his name was Roy.

Roy was a dedicated believer, a son of God, part of the Christian lineage who would receive an eternal inheritance. It was by making Christ the cornerstone of their life and marriage together that a powerful bond was forged between them. The physical bond was only broken by his death, but not the emotional or spiritual one. Through misty eyes Betty shared that one day she will not only see the wondrous face of her Savior, Jesus, but she will see the precious face of her Roy.

Andrea admired, and even secretly coveted what Betty had. She possessed the inner strength that helped her walk through the loss of her beloved husband, along with the heavenly confidence that gave her assurance that one day she would see him again. It was clear that there was an empty space in Betty's environment, but her life was full, her soul satisfied, and her heart was lifted up and floating on the currents of glorious expectation.

Even though Andrea had brought portfolios home to work on that night, she couldn't get the story of Rahab out of her mind. The reels of her mind kept replaying it. As the story was repeated in her mind, Andrea felt a deep need to read it for herself. However, she did not own a Bible.

As she thought about where to obtain a Bible, a memory darted out from behind one of the many curtains of her mind. It was a memory of actually taking a Bible from one of the many motel rooms she had stayed in. In most cases she ignored the Bible that had been placed in the night stand by her motel bed, but it was during one of those times her curiosity was peeked about the foreign book. She picked it up thinking that one day she might even read it to find out what was so important about it. She put it in her baggage and brought it home. In a hurry, she had placed it in one of her many drawers, but she couldn't remember which drawer it was in. Was it in a kitchen drawer, a dresser drawer, a desk drawer, or a utility drawer of odds and ends?

She decided she needed to look for it. It took about twenty minutes before she finally located the book in the very back of one of her desk draws. It had a hard red cover, and it was marked as belonging to the Gideon's. As she opened the book, she realized she had no idea where to find the story of Rahab. As she thumbed through the book, she became overwhelmed. Where would she begin to look for it?

She closed her eyes, opened the Bible and put her finger on the page. When she looked down she read the following reference, "For what is a man profited, if he shall gain the whole world, and lose his own soul? or what shall a man give in exchange for his soul?" The words went into her spirit. It awakened a conversation that she had had with someone recently. She struggled to remember who the source was and what the words were. Oh yes, it was the voice of her boss who warned her against bartering away her soul for that which was vain and loss.

She closed the Bible and her eyes once again and randomly opened it. She put her finger on the page. The words she read brought further indictment, "Destruction and misery are in their ways: And the way of peace have they not known: There is no fear of God before their eyes."

The Bible was clearly giving her an outline of her life. She had actually been selling her soul to gain something that seemed to become more elusive each day. She had walked in the way of destruction, bringing misery to her life and others. There was never a time in her life when she felt peace. And as for God, until she met

Betty she had no consciousness of Him. How could she fear what she didn't know?

Andrea closed the Bible. She had hoped to find the story of Rahab, but only found an indictment being brought against her. In her weariness, she felt like a hopeless case. When it came to God and the Bible, Betty spoke of love, forgiveness, and something called, "Redemption," but all Andrea could see was judgment. However, she had no idea what judgment meant.

She did the only thing she could do and that was close the Bible, shut her eyes, and randomly open it to another reference. Surprisingly, it seemed that the book was mysterious and supernatural for the next reference answered her question, "And fear not them which kill the body, but are not able to kill the soul: but rather fear him which is able to destroy both soul and body in hell."

The concept of "hell" had always been a joke in her mind. But, this strange book made it clear that there was a hell. As the reality of hell took a quick bow in her mind, she became suddenly aware of how estranged she was from the reality of God and His book. She felt unnerved, scared, and exposed. All she could think of was the fact that she had been selling her soul, but to what and for what? The book told her she was selling her soul to the world in order to gain it, but the consequences for obtaining it would be the judgment of hell. Perhaps what occasionally looked back at her in the mirror was a soul that was lifeless, empty, and alone in its misery.

She found herself pacing back and forth like a caged animal, tormented by unseen bars that had isolated her from any hope. As she looked within, she knew she would see nothing for her dreams had been shattered long ago, leaving her empty; and, as she now looked without, her purpose for being lay in a heap of disarray, leaving her in utter despair.

Andrea knew she badly needed sleep. She knew that she was "running on fumes" and she was losing her sharpness to properly function, but sleep eluded her as her mind wrestled with her plight. She didn't know where to turn. She felt the need to confess her wrongs, but who could forgive her? She wanted to be cleansed but no physical water could bring inward cleansing. She wanted rest, but the torment of the past was driving her on tumultuous winds of emotional upheaval.

Sleep did finally come, but it proved to be restless like the stormy waves on the ocean. Her emotions were tossing her back and forth as her mind jumped from the different indictments that were brought against her by the Bible.

143

When the alarm woke her with a jolt, she wasn't sure whether she should rejoice because it raised her from a state of torment, or if she should feel sorry for herself instead because real rest had eluded her. Regardless of how she felt, she had to put one foot in front of the next. She had to get through this day. She would see Betty and ask her where the story of Rahab was in the Bible, and perhaps she would schedule a time with Roma to get the latest scuttlebutt in the office.

The morning for Andrea proved to be unbearable. She could not think clearly, yet she had to function as if she was on top of the world. She managed to set up a time to meet Roma at their favorite bar after work, and met with Betty for lunch.

At lunch time, Betty looked at Andrea with grave concern. "Are you getting enough rest?" she inquired.

Andrea smiled, "I sort of had a bad night." As if to escape overelaborating on the lack of sleep for some time, she went on to ask the question she had been waiting all night to ask, "Hey, I was wondering where I could find the story of Rahab in the Bible?"

"You have a Bible?" Betty's question was tinged with disbelief.

"Yes, I do have a Bible!" Andrea answered. However, she was not about to tell her she had stolen it from a motel room because of a passing fancy.

With a twinkle in her eyes, Betty gave Andrea the Scripture references that had eluded her the night before. "You can find Rahab's story in Joshua 2 and 6 of the Old Testament, and find her part of the lineage of Jesus in Matthew 1:5 in the New Testament. It shows that she was married to Salmon and was the mother of an honorable man named Boaz."

Andrea had to know one thing, "Betty, what does it mean to sell your soul?"

Betty's eyes became intense, but remained soft. "Well Andrea, there's no easy answer to your question. The best way I can explain it to you is that your soul represents a type of anchor as to the person you can be. It houses your will, intellect, and emotions, which will culminate into your personality. It is unseen, but it is influenced by the perceptions you adopt, and will manifest itself in the attitudes you take on about God and life.

"When you lose sight of why you were created, which is to serve and glorify God, you begin to unknowingly cut the line of that anchor to the conscience of your soul to do your own thing. You will eventually trade that which could distinguish the quality of your person and life, such as integrity, morality, convictions, and beliefs, to gain something that is worldly, fleshly, temporary, and empty.

"People who sell their souls will find themselves adrift on the ocean of life where they seek the meaning and purpose of life by looking to things that have no identity or lasting purpose. When they lose themselves in the empty vacuum of such things, they lose sight of what is important and become lost in a world that has no real substance. In the end, they will take on lifeless images according to the world they operate in, but these images will eventually fade, collapse, or fail in time."

Andrea knew that Betty was describing her present state. In her attempt to control the waves of life, she had become lost. Because she sought her identity in that which was lifeless, she had been sucked into a vacuum of nothingness, leaving her with no real identity. What she exhibited to the world was an image that had no life or substance behind it. She had become one of those lizards—a chameleon—that changes color according to its environment, attitudes, and games.

As a savvy business woman, Andrea had quickly learn how to blend with the terrain around her, by adopting a right image, adjusting the presentation of herself according to the crowd, and learning to identify and play the appropriate game. However, she realized in her clever attempt to beat the system and come out on top, she had sold her soul. And, what would she gain from doing so? Some title that would eventually fade, a brief point of recognition that would quickly give way to another game, and a lonely place at the top if she did manage to reach what she was now beginning to see as a "impractical" goal.

As Andrea was contemplating this new revelation, a voice broke through the intensity that surrounded her. It was Kyle. "Sorry to interrupt your conversation, but I wanted to ask Betty about some paper work."

"You didn't interrupt Mr. Davidson, Betty cheerfully responded. "In fact, your timing could prove to be impeccable. You might be able to bring some more insight into our conversation. Ms. Bigelow was asking me about what it means to sell your soul. Men have a tendency to bring concision to such in-depth matters."

Kyle nodded towards a chair to see if he would receive the proper invitation. "Yes, please sit down. I would like your take on the matter." Andrea replied to his gesture.

Kyle eased himself into the chair and looked from Betty to Andrea. Andrea saw that Betty ever so lightly nodded her head at Kyle as he looked her way.

He then looked intently at Andrea. Once again she didn't feel that he was judging her, but that he was trying to determine what approach to take to answer her question.

Apparently, he rightly surmised the best approach to take with her was complete, unadulterated honesty. "To put it bluntly," Kyle firmly stated, "selling your soul means prostituting it to what would be considered the highest bidder. In essence, it is selling it to the world to receive its wages or benefits that in the end will prove to be enslaving, miserable, and worthless."

Andrea a bit taken back by his bluntness, asked, "Have you ever sold your soul, Mr. Davidson?"

He paused slightly before answering her, "Yes I have to a certain point. My parents were Christians, but as a young man I was attracted to the world. It seemed that it promised what was exciting. I had great plans and expectations for myself, and I figured the world was the way to secure them. Since my uncle owned an investment firm and I was good with numbers and had somewhat studied economics and the stock market, I saw it as easy street to make my aspirations come true."

"Who wouldn't take such advantage of an opportunity if the person was in your place?" Andrea interjected. As she heard herself openly admit that anyone who had any common sense would take advantage of such an opportunity, she had to look at her own attitude towards such individuals. She resented them because she was jealous of the breaks they had in life and coveted their positions and lifestyles.

"True Ms. Bigelow, but my uncle did not believe in handing me anything. In fact, to prove he wasn't going to show favoritism to his nephew, he made it as difficult as he could on me. He started me from the lowest position in the firm, and either ignored me altogether or he rode me over petty matters in front of the other workers.

"At first I resented and hated him for what he was doing to me. I almost walked away, but I decided that I could let it beat me or I could beat it. Even though my motive was born out of the arrogance of self-sufficiency to prove myself, I'm now thankful to my uncle. In the long run, I learned great work ethics from him which taught me about self-respect. It developed initiative in me along with the motivation to pay my way through college to gain a greater edge in competing for better positions. My college experience taught me to look for, as well as value and take advantage of, worthwhile opportunities."

Andrea realized her first conclusion about Kyle was wrong. He wasn't handed a silver spoon. It was apparent he had to work his way to the position he was now in. She wanted to learn more about Kyle's adventure climbing the corporate ladder and knew from past experiences how to cross examine him with statements. "Apparently, you did win your uncle's approval because of the position you now hold."

"I did, but not without difficulties and hitting some personal crises," Kyle admitted. "Even though I worked hard, earned my college degree, and showed my willingness to work my way up in the firm, my uncle would play with me by dangling prospects in front of me, only to rip them out of my grasp at the last minute and offer it to another. Every opportunity that came my way came in the form of a minuscule drip of necessity. But, the small open doors of necessity are what provide opportunities; that is, if you are willing to let your pride be walked on."

"It doesn't seem fair," Andrea stated. "Obviously, your uncle could trust you. Why would he treat you in such a way?"

"I had to come to the conclusion there is not much fair in life Ms. Bigelow. The wisest man of all before Jesus Christ made an important statement that put it all in perspective. However, this is my paraphrase of it, 'Princes end up walking like servants, while fools are riding horses of importance.' In other words, the world is upside down in how it operates. Today we see this scenario in all walks of life. It seems there are more fools holding the reins of this world, thereby oppressing and subduing those who have the potential to conduct themselves like royalty."

"It's amazing you're still working for your uncle," Andrea thoughtfully stated. "He sounds like he fits into the category of being a fool."

"My uncle thinks the contrary," Kyle replied. "He thinks he is a very clever man. He clearly rides his own horse of importance. If a man is a fool it is because he doesn't believe there is a God. Such a man thinks himself to be important, a king, a ruler, but in reality he is a slave to his own greed, lusts, and delusions.

"My uncle believes there is a God, but he believes that he earned what he now possesses. I had to learn the contrary: that everything we have is a matter of God's grace. My dealings with my uncle eventually taught me that important fact."

Kyle almost smiled to himself, "I had considered trying to prove to myself in such a way that I could win my uncle over by cunning, clever ways, but my uncle must have recognized my games because he would pull the rug out from beneath me every time I tried to be clever. I finally came to the end of myself and realized I would never win my uncle's approval, and that I would have to wait for those oozing drops of opportunity to come my way for any type of advancement. After all, the more I tried, the wearier I was becoming with it. One day my temper hit its peak over another thwarted opportunity. I went to my uncle's office and gave him the facts and told him what I thought of his practices in regards to me. At that time I didn't care if he was my uncle or whether I would have a job when it was over."

Andrea had become quite intrigued with his story. "What happened?" she interrupted.

"My uncle gave me the position. I realized he was looking for honesty, not games. He didn't want me to consider matters from a family relationship perspective, but from a professional one of character and ability. Most people don't work for their relatives and if they do, they should not expect preference. Sadly, it was my uncle who made an honest man out of me in the business arena. Although I was willing to sell my soul to reach my goals, my uncle wouldn't allow me to. It took me awhile to realize that he was waiting for me to honestly stand my ground with him as a way of earning both his respect and trust.

"Eventually the frustration, dissatisfaction, and emptiness in my high position and life brought me back to Christ, to realize His ways are not obsolete. Since then, others have also challenged me to consider my ways on both a personal and professional level. Are they centered on what God wants me to do or are they left of center according to the way the world operates? I'm thankful that my uncle didn't require my soul, but my honesty. I would have been fool enough to sell it to him, thereby, losing my way. Since then I realized there is nothing worth selling my soul for, and... I do all I can to guard it."

Andrea knew what Kyle spoke was the truth, but it was also strange. She realized how the world is reverse. Honest ways should never be strange, but in the world of corporate America they have often times been sacrificed and made foreign to its many practices. In some companies, it has become a club where the major activity involved scratching each other back and catering to the fragile egos that sit atop thrones of arrogance.

Kyle's concerned tone broke through her thoughts, "Are you alright Ms. Bigelow?"

"Yes, what do you mean?" Andrea answered in an almost confused tone.

His soft eyes were concentrated on her. "I think you've been working too hard, you need to take the rest of the day off."

"I can't take the rest of the day off," Andrea protested wearily. "I have some portfolios to finish."

"Cory Jackson is caught up with his work. I'm sure he'll be glad to take some of your files and complete them," Kyle replied with a slight smile on his lips.

Andrea knew there was no way that Kyle could have known her attitude about her main competitor, Cory. She felt herself close to flying off the handle at him for even suggesting it. It was at that moment, she realized she was emotionally ready to lose it. Her nerves felt like stretched rubber bands, ready to break at any moment. She could feel a dark shadow overtaking her mental faculties. It seemed that everything around her was receding in some far away background. Her alarming state brought both uncertainty and fear to her.

It took everything in her to pull back the scream that was ready to lash out at her unsuspecting supervisor. Andrea knew she had to keep it together and show some wisdom. "I'll consider how much I have to do, and I might just turn some over to him. Thanks for suggesting it." However, Andrea's voice sounded strange to her own ears, almost as if she was speaking through some tunnel.

She steadied herself as she stood up and excused herself to resume her work day. She felt somewhat faint and decided to take a slight detour to the women's restroom. It had a couch she could rest on, and hopefully collect her thoughts.

As Andrea reclined on the small couch, her mind was spinning. It seemed like her thoughts were colliding with one another. As the demolition derby was taking place in her mind, she closed her eyes. She tried to pull her thoughts together but the chaos that was taking place was heighten by her frayed nerves that were already stretched beyond their capacity.

She was exhausted and felt her body succumbing to a restless state. She found herself descending into a tormenting dream world. Voices were fading in and out eluding her understanding, while memories were springing up to mock her. Her body was heavy from weariness, but her mind was in a free fall of anxiety, and her thoughts were erratic. She needed sleep, but she couldn't escape the insane world of her spinning mind.

Andrea became aware of activity around her. She was aware of voices, but could not open her eyes to see who was speaking. However one disconcerting voice managed to stir her and it was the voice of Roma. "Andrea, Andrea, are you alright?"

Andrea finally managed to lift her heavy eye lids, forcing her eyes to focus on Roma. She positioned herself by propping upon one elbow. She realized there were three other concerned faces looking at her.

"I'm fine, I'm just tired," Andrea stated to hopefully relieve every one of their concerns.

"I'll see that she gets home," Roma assured the others.

Roma helped Andrea get to her feet and steadied her with her body. She guided her down the corridor and through the office entrance doors and out to her car. Roma helped her into the passenger seat.

Andrea laid her head back against the head rest. Roma slid to the driver's seat looked over to Andrea with a question mark, "Perhaps I need to take you to a clinic or something to have you checked out."

"No, just take me home, I'll be fine, Roma." Andrea responded, faintly smiling while patting her arm. "I just need some rest. While you take me home, why don't you bring me up to date on the latest office scuttlebutt?"

Andrea's comment opened the floodgates of information. Some of Roma's information fell to the wayside as Andrea's mind remained muddled and Roma's voice seemed to fade in and out. However, there were two bits of information that penetrated her confused mind. Their former boss was facing legal charges, but his wife was still sticking by him. Andrea was relieved to hear that his wife was not abandoning him, but she also felt guilt rise up with a flood of indictments that caused her already tattered emotions to vibrate at uncontrollable heights. She wouldn't blame his wife if she hunted her down and scratched her eyes out. However, the one bit of information that sent shock waves through her being was that Kyle Davidson was engaged to be married.

Andrea realized that she was quite attracted to the honest ways of this man. He somehow maintained the integrity of his Christian testimony in the midst of temptation. It was clear that he was also ensuring that he remained true to his fiancée. In a way it was disconcerting to her, but it also was pleasing for her to know he wouldn't compromise what was right. She was glad her seductive games failed to penetrate his resolve to remain true to himself and his future wife.

When they arrived at Andrea's apartment complex, Roma once again helped Andrea to her apartment. She aided her in getting into her pajamas and put her into her bed. She asked Andrea if she could get anything for her. Andrea remembered telling her that she had a slight headache and needed some type of over-the-counter medicine that would address her headache and help her to sleep, but she had none in her apartment. Roma agreed to go to the drugstore a few blocks away and purchase something for her.

Andrea's thoughts were still the scene of a demolition derby. The one thought that continued to triumph above the others was the fact that she had sold her soul. It was loud and condemning. How could she redeem her soul back? She had forgotten to ask Betty. Oh, how she wanted to get rid of the tormenting thought that was crashing against her very resolve.

In spite of the torment, the idea of being thirsty was beginning to gain her attention. She pushed herself up from her bed and slowly made her way to the bathroom, steadying herself by holding onto the furniture. She picked up the drinking glass on the counter and looked into the mirror. Hollow eyes stared back at her. She blinked, but the look remained. It was not only an empty, lifeless look, but it was a haunting look. Where was her soul?

Suddenly, she loathed the image peering back at her. It had become etched in her mind. She wanted to wipe it out and everything attached to it from the fake smile, along with the latest fashionable clothes and hairstyle. It all hid a very imperfect, confusing, frightening world. Anger rose up in her and she began to scream as she pounded the mirror with her hands and arms, but the lifeless image remained intact.

Her muddled mind suddenly remembered that for protection she kept a bat beside her bed. Somehow she found the strength to make her way back to her bed, retrieve it and return to the bathroom. She was determined to wipe that horrible image from the mirror. She took one more look at it and swung the bat, not once but twice, three times. She heard glass shattering and falling onto the counter and into the basin. She looked at the mirror. The image was no more. However, there were pieces of glass lying on the vanity and in the basin that were still big enough to reflect miniature aspects of the image. Out of rage, she dropped the bat and began to pound her fists on the broken glass on the counter and in the basin. She laughed wildly as she heard the glass crack and crumble into smaller pieces, but then as suddenly as it began the storm ended. Andrea stood trembling, staring at the shattered glass that lay all around her. Tears began to form, turning into miniature streams as great sobs rose in her throat. Blood was beginning to trickle from her hands to her wrists and arms from the small shards of glass that were now embedded into her hands.

When she saw the blood, she leaned back against the wall and cried uncontrollably. She slid down the wall and landed in a heap onto the glass that littered the floor. Suddenly she heard herself laughing again as she looked at the chaos. In the emotional swings of her insane reality, she became aware of a shocked Roma who looked down at her in utter disbelief. Andrea watched her dial a number on her cell phone. Roma's voice seemed muffled by her own intermittence of uncontrollable laughter and wailing.

Andrea didn't know how to control herself. Her world was out of control and she felt darkness enshrouding her. The frightening darkness eventually took hold of her, silencing her uncontrollable outbursts. Andrea stared into the abyss of eerie silence shocked and disconnected from any reality. The darkness was winning and there was nothing she could do about it. Inwardly she felt mute, but she also sensed she was becoming enslaved in a reality that was dark, strange, and alarming.

***

Andrea felt herself in a dream world. She slightly opened her eyes and saw a couple of people conferring with each other. She was wondering where she was. She quickly surmised that it was not heaven, but then how could it be earth? As she looked around, there was one face she did recognize. It was Betty's strong, but warm face. Andrea quietly let out a sigh of relief. Betty smiled when she realized that Andrea had opened her eyes and was looking at her.

Betty had been sitting in a chair, but stood up and made her way to Andrea's side.

"Where am I?" Andrea whispered.

Betty smiled, "You're in a hospital. You had a complete breakdown brought on by physical and mental exhaustion, but you're going to be alright."

She desperately wanted to grab Betty, but her hands were bound by bandages. "I have a question to ask you, Betty. I must know." Andrea stated in her strongest tone. "How can I buy my soul back from the world? Who has the means to forgive me for all my wrongs?"

Betty took hold of her bandaged hand, "You can't buy your soul back Andrea because there already has been a payment made on your behalf to purchase your soul back by God Himself to open up the way to forgiveness. He sent His Son to redeem your soul. Redemption points to God buying back the soul. All you have to do is with a sincere heart ask Him to forgive you for neglecting and selling your soul, and like Rahab, become identified to the red scarlet cord of redemption. You can grab a hold of the scarlet cord provided by God in Jesus by asking Jesus to save you from your sins, as well as your selfish ways, and the endless traps of the world so He can once again claim your soul for His good purpose and glory."

"I don't know how to ask Him to forgive and save me," Andrea despairingly replied.

"I'll help you by praying with you Andrea," Betty assured her.

Andrea followed Betty in prayer. When Andrea asked the Lord for forgiveness of her sins, her guilt began to lift. As she sought Him to cleanse her from her dull conscience towards wicked ways, shame vacated the premises. When she asked the Lord to be purged of the world's influence in her life, condemnation fled. And, when she requested the Lord to flood her empty soul with His Spirit, she felt His loving warmth enfold her inner being, as peace took center stage in her mind, and joyous contentment inundated the empty vacuum of her soul.

After the prayer, Andrea knew that it was well with her soul. Jesus had a firm hold of it, and her life would never be the same. In her mind, she knew if she held close to Jesus that vanity would not be able to haunt her as before, loneliness would not be able to taunt her, and emptiness would never be able to claim her again.

Andrea could tell that Betty was pleased with what had transpired. She smiled at the older woman, and in a low voice, thanked her for not giving up on her. She admitted that she was quite tired. Betty smiled and wished her sweet dreams as Andrea closed her eyes, submitting to the sweet, peaceful rest of heaven.

After a week of complete rest, Andrea was up and walking around the hospital corridors, regaining her strength. She was aware that she was within a day from being released from the hospital. Betty had been a regular visitor, encouraging her with the Word of God. For Andrea it was a special day because Betty had escorted her out into the hospital garden to enjoy the sweet breezes of the fresh air. She then had gone to the cafeteria to get some coffee for the both of them to enjoy together in the lovely outdoor setting.

"How are you doing, Ms. Bigelow?" Andrea immediately recognized Kyle's voice.

She looked towards his voice, noticing that he was now standing near her, "I'm doing much better Mr. Davidson. Thank you for asking."

"Betty told me where I could find you. I came here with a mission." He sat down on a bench next to her. "First I came to see how you're doing, and second, to ask you a very important question."

Andrea could not imagine what the question would be. "Question,.. what question?"

"I was wondering if you would accept the supervisor position for this local office?"

153

Andrea was absolutely stunned. "Why would you ask me to accept such a position," she paused, "especially after my recent conduct and breakdown?"

Kyle had a twinkle in his eye and a light heartedness in his answer, "You have to promise me you will never work yourself into such a state again. But, to answer your question, why would I not ask you, you are the most qualified to take on such a responsibility. But, I think you should know that Cory Jackson will be your assistant. How will that work out for you?"

Andrea felt a twinge of guilt about her past biased feelings and conclusions about Cory. "How does he feel about me being a supervisor?"

"Oh, he wholeheartedly agreed you would be the best one to fill the position. He has long recognized your abilities and commitment. Well, do you agree to accept the position?"

Slowly and thoughtfully, Andrea gave Kyle her answer. "I do so with trepidation. You have probably guessed that I have been greatly humbled by this recent situation, and like you, I realize that nothing gets done without the grace of God. With Him, I know that I will be able to do the best job possible for this firm."

"That's the answer I was hoping for Andrea."

Andrea was surprised that he called her by her first name. "Thank you, Mr. Davidson."

"Call me Kyle." Pointing upwards towards heaven, "I understand we are part of the same family, the family of God." He stood up to leave. "Well, my job has been completed here and now I have to get back to corporate office. Betty will be staying on at your office for a bit longer to help you get properly settled in your new position, and if there are any questions about company procedures and policies, she also has my number."

"Thank you Kyle." Andrea looked up at him with a smile. "Oh, by the way, according to Betty, I understand that congratulations are in order for your upcoming marriage. She is a fortunate individual."

Kyle smiled at her. Andrea had to get something off her chest to ensure a clean slate. "Kyle, I want to take this time to ask your forgiveness. At first I tried to influence you in an ungodly way. I guess I lost my touch because," she hesitated to go into details, "thankfully it didn't work."

"You did not lose your touch," Kyle replied, "I recognized you were trying to seduce me. The temptation was real and might have worked, but I knew I had to flee all temptation like the Old Testament hero Joseph did when he was tempted by his master's wife. I also chose to remember what it would cost me if I gave way to it. It would first cost me my relationship with God, and then my future life with my bride-to-be, along with a healthy environment in my soul, and an unsoiled conscience--a conscience that in the end would torment me for such wicked foolishness. Ultimately, I would have to sell my soul." He paused, "Know that you are forgiven. All past matters are under the precious blood of Jesus."

"Knowing all that, why would you agree to entrust me with the supervisor's position?" Andrea asked in surprise.

"I admit that I wasn't sure about your character, but I did notice that when professional procedures were finally in place, you quickly complied and worked within their boundaries. There was a point, I felt that your original motive towards me somehow changed or ceased to be a priority, and your efficient professional side took hold and began to shine through, highlighting your abilities and talents."

Andrea was surprised at Kyle's perception. It was true that she had started out with dishonorable intentions, but eventually the procedures put in place brought order even to her life and caused her to refocus her attentions.

Kyle continued, "I also have a bit of parting advice. You have much worldly ambition, Andrea. A very wise mentor put ambition for me in this light. Ambition is dangerous because the "am" of it requires *you* to become the driving force to bring your goals about, reducing the Great I Am, God Almighty to a footnote in your activities. The "bit" of ambition represents those bits of your dignity that you must often offer up to acquire the crumbs of worldly success, producing an unbecoming state. This is when a person can easily sell their soul. You must change the focus of worldly ambition to that of doing what is right in all matters. You do this by keeping your feet firmly planted on what is honorable, truthful, and real, and always being mindful as to what is important and what needs to be important so that you do not lose your way."

Andrea nodded her head in agreement as she allowed his wise advice to penetrate deeply into her soul.

"I also appreciate your congratulations," Kyle added, "but I'm the one who is fortunate. I've known my lovely bride-to-be since high school. She has stuck by me through the chaotic and worse times of my life. She has shown me the incredible love and patience of Jesus Christ when I've been at my worst. In fact, after years of wasted vanity, she was instrumental in me coming back to Jesus." He once again smiled at her. "Well, I must go. May God bless you beyond measure, Andrea Bigelow."

Andrea looked into his kind eyes and smiled, "Thank you, and the same blessing back to you Kyle Davidson."

Kyle reached out his hand to her in friendship, and likewise she offered hers. He lightly held it and slightly nodded his head at her in acknowledgment that he had received her blessing. He then gently let it go and begin to walk away.

Andrea longingly watched Kyle's retreating figure. He stopped long enough to say a few words to Betty, who just happened to meet him on her way back with the coffee, safely secured in a carrier.

Betty's smile was extra wide when she reached Andrea.

"You knew all along about my promotion, didn't you Betty?" Andrea inquired.

"Yes, I did but it wasn't my place to tell you." Betty said with a pleased look on her face. "What are you thinking about now Andrea?" Betty had noticed the small longing glint in Andrea's eyes.

"I was wondering if there are any more single men out there like Kyle."

Betty smiled, "You know, I have a single nephew by the name of Joel. He is the same age as you, and since he is a committed Christian, he is looking for the right Christian woman, but as of yet has not discovered her."

Andrea chuckled, "Oh, Betty you're such a dear."

"I'll tell you what," Betty said in an enthusiastic tone, "it's getting a bit breezy out here, and it's probably time for you to return to your room. And, as we make our way back to your room, I'll tell you all about Joel."

Arm in arm Andrea and Betty begin walking towards the hospital. As Betty was highlighting her nephew's traits, Andrea was basking in her new life. She realized that she could not change the former habits of her thinking and ways overnight, but she had met the One who could transform them. Granted, she was brought to the lowest place possible, but that is when she discovered that she had only one place to look, and that was up.

Andrea's heart was rejoicing for she was on a new adventure. She knew that a different life awaited her. Although challenges and temptations lay before her, she also had the assurance that the false image that haunted her for so long was not only shattered that terrible night, but because of her adoption into a new family, it would never find a lasting platform in which it could be erected to haunt her again. The glorious truth was that her once dead, empty soul had been reclaimed through redemption and then infused with a complete heavenly life that had no room for the lifeless, worthless, and insidious counterfeits of the world to once again fully reign.

For the Son of man
is come to seek and
save that which is lost.
(Luke 19:10)

Lost

Sonja Templeton allowed herself to breathe again. One minute she was crossing the street, the next she was being forcefully shoved by unseen hands. Even though the events were fast moving, time seemed to actually shift down into slow motion for her. She heard the screeching wheels and felt hands pushing her towards a couple of unsuspecting bystanders who witnessed the events. They had actually managed to catch her with their braced bodies and outstretched arms, stopping her from falling face first onto the sidewalk. Stunned and confused, she was doing everything she could to regain her composure as she looked around. It was then that she saw him—the still body of a man lying at the base of a light pole on the corner of the intersection. She gasped as she saw that his lean body appeared to be almost wrapped around the pole.

The hands that had caught her were beginning to relax their hold as she struggled to gain her composure. Sonja fought to understand what had just happened. She felt shock begin to take hold of her present reality, causing a surreal environment, as she struggled inwardly to push back tentacles of fear that were beginning to cling to unraveling emotions.

By this time a few people were kneeling down to see if they could help the man who was motionless on the sidewalk. There were no sounds or movement coming from him. Sonja felt herself almost holding her breath. Was he alive, and if so how badly was he hurt?

Still stunned, she heard herself ask the question that was emerging from the unsettled chaos of her emotions, "What happened?"

One of the men who had helped stop her momentum excitedly answered her question. "There was a driver who was speeding around the corner. Apparently, the man, who was behind you, saw that you were about to be hit and somehow to push you out of the way, but as you can see he wasn't as fortunate. He was hit and thrown against the pole!"

Her day had started out in typical fashion. As a real estate agent, she had to check her calls, follow up for her clients as to the progress of their loans, and have lunch with perspective clients from out-of-town. In fact, she had just finished lunch with one such client and was on her way back to the office when her normal day was disrupted by what now seemed like a surreal event.

She thanked the two men who had graciously stopped her fall before making her way to the crumpled figure on the sidewalk. As she walked toward him, she breathed a prayer that was short and to the point, "Lord, you have already given Your life for me, and I ask that this man's life be spared and that you raise him up and bless him for the sacrifice he has made to save me." As she stood behind the people who gathered around the man, she heard sirens in the distance. A policeman emerged from the crowd and directed the people to step back from the lifeless figure. He leaned over to see if the man was breathing. The look of relief that lit up the policeman's face gave mute evidence that he felt a pulse.

A second cop emerged, and was directed by another officer to seek out those who witnessed the accident. The men who had stopped Sonja from being injured, stepped forward and gave their report concerning the events that had unfolded before them, as well as a description of the vehicle that had been involved in the hit and run accident.

It was then that EMTs stepped on the scene. From that point, Sonja became a part of a whirlwind of events that seemed to escalate as the EMTs begin to work on the man. The police took down her name and address and questioned her about what she knew, but she couldn't offer any real details except that the man had apparently pushed her out of harm's way. An ambulance finally made its way through the clogged intersection to take the man to the nearest hospital.

Sonja walked up to the EMTs and asked about the man's condition as they checked him out. They admitted that he probably had a bad concussion, maybe broken ribs, and possible internal injuries. She also wanted to confirm the hospital he would be taken to.

She was aware that she could walk away with a grateful attitude from this "Good Samaritan" who had demonstrated such a heroic act, but as a Christian she felt obligated to see if there was any way in which she could help him. She felt a real need to make sure he would be alright. She waited until the heroic stranger was lifted on a gurney

160

and put into the back of the ambulance before she executed her next move.

On her way to the parking garage adjacent to her real estate office, Sonja called her workplace to see if she had any phone calls or pending appointments. When she found out that she had none, she briefly recounted the events that had taken place to the receptionist and informed her she wouldn't be in the office for the rest of the day.

Sonja continued to silently pray for the injured stranger while making her way to the hospital. She was thankful that she was missing the worse of the city's rush-hour traffic. As she walked into the entrance of the hospital, it suddenly dawned on her that she didn't even know his name.

She made her way to the emergency room and inquired at the desk about the man that had just been brought in from a pedestrian accident.

The nurse's face lit up as she quickly assessed the middle-aged woman. "I hope you're family, because the man had no identification on him."

Sonja shook her head no. "I'm sorry, I am here because he was hit by a car saving my life. I just want to know how he is and what I can do for him."

The nurse shook her head in disgust. "The only thing you probably could do to help him is take full responsibility for his situation, like paying the hospital bill."

Sonja knew that was impossible. "Sorry, I'm a single woman who has various other obligations to financially take care of."

In a terse manner, the nurse responded, "Then, there's nothing you can do for him."

Sonja wanted to react to the nurse's attitude, but refrained herself from telling her what she thought of her selfish display of being inconvenienced by this man. However, Sonja couldn't stop herself from making a point.

Sonja's brown eyes fixed on the nurse's face. "I'm sorry, but I thought a hospital was a place for the sick and wounded in spite of a person's status."

The nurse scowled. "Hospitals can't run without money. Like you, I had such notions in the past, and that's why I became a registered nurse. But, I discovered early on what you are about to find out-- hospitals, for the most part, are operated like big business. They aren't about health, but about making the almighty dollar."

Sonja, suddenly found herself feeling sorry for the nurse. Clearly, the nurse started out with noble expectations and an honorable calling, but because of worldly systems hospitals have to operate within, these organizations have been forced to calculate everything in terms of financial consideration and not according to individual health. Obviously, this caused this registered nurse to lose her vision for helping others and her passion to maintain the honorable intent she started out with, thereby, becoming embittered.

As Sonja continued to look at the nurse, she noticed her nametag, Karen Gibbs. She felt something rise up in her, compelling her to speak to the nurse's heart and conscience. "Karen, regardless of how money-oriented hospitals may become in light of the masses that come through their doors, you mustn't allow yourself to become lost in their indifference.

Noting that the nurse's eyes were fastened on her, she continued, "Don't forget why you are here. God gave you a gift of mercy to enable you to fulfill your calling as a nurse. You can always personally maintain your compassion for the hurting, and demand of yourself the type of excellent commitment towards the injured that will ensure you do not betray your compassionate heart or your incredible calling."

Sonja's words penetrated the cold wall of Karen Gibbs' heart with an inoculation of truth. Her dark eyes widened as the scowl melted from her face, and tears pooled in her eyes.

Before she could respond, Sonja heard a voice from the side call out her name, "Ms. Templeton, I'm glad to run into you."

It was the policeman who had interviewed her. When Karen heard his voice, she lowered her head and busied herself by fishing in her purse in an effort to keep him from seeing the tears that had welled up in her eyes.

Quickly regaining her composure Sonja walked up to him. "Do you know how he is?" She inquired.

"Well, he became somewhat conscious in the ambulance and is now floating in and out of consciousness, but when he is the most conscious, he is giving the hospital staff a bad time. They have managed to get x-rays and give a limited prognosis on his condition. Even though he has a bad concussion, his ribs are broken, and his one kidney possibly bruised, along with bruises up and down his right side, this man wants out of the hospital in a bad way."

"Out of the hospital!" Sonja exclaimed. "Who is he and where's his family?"

"That is the problem. The best we can figure is he's homeless and has no family. He clearly has no business going back out on the streets. The doctor informed me if anything happens to him in his present state, it could be irreversible. But, the hospital has no legal right to hold him."

Even though she had no idea what she would do, she had to see him for herself. "Would you mind taking me to him?" Sonja asked.

He glanced at the other officer, "George, I'll meet you out at the car after I take Ms. Templeton to see the victim."

Sonja followed the officer to the emergency room where they were trying to contend with the stranger. When she arrived it was obvious that he was floating out of consciousness into a restless state. The emergency team looked somewhat unraveled by the man's aggressiveness.

Sonja could see that in his agitated state, the man was fighting against giving way to rest or sleep. As he nodded off into a semi-conscious state, his head literally jerked as he loudly demanded, "Let me out of here!"

It was clear that he wasn't ready or able to listen to reason. Since he had nowhere to go, the thought hit Sonja that putting him in a different setting might possibly allow him to rest and heal.

"What would it take to take care of him?" Sonja asked.

The officer stared at Sonja while the hospital staff began to look relieved at the thought of the man being taken off their hands. "You're not thinking about taking him home?" the officer asked.

"Why not? There's an empty apartment attached to my house that has a bathroom and side entrance that I have rented out in the past and it might be a good place for him to heal. I could keep an eye on him and hopefully make sure he does what he needs to do to get well before he goes back to his life, such as it is."

"Do you have a husband?" the officer inquired.

"No, but this man is greatly hurt and even though he is homeless. I don't feel that he's dangerous. Right now he looks like a man who is afraid of hospitals and doesn't want to be in one," Sonja replied.

The officer couldn't keep from stating his objections. "Ms. Templeton, it's not a good time to be a 'Good Samaritan.'"

"'Good Samaritan!' Sonja exclaimed. "This man is the one who sacrificed himself on my behalf. We don't know each other except by his one act, and I must be willing to reciprocate in like manner. It's not the act of a 'Good Samaritan,' rather it's the Christian act of doing what I consider to be my reasonable service. Besides, I believe he'll heal better outside of this environment."

The doctor quickly agreed with her. "We cannot really do any more for him than you could at your home. We can give him a pain shot and send you home with some pain meds, but he needs rest and time to heal, and he is clearly fighting against us."

Secretly, Sonja agreed with the concerns of the officer, but she felt responsible towards the stranger. The suggestion that she take him to her house seemed foreign and ridiculous to her as well, but she knew it was her voice that spoke it. She sensed that she was in an unseen current where the unfolding events were beyond her control. For some unknown reason she was being swept into the same boat with this stranger and they were about to take a journey together.

Looking at the doctor, Sonja verbally formulated a plan, "I'll get my car and pull it around to the front door. It's up to you and the staff to get him to my car. Once he's in my car I'll take responsibility for him."

Sonja pulled out her cell phone as she headed towards her car. The first person she called was her daughter, Darcy to let her know she was bringing someone home who would be staying in the small side apartment. Darcy was excited about the prospect until she found out that the stranger wasn't going to be a paying guest. In fact, he would have to be taken care of. Sonja hurried and gave the facts to a loudly objecting Darcy who became more than concerned when she heard about her mother almost becoming the victim of a hit-and-run accident.   Over her mother's insistence, she continued to grumble about the unknown factors that loomed ahead of them.

After Darcy gave up, Sonja called her next-door neighbor, Josephine Croswell. Josephine's husband, Wade, was a policeman. Sonja concluded that between her, Wade, and Darcy they could get the man into the house. Sonja also knew it would be wise on her part to let Wade in on the situation to monitor the stranger's behavior. She quickly filled in a disturbed Josephine on the details. Josephine agreed to have Wade waiting and present to see that the man was settled into his new environment.

As Sonja pulled up to the front emergency entrance, she could see that the hospital staff had managed to get the man into a wheelchair and were waiting for her. The officer was still monitoring the situation. She positioned the car in front of the wheelchair, a nurse opened the passenger door of the car, shoved the seat as far back as she could, while a couple of orderlies, along with the cop steadied the man enough on his feet to stuff him into her small car. She had not realized how tall the man was until they wrestled his long legs into the front and pulled up the headrest as far as they could so they could lean his body back into the seat, resting his head back on the headrest.

The injured man groaned a bit through his ordeal but seemed to relax into a restful state as his body came to rest in the car seat. Sonja silently prayed that he remain so until she reached home.

However, before she reached her destination there was one point when he became somewhat aware of his environment. He tried to focus his dazed eyes on her. "Where are we going?" he whispered through cracked lips.

"Home," Sonja answered.

Sonja realized it was her home and not his, but the very word made him relax and fall back into a state of rest.

As she slowed to a stop before the front sidewalk of her house, the requested crew made up of Josephine, Wade, and one of their men friends were there to greet her. Darcy's face betrayed reluctance and anger, while the others mirrored both concerns and questions.

The five of them managed to pry the stranger out of the front seat and haul him into the side apartment. Darcy had prepared the bed for the stranger and he was gently laid on it. The two men agreed to undress him and put him under the bed covers.

After the men left the room, Wade asked the obvious, "Are you sure about what you are doing? You know you are not only exposing yourself to this man, but Darcy and Jared?"

Jared was Darcy's son. He was only seven and very impressionable. Intellectually, Sonja wasn't certain about her decision to bring a complete stranger, and a grown man at that, into a home with two single women and an impressionable child, but she had to acknowledge, that as a Christian, she had a compelling sense that it was the right thing to do even though to others it looked like an insane and possible suicidal act. As a result, any anxiety she felt was quickly subdued by a peace that passed her personal understanding.

She looked Wade in the eyes, "I realize that my action doesn't make sense, but due to the circumstances I didn't see any other way."

"Well, I'm next door and if you need anything, call!"

With a sigh of relief and a smile on her lips Sonja acknowledged his kindness and concern, "Thanks Wade."

The stranger's groans interrupted their conversation. Sonja excused herself to see if she could make him more comfortable.

The light by the bed was turned on the lowest setting. As Sonja walked up to the helpless figure in the bed, she realized that it was the first time she was actually able to study him. His appearance was conducive to that of a street person. His hair, which was black with silver highlights, was shoulder length. His beard, which was mostly silver, was straggly. However, it was his face that caught her attention.

Even though his beard hid much of his face, she could tell he was handsome and she sensed that he was intelligent and probably not much older than she, In fact, he didn't remind her of a street person, but then she silently had to admit that she didn't know what a street person really looked like. Other than his outward appearance, she concluded that no one could have classified him as being from the streets.

His arms and hands were outside of the blanket and neatly placed by his side. His biceps were muscular and his hands large and strong, but they did not appear to be the hands of a laborer. There was no dirt under his fingernails and for the most part could have belonged to a businessman.

Sonja was once again reminded of how life is fragile and unpredictable. Until this afternoon, she didn't even know this man existed. Perhaps she had even passed him on a street, but he had remained part of the faceless humanity to her, who, for the most part, would remain nameless and insignificant. He had simply been walking behind her in the same crosswalk when an unexpected event flung them into the same path. Not only did their paths cross in that moment, but their lives were becoming intertwined.

Sonja turned on a night light and shut off the three-way lamp. She could see that the stranger was resting comfortably. She didn't want to disturb him. It was time to fix dinner, and she would take the opportunity to prepare nourishing broth for him for when he was ready for it.

The dinner table remained quiet, except for the inquisitive Jared who asked about the stranger in the bedroom. Darcy was somewhat abrupt with him, but Sonja tried to whittle back some of her brusqueness by explaining to the wide-eyed youngster how the stranger had saved her life, and that it was only right to help him until he got back on his feet. Sonja also explained to Jared that he might have to cut back on some of his more noisome activities until the man regained his strength.

After the dinner dishes were cleaned up, Sonja went to check on her patient. She quietly pulled a comfortable chair closer to the side of the bed, positioning herself so that she could monitor his condition. She even placed a blanket from the back of the chair over herself. She felt the need to make herself available to answer questions or provide nourishment if he should awake.

As she sat quietly in the dimly lit room, she wondered what the man's name was and about his history. After all, everyone has some type of story, a history that explains why they end up in the condition or situation they become entangled in.

She had such a history. How vividly she remembered both the sweetness and the bitterness of her past. She had a good childhood. Her parents were devoted to one another and ensured that when her tender heart was ready at age eight, she became part of a spiritual legacy that began with an old-rugged cross. It was then that she believed and personally received the message of salvation and hope provided through God's Son, Jesus Christ. The precious message of the Gospel was not only believed and upheld by her parents, but also by the Bible based church her family attended.

Her teenage life was full of school and church activities. At nineteen her life seemed to become set in stone when her path crossed that of the handsome Hunter Corban. She met him at church while attending college, and they instantly connected. His exuberance to be a missionary on the foreign field caught her attention, and according to him, her countenance caught his. He often told her she had the countenance of an angel and that he could almost see a soft heavenly glow surround her serene face that appeared to be perfectly framed by her blond hair.

Even though it flattered her that Hunter would see such a countenance, she had to secretly wonder if his eyesight was a bit off or perhaps he was seeing her through some unseen glasses that the Lord had put there in order to bring them together. It was clear to them early in their courtship that God had brought them together and that the marriage union would simply verify their God-ordained bond.

Once married, they both shared in the same focus of getting onto the mission field. They prayed about where God wanted them to go, and felt that they were being called to the Philippines. Even though they would have to make sacrifices, they knew that Hunter would have to finish his education of becoming a doctor if he was going to be of any use on the mission field.

Within the first two years of their marriage they were blessed with twins, Dawson and Darcy. Although it required Hunter to work harder in the labor field and in his studies, he made sure that Sonja was a stay-at-home wife and mother. However, Sonja felt she could somewhat adjust her time if she became a real estate agent. It would allow her to do work at home while still bringing in some money.

With God's help, Sonja managed to effectively juggle her various responsibilities with the help of her mother. She wasn't away from home very often, and if she was, Hunter was there to fill in or her parents were more than willing to watch the twins. She thoroughly enjoyed being a wife, but she loved being a mother. The twins were a handful, but they brought such joy to her.

As a couple, both Sonja and Hunter enjoyed watching as their twins developed their own personality, likes, dislikes, and temperaments. Dawson was more sensitive and Darcy more imaginative. Dawson only had to be warned once when it came to discipline, but Darcy would test her parents' resolve by moving the line of their authority. Darcy was the more dominate, while Dawson was more kicked back. They rarely fought because Dawson would concede in most areas that he considered non-essential, but when he felt strongly about something, Darcy found him pushing her back. After they got a bit older, Darcy learned after a couple of brushes with him that at such times she better back off and leave him alone.

Just before Hunter finished the last phase of his education, the couple applied to various mission boards to begin the process of moving forward to fulfill their calling. Since their target was the Philippines, one mission board accepted their application. They began the process of jumping through the various hoops of preparation for the mission field. There were some classroom requirements that involved linguistic instruction, along with field experience where they would actually be put in a situation that would give them a taste of the life they were about to embark on. They also had to begin seeking financial support from churches and individuals. The learning part was easy for them, and the field experience proved adventurous to their children, but seeking support was intense and time-consuming. However, Hunter's ability to preach the Gospel and reach out to people in a personal way helped them obtain the support that they needed.

The twins were five and Hunter and Sonja Corban were within a few weeks of embarking on full-time missionary work when an unpredictable storm of life touched down in their midst, leaving utter chaos and destruction in its path. On that night Hunter was running late and the clouds in the sky threatened to drop a deluge of water. The winds had been whipped up into a frenzy. When the rain finally came down in torrents the strong wind caused it to hit from an angle. The pounding rain, along with the nighttime conditions, would prove hazardous to anyone who found themselves in the midst of the storm. For those on the freeway, it became a death trap. That night three lost their lives in a ten-car pileup, including Hunter Corban.

Tears streamed down Sonja's cheeks at the remembrance of that awful time. She wanted to scream out the "Whys?" Like the writer in Psalms, she wanted to reason with God as to how could Hunter

Corban praise or serve Him if he was dead? However, he was dead and all Sonja could do was fall back on the book of Job.

Job's losses and suffering didn't make sense to him or others, but God was still in control. She had to trust the character of God in spite of the loud indictment that circumstances were bringing against her resolve concerning the wisdom and justice of God. She had to hold tightly to what she knew about God in His sovereignty and faithfulness, and she had to cling to His many promises of comfort and hope to walk through the deep abyss of sorrow and depression.

Sonja put one foot in front of the other, knowing that God would bring healing in due time. She kept going forward for the sake of her children who represented the sweet union she had with Hunter. She couldn't sit in the middle of the road of despair in resignation to be swallowed up by the consuming bellows of sorrow washing over her soul. She wouldn't allow herself to lie down in the waters of self-pity or succumb to the repugnant grave of skepticism and bitterness.

Life went on and she had to remain in its unpredictable current if she was to obtain comfort and healing. Sonja knew that in the end her faith in the Lord would be confirmed, but she had to walk through the aftermath of the storm. Even though the loss left a great rift in her life, the ever flowing current of life would go on, filling up any holes and erasing any indelible footprints left on the shores of her heart by the healing balm of God's touch and time.

Memories of her life with Hunter often left her feeling vulnerable and lonely, but she noticed that time eventually brought healing to her soul. For the sake of her children she continued on with an open heart to life and an open mind to the Holy Spirit's sweet leading. The three of them became established in a local church. It was in church that she met Jake Templeton.

Jake was the son of the preacher, who was also the founder of the Bible-based church the three Corbans were attending. When Sonja first noticed Jake, it was merely a casual glance. The woman next to her quietly informed her of who he was and that he was divorced and had a son and two daughters. She also informed her that she better beware of him. Since Sonja was not interested in getting involved with any man, Jake wasn't even on her radar, and she quickly pushed aside the woman's warning as being unwarranted.

However, their paths did cross each Sunday in the foyer. Jake proved quite charming and seemed harmless enough to Sonja. He was a teacher at a local High School. In each encounter she found herself talking more freely to Jake. He seemed sincere enough about his faith, sad about her loss, genuinely interested in her children, and struggling over his divorce. When she met his children, she fell in love with them, and they with her. As an attempt to silence any concerns she may have about him being divorced, he explained that his wife had rejected the Christian faith and no longer wanted anything to do with him or his "religious" family. Since she confessed to be an unbeliever and asked him to leave, scripturally he had grounds for a divorce.

Each encounter with Jake finally led up to their courtship. Early in the courtship he wanted to marry Sonja, to not only help support her and the children but bring two fragmented families together as one. However, Sonja knew that her heart still belonged to another. In her mind she could not reconcile being half-hearted towards Jake in a marriage relationship. Although she was honest with Jake, Jake cleverly challenged her about her idea of love. He acknowledged he would never be a Hunter, but he was Jake, his own person, and her feeling of love for him would also be different. And, though Sonja's feelings of love were not present for him like it was for her first husband, he asked her if the past would keep her from being committed to him in marriage.

Sonja admitted that she could see how she could make a commitment to him in a marriage bond. He then challenged her to give him one substantial reason why they should not marry. In the court of logic and reasoning, Sonja could not present any real objections.

Jake and Sonja were married in a quiet ceremony conducted by his father at their church. All seemed to go well until Darcy hit her teenage years. Darcy had a tender heart towards the Lord, but as she got older, she became skeptical towards religion in general. Although her attitudes had been changing, they came to full bloom when she hit thirteen.

As Sonja sought help and wisdom from Jake to challenge and curb Darcy's behavior, he came across as indifferent, telling her it was a stage she would grow out of in due time. However, Darcy's behavior escalated into smoking, drinking, drug usage, and eventually sexual promiscuity. Each time Sonja sought Jake's involvement in the situation with Darcy, she was met with indifference, and if she pursued it, his response would turn into scoffing and mocking.

His attitude came out even more so in one of the last conversations they had about her. In frustration, Sonja had once again appealed to Jake, "I don't understand you, Jake. There was a time you seemed close to Darcy, and no doubt could speak into her life, but now you treat her as a stranger. Why don't you fight for her in some way?"

Jake's real attitude about Darcy finally reared its head, "I think it's a waste of time trying to reason with her. She has made her choices and now she's going to have to live with the consequences of her decisions."

Sonja was somewhat taken back by his attitude, but at the same time she had just had a glimpse into his thinking, "Would you feel the same way if it was one of your children?" she asked.

Thoughtfully, Jake replied, "I can't honestly answer that since she's not one of my children. I understand why you continue to try to help her, but to me she is a lost cause."

By this time Sonja was horrified at his thinking, "Jake, Darcy may be a lamb that has lost her way, but my daughter is not a lost cause to me or the Lord!"

Jake shrugged his shoulders and as he was turning to walk away, he put the final connotation to confirm his impenetrable attitude towards Darcy, "Whatever."

After their last conversation, Sonja kept her heartbreak and struggles concerning Darcy to herself. The one who tried to help was Dawson, but he was only Darcy's twin brother. He had tried talking to her about her actions but hit a stone wall. He was decisively benched, forced to helplessly watch her self-destruct from the sidelines.

When Darcy turned 16, the consequences of her behavior hit her along with Sonja and Dawson like a freight train traveling down the tracks at high speed. She became pregnant. The father was James Hampton, an alcoholic who dabbled in drugs and sold them to feed his habits. He was known to be aggressive and mean-spirited. In fact, Darcy had served as his punching bag a few times. Even though there was violence in their relationship Darcy insisted on marrying the father of her child, and assured her mother and brother that when he was not drunk or mixing drugs, he was a nice guy.

Sweet, sensitive Jared was the product of Darcy and James' union, but the marriage was a disaster. Sonja knew that unless there was a sincere change of heart in both of them, that there would be no change in behavior. The old ways were clearly brought into their marriage and the fallout continued to manifest itself in drugs and violence. For a while Jared lived with Sonja and Jake and eventually Darcy even sought shelter for herself at their home in an attempt to escape from her husband's cruelty.

It was when Darcy lived at the Templeton's home that an incident occurred which ripped open the façade that had hidden a deep wound under a darkness of silence. One day when Darcy was at the Templeton's home alone, watching her infant son, Jake's son, Dexter came over to see his father. When he realized no one was around, he started making advancements towards Darcy. She resisted, but he became more aggressive, they ended up on the floor in a struggle. The struggle became intense as he made his wicked intentions known. Like Ammon, the son of King David, who lusted after his half-sister, Tamar, Jake's son would not be denied from tasting Darcy's fruit.

Before he could have his full way with her, Sonja walked in on the situation. As if it was yesterday, she still could remember the sickness she felt and the utter disgust of the revelations that followed.

Sonja could still hear her terse voice cut through the room, "What's going on here?"

Dexter was the first one to chime in as they both quickly got up from the floor, "She was making overtures at me and I was fighting her off."

Darcy may have been struggling in her life because of bad decisions, but she was not a liar. It was also obvious by her ragged appearance who was telling the truth. "What?" screamed Darcy. "You liar!" She whirled to face Sonja. "Mom! He was trying to rape me!"

Dexter was ready with his defense, "Come on Sonja, you know your daughter's reputation. It is certainly not a pure one. I'm engaged, I wouldn't risk ruining that relationship for someone like Darcy. I'm not that dumb."

Darcy angrily moved towards Dexter, both hands in fists, cursing him for lying. Sonja quickly positioned her body between Dexter and Darcy in an effort to stop and silence her.

Looking straight into Dexter's face, Sonja began the cross-examination, "I have a question for you Dexter."

In a smug tone Dexter responded, "Sure, what is it Sonja?"

"If my daughter was the one making the overtures and you were innocent, why didn't you have the moral strength to flee from her like Joseph did Potiphar's wife? It's obvious you're the bigger and stronger one between the two of you, and clearly you think you're also stronger on the moral and physical fronts."

Dexter stood firm, "I told you I was fending her off."

Sonja glared at him, "If you were fending her off why were you the one on top of her, holding her down with your chest and one arm, while your free hand was reaching down where it had no business being?"

Dexter turned red, while pointing an accusing finger at Darcy. "All I know is no one will believe her."

Doing everything within her power to hold her temper and tongue, Sonja had a final barb that she was going to carefully aim in order to nail him in his coffin of lies and guilt. "I have one suggestion for you Dexter."

In defiance he said, "What's that?"

Standing her ground, she tersely said, "I suggest you adjust the zipper on your pants before you display any more incriminating evidence."

It was obvious that Sonja's statement unraveled Dexter in a way that stripped him of any further defense or justifiable explanation. He abruptly turned away to take care of his clothes.

However, Sonja was not finished with him. While maintaining a semblance of grace she firmly made her final statement as she glared at him, "You're lucky you're still standing. I've considered you a son in the past, but you have just preyed on my daughter, and now all I feel is like a mother bear who must protect her cub. If your actions had not initially shocked me, I might had found the nearest object and used it on you!

"There are four things I know right now, Dexter. First, you are a liar, secondly, you wouldn't risk your upcoming marriage unless you were foolish enough to believe that you could get away with it at the expense of my daughter's credibility, third, the just God of heaven knows the truth and one day it will be declared from the roof tops, and fourth,…GET out of my house, you are no longer welcome here!"

Dexter backed away from Sonja as If she had physically slapped him, and turned to quickly walk out the door.

Sonja turned around to look at Darcy. "Has he ever tried to do this to you in the past?"

With torment-filled eyes she looked at her mother, then lowered her gaze to the floor, "No, not him, not until today."

"What do you mean, 'not him'," Sonja shot back at her.

Heading towards the back bedroom, Darcy shot back over her shoulder, "Never mind, I need to change my clothes."

That night Sonja informed Jake about the events. Jake once again remained aloof when she asked him what he was going to do about Dexter. "What do you want me to do? You know boys will be boys."

Sonja was appalled. "What do you mean 'boys will be boys'? He tried to rape Darcy."

"That was according to her word. I just think he misread her and she misread him."

"Misread?" Sonja stated in complete shock, "I witnessed it! He was on top of her trying to rip open her pants! There is no misreading that!"

"You're making a big deal over nothing Sonja," replied Jake.

In disbelief, Sonja asked the question that had been dogging her since Darcy started to rebel "I don't understand you Jake. Before you married me, you promised to treat my children as your own. Do you mean to tell me you would quietly sit back and allow your daughter to be violated without taking a stand?"

Jake's voice dripped with cold indifference. "Well that is the whole crux of the matter. Dexter is my son, while Darcy is your daughter."

In a steady but seething voice, Sonja made her statement, "So that's the score."

With casual indifference still reigning, Jake replied, "Yes, it's the score. Did you expect it to be any other way?"

Even though Sonja's emotions resembled hot lava, she still felt the need to press the matter further. "Why did you give me the impression you wanted to be a responsible, loving father to my children?"

Jake stared at her as if trying to calculate the best way to respond. Based on his answer, he must have concluded that he might as well be truthful because it was obvious that things were quickly unraveling. "There was no other way to get to you, but through your children."

Sonja couldn't help but ask, "Why did I suddenly become your prize? I'm sure it was not because of love."

It seemed that once the door was opened up by honesty that it gave way to the floodgates of truth. Sonja could clearly see that Jake was being swept along by the some type of current, "It was all about image. You would make me look good, fit in the religious scene as far as my family, and give me a respectable status in the community, especially after my messy divorce."

Sonja knew truth without love could be cruel. Even though it was sharp, tearing away any hope that the two families would be a functioning Christian family, she was thankful it didn't rip her heart. She realized that in the ten years of marriage, she never gave Jake her heart and had carefully guarded it. Yes, she had striven to be a good Christian wife, but that didn't take heart, it simply required integrity before the Lord.

Sonja had to concede to the truth, "You're right nothing has been really ours has it Jake? It has been yours or mine, and in material matters, mostly yours. It's obvious that our marriage is nothing more than a sham. However, what I want to know is that since your reputation and image was so important to you, why did you just now let this knowledge out as to your real intention for marrying me?"

Looking at her with curiosity, "Just what do you mean, Sonja?"

"Don't you know Jake? When someone plays on the innocence of children and selfishly takes advantage of the vulnerable affections of individuals such as me, such actions makes the individual a predator, a wolf. How will such a classification play out for you as far as your reputation and image unless you don't care if the information gets out," she paused, "or, you are sure that I will keep this façade up because I don't believe in divorce?"

Jake was taken aback by her latest summary of him. At the time Sonja didn't realize that her assessment of Jake would be confirmed beyond any reasonable doubt.

Sonja added, "But just to let you know your son is not welcome in my part of the home until he owns up for his vile actions and repents."

Jake actually raised his voice, "What do you mean Dexter is not welcome in your part of the house! I want to remind you I pay the mortgage on this house and since I'm the man of this household, I have the final say. Do you get my drift?"

Sonja was ready for his power play. He had played it occasionally in the past. As a real estate agent she provided just as much, and occasionally more of the money for the lifestyle they both enjoyed. She would set the record straight and take a stand at the same time. "I want to remind you that you have just set the rule as to what is yours and what is mine. I have clearly paid my fair share of the mortgage, but if I have to protect my daughter from your son, I'll go to the police and file a complaint and a restraining order against him to ensure he never comes around here again. So, do you get my drift?"

It was clear that Jake was beginning to lose ground. "That would be a scandal and just how would that make my family and the church look!"

Shaking inside with utter disgust and anger, but still keeping her emotions in check, Sonja's determination remained unmoved, "Frankly, I don't care about the 'image' of your family and the church. Right now you're the one who needs to count the cost because my daughter was a victim of a violent act committed by your son and I will not silently stand by and let it happen again! If you don't want your 'family's image' tarnished, then I suggest you deal with your son pronto!" She turned and walked out while Jake's face turned various shades of red and blue.

That night Sonja bunked with her daughter. She wrestled before the Lord. "What has happened to my family, Lord? In the beginning, there seemed to be such great hope for all of us."

She looked at the sleeping Darcy. "What happened to my daughter? She had such a tender heart towards you. What made her hard and rebellious?"

In the silence of the night, she heard His voice. "Are you sure you want to know?"

Sonja felt the tentacles of fear grip her. She sensed that the knowledge was going to cost her, but she had to know for the sake of

175

daughter. She knew there could be no healing until whatever was hidden came to the light of truth.

"Yes, Lord, I want to know."

In a flash the Lord showed her what had been hidden in the darkness. She wasn't shocked by it; rather, everything became clear. But, as the truth set in, her emotions began to smash against her resolve. She wanted to scream, mourn, and lash out at something in rage. She felt waves of nausea hitting her stomach, slamming her heightened emotions against the rocky cliffs of repulsiveness. She wanted to shake those awake who were involved in the tangled web to confirm everything, but pulled herself back. The truth would come out soon enough, but she needed the Lord's wisdom and strength to walk through it. She needed to be prepared.

She quietly rose from the bed and went to a quiet place. There she prayed, pouring out her heart to the Lord, letting her sorrow spill out on the hallowed ground that was being bathed by her tears. She wrestled with the "whys" as she struggled to let go of her rights to understand the "how's" of it. "How could this have happened, how could God let it happen?"

She knew if she didn't let go of her rights to understand and put the "whys" and "how's" of it on the altar to be consumed by the sanctifying fires of God that the fire of her anger would become raging and destructive, the seeds of bitterness would take root in her soul, defiling everything, and feelings of resentment would take a life on of their own, digging deep trenches of anger and regrets.

Sonja also knew that there were victims, but she had to avoid becoming one. She had to maintain the integrity of her own life before the Lord, and raise a standard of truth if there was ever going to be any resolution. If she gave way to the sins of the old man, godly wisdom would take flight and elude her, truth would fail to be liberating to those who had been taken captive, and there would be no promise of healing, life, or restoration.

As she struggled with the "how's" of the matter, she was reminded of a warning put forth by the woman in church, but Sonja let it fall to the wayside. She had no one to blame but herself. If she had only listened, and if she had only taken the warning to heart, the face of the present would be different. However, she couldn't change the past. She had to take the sting away from the regrets that were beginning to come at her in the form of accusations and guilt. To ensure that regrets didn't become a heavy chain that hung around her neck, she had to confess her own failures before the Lord, recognize her weaknesses, and allow the Holy Spirit to teach her lessons that would prevent her from falling into the same traps in the future.

However, she had to ask the Lord one more question. "Why didn't I see what was happening? Am I that blind or was it a point of living in some type of denial?" Sonja felt both confusion and failure. It was then that Titus 1:15-16 came to her, "Unto the pure all things are pure: but unto them that are defiled and unbelieving is nothing pure; but even their mind and conscience is defiled. They profess that they know God; but in works they deny him, being abominable, and disobedient, and unto every good work reprobate."

To Sonja, all things were pure. She would have never suspected or thought in such wicked terms. No wonder the Bible states that the children of the world are wiser than the children of God. The children of the world understand that there is no real purity when it comes to the functions of the world. The world operates according to self-serving agendas, ignoble priorities, and reprobate works.

Sonja realized that when it comes to purity, it is necessary for Christians to maintain it and guard it in order to see God, but they need to recognize that they operate between two extremes. Purity that lacks the touch of reality will be void of any real discernment. It will give a false sense to those who hold to it but can prove down the line to be ignorant about the works of darkness. Such ignorance will allow a door to be opened, letting the vilest things to come in to rob innocence, betray what is holy, while killing hope and ultimately destroying people's lives without being detected.

The other spectrum of this scenario is when Christians consider matters strictly from their religious premise; they will have no real reality or discernment in which to judge matters. These individuals can become self-righteous, suspicious, and judgmental, often wounding true servants of God with unfounded conclusions, gossip, and accusations.

Sonja knew God was not convicting her for being pure towards the world, but He wanted her to understand she must not forget the wicked spirit that influences the deviant ways of the world. She needed to learn to test the spirits to know how to properly look at something and how to approach it.

As Sonja let go of the "whys", the "how's", her personal rights, past failures, and regrets, she felt the cleansing waters of the Spirit flow, bathing her soul with forgiveness and reviving her spirit with new life. She could sense the Great Physician touching her broken heart and frayed nerves with His sweet virtue, and making her resolve strong towards truth.

Even though she spent most of the night in prayer she felt fresh when morning finally arrived. Sonja also sensed that once the truth came out the fallout would be devastating. Inwardly, she was aware that the Lord would hold her up, but she had to brace herself mentally and emotionally. She quietly slipped back into bed, and although the latest revelation had initially proved to be overwhelming and tormenting, she fell into a restful sleep.

Sonja woke to broad daylight and quickly dressed. She then prepared herself for the battle ahead. She knew if she gave into the flesh in even small ways, it would result in greater devastation. She called the office and told them that her plans had changed and that she would take care of business from her home. Jake had already left for the day, giving her the liberty to begin untangling the web. The first person she had to question was Darcy.

Jared was already at the scheduled daycare, while Darcy took a day off from work to do some business. She was sitting at the island in the kitchen, catching a late breakfast.

Darcy looked at her mother, "Did you sleep well?"

"Yes and no," Sonja replied. "When I finally got to sleep, I slept like a baby."

Darcy looked at her mother who was intensely staring at her. "Mom, is there something wrong?"

Sonja proceeded to tell her what the Lord had revealed to her. Darcy showed a mixture of shock and relief as Sonja related the events of the night before. "Darcy, all I need to know is whether it is true or not."

Tears begin to form in Darcy's eyes. "Yes, it's true."

In a calm manner, Sonja had to ask the obvious question, "Why didn't you come to me and tell me?"

Darcy looked down in shame and then put her head in her hands as the tears began to freely flow down her checks. "He was blaming me for what was happening."

Sonja gently took Darcy's arm, "Blaming you for what happened? How can that be, you were how old?"

"It started when I was nine and it continued until I married James." Through a muffled voice, Darcy shared the events that had ripped her life apart, causing her to become lost in a world of hurt, shame, perversion, and rebellion. It caused her to feel that the only thing she was good for was to be used up by men and then discarded like a sack of smelly garbage after they had finished partaking of her fruit. She felt dirty and began to see her womanhood as a curse that caused bitterness to her soul. She told how her child-like affections, even at a young age, were misconstrued to be a come-on by her predator. She was also told that if she ever told anyone she would be responsible for breaking up a family and causing much unhappiness and shame for her mother.

Sonja's heart broke for her daughter. She wanted to take justice in her own hands and destroy the predator that had exploited innocence, tender affections, and child-like trust. However, she would have to put her feelings aside and minister to her hurting daughter. She walked over to Darcy, enfolded the hurting lamb in her arms, slightly rocked her back and forth as tears flowed from both. She wondered how anyone with any kind of conscience could twist, pervert, and bury such a precious lamb as her daughter with such vile burdens. She now understood the source of Darcy's destructive behavior.

"Mom, my life is spinning out of control. I feel like I've been marked in such a way that I attract every pervert and loser imaginable. I just don't understand. I don't know how to get off this treacherous merry-go-round."

Sonja recognized the footprints of the enemy of God all over her daughter's life. Her daughter's sweet heart had been broken by demonically inspired actions of a wicked person who had to be devoid of conscience. She silently rebuked the devil and gave him notice that he could not have her daughter. She was dedicated to the Lord, received His salvation as a young person, and her heart still belonged to Him.

Darcy's voice interrupted Sonja's silent prayer, "You know, the last person I ever wanted to be hurt was you. I love you so much and I have always wanted you to be happy."

"I know Darcy, but it's not up to you to ensure my happiness. Your silence deprived me of the most important responsibility I have as a parent besides teaching you right and wrong and that is to protect you. I'm so sorry I was so naive that I didn't figure out what was happening to you. Forgive me for not listening to all the warning signs."

"Warning signs?" asked Darcy inquisitively and even repeated it as she looked up at her. "What warning signs, Mom?"

"The changes in your behavior."

The mother and daughter team spent the remainder of the day sorting through the tangled web of their lives and relationship. When Darcy questioned Sonja about what she was going to do about the matter, Sonja assured her that she would take care of it.

An hour before Jake was to arrive home, Sonja excused herself and encouraged Darcy to wash her face and put some cold water on her swollen eyes.

Sonja began to prepare for her next stage of untangling the web of lies that had been choking the life out of her daughter and causing confusion and despair for her. She knew that she couldn't entertain her angry feelings or give way to the deepest desires of making the culprit pay to the fullest. She couldn't give way to her lower nature, thereby, succumbing to the same vileness as the culprit. She continued to remind herself that God is a just judge and all vengeance belongs to Him.

All she could do was ask the Lord to hold her heart, guard her tongue, and keep His hand on her at all times. She couldn't make the situation personal; she had to make it about truth, truth that would cut through lies, truth that would cause the darkness to part, truth that could bring liberty and healing.

When Jake walked through the front door, he was greeted with his personal belongings sitting at the front entrance. Sonja was sitting at the dining room table waiting for him.

He huffily walked into the dining room, looking disgusted, "Sonja, you're carrying this matter with Dexter too far!"

Sonja stood up with a new resolve, "I discovered something of great importance last night."

"Sonja, let's not play any guessing game. Just tell me what's going on. "His tone and mannerisms gave evidence of his frustration.

"Well, Jake I discovered that the acorn doesn't fall far from the tree."

Jake's face turned red, "She told you, didn't she?"

"Who told me what Jake?"

"Whatever she told you, you can't believe a word she says."

Even though Sonja wanted to tear Jake apart, the Lord was honoring her prayers, giving her calmness to continue to confront him without any physical affront. "Who are you talking about Jake?"

"Why, your liar of a daughter, Darcy!"

"Jake, my daughter didn't tell me anything, she simply confirmed what had happened, but you on the other hand you clearly have been telling me plenty. With your attitudes and now your words, you have confessed your actions.

Cautiously, Jake asked, "What actions?"

"That you've been molesting Darcy for most of our marriage."

Jake opened his mouth to protest, but Sonja put up her hand, "Enough with the lies, Jake! The light of truth has been turned on, and what will be interesting is to hear what you have to say in defense of your vile actions of betrayal, and of exploiting an innocent child, my child!"

His answer was quick, as if rehearsed. "Innocent child? Why, she was coming on to me! Sorry, but any man presented with such temptation wouldn't be able to resist it."

Waves of revulsion hit Sonja's stomach, making her feel like vomiting, forcing her to swallow down the gall before she could speak. "First of all, Darcy's affections toward you were that of a vulnerable adolescent towards a man who said he would be a father to her. Only a self-serving, perverted infidel would choose to classify such affections as being a come-on,'" she paused to push back the tidal wave of emotions that were crashing against her resolve. She swallowed hard, "As far as you being 'any man,' in regard to temptation I want to remind you that you're supposed to be a Christian who should flee such abominable thoughts and actions."

Jake laughed nervously, "Call my actions what you will but as far as being a Christian man, I never had any intention of trying to live up to your idea of a Christian man."

Almost surprised at his insane logic, Sonja shook her head to see if it wasn't just some bad dream. However, she wasn't done probing into his insane thinking. She pushed the point, "My idea of a Christian man? The Bible clearly states what the Christian life looks like, spiritually and morally. What are you, a Christian in name only?"

"When have I ever referred to myself as a Christian?" Jake asked. "I don't have to claim being a Christian because people assume I'm a Christian since I've grown up in church and my dad's a pastor and runs it. In fact, most people including my parents hope I take my father's mantle in order to keep the church in the family, you know, establish a dynasty."

Sonja suddenly felt frightened as she began to see further into Jake's reality. He was right. He had never really declared himself to be a Christian. She was guilty of assuming he was a believer, but she wasn't about to drop the matter. "This is probably not important to you, but 'calling' in the kingdom of God is not a business that is meant to be passed down to family members, but to those who have been truly called by God. However, since you brought it up, do you consider yourself a Christian or not?"

"I guess so," he said nonchalantly. "After all, I accepted Jesus as a young person. My family runs a church and I know God loves me and love covers a multitude of sins," he paused, "and besides He wants me to be happy."

Once again Sonja was taken back by his insane reasoning, but she knew she had to delve deeper into his unreasonable world, "Do you believe God wants you to be happy at the expense of exploiting vulnerable women and girls, using them for your own self-serving perverted purposes?" By this time her words were almost tumbling out of her mouth, "And, what concerns me is if you have justified vile, illegal actions with my daughter, who else have you exploited, perhaps your daughters or maybe vulnerable students?"

Jake turned red. "Call my actions what you will, but I would never do that to my daughters or students, I'm not that type of man!"

Sonja could see that he really believed his perception about himself. It was then that she realized he pursued her to get to her daughter to fulfill some sick lust or fantasy. Once again, she had to push back the repulsion that was consuming her stomach, but she couldn't allow herself to be silent. "So I gather you've only done it to my daughter to fulfill some perverted lust, while covering your backside. My, aren't you clever! You can declare that Darcy lied and since there are no other known victims, your family and the church will choose to believe you, and even though the police will file a report at my request, the prosecuting attorney will probably not touch it since my daughter's reputation will be used against her in a court of law," she paused to shake her head in disgust as the scenario ran across the screen of her mind, "as my daughter is once again sacrificed for the sake of your, delusional, sick appetites and image."

Looking smug, Jake replied, "That's how the game is played. And, as far as my family, you know the saying, 'blood is thicker than water.'"

By this time Sonja wanted to take justice into her own hands and put the predator out of his miserable, wretched state, but she knew that would not solve any problem, it would only add to the misery of the situation. With a sad, but firm tone, she continued her exhortation, "Sadly, you are right, Jake. I'll file a report with the police, probably for future purposes, just in case you are foolish enough to ever slip up again, and since my daughter has already been a victim of your predatory ways, she doesn't not need to be subjected to one of your legal piranhas as he publicly rips her to shreds to protect your abominable acts. As far as family defending you, I'm sure of that. But since you have no fear of God, there is one fact you have failed to consider, Jake."

A question mark formed on Jake's face as she continued, "Your clever ways may keep you from paying the consequences at this time, and your family ties will temporarily keep you in good standing, but there is a day coming soon, and if your abominable sins are not under the blood of Jesus, you will be held responsible by the just court of heaven for every offense committed against God and my daughter, and if your abominable actions cause my daughter to stumble into hell,

Jesus' words in Matthew 18:5-6, will come to bear upon you at that time, 'But who shall receive one such little child in my name receiveth me. But whoso shall offend one of these little ones which believe in me, it were better for him that a millstone were hanged about his neck, and that he were drowned in the depth of the sea.' Right now you have a millstone hanging around your neck and all of your clever attempts and religious affiliations will not keep you from being dragged down into the depths of the lake of fire by God's wrath that presently abides on you."

Sonja could tell that her words cut through his delusion. Fear gripped his eyes and face, and his mouth flew open in astonishment.

In a commanding voice she had one parting shot to make, "Now, get out of my house, Jake. The next person you hear from on my behalf will either be the police or my lawyer." She left him standing in the dining room with his mouth hanging open.

A report was filed concerning Jake's vile behavior, and thankfully a lawman even believed Darcy, but he, along with Sonja, and the legal counsel came to the conclusion that Darcy couldn't emotionally handle the rigors Jake's attorney would put her through about her conduct and reputation. She was already damaged enough and they all knew that they could not allow her to become more wounded; therefore, no official charges were brought against Jake.

Somehow the information about the molestation was leaked by an unknown source, but it caused people to take sides, pitting almost everyone against Darcy, along with Sonja for standing with her. Sonja had been close to Jake's oldest daughter, but the truth caused a separation between them along with other people that Sonja had considered friends. Darcy, Dawson, and Sonja were banned from going to Jake's father's church. There were even threats of suing Darcy and Sonja for slander, but Sonja knew that such threats would not go anywhere because Jake couldn't afford for the truth to come out in a court. Cleverly, Jake played the noble victim of slander, citing that it would not be the Christian thing to take either one of them to court.

Sonja and Jake did get a divorce, as well as Darcy and James. But, the ripple effect for Sonja was far from being over. The divorce caused Sonja to become more of a scorned woman because she did not stand by her husband who was being supposedly "falsely accused" by her daughter.

The house was sold, and Sonja was given half of everything which allowed her to buy the house in a bedroom community away from what happened with Jake and close enough to her real estate job in the city that she didn't have to travel far to do business. It was a house that needed various things fixed but she had fallen in love with it the first time she saw it. Due to financial restraints as well as time and abilities, the house was not taking shape as fast as she hoped.

However, there was one other sorrow Sonja had to face that she hadn't counted on. She knew that she would lose friends and standing in the community, but Dawson became a victim as well. It devastated him when he found out what had happened to his twin sister. He wanted to physically pass judgment on Jake, but knew that it would add greater sorrow. He became tormented by the fact that he didn't protect his sister. The whole situation constantly replayed itself on the screen of his mind. Two weeks after graduating from high school, he decided he could no longer be reminded of what he perceived to be failures on his part. He left in the night, leaving a note that expounded on his failures, as well as his inability to handle it any longer. In a way he had become lost in guilt, failure, and helplessness. Since he didn't know where he was going or what he would be doing, he didn't leave an address.

Greater sorrow was added when Sonja didn't hear from him. She didn't know where he was and how he was doing. Her dear, precious Dawson had been lost to her for the last six years. As she sat in the dark room with the battered stranger and wondering where Dawson was, she quietly prayed for her lost son.

At the end of the prayer, she softly spoke the words that were on her heart as the tears flowed freely down her cheeks, "Oh Dawson, where are you? If only you could have stayed around, we could have all healed together as a family. If only Dawson, if only…"

The last, "if only" caused her to close her eyes as she gave way to weariness, leaving the silent tears to dry on her cheeks.

***

Sonja sensed someone was staring at her. As she opened her eyes, she became confused about her location. She blinked to bring clarity to her vision and realized she was in the small apartment. Her neck felt stiff and her back ached, causing her to realize she had fallen asleep in the chair.

Then she remembered why she was in the suite. She looked towards the stranger, only to be greeted by the bluest eyes watching her she had ever seen.

"I'm not in heaven am I?" the deep voice inquired.

Sonja smiled, "Not unless it's a known fact that angels can fall asleep while on duty."

"You remind me of an angel, your countenance that is," he paused while blinking his eyes. "But, I knew it couldn't be true. But, I must ask where am I and what am I doing here?"

His remark about her countenance reminded her of another time, another place, and another man. She quickly pushed aside the temptation to take a detour down memory lane. She also wanted to pursue the man's implication that he didn't expect to wake up in heaven, but she refrained by first introducing herself and answering his questions.

Sonja noted that a faint shadow of relief passed over his face as she responded to his questions. It was obvious that he was still a bit dazed. "Ms. Templeton, it was kind of you to take care of me, but it's not necessary."

"No one knew your name or where you lived, so it was only right for me to bring you here. But, if you have a family and home I'll be glad to contact them or take you to where you live."

"That won't be necessary Ms. Templeton. I'm part of the lost people."

"The lost people?" Sonja inquired in the hope of confirming what she already suspected.

"You know the street people who become lost in the masses during the day, and lost in the night as we each strive to survive the coldness and indifference of our world. Those who are lost have no name that is of any importance and in most cases no permanent home." He closed his eyes before continuing. "You've done your good deed, now you can take me back to the streets where I belong."

Sonja was not about to be put off by the stranger. "Call me Sonja, and what I'm doing is not a good deed, but the least I can do. You'll stay here until you get on your feet and are able to walk out that side door or catch a ride with me to the city. As far as being lost because of your situation, I want to remind you that you aren't lost to God; He knows where you are and who you are. Now you have a choice. You can give me your name or I will be obliged to address you as, "Sir."

He opened his eyes as his lips curved in a half smile. "My name is Richard Blackwell. I'll only call you Sonja if you'll call me Richard."

"You have a deal Richard! Now, would you like some broth or solid food?"

Before he could answer, they both heard the doorknob quietly turn. Darcy peered around the door. "Come on in Darcy and meet our guest." Sonja beckoned with her hand.

Darcy slowly walked in while suspiciously eyeing the man in the bed. "Darcy, this is Richard Blackwell, and Richard this is my daughter

Darcy. Darcy and her son Jared live here as well. Between the two of us, we will be checking on you to see if you have any needs."

Sonja could tell the man recognized Darcy's suspicious air and his response revealed that he wanted to somehow put Darcy at ease.

"Nice to meet you Darcy. You're both very kind, but I'll do my best not to inconvenience either one of you. I hope to only be here a couple of days."

Likewise, Sonja wanted to put Richard at ease. "We'll see in a couple of days if you're able to leave. But, right now I need to know. Do you want broth or solid foods?"

He conceded by answering her question, "Is there any way I could have solid food, like some eggs? And, I don't care what form they come in either."

Smiling while taking Darcy by the arm, Sonja glanced over her shoulder towards Richard, "Eggs coming up."

Frowning while standing in the kitchen watching her mother prepare the eggs, Darcy voiced her concerns, "Mom, we don't know this man, he could be a murderer or some pervert."

"Darcy, I understand your concerns, but I don't sense he represents any danger to us. If he does I'll have Wade come over and promptly escort him out of here."

As usual Darcy had a rhetorical response, "Well, that's all good and well, but if he does something wrong, it'll be too late to escort him out of the house."

"Darcy, since you are a better judge of character than myself, what do you sense about him?"

Sitting at the kitchen island, meditating on what she sensed, she finally looked at her mother, "First, I think he has beautiful blue eyes and a nice smile, and I suspect under all that hair he is probably a very handsome man."

Sonja smiled, "I'm not talking about his looks. What do you sense about his person or character?"

"I don't sense we are in danger, but I'm confused" she confessed. "He doesn't appear to be a street person. What's up with that?"

Sonja's response simply mirrored the scenarios she had already played out in her mind, "Perhaps, he's running from something personally or hiding because of something he can't reconcile in his mind. It's hard to say, but we both don't sense that we are in danger because of his presence here."

When Sonja took the eggs to the room, Richard was pale.

"Are you alright?"

"Yes, I just made a trip to the bathroom. I must admit it was pretty painful. I might be here a bit longer than I previously thought."

Richard was true to his word. He tried not to be a point of inconvenience. He slept much of the time and when he did move around, he was met with a great deal of pain. Even though everything he did resulted in pain, he never complained and tried to ask as little as possible from Sonja and Darcy.

On the third day of Richard's stay, Jared came up missing. Darcy was in a panic as she looked for him in all of the familiar places. Sonja also frantically joined the search. To Darcy's relief, but dismay she found him in Richard's room talking a mile a minute to the stranger. Clearly, fear was motivating her, and as a result she over reacted by harshly reproving him. Her over reaction caused Jared to recoil in hurt and shock.

Sonja understood Darcy's concern, but felt sorry for Jared. However, Richard seemed to read the situation and in a surprising way he actually defused it.

"I'm so sorry Darcy, he peeked in my room and I invited him in without first encouraging him to ask your permission, or at least let you know where he was."

He then looked at Jared, "It's alright son, your mother was concerned because you're not supposed to talk to strangers without her knowledge and permission. I'm sorry Jared, I got you in trouble, but I want you to know it was nice meeting you and talking to you. Next time, and I hope there will be a next time, you need to ask your mother if it's okay for you to come and talk to me. Agreed?"

Jared shook his head in agreement and looked up at his mother. Sonja could tell that Richard had wisely recognized Darcy's concern and put her at ease. It was then that Darcy was able to establish some basic rules with Jared, "Yes, you can come in and talk to Mr. Blackwell after you first ask my permission, and secondly, after you see if he is up to you visiting him."

From that point on Jared was a regular visitor to Richard's room. At first they talked about everything, but then it graduated to playing games. Richard taught Jared checkers and started exposing him to Chess, while Jared exposed Richard to the world of video games. They also started reading stories and doing homework together, something that Darcy was too busy to do and Sonja was unable to do because of her schedule. It was obvious that Richard needed Jared and Jared needed Richard. They both began to blossom in their attitudes, which caused the cautious Darcy to even let Richard watch Jared occasionally when she had to do errands.

It was on the third week of Richard's stay that a leak was discovered under the kitchen sink during Sonja's absence. Darcy tried to figure out how to fix it on her own, which resulted in frustration and a few choice words flying around in the atmosphere. Richard being aware that something was going on in the kitchen area, cautiously made his way out to the scene of the problem to find out if there was anything he could do.

Darcy later admitted to her mother that she was glad that he was there because that is when one of Richard's incredible talents was discovered: he was a handy man. Even though it was still painful for him to bend or do any strenuous labor, he still did what he had to do to take care of the problem. He instructed Darcy as to what needed to be done, and between the two of them they managed to conquer it.

From that point on Richard started to do the odds and ends jobs around the house. The better he became physically, the more taxing the projects he conquered. Before long, the house was taking shape. The thing that amazed Sonja is that it didn't cost her a dime except for some special paint and new toilets. Richard utilized the variety of materials located in a small shop in the back of the house where building supplies had been stored by the previous owner to fix up the house. Due to being relocated by his work, the former owner had to quickly sell the place, agreeing to leave all of the material behind.

Every day Richard worked on something new. Before long, faucets were replaced, new toilets mounted, and granite countertops installed in the kitchen and bathrooms There was molding carefully put in place around the ceilings, along with new wood flooring put down in the kitchen and dining area. Old carpet was replaced with new carpet. Within a few months, Sonja watched the house take on new life as her vision for it was being completed before her eyes. She rejoiced because it was an answer to prayer. Who would have thought that God would use some homeless person to renovate her home for her and her family?

What was amazing was that renovating the house became both a family affair and a neighborhood affair. When Jared was not in school or doing homework, he became Richard's regular helper, while Sonja helped on her days off and Darcy occasionally offered her services when she was not being pressed by her other responsibilities such as schooling and work. Richard showed great patience in teaching Jared the art of construction. He gave him his own small carpenter's belt with tools that fit his hands and taught him how to handle and take care of them. He closely supervised everything Jared did, giving Darcy some free time to herself when she felt overwhelmed by life. The two women had to admit to each other that they learned a lot from Richard's patient instructions as well.

Then there was the involvement of some of the neighbors. One day Wade caught Richard sitting out on the front porch and took the opportunity to strike up a conversation with him. Sonja had no idea what they talked about but Wade and Richard seemed to develop an instant friendship during that encounter. When there were heavy projects, Richard sought Wade's help, and Wade would seek the help of the other neighbors who were taking an interest in what was going on.

One day when Richard was out playing ball with Jared the two women voiced the down side to what was happening. Darcy was the first one to broach the subject while watching the two of them tossing the ball back and forth from the kitchen window, "Mom, what's going to happen when Richard leaves? We've all grown to appreciate him and Jared is quite fond of him."

Sonja silently knew that Darcy's choice of words was a means to take the sting out of the reality that they had all grown quite fond of Richard. In fact, Sonja had been ignoring the fact that her feelings were not just a matter of having a fondness for him, but she was finding that she was very attracted to him. She did her best to push the attractions aside and set her affections on the things of heaven, while striving to keep a realistic handle on the confusion that surrounded this mysterious stranger. She knew his name and benefitted from his intelligence and ability. She had witnessed a gentle, sensitive side that manifested itself in kindness, consideration, and manners. However, in spite of having some conversations with him, he never shared anything about himself with her. She still didn't know his history or why he was among the street people.

Sighing, Sonja replied, "I don't know what is going to happen, Darcy. No doubt he has become a big part of our lives, but he has a life somewhere else. It would be natural for him to go back to it."

Alarmed Darcy responded, "You mean back to the streets?"

Thoughtfully, Sonja voiced her conclusions, "No, I suspect he has a home somewhere else besides the streets."

"If that's so, why was he in the streets and why would he stay with us?"

Just as Sonja went to answer, Richard and Jared came in from playing ball. Although dirty, Jared was happy. The ladies could tell he was enthralled with Richard.

Darcy interrupted Jared's happiness by reminding him of his least important activity before lunch, "Jared before we eat, you need to clean up. Follow me to the bathroom."

The smiling Richard seated himself on a stool at the island, while watching Jared reluctantly walk towards the dreaded bathroom.

It was unusual for Richard to sit at the dinner table and kitchen island. He had rarely interacted with them on a personal level and always took his meals to his room. Occasionally, Jared joined him.

"He's sure a great kid, isn't he?" Richard commented more to himself than to Sonja.

Sonja took the opportunity to agree with him, "Yes he is, but I'm a partial grandmother."

Richard smiled at her. "You know he has been a great help to me in more ways than one."

Sonja took the small window of opportunity to voice her concern, "It's obvious Richard, that he thinks the world of you. Have you ever thought what will happen to him when you go back to your old life?"

"Yes I have," Richard thoughtfully replied. "I don't want to lose touch with the little guy. But, I'm afraid that if I go back to my former world, I'll become lost in the darkness of it again, and end up drowning in despair and hopelessness."

"You can stay here as long as you want," Sonja interjected.

Looking at Sonja, "That's kind of you but that would not be fair to you."

Curious as to his reasoning, Sonja couldn't help but ask, "What do you mean it would not be fair to me?"

"Well, you're a good Christian woman, and certain neighbors are already talking about me staying here. Even though it is all above board, it gives the appearance of evil to others who do not know the caliber of person you are, and who naturally give way to their suspicious, small minds."

Sonja was shocked that Richard acknowledged her Christianity and displayed knowledge about the Bible. "You know the Bible?" She paused and looked at him, "Are you a Christian?"

He studied her for a second before responding, "I have some background in the Bible. I'm sure you know that just because a person has some religious or Bible background, it doesn't make them a Christian."

Sonja could tell by his mannerisms that he allowed her to catch a glimpse of a small aspect of his life. It was becoming increasingly obvious that he was an honorable man, but it also became clear that he was quickly closing the curtain on any further insight.

"Well, it's kind of you to be concerned about my reputation, Richard, but I assure you that my reputation has already been pretty much trampled on. If it wasn't for Darcy and me, I don't know who else the gossipers of this neighborhood would entertain themselves with." She paused and continued her evaluation, "You know such people often operate with a 'soap opera' mentality and thrive on the insignificant details of others' lives, or garbage that their imaginations can conjure up about those who have unsuspectingly become entangled in their web."

"I understand about the nature of gossipers, Sonja," Richard stated, "but I don't want to provide them with any more rocks to throw at you and Darcy. Since I'm the source of their gossip, it's up to me to silence them. According to my way of thinking there are two recourses that can be taken. The first one is obvious. It's clear to all who see me that I'm well enough to leave here, but I admit I don't want to go, especially at this time. I feel I'm getting on my feet in more ways than one." It was at this point he suddenly took a deep breath and became eerily silent, stopping short of expounding on the second option.

"What's the second recourse," Sonja asked.

Looking at her, "Well, it involves your cooperation."

"My cooperation?"

Richard's face took on a serious, intense expression as he looked into her questioning brown eyes, "The only other recourse that would solve more than one problem is that we get married."

Sonja suddenly understood what the expression of being 'floored' meant." She felt like all the wind was taken out of her. Her head spun, she felt like almost passing out, producing a sense that she had fallen through some hole in the floor. Instead of there being an emotional freefall, she felt like she was floating downward into some surreal world. After all, such things only happened in the movies, not real life. She wanted to shake her head to make sure she wasn't imagining the event or pinch herself to ensure she wasn't dreaming. As she struggled to gain some semblance of reality, she could tell that it was not a dream nor was it some sick joke that Richard was using to test her humor. His facial expression and mannerisms made it clear that he was serious about marrying her.

As she tried to once again tune into the reality of her environment, she could only guess at the expression on her face. She knew that her mouth was hanging open in shocked astonishment. It was clear that Richard was observing her reactions.

"I realize this is probably a shock to you, but I'm serious about my proposal." He paused, looked down as he formulated his next thought, and then looked up at her, "I know everything seems backwards, since there has been no real courtship. I also recognize that the idea of love, which to me has been exploited by the world, as well as the notion of romance are both missing from the equation, but I do respect you and consider you a friend and since you're a Christian woman I hope you'll pray about my proposal before you make any real decision. I also want to assure you that I will stay right where I am in this apartment, keeping our relationship strictly platonic, and if at any time you want out of the agreement, you'll be able to get an annulment."

He stood up from the stool, and began to walk to his room. She watched as he hesitated a moment, but stopped and turned to once again look at her. His eyes met hers, as he softly said, "By the way thank you for not laughing or mocking my proposal." After expressing his gratitude, he went into his room and quietly closed the door.

Sonja was still standing in a state of shock when Darcy came into the room. When she saw her mother's face, her question revealed a mixture of curiosity and concern. "Is something wrong, Mom, you look like you're in complete shock."

It was then that Sonja discovered another symptom of being "floored;" that of being speechless. After putting her hand up as to stop any further momentum on the part of her daughter's concern and questioning, she was able to formulate and communicate a short message to her daughter, "I'm fine, I need you to finish lunch. I'm going to my room right now," and upon taking a deep breath, she finished her sentence, "and I'll tell you later what is going on."

Sonja couldn't stop the inner turmoil as she made her way to her sanctuary. It was in her bedroom that she had made a place of personal worship. It was there that she studied the Word of God at her desk, meditated on it truths, poured out her heart to the Lord, and constantly sought His wisdom and intervention.

When she first entered the room, she didn't know what to do, whether to sit, kneel, or pace until all her excess anxiety had subsided. As she wrestled with confusion, that familiar gentle voice penetrated her flighty state, "Be still and know that I am God."

She knew that in her present anxious, confused state the Lord couldn't speak to her. She had to let everything land, from her emotions to her confused thoughts, and perplexed feelings. Even though Richard's proposal was out of the ordinary, she knew that she wasn't closed to it. However, she had to discern between her attractions for him, her fears about him, and any whimsical notions she may still have about love, romance, and marriage.

192

As she sat down, she asked the Lord to straighten out the "roller coaster ride" that was producing such a rush in her emotions. When she married Hunter, she knew he was the right man for her, but when she married Jake, she assumed he was the right man because he fit the image. But, as far as Richard was concerned, she had no idea if he was the right man because he certainly didn't fit any "normal" scenario. In fact, he represented that which she would consider contrary to any acceptable marriage before God.

As she settled her nerves, she had to face her fear. She was afraid that Richard was not the right man, but she was also afraid that he might be. She knew that she had to silence the dichotomy of her fear. After she admitted her fear to the Lord, and gave it to Him, she had to confront her attraction for Richard.

Why was she attracted to him? She had to discern the source of it. It was true he was handsome even with a beard and shoulder-length hair, but her attraction was not fleshly. It also was obvious that he was a strong man in many ways with a good personality, but she knew that such attraction could be surface and temporary. She realized that she was attracted to his spirit which expressed itself in wisdom, as well as to his mannerisms, which showed graciousness and kindness. She had clearly seen that he was a man of integrity who was bent on doing right and being honorable. It was clear that she was attracted to his person, and not his looks and abilities. Although her attractions were honorable and a basis to ensure a good foundation for a relationship, they didn't confirm whether marriage between them was God's will.

Once she could step outside of any personal agenda and make the situation a matter of God's will, she was confident that she could seek Him in order to find out His mind and purpose about the matter at hand. As she quietly sat before the Lord to hear what the Spirit was saying about the proposal, she had confidence that the Lord was faithful to show her His will. When she began to discern His voice, she was astounded at the revelation that was imparted to her, but than a peace came over her. In spite of God confirming His voice to her, she still wanted confirmation from other sources.

It was after Sonja's great wrestling match before the Lord that Darcy knocked on her door to see if she was alright. Sonja invited her into her room.

"What happened in the kitchen Mom?"

Looking at Darcy's inquiring face, Sonja was ready to share the event, "Well, you wouldn't believe it, but Richard asked me to marry him."

Darcy looked shocked, and then an excitement began to part like a curtain across her face, "You are going to accept aren't you?"

This time it was Sonja's turn to be surprised. "We don't know anything about him, but you trust him enough to make him part of our family?"

"Yes I do, and I think he's a wonderful man," Darcy paused before concluding, "and, I don't think you could do any better than marrying Richard."

"What about love? Shouldn't that be part of the equation," Sonja asked?"

"Sorry, but I think the notions about love are overrated, and the presentation of romance is not always realistic. I know you like him and I'm pretty sure you're even attracted to him."

Sonja felt like she was hearing an echo coming from Darcy. Richard had used some of the very same arguments with her.

To ensure she heard right, Sonja asked for confirmation, "Let me get this clear in my mind. You wouldn't have any objections to me marrying him?"

With enthusiasm Darcy reaffirmed her conclusion, "Of course not, I think you both are perfect for one another."

That night after dinner was prepared Darcy was ready to fix a plate for Richard when Sonja stopped her. "I need to talk to him before we hand him his meal."

Sonja went and knocked on Richard's door. When he opened the door, Sonja looked into his surprised clear blue eyes. Since he was able to take care of himself neither woman had really entered his room. Darcy always delivered his food usually just inside of his door.

"Richard, may I come in? We need to talk for a moment before dinner is served."

Richard beckoned her to sit in the chair she sat in the first night he was brought to the house. Sonja was pleased to see he kept everything clean and tidy.

She sat down as he sat on the edge of the bed with his hands folded together, "I must know Richard if you are still serious about your marriage proposal to me."

His blue eyes met hers as he leaned towards her. His reply was quick and firm, "Of course, I am. Do you think I would change my mind?"

"Well, let's face it you have had some time between your proposal this afternoon until now to reconsider it. After all, marriage is a big step and change in life. I don't believe in divorce, except where Scripture

194

allows; therefore, in my mind the two of us would be in this relationship the duration of our lives together."

"I don't believe in divorce either," Richard responded. With great seriousness in his voice, he reaffirmed his intentions, "I'm ready to spend the duration of my life with you in this bond, but remember I have provided you with an exit plan. If you feel it's all wrong, you can choose the route of annulment because at that point it still will be a marriage in name only."

Sonja could not help but express her curiosity, "Richard, I still am not sure why you would open yourself up to a relationship that offers you very little and may end in failure. It sounds like initially you will be the one making most of the concessions in this matter."

"Sonja that is my choice and my concern."

Sonja was carefully studying Richard's facial expressions and body language. She took a deep breath as she realize that she was about to jump into the situation with both feet, "Well, if you are going to be part of this family, you need to start sitting at the dinner table with us."

Richard was at first stunned by the implication, "You mean you'll marry me?"

"Yes Richard, and until we do take the vows, I want to remind you that you can back out at any time and I would understand."

By this time Richard began to mirror excitement and hope as he stood up. "You know that goes both ways. I will arrange everything. All you'll have to do is jump through a few hoops, sign the license, and take a vow."

"Well, I take it that you'll be coming to dinner from now on?" Sonja asked.

"Yes I will." Smiling, while offering his arm to her, "Ms. Templeton, may I have the pleasure of escorting you to the dinner table."

Taking his arm, while getting up from the chair, "Yes you may, Mr. Blackwell."

As they walked together into the kitchen, Sonja sensed that the door to an old chapter of her life was closing and a new one was about to be written.

***

True to his word, Richard made all the arrangements for their marriage. In the midst of swirling activities, Richard sat at the dinner table. He always respectably bowed his head for prayer and even accompanied them to the small church close by. Although, he listened carefully to the minister, he never made any comment about what he heard.

Within two weeks of his proposal, Richard and Sonja were standing before a minister in her home on a Saturday afternoon with Wade and Josephine Croswell serving as the witnesses, while Darcy and Jared watched happily.

Even though she didn't know where he got the money, Sonja was aware that Richard had purchased a wedding ring for her and through Darcy she found out that it was gold with a diamond setting; and, with a bit of maneuvering on her part, Sonja also found out his ring size. This information allowed her to purchase a gold band for him.

When they exchanged rings, Richard was surprised that she had secretly purchased a gold band for him and she was pleasantly pleased with the ring he had chosen for her. It seemed he had correctly surmised her personal taste about jewelry.

When the minister pronounced them husband and wife, and told Richard that he may kiss the bride, he leaned over and gave her a tender kiss on the cheek. Although the kiss was not typical for the occasion, the gesture of it caused Sonja's heart to leap. It gave her a peaceful assurance that Richard indeed would cherish her as his wife, honor his vow to her, and continue to be an asset to the family.

After the ceremony and all the congratulations were given, cake and beverages were provided. Darcy had purchased a cake and Josephine provided the beverages. It was then that Sonja discovered the minister served as a Christian clergyman to the fire and police departments. Sonja guessed that Wade had something to do with securing him for the wedding.

After the wedding activities, life went back to normal, except Richard was going to become a greater part of the dynamics and working of the family. Sonja wasn't sure how the face of the family would change, but due to the changes that had already occurred because of him, she had peace about the outcome.

The initial change took place at the family dinner table. For Darcy, Jared, and Sonja to sit down together and have a meal at night proved sporadic because of the women's schedule. But, since Richard started eating dinner with them, both women made every attempt to ensure that each member of the small family was present and accounted for. What began as an attempt to make Richard feel comfortable at the dinner table quickly became a pleasant time for each of them. Beginning with a different family member each night, Richard would ask each of them about their day, which produced more communication at the family table. Sonja was even surprised about how the conversations about daily activities sometimes turned into discussions or stories. Even though Richard assured them that his daily activities were not as interesting as theirs, Sonja suspected that he was not yet prepared to totally let them in.

The second change is that they did things together on the weekends. On Saturday they usually did something fun and it was Jared who often inspired the activity. One Saturday it was a picnic at his favorite park and another time miniature golf. Jared liked the bumper cars, but Sonja always bowed out from participating in such activities.

The third change that was taking place involved Sonja's feelings for Richard. She had been silently attracted to him, but she became aware that her feelings were taking on a different dimension. The different currents of emotions she was feeling were hard for her to identify. Perhaps it was fondness or maybe it was that "L" word that embraces a broad spectrum of feelings from obsessive lust to youthful passions. She knew that she didn't want a surface love based on lust or an unrealistic adoration that was inspired by youthful passions. She wanted a love that had a solid foundation that would develop deep roots, a love that had character to withstand challenges, while still preferring the other's best interests because it was committed to genuine self-denial and sacrifice. She wanted a love that would give way to what was right and honor that which was reckoned as sacred by the God of heaven. She could tell by Richard's character that he might have the means in which to possess that type of love, but until she knew where he stood, she had to keep her feelings to herself.

Richard had informed Sonja that he had a job. Although he remained mysterious about it, every day he left for the bus and returned at night at the same time. She volunteered to drive him to work but he politely turned down her offer.

Almost three months after their marriage, Sonja felt uneasiness in her spirit throughout the day. Occasionally, she would offer up a prayer, seeking God's illumination, wisdom, and intervention. She sensed something was about to happen, and that only God could ensure the outcome of it.

That evening as they sat at the dinner table, they were interrupted by the doorbell and loud knocking. Darcy was the one who made her way to the door. Sonja knew something was terribly amiss when she heard Darcy tell the unexpected guest that he was not welcome. Next she heard what she thought was door being kicked, but before she could move, she heard it kicked open. By this time Richard was out of his chair, running towards the front door.

197

Without having to guess, Sonja knew who the unwelcome visitor was: James Hampton. He had threatened to kill Darcy a few times and kidnap Jared when he was under the influence of alcohol and drugs. As a result, they had a restraining order against him. He was not allowed to come near their home, work places, or Jared's school. Yet, here he was pushing his way into their home, spewing out threats and obscenities.

Jared had jumped up to follow Richard to the front door, but Sonja quickly grabbed him with her left arm while dialing 911 with the other hand. Jared wiggled loose of her hold when she was talking to the 911 operator and made a beeline for the front entrance. Sonja followed suit while giving the 911 operator as much information as possible. Within seconds the four of them were standing face to face with James, who was tossing a knife from one hand to the other, threatening each of them with bodily harm and death.

Sonja could see by his eyes that he was insane. Darcy was positioned behind Richard. In a very calm voice, Richard asked Jared to take his mother and grandmother to a safe place. It was clear that Richard recognized the protective nature of Jared towards him as well as the two women of his life. Richard was using a type of psychology on Jared that as the man his first responsibility was to get the women out of harm's way.

When Jared went to grab his grandmother's hand she made a motion for him and Darcy to seek safety. Darcy knew the look on her mother's face revealed that she wasn't not about to be moved regardless of her husband's instructions. What followed caused Sonja to feel as if she was watching a violent movie. Even though she consciously knew what was going on, she felt as if she was a simply a spectator.

As Darcy and Jared fled the scene, James, wild-eyed and sinister made his intentions known. "No matter where you hide Darcy, I'll find you!"

"You have to go through me first," Richard interjected.

"Just who do you think you are? Why are you even here? Darcy is my wife and Jared my kid. Stay the h—l out of my way!" he yelled.

Calmly Richard stated who he was, "I'm married to Sonja. I belong in this house more than you do. As I said, you'll have to go through me to get to any one of the three people in this house."

An evil sneer spread across his face as he roared at Richard, "That won't be a problem!" He took a step forward as he swung the knife at Richard's mid-section.

Richard quickly stepped back and pulled his stomach in as the knife wisped in front of him. When James brought the knife back he caught Richard's lower arm. However the momentum of the knife threw James off balance. Seeing his chance, Richard grabbed James' knife arm, bringing it down hard against his leg. Sonja could even hear the breaking of a bone in James' arm causing him to cry out. Before she knew it Richard had James in a neck hold, bringing him down to his knees. He had pressed his left arm firmly across James' neck and his bleeding arm behind his neck as if ready to twist it. James tried to use his good arm and hand to loosen Richard's grip, but it was clear Richard had him in a firm hold.

Sonja could see that blood was flowing from the cut on Richard's arm onto James and the floor, but he seemed oblivious to it. She could also see that Richard was seething with anger, almost shaking as he was trying to hold it together. Since Richard had the upper hand, it was time for him to put James in his place. "So who has the problem now?" he declared as he tightened his grip on James' neck. It was obvious that it was becoming harder for James to breathe. Richard continued, "I could rid my family of you ever trying to harm them again. I could send you to hell right now by choking you to death or even breaking your neck. What do you think about that you scrum bag? And, if I'm not comfortable with ridding the world of a piece of scrum like you, I could break your neck in such a way as to put you in a wheelchair forever. Which one would you prefer?"

Sonja could tell that the reality of his situation was setting in for James as he struggled for each breath. Fear filled his eyes as he realized that Richard held his life in his hands. Sonja could hear sirens, and as James began to turn blue she suddenly realized she needed to cease from being a spectator and become part of the scene. She touched Richard's bleeding arm and as he looked at her, she heard herself asking him to let the police take care of James.

It took a second for her words to penetrate Richard's anger, but once they sunk in he began to loosen his grip on James' neck. As he relaxed his grip, Richard still held his arm against James throat and spoke into James' ear an ominous warning, "You're fortunate my wife is a merciful woman, but if I ever hear of you threatening my family again in any way, shape, and form, I will chase you down like the rabid dog you are and I will make sure it'll be your last encounter with them. Do you understand me?"

Still trying to catch his breath, James shook his head yes. As Richard let go of him and stood up straight, he did one final act of aggression against him. As James leaned back on his knees gulping for air, Richard placed his foot against the upper part of James' back and slammed his face into the floor. "You stay right there until the police take you away." Richard paused, and then added, "and, I don't want to hear a peep out of you!"

Sonja could tell that James' broken arm was becoming the center of attention to him. It was clear he was in pain, but he knew he better hold it in. He didn't want to risk bringing any more unwanted attention his way.

Sonja grabbed Richard and steered him towards a chair in order to tend to his cut. "Richard, you're going to need stitches, it looks bad."

Richard took his eyes off of James and looked at the deep gash in his arm. "Oh, it'll be alright." Sonja positioned his arm in an upright position and went to the kitchen and grabbed some towels to wrap it. By the time she reached Richard, Wade along with his partner came through the door. Wade looked at the blood flung around the room, Richard's arm, and the prostate James and instructed his partner to call for assistance from the EMTs and for an ambulance.

As Sonja gently wrapped Richard's arm, Richard spoke to Wade. "I'll be pressing charges against this man. He needs to be put away before he kills someone."

Wade kneeled down to look at James, "Well, we meet once again."

Almost pleading and screaming, James' fear was finally released, "Get me out of here! This man tried to kill me."

Smiling, Wade responded, "You're fortunate you're alive to tell about it," he paused to let his latest statement sink in before continuing. "You really have done it this time, James. I can see that your bullying ways didn't fare well for you tonight. You met someone bigger than you," he paused, "who clearly is not going to let you get away with it. And, for your information, breaking the conditions of your restraining order and being charged with a couple counts of aggravated assault means you are looking at some time in the big house."

James groaned from both the pain and the latest information. He had been shown lenience many times previously due to his addictions, which were the driving force behind his violent aggressions. He had been sent to various programs, always promising to mend his ways. However, this time would be different. He would face the full weight of consequences for his actions and the looming prospect was sobering to him.

The EMTs came through the door. They quickly saw that there were two individuals that needed tending to. The first EMT came to Richard and examined his arm. "He'll definitely need stitches."

The other EMT turned James over on his back and gently examined his arm and the bruise that was forming on his right cheek due to being shoved hard against the floor. "This man has a broken arm," the EMT declared, "We need to put a splint on it for his ride to the hospital."

It was upon hearing about his broken arm that James nodded his head towards Richard and whimpered like a little boy, "He's the one who broke my arm."

Wade piped in, "And, when did that happen, James? You see I need to write out a report. Did he break your arm before or after you threatened him and his family with a knife, which ended with you assaulting him with it?"

From that point on, except for a few groans James remained silent.

The ambulance drivers came and wheeled James away, while the EMT who attended Richard instructed Sonja to take him to the emergency room to have a doctor do a more thorough examination of the deep cut and to stitch up his arm, but Richard would not agree to it.

"Sonja, you need to stay here and clean up this mess," he told her. "I don't want either Darcy or Jared to see it."

It was then that Wade volunteered to take Richard to the emergency room, as well as make sure he returned safely home.

Richard followed Wade out the door to the patrol car. Sonja realized that her foreboding sense had lifted. Although a bit shaken, she thanked the Lord that Richard was there to intervene and that no one was seriously hurt.

She began to clean up the mess. It was twenty minutes after the whole matter ended that Darcy came out of hiding. Her eyes were wide with concern as she looked at the remaining blood that Sonja was wiping up. "Is everyone okay? Where's Richard?"

Sonja quickly calmed her concerns with the assurance that Richard simply had been cut on the arm and was at the emergency room to have it stitched up. She then proceeded to tell her the whole story. By the time she was finished telling the story, the blood had been cleaned up and everything put back in its place and now they could call Jared out of hiding.

Sonja waited for Richard to return home and had to fight growing anxiety by praying. It began to get later and later without any word from him. Even though both Darcy and Jared wanted to see Richard to make sure he was alright, he still had not arrived home by the time they both went to bed, which was a 9:30 ritual for the whole family.

When she heard the key in the door around 10, she let out a sigh of relief. He walked into the entrance and started towards his room, when he noticed her sitting under a blanket in her favorite chair in the living room. He seemed surprised that she was waiting up for him. "Are you okay, Richard?" she asked. "After all, you were gone quite a while."

He wearily flopped down in the big easy chair before commenting. "I went to the emergency room and they fixed me up in no time," he lifted up his bandaged arm, "but then I opted to go to the police station to file a complaint against James. I'm sorry; I should've called you to let you know where I was."

His actions made sense to her since it was obvious that he was bent on seeing that the appropriate charges would be filed against James. "Would you like something hot to drink? I can fix you some coffee," she slightly paused, "or since I just fixed myself a cup of tea, maybe you would like to join me and have a 'spot of tea' as they' say?" Sonja inquired with a smile.

"It's late and I don't want to inconvenience you, but tea does sound good."

Sonja went into the kitchen and put the teakettle on the stove. Richard followed her and sat at the island. Even though Sonja knew very little about the man she married, she sensed he had something to say.

"Is there something on your mind Richard?" Sonja asked.

In a thoughtful tone, Richard responded, "I know it's late, but could we talk for a while?"

Sonja's emotions plunged to the pit of her stomach, causing a rush. She felt both excitement and trepidation. Perhaps she was about to be let into this man's world, but what would she discover? She managed a smile, "Sure, why don't you go back to the living room, I'll bring the tea, and then we can talk?" He nodded in agreement and headed for the living room.

As she prepared the tea, she quietly prayed. The unknown was unnerving, but the quiet assurance of God being in control assured her that all was well and took the edge off of the unknown. She didn't know what was before her, but she sensed that God wouldn't let her down.

She set Richard's tea on the corner table beside the chair he was sitting in, then settled herself in her chair, and once again pulled the blanket over her lap. She took a sip of tea, waiting for Richard, who seemed to be mulling something over in his mind, to begin the conversation.

"You know, Sonja, I was going to leave you a note tonight in regard to my plans. However, I've been wanting to talk to you for some time, but..." he became quiet again.

Sonja knew she had to be patient, but her nerves were being jerked by the anxiety she was trying to keep at bay. She finally heard herself calmly say, "But, what?"

Richard looked at her, "I'm afraid that if I bring the past together with the present, that what I have now will dissipate like a mist, and I don't want to lose what I have here," he paused as he looked down.

"Richard how would you lose the present life to your past life?" Sonja inquired, while battling to keep her flitting nerves intact.

Once again he looked at her, his blue eyes searching her face. "I guess the real issue Sonja, is that I don't know how to bring them together. You see I became lost to my past, and until I came here I had no concern for the present and no hope for the future. I was living in a surreal reality that made me numb to the past, while the present held no real distinction because there was no day," he paused, "only the night, a long endless night of sorrow, despair, and hopelessness."

He stopped, took a sip of the hot tea, and then leaned forward to look more intently at her. "What's sad is that even the good things about my past became lost to me as I lived in the shadows of an insane world that had no absolutes. On the streets, survival is the name of the game. In the survival game, each person stakes their own small territory and sets their own code in light of what it'll mean to survive. It all makes sense and yet," he paused as to collect the right words, "it's all so senseless."

Sonja suspected that he was talking about haunting experiences that he had witnessed while on the streets. She needed to share her observation with him, "It's obvious, Richard, that the streets are not your home. How did you end up there?"

Focusing on her face, he answered her, "It was a special assignment."

"Special assignment?" This new revelation made Sonja grapple with what she was hearing. "What do you mean Richard?"

"I'm in law enforcement, actually a detective, but due to circumstances, I accepted a special assignment to bust a notorious drug dealer who preys on street people. Needless to say this drug dealer uses the streets as his personal platform to disburse his drugs to various parts of the country."

Sonja wasn't really stunned at the disclosure because it shed light on some of the events that had happened, but it did bring an element of surprise with it. "Wade knows that you're in law enforcement?"

"Yes, he does."

"And, you've been working…"

"Yes, I have been at the police station helping to work cold case files until I felt strong enough to finish my assignment."

To Sonja the solution was obvious, "Since it's so overwhelming for you to be on the streets, do you have to see this assignment through?"

He slightly smiled, "The streets are very depressing, but that's not my problem. You see I went into the streets to become lost in the first place, to get rid of my pain once and for all."

Sonja became somewhat alarmed by his statement. "What are you talking about?"

Sonja could tell that Richard was rolling back the years in his mind before speaking. He slowly began to share his story, "I grew up in a Christian family. I had a good childhood and planned to be a policeman at a very early age, even though my father ran a construction company and taught me the trade during my teen years. My parents knew that law enforcement was dangerous, but they never discouraged me. They always told me as long as I kept God the center of my world that I would be able to keep everything in the proper balance.

"I even married a Christian woman by the name of Kathryn, who was willing to share my life in law enforcement. We had a wonderful marriage that produced two beautiful daughters, Krista and Karina and a son, Ross. I always felt that God and I were tight, but I didn't realize that my faith towards God had never really been tested in fiery ovens of sorrow.

Sonja wasn't surprised at the new revelations. Her suspicions about him not being a street person but having a past life were now being confirmed, but at the same time she felt anxious about the fact that he had a wife and children.

"Then that terrible day happened." Richard's voice faded as he closed his eyes as if to shut out memories too painful to bear."

Sonja held her breath, and then heard herself softly ask, "What happened Richard?"

Richard swallowed hard before he continued his story, "My children were away on a Christian retreat for young people and my wife was home alone. When I drove up to the house, it was dark. I knew something wasn't right. I took my gun out the holster and crept to the door, only to discover it was slightly ajar. As I entered the house, there was an eerie silence and a menacing sensation. I slowly made my way through the house and it was in the kitchen that I found the murdered body of my beloved Kathryn."

Sonja felt all of her pent-up breath suddenly exploding out of her lungs as a great wave of sorrow rushed in. Like her, Richard had tragically lost his beloved. She understood the methods in which death claims its victims affect people differently. Death caused by illness is considered natural regardless of how much it ravages someone. On the other hand, Hunter's death, which was the result of a car accident, was considered a tragedy, but murder in a society governed by moral laws is a violent atrocity committed against the decency of all humanity. Even though death creates a vacuum in the lives of loved ones, the means in which it occurs can actually create a deep tormenting, mental rut in people's minds that prevents them from being healed. It would become obvious by Richard's action that he had been clearly taken captive by the unanswered questions that were left in the wake of the evil events that had claimed his wife.

Sonja knew that such torment was especially true in such cases where violence occurs. The imagination can take flight as to what the loved one felt and experienced. The possibilities create tormenting images, haunting those left behind as they try to fill in the blanks and pick up the pieces of that which seems so cruel and senseless.

As Sonja focused in on Richard's tormented expression, she watched as he struggled to come to terms with the haunting reality that was being replayed across the screen of his mind. He fought back tears that threatened to make a grand entrance, and breathed deeply as he pushed his way through the emotional tidal wave that affronted him.

Sonja knew that she had to remain quiet. There was nothing she could say that would take away the pain that was consuming him. How well she remembered her own pain and the disturbing prospect of going on without Hunter. No one could really take the pain away. It was there to cut deep into her soul, especially at night when the silence became deafening as she strove to hear him breathe one more time, remember his tender touches of love and assurance, and feel the warmth of his presence close to her. At such times she had to settle for memories that left her feeling bitter-sweet, bitter because it would never be again; and sweet because the joy their relationship had brought her made her present pain bearable.

Even though Sonja had not felt the bitter-sweetness of her loss for years, she was now being reminded of it as she watched Richard reliving the emotional tidal wave that flooded his inner being.

Richard looked at her and once again found his voice to continue his story. He closed his eyes to replay the dreadful memories. "After her death, I found myself becoming lost in a deep abyss of guilt and self-pity. I blamed myself for not being there to protect her. Here I was, a policeman, sworn to protect society, and I failed to protect my wife.

He gave a ragged sigh, and continued. "And, after I had indicted myself and put myself on trial in the courts of my mind, I couldn't help but blame God as well. Why did He allow this to happen? After all, I had always tried to do everything right, and yet he allowed my wife to be brutally murdered. Where was He, didn't He care, didn't He hear her pleadings whether silent or aloud? It seemed so ironic to my logic that everything I believed, thought, and perceived about God began to mock me.

"I began to slide back into a hopeless state and became lost in a dark world of shadows that eventually turned into thick darkness that almost suffocated me. I had no hope because God had become an imposter in my mind and my faith in Him a sham. Underneath, I knew I had no real case against Him, but I wanted to blame someone besides myself. I wanted the right to feel anger and to hate. I wanted to destroy those who killed her and I had to steel myself against having a conscience that would halt my plans of vengeance.

"However, the police couldn't solve the crime. After a year of almost being driven mad by torment, I became desperate to execute punishment on someone, on anyone and when this assignment came up I figured I could exact my revenge on some ruthless thug. Admittedly I was formulating another maneuver in my mind. Due to the danger the assignment posed, I also saw it as a possible way out of my pain and despair. I could go out in a blaze of glory while taking a murderous drug lord with me without anybody being any wiser to my secret death wish."

He opened his eyes and looked at her, "I almost got both wishes. He smiled, "Pushing you out of the way of the car almost made my death wish come true and I almost executed judgment on a thug tonight."

He shook his head, "Sonja, it would have been so easy for me to break James' neck," he paused for a moment, then continued, "and that scared me." He lowered his eyes, and in a husky voice said, "And, now you probably think badly of me."

Even though Sonja had maintained a calm appearance, behind the scenes she felt her emotions were being taken on a roller coaster ride. He became silent. This is when Sonja felt she could speak, "Why would I think badly of you?"

"Because, my actions probably frightened you."

"On the contrary Richard. Your actions didn't frighten me one bit because underneath I know you aren't an angry or violent man."

Surprised he asked, "How do you know that?"

206

"It's how you have treated Jared, Darcy, and me. You've shown such consideration," she paused to compose her thoughts. "And, a person full of anger is self-absorbed, is unreasonable, and has no regard for others unless he can use them. But, my question is what changed you from the despairing, lost man to who you are now?"

"You guys changed me," he smiled. "It started with Jared. He reminded me there is hope, while Darcy sort of served as a mirror of my own fear and skepticism. As I became involved with renovating the house, I forgot about myself. And, as I learned about your own predicament, I realized what a boob I had become."

"My predicament?" Sonja quizzed.

Shaking his head, "I know about the situation with your ex-husband and what he did to Darcy and about your son, Dawson. I even thought for a while, that the Lord kept me alive so I could take your ex-husband out. That goes to show you how out of touch and insane my reality became. However, as I observed you, you displayed great forgiveness and peace. It occurred to me that if you could forgive the likes of your ex-husband and not be tormented by what happened, than I also had hope to find such peace. I already know the answer, but I have to ask you, how did you manage to walk through what happened?"

Sonja smiled, "You do know the answer Richard. It was my relationship with the Lord that enabled me to go through that deep, dark valley. When the Lord showed me what had happened, guilt was standing at the door of my soul and condemnation was knocking on it, ready to come in to torment me. In my mind I should have known what was happening to my daughter, but the Lord showed me that I'm not all-knowing.

"Let's face it Richard, we condemn ourselves for not being God. We want to see ourselves somehow saving the day, but there's only one who is Savior, and He didn't come to just save the day for one person, but to save each of us from our sinful selves and eternal damnation. He came to bring hope to our insane worlds and silence the mocking, tormenting ways of guilt and shame that we feel towards those things we cannot control or change. He came so we could have peace with the only true God, so we could trust Him with our lives, and accept what is, as well as the outcome of that which leaves us devastated.

"Richard the Lord has been faithful to slowly bring healing to my family. I know that one day He'll bring my son home. Until then, He has become my place of refuge and rest for me. You know, don't you, that He has been waiting for you to come home ever since you became lost?"

Richard looked at Sonja with tears in his eyes, "I want you to know that the incident with James revealed to me where I was heading if I didn't change my path. As a result, tonight while I was at the police station, I repented of my backsliding ways and found my way back home. I also know the Father received me with open arms."

Sonja wanted to jump up and yell, "Praise the Lord," but she knew that she had to keep such rejoicing to herself, because she sensed there was more conversation to come and she didn't want to break the flow.

Richard smiled at her, "I sense by the smile on your face you would like to celebrate in a more visible way."

"You're right Richard, but I also sense this conversation is not finished."

"You're right, it's not finished. There are four things I must relate to you." He then stood up and came towards her. He handed her a piece of paper with a phone number. "First you need to call this phone number tomorrow. Secondly, my children know about you, Darcy, and Jared, and my oldest daughter, Krista will probably be contacting you within the next couple of days. The third thing is that I'm leaving tonight to go back on the streets to finish the assignment. I don't know how long it'll take, but I will not be able to contact you until it is done."

He took an envelope out of his back pocket and handed it to her. "I've made you my beneficiary. You will receive my insurance and so-forth if anything happens to me."

By this time Sonja felt like she had fallen off a cliff. One minute she was ready to celebrate and the next she felt like she was in a freefall ready to crash into the ground.

"The fourth thing I want to say to you is thank you. You took a big risk in marrying me and letting me into your family." He chuckled, "And, I don't know what possessed you to do it—but,"

Sonja could no longer remain silent; she jumped up to face him interrupting his words. Surprised, he took a step back. "Richard, this may not make any sense, but I married you because the Lord instructed me to do so, and now I know why. Please don't tell me I could be a widow again!"

Richard looked a bit stunned, he gently took her hand, "I've been hoping you feel the same way about me as I do you."

She grasped his strong hand with both of her hands as to not let him go. She felt a tingling sensation flow through her body as a flush spread over her uplifted face.

She looked into his soft blue eyes to soak in his words, "Sonja, I never thought it was possible to ever love again, but I want you to know I have fallen in love with you."

It seemed to Sonja that time was standing still as she tried to take in and savor the moment. "Richard, I'm in love with you, and I don't want to let you go."

Richard leaned over as he began to enfold her into his arms. His lips pressed against hers with sweet tenderness. She felt an oneness with him, a feeling she had not felt since Hunter. Assurance arose up like a phoenix in her inner being. She knew without a doubt that God had ordained and orchestrated their union, but she felt confusion and fear waiting in the outer fringes. In her mind, they had just found each other and now they must be parted by a dark uncertainty. She struggled to calm herself as she reasoned that the Lord surely wouldn't take him away from her, not now. She found herself clinging to him as her body completely relaxed in his arms while her head came to rest on his chest.

Richard's voice interrupted the moment, "If I don't go now Sonja, I'm afraid I'll never leave."

Although Sonja already knew the answer, she still had to ask it even if it only meant extending their time together for a few more seconds. "Why do you have to go?"

"I started this and I must finish it."

Sonja knew she had to let him go. God had brought this man into her life, but now she must entrust him back to Him. As she slowly released her arms from around him, she could feel him letting go of her. She looked at him, "What will I tell Jared and Darcy?"

He put his right hand on her cheek. She leaned her face against his hand and grasped his other hand, "You can tell Darcy the truth, and I've already told Jared that I would be leaving to finish some business, but that I would be coming back."

Sonja couldn't help herself. She tilted her head back and looked into his eyes. She needed to cement his words in her soul, "You're coming back?"

Richard smiled, "What do you think?" He leaned over and kissed her once again and backed away from her before turning to walk out into the night air.

When she heard the door close, she ran to the front window. She watched Richard walk into the night to catch the last bus to the city. She soaked in as much as she could of him as the light from the street lamps highlighted his figure. As he faded into the black shadows, she took comfort that he was no longer a child of the night, lost in gross

209

darkness, but now he was once again walking in the glorious light of Jesus Christ.

***

Sonja had a restless night. She struggled to get her mind around all the information she had learned. She also didn't want to sleep unless she woke up to discover what happened between her and Richard was nothing more than a dream. She struggled to put down the anxiety that was mounting due to the possibility of losing him before they could really make a life together. She feared that the moments she had shared with him would quickly fade into uncertain shadows, but she also was aware that everything could easily turn into a nightmare. Unlike Hunter, she only had a few precious memories of Richard to hold onto.

She finally dozed off to wake to a new day. In spite of knowing that the night before had changed everything for her, she reluctantly got out of bed to start her regular activities. She knew life had to go on regardless of new shocks waves that had rattled her world the night before.

Wondering if it was all a dream, Sonja drifted into the living room where she glanced at the easy chair where Richard had sat the night before. His teacup still sat on the coaster where she had placed it. She walked over to it and noticed that it still had some tea in it. She picked it up, clasped both of her hands around it and closed her eyes to try to recapture the feel of his arms and lips, the smell of his cologne, the expression of his eyes, and the tone of his voice.

Darcy's voice interrupted her mother's reminiscing, "Mom, are you alright?"

Sonja looked at Darcy, "We have a lot to talk about before Jared wakes up."

Looking alarmed, Darcy volunteered to fix breakfast while Sonja filled her in on the latest information.

Sonja sat at the island while Darcy prepared biscuits and put bacon in a pan. At one point the information almost caused Darcy to forget the biscuits were in the oven and the bacon needed to be turned over. Somehow the breakfast survived Darcy's shocked fascination towards the latest revelations about Richard, and both Sonja and Darcy were able to avoid partaking of burnt offerings.

Sonja looked at her daughter, "I admit, I wondered who told Richard about Jake."

Darcy's face turned a shade of red, "I've got to admit that Jared spilled some of the beans and I filled in the blank spaces." She looked at Sonja, "Mom, I just felt he was a trustworthy person and I could share with him as to what happened and how I felt about it without him judging me. You know what he did?"

A question formed on Sonja's face. "No, tell me.

"He apologized to me on behalf of all men, and told me that Jake had no right, no grounds, and no excuse for what he did to me, and he needed to be hung from the highest and nearest tree. He also told me I was a beautiful person and that I must never let some wicked infidel like Jake or James define my worth as a person and as a woman."

Sonja was becoming more convinced that her assessment of Richard's character and ways were correct.

"Mom, what about that phone number, shouldn't you call it and find out where it leads to."

Sonja shook her head in agreement. She suspected that it could be one of his children. She went to the bedroom and located the mysterious phone number on her side table. She grabbed her cell phone and headed back to the kitchen. She sat back down on the stool, entered the number and waited for someone to answer it.

After the fourth ring someone said "hello". When Sonja, heard the voice she froze. Once again the voice said hello, giving Sonja time to find her tongue, "Dawson, is that you?"

"Mom, I can't believe it! How did you get my phone number?"

When she heard the name Dawson, Darcy's hand flew to her mouth in complete shock.

Sonja suspected that Richard had used the tools and training of his profession to locate Dawson, but she would wait for another time to explain who gave her his number. "Dawson, where've you been for the last six years?" Sonja cried.

"It's been that long? Mom, I'm so sorry. I wanted to get in touch with you so many times, but as time passed, I convinced myself that the door was shutting tighter against me having any real communications with you."

"How can you believe such a thing Dawson?" Sonja exclaimed as tears began to pool in her eyes. "The door of my heart would never be shut against you. You're my precious son. How could you even think that?"

Sonja could tell by her son's voice that he was also choking back tears, "I failed to protect Darcy and to become a point of strength when you needed me the most. In fact, I just ran from the all mess like a weak coward."

"You're not a weak coward, Dawson; you simply became lost in the overwhelming tidal wave that hit our family. You bought a lie of the enemy that somehow you failed to protect your sister from something you had no knowledge of or control over." She paused, "As you accepted the lie, you took on guilt and shame as the feeling of failure tethered you and pulled you down into an insane reality of hopelessness. It's time you break free of that tether and come home where you are loved and you belong."

By this time Sonja could tell that Dawson was unable to hold back his tears. They flowed freely as he admitted that he wanted to come home.

"Dawson, when can we expect you home?"

"I've a couple of things to wrap up here Mom. I know my former boss over there really liked my work, so I'm going to call him to see if he has any openings for me at his company. These activities, along with travel time, will take me a couple of days."

"Then we'll see you in a couple of days and then we can talk and catch up on everything that has been happening, but meanwhile will you please keep me informed of your progress?"

"You got it Mom. I promise."

When Darcy overheard that her brother was coming home, she couldn't hold herself back any longer. She tugged at her mother's arm to give her the phone. Sonja conceded and knew it was time for her to give the siblings some time to themselves. As she left the room, she could hear Darcy's excitable voice chiding Dawson, but at the same doing her "sisterly interrogation."

Sonja retreated to the living room, as tears of joy cruised down her cheeks. She silently praised her faithful God. Her son was coming home! The Lord had indeed heard the prayers of her heart and set up unusual circumstances that would culminate in Dawson's return.

She also gave Richard to the Lord. She wanted to hold onto him, but she knew the safest place for him was in the Lord's hands. She had to trust Him with the outcome. Meanwhile preparing for her son's homecoming would occupy some of her time until he arrived.

Jared came out of the bedroom and asked Sonja what his mother was excited about. "She is talking to your Uncle Dawson, and guess what?

Jared eyes widened, "What?"

"He's coming home very soon."

Even though Jared was a baby when his uncle left, she and Darcy talked about him like he was on some great adventure and would one day come home.

With a big grin, Jared squealed, "My uncle is coming home?"

"Yes he is Jared."

Jared's twinkling eyes searched the room. Sonja saw that his face became concerned. "Where is Grandpa Richard?"

"He had to go away for a few days. I guess he already explained this to you."

Jared shook his head yes. "Ya know, Grandma, Uncle Dawson and Grandpa Richard could come home at the same time. Wouldn't that be great?"

She gathered Jared into her arms and held him as tightly as she could. It was as if the Lord was giving her an assurance that Richard would be home soon through her grandson. In a low tone, she replied, "Yes Jared that would be indeed."

The next couple of days proved to be long but busy. Sonja occupied her mind with little details, but the silence of the night mocked her. She wrestled to bring her thoughts under control so that her imagination wouldn't have a platform in which to inspire any false hope or vain, tormenting possibilities. She knew that she had to keep her wits about her to prevent herself from giving way to utter anxiety.

True to his word, Dawson kept both her and Darcy updated. Between phone conversations, he was informed about Richard. At first he seemed uncertain and suspicious. He even asked his mother if this Richard guy would be upset if he was around for a while. Even though Sonja could not speak for Richard, she assured Dawson based on his character that he would consider their home, his home. It was only after speaking to Darcy about Richard that Dawson finally informed his mother that he would withhold judgment about him until he was able to personally meet and talk with him.

On the day that Dawson was to arrive, Krista Blackwell phoned Sonja. Even though there was some nervousness on both of their parts, the barrier of the unknown was quickly broken when both ladies admitted to the other that they were anxious to meet the other. They set up a time and place on the following day which was Saturday in which members of both parties, if they so desired, could have lunch. In fact, it was Krista's suggestion that they go somewhere were Jared could enjoy himself. They picked a place where there were games for both children and adults.

Dawson arrived early on Friday and it turned out to be a homecoming that would not be forgotten. There were tears of joy, long hugs, and laughter. There was so much to talk about from obvious changes to not so obvious. The greatest change for Dawson was Jared, but for the women, they acknowledged that the fiery oven that

Dawson had been in for six years had brought sobriety and a level of maturity. Even though he was raw in places due to unresolved issues, it was obvious that he had refused to surrender to all of the nagging lies and accusations.

After Darcy and Jared went to bed, Dawson and Sonja kept the lights burning late into the night. Dawson shared with Sonja about his six years, from the cities he traveled to, the jobs he worked at, and torments he had to face down. However, his greatest regret occurred when he realized that he had dropped the ball at the most crucial time when his mother and sister needed him the most. He was so busy looking backward at what he missed, that he failed to be faithful with the opportunities that loomed before him to be a real support to both his mother and sister.

"Dawson, you have been bruised by the sins of others," Sonja stated. "However, for healing to come, you have to quit making the same mistake by continually looking back at missed opportunities that are long gone. Learn from your past regrets so you can face present challenges. Regrets will always cause you to look backward, preventing you from seeing what is right in front of you. You have a life, but it's in front of you, not behind you."

Thoughtfully, Dawson nodded his head, "You're right Mom, but I don't know how to get off the elevator of regrets. I have been going from one terminal of despair to another in search of the right flight that would take me far from my past failures, but no matter what I tried I could never get away from them."

Sonja took Dawson's hand in hers and looked into her son's hazel eyes, "Son, there is only One who can deliver you from past regrets. Remember it is because you took your eyes off of Him in the first place and put them on the circumstances that you lost your way."

Dawson smiled, "I know that only Jesus can deliver me from the failures and pains of the past. I guess that is another reason I didn't come home because I didn't want to be delivered from my wilderness. I felt it was a good way to punish myself, but I'm tired of seeing and feeling the same barren terrain in my life. I'm ready to come home for good."

Mother and son had a good prayer session as Dawson in brokenness sought forgiveness from the Lord for his wayward ways and detours, while his mother prayed for his complete healing and restoration. Dawson even prayed for Richard's safety while his mother took the opportunity to ask the Lord to bring her husband home. Later, they both admitted that they felt the sweetness of God's Spirit as He enfolded them in a cocoon of love and peace.

The next day Darcy, Dawson, and Jared all went as a united front to meet Richard's children. Krista had told her what she would be wearing as a point of identification and Sonja informed Krista what she would be wearing. When the three of them walked into the establishment, Sonja quickly scanned the people. A lady stood up, waved at her and started walking towards them.

When she reached Sonja, she took both of her hands. "Sonja, I'm Krista."

Sonja smiled at her as she held her hands. She wanted to see if Krista possessed any of the traits of her father. However, if there were physical similarities it wasn't obvious. Krista was dishwater blond and had brown eyes. However, she saw a bit of Richard in Krista as to how she handled herself. It was clear that Krista had character and knew how to carry herself with grace.

Krista was also studying Sonja, "Sonja, Dad did a good job of describing you because I recognized you when you first came through the door."

Sonja was a bit surprised and pleased that Richard had gone to some lengths to describe her to his daughter. But, she began to wonder what context required him to describe her in the first place. Sonja introduced Krista to the twins and Jared.

Krista seemed genuine in her excitement to meet them. She then led them over to the table where Karina and Ross were patiently waiting. They both stood up as introductions were conducted. Sonja recognized that Ross might look like a clean shaven Richard. Karina had his smile but had brown hair and brown eyes.

They all sat at the table making small talk to break the ice of uncertainty. It was Jared who piped in while looking at the three Blackwell siblings, "Are you my aunts and uncle?"

Darcy seemed embarrassed, while Sonja realized that her daughter wasn't the only one at the table that was trying to refrain from smiling. She could tell that both Krista and Karina were struggling to maintain a straight face. It was Ross who broke the silence.

"Well, Jared that depends on what a man by the name of Richard Blackwell is to you. For instance, what do you call Richard?"

In innocence and seriousness, Jared answered him. "He's my grandpa."

Smiling at Jared, Ross set the record straight, "If Richard is your grandpa then I'm your uncle and Krista and Karina are your aunts."

"Good!" Jared exclaimed.

"Why is it important for you to have more uncles and aunts?" Dawson asked.

"Wel-l-l-l-l, he drawled, my friend told me the more uncles and aunts I have the more fun and presents I can have."

That is when the smiles broke into laugher. It was obvious to everyone that Jared was an innocent opportunist that unknowingly broke any remaining barriers that existed between the six adults.

As Sonja watched Jared laughing with the adults as Ross ruffled his hair, it reminded her of the Scripture that says a little child shall lead them. She became aware long ago that adults were too caught up with protocol, images, and impressions to be transparent and unassuming. They spend a great deal of time testing the waters before committing themselves to others, but for a childlike Jared, innocence serves as the transparent light as to the unabashed sincerity of a child's soul. No wonder Jesus stated that before one can inherit the kingdom of God, he or she must become as a child.

The happy group started freely asking questions. The three Blackwell's found out about the Corbans and vise versa. Sonja learned that Krista was a teacher who worked in the same school district as Jake; Karina was a veterinary, and Ross a fireman. She sat back as each one shared about different aspects of their life while eating lunch. Ross shared some of his adventures working construction for Richard's father, while Karina talked about riding her stick horse named Rowdy and playing cowboys on the farm belonging to her mother's parents. Krista liked books and working indoors and avoided tomboyish activities. For Sonja, each piece of information was creating a mosaic. Since some of it was like storytelling, even Jared became fascinated by some of the childhood memories the five different siblings relived. There were even suspenseful moments when they talked about the times they spread their wings to embark on new endeavors, followed by laughter at comical consequences that often emerged from their adventures.

When lunch was finished, Jared asked who was willing to play games with him. Dawson, Ross, and Karina quickly took him up on his invitation, while Darcy reluctantly agreed to share the looming adventure that was beckoning the imaginative youth.

Sonja and Krista silently watched Dawson set the pace for the four adults as Jared pulled him towards the world of new challenges and adventures. The conversation between the two women that followed was about Richard, except for a reference that Krista knew Jake and that she had harbored secret concerns about him. She smiled at the curious Sonja, as she explained that Jake had made overtures towards her a couple of times until he found out her father was a policeman.

Sonja couldn't help but ask the question, "One has to wonder how many other women has he flirted with, and does his present wife know about it?"

Krista smiled, "I don't think so, but eventually he's going to be caught in his own trap and the truth will come out about his real character."

Krista then shared how she and her two siblings felt they lost both parents when her mother was murdered. However, a couple of weeks ago, their father had contacted them and met with them to ask for forgiveness for his selfishness and to bring them up to date about the changes and marriage that had occurred in his life. Although shocked, each of the Blackwell siblings rejoiced because they knew their father had come back from the dead.

Sonja filled Krista in about her father's stay at her house. She talked about how mysterious he had been about his life and what led up to their unusual marriage, as well as the happenings and conversation they had the night he left. Then she added, "You know your father has made me the beneficiary of his policies? I think he should have made you three the beneficiaries."

Krista shook her head no. "Sonja, we're already taken care of. Dad was concerned about you, Darcy, and Jared. All three of you are very important to him and I'm thankful for all of you because you had a big part in bringing my father back to the three of us."

Sonja looked at Krista, "I would trade all the policies in the world just have your father sitting with us right now."

"I know you would Sonja."

The sound of laughter filled their ears as Ross, Dawson, Darcy, Karina, and Jared came towards the table. It was obvious they had some fun adventures and were talking about it. It delighted Sonja's heart to hear the joy resonating between the five of them. Loss and tragedy were part of their history, but laughter now filled the moment. In the middle of them was a small figure almost dancing with glee as he spotted his grandmother and ran to tell her and his newest aunt Krista about his most recent adventures.

***

On Monday morning Sonja was awakened by the ringing of her cell phone. When she picked it up, she heard Krista's excited voice. "Sonja, have you heard the news?"

In a sleepy voice, Sonja replied, "No, I just woke up. Is something wrong?"

"Oh, I'm sorry for waking you but the news station is reporting that there was a big drug bust on the streets sometime during the night that was international in scope. I don't know how to tell you but they said that a policeman was shot, as well as the drug dealer. They didn't release any names or the condition of either man."

Sonja's heart dropped. She shook her head as to push back the reality that was now hitting her in the face with the fear that she had been wrestling with for the past five days since Richard walked into the night towards an unknown destiny.

"Sonja, I'm sure you'll be contacted one way or the other, and if you hear anything, call me anytime. I will keep my phone on."

Sonja assured her that the minute she heard anything, she would let her know. After she hung up, she got out of bed and kneeled down beside it. She remained silent, knowing that it was time for her to be still and know that God is God, sovereign in all He does, perfect in His ways, and capable of bringing forth that which is eternal. Her soul had to come to rest on His goodness, trust His faithfulness, and maintain the assurance that He works all things out for His glory. It was only then that she could humbly submit to His will and once again offer to Him in sweet surrender, her beloved Richard.

As she stood up from the bed in renewed confidence, her phone rang again. She hurried to it to find an unidentified number. She held her breath and answered it. It seemed as if time stood still before she heard a tired, but familiar, voice, the voice of her beloved Richard.

"Sonja, it's Richard!"

With great relief, while trying to corral her pent up anxiety from heightening her concern, she exclaimed, "Richard are you alright?"

"Yes, I'm calling you to let you know it's over and I will be coming home, but a friend of mine was shot."

"Yes, I heard about it. I'm so sorry, will he be okay?"

"I don't know. I have to finish filling out reports, but afterwards I'll be going to the hospital to sit with his wife until we know the score on his condition."

"I'll be praying for God to guide the doctors where your friend is concerned," Sonja assured him, "as well as for comfort and strength for his family and you."

"Thanks Sonja, I knew I could count on you praying, and hopefully I'll see you very soon."

"I'm praying for that as well," Sonja stated, then added, "oh, by the way, Krista heard about the bust on the news and is very concerned. Do you want me to call her or do you want to touch base with her."

"So, you've met Krista?"

Sonja felt the need to give him a short summation of what she perceived not only about Krista but the other two as well, "Yes, I've met her as well as your other two children. I think Krista is lovely, Karina is lively, and Ross is a gentleman like his father."

Richard let out a sigh, "I'm so glad that the gap has been closed between my past and present."

"Yes, and thanks to you, Dawson finally came home!"

Richard's tired voice became animated. "Oh Sonja that is great to hear, but I can't take that much credit for it. Thanks to the technology of today, so much information can be obtained by just pushing a button. I'm anxious to meet him."

"About Krista, do you want me to call her?"

"No I'll call her. By the way, I love you."

Sonja's felt her heart leap with joy, "I love you too Richard."

After Sonja hung up, she quietly praised the Lord for giving Richard back to her and prayed for the injured officer and his family.

She went to the kitchen to prepare breakfast. Although a little apprehensive of how Richard would respond to him, Dawson shared in the joy of the other three about Richard coming home. He became even more light hearted when he found out Richard was excited about meeting him.

In Sonja's mind there was a lot to do to prepare for Richard's homecoming. She had learned some of his likes and dislikes and knew he loved Shepherd's Pie. She decided to not only prepare it for him, but also invite Krista, Karina, and Ross to join them.

It was about three in the afternoon when she received another call. Richard's deep voice greeted her.

Holding her breath, Sonja asked the obvious question, "Is everything alright Richard?"

With a sigh of relief, Richard responded, "Yes, my friend is expected to make a full recovery. However, Sonja, I have a favor to ask you."

Sounding a bit alarmed, she asked, "What is it?"

"I'm exhausted. I just missed the bus and don't want to wait for the next one. Would you consider coming and picking me up?"

"You bet! I will be there!" Excitement bubbled up in her inner being. Richard was finally coming home. "Depending on the traffic it will probably take me 20 to 25 minutes to get there."

He told her he would wait for her in the waiting room closest to the front entrance and then added, "By the way an old friend of ours wanted to me to tell you 'hello'."

219

Sonja couldn't think of any old friends that the two of them shared. Richard chuckled, "I have to admit I don't remember her, but she remembers both of us. In fact, she is a nurse here and her name is Karen Gibbs. She told me you really helped her at a pivot point in her life when I was brought in after the accident. She also told me to thank you for the reality check you gave her and congratulated us on our marriage."

Memories of that day came back to Sonja. She remembered how everything was running amuck and as a result, she would not tolerate an unbecoming attitude in a nurse. It never ceased to amaze Sonja how God takes small moments and imparts life-changing truths into them and changes the course of an individual.

"I remember Karen, and if you see her be sure to give her my regards. I'll see you very soon."

It seemed like it took forever for Sonja to get to her destination. She walked into the front entrance and asked the receptionist where the nearest waiting room was. As she walked into the waiting room she only could see one man. He was somewhat spread out on a couple of chairs sleeping. Sonja began to wonder if there was another waiting room. As she looked towards him, it was obvious that there was a bandage on his left arm, catching her attention.

There was also something familiar about him. Curious, she slowly walked in his direction. She noted that he was clean-shaven with neatly trimmed hair. His clothes were casual, but clean. Then she noted that his dark hair had some silver in it. Suddenly, it hit her! The man was an older version of Ross. She stopped and stared at him, trying to wrap her mind around the truth, trying to seal it as being so. The sleeping man was Richard. Clearly, he no longer harbored the garb and looks of a street person. As she admired his new look, she concluded that he was more handsome than she had previously imagined. Finally, the sleeping man stirred, causing her to remember her real mission.

In an unsure tone, she called his name. "Richard?"

The man's eyes flew open. Sonja was looking into familiar clear blue eyes and when he spoke, she was hearing a familiar voice.

"Sonja, you're here!" He quickly stood, reaching for her and pulling her to himself in a warm embrace. As he looked down at her upturned face, he slowly lowered his head until their lips met.

"I'm so happy to see you! He whispered into her ear. Sorry, I fell off to sleep while waiting for you."

She smiled at him, "That's alright it gave me time," she paused, "to...."

"To what?" he asked.

"To get used to the new Richard."

Sonja could tell that his initial confusion gave way to understanding. He chuckled.

"I guess I should've warned you that I finally got to shed that old role this afternoon. It clearly wasn't me." Laughing, he added, "but if you liked the old me...."

Sonja giggled, "Oh no, I like the new you just fine, I just have to get used to it."

He grinned, "Hopefully, it won't take too much time for you to get used to my new look."

"I'm quickly adjusting to it, but I also wanted to warn you about something," Sonja stated.

With a questioning expression, "What's that?" Richard asked.

"I hope you don't mind, but I had to move you out of the apartment in order to move Dawson in there until he gets on his feet."

Taken aback, Richard asked, "Where did you move my stuff?"

Sonja sheepishly smiled, "I hope you don't mind, but into my...now our room."

Richard grinned, "If you don't mind, I won't either." He then paused. "Mrs. Blackwell, it's time to go home."

Sonja's smile widened. "Indeed it is Mr. Blackwell. Indeed it is!"

But he that heareth,
and doeth not, is like a man
that without a foundation built
an house upon the earth; against
which the stream did beat
vehemently, and immediately
it fell; and the ruin of that
house was great.
(Luke 6:49)

Ruined

Jill Lansing was trying to ignore the knocking on her door that clearly demanded her response. The room had become her hiding place even though the events of her life were echoing in her tormented mind. She shook her head as she silently admitted that although she was in her early forties, she was a runaway. She had run away from home, and had no intention of going back to the cesspool she had escaped from.

The darkness of the room mirrored the dark hole of her life; she did not feel emotionally equipped to allow any light to shine on it. She struggled with what had happened. She had such high hopes when at the age of 20 she married Jack Lansing, the aspiring young minister.

She first came to Christ at 16 when she attended a camp meeting for youths. The day she was born anew into the unseen, eternal kingdom of God remained sweet, but her present life was sorely bitter.

Aspects of her teenage years had laid in ruin due to her parents' divorce, but the reality of who Christ was and what He did for her brought great healing and comfort to her confused soul. The weight of despair, failure, loneliness, and hopelessness had fallen off her back to be replaced with a sustaining anchor of joy and childlike faith. It was for this reason that she not only embraced the reality that God had come in human form to take her place on the cross to save her from the dictates of sin and the consequences of spiritual death, but she greatly appreciated the freedom it brought to her soul. She had fallen in love with His Word and wanted to serve the One who gave all so she could be reconciled back to God.

At her vulnerable age, she considered how she could serve the Lord, and surmised that the only way was to marry a pastor. She knew that she would have to be in the right place to meet such a person. It was for this reason she attended a Christian college.

That is how she met Jack. He was the most popular man on campus. The girls saw the tall blond-headed strapping young man as a worthy catch, the guys wanted to be associated with him, and the teachers saw him as a protégé who could be entrusted with a spiritual legacy.

Jill would never have imagined that this popular aspiring minister would even give her a glance, but one day she found herself literally falling into his strong arms. She had tripped on the steps leading away from the library, and he caught her. As she looked into his clear brown eyes, something clicked. It was from that chance meeting that everything escalated. It began as a friendship, where over coffee and tea they talked about the things of God, and then it graduated into romance that finally expressed itself in the two of them coming together as one into a covenant marriage.

They both discovered the difference between a vow taken at marriage and actually making a covenant when they were going through pre-marital counseling. A vow ceases after it is broken or is fulfilled, while a covenant is perpetual. It serves as a witness and testimony that is to be passed down to the next generation. Although they both valued the vow of faithfulness, they wanted the godly principles of marriage to be a living witness to their children with hopes of it being implemented as a legacy to the following generations.

At first it seemed like her life with Jack was a fairytale. They both had great expectations when it came to serving Christ. Together they would serve His Church in America. Because of his dynamic charisma and enthusiasm, Jack had quickly managed to quickly acquire the position of youth minister at a large church and was aware that he was being primed to take his turn at being an associate pastor, and eventually if everything went as planned, the head pastor.

As she looked back, she realized that as a couple they were living the American dream. Although they had financially struggled in the beginning and had two beautiful children, Jack Jr. and Deborah early on, they were realistically prepared to work, be financially responsible, and wait patiently for opportunities to advance them forward in their goals. As expected, opportunities did present themselves through the ministry. As Jack's responsibilities grew in the church through popularity and availability so did their financial status. They eventually acquired a beautiful home and a nice car.

However, something began to happen in their home. Granted, their image as a family was impeccable. Jack successfully climbed the "church ladder" and at the age of forty became the head pastor. They were considered by onlookers to be the perfect family, but Jill became aware that something was amiss in their home, creating a consuming darkness that began to suck the life out of their marriage and her inner being.

At first it was subtle. She couldn't even distinguish the moment it started, but as the web grew and began to ensnare her home the fruits of it became obvious. Initially Jack distanced himself from her. His mind seemed preoccupied and she had accredited his preoccupation with the pressures of the ministry, but it began to invade their intimacy.

Like most couples their intimacy had been special and sweet at the beginning. They enjoyed being husband and wife. They delighted in each other's company, and valued the small things of life such as a quiet walk in the park, watching God's "paintbrush" create a beautiful sunset, and holding each other in the silence of the night as they talked of future plans and spiritual lessons they were learning in their studies.

When the children came, they rejoiced in the miracle of life as they watched each child experience the different stages of maturity. They had decided early in their marriage that they would have a date night to ensure that their relationship would not become one-dimensional, where the total focus, conversation, and point of agreement centered on the children or ministry. They realized that if they didn't maintain their relationship in a constructive way, they could lose a sense of each other.

However, their desire to keep their marriage in the right perspective was sacrificed in the name of ministry and escalating responsibilities that came with growing children. Jack's ambition to become head minister became almost obsessive causing him to spend many hours away from home and family. At first Jill felt such a sacrifice was a privilege because it was for the sake of furthering the kingdom of God, but as the emotional needs of family were becoming the daily causality, she begin to wonder whether all the sacrifice was truly for the Lord or if it was for Jack's ego that seemed to be growing with each promotion. Outwardly, he came across humble enough to the congregation, always saying the right things and preaching against the wrong things, but at home, he became impatient, at times demanding and demeaning to both her and the children. It seemed nothing was good enough for him, which ultimately reared its ugly head against her, making her feel she was no longer good enough for the now upcoming spiritual leader who was being noticed by the church leadership and community.

The first thing that was blatantly sacrificed in their personal relationship was the tenderness that had existed between them. At first their kisses had been sweet, but one day Jill noticed that when Jack kissed her it was something he did out of tolerated necessity. There was no real desire and pleasure in showing any real affection towards her. In the confines of their bedroom, he seemed to be absent. Any physical interaction between them came out of mechanical duty that clearly replaced any emotional connection, and if passion did manage to make an appearance, it came in the form of perverted lust that not only left her confused, but feeling like a prostitute.

She struggled with the fruit that was coming out of the inner core of their relationship, but who could she go to? After all, she was a pastor's wife and the unspoken rule was she could never let any dirty laundry be aired in front of others for fear of bringing a reproach to Christ.

There were a couple of reasons for this unspoken rule. First, there were tender souls that were like lambs who still were in the stage of iconic worship, and sadly, her husband was the center of much of their personal adoration. She could not bear the idea of becoming a stumbling block to such vulnerable people. The second reason was that it would hurt the image of the church, possibly causing it to become a point of ridicule to the observing public, losing valuable credibility.

Jill did what was required of her. She kept up the front of a loving, supportive Christian pastor's wife, while her life spun out of control, flinging her into a deep pit of loneliness and hopelessness. She struggled, trying to think what went wrong. At first, being the loving, supportive wife of Pastor Jack Lansing was natural, but as the unidentified darkness began to engulf their home and her soul, she had to tap into her sense of duty and personal strength to keep up what was becoming a hypocritical show in her mind. It was as though she stood behind a window that allowed her to see out, but no one could see her. It was clear that behind the perfect image was a life that was being torn apart.

She had tried to be a perfect wife to establish her personal worth in the scheme of things, but Jack's attitude of dissatisfaction towards her behind closed doors, caused her to fling herself into her mother role. If she could not be a perfect wife, she would be a doting mother who would somehow compensate for the absence of a father figure. However, her mothering skills came into question when Jack Jr. became rebellious and joined the military right out of high school, and his younger sister, Deborah, became despondent in her freshman year.

Jill had turned over every stone to figure out what she did wrong as a wife and now as a mother. It seemed that all of her dreams were now in broken fragments that mocked her, her hopes were shattered, and her expectations lay in ruin. She no longer had any real identity and had somehow become lost in her present reality. Everything about her seemed to speak of failure. Her worth as a woman had been called into question, her role as a wife appeared to be disastrous, and now her mothering skills were crumbling in utter failure. She found herself falling into a hopeless vacuum, leaving her empty, uncertain, fearful, and depressed.

As the tentacles of depression gripped her soul, she found herself spiraling downward into a world of complacency. She wanted to hide her head under the blankets when the sun came up to avoid facing the same emptiness. She dragged herself through each responsibility, only to wearily collapse on the couch to get lost in her favorite TV shows.

Since she was emotionally empty, dissatisfied with life, and living in a surreal reality, she tried to fill the endless vacuum with food. Food would awaken her emotions and make her feel alive, causing her indifferent reality to take on a euphoric atmosphere. However, when the temporary euphoria wore off, she was faced with the feeling of leanness in her soul. Heaviness turned into guilt. The reality of her out-of-control life and destructive pattern showed in her clothes that ceased to fit her bloated body, while dullness replaced the sparkle in her eyes.

Others could see that something was terribly wrong. The head elder's wife, Luann Anderson met with her a few times to see if she could minister to her. When she asked Jill what was wrong, Jill remained silent. How could she tell her what was wrong, when in all reality she didn't know herself? All she knew is that darkness was engulfing every aspect of her life. She sensed that it was hiding something sinister, but how can one address a matter until it has been revealed by the light?

It was at their last meeting together that Luann asked Jill how she could pray for her. It was then that a small light penetrated Jill's despair and provided her with an answer. "Pray that the light comes on in the darkness so that all will see what is going on."

Jill had no idea how swiftly God would answer that prayer. She always knew that light was an amazing source. It could part any blanket of darkness, bring warmth where coldness reigned, give guidance in lieu of confusion, and even bring a type of purging. However, for Jill it lit a fuse resulting in an explosion that ripped through the fiber of her being and home.

The fuse was lit when 17-year-old Deborah, a new high school graduate, tried to take her life. It became obvious that her suicidal

227

attempt was a call for help, which forced the light to penetrate the great darkness of the Lansing home. Jill's confusing reality began to make sense when the truth came out shortly after her daughter's suicide attempt as Deborah broke down in front of her in her hospital bed and confessed the source of her despair. The dots suddenly connected, revealing an onslaught of endless debris left behind by the tidal wave of wickedness that had been wreaking havoc in their lives and home. The emotional decay emitted a stench that caused her soul to feel sick.

Even though Jill was shocked at her daughter's revelation, she managed to keep a calm composure. However, behind the appearance of her steady self-control, her emotions felt like they were on a gigantic rocket that had just been launched by the latest revelation and she had no idea where it would fall. Anger soared to great heights, threatening to explode like fireworks while at other times feelings of rejection and betrayal plunged her into an emotional abyss. There were even moments when confusion caused her to hit plateaus of numbness where she felt clueless about how she was supposed to feel.

With the light revealing the source of the darkness, Jill found some semblance of liberty and relief. The source of the breakdown taking place in the family was not her inability to live up to some unbearable, rigid code or make her family happy, but it was Jack, the aspiring pastor's dirty little secret. Both Jack Jr. and Deborah had accidentally discovered his secret sin. They had carried the secret to keep her and the church from knowing, thinking it was the only way they could protect those who were ignorant and innocent.

However, the secret was gut-wrenching to the siblings. Discovering it had caused her husband Jack to fall off the pinnacle of admiration in the eyes of their son, shattering any authority and respect the junior had for the senior. It ended up causing Jack Jr. to adopt an attitude of skepticism and mocking towards God and life. When it came to their daughter, her father fell off his white horse, crushing the adoration Deborah had felt for him, leaving her feeling betrayed, insecure, and depressed.

Jack had been away at a minister's conference when Deborah attempted suicide. Since Deborah didn't want to see her father, Jill waited for 24 hours before informing him. She didn't want to talk to Jack; and since she knew his schedule, she avoided talking to him by leaving a message on his voice mail. She also asked Luann's husband, Delbert to inform Jack about the situation. Whether it was out of show or real concern, Jack grabbed the first plane home. Before arriving home, he tried various times to call Jill, but she had let her voice mail pick up each call. Jill didn't want to talk to him on the phone. What she had to say to him had to be said in person.

Jack's first stop was the hospital. By this time the light had been completely turned on, and Jill was ready to knock all of the props out from underneath her husband's pompous exterior that had been erected by excuses and finger pointing. She hoped that by confronting him with the truth, it would cause him to not only stumble under a load of guilt, but fall in utter brokenness of repentance.

Secretly, she admitted to herself that she no longer knew Jack. The old Jack would repent, but the current Jack seemed impenetrable, cruel, and cold. Clearly, he had become a different person, and she didn't know if there was enough of the old Jack left that could be salvaged. When he walked into the waiting room where she was taking a break from sitting with Deborah in her hospital room, she saw his white face, and a small flame of hope flickered in the midst of the dark blanket of despair.

"Where is she?" he asked Jill in frustration.

There was no way she could smooth over the harsh reality that had occurred; therefore she concluded that honesty would be the best policy. She stood up to confront him, "She doesn't want to see you Jack," was Jill's matter-of-fact response. She went on to explain Deborah's plans. "In fact, to avoid seeing you before she has properly processed what has happened to her, she's getting ready to go with her best friend, Jacklyn and her family up to their house at the lake for a month."

"What do you mean she doesn't want to see me?" he coldly retorted as he walked close to her. It was clear that his anger was about to boil over. Although he had not been physical with her in the past, she found his aggression taking center stage when he forcefully bumped her with his body, throwing her off balance. She found herself falling backward into one of the chairs in the waiting room.

He bent over Jill, and it was clear his unabated anger had tremendous momentum. "I'm her father! In fact, where do you get off by not immediately informing me of what was happening in my own home? And, just where does Deborah get off by making plans without my knowledge and approval? She is only 17 years old and still under my roof. I'm the head of this family," Jack paused, straightened up his stance and stepped back from Jill before adding another point of irritation to him, "and, it was stupid of you to air our family's wash by involving the head elder of the church! What will the leadership of the church think when they hear about what has happened, and how it has been handled?"

Jill could see that Jack's reputation was still more important to him than his daughter's present plight. It was obvious that Jack had long lost sight of what was valuable; therefore, she ignored his ramblings and stayed her ground. She stood up from the chair to face him with greater determination. "This is not about you Jack and your precious reputation, but the welfare of our daughter. Her feelings must be considered first and she doesn't want to see you because apparently you're the source of her confusing, despairing situation.

"As far as not personally informing you about this situation, I was trying to wade through the fallout for myself. I was also trying to be sensitive to Deborah. Since her emotions were raw and she was insistent about not seeing you, the doctor and I both agreed she needed time to figure out how she felt. As already stated, her well-being is my first and foremost concern and responsibility at this time."

Jack's face paled, but he retained his offended pose while venomously spewing out his next sentence. "I don't know what you mean that I'm the source of her-r-r...situation."

"You really don't know why you're the source behind her plight?" exclaimed Jill. "Come on Jack! You brought something sinister into our home and not only opened our home up to grave darkness by exposing yourself to wickedness, but our children as well, causing them to lose all respect and trust in you," she paused before finishing the statement, "as a result their great hero has fallen in their eyes, causing much emotional distress to their souls."

Jack's face began to turn red. Jill could tell that he was struggling to maintain his claim of ignorance about the situation, as well as the upper hand in the confrontation. "If something is wrong in our home, with me or the children, it's your fault!" Waving his hand towards her, he continued his searing accusations, "Look at you, how far down you have come in your upkeep. You're a disgrace as a pastor's wife and a bad example as a mother to our children!"

Jack's accusations were hitting the mark. It felt like he was pouring salt into open wounds, cutting deeper into the raw gashes that already promised to leave deep scars in her heart. His attitude was serving as a confirmation to what she needed to do for herself. But, for the present, Jill knew she had to stay her ground for the sake of Deborah.

Keeping her composure, she looked right into his angry, red face and with a calm voice firmly stated what she had already established, "You can blame it all on me as much as you want, but the fact is YOU are the one she doesn't want to see!"

Her emphasis on the word "you" caused him to take a step back as if he had been slapped. Jill could tell her last statement had made an inroad into his impenetrable armor. She knew it was the right time to make another point that had haunted her for so long. "Jack, I'm sorry I have failed you as a wife, but if you think that my failure has caused such hardship on you, I believe I have one up on you." With a trembling voice and tears filling her eyes, she carefully aimed the arrow of truth at his sagging resolve, "Over twenty-three years ago I married a wonderful man, who not only proved to be a loving, supportive husband but a committed father, but somewhere along the way the children and I have lost him, and Jack, I was wondering if you could tell me where he went because we sure do miss him."

Jill's words hit the mark. Jack not only staggered backwards, but he fell back into one of the chairs. His shoulders slumped over and he put his head into his hands. Even though Jill had scored a victory, the bitterness and despair that were now freely flowing through her soul robbed her of any feelings of relief. The fact was that her family still lay in ruin.

Before she left Jack to face his own demons alone, she knew that she still had to be a Christian and do what was right. "I'll inform Deborah you came to see her."

The faintly muffled response caught her by surprise. "Thank you."

As she walked past the slumped figure of the man who had become a stranger to her, she knew in her heart that her decision to take a leave of absence from her present situation was a necessity. Everything had become too hard to bear and could easily prove to be confusing. Even though Jack had not been physical with her until the scene in the waiting room, she knew instinctively that his dissatisfaction had escalated along with his frustration which was manifesting itself in not only anger but violent tendencies. It was clear that he was losing control.

As a pastor's wife she was aware that such dissatisfaction and violent tendencies could easily turn into physical abuse. She remembered a couple who came to their church. They had two daughters. Although they looked normal, the wife's mannerisms implied the contrary. She seemed as if she was walking on a narrow tightrope. Fear and rigidness comprised her unseen boundaries as she appeared to be doing an incredible balancing act on the formidable tightrope.

As in every situation, that which is hidden behind closed doors will eventually be made manifest by the light. One day the couple didn't show up for church. One of their friends secretly admitted that the man

231

had almost killed his wife the night before in one of his rampages. She was in the hospital, he was in jail, and their two children were with their grandparents.

Jill was surprised as to the response of the different people in church, especially the one from her husband. Here was a hurting family being torn apart by sin. Not only did they need healing, but they needed reconciliation as a family. Instead of taking the side of righteousness, her husband remained silent and indifferent about it while other individuals began to take sides on the basis of who they perceived to be right or wrong. There were those who clearly felt empathy for the wife and the children, but there were those who felt sorry for the man. Some of those individuals blamed the wife for the man making her his personal punching bag, while others, such as some of the women took the pose of a motherly figure towards the abuser. These women wanted to take him under their wings as if he was a little boy who needed understanding and coddling.

The one person who took a definite stand for righteousness was the head elder, Delbert Anderson. He understood that there was a scriptural protocol when it came to the kingdom of God. For there to be healing and restoration in the family, there first must be repentance from the man. To act indifferent or to coddle such action would be the same as partaking of the sin. Delbert clearly stated that there was no excuse for such behavior. He exhorted that such action was akin to hate and murder and must not be ignored or tolerated by the family of God.

It was agreed that certain wise men from the church would counsel the man in an attempt to bring healing and reconciliation. As pastor Jack was present during their different meetings with the man, but it was noted by those present that he remained quiet and aloof.

In light of the recent revelations, Jill knew why Jack had remained quiet. He had no real authority to speak into the man's life. Although Delbert had gained Jill's respect and trust for raising the standard of righteousness during that time, she still didn't feel at liberty to turn to him about the situation threatening to ruin her own family.

She knew that in her present weak state she needed to gain some perspective before "airing their dirty laundry." Like her daughter she also felt the need to step outside of the depressing environment of their home. She knew that the real issues could end up being sidelined by misdirected sympathy, misappropriated compassion, and misguided love by guilt, fear, and vulnerability.

Jill had carefully packed her suitcase while forming a plan before Jack arrived home. To avoid any unnecessary scenes, she even left him a note, informing him of her plan to take her own sabbatical. At first she was at a loss as to where she could go to be free from Jack and the other so-called "concerned individuals," but one person came to mind, a person who would open her doors wide to her. Jill had already discussed her plans with her daughter, knowing Deborah would be in her own place of safety and rest. Once her daughter was on her way to her safe haven, Jill would be free to escape. She knew she had to escape; she had to run, and flee the heavy sorrow that was enveloping every aspect of her soul.

***

The banging on the door brought Jill back to reality. She had fled and sought refuge at her dear friend's, Marjorie Kirkpatrick. Marjorie had been a good friend of Jill's mother, but due to the fact that she was only eight years older than Jill, she had become like a big sister to her, especially during the time that Jill went through the divorce of her parents. Later, the two became best of friends as Jill neared adulthood.

Not only did the two women share a history together, but they were also born again into the kingdom of God the same year. The two new converts were excited when they compared notes as to their new status in the kingdom of God. They were now officially adopted sisters, sealed by the Holy Spirit, and united together in a spiritual, heavenly family by the blood of Jesus. Their previous friendship had brought meaning to their lives, but they both knew that their new bond would put their relationship on a more excellent plain, assuring them of an eternity of uninterrupted unity and fellowship.

When Marjorie married Lloyd Kirkpatrick, Jill had served as her maid of honor. In Jill's mind Lloyd and Marjorie were the perfect couple. Both were strong believers, and appeared to possess the same vision for the future. He was a third generation dairy farmer who wanted to share his blessings with those of the kingdom of God. He also wanted many children in his quiver to love and spiritually mold. Likewise, Marjorie wanted to support the furtherance of the kingdom of God, and like her husband, loved children. Lloyd was a hard worker and Marjorie an entrepreneur. She understood marketing, and together they figured that they would expand the dairy where it could support a big family, as well as benefit the work of God in other harvest fields.

However, their vision went through a revolutionary affront. Due to overreaching government regulations and the stranglehold that many of the industrial dairy farmers had on the market, they almost lost their independent dairy farm and barely avoided bankruptcy. However, the gifted combination of the two eventually turned the tide. Instead of putting all their resources into what appeared to be a failing dairy business, they branched out into other markets.

A good business person seeks out and finds a need and then capitalizes on it. Marjorie did her research and discovered that the companies around them needed many pallets to move and transport their products. It was then that Lloyd and Marjorie obtained the necessary equipment and the contracts to begin a new enterprise. They started out making pallets in one of the small rooms in the dairy. The new enterprise not only paid their bills, but allowed Marjorie time to explore other avenues as far as the dairy operations. Eventually, she discovered other small businesses that needed milk to produce their products. In the end, her business savvy turned both operations into prosperous enterprises. They eventually had to build a separate building in order to fill the onslaught of orders for pallets and they upgraded and expanded the dairy business, allowing them to bless others individuals with much needed employment in a depressed area.

However, the greatest affront to their Christian life and marriage didn't come from the financial challenges. They had one daughter, Diana, but due to complications during her birth, it was decided that it would be a great risk for Marjorie to have other children. Although Marjorie never mentioned how the ruin of one part of their vision as a couple affected their relationship and marriage, Jill sensed it was a bitter pill for both of them to swallow. However, Marjorie and Lloyd found reason to rejoice in the precious gift God had given them and turned much of their joy, attention, and affection to their sweet princess.

Just as Lloyd and Marjorie were getting somewhat on their feet financially, they discovered that their sweet princess, Diana had Leukemia. Although at the beginning the prognosis sounded positive, it was short-lived. For the next two years, this family saw a great deal of the inside of hospitals rooms. New terminology was added to their vocabulary. Blood tests and transfusions became the normal procedure in the up and down emotional chaos that was now gripping every aspect of their lives.

In spite of the great interruptions, the Kirkpatricks managed to keep both of their enterprises on track. They later accredited such success to God showing them amazing favor from various factions. Dedicated workers from inside of their different businesses stepped forward to take the helm and steer each business through the personal crisis. Business associates showed incredible lenience and understanding towards the small inconsistencies in business procedures that occurred as those in uncharted waters struggled to fill big shoes.

Sadly, after two years of intense struggles, at age seven, Diana gave way to a sweet sleep to never wake again on this side of eternity. Both of her parents were with her. They had watched their sweet princess being assaulted by an unseen killer. All three had fought an incredible battle, but in the end, death would claim another young, innocent victim.

Jill knew there was no way she could enter into the deep sorrow that clearly consumed the couple. She had never experienced such a loss; therefore, she instinctively knew she could only let her presence and prayers be known to the couple. Although miles separated them, there was closeness between Marjorie and Jill that connected them spiritually.

Even though the Kirkpatricks walked through the deep valley of despair, they allowed God to turn what was intended to destroy them into something good. Out of their despair a ministry formulated in light of their original vision, and grew. They became foster parents to many children and even adopted eight of them. They raised the children in the love and nurture of the Lord. They trained each child to walk in the ways of righteousness. Although a few went their own way, many of them chose the ways of God and proved to be an asset to their churches and communities. Some even went on to serve the Lord in the different mission fields of the world.

Now like a lost child, Jill had sought refuge at their home. Even though miles and different paths had created a physical distance between them, Jill never lost touch with Marjorie. Granted, she and Jack had visited them a couple of times in the first years of their married life, but after their last visit, Jack's attitude towards them changed. Although he never offered any valid explanations for the change of attitude towards them, he did offer one excuse after the other for why they didn't have time to visit them.

Jack's attitude did not deter Jill from keeping in touch with her dear friend. They would e-mail, text, and occasionally speak on the phone about family happenings, events, and new spiritual insights they had gained through their Bible studies. Even though it had been a great struggle for Jill to keep the line of communication open to Marjorie, she knew that she couldn't neglect the life-line between them. Marjorie represented the one person who was anchored to the Rock of Ages and who could bring stability to her tumultuous life.

In the safety of the room, Jill could begin to clearly see how the great spider, Satan had gained a foothold into her home, sucking much of the strength and life out of her family. It was clear that her family needed an extraordinary dose of healing, forgiveness, and restoration, but before such liberation could take place, truth had to take center stage, emotions had to be corralled, and wisdom from above had to be implemented. She knew that only God could take the ruined aspects of her family and bring healing and wholeness to it. However, she was weary with it all. Jill had no strength, no vison, and no hope where her marriage was concerned.

The battle she had been fighting had robbed her of all her resolve, the depths of her despair had killed much of her incentive to continue to fight the battle, and the neglect and abuse she had experienced in her marriage had practically destroyed any real desire to care. Jill discovered that it takes energy to confront the various challenges of life, and she had none.

She had tried to ignore the pounding at the door, but the concerned voice of Marjorie on the other side of it made her realize she had to respond. "Jill, are you alright?"

"Yes Marjorie, come in," Jill replied.

Marjorie entered the room holding some neatly folded clothes over her arm. Her presence brought some measure of comfort and reassurance to Jill's tattered soul and frayed nerves, but her searching eyes caused Jill to look down to the floor. Even though she trusted Marjorie, she wasn't ready to talk about the deep sorrow that was consuming her.

On the drive from the airport to the Kirkpatrick's home, Marjorie apparently sensed Jill's fragile state and refrained from questioning her. However, Jill knew that Marjorie would not continue to tolerate the silence. "Are you ready to tell me why you're here?" Marjorie inquired.

"Not now, Marjorie. I'm still trying to process everything," Jill responded in a pleading voice.

Jill sensed that her state was so vulnerable that if she started talking about the situation she would totally lose it and there would be nothing left to salvage of her emotions and state of mind.

In an understanding, but firm voice, Marjorie inserted the obvious into Jill's fragile reality, "I'm sure you'll know when the timing is right to talk about whatever is ripping you apart, but meanwhile, you can't hide in this room and drown in the despair of it. The type of darkness you're in can only breed greater darkness. You need to seek the light if your perspective is going to change."

Jill let out some of the frustration that was bubbling up through her heightened emotions. "What am I to do Marjorie? I'm so confused right now." Her voice hinted at begging.

Marjorie was ready with an answer, "Well the first thing you have to do is get to work!"

"Get to work!" Jill responded in disbelief. Marjorie was coming across as a heartless, unconcerned friend. She began to wonder if she had made the right judgment call about her choice of refuge places.

"Work is a privilege and would change your focus Jill." Marjorie explained. "It'll take your mind off of whatever is going on and give you some time out from running around in a mental rut that is being dug deeper by the despair that is consuming you."

Jill reluctantly had to silently admit to herself that Marjorie was right. However, she also knew Marjorie ran a tight ship and couldn't see where she could serve as a benefit. "But, what can I do around here?" she whined.

"Why, you can work in the diary," Marjorie replied with a knowing smile.

"The dairy, you know I'm afraid of cows," Jill responded shrilly.

"I've never understood your fear of milk cows, Jill, you know they don't bite," Marjorie stated.

Jill didn't want to admit her fear of bovine came down to two factors: They were big and they could intimidate you with their stare. Jill quickly came to her own defense, "They may not bite, but they can kick you!"

"Then don't stand behind them and they won't be able to kick you," Marjorie responded factually.

"They can also run over you if they have a mind to," Jill retorted.

Marjorie replied light heartedly. "I would then strongly suggest you don't stand in front of them either." Marjorie paused before continuing on as she observed Jill holding herself back from throwing a tantrum, "Besides, you're not going to milk them Jill, we have machines for that and you won't have to worry about herding them to the facilities because they know when it is milking time. All you have to do is help clean the dairy and maybe bottle-feed a few calves that are smaller in size than you are."

It became obvious to Jill that she wasn't going to win the argument. However, she would not willingly concede without first trying to hide behind her ignorance and inexperience, "I've never cleaned a dairy before or bottle-fed a calf, nor did I come prepared to do such things."

"Don't you worry. I've brought you some clothes, and Belinda will teach you everything you need to know," replied Marjorie as she handed the clothes to Jill. As she closed the door, she looked over her shoulder and clinched the deal, "See you at the dairy."

Belinda was the Kirkpatrick's adopted daughter, but she had not been part of the clan when the Lansing's had last visited them. At the time of their last visit, Jack Jr. was seven and Deborah was four. Even though the two Lansing siblings were both young, they had retained fond memories of their time with Aunt Marjorie and Uncle Lloyd and all the children. They had been included in many of the farm activities. They were excited about the cows, horses, dogs, cats, chickens, and the other array of animals, and as a result showed great disappointment in the following years when their father was unreceptive about taking time out for another visit.

Belinda was the same age as Jill's son, and was studying to be a veterinarian assistant. She was a beautiful, poised woman with a lovely countenance. Swirls of dark hair flowed freely down to her shoulders, while highlighting her blue eyes and the freckles that dotted her cheeks. She was petite, but when Jill initially met her at the house, she suspected that her outer stature did not represent the strength and abilities of her inner person.

Jill laid out the clothes wondering if she would fit into them. To her relief the clothes were a bit loose and comfortable. As she entered the front room, she found Belinda sitting in a chair waiting for her.

Belinda looked up and smiled at her, calming her nerves. "How did you get elected to be my babysitter?" Jill inquired light manneredly.

Belinda smiled at her, "I volunteered. I've wanted to get to know you ever since I learned about you from Mom. Now I have an opportunity to do so," she paused as she looked into Jill's eyes. "I realize this time is difficult for you, but I think we'll actually have fun together."

Belinda's summation turned out to be correct. When she was teaching her to wash down the cement floor with disinfectant, they were swapping stories about Belinda's adoptive parents, laughing about some of the more comical incidents that had intruded into moments of drudgery and seriousness, to not only add humor but also provide legendary material that would never lose its savor when retold. When they were washing certain articles that were used in the milking process, they were exchanging information about family, and when she was learning the art of preparing for and bottle-feeding the calves, Belinda shared about daily activities around the farm and the pallet business.

Jill began to feel a sense of normalcy return to her world. Marjorie had been right; the work had taken her mind off of herself and caused her to focus on ordinary matters. To her surprise the activity that brought her the most pleasure and comfort was feeding the calves.

They were needy little creatures with soft muzzles. Taken away from their mothers not long after their birth, they were totally dependent on the mercy of their owners. Their innocent eyes revealed a certain purity and trust. As they zealously sucked on their bottles, Jill felt a trickle of life flow back into the empty vacuum of her soul. She suddenly found herself connecting to the calf's vulnerability. There were feelings of motherly protection peeking around what had become a blanket of darkness, despair, and failure. Joy surfaced towards the calf as she watched his life and personality manifest itself in how he retrieved the milk from the bottle. It was then that Jill decided that she could possibly like cows after all.

The work had revived her spirit and her soul, bringing ease to her at the end of the day. Instead of staying in her room during dinner as she had for the last couple of nights, she joined the family at the dinner table. There were Lloyd, Marjorie, Belinda, and two sons, Dale and Mason.

Dale was in his mid-twenties, single and was the overseer of the pallet business. Mason was in his early twenties, and was the one who made sure everything worked in the dairy. He was newly married, but his wife was visiting her family due to a sick grandfather.

The dinner table of the Kirkpatrick's was full of discussion and laughter. Jill found herself sitting back and enjoying daily conversation of a family that made such interaction seem natural. She couldn't remember the last time her family had actually sat at the dinner table and simply enjoyed each other's company.

Jill was surprised that they never discussed business at the table; rather, they discussed the happenings of their day. She suspected that they started to tell comical stories about their lives for her benefit. Occasionally Jill was aware of Marjorie glancing her way to see how she was responding to her environment.

When Jill seemed the most relaxed, Marjorie started to tell a particular story about Jill that she had forgotten. It happened during the time Marjorie and Lloyd were engaged and she was trying to be a mature teenager in an adult world. The newly engaged couple was asked to help a friend move some sheep into a penning area before being moved to higher ground for pasturing. Marjorie invited Jill to go along. As Marjorie began to tell the story, embarrassing memories of that infamous day started to rise up out of the recesses of Jill's mind. She remembered at the time as seeing the invitation from Marjorie as a break from her other dismal existence at home and in ignorance jumped at the occasion to get away from her setting.

239

It had been raining the day and night before, leaving the ground muddy. Lloyd, Marjorie, and the owner of the sheep, Kelly Hollister, along with a Border collie had managed to herd the muddy sheep into a controllable mass. To stay out of the way, Jill was standing inside of the gate of the designated pen, waiting impatiently for the dreary exercise to be over with. As the sheep begin to enter through the gate they naturally became bunched together. Apparently, the Border collie that was guarding the outer edge of the flock perceived that one of the sheep was straying too far outside of the invisible perimeter. At that point the dog nipped at the hind leg of the sheep to get it back into line, causing it to jump into the air, coming down on the back of another sheep. The sheep that was hit by the flying ewe became startled and jumped on the back of the sheep next to it, and proceeded to scramble across the backs of the other sheep who were becoming alarmed.

As Marjorie put it, "To make a long story short, Jill was standing right in line with the frightened sheep who was making tracks across the backs of the other sheep." The frightened ewe actually jumped right into the arms of a startled Jill who went flying backwards onto the muddy ground. Even though the ground abruptly stopped Jill's descent, the sheep was still in motion as it leaped from her chest and continued its flight to furthest part of the pen. At this point Jill's arms were frantically flailing in the air, as the other excited sheep begin to show signs of confusion and chaos around her.

Marjorie had been standing not far from the same side of the gate that Jill was located at, and had fortunately witnessed the fiasco taking place. She began to push the sheep to the other side of the entrance as she made her way towards the downed Jill who couldn't even sit up in the midst of the excited sheep that were flooding through the gate and scrambling to whatever opening they could find in the pen. As Marjorie pushed and shoved the excitable sheep away from the side of the entrance, she made her way to Jill. Reaching down, she grabbed a hold of Jill's waving arm, pulled her up and swung her towards the side of the pen.

Jill grabbed the side of the pen while Marjorie continued to stand between her and the excited sheep. Jill remembered that between the ewe and the ground, her breath had been knocked out of her. She clung to the side of the fence while trying to fill her lungs with priceless air. Looking down at her yellow cashmere sweater, she stared at the muddy hoof prints that had just ruined some of her best clothes. She was also aware that mud was caked to her long brown hair, as well as her back and arms.

It was at that point that Jill felt something else, the fiery hot flow of anger, tumbling up like lava. It made its way from the pit of her being, up her torso, bubbling up to the opening of her lips, and hit the top of her head with such a velocity that she thought she was going to explode. She wasn't sure if the alarm that was going off was strictly the result of her anger or her blood pressure, but she knew by the sight of her knuckles turning white as her hands griped the side of the pen that the momentum of the situation was ready to erupt.

After all the sheep were in the pen, Marjorie tugged at her arm, signaling her it was time to let go of the side of the pen and exit it. As Jill followed Marjorie out of the pen, she wanted to scream at her for having the audacity to invite her to such a lame exercise, kick every sheep that got in her way, throw a stick at the dumb dog, push the almost smiling Lloyd in the mud, and tell their concerned friend, Kelly what he could do with his stupid sheep in no uncertain terms.

Jill could tell that Marjorie knew she was in a foul mood. Marjorie quickly evaluated Jill's physical condition and determined that in spite of the mud and a few bruises Jill would live, and stated as much to the two men. Lloyd was still trying not to smile and their friend took on a pose of relief after hearing Marjorie's diagnoses. However, Jill wasn't so sure that everything was alright. She wasn't certain that at the end of the day that there wouldn't be some casualties left behind. Her problem was that she didn't know which one deserved her wrath. Marjorie had saved her life and Lloyd was simply a bystander who was trying not to let on that the whole situation was amusing to him.

She was also doing her best to act mature as a young teen and impress not only Marjorie and Lloyd but Kelly, but at that moment she felt the incident was revealing the youth of her years. She wanted to throw a tantrum. She couldn't let Kelly have it because he showed too much concern for her well-being, and as far as taking it out on the dog, he appeared as if he could defend himself, and the sheep were too flighty to stand still long enough to accept punishment. She was indeed left in quandary as to where her anger could be released. As a result, she silently stood there with steam running out of every pore of her body.

As Marjorie was telling the story, Jill was reliving every emotion she experienced during the ordeal. She could tell that those hearing the story wanted to laugh, but they refrained from it as they looked at her countenance.

Due to her reliving the incident in her mind, Jill wasn't aware that she was showing any reaction. It was at the point of Jill reliving her dilemma to figure out what to do with her anger that Marjorie interjected that Jill should finish the story.

"Finish the story?" Jill answered, "You pretty well told all of it!"

"Come on Jill," Marjorie coaxed, "you need to share about your part."

"My part," Jill exclaimed, "I was absolutely livid!"

"I know you were," Marjorie smiled and turning to the others, "you should've seen her face. Standing there shaking as she clenched her hands into fists, even though she was bravely wearing the medals of cloven hoof prints on her chest. I might also add that in spite of being caked in mud on her backside from head to toe, and one of her artificial eyelashes clinging to her cheek, her face was radiating a bright red that extended from her neck to her forehead."

"And, I must say you didn't help the situation, Marjorie," Jill added. "Remember what you said? You looked at me and declared that you actually witnessed something new that day. Jill paused, "You must have been baiting me to ask you what you had witnessed."

Mischievously, Marjorie interjected, "I don't know what you're talking about? All I remember was you huffily walking towards the car, as pieces of mud fell off of your clothes."

"Come on Marjorie," Jill retorted. "When I took the bait and asked you what you had witnessed, you said that it was the first time you ever watched someone like me parley with a sheep!"

Up to this point everyone at the table had been refraining from giving way to any real fit of laughter as the events unfolded, but Jill's last statement opened up the flood gates of laughter. It immediately became contagious because even the refined Marjorie was chuckling. As the laughter enfolded the group, Jill began to see the whole situation from the grandstands of a spectator, rather than a participant, and laughter caught hold of her. Within seconds everyone was roaring, and some even had tears in their eyes.

For the first time in months, Jill was being reminded of how laughter was medicine for the soul. It clearly was serving as a valuable form of release from under the depressive blanket that had enfolded her for so long.

That night, Jill had one of her best nights. Her sleep was restful and deep. She wasn't fitful and agitated. As she succumbed to the sweetness of peaceful slumber, she could feel her soul let go of the torment and her spirit set free to simply rest in the cradle of God's abiding arms.

***

Jill quickly settled into the routine of the dairy farm. Even though she was doing the same job every day, it brought contentment to her soul. She actually felt accomplished at the end of the day. Within a few days, she could tell that her body was changing as well. She actually felt better.

Although her daily interaction with the Kirkpatrick's proved to bring satisfaction and joy to her, it reminded her that her family lay in ruin, and that the full force of the sorrow that had plagued her was being put at bay for the time being. She still was at a loss as to what to do, and yet she didn't want to break the peace that had settled on her life by exposing the darkness that had brought her there.

Just as she was settling into her responsibilities around the diary, Marjorie came to her one day and told her that one of their truck drivers had to take time off for personal matters and she needed her to drive some pallets to a shipping dock outside of town.

Jill was a bit stunned at the prospect, and stated as much, "Marjorie you know that I have never driven a truck before. Why can't one of the others like Dale, Mason, or even Belinda?"

"They are all going to be busy with driving other trucks, Marjorie commented. "Besides, driving is driving, Jill. I know you know how to drive a car. All you have to do is get in and drive the truck," Marjorie answered in an impassive way.

"Driving a truck is a bit different than driving a car," Jill whined.

"You complicate everything Jill. It's a breeze to drive a vehicle; it's like riding a bike."

"There is only one problem with that example," Jill vehemently stated. If you are inexperienced at riding a bike, you can easily fall off the bike and hurt yourself."

With great diplomacy, Marjorie defused some of Jill's resolve, "You're an intelligent person, and I have the greatest confidence in your ability."

"Perhaps, I could drive a truck with a bit of practice as long as it is an automatic," Jill verbally conceded.

"It is a stick shift, but that will be no problem for you. Remember, as believers we can do all things through Christ who strengthens us."

Adding the Lord to the equation didn't silence Jill's anxiety. "No way can I drive a truck with a stick shift," Jill flatly stated.

Undeterred, Marjorie was not going to accept no for an answer. "Jill, a new adventure would be a nice change for you. It would give you a new experience, and such experiences are good for enlarging your horizon."

It was clear to Marjorie that Jill was not accepting her reasoning. It was then that Marjorie delivered her main challenge. "Jill, I'm sure you have heard the story about the two men who came upon a deep impassable river."

Once again Jill felt she was being set up, but she was curious about how Marjorie was going to maneuver around the facts. "No, I don't know that particular story," she huffily retorted.

"Well these two men came up to this wide, deep river. One was named "Can," and the other's name was, "Can't." They needed to cross over to the other side to take care of some important business. When Can't considered the river, he quickly resigned himself to simply sitting on a log alongside of the river bank in a melancholy state of wishful thinking in hopes a solution would somehow fall out of the sky or come his way, but Can would not accept such resignation. He began to look around for some means to solve the problem. Sure enough he found scraps of driftwood that could float and strong reeds that he could use to tie the wood together. He also noticed there was discarded sheet of plastic that he could put on the top of the raft to keep it somewhat dry, so Can set to work building his raft.

"When it was all finished he invited Can't to come along, but since Can't wasn't sure whether they would make it safely across the river, he opted to wait for a sure thing and with a great deal of remorse declined. He sat on the bank of distress as he watched Can successfully cross the river and continue on his way."

Jill suspected that she would regret asking Marjorie the obvious, but curiosity had clearly taken hold of her. "What happened to Can't, didn't Can send someone back to help him?"

"Oh, there were many who came along and offered Can't help, but because he had no initiative, he was not prepared to make the necessary trek to some type of crossing; and, since he lacked imagination, he could not see any sure way of successfully crossing the river. Since he also was afraid to risk whatever he had left to cross over, he just sat there."

"Well, what happened to him?" Jill asked.

"Well, he eventually became petrified in his state and in the end became a bump on a log that people still pass by to this day."

Jill shook her head in disbelief, while trying to hold back a smile. Silently, she knew Marjorie had a point. She had to quit being afraid and once again face what seemed impossible to conquer. She had to face the rivers that signified failure and loss to her, while trusting the Lord with the outcome so she could move on. And, even though the stick shift seemed daunting, it was not an impassable river she was facing. She resolved that she was not about to become a "Can't" who would eventually become some fossilized bump on a log to those around her.

"Okay, I'll drive the truck, but you'll have to teach me," Jill flatly stated.

Smiling that she had made a point and confident that she could teach Jill how to handle a standard transmission, Marjorie was quick to reassure her, "Oh, it will not be a problem. I'll have you driving with a stick in no time. In fact, your first lesson starts now."

Jill slowly followed Marjorie to the truck. Even though it was not a semi, it seemed monstrous enough to her. As she opened the door, she realized that it was hard for her to get her foot firmly on the running board. She had to reach up, grab the handle outside of the door, and practically pull herself up onto the running board.

As she sat behind the steering wheel of the truck, she struggled to adjust the seat to her small frame so she could properly put the seat belt on. It was after she was correctly positioned behind the wheel that she realized the power a person can feel when they are sitting higher than other vehicles.

Marjorie's voice interrupted her thoughts as she settled into the passenger side of the truck, "Now Jill, your left foot must be used for the clutch while your right foot must be used for the gas and brake. You must hold the clutch down when you go to start, shift, or stop. You must learn to feel the clutch when it comes to letting it out. Once you learn the feel of it, driving a standard shift will prove easy.

Even though instructed otherwise, Jill had always used her left foot for the brake. She suddenly realized why her driving instructor had told her to use only her right foot to execute both the brake and gas pedals. She now had to rethink a bad habit in order to drive the truck, which made her wonder how many other bad habits did she have to rethink in order to advance forward in her life.

"Now Jill, look at the alignment of your gears," Marjorie instructed.

Jill looked at the order of the gears.

"Note the number "one," you are going to have to shift it in first gear, while holding down the clutch and brake. We are going to now start it. Of course, you can only start it in park or neutral, preferably in park. Put the clutch in, as well as push down on the brake."

Jill pushed down on the clutch and the brake. The truck started up right away. Under Marjorie's watchful eye, she managed to shift the truck into first gear with minimal struggle.

"Now, slowly but steadily let out the clutch as you take your right foot off the brake to put it on the gas."

Jill tried to follow Marjorie's instructions, but when she let out the clutch while trying to put her right foot on the gas, the truck leaped, jerking both Marjorie and Jill, and then died.

"You let out the clutch too fast, Jill. Let off of the clutch slowly while taking your right foot from the brake to the gas. You must simultaneously let up on the clutch while quickly repositioning your foot from the brake to the gas."

Jill tried again, with the same results. "This is stupid, I'll never get it," whined Jill.

In a calm but firm voice, Marjorie set the record straight, "The process is not stupid, Jill. You must not let frustration rule you because you're struggling to get the technique down. Start it again!"

"There's too much to remember," Jill complained. "It's much easier with an automatic."

With a firmer voice, Marjorie kept up her insistence, "You need to keep doing it until you get it right. That's true for any project or responsibility"

"I've tried, and you can see how miserable I'm at it," Jill stated, almost bordering in self-pity.

Marjorie sat back in her seat and looked at Jill with determination. "Jill, have you ever heard the story about the two men who were trying to build a cabin?"

Jill could see another story coming on, but she figured she would humor Marjorie by listening to it while giving herself some precious time from facing what appeared to be the inevitable. "No, I have not Marjorie, so why don't you tell it to me?"

"There were these two men who wanted to expand their experience by building a cabin. Their names were "Try" and "Do." They did all the preliminary work by locating and securing the property, figuring out the dimensions, and then purchasing the necessary materials.

"The problem was that neither of them had ever built anything. Try was zealous and ready to jump right into the project. Do, on the other hand had taken time to find out how the experts build houses. He read books and watched their techniques on the internet. When Do felt he was equipped enough to build the cabin he set a date with Try to begin the process. Do started with the foundation, while Try wanted to quickly see results; therefore, he wanted to do the structure. Do was willing to let Try build the frame while he did the foundation. Try as he might, everything he did proved to be disastrous. His attempts ended up being uneven or fell apart. Eventually Try flung his hands up in the air and declared that he had at least tried, but nothing worked for him;

therefore, he abandoned the project to pursue other avenues he was more comfortable with.

"However, Do continued to meticulously build the cabin and when he made a mistake, he went back to the drawing board until he figured out the most constructive way to do it. Eventually, he succeeded in finishing the cabin and was able to enjoy his accomplishments."

Jill was waiting for the punchline, but Marjorie showed no sign of giving one.

"Well?" Jill asked.

"Well what?" Marjorie retorted.

In an irritating voice, Jill asked, "Isn't there some great punchline to the story?"

"What do you think the punchline is Jill?" Marjorie inquired. "As Christians what attitude must we adopt towards challenges to ensure excellence in what we do?"

Thoughtfully, Jill tried to summarize the moral of the story, "Well, Try never got anywhere in life. I suppose he spun his wheels in everything he did but never had any real accomplishments to show for his activities because he never finished anything. And, most likely he probably became some morbid figure that bemoaned his plight in light of Do's accomplishments. As Christians we have a responsibility to do right in order to bring glory to the Lord."

"Very good Jill, but you're leaving out some very important facts: the reasons for Try never finishing anything. Try was the type a person who was half-hearted in everything he did. He easily became bored with activities that did not fall into place according to his feelings, ideas, and time schedule. He had fickle zeal that had no passion or stamina to it. Try perceived that as long as he tried something a few times that was good enough because he had no real intention of doing it right in the first place. In his mind, life had to accept his tries even though his half-hearted attempts would never get the job done. He didn't care to take time to learn what it would mean to get something right. He was busy giving the outward impression but always dropped the ball before he completed anything. As a result, Try was always left outside of the real successes of life with his many failed attempts eventually mocking him."

Marjorie studied Jill's thoughtful face. "Jill, you have lost your passion to experience new aspects of life. You had no intention of seeing this situation through. You thought you would console yourself that you tried, and at the same time show me what a failure you are at this so you could get out of learning it. The real issue is that people who try are never trying to do what is right; they are simply doing what

247

is comfortable and convenient so they can always console themselves for their failure to do right and complete a matter.

"Doing right may experience failures along the way but for believers such as you and me, each failure should be used as a stepping stone to successfully finish the task at hand. The Do's of this world welcome new adventures and new experiences. They are always on a learning curve but they welcome and embrace every new challenge as a platform to become enlarged as a person."

Jill painfully knew that Marjorie was right. She had allowed the adventurous spirit of initiative, along with enthusiasm for new experiences, and the passion to discover new depths ebb from her life, causing her to digress into a morbid state of narrowness and nothingness. She had tried so many different angles to right wrongs without success that she had given up and saw no more need to try again. It seemed noble, but the harsh reality was that she had been doing everything in her own strength, and trying to figure how to do it her own way rather, than seek wisdom and strength from above.

Jill knew she needed to break free from her morbid state. She resolved to go forward and eventually become a doer of what was right, regardless of how many times she needed to pick herself up and try again until she got it right. With new determination, she pushed the clutch down to put it in park and then put her foot on the break to start it. She silently said a prayer and shifted it in first gear, while working the gas pedal. The third time proved to be a charm. Jill managed to avoid killing the engine, but her clutch work was far from smooth. The truck leaped forward a couple of times before it started to advance forward. As they neared 15 mph, the engine started to roar.

"Jill, when you begin to hear the engine roar like that it is time to shift it in the next gear," Marjorie instructed. "Put your foot on the clutch and push it all the way down to the floor, while lifting your foot from the gas, shift it into the second gear and then slowly let up on the clutch as you once again push down on the gas pedal."

To Jill's surprise she managed to shift it into second with only minor jerking. "I haven't given you a whiplash yet, have I Marjorie?" Jill giddily inquired.

Marjorie smiled at her, "You're doing fine, stay the course."

Jill felt proud of herself. They were going down the country road at the speed of 20 mph and the speedometer was slightly climbing.

Marjorie interrupted her brief celebration, "Jill, when you get to 25 mph, the engine will start roaring again and you will have to shift into third gear."

Jill decided that she needed to accept the upcoming challenge. As she hit 25 mph, she pushed the clutch all way down while letting up on the gas. This time the shifting was almost flawless in its execution.

Jill was beginning to enjoy her new adventure. She felt as if she was flying down the country road at 30 mph. As Jill looked ahead, she could see a curve in the road and a speed sign that read 20 mph. At that time she knew she needed to act and even though Marjorie started to instruct her about properly slowing down, a panic attack begin to take possession of her faculties. Her mind became confused as to what she was supposed to do.

As they passed the sign Jill was aware that Marjorie was excitedly telling her to slow down. She heard the words, "clutch, brake, and shift down," but confusion and fear had caused her to become frozen.

The next thing she was aware of was the truck going off the road, launching down a slight embankment. As Marjorie was wrestling Jill's right leg in order get her foot off of the gas, the truck crashed through a white wooden fence. Jill then became aware of the truck lurching slightly upward and forward after hitting a small mound, making a loud thumping sound as the front tires hit the ground. Through it all Marjorie had a hold of Jill's frozen right leg as the vehicle rolled through a herd of panicked cows that had parted like the Red Sea. The truck finally came to a stop in front of a water trough.

Jill was holding tightly to the steering wheel while staring at the feeding tough. She was only slightly aware that the motor was silent. She managed to look towards Marjorie who was now sitting upright in the passenger side of the truck.

Marjorie's face was an ash color, her lips were almost missing as they formed a tight line and her eyes were wide open. The one thing that caused an eerie atmosphere is that she was silent. It was as though she was frozen in time.

"Marjorie, are you alright?" Jill reluctantly asked, not sure of the response.

Even as Jill waited for some response, Marjorie remained still.

As if almost pleading with her, Jill broached the silence once again, "Are you alright Marjorie? Say something!"

Without looking at Jill and in a strained voice, Marjorie answered, "Get out of the truck. We need to make sure the cows do not get on the road."

It was clear that Marjorie had released her seatbelt during the fiasco. She simply opened the door, got out of the truck and almost slammed it.

As she undid her seatbelt, Jill looked around and could see the agitated cows appeared to be glaring at the truck, some protesting loudly at the loud object that had so rudely interrupted their calm world. Even though Jill didn't like cows, she knew she better get out of the truck and follow Marjorie to the place where the truck had left a hole in the fence.

As she piled out of the truck the cows watched her walk up to Marjorie. Those that were not protesting seemed to have a condescending look. Silently, she had to agree with them. The whole incident must have appeared foolish-even to a cow.

Jill noticed that Marjorie was on the phone. She assumed that she was talking to Lloyd or one of her sons.

When Jill reached Marjorie, without looking at Jill, Marjorie informed her that Lloyd and the boys would shortly be on their way with another vehicle and the means in which to temporarily fix the fence until it could properly be reconstructed. Marjorie went to the opposite side of the gap in the fence while Jill held her position at the other side of the opening. An eerie silence hung between them. Within fifteen minutes Lloyd, Dale, and Mason showed up in two vehicles, with necessary supplies in the back of a pickup.

Without saying a word, Marjorie walked up to Dale and reached out her hand for the keys to the vehicle he was driving. Jill could see that the men wanted to laugh, but after one look at Marjorie's face they wisely kept their lips tightly sealed. Dale obediently handed her the keys without saying a word.

Marjorie's stern voice broke the silence. "Come Jill!"

Jill followed Marjorie to the vehicle like a puppy that just got in trouble. As she walked by Lloyd, his eyes were smiling and it was clear that he was trying to hold in the laughter that was threatening to make itself known. When he caught Jill's eye, he smiled. Jill slightly smiled back at him.

As Marjorie was driving away from the scene, Jill looked in her side mirror and saw Lloyd lying over the top of the pickup laughing, while Dale was bent over and holding his stomach. His whole body shook with amusement. Mason was slapping his knee, his head rolling back and forth, his mouth wide open, letting out howls of laughter.

The three men's merriment caused Jill to smile, but she dare not look at Marjorie. She put her hands in her lap and stared straight ahead, while Marjorie remained silent as she drove home.

Once home Marjorie exited the vehicle. Except for the door almost being slammed, the silence was deafening. Jill, like an obedient dog, followed Marjorie into the house. Marjorie busied herself to fix lunch, while Jill sat at the island silently watching her.

Jill decided it was time to break the silence, "I'm sorry, Marjorie, I froze, I suddenly found myself confused at what I was supposed to do. I know that there's no excuse for what I did," Jill paused. "I now realize I should have been going slower until I was more familiar with the truck and the road. I'm relieved that neither one of us were hurt."

With her back still towards Jill, Marjorie finally broke her silence. "It's not all your fault. I shouldn't have encouraged you to shift into third, but I was caught up with your enthusiasm to conquer the stick shift and forgot where we were as far as the road."

"I have to admit, I was beginning to enjoy myself," Jill smiled.

"You were doing quite well," Marjorie said before letting out a sigh, "that is until we made an unexpected visit to that pasture."

"I was wondering what it was like for those cows to have an upfront view of our mishap," Jill stated lightheartedly.

"If they could talk, I don't think they would be able to give you much detail because they were running for their lives." It was then that Marjorie turned and cracked a smile at Jill. I have to admit, I might be able to figure out what happened, but I'm not sure I could tell others what was going on because I was holding on to the left side of your leg as I tried to maneuver your legs and feet and reach the pedals myself.

"I actually felt myself being almost thrown across your lap because I had undone my seatbelt at some point. I was afraid of being wedged between you and the steering wheel. I have to admit as I grabbed the left side of your leg, I just held on to the lower part of the gear shift, to brace myself. I was praying for our safety and thanking God that I was ignorant about the route the truck was actually taking. "

Jill started giggling. "And, I'm also wondering who actually turned the ignition key off, stopping the engine. After all, my hands were glued to the steering wheel."

"I could have, but I don't remember it. Even though we might have been entertaining the Lord and His host, God had to have mercy on us and must have instructed one of our guardian angels to turn it off."

"You know Marjorie another legend has been borne today in the heartland of the Kirkpatrick's that no doubt will receive a lot of play around the table for a long time to come."

Marjorie started laughing, "I'm curious as to what kind of spin Lloyd, Dale, and Mason will put on it since I didn't tell them much about what happened." She stopped as she let out a few laughs, "You know I am tempted to not tell them anything to see what kind of story they come up with."

251

"Shame on you Marjorie, won't that drive them crazy?" Jill inquired as laughter bubbled to the surface.

"That is the whole point." It was upon her last sentence that Marjorie began to follow the intensity of Jill's laughter. They both laughed until tears started running down their faces and their sides began to hurt.

Their laughter died down, but tears remained. Suddenly Jill did something that shocked herself. As she looked at Marjorie, she finally let the cat out of the bag, "Jack has been involved in hard core pornography for some time."

Marjorie froze, suddenly serious. Without a word, she moved toward Jill, put her arms around her and held her.

Secure in Marjorie's arms, the words begin to flow from Jill's lips as tears began to trickle down her cheeks. "I don't know what to do Marjorie. I knew something was wrong, but I couldn't put my finger on it. It all came out when Deborah tried to commit suicide. Both the children knew a long time before me and it has practically ruined them."

Marjorie gently let go of Jill and sat down next to her. She took both her hands in hers, and looked steadily into her eyes. "Do the leaders at the church know?"

"I don't think so. But who knows? It seems like the wife is the last to find out about such things," Jill wearily stated. "I feel so-o-o...."

"Dirty, like a prostitute in your own home," Marjorie finished her sentence.

Shocked, Jill asked the obvious, "How do you know how I feel?"

Marjorie took a deep breath, "Lloyd was into pornography when we were first married."

The revelation almost caused Jill to fall off of her chair. "Oh no! I had no idea. I'm so sorry Marjorie. I always thought you were the perfect couple."

"You never know what goes on behind closed doors, Jill, but sins like pornography are a shameful secret that is often kept hidden by the offender and the ones being directly affected by it. This allows such sins to grow, consume, fester, and eventually destroy."

"How did you handle it, Marjorie?" Jill asked.

"I confronted Lloyd and told him I would not expose our daughter or myself to such a repulsive practice. I also went to the leadership of the church. Most of them remained mute except an elder, and Kelly Hollister."

Looking at Jill, "You remember the one with the sheep?"

Jill nodded her head.

"Well, they confronted him, but he was quick to justify that it was a natural manly practice. His justification to hold onto his pornography caused me to take steps to leave him in his cesspool and file for divorce."

"It's obvious you didn't leave him, so what happened?" Jill inquired.

"Diana's illness," Marjorie said with a far-away look. "When we found out how sick our princess was Lloyd became sober. He even saw Diana's illness as God punishing him, and began to make bargains with God about sparing our daughter, which included giving up pornography."

"Do you think God was punishing him, Marjorie?" Jill asked.

"Of course not, Jill! That would mean I was being punished for Lloyd's sin as well. God holds every life in His hands and knows our days. He gave our daughter as a gift to us and required her back after a few years on this earth, but I do believe the Lord was using it to get Lloyd's attention. You know what amazed me?"

"What Marjorie."

"That Lloyd could justify his sin before men, but when it came to God, he knew it was wrong and that God could never bless him in it. Inwardly, we know the truth about the holiness of God. So he tried to bargain with God, confessing what a stench his sin was to heaven as a means to try to change the outcome."

"What happened to Lloyd when God took Diana home?"

"It broke him into a million pieces. At that point he had to make a decision: to live in a world of shame and guilt while becoming bitter and hateful to God, or repent and grow up as a man before the Lord and truly receive His forgiveness and healing. Thank God he chose the latter because the Lord was able to heal and save our marriage."

Looking more intently at Jill, Marjorie added "In fact, our marriage came out better, healthier. And, from the travailing, loss, and sorrow of everything grew the vision of adopting and fostering children."

Considering Jack's attitude in light of Lloyd's repentance, Jill had to confess the obvious to Marjorie, "I can tell you now Marjorie, Jack was shaken by Deborah's attempted suicide, but he wasn't broken by it."

"Jill, Jack's sin must come to the light. He has no business standing behind a pulpit and profaning God's name and Word with unholy lips and wicked practices. The leadership of the church must be informed." Marjorie paused, "This is bigger than the reputation of a church, a soul is on the line here. The Greek root word for fornication is "porn." This implies that all acts of fornication are considered pornography to God, and we know fornicators will not enter the kingdom of God. Hopefully, there are strong godly leaders in your church who will do what is right in regard to Jack's soul."

Jill knew Marjorie was right. The one church leader she could trust was Delbert Anderson. She knew that she had to inform him, but once she fulfilled her Scriptural obligation, the ball would be in the church's court as to any action that would be taken.

Marjorie interrupted Jill's thoughts, "Jill, I would advise you that after dinner you share this information with Lloyd. He works with people who are addicted to pornography. No doubt, he will even give you more insight."

Jill nodded in agreement.

That night after dinner, Jill's mind was temporarily taken off of the mission before her as the men and Belinda tried to patiently wait to find out what happened with the truck. It was Mason who first brought up the subject.

"Mom, what happened with the truck this afternoon?"

Looking non-committal, Marjorie answered, "What do you think happened?"

Mason carefully collected the facts before answering, "Well, it's obvious that truck left a gaping hole in the fence and tore up some of the pasture land, but as to why or how it happened, we can only speculate."

With a mischievous look in her eye, Marjorie continue to carry out the plan she had concocted earlier, "Why don't you tell me what you think happened?"

Dale was the one who piped in next, "Was there a cow in the road?"

"No there was no cow in the road; they were all confined within the pasture."

Mason followed Dale's train of thought, "Was there a rock or some other object in the road?"

In a lighthearted manner, Marjorie answered Mason's inquiry, "No there was nothing in the road."

By this time Dale and Mason were digging deep to find the reason behind the fiasco with the truck. Jill noticed Lloyd sat back with a smile on his face while Belinda listened with a curious look. She suspected that both of them recognized what Marjorie was doing.

"I know what happened," Mason declared, "a car ran you off the road."

"No, there was no car," Marjorie assured him.

By this time both brothers were becoming frustrated. "Come on Mom, tell us what happened," Mason almost pleaded.

Marjorie looked at Jill with a wink, "Should we put them out of their misery and tell them?"

Jill winked back and nodded her head.

"Well, the truth is, I was teaching Jill to drive the stick shift. She was doing quite well but I had not properly prepared her to shift down when we came to a curve in the road and we ended up entertaining the cows."

Jill could tell that the men were already imagining the scene. They started to chuckle. It was then that Marjorie began to share how Jill became frozen by confusion and in the chaos she had released her seatbelt to lean over to lift Jill's foot from the gas when she was practically thrown across her lap, thereby, missing the truck's performance. That is when Jill filled them in about the truck running off the road, descending down the embankment, hitting the fence, then being propelled through the air by a small, grassy mound and finally coming down in the pasture. The startled cows parted and began to flee for their lives, with the truck finally coming to a stop in front of the trough. By this time everyone at the table was in stitches, including Jill. Now that all the pieces of the puzzle were put together, it was clear that the event possessed the stuff legends are made of.

After everyone had gone to their perspective places after dinner, Jill, Marjorie, and Lloyd sat in the living room while Jill informed Lloyd what was going on with Jack. What surprised Jill is that Lloyd was not shocked by the revelation.

"You don't appear to be surprised by this information, Lloyd," Jill stated.

Lloyd looked at her as he was considering what he should say. He let out a breath, "Jill, I'm not surprised because I suspected that Jack was playing with pornography when you last visited us some thirteen years ago."

This time it was Jill who was surprised. "Jack was into pornography that many years ago?"

Nodding his head, Lloyd sadly confirmed her statement, "Yes, he was. Perhaps it was on the outside fringes of being what we now refer to as, "hard core," but pornography represents a door that once opened, even by what seems innocent, is like opening Pandora's Box. From that point on a net of defilement begins to be thrown over those who open it. Their affections become entangled in lust, their imagination becomes ensnared by the profane, their appetites become enslaved to obsession, and their sense of right and wrong becomes hijacked by a seductive delusion that eventually causes them to become totally divorced from reality."

255

In a bewildered voice, Jill responded, "Lloyd, I don't understand, Jack is a Christian, he's a minister, how can this be?"

"Jill, according to statistics, the percentage of pastors who dabble in pornography is at least 50%. It is the latest addiction that is now entangling our society in the most destructive way."

"Fifty percent," Jill cried, "Oh, God help our churches. This can't be good for God's sheep, the pastor's family, and the name of Christ."

Lloyd sadly shook his head, "Jill, sacredness has been offered up to the gods of pleasure in our society beginning with the affront against marriage and family and the abortion issue. When you stomp on the sacredness of life by claiming rights to live any 'ole' way that you desire without having responsibility for personal actions, then sacredness in other areas will be sacrificed as well. People will be dulled down to morality and eventually worldly excuses will make more sense than moral rightness because it feeds and justifies lust.

"When I was in pornography, I eventually lost all sense of guilt. My conscience became seared as I justified my right to seek what I considered 'earned' pleasure. I convinced myself that since I worked hard, I had a right to have some type of outside activity from work and home. To me there was nothing wrong with looking at a beautiful, sexy image on the page or the internet. After all, I wasn't doing anything physically wrong but what I failed to realize is that those images were setting aflame my lust and imagination. I lived in denial about my wicked imagination even though at times I fantasized that some of those faces and bodies I had mentally partaken of were attached to Marjorie during intimacy with her. Underneath, I knew I was conning myself, but I managed to convince myself intellectually that I wasn't breaking my marriage vows.

"When Marjorie confronted me, I thought she was making a big deal out of nothing, and actually felt misunderstood and sorry for myself. In my mind, she should understand that it was a man-thing and I wasn't doing anything really wrong, but the sick truth is I was defiling the marriage bed.

"In the end I became so self-absorbed that I didn't care what I was doing to my relationship with God or to the family He had entrusted to me. I shrugged at the domino effect that my sin was having on my family and my soul. To put it bluntly, I was a selfish, arrogant jerk who chose to remain indifferent to my reality, while clinging to a sinking ship of spiritual ruin and emotional despair."

Jill was quietly taking in everything. The confusing lose ends of her life were beginning to come together in a clear picture.

"The question is Jill, what do you plan to do about it?" Lloyd asked.

Jill knew she could somewhat soothe her fragile conscience because she had truly been ignorant, but she also realized that she had been wrong in her thinking. She wanted her answer to Lloyd to reflect that important factor. Looking at him she carefully chose her words, "I've been in the habit of trying to protect Jack and the church's reputation. I realize now I was wrong. My sin is that of idolatry, exalting the institution of marriage and the church above God's Word, and hiding the darkness of grave sin from the light. As we all know, I ignorantly partook of the delusion and wickedness of this sin."

She took a deep breath, and then continued. "God's Word is clear that sin can only take root and grow in darkness. It must be brought to the light, especially for the sake of the one in the offense," she paused as she reflected on what she had been learning. "Once sin is brought to the light it can become a point of edification as it serves as a visible source of instruction and warning to others."

"Very good, Jill," Lloyd said with a sad smile. "You have learned some valuable lessons, but what are your plans?"

Jill knew what she had to do. "I'm going to inform the head elder of what is going on. It's clear that Jack needs to be held accountable for his actions by those who are in authority in the hope that he will repent and become reconciled back to God. Even though the latest events have shaken him, he has not paid any personal consequences. Until he does, he will most likely fail to see any need to deal with his fornication."

"You're right Jill," Lloyd affirmed, "Jack not only needs to be held accountable, but he needs someone who will continue to hold his feet to the fire."

Jill looked at both Marjorie and Lloyd, "I want to thank you both for letting me come here. I was badly broken and you have provided a sanctuary for me to find healing and peace." She paused, "I don't know what's going to happen, but I'm going to continue to go forward in this journey. Even if Jack gets his act together I know that we can't go back home. I'll be looking for a job around here so I can support Deborah and myself— that is until God can put our family back together in the right way." She paused, "I know that the Lord will ultimately bring each of us through this terrible wilderness if we allow Him to."

Lloyd smiled, "We're both glad we could be here for you and to help you and your family in any way we can as you walk through this deep valley. You're welcome to stay here as long as you need to."

Gratitude, like a river of refreshing water, suddenly flowed over her soul. She didn't know what the future held, but she knew that the Lord would work out all the details according to His plan and glory.

***

The next morning she called Delbert. The head elder was glad to hear from her. The typical greetings took place between them, along with sincerity on Delbert's part to inquire how she was doing. Jill always appreciated the integrity of this quiet, but strong man. His heart was pure and his desire to do what was pleasing to God honorable. In hard places she could tell that he was most interested in pleasing God and not man. Even though he occasionally walked a precarious line, he showed wisdom and grace.

It was after his inquiry and her answer that Jill took a deep breath. "Delbert, the reason I called you is to inform you as head elder as to what is going on in the Lansing home."

Delbert's voice revealed a relief, "I appreciate that Jill. I know there is something going on but until I know exactly what it is, there is nothing any of us in leadership can do to address it."

Jill was anxious to get it out in the light. "Well, I'm going to get right to the point. Jack is into hard core pornography, and what I know by recent uncovered facts, he has been in it for some time."

Jill wasn't sure what was going on at the other end of the line because she was met with a long silence. She wasn't taken by surprise by the silence because Delbert was very methodical about how he approached a matter, but she began to feel anxiety creeping in before the silence was broken.

"I suspected as much Jill, but I needed confirmation. Now the leadership of the church can take constructive actions."

Jill wanted to give a better explanation, "Delbert, I wasn't aware of his sin until recently, but the children have known about it for some time. It has been a dirty little secret that has been slowly ruining our family."

Delbert paused before he delivered vital information, "Jill, I think you should know that Jack Jr. finished his military obligation and came home. His father and he had quite a confrontation that ended with the police being called. Even though we have put Jack Sr. on a type of administrative leave until we can untangle the mess, neither of the Jacks are giving any details. I think that Jack Jr. got the short end of the stick. He has a black eye and a split lip and right now he has been staying with us."

The latest information shook Jill to the core. "Oh no! I had no idea he was going to be discharged from the military. He hasn't communicated with us for a long time. I don't understand why he didn't call me! He has my cell number."

"All I can tell you is that he has been in contact with Deborah. They both decided you needed this time away from the family dynamics. In fact, Deborah will be here in a couple of days to see her brother."

Jill knew what she needed to do. The three of them needed each other and it was time for healing and not separation. "Delbert, can I ask you for a favor?"

"Sure Jill, what is it?"

"I'm a ten-hour drive away from you. If they agree, would you consider driving Jack Jr. and Deborah here?"

"It would be my honor to do so."

Jill went to Marjorie and gave her the details. "Marjorie, I hate to impose on you, but I feel that the children need to be with me to begin the healing process. I was wondering if. . ."

Before Jill could finish her sentence, Marjorie jumped in, "Of course, all three of you are welcome to stay here until you get on your feet. It will be good to see Jack Jr. and Deborah and get to know them as young adults."

Jill immediately called Deborah. Deborah was glad to hear her mother's voice. When Jill informed her that she knew that Jack Jr. had come home and there was some type of altercation, sadness entered the tone of her daughter's voice.

Deborah had always fondly called her older brother "Jocko." "Mom, Jocko and I were going to wait a while before we told you about what happened. But, from what I gather, it was bad. Jocko said that Dad looked terrible and their conversation was strained from the start. They talked about everyday matters, and somehow it finally graduated to the big elephant in the living room that no one was willing to talk about.

"I guess during the conversation about the domino effect that was taking place due to Dad's problem, Dad got so mad he physically attacked Jocko. Jocko shoved Dad away from him so that he could leave without any more violence. Then Dad tackled Jocko on the front lawn. Jocko wouldn't fight back because he was afraid he would hurt Dad, so he took quite a whipping. Neighbors who witnessed the event, called the police. Dad ended up in police custody, but Jocko wouldn't press charges, so they let Dad go. Dad has locked himself in the house and has only communicated once with Mr. Anderson. I guess the incident was in the newspaper, forcing the church board to give Dad a leave of absence until further notice."

"You should have called me Deborah," Jill admonished.

"We wanted to but we knew that you were trying to wade through the situation with Dad and me."

Jill appreciated the desire to give her space, but it was time to work it out together. "Deborah we need each other right now. And, guess where I am?"

Deborah caught the intrigue of her mother's question, "Where are you?"

"Right now I am staying with Aunt Marjorie and Uncle Lloyd."

"Really!"

"Yes, really! And, guess what?"

"What?" Deborah excitedly inquired.

"All three of us have an open invitation to stay here. How would you and Jocko like coming here and staying at their place with me until we all figure out what we are going to do?"

"Are you kidding?" Deborah exclaimed. "Both Jocko and I have wanted to go back there for years! Even though I was only four, I've never forgotten them and their farm."

Jill got caught up with Deborah's giddy excitement, "I've made arrangements with the Andersons to bring you both here. So, just imagine! In a couple of days, we'll be together!" And, Jill had to add the obvious note of a mother's heart, "And honey, know that I love you and tell your brother that I love him and if he needs to talk to me to call my cell phone at any time."

Jill had a lot to do in a short time including conquering the truck. They still needed a driver for the next day. Since Marjorie was busy with business in town, Jill approached Belinda about helping her tackle the task while they cleaned the dairy.

Looking at Jill with a smile on her face and a twinkle in her eye, she said, "Why not, I could use a bit of excitement in my day."

Jill silently hoped there was not too much excitement. As they approached the truck it didn't seem as intimidating to Jill as the first time. Since she had previous experience with it, she knew what had to be done. She wanted to smooth out the rough edges so she could naturally drive it without it jerking forward or her succumbing to fear and confusion.

Belinda's easy manner was calming to Jill. The first couple of times there was a bit of jerking, but as Belinda encouraged her to take her time, and directed her to spots that wouldn't present any unexpected challenges, Jill was able to get the rhythm down when shifting gears. Even though her practicing took most of the afternoon, Jill felt she would be capable of driving the load of pallets to the shipping dock.

The next day, she was ready to take her spot in the caravan. Belinda had instructed Dale to put Jill's truck second to the last. When

Marjorie saw Jill standing beside her loaded truck, she gave her a questioning look. Jill looked at her with a smile and nodded her head.

The drive to the docks proved to be quite pleasant for Jill. Each driver was considerate of her and took their time going the six miles to their destination. When they arrived, Jill walked from the landing dock to the office where she noticed a poster that advertised for a bookkeeper.

Jill had been trained and worked in bookkeeping before motherhood. As she read the sign, she heard a voice behind her, "Jill Carter, is that you?"

Even though Carter was her maiden name, it was natural for Jill to respond. She turned around to see a familiar face, and suddenly realized it was Kelly Hollister.

"You're Kelly Hollister, right?"

"Right," he said with a big smile.

Looking at the poster then back at her, "Starting pay is only $15.50 per hour, but in 90 days if a person works out it will go up to $18.50. Would you be interested in this job?"

It all sounded great to Jill but she had to defuse her excitement. "As long as it doesn't have anything to do with sheep," she grinned mischievously.

A past memory awakened in him, and he laughed, "You won't even be required to count any sheep."

Jill laughed. "It's been awhile since I did bookkeeping, but I'm up to the task of sharpening my skills once again."

Kelly reached up and took the poster down, "You're hired."

Shocked, Jill echoed her surprise. "Just like that?"

"Since I am the owner and boss of this particular business, it's my prerogative to hire those whom I will, and I've just hired you."

Her response was to hug him, but knowing she was a married woman it would not be proper; therefore, she refrained herself. She clasped her hands together and in a choked voice, stated her gratitude, "Thank you, you'll never know what this means to me."

"Well it's for my benefit I assure you. Since this is Wednesday, why don't you start Monday morning?"

"That would be perfect Kel. . . uh, Mr. Hollister"

Grinning he said, "It will always be Kelly to you, Jill. See you Monday." He turned and walked back into the office.

Her spirit danced and it felt like her soul was floating as she approached the truck in a surreal state. As she drove back to the dairy, she realized if it was not for "Can," who accepted the challenge of the truck, she would have failed to "Do" what she needed to do, and would have never been in the right place at the right time to receive the job.

Her first mission when she arrived home was to inform Marjorie of God's perfect timing in relationship to getting a job. Marjorie was not surprised but she was quick to rejoice with her.

"You know Jill, there is a two bedroom apartment over the garage. Dale has been living there, but after a family meeting, we all agreed that it would fit you and your children nicely until you get on your feet. Dale will be moving out of the apartment into the basement where Mason lived up until his marriage."

Jill was overwhelmed. Her prayers were being quickly answered. Things were moving fast for her. It was indeed wondrous to her soul and brought awe to her spirit. It had been such a long dry spell for her. The spiritual wilderness she had been in left her feeling barren, but the Lord was now uncapping the living waters in her inner being. The waters not only brought hope to her but healing and peace. It was like experiencing that initial exciting love she had when she was first saved. It was clear that God had not left her; rather, He had silently been there all the time, nudging her on when she was ready to give up, while adjusting her feet to stay within the narrow path to finally bring her to a place of deliverance.

The next day Jill tried to busy herself until the arrival of the Andersons and her children. She quietly prayed for God's wisdom throughout the day. She knew that it would take wisdom to ensure that a healing process would take place for Jack Jr. and Deborah.

When Jack Jr and Deborah arrived, Jill hugged them tightly. It was a tearful reunion for all three of them. When she could finally look into their eyes, she noticed that sadness permeated Jack Jr.'s brown eyes, but she could also see that hope was beginning to part it. Deborah actually looked like some life was coming back into her big hazel eyes.

Marjorie and Lloyd along with the Andersons stood back giving the three Lansing's the necessary time to greet each other. When Deborah saw Marjorie and Lloyd, she ran to them and greeted both of them with a big hug, causing Lloyd to let out a joyous laugh that left Marjorie smiling. When Jack Jr. initially walked up to the couple, he refrained from showing too much emotion. He took Lloyd's hand and firmly shook it with both of his hands as he looked into his face, but when he came to Marjorie, he stood in front of her for a second, then he leaned over and embraced her, while laying his head on her right shoulder. Marjorie held him tightly as Jack Jr.'s body shook from the tears that were now freely flowing down his cheeks. Deborah not wanting to miss comfort and assurance stepped up next to Lloyd who put his arm around her shoulders and pulled her close as she put her arm around his waist. They both quietly stood and watched the interaction between Jack Jr. and Marjorie.

Jill realized how much her children needed this couple. They would have brought much needed stability and wisdom to their lives. In fact, if Jack Jr. and Deborah would have confided to anyone, Jill was sure it would have been to either Marjorie or Lloyd or both. It had not only been unfair to keep them away from benefitting from Marjorie and Lloyd's kindness and example, but it had also been cruel. Even though Jill was trying to be a submissive wife to her husband by honoring his excuses, she realized she failed to fight for the welfare of her children.

Jill remembered the Andersons were quietly observing the interactions. She turned and walked over to them. She hugged Luann and shook Delbert's hand. Delbert and Jill both exchanged looks that indicated that they shared knowledge that brought a certain understanding as to the events unfolding, and were about to visibly unfold in the future.

After Jack Jr. let go of Marjorie, she ever so slightly touched his cheek with her right hand. Jill could see the kind, but determined look in Marjorie's eyes. It was as if she was assuring him that he would never be hurt again in like manner if she had anything to say about it.

Then Jack Jr. remembered the Andersons. He put his arm out to Marjorie and escorted her to where they were standing. Lloyd and Deborah, arm in arm followed behind. Jill introduced the Andersons to the Kirkpatrick's. Dale and Belinda joined the exchange of greetings.

Dale and Jack Jr. remembered each other and warmly greeted one another with a friendly handshake. When Dale saw Deborah, he smiled. "Jack, this can't be the four-year-old little girl who managed to irritate us to death with all of her antics of trying to catch every wild kitten, cuddle every dog, hug every calf, ride every horse, and introduce herself to every cow."

Jill was reminded that unlike herself at age four, Deborah was fearless of the animals around her. She loved them and wanted to tame, rehabilitate, and make every one of them her pet. She remembered that Deborah had kept the other Kirkpatrick children on their feet to make sure that she would not get herself in too much trouble around the farm.

Laughing Jack responded, "It's her alright."

As if to act insulted, but smiling at the same time Deborah was quick to reply, "I'm that girl, but as you've noticed I'm no longer four years old!" Leaning forward as if to confess something of great importance, "But, I have to admit, I still want to tame all the wild kittens, hug every dog, love on every calf, ride every horse you have, and introduce myself to every cow. I have just one question, when can I get started?"

By this time everyone was enjoying the exchange taking place. It was as if the bad years never existed for Jack Jr. and Deborah. They were care-free and picking up where they had left off as if it was just yesterday.

Belinda's voice broke through the teasing, "You can start right now. In fact, you can take your mother's place in feeding the calves."

Then Belinda was introduced to Deborah and Jack. The final introductions were barely finished between Dale, Belinda, and the Andersons when Deborah piped up, "Can we go feed the calves now?"

"Sure, why not," Belinda answered, "what about you two guys helping out?"

"I'm game," Jack quickly stated, while trying to hide his excitement.

"Well, you know I work with pallets, not calves," Dale exclaimed.

With a smile and a determined look like her mother's, Belinda quickly set the record straight, "It would be good for you to be reminded about the other side of the operations around here."

Grinning mischievously Dale answered, "I might argue with you about that Belinda, but since Jack is an old friend of mine, I wouldn't like leaving him to the likes of you two."

Even though Deborah had only been four years old when she had last been on the farm, she remembered where the calf pens were located. As she ran in the direction of the pens, Dale and Jack Jr. started talking about the memories they had of each other as Belinda listened to their adventures. At times you could hear her children laugh as they relived something that touched their funny bone.

To Jill, hearing her children's laughter was medicine to her soul. Life had been so terribly serious for Jack Jr. and Deborah, robbing them of their childhood innocence and causing them to feel the depths of despair at an early age.

Marjorie's voice interrupted Jill's thoughts. "It's time to fix dinner. Luann and Delbert would you stay for dinner, and stay the night as well?"

"We couldn't impose on you," Luann objected. "We were just going to get a motel room."

"There's no need to get a motel room, and you are not imposing. We have plenty of room," Lloyd assured them and then added, "Delbert, would you be interested in seeing our operations, while the women do their thing?"

"I thought you would never ask. I've always considered myself a country boy," Delbert exclaimed excitedly.

"Let's get to it."

As the men walked towards the dairy operations, the women walked into the house to start dinner. It was amazing how the three women seemed to work as one while enjoying each other's company. Jill watched how Marjorie and Luann immediately found common ground and began to bond. The three women talked about homes and family, as well as funny moments that come with learning and growing. Eventually they talked about their spiritual walk. It was clear that both Marjorie and Luann were being respectful to Jill by staying away from the subject of Jack Sr. Jill knew that the subject would come up soon enough, but she wanted to enjoy the sweet fellowship she was having with the two women.

At dinner, Jack Jr. and Deborah were reminded of the entertainment that was provided at the Kirkpatrick's table. It was obvious that the Andersons clearly enjoyed it as well. As usual the dinner table represented story time. Jill somehow knew that her incident with the sheep and the truck were probably going to become the main attractions for the evening. Sure enough the stories were once again retold. The laughter over the sheep story hit some high decibels, but the one about the truck sent the decibels through the roof. Jack Jr. laughed so hard he almost fell out of his chair, Delbert had tears in his eyes, Luann had her head in her hands, as her body shook with laughter, and Deborah held her sides while tapping her foot against the floor.

Jill realized that people had different ways of expressing laughter. And, she was beginning to see why Proverbs declares that a merry heart is good like medicine."

As the laughter died down, Jack, with tears still in his eyes, had to ask the question, "Aunt Marjorie, how did you ever manage to get Mom behind the wheel of a truck with standard shift?"

"I'll answer that question," Jill interjected. "She told me the stories about "Can" and "Can't" and "Try" and "Do.""

Jack Jr. and Deborah looked at Marjorie with question marks on their faces, and Jill could tell the Andersons were displaying measurable curiosity as well.

"How many times have we heard those two stories?" Dale asked Belinda.

"I admit I've heard them a few times through my life," Belinda replied with a smile.

"Marjorie, why don't you tell the rest of these people those two stories," Jill suggested.

Marjorie complied and shared both stories. Even though there were a couple of smiles and a few giggles, Jill could tell that it caused her children and the Andersons to pause to consider the significant meaning behind them.

After dinner, the younger generation went downstairs to play some games, while the remaining five adults sat in the living room to discuss the latest information. Delbert informed the group that Jack was asked to step down from the pulpit indefinitely to deal with his sin of pornography and try to bring reconciliation with his family.

When Jill inquired how Jack took it, Delbert related that he did not deny what was going on, and took it in a quiet, but defeated way. That very day Jack waited until he knew everyone was gone and had cleaned out his office and left the key on the desk. He had not been in contact with anyone except for Delbert.

Delbert looked at Jill, "Jill, I think you should know that Jack asked where you were. He made it clear to me that he wants to talk to you in person."

Jill took a deep breath. She knew she had to face him eventually. She looked around the room as if to ask each one the question. "What do you think I should do?"

As they looked around at each other, it was Lloyd who was the first to speak. "Jill, you need to meet with him. As Christians we are to be ministers of reconciliation. The real reconciliation that needs to take place above all else is the restoration of Jack coming back into a relationship with his Creator. Until that relationship is right, any attempt to put back his other relationships will be like putting a Band-Aid on a bleeding artery at best. You are the only one now who may be able to hold the line of truth with him."

Jill knew that Lloyd was right, "Lloyd, you may be right, but I'm not sure that it will make any difference."

With gentle firmness in his voice, Lloyd set the record straight, "Jill, the details belong to the Lord, you will simply be a mouthpiece, and what Jack does with it is between him and God."

Jill looked at Delbert, "You can call Jack tonight and inform him where I am, and that I'll be glad to meet him here at 5 p.m. tomorrow."

Delbert nodded his head as if to say it was already done.

That night the three Lansing's met in the apartment above the garage. Twin beds were made up for the two women and the other room had a double bed that was clearly calling Jack Jr. However, there was much to discuss. Jack Jr. informed Jill that Dale had offered him a job at the pallet mill and hoped she would not mind.

"Why would I mind," Jill asked.

"Besides learning how to build pallets, I'll be taking over your job of driving the truck," Jack stated with a grin.

"Oh, please do so, Son!" Jill laughed.

"I want to stay here and help around the farm," Deborah piped in.

"What about your friends back home?" Jill inquired.

"I'll miss them, but I'll renew some old friendships and make some new ones. I see a new beginning here." She paused, "You know I love animals so I talked with Belinda about being a veterinary assistant. She thinks I would be a great one. So I'm going to apply for scholarships and register at the same university she is attending."

After the excitement of the future began to wind down, the two siblings started sharing with Jill about their experiences surrounding their father. She listened as the brother and sister shared about the nightmare that had emerged because of their father's sin. That nightmare included an array of confusing emotions that ended in shock and hurt, which ebbed into disappointment, then materialized in anger, ultimately pushing them into a pit of hopelessness. Out of their honesty came some cleansing tears that emerged into a healing balm of forgiveness and a sweet bond of fellowship that was knitting the three together.

It was Jack Jr. who asked the question, "What will happen to Dad?"

"I don't know son," Jill answered matter-of-factly. "The ball is in his court."

"How can we help him Mom?" Deborah inquired, and then added, "I still love him."

"And that is how it should be for both of you," Jill stated. "All we do know is to pray that he will desire the light over his present darkness, repent, and seek the necessary help to overcome the addictive hold of this sin on his soul."

Staring at the tip of his shoes, Jack Jr. confessed his struggle, "You know Mom, I have had a terrible time not hating Dad, but when we had that last confrontation, I realized he is like a lost little boy. Even though it pained my soul that he would physically attack me, I felt sorry for him because he has lost everything important to him and now has no one in his corner."

"Have you forgiven your father, Jack?" Jill questioned.

"Yes I have. I recently recognized that my bitterness was doing me much more harm than it was him and that I had to let go of my hurt, disappointment, and anger."

"What about you Deborah," Jill asked.

"Yes, I have Mom, and I have also let all my pent up anger go." Deborah paused, "The hurt and disappointment was great and almost consumed me, but this latest incident with Jocko made me realize that Dad is also a victim. It was obvious that Dad is consumed by his sin, but it was not my sin, and I needed to step outside of the circle of destruction in order to become an overcomer."

Jill could see that the spiritual investment made in her children's lives was paying valuable dividends. "I'm proud of both of you." Jill said as tears welled up in her eyes. "You've made good decisions in the midst of a great tragedy. Tonight, I know we're all going to be alright because God is taking what was intended to ruin our family and is turning it around for His glory, and we are going to come out better for it."

They all came together for a group hug before going off to bed where they at last enjoyed a restful night. Jill's dreams were no longer filled with nightmarish realities, but with the sweetness of hope.

While busying herself with the regular tasks the next morning, Jill spiritually prepared herself by quoting Scriptures and praying for her upcoming meeting with Jack. There was a lot on the line, and Jack held the ball. Jill silently questioned whether he had the inner character to carry the ball full court to change the outcome of the game. It was clear he had to get this one right or he would know greater bitterness and failure.

Jill fixed herself up for the meeting. As always, the senior Jack was punctual. When Jill saw him, he was clean shaven and dressed in jeans and a casual shirt, but looked worn-down. She watched him walk up to her, and even though he looked haggard, his smile indicated he still had some charm and charisma left.

He reached out, took both of her hands in his, and leaned down to kiss her. Jill turned her cheek to him. His kiss was cool and light. Still holding her hands he backed up. He kept looking at her as he greeted her awkwardly "Hi Jill, it's nice to see you."

"Hello Jack."

"You probably know why I'm here."

"No I don't Jack. I was informed that you wanted to talk to me, but I do not know what about."

"You heard I was released from my position as head pastor."

"Yes, I did hear that," Jill commented in a non-committal way.

Jill's factual manner with Jack seemed to unravel whatever self-confidence he may have had. Jill knew that Jack expected her to probably show some type of emotion towards his plight, but she knew that she had to stay away from emotional traps. They both began walking towards the empty cow pasture.

As she expected, Jack begin to smoothly present his case. "Jill, I know I have a problem, but if you and the children come back, I know we can work it out together and I could most likely get my position back."

Jill could not contain the disgust in her voice. "There's a problem, Jack." Her voice rose as she questioned his understanding of his offense towards the Lord and his family. "Is that all you consider your abominable sin of fornication to be?"

Jack stopped dead in his tracks. She watched as his face turned purple then red. Finally, in a measured tone he replied, "It's not all that bad."

By this time, Jill was doing everything she could to not yell, "Your problem is 'not bad,' but yet it's destroying your family and is costing you your position. I guess everyone involved from your family to the leaders of the church are being too hard on poor, Jack."

Jack's tone was defensive as he hid behind a prior accusation. "Well things wouldn't be as bad as they are now if our personal laundry was kept in the family. We could have worked it out."

Jill shook her head firmly in disagreement. "Really Jack! How has that worked for us as a family, you hiding your sin beneath a cloak of hypocrisy so no one knows the depth of darkness that has been consuming the Lansing's' home? And, I might add, who put a big fat light on your problem when you decided to beat our son up on our front lawn?"

Jack's voice rose to a high pitch. "Well, he provoked me!"

"And, Jack, just how did he provoke you, by being honest with you?"

It was apparent Jack was landing on any excuse he could, "Well, no son should talk to his father like that!"

"I don't know how our son spoke to you, but I do know one thing, any good Christian man and father would not have taken occasion to beat up his son who was struggling over his father's sin!"

Jill could tell by Jack's face she had made a vital point. However, after a few seconds of silence it was obvious that Jack would not be deterred from his mission. "Well, I came here to tell you I'm willing to work it out with you and the kids." He paused, shifted his gaze to the tree-studded hillside behind Jill, and then retorted, "You know, just let bygones be bygones."

Jill felt her blood pressure rising and threatening to explode into a million pieces that would bury him in an onslaught of debris. She wanted to become sarcastic about his fake nobility, but she knew it wouldn't do any good. It was clear Jack wasn't getting it. Whether he loved his sin more than God and his family, or if he was in complete denial or both, it was apparent he was not prepared to be honest about his sin, and brutally confront it. She realized that she was emotionally sliding downward into his miry cesspool, and she had to change tactics if she was going to avoid wallowing in the stench of it.

Jill decided the best tactic was to lay out her conditions. "There is only one problem with letting bygones be bygones, Jack."

"What do you mean?"

She looked at him, her eyes alive with the fire of her convictions. "I'm wondering whether my honesty about my conditions will provoke you, or are you strong enough to keep it together?"

Jack's face turned red once again. "I know how to handle my temper. You tell me what the conditions are. I'm quite sure that I can meet them."

"Jack, the problem you have is bigger than you and me. However, I will no longer prostitute myself to protect your image or keep you as my husband."

The redness of his face deepened. "Just what do you mean, prostitute yourself!" Jack exclaimed.

"Jack, until you get rid of the endless harem that you've acquired and brought into our bedroom every time you turn on your computer, there will be no marriage or future for us." She paused, "I don't know how this wicked, perverted practice is beneficial to you, unless you prefer to lust after and taste of forbidden, deadly fruit to fill some sick fantasy," she paused before continuing her indictment, "as well as using it to continually judge me as inept in order to justify your wickedness to live in denial as to the evil you are steadily partaking of."

Jill could tell that Jack recognized that he had opened a door of truth that could not and would not be closed by any logic or form of justification.

Jill continued, "I'll not share my bed or my life with others when it comes to the marriage bed. You are an unfaithful husband who has made a mockery out of our marriage vows and shown utter contempt towards the covenant you made with me before God. Your unfaithful actions are causing me to wonder just how far you have gone in acting out these wicked fantasies."

Jack fixed his eyes on the ground.

Jill recognized that he was probably hiding a lot more than she realized. "Perhaps I don't want to know after all Jack! But, this one thing I know for sure, I'll not play second fiddle or any other fiddle in your life just to have sick leftovers. I'll not share your affections with outlandish sexual images, compete for your heart with its insatiable lusts, try to stand against the perverted imaginations of your mind, and accept whatever unmerciful crumbs you throw at me to keep me quiet when the loneliness and torment become too loud and unbearable for me."

Jill's words were turning Jack into an emotional pretzel as they hit their target. It was apparent that he didn't know how to undo the knot his emotions had been tied into by truth. Jill could tell he was struggling to keep some semblance of control.

Although flimsy, he played the only card he had left. Clearing his throat, he boyishly intoned, "Don't you want our marriage to make it?"

"What marriage, Jack? You have sold your spiritual birthright for a pottage of scum. You have been caught up with all those women on the internet, and by your reaction it's obvious in other seedy places as well, while selling bits and pieces of your soul along the way so you could taste forbidden fruit.

"And, in the process who have you dishonored besides yourself and me? Who were those women you lusted after and came into an unholy agreement with? Like your daughter, Deborah, they were someone's daughter or sister, perhaps someone's girlfriend, wife, or even mother. How many people have you dishonored by partaking of their fruit with your lustful flesh and eyes?"

As Jill spoke, Jack continued to hold his head down like a boy whose hand had been caught in the cookie jar. In the past, Jill would have felt sorry for him and tried to comfort him like a mother, but she was not his mother, she was his wife who had been betrayed by his unfaithfulness. She was not through with her exhortation.

"Even when you were with me, you were absent from me. Even though I have not understood what was going on, I have sensed for some time that you wish I was someone else, or that you could be free to live out some perverted fantasy. Although you needed me to keep up the front for the church, you either resented me because I could not fulfill your unrealistic fantasies or you despised me because I stood in the way of you pursuing it.

"Do I want our marriage to make it? Yes I do, but we don't have a marriage. We have a ruined mess, a sham, and as I stated back at the hospital, my husband has been gone for a long time. And, now I want to emphatically state that I will only accept back the man I married, no doubt broken by his sin and wiser and more sober for it, but changed, cleaned up, and restored."

271

By this time Jack was close to tears. "What do you want me to do Jill?"

"Come on Jack! As a Christian you shouldn't even have to ask that question. Let me ask you, are your tears that of self-pity because you got caught and are now paying the bitter consequences; or, are they tears of brokenness because of what your sin has cost God and your family? If I need to answer that question for you, then I must conclude that you aren't even close to the place of repentance. You of all people know that your greatest offense or sin has not been against our marriage or our children or the church, but against God Almighty."

Jack's shoulders slumped, his fists clenching and unclenching nervously, as he muttered something to himself.

Jill's voice was firm. "Jack, you must get your relationship right with the Lord, before you can ever expect reconciliation with me or your children."

In a voice filled with self-pity, Jack mumbled the next question, "What am I to do, Jill, I have lost everything?"

Again another door was cracked open for Jill to push wide open and walk through, "Jack, I suggest you start with brutal honesty. What do you mourn the most, the loss of your position or your family?"

Jack lifted his eyes and looked into Jill's face. He stood silent for a moment. "Honestly Jill, right now I mourn the loss of my position the most."

With a sigh of relief, Jill looked into Jack's eyes. "Thank you, Jack."

Surprised and confused, "For what Jill?"

"It's the first time you've been honest with me in a long time. You have just risen a mirror up that will give you a pretty good idea of where you are right now—that is if you care to look hard and long at it. If you do, perhaps it is a start for your spiritual healing and restoration, and reconciliation for us."

In a voice of resignation, Jack once again tried to receive some kind of commitment from Jill, "What do you want to do? You want me to move out of the house so you and the children can come back there to live until I..."

"Sell the house," Jill flatly interjected.

Shocked, Jack exclaimed, "Sell it? Don't you want to live there?"

"No I don't. I have a new life here and a new job. I'll never go back there."

"Well, what if we get back together, Jill, and I manage to get my position as head pastor back? We won't have a home to go back to."

"Because of your sin, you won't be able to go back either, Jack. Right now, you have only two ways in which to go, and you must choose one of the ways. You must go forward in true repentance towards a new life in Christ, or you must choose to serve the tyrannical master of your flesh that will lead you into the pit of destruction, but either way, you'll never be able to go back to what was."

Jill paused, "Go home Jack, and make up your mind. You cannot remain on the fence as you grab at both worlds to maintain your right to walk in wickedness, while giving the impression of being righteous. Perhaps you need to go home and freely serve the gods in the plush valleys or Sodom and Gomorrah until you become sick in your soul by the loathsome taste they will leave in your mouth and the leanness such idolatry will leave in your spirit and soul. Perhaps then you will be desperate and broken enough to look upward for forgiveness and restoration and determined enough to seek out professional help from others who will hold you accountable."

Jack stood in stunned silence as Jill continued, "But, I suggest you do it soon because I plan to go forward in my life, personally and spiritually, and as long as you remain in your present cesspool, you will be left behind. There's only one way to go forward and that is to come back into a right relationship to God, through genuine repentance." She paused as she intensely looked into his eyes. Jill could feel her eyes narrowing, "I warn you that you can't continue to resist the Holy Spirit's conviction without becoming harder towards the truth.

"You know, Jack, repentance is a place of humiliation and if you try to come to the place of repentance without the fruits of repentance, turning from your sin in complete brokenness with the determination of doing right, like Esau, you could completely miss the place altogether."

Sensing God's grace suddenly flowing through her, she felt genuine sympathy for the broken man standing before her. It allowed her to speak her parting sentence to him in a sad but firm tone, "But, there is one thing for sure, Jack, you cannot serve hell and please God at the same time."

Jill turned away from a despondent Jack to make her way back to the house. She felt great pity and heaviness for Jack, but at the same time she felt her spirit was soaring in a new freedom and her soul cleansed and giddy. As Jesus' words echoed in her soul, she knew that she had indeed become a recipient of one of His most powerful statements. It was clear that His precious words were compelling her forward with expectation and renewed hope as she quietly repeated them, "You shall know the truth and the truth shall make you free."

For if we have been planted together in the likeness of his death, we shall be also in the likeness of his resurrection. (Romans 6:5)

Resurrection

Hannah Bailey sat alone in her dark bedroom, alone with her thoughts. Her long, black hair was tousled, and her eye makeup smudged, but she didn't care. What started out to be her refuge, had become a tomb. It seemed as if the walls were hollow, echoing the sound of her breathing, as she spiraled downward into an endless cavern of loneliness.

She felt as if everything was upside down in her life. She had lost count as to the many times she had tried to make sense out of the happenings that not only consumed her thoughts, but always caused them to merge into tormenting memories. Like a powerful, rushing river, she was forever being swiftly swept away to face the cascading falls that would cast her deeper into the watery abyss of despair and hopelessness.

Like all women in the youth of her life, Hannah had dreams. They seemed harmless and innocent enough. Her dreams had inspired her to scale pinnacles of ecstasy, float through rivers of possibilities, and endlessly swing in her imagination from one dream to the other while hanging on to the limbs of expectation. Now as the memories ran across her mind like ticker tape, she realized that life had a way of revealing the vanity of such pinnacles, drying up the rivers of possibilities with dams of human frailty, and cutting the branches of expectations with sharp edges of reality.

As she tried to find an exit to avoid going down the same river and hitting greater depths of despair, she once again felt entangled by her emotions. After all, her emotions served as the current in this river that had at first entangled her like seaweed, making her susceptible to the currents and various waves that entered with the different happenings of her life. Eventually, her emotions became such an overpowering torrent, that she found herself being carried off by their momentum.

Once again she felt like she was in one gigantic whirlpool that was dragging her down by an unseen force. In the past, she had clung to her dreams, but now in the darkness of her despair there was nothing substantial to hang on to. She was helpless, and found herself at the cruel mercy of the force that enslaved her.

What events brought her to this place? Buried deep in the recesses of her mind she knew the answer. It was an answer that haunted her. It failed to soothe the rawness of her emotions or calm the raging storm that moved through her inner being. However, the answer was there. She was in her present state because of "love."

Most of her life, Hannah felt like a little girl who had to be perfect, serve the ideas of others, especially those of her mother, and comply with a smile, while resentment seethed beneath the surface. She often felt stifled from discovering who she was, and when she insisted that she must be set free from her cage in order to soar, she was often met with failure in her attempts to secure her idea of life. She had always feared that one day her resentment would bubble to the surface and erupt, leaving her alone and devastated. Just as she suspected her fear came to pass in the most unlikely way. It didn't happen because her mother pushed her too far or life became overwhelmingly boring or unsatisfying. It happened because of love.

"Love," that one word in which fantasy rides on the high waves of dreams, perpetual romance becomes the desired manifestation, and hopefully, happiness the end result. It's where expectation finds its inspiration, and hope seems indelible and certain, even in light of tragedy.

Now as Hannah looked back into the mirror of time she had to wonder if she knew or understood what constituted true love. Even when love ended in tragedy in the stories and movies, it was often for the sake of nobility, making love honorable and worthy. However, there was no honor in the tragedy that love had brought her way. The romance she had encountered was a passing fancy, a masquerade that left her disillusioned. Her expectation towards love now lay in a ruinous heap, and any hope of experiencing lasting happiness had been drained from her.

Perhaps the exit she longed to find was camouflaged by what she thought love was. Maybe the real exit to her plight rested with discovering what love is because she had clearly experienced what it was not. Mentally she didn't want to attempt to explore such a thesis, while her heart felt like shattered glass. Emotionally she was so raw that any more disappointment would cause what inner resolve she had left to be reduced to a vapor that would evaporate with the next breeze. However, it was her notions about love that brought her to this insipid, hollow place. Something had to be done, something had to change, or she would become bitter and eventually go mad.

With everything in her, she began to line up her thoughts as a means to bring order to her memories. She had to start from the beginning. Her initial notions about love came from stories like Cinderella. According to fairytales, once the initial obstacles were overcome and love finally unveiled, it would prove to be simple, pure, and easy. However, the initial love she encountered proved to be anything but easy, its simplicity became lost in uncertainty and its purity dissipated in whirlpools of speculation.

Perhaps the reason her first love proved to be anything but easy was because love requires risk, courage, and honesty. Her first boyfriend represented a missed opportunity because the initial idea of being involved with him had not seemed plausible to Hannah. She had imagined that her lover would come and fight any obstacle to deliver her out of the dungeon of her small existence. In her naiveté, she didn't understand that it was up to her to initiate those first steps. She had to put value on what she desired before she herself could courageously take hold of the opportunity that lay before her.

However, Hannah could not see herself around the ever-looming obstacle of her overbearing mother's judgments and lectures. Subsequently, she never attended the senior prom with the one young man who seemed willing enough to risk her mother's scrutiny. Because she failed to risk the critical eye of her mother, her missed opportunity turned into the unresolved crescendos of "if only", while her resentment turned outward towards her mother. Meanwhile, life continued to march on leaving her behind.

At age 29, this man would walk back into her life. It would be apparent from his overtures that he was still interested in her. His willingness to reach out to her in spite of the past failure began to open a narrow window of possibilities and hope into her small world.

Every encounter with him seemed like chance. Did not "chance" bring many forlorn lovers together? Was "chance" throwing them together? He proved to be sweet, fun, and sincere. He seemed to really care about her. When the opportunity came to attend a social function with him, Hannah was not about to make the same mistake she had in her senior year. She would risk the opposition of her mother.

Opposition did come, but Hannah discovered that by risking it she found enough strength to hold her up in such a confrontation. Even though she felt some trepidation in facing her mother, she also experienced blessed liberty and a proposal of marriage from him. She accepted and once again braced herself in order to stand up against the scrutiny of her mother.

In spite of her mother's half-hearted approval of her forthcoming marriage, it never happened for he backed out. The reason seemed silly to her at the time but now with hindsight she realized he didn't really fit into her life. It dawned on her that their relationship had been based on the "what if's" of the past.

Missed opportunities cannot be recaptured to resolve what could have been, and what existed in the past will not always fit into what the present has become. They were both unprepared to enter into a realistic relationship. Although she was hurt, she was not devastated. She had to honestly admit that it was her pride that was hurt and what she dreaded the most were those infamous words that would surely come out of her mother's mouth, "I told you so."

Hannah's next love was a drifter. However, he brought excitement to what seemed like a dull existence. He stirred up her feelings into heights of ecstasy, but his mixed messages quickly sent her down into the dumps. She didn't know if she was coming or going with him. At times she felt like an emotional yo-yo. He had the uncanny ability to lead her along with certain looks, and then throw a curve ball at her by flirting with another woman. He seemed like a restless wave on the ocean of life, and admitted that he wasn't ready to be corralled by any woman.

At times Hannah was willing to let it be. She kept a casual friendship with him, but he always threw caution to the wind in such times by openly pursuing her. What caused the greatest confusion to her was his kiss. Every time he kissed her, bells, whistles, and fireworks would go off, setting aflame her feelings for him. She was aware of his restlessness, but felt that the love of a good woman would give him enough reason to settle down.

Surprisingly, it was during this fickle romance that three other men were also vying for her affections. One was sturdy in his character while the other two were flashy like the drifter. The sturdy one was like an old shoe that comfortably fit as a trusted friend, while the other two possessed questionable intentions. One was attracted to her standing in the community, and the other to her inheritance. Although these two had their different points of attraction, the idea of being used for possible self-serving gain eventually turned her off to both of them.

Unwillingly, as she looked into the mirror to see her own selfish ways, she had to realize that she had taken for granted and used the friendship of the one she viewed as the sturdy "old shoe" in her life.

How many times did she seek that "old shoe" out for companionship when it was convenient? She had no real attraction towards him, while with the second man there was a temporary attraction until she realized that his intentions toward her were dishonorable.

Meanwhile, the pursuit of the "old shoe" and the "dishonorable suitor" lit the feet of the restless soul of the drifter and off he went. Although he came back a year later to start up with Hannah where he had left off with her, she was guarded. He had not bothered to keep in touch with her. The lack of investment caused the fiery passion to be completely distinguished, and when she kissed him to see if the passion could be relit again, she discovered there was nothing there.

Admittedly, nothing substantial had ever been present in their relationship. Hannah quickly learned that feelings are fickle; they come and go according to circumstances. They are self-serving and lack any real commitment. Without any foundation of commitment and trust, feelings of this nature will go out with the changing tide, leaving no anchor behind in which to establish a relationship that will move forward into maturity. She concluded that genuine love had to be an anchor that proves enduring and lasting.

As she thought about these different relationships, she realized each one made her soul restless. She wasn't willing to settle for an "old shoe," that was void of attraction nor was she willing to accept leftovers from the drifter. It was then that she realized a relationship based on mere feelings must be constantly stirred up with passion. Such feelings have a short fuse and will prove to be temporary in the end. Clearly, love is more than passionate feelings. If these fickle feelings find no other outlet except to be restless, they will always be seeking, always be on the move to find something, to find anything that will catch the seeker's fancy and sentiment.

Now she came to the latest relationship. As the memories began to march in front of her, the anger, the pain, and the bitterness once again welled up in her like a volcano and spilled out in a torrent of rage. How could this have happened? And, yet she knew how it happened. She was desperate to have life and love on her own terms, making her vulnerable. She was impatient to experience her future, making her a target. She was ripe for the picking. And, pick he did!

He had simply stopped in her small community to have his car serviced. Supposedly everything about their meeting was a matter of fate. She had been standing and talking with a few of her friends on the sidewalk, when it seemed he immediately identified her as being the "one". He swooped down like a bird of prey, plucked her up in a whirlwind romance, and carried her off into a world of excitement. It happened so fast. One minute she was single, the next married.

She shook her head as she wondered what she was thinking. However, she had to admit her mind was not engaged, for her heart was flying high. It seemed all of her expectations were being realized in this strong, tall handsome stranger. His blond hair gave the appearance that he already wore a crown, his mannerism spoke of high society, his attention towards her implied perpetual romance, and his kiss was like currents that could lift her in ecstasy.

At one point the thought that, "it was all too good to be true" flashed before her, but the momentum she was in was too great for her to give such a warning any real consideration. After all, it's the life she always wanted, the type of love she desired, and how could it be wrong? But, wrong it was!

He was a swindler. He cleverly swindled those who had money and would not bother with prosecution because it would amount to nothing more than pocket change to his intended victims. As the facts were brought to the light about his devious ways, it became clear that such pocket change amounted to thousands of dollars. She had been the "one" alright—the one to be part of his latest scheme concerning her own mother and her mother's business associates. After all, her mother would not prosecute her son-in-law. Hannah, in her innocence and naïve state, had allowed her trust to entangle her into the plot, buying into the lie.

In her first relationship her pride had been hurt, and in her second relationship with the drifter her feelings grew cold, but in this relationship, her very being had been crushed. He put it best, "She had been a beautiful, fragile glass and he had broken it."

The harsh reality is that when the truth came to the light, she was married to a dead man. He had borrowed a name from a dead man and his identity amounted to nothing more than a façade. Everywhere she turned in relationship to him, she found herself falling into confusion and emptiness. The man she had married was a fake and the man she was married too was a stranger. He had used her like a condiment to put the right touches to his latest scheme to get her mother involved with a false investment company.

Although he claimed he loved her and regretted using her, the point is he still used her in his scram. When his scram was uncovered, he claimed he was going to cease from such activities and go straight. The problem was that he didn't see that his conniving ways were plainly illegal and morally wrong. He did not regret his activities, he just regretted that he had been discovered and had hurt her. Even though he claimed to make things right with past victims, he fell short of setting the record right where her mother was concerned. Later she would find out that he was not completely forthcoming about setting matters right.

Regrettably, she had put a scheme together to give him a taste of his own medicine. She knew she was lowering herself to his level, but her unabated hurt and anger had caused a cold wind to blow across her broken heart and raw emotions. In her mind, she would swindle him to obtain money from him to repay her mother before she caught on to his devious activities. She secretly admitted to herself that since her relationship with her mother was difficult, it would be easy for her to let her husband take advantage of her and her associates, but realistically she knew that she was brought up to be honest and responsible.

She learned you cannot con a con. Even though her husband knew what she was doing, he played ignorant. She received the money and managed to cover up his scheme before her mother and business associates caught on to his games. When she informed her husband what she had done, he had told her he was already prepared to do right. Later, she discovered that he had put the money aside but was waiting to see what would happen in their relationship. No doubt, he would have paid it back to regain her confidence, but most likely would have kept it if he felt the relationship wasn't going his way. Even though she had lowered herself to his deceptive ways, she felt she rightfully forced him to pay back the money that he had received from his latest scam.

Clearly, he had hoped that what she had experienced in their whirlwind romance would outweigh the fact he had used her love in an unbecoming way. It amazed her that he had the cleverness to patiently set up his victims to be swindled out of money, but he didn't have the foresight to count the cost when the dam, holding back the consequences, would finally break through the thin veneer of his lies. She knew she still loved him, but what was shattered was not her love for him, but the glue of trust that holds love together had been weakened and shattered.

Since she found out about being a silly pawn in his game, her love for him became chaotic. Feelings from every spectrum flooded the terrain of her heart, overwhelming her soul with scorn. Admittedly, she did not know how to feel about anything. The only thing she was sure of was that he had betrayed her trust. He clearly played on her love for him, using her heart strings to set her up, and her naiveté to seduce her into his game; but, it was the betrayal of her trust that torpedoed the flimsy foundation that held up their infant relationship. Without trust there was nothing to hold up what was, and there was no anchor to attach to any real foundation to secure any future relationship. When the light of truth was put on their relationship it fell into utter ruin like a house of cards.

Even though she learned his real name, she still had no idea of who he was. He appeared to have no past; therefore there was no starting point to build on. Did he really know who he was? After all, he lived another man's life. How could she be sure of his real identity, and with all the unanswered questions, how could there be any future for them? She fought from becoming part of the nothingness she fell into when she tried to wade through the mystery. She was not good at mysteries and intrigue, even though her life had taken on both elements when she got involved with him.

Did it really matter? Legally, she had married a dead man. Even though divorce was mentioned, how could she obtain a legal divorce from a man who bore another's name? Ironically, a car accident took care of the legal challenges. He not only loved fast living, but fast cars. The latter left him a statistic.

Fortunately, he died under the umbrella of his correct name, leaving her the sole beneficiary of all of his earthly goods. As she discovered, his past was muddled. Born in poverty, raised by a young, immature widowed father on the streets of a big city, and orphaned in his teenage years due to substance abuse, he hotly started to pursue the American dream. He had decided to never be poor again. Due to his street education, he bypassed the hard work and took the fast lane of high class fraud.

Hannah could not fault him for wanting better, but when one resorts to taking the low road, that individual will ultimately miss the high road, and fall into ruin. Now she was left with the fallout of something she didn't understand, and something that was not of her own doing.

As Hannah looked out the window at the snowy landscape, she realized that the loneliness she felt was mainly due to her heart being left cold by the circumstances. She instinctively knew that she could not let her heart remain in such a chilled state. She was not wired to function in such a way. If her heart didn't change she would become a stranger to herself. But, what could melt her icy heart?

She remembered that the community was ready to kick off the Christmas season that very night. She was brought up in religion, but it was not a reality to her heart. She celebrated the birth of Christ on Christmas and His resurrection at Easter, but she never really gave it much thought. The religion she possessed was so proper, so rigid, and something she tacked onto her life on certain days, at specific times, but it was not part of her way of life.

In that room she realized she was alone because she had no one to turn to, no one to make sense out of her jumbled life. How many times in church did the pastor exhort his congregation to turn to the Lord in times of need, seek Him in times of uncertainty, and to wait before Him until a matter was resolved? Yet, she had not turned to Him because He was a matter of theology and not someone who would personally become involved with the foolishness of her plight.

As she thought about the void in her spiritual life, something began to stir in her. Call it a need, an impression, a flickering flame, but she felt a compulsion to cry out to this unseen God in desperation, to seek Him in her confusing mess and to fling herself on Him in utter helplessness. As she cried out, the idea of a sweet baby in a manger began to take hold of her. God had given the gift of His Son to the world. He knew His Son would die, but what did the famous scripture state, "For God so loved the world that He gave His only begotten Son." And, why would God give His Son? So man could be saved, so he could receive eternal life.

It suddenly dawned on her that she had been seeking the wrong things in the wrong places. God sent His Son into this world to bring life. It is by finding the essence of real life that one can discover true love. She had been looking to others for love to find her life; instead of looking to God to find her life in order to secure lasting love. She realized that when she looked for what she thought she wanted, she actually overlooked what she had need of--to experience the love her heart truly desired.

The error of her thinking and ways became a sharp sword of truth that penetrated the coldness of her heart. As the truth went deep, she began to feel undone before a loving but holy God. By doing her own thing, she was shunning what was true and right according to heaven. She could blame all of her trials on others, but it was her foolish, immature thinking and ways that brought her to this barren place of despair, sin, shame, guilt, and brokenness.

In her state she could do nothing but fling herself on the Lord. She had failed Him and there was no way of getting around it. She needed His forgiveness, His grace, and His restoration; she needed to be saved from herself. She began to cry out for mercy, seek forgiveness, and ask for deliverance from all those things that had beset her, bankrupt her, and left her wounded and broken. As her tears flowed, she felt gentle warmth envelop her. It was as if each tear was merging into a stream of cleansing water that rushed over her like the billows of the deep. Each wave brought a wondrous flow of love, mercy, and grace to wash away the debris from her broken life.

She could not say how long she was in the water of God's love, feeling the currents of His mercy and grace, while experiencing the strong anchor of humility, but she knew she was cleansed and for the first time, she was experiencing Jesus' life pulsating through her inner being. She wanted to jump with joy and declare her discovery as to the identity of the real gift of Christmas. Then she remembered the Christmas celebration that was about to begin. She saw her opportunity to rejoice with others by singing Christmas carols.

She hurried to the coat closet to seize her coat, grab her boots, and locate her gloves. Before she knew it she was on her way to the local park. She felt as if she was walking on air.

***

With new buoyancy in her walk, Hannah was ready to meet the world once again, even if it was the small world of her community. It seemed lately as if the place she grew up in had become a big anchor around her neck. Since her disastrous relationship with her now deceased husband, Hannah had stayed away from the attention of the townspeople. There were always rumors and suspicions that followed in such matters. She felt the whole community would be looking at her with pity or scorn, but now she didn't care about the possible side glances or the whispering that might follow her. She thought to herself, *Let them look and hopefully they will see a new Hannah, a Hannah who has been awakened, raised from the depths of hopelessness, and resurrected to discover a new life of healing and hope.*

As expected, there was a throng of local citizens present for the festivities beginning at the town's Christmas tree. They were ready to celebrate and so was she. And, sing she did! With everything in her she sang of the babe who was born in a manger, of a Son sent from above, and of the glory of heaven declaring the entrance of the Savior into the world. She sang of the shepherds and the three wise men. She was caught up with such rapture that she didn't notice those around her. She was in another realm.

Before she knew it, the singing was over, but not her joy. As she walked towards the town's gazebo, looking at the wonders of the Christmas lights, she became aware of someone behind her. She turned just in time to bump into Phil.

Phil Jones had been the one man who often stood on the perimeter of her romantic notions. Even though he could blend into the crowd of normalcy, there were aspects to his looks and mannerisms that caused him to eventually stand out. He stood straight, reflecting a sturdy, lean build. His face had sharp features to it, but each feature came together nicely, and the sharpness was softened by his gentle countenance. She had been attracted to him, but he only let her in so far. He had lost his wife and had not been prepared to risk getting involved in another relationship. Although she felt he was attracted to her, he wasn't willing to pursue it.

When he discovered what had happened to her in her latest relationship, he had reached out to her with friendship and kindness. He had quietly offered her a listening ear. Although she was not willing to share any details with him, she had greatly appreciated the strength he indirectly brought to her fragile state.

With a questioning look he asked her, "Where are you going, Hannah?"

Hannah looked into his kind brown eyes. With gaiety in her voice, she answered, "I was just going to the gazebo to get a closer look at the Christmas tree and decorations."

Phil offered her his arm. She accepted his invitation and they walked together to the impressive and colorful display set before them.

The silence was interrupted by Phil, "Something is different about you Hannah."

It amazed her that he would even notice. She glanced at him, "I hope whatever difference you're detecting is good."

"It must be good, because you have a sparkle in your eye and a glow on your face." Phil paused as if to study her with a sideways glance and went on, "I've been worried about you. You almost seemed like you had given up on everything."

As they made their way up the gazebo stairs, he paused again as if to choose his words carefully. As they stepped onto the platform, he gently let go of her arm so he could face her and finish his train of thought. "I know this business with your late husband has been extremely difficult for you, but-t-t...you're too young and beautiful to let this keep you down forever."

Surprised that he would let her see his concern for her and notice her in such a way, she murmured, "It's very kind of you to have such concern, and I truly have appreciated the friendship you have shown me. But, please be assured that I'm fine."

285

However, not wishing to leave it at what she considered to be a mediocre description of her condition, she added, flashing him a smile, "I'm not simply fine, but I'm better than ever!"

Phil looked at her whimsically.

She continued, "You see Phil, I finally found what I was looking for." She sighed as she collected her thoughts. "I was looking for love and tonight I found it in the most surprising way."

Confused by her statement, Phil pressed her, "You found love tonight, so soon, I don't understand Hannah?"

Hannah could see the confusion in Phil's face. She took his hand and patted the top of it with her other hand as a means to calm him in his state.

"What I'm trying to say, Phil, is that I found everything I was looking for in Christ. Everything I have desired can be found in who He is and what He did for each of us on the cross. Tonight I found love in the form of forgiveness and restoration. In forgiveness I found salvation and in salvation I found hope."

After her explanation, Hannah noticed how Phil's eyes had a faraway look. It was as though he had become lost in another time.

"Phil! Phil, what are you thinking about?"

By calling his name, Hannah brought him back to the present.

"I'm sorry Hannah. I was remembering when I lost my wife. I became angry at God, as well as lost in my grief. However, in the back of my mind, I knew Jesus was the only One who could get me through my ordeal."

Stopping for a brief second to check the emotions welling up in him, he continued, "It took me awhile before I finally turned back to Him, but I knew until I did that the inner vacuum that was becoming larger and larger would eventually swallow me into an abyss of hopelessness."

By this time emotions were causing Phil's voice to waver and Hannah detected tears escaping from the corner of his eyes. They left a glistering trail on his cheeks that reflected the Christmas lights.

Trying to gain control of his voice by taking a deep breath, he preceded to share with her what had been pent up since the death of his wife. "It was only when I turned back to Him that I found healing for my broken, empty heart. The journey hasn't been an easy one, but it has proven to be a blessing in different ways."

Hannah was surprised when he looked deeply into her eyes, causing her to feel as if he was peering into the secret places of her heart. "Hannah, I have some idea of what you have been going through. It's true I didn't experience the betrayal as you did, but the loss of one you love is a great loss. I have been praying for you that God would meet you and make the Lord Jesus Christ real to you. I knew that Jesus was the only One who could bring peace to your soul. Obviously, He has answered my prayer. I know He has answered my prayers in the past, but to know how He touched you tonight is proving to be humbling and overwhelming for me."

Hannah was shocked that Phil would pray for her or that he had that type of spiritual depth to him.

Now that the dam was open, Phil was not about to be silent. He wouldn't be deterred from getting off his chest what had been burdening him down.

"Hannah, you know I'm attracted to you." Phil struggled to avoid tripping over his words while at the same time making an attempt to spill out the thoughts of his heart. "Well, to be honest with you, Hannah, I'm quite fond of you, but I knew you were restless, looking for something I could never give you. I felt that I would never measure up, and unless such restlessness was out of your system you would always live in the "what if's" of a fantasy world. I realized that this last relationship was the knife that cut away the root of such dreams, and it greatly devastated you. But, it actually gave me some hope where we are concerned. For your difficulties, I'm sorry, but can you consider what has come out of it?"

Hannah's emotions were flip-flopping like a fish out of water. In spite of her emotional roller coaster, she was sure of two things: that she couldn't trust her emotions and that Phil was right in his evaluation about her. She now understood why he avoided her, and in those rare times when he attempted to move towards her, he backtracked to once again hide behind his wall.

Phil's voice broke through the roller coaster ride she was on, "Hannah, what are you thinking? I hope I haven't brought any more confusion to you."

Hannah looked into his face and smiled. "I'm reminded of a simple truth, 'When we look for what we think we want, we can overlook what we have need of, or what is important.' Tonight I was reminded that often the life we seek is right in front of us."

As if almost afraid to breathe, Phil asked her, "Have you found your life?"

She sighed, "Let's just say I have found the source of life in God, and I believe He is the one who is preparing me for the life He desires to give me. And, does that mean the life He desires to give me has something to do with you? That's a good possibility but only time will tell."

Phil shook his head in agreement and added, "Meanwhile, where do we go from here?"

With a smile on her face and a twinkle in her eye, Hannah said, "Well, Phil, we have a good start. We have become good friends during my various ordeals. Good, healthy marriage relationships usually find their foundations in good friendships."

Hannah could tell by the look on Phil's face that he was agreeing with her assessment. He took her hand in his and smiled as he looked up at the arched entryway under which they stood. She followed the direction of his gaze to discover that they were standing under mistletoe.

Phil looked at Hannah, "Should we break tradition?"

Hannah smiled, "We should never break a longstanding tradition."

Phil grinned. Then he gently put his hands of her shoulders, looked into her eyes and softly said, "Merry Christmas, friend." Tenderly he slowly leaned over and gently kissed her on the cheek.

But we are all as an
unclean thing, and all
our righteousnesses
are as filthy rags; and
we all do fade as a leaf;
and our iniquities, like
the wind, have taken us away
(Isaiah 64:6)

Damaged Goods

Amy Lawrence stood glaring at Ted Larson. The son of the richest man in town stood before her with a smirk on his face. Although he was a strapping young man with the looks of the iconic celebrity, Brad Pitt, he often boasted a prideful, cruel demeanor that caused his countenance to take on a dark sinister appearance. Ted had always been a snob who cleverly bullied people with his elitism, mental games, and cruel mockery. When she first met him in church, she knew he was not someone she desired to befriend regardless of his looks or status. Eventually, she distinguished that it was that darkness that had initially caused her to take note of his mannerisms which repulsed her.

She was also very aware that Ted was clever in his usage of words. Like the sport he effectively played in college, he was also a "tennis player" when it came to delivering certain jabs, while at the same time proving to be a savvy lawyer in his presentation. He knew how to plant innuendoes into the minds of people so that any false accusation or fallout couldn't be traced back to him. He used every occasion as a courtroom to present his case to strip and whittle down anyone who didn't meet with his approval. Therefore, the stinging words that followed his smirk were not surprising to Amy. She knew that he meant them to resonate through the college dining hall for those who desired to dine on any juicy gossip.

In a clear voice he sent his first jab, "Your old man deserved to be fired as a minister. After all, how can he be an effective minister when his daughter is, what should I say," he paused long enough to let his barbed words sink in, then finished with, "questionable in her moral activities, if you know what I mean?"

"No I don't know what you mean Ted, unless you are a firsthand witness of--or a participant in, the questionable conduct you are making reference to?"

Amy was surprised to see that her retort actually stunned Ted for a second. However, she knew his caliber. He couldn't let anyone get the best of him. She braced herself, while trying to patiently wait for him to slam the ball back in her court.

She had not planned this confrontation, but in his backhanded way he had successfully challenged her in this most inappropriate place. He meant to entertain himself at her expense with his famous cat and mouse game. She had watched him set different people up many times before, and go in for the kill as he pounced on them.

Even though the outward battle was proving intense, there was a greater battle going on within her. Amy sensed fear beginning to peek around the corners of her emotional chaos. She felt hatred seething through the open cracks of the fragile walls of her restraint. She wasn't sure how long she could keep her attitude and response in check. However, as the flow of her hatred began to break down the restraint of her resolve, it started to fan her anger into a consuming fire that she knew couldn't be easily controlled once it broke down the remaining part of her protective wall.

Her hatred momentarily shocked her and brought her back to her senses. How could a committed Christian girl hate with such passion and still consider herself godly? She realized at that second that she didn't fear Ted; rather, she feared the momentum of her own anger towards him. She was frightened that if she allowed it to be unleashed, she could end up doing the unthinkable. What escalated her concern about her anger even more so was that she realized she didn't care about what happened to her or the possible consequences that might follow. It was almost as if a blanket of numbness had been thrown over her conscience and reasoning. Everything in her wanted to wipe that smirk off of his face at any cost and make him pay for the damage he had brought to her and her family.

As she fought to lasso and take captive every emotion, feeling, desire, and thought that was parading in front of her, the smirk Ted had managed to maintain on his lips began to slowly crawl behind a look of uneasiness. Amy had no idea what her face was reflecting, but she could sense great flashing intensity in her brown eyes. Her usual full lips were compressed into a thin line of unadulterated determination, and her face had to be flushed because she could feel the combination of her hatred and anger caused the temperature of her emotional momentum to rise into a crescendo that was greater than any anger she had felt in the past. It was not only hitting the "top of the charts" but it was spilling over the borders of her resolve, creating a reservoir that was quickly filling up with tumultuous emotional waves.

It was clear that the dams of her resolve were falling apart and she had to quickly act to prevent devastation. She decided she needed to step on top of her emotions and wait for his next move.

At that point, it seemed like time was standing still for her. The events of the last two months were flashing in her mind. These events were threatening to destroy the very fabric of her and her family. Instead of slamming the ball back at her, Ted lopped one in her direction. It was his attempt to defuse the matter and keep control of the situation by taking on an innocent stance in order to claim ignorance.

"I don't know what you mean, Amy. My father was doing what he thought was right for the sake of the reputation of the church. I had nothing to do with it."

"Don't act innocent with me, Ted Larson," she said in a low tone to keep from screaming. "I know who informed your father about the so-called 'rumors'. And, don't bother to appear noble by trying to act as if you're trying to protect the reputation of some unknown third person. You know whose reputation is being smeared by you, MINE!"

She sent an ominous warning to him. "But, for being so smart, Ted, I must say that it was the dumbest thing you've ever done. Now the truth can come out and we'll see who is left standing with reputation intact."

For one second, fear made a fast appearance in Ted's eyes, but was quickly replaced with a hard glint. "I don't know what you're talking about Amy?"

"Oh, yes you do! Apparently it's not enough that you've tried to destroy me, but now you're after my whole family. I've remained quiet until now, but no more...NO MORE, you hear me Ted Larson?"

Ted shot back with an intimidating tone, "Don't you threaten me! Who do you think you are? You don't know who you're dealing with!"

To Amy, Ted's remark was like an open door, and she saw her opportunity to slam dunk him with one final swoop. "I'll tell you who you are, you're a coward, a thief, and the lowest type of snake there is, and the whole town will know it before this matter is over with."

It was clear that Amy's remarks were hitting the target. Ted's countenance became dark, his eyes flashed with anger, and one side of his lip curled up at the edge. As he began to speak the tone of his voice betrayed his internal rage in spite of his best efforts to control it.

"I'm warning you! If you try anything, or say anything, you'll answer for it."

With a calm but weary voice, she said, "What can you possibly take from me or my family that you already haven't taken? Just what will you do to harm me or my family more than you already have? Thanks to you, we are paying for something I don't understand." She grappled with trying to control her tone and emotions, but she couldn't stop the flow of words that were coming out of her mouth. "I may not understand your motives, but I know a couple of things. I know according to your past pattern you'll continue to make us pay, but I know this time you'll be going down with us. The day of reckoning is coming Ted Larson, and all the money in the world is not going to spare you or your father from paying the consequences."

Upon her last remark, Ted started towards her. She knew according to the look on his face that she was possibly in harm's way. Amazingly, she wasn't afraid. Let him show his violent side and she would have another reason to talk to the police. The truth is, she didn't care what he did to her. In the back of her mind, she knew he needed to be stopped, and if it took her body to be battered or rendered a corpse, so be it.

Before Ted could reach her, Jonathan Davis stepped in front of her and positioned himself between the two of them. Jonathan was a known friend of Ted's. He was a college football player who stood 6'4" and weighed 225 pounds of pure lean muscle. Besides having a physique that made him stand out, he also had beautiful dark red hair that was always trimmed and nicely combed. His clear blue eyes proved to be a perfect match with his hair. They both highlighted a handsome face that often mirrored kindness and compassion that were clearly inspired by his Christian faith.

Amy had wondered how Jonathan could be Ted's friend. They were opposite in every way. She observed that Jonathan would often keep Ted honest. It was obvious to most that if anyone could reason with Ted it would be Jonathan. When the football player was around, Ted could prove to even be cordial. She believed that the only reason Ted came to any Christian activities was because Jonathan encouraged it.

The tone in Jonathan's voice told her that Ted's advancement towards her was thwarted. There would be no physical encounter taking place between them today. The confrontation was over.

"Ted, enough! You need to cool off," Jonathan exhorted.

Amy could tell that Ted didn't want to drop it, but he realized Jonathan was not about to budge. His body was firmly established in front of her and posed to stop any further encroachment on Ted's part.

Ted nodded his head in resignation, turned around and walked out of the dining room. It was then that Jonathan turned around to face Amy. Even though his blue eyes penetrated into her soul, she didn't feel any judgment from him. She knew in the back of her mind she had probably made a fool out of herself, which in turn made her feel alien and undeserving towards the kindness he was expressing in his look. She found herself looking away from him.

"I'm sorry you had to witness this..." She paused as her mind fumbled with different words trying to find the right one, "... unpleasant situation Jonathan, but I want to thank you for putting an end to it."

She looked up and briefly smiled at him, then turned around and began to walk away.

However, she could not escape his penetrating eyes or his questioning voice, "Where are you going Amy?"

Amy stopped and looked down at the floor. "I'm going home."

"Do you need a ride?" Jonathan asked.

She turned once again to face him, "Thank you for the offer, but the transit bus will do, and you need not bother."

He smiled, "It wouldn't be any bother to take you home. After all, you've been through quite an ordeal." Jonathan paused and added, "Besides, I want to make sure you get home alright."

Amy felt herself numbly shaking her head in agreement with him.

Jonathan walked up to her and gently took her arm to guide her. As she walked beside him, she found herself feeling protected for the first time in days. It was as if she could relax and allow herself to let go of all of the tension that had been building up in her for the last couple months. Admittedly, she felt like she had been a windup toy, but during the confrontation, she began to quickly unwind. It was at that point she also realized that without the tension, she was beginning to feel a certain vulnerability that caused her to feel insecure.

He led her to his vehicle and opened the door for her to get into the passenger side. Once he made sure she was in, he closed the car door. She was touched by his act of respect and consideration. He was treating her like a respectable woman. It touched a nerve that caused tears to well up in her eyes. As he gracefully folded himself into the driver's side of his Jeep Cherokee, she turned to look out the window to hide the evidence of her unexpected sentiment. She silently chided herself that she was being silly about it.

As Jonathan put the key in the ignition, he noticed Amy focusing her attention out the window. Instead of starting his Jeep, he settled back in his seat.

"Amy, are you alright?"

Still feeling numb and vulnerable, Amy responded with a quiet tone of uncertainty, "You're probably wondering what that was all about back at the dining hall."

"It's none of my business, but if you need a friend to listen to you or a shoulder to lean on, I have both a good ear and a pretty big shoulder."

Puzzled by his response, she turned to look at him and blurted out, "Aren't you a good friend of Ted's?"

Jonathan half-way chuckled, "I've shown myself friendly to Ted, but our relationship is based more on a mutual understanding. When Ted decides he can use me or is lonely, he then seeks me out for companionship."

"I wouldn't say that is much of a friendship, would you?" Amy asked.

"It isn't, Amy, but I know Ted needs a friend. I've always felt that one day his world will cave in around him. The so-called 'friends' he has right now are users like he is and will abandon him when the waters get rough. I want to be there for him so that I can speak the truth into his life about the direction he's going and his need for Jesus to truly be His Lord and Savior."

Jonathan stopped to let the words sink into Amy's understanding before he continued. "From what I witnessed between the two of you in the dining hall, it sounds like his world is about to cave in around him."

Amy struggled with what to say to this gentle man. She wanted to believe that Jonathan could be a friend she could trust, and that he was honorable. As she struggled with what to do, she had to ask herself, "*What could a man understand about my plight,*" but she couldn't ignore the obvious. His act of kindness was still fresh in her mind. She knew she needed a friend, someone she could talk to. The truth is she felt like she was ready to lose it if she didn't rid herself of the heavy burden that was weighing her down.

At this point she decided to test Jonathan. She would pose some questions to him to see how he handled them. Each test he passed, she would bring him further into her plight. If he proved to possess the sincerity to be her friend, she would then let all the chips fall as they may. She knew in time the truth would come out, and many who had any interest in the matter would choose sides according to preferences and biased opinions. In her mind, if Jonathan was willing to listen and wade through the matter so that he could choose which side he wanted to be on. She would simply give him the facts from which to glean.

Amy presented her first test. "I'm not sure you want to know the truth, Jonathan. You may not like it, and besides that, you may have to choose a side."

His response showed he possessed wisdom. "Amy, the only side I will choose is the side of righteousness. Things happen among people. If sin exists, as believers we can judge the wrong of it, but when it comes to taking sides, there is only one side a Christian can take and that is the side of Christ. It must exemplify His truth, His ways, and His righteousness in the end."

Jonathan's response had a calming effect on her frayed emotions. In Amy's mind she had to admit that he passed the first test.

She wanted to somehow prepare him for the ugliness that was ripping through the very fabric of her being. "It's not a pretty picture Jonathan. You will not be able to forget what you'll hear today, and it might influence how you look at others, e-e-e-especially me."

Jonathan's reply showed he had a realistic view of the world, "Life is life and at the core of it are darkness, tragedy, and destruction. But, until a matter comes to the light, there is no hope of changing the course or end results of it. Truth illuminates a matter so there can be healing, forgiveness, reconciliation, and restoration."

To Amy, it seemed as if Jonathan recognized the moves she was making to prepare him. It also appeared to Amy that he could handle the secret that was robbing her of her inner peace.

As she wrestled with the decisions before her, Jonathan added, "Amy, you don't have to prepare me for whatever has happened. I may not like what I hear, but it's not my place to carry any judgment towards you or Ted. I simply want to be your friend," Jonathan paused and added, "and encourage and help you in any way I can."

Jonathan's last words seemed to serve as a sign that it was time to spill the beans. The last bit of Amy's resolved melted away into an abyss of silence. She either had to share her secret or flee from the vehicle to stop the matter from coming out.

She struggled with how to begin. She wanted to summarize it and avoid giving the whole ugly situation any real undue attention. She didn't want pity or placating sympathy. She wanted her dark perspective challenged in hopes of finding answers to the endless "whys" parading in front of her. She also needed realistic advice that would break through her confusion. She wanted someone to hear the struggles of her heart.

Amy took a deep breath and slowly began her descent into the hellish nightmare. "Well-I-I-I-I, it started two months ago. I was out with my Christian friends, enjoying dinner before attending a Christian concert with them. We were joyfully fellowshipping when I noticed Ted out of the corner of my eye. At the same time one of my friends also noticed him and invited him to sit with us. He sat in the chair next to me. Even though I've never been comfortable around him, I've always tried to be cordial to him."

She paused as she collected the facts in her mind, and then proceeded. "I had to excuse myself and go to the restroom. When I returned, my friends were talking to Ted about going to the concert. I sat down and finished my coke and got ready to leave. It seemed that within a matter of minutes I began to feel dizzy. My friend noticed something was going on with me and asked me if I was alright. I knew that they were ready to leave for the concert. Since I had my own car, I told her that I didn't feel right and to go on without me. In my mind, I would wait a few minutes to see how I felt and if I became worse, I would go home."

Once again Amy had to stop to collect her thoughts. "To be honest, I don't remember what happened after that. All I know is that I woke up in my car confused, sick, and my clothes in disarray. I didn't know what time it was or where I was, but I had a sick sense something terrible had happened to me, and nothing would be the same ever again."

Amy didn't have to say anything more to Jonathan. She could tell he had come to the right conclusion. His face paled. She had been the victim of "date rape", but the truth was there was no real date; nevertheless, she had been drugged and raped.

In a hushed voice, Jonathan asked, "Was it Ted?"

"I suspect it was him because he was still sitting next to me when I started becoming dizzy. I remember him telling me, 'I'll take care of you.' Boy, did he ever take care of me!"

Amy's voice trailed off as she was reliving how she felt in the car when she awoke to find herself lost in a dark hole—afraid, feeling violated in some way, and sick.

Jonathan's kind voice pulled her back to the present, "What happened next, Amy?"

"I felt around for my purse in the darkness of my car, found my phone, and called my parents. They came and took me to the hospital. When I told the hospital officials what happened, they called the police. A rape kit was produced, and the nurse took my blood to have it tested. Even though I was still somewhat confused when the doctor told us the results, the words that stood out to me are that I had indeed been violated. The next thing that caught my attention was when they asked me if I wanted the morning-after pill to ensure that there would be no unwanted pregnancy."

Once again Amy became lost in a tangled world of haunting memories and unbearable decisions.

Jonathan continued to gently prod her, "What did you do when you were confronted with what must have seemed like unspeakable circumstances?"

"'Unspeakable' doesn't touch what I was faced with. I knew I couldn't take the morning-after-pill because two horrific wrongs will never make a right. I knew I had to trust God with the outcome even though I knew in the back of my mind that if I found I was pregnant I would probably regret my decision. And now,..." her voice trailed off as she became entangled in the haunting whirlwind of sick feelings, unbearable sights, and cruel sounds that continued to bombard her.

Tears were once again threatening to make their appearance. "True to my fears, it appears to be a reality. I think that I'm pregnant."

It was obvious to Amy that Jonathan struggled to veil his emotions and thoughts. However, her last statement seemed to leave him breathless. It was as though a pin had been put in a balloon.

"Jonathan, I'm afraid." She stopped to collect her thoughts. "It's amazing how brave you can be when you don't have to face the reality of a matter, but when you become another statistic, you find out what you're made of. I've discovered that I'm not strong because I now wish I had taken the easy way out. I'm not honorable because I have to fight from hating Ted and doing everything in my power to destroy him. I even questioned my own Christianity."

Amy could see that Jonathan knew she was fragile and she sensed that he wanted to comfort her with the right words, but he was struggling with what to say. She suspected he didn't want his words to come across as being hollow and indifferent, stripping her any further. She sensed he was quietly praying.

When he finally began to speak, it was clear that he was choosing his words carefully. "If I was in your position, Amy, I have no doubt I would feel the same way. The test that comes to Christianity does not come along the line of pretending that we, as believers, are beyond, or immune, from feeling the harsh impact that comes with the trials of being human in a wicked world that rarely plays fair. But, what we must do is honestly face these overwhelming feelings and seek God to preserve our souls and character in such times. He's our source of strength and we can only take courage when we decide to do the right thing, even though later it makes us second guess ourselves and we may end up looking foolish to others for doing it."

To Amy, Jonathan's words brought hope to her heart. As a pastor, her father, Luke Lawrence, always reminded her that it's easy for Christians to forget they are human. They are emotional creatures, and since they are not immune from the temptations, tests, and tribulations of this present world, they are going to taste the bitterness of it as well. He often reiterated that the test of Christianity does not rest in how one feels about a matter, but what one does with it when it comes to decisions, attitudes, and actions.

Jonathan's voice intruded into her thoughts. "What do your parents think about all of this? Is this why there is a conflict between Ted's father and your father?

Amy shook her head 'no' before answering. "My parents have been very supportive, but they don't know that I suspect that Ted is the violator and that I'm pregnant."

"You didn't tell your parents about Ted and the possible pregnancy!" Jonathan response showed he was surprised that she had kept them in the dark about these very important facts.

"I'm pretty sure about being pregnant, but it has not been confirmed. As far as Ted, I know how his father felt about my father's preaching on such subjects as sin and hell, and I guess I was trying to protect my father's reputation. Mr. Larson always chided my father for not being more tolerant. After all, who will come to a church if people hear negative things being preached from the pulpit even if it is part of the salvation message?"

Amy paused before continuing. "Ted apparently gave his father the necessary tool to call a board meeting to bring to light the rumors of indiscretion of the 'only daughter' of the pastor as a political ploy to discredit my father and demand his resignation. It became the necessary proof to me that Ted was the violator. After all, the only ones who would know about the "violation" besides the hospital staff and the police were my parents, the violator, and me.

"Ted overplayed his hand when he did what he did. He didn't realize I held the trump card. He didn't foresee that evidence would be obtained as the means to identify the perpetrator of this act, and now it appears that even more evidence will be available in seven months."

Jonathan interjected what would be obvious to her. "Your parents have a right to know. In fact, they need to know in order to help you to do what is right. The truth must come out, and regardless of the conflict that has played out between Ted's father and your father, I know by what you've told me about your father that in the end he'll do right."

"I plan to tell my parents about both matters," Amy responded. "But I wanted to make sure my motives towards Ted were right when I told them. I have scared myself many times because I really want him to pay in some way, but vengeance belongs to the Lord. I know I need my parents to help me walk through this situation, because at this point I just don't trust myself to make the right decisions."

In spite of her emotional struggles, it was clear to Amy that her Christian virtues were truly winning out in spite of the terrible circumstances. Such knowledge brought some relief to her in the midst of her up and down rollercoaster ride.

"Amy, if there is anything I can do, just let me know."

"There's something you can do for me, Jonathan."

His response was quick, "What is it?"

"Why, why did he..." she shuddered as she said his name, "T-T-T-Ted, do this to me? I never did anything to him. Why do people, or should I say men do terrible things to women who are vulnerable? I've read how when armies attack and defeat a group of people, the victors usually humiliate those they have conquered by violating the women and children. If that is not bad enough, why must men do it within their own society? Who are they humiliating at that point?

"Why do people do terrible things to one another, she groaned. How can they do such . . . ." Amy struggled with her thoughts. It was clear that there were no words to describe the destruction.

She could tell once again that Jonathan was trying to choose his words carefully. "You have asked a lot of questions, Amy. You know as well as I do that at the core of the depraved ways of men is sin. Without civilization man would be nothing more than an animal in his actions, and without God, he is nothing but a moral despot in his ways. Mediocrity will make him dull, sensationalism will make him emotionally fickle, fanaticism will drive him into insanity, obsession will drive him into utter torment, and fear will enfold him into nothingness, a hopeless cycle."

It was obvious to Amy that Jonathan was a philosopher, one who thought deeply about the matters of life. He had sought answers to the "whys," and somehow discovered bits of God's wisdom.

He continued, "The Bible is clear when men violate women, they disgrace their own manhood and betray themselves, for woman was taken from the side of man, and he is to cherish her in the same way he would his own life."

301

He looked at her more intently, took a deep breath and continued, "As for Ted, I can only guess why he committed such an atrocity against you, your womanhood, and your testimony. Maybe he was spoiled and selfish enough to justify taking what he secretly desired, or perhaps he had a fetish to conquer the one person who was not impressed with him, the one person who couldn't be bought or seduced by his good looks, surface charm, and status quo in society. Perhaps in a sick way he's hoping in the end he'll get caught because he knows you wouldn't take such an offense lying down. It's hard to say."

Amy couldn't help but interrupt, "How could he feel good about conquering me in such a deceptive way? Where is the victory in all of this for him, and wasn't my humiliation enough for him? Why did he set out to destroy my family?"

"I think Amy, that it could be the same scenario as David's oldest son Amnon and his half-sister, Tamar. You remember that situation. It's where Amnon secretly lusted after Tamar. He managed to deceitfully get her to himself and ended up violating her. Once he had his way with her, his lust and expectation turned into intense contempt towards her."

He pursed his lips, a slight frown forming on his brow. "My take on it is that at the end of Amnon's wicked action, he was left with an empty victory because the lust fled, the expectation of what could be eluded him, and what he was left with was the awful reality that what he once valued about her, he had not only tainted or destroyed it for another, but for himself."

Amy couldn't help but ask him the question that had been in the back of her mind, "Jonathan is there any really good men left? I know that my father is a wonderful man and I believe my parents are raising my brother, Ben, to be an honorable man," she paused, "and, I don't want to exclude you from such a group, but I've met very few honorable men in my generation."

Jonathan had a slight smile on his face. "Thanks Amy for including me in the list of honorable men. I admit that the pickings among men may seem slim, but it's also true when it comes to finding godly women. Some of the women I have encountered in college are aggressive or manipulative. They seem to see men as slabs of meat that must be examined, or stallions that must perform a certain way. Since they don't demand integrity from themselves, they aren't interested in the character of the men they are pursuing."

He paused briefly to give his last statement a chance to sink in before continuing. "I personally take courage in the fact that no matter how many of our generation are chasing after the gods of lustful pleasure or are bowing before the idolatrous altars of self-serving pursuits, there has to be at least 7,000 believers who have not bent their knees to the Baal of this age." With a smile, he added, "You know what that means for misfits such as us, we don't have to swear off altogether the opposite sex and marriage."

Amy had to smile at his reasoning and quietly agreed with him. It brought some understanding to the unrefined edges of her intense feelings. She knew that it was hard for committed Christians of either gender to find likeminded believers to fellowship with, let alone share their lives with in such an intimate relationship.

She suddenly felt weariness covering her body like a blanket. Jonathan seemed to sense that all of her emotional reserves were completely drained.

"Regardless of how enlightening our talk has been Amy, I need to take you home. Your chariot awaits and all you have to do is point me in the right direction."

Amy closed her eyes during the ride home. Her thoughts were going in every direction. When the car came to a stop, Amy knew she was home. Jonathan got out and opened the door for her. As she turned to exit the vehicle she looked up into his face.

"Jonathan I always wanted to meet the right man and have a godly family. Now, I wonder what decent, honorable man would want a questionable woman with a child. You know what they call women like me." She looked down at the ground. "They call me 'damaged goods.'"

"Amy, look at me."

Amy looked up at him. "Don't let this matter rob you any further. Seek to forgive Ted, because unforgiveness will bring you down to his level. Choose the righteous ways of Christ and He will give you the grace to forgive him from the heart. Meanwhile, know that there is a right man out there for you, and he'll see you for the wonderful person you are.

"As for being 'damaged goods', Amy, we all are 'damaged goods' because of sin. That is why Jesus came and died on the cross. He took our place so that we could be made into a new creation. Remember, it's His blood that cleanses us, His life in us that makes us a new creation, and His Spirit that will bring us to perfection. Amy, in Christ, nothing has changed, you still are His prized, chaste bride."

Tears came to Amy's eyes. She knew that every word Jonathan spoke was true, for the Bible said so. Therefore, by faith she had to quietly say "amen" to it.

"Thank you for reminding me what I have in Christ. No person or violent, profane act can ever take that away from me." She took his big right hand and cradled it between her small hands and smiled, "Good bye."

He nodded slightly. She let go of his hand and slowly began walking towards the house. There was still unfinished business she had to attend to.

***

Amy was feeling uncomfortable. The due date for the baby was close at hand. Everything in her body ached, but today it was different because no matter what she did physical comfort could not be found.

She had to get her mind off of herself. She started looking back on the past seven months since her last encounter with Ted in the dining room of the college. Although her emotions could quickly change and wash over her like a tsunami of anger and despair, she still was able to find consolation because of her faith in Christ and her family support.

After that day of confessing all to Jonathan, Amy shared everything with her parents. Even though she could tell that her father was enraged by the knowledge that the predator was most likely Ted, he kept it under control. And, the support and love both of her parents showed her when she admitted that she was most likely pregnant, took the edge off the anxiety she had been feeling about it. Luke and Lydia Lawrence both surrounded their daughter and as they held her between them, they assured her that they would see her through the ordeal and that even though the circumstances were not pleasant, they would openly welcome the unexpected gift of God into their family. She knew then that her family would be helping her to raise the child in a loving, nurturing home.

After much prayer and consultation among themselves, they agreed that the police had to be informed as to Ted's possible involvement. When the investigating officer was given the story and identity as to the suspected culprit, Amy and her parents could tell that he wasn't sure how much progress he could make to bring resolution to the case. After all, Ted's father, Wilber Larson was a big man in the community. He was a mover and when something stood in his way, he would simply shake it until it was brought down.

It was clear that Wilbur Larson was establishing a kingdom for himself and his only son in the community. Up until five years ago, Ted's mother, Margaret spent much time in the public eye promoting her husband's agenda. Rumor had it that her social life and the personal demands of being married to a mover and shaker caused her to become entangled into the world of alcohol and prescription drug abuse. Wilbur ceased to speak of his wife, and it was clear he was directing all of his attention towards his son. He had high expectations for him, and he expected Ted to continue his legacy. It was clear that he would not lie down and let his only son face any real legal prosecution.

Amy knew that it was not unusual for families like Ted's to wear fragile veneers that simply hid dark secrets and kept the light from exposing any skeletons in the closet. Even though at times she found herself raging against Ted, she would find herself the next minute almost feeling sorry for him. She sometimes shook her head at the emotional fickleness she constantly experienced. She hated the fact that so many times she felt her emotions were out of control.

She learned that the police did question Ted about his presence and possible involvement in the case. Even though he could not deny the fact that he was present that night, he did deny any involvement in the rape and implied it was probably a matter of promiscuity on her part with some secret boyfriend, while his father clearly took offense that his son was being subject to such an investigation, and threatened to sue Amy's family for libel. The accusation he threw at the police was that the reason Amy and her family were targeting Ted was because the former pastor of his church, Luke Lawrence was trying to get back at him for his part in stripping him of his pastoral position. The police told Ted that he could clear the matter up by providing the police department with his DNA, but not surprisingly, he flatly refused.

Amy knew because of the situation that she couldn't continue to physically attend college. Thanks to technology she was able to continue her studies via the computer. She didn't have to worry about running into Ted or about contending with the stares and gossip that would have ensued by those who were familiar with her.

Being able to stay home and continue her studies also gave her time to wade through the different periods of darkness that swept over her. When she realized she was pregnant, she became fearful that she could not love the child in the right way. One night the fear was so overwhelming that she finally confessed it to her mother.

She would never forget her mother's response. "Amy, right now the circumstances surrounding this child's conception is clouding how you feel about the life that is in you, but keep in mind that child is a part of you. And, once the baby begins to grow, so will your affections for the child. And, when the baby finally moves within your womb to awaken you to the fact that you are carrying life within you, much of your confusion will give way to an expectation. You will cease to fear about not loving your child and will begin to become concerned about being the best parent you can be. And, when you finally hold that precious life in your arms, the love and joy you will feel will cause all past pains, fears, and doubts to completely flee away."

She now had to agree with her mother. The more she became aware of the life that was growing inside of her, the desire to nurture and become personally acquainted with this precious child grew. She would never forget the first time she felt the baby kick. A surprised expression broke out on her face as a gleeful exclamation came from her lips.

Another person who caused excitement in Amy when it came to the baby was her brother, Ben. Ben was only ten but he became ecstatic about being an uncle. His first request was that he wanted to choose the name. When questioned about his preference as to the name, Ben stated that he wanted to name the baby, "Tom." When asked why, he admitted that he was quite caught up with Mark Twain's Tom Sawyer. He hoped that as "Tom" grew, he might embark on great adventures with him.

Amy wanted to wait for the birth to discover the child's gender and didn't want her brother to be disappointed. When Ben was told that the baby might be a girl, he became silent. It was clear that it never entered his mind that it could be a girl.

For the next couple of days Ben remained quiet about the matter. No one knew if he had simply dropped the subject. One night as they were sitting at the dinner table talking about preparing for the baby, Ben interjected, "Thomasina".

Everyone stopped talking as all eyes focused on the young boy. Amy's father, Luke asked Ben to repeat what he said.

Ben replied, "Thomasina! That is what we will call the baby if it is a girl."

Amy could tell by the look on Ben's face that he felt he had presented a viable solution to the matter of a name for a girl, while still holding true to his dedication to Tom Sawyer.

Smiles broke out on each face, and Ben was complimented for his tenacity in solving the matter.

In the midst of the healing and light-hearted times, guilt always cropped up to make its appearance. Amy felt guilt towards her father losing his pastoral position. Even though the circumstances were not of her doing, the "if only" plagued her. No matter how many times she relived what happened in order to try to figure out what she could have done differently, the reality remained the same.

One day she confessed her guilt to her father. She always knew her father to be wise. He always accredited such wisdom to the throne of heaven, but what transpired between them was seasoned with grace. Amy's father admitted that he felt all the human emotions of rage and revenge any father would feel about a daughter being violated in such a way, as well as anger towards the unfairness in losing his position.

He told how he knew he couldn't give way to such emotions, and as he ascended into the dark valley of testing that lay before him, he knew that God would not fail to walk through such dark times with him. He also had the assurance that the Lord would take what was intended for evil and turn it around for good.

As the Lord faithfully walked through this dark time with him, he realized that he had lost sight of what was important to the Lord as pastor of the big church. It is not that he failed Him; rather, it was the reality that he became so caught up in the politics of the church that he lost sight of practical ministry to the needy, and lost his fervor to evangelize.

He shared how the Lord used the situation to renew his vision and give him purpose. Like Paul he had to find his own form of tent making to provide for his family, but the Lord opened the door to not only a job, but to a new outlet for ministry. As janitor of a local school, he was able to serve as a living witness of his faith to those around him and make himself available to the young people, some who found themselves attracted to his life.

He realized that if the following generation was not challenged to pursue a vision of a higher calling, and a more excellent way, it would end up producing more Ted Larson's: young people who are like waves on the ocean with no spiritual compass, purpose, or direction. And, thanks to Jonathan, he led Amy and her family to his small church where they found refuge and another open door. Within two months of them attending it, the pastor retired after many years of faithful service, and the church asked her father to accept the position. Not only did Amy's father embark on a new mission field, but God opened up a church where young seeking hearts could come and find love, answers to their questions about life, and a solution to their spiritual plight.

As for Jonathan, just the sound of his name produced such sweetness to Amy's soul. He had proven to be a good friend. In fact, he visited almost every day to encourage her in her studies and ensure proper exercise by walking with her. They had shared much about their personal lives. She discovered that he was Jonathan the III. He apparently carried the names of his grandfather and father, who had clearly established a powerful spiritual legacy in his family. It was obvious that the legacy had influenced his life and it was what she admired about him the most. She also appreciated his sense of humor and even though he was a giant of a man, he was tender in heart and gentle in touch.

It was clear that her family thought a lot of him as well. Her father and Jonathan had many in-depth discussions about spiritual things. He often helped her mother with "handyman" jobs, and Ben acted as if they were best friends. According to Ben, they had shared adventures and even a few secrets.

Amy knew she had avoided admitting to herself her real feelings for Jonathan since she wasn't sure how he felt about her. She was aware that her feelings went deeper than just friendship and suspected the same about his feelings but until he verbally expressed it, she would have no choice but to keep hers hidden.

There were a couple of times it appeared as if he was about to kiss her, but each time he appeared to rethink his act and gracefully backed away from her. Those times left her wondering and guessing, making any advancement in their relationship uncertain. This uncertainty grew in light of future events. It was his senior year, and he would be graduating from college as a CPA. He had already acquired a job with a large firm located a couple of hours drive from her home.

The doorbell interrupted Amy's reminiscing. She heard a man's voice insisting on talking to her father. She became aware that Ben had answered the door and the man's voice seemed almost threatening. She heard her mother's brisk footsteps and then her voice firmly asking what she could do for him. Amy entered the room just in time to see Wilbur Larson practically push his way past Ben. He looked like a charging bull, ready to run over anyone who dared to get in his way.

Larson insisted on seeing Amy's father. His reason was to settle the issue between Luke's daughter and his son once and for all. After all, even though no legal actions had been taken towards his son, suspicion was still hanging over his son's head.

Upon hearing the commotion, Amy's father came to the living room, followed by Jonathan. Jonathan was in the habit of coming through their side door especially if he first encountered her father working outside.

When Wilbur Larson saw Amy's father he charged towards him, "Luke, I thought you were a better Christian man."

Amy's father calmly responded. "Wilbur, I don't know what you mean?"

"I figured you might try to get back at me for getting you fired from the pastoral position, but I never thought you would go after my son. This accusation that is now hanging over his head is threatening to ruin his reputation and future career. You need to agree to drop this accusation against my son right now, or I'll sue you for libel."

Amy could tell her father was trying to keep calm, but his eyes told her that he was struggling to hold his temper in check. "Wilbur, this matter has nothing to do with you and me. It is between your son and my daughter. All suspicion and any threat of legal action can simply go away if your son would agree to DNA testing. If he's not guilty then he has nothing to worry about, but if he's guilty he needs to owe up and face the consequences."

Larson's reply revealed an escalation in frustration. "You know your daughter is lying. She has never liked my son and she is trying to cause all kinds of problems for him. As her father you need to force her to tell the truth."

Initially, the elder Larson had not noticed Amy. She was standing behind him and his focus was on Luke, but he noticed Amy's father's looking behind him. Larson turned around and saw her. The minute his eyes landed on her, it seemed as if he lost all train of thought. It was then that Amy realized that Larson had no idea that she was pregnant. Amy had sworn her closest friends to secrecy about her pregnancy, and since she did her college courses at home, many didn't know about her condition. This included Ted and his family. Wilbur stood absolutely stunned and appeared to become unsure of the situation.

The ringing of the doorbell jerked him back to reality. Amy's mother answered the door. It seemed like the surprises were not over, for it was Ted and his mother. Ted came straight up to his father and asked him what he thought he was doing.

The elder Larson looked at his son, "How did you know where I was?" He then began to bristle at his son's intrusion, "I'm trying to resolve this matter, something you have failed to do, or I should say refused to resolve!"

Ted was ready with an answer, "To answer your first question, your secretary told me that you were heading for this address. And, just, what do you mean about clearing up this matter?"

"What do I mean? Ted, this matter hanging over you will keep you from your future plans. I'm here to stop it once and for all."

"You know I'm not guilty Dad, and I would be glad to stop this nonsense, but as you know," he gestured with his hand towards Amy's parents, "their daughter has it out for me. I would reason with her if I could, but there's no way I can resolve this because I have had no access to her since that day she falsely accused me at college."

"Oh, there is a way you can resolve it, Ted" Jonathan interjected. "Allow the proper authorities to have your DNA."

Ted retorted sarcastically, "Jonathan, how nice it is to see my former friend in the enemy's camp. Now I know where you've been hanging out. What business is it of yours whether I prove my innocence or not."

"Come on Ted! You and I both know why you refuse to take the DNA test," Jonathan challenged him. "It's because you're GUILTY! I don't know why you thought you would get away with it, or maybe in some sick way you want to be caught, but we both know you're guilty, and for the first time in your life, you need to be man enough to face what you have done."

The color began to drain from Ted's face. "You are incorrect about your conclusion Jonathan."

"No Ted, you're WRONG, and the truth is about to come out."

Suddenly Ted became aware of his mother. Her face was white and her body was shaking. He could tell she was staring at something to the side and behind him and whatever was in her sights was unnerving her.

Ted turned around to see Amy who had quietly listened to the Larson men once again attack her character. Amazingly, the Lord had kept her both calm and quiet. However, when Ted saw her in her delicate condition, he stepped backward in a state of disbelief.

Seeing Ted's reaction, Jonathan once again challenged him, "Yes Ted, there's a child involved. And, that child holds the DNA of the father. Don't you think it is time you owe up to what you did to this godly woman, and set the record straight as to who did what to whom, and be man enough to face the consequences?"

The elder Larson had seen his son's reaction to the sight of Amy, "Ted, you're going to take the DNA test to prove to everyone that you're not guilty of what you have been accused of."

Ted numbly shook his head 'no.'

"Ted, as your father I am ordering you to take the test."

Finally, Ted shook himself out of his shocked state, and revealed his frustration. "I will not take the test!" he shouted as he looked at his father.

The elder Larson's face was turning dark red, "You will not defy me! You'll take the test or you'll give me one good reason why you are refusing. And, it better be good!"

It was as if the words almost exploded out of Ted, "It's because I am GUILTY! I did drug and rape her, and now she is apparently carrying…my child." As he looked back at her he almost sounded sorrowful when he added, "A child, the only decent pure thing that will come out of this mess," he paused, "that is as long as, WE, the miserable Larsons stay out of its life!"

Wilbur Larson was stunned, his reality suddenly surreal. He finally asked the one question Amy had been wanting to ask Ted from the beginning of the nightmarish ordeal, "How could you do such a thing?" While shaking his head, he then continued with other indicting questions, "How could you disgrace your mother and me? How could you ruin your future, and our plans?

Ted's face turned from disbelief to contempt as he looked at his father, "Our plans! It has always been about what you want, but you have never considered what I want. And, as far as why I did it, didn't you always tell me that if I wanted something bad enough, all I had to do was take it? After all, I am a Larson. Well, I wanted Amy, because I couldn't have her. She was a Christian through and through, and other than being gracious to me she would have nothing to do with me. I waited for the right opportunity and when it presented itself, I took what I wanted just like you always told me to do!"

The events that followed took but a few moments, but to Amy it all seemed to be happening in slow motion. Wilbur Larson flew into a rage. He took his left arm and flung it up and around hitting Ted on the right side of the face. Ted flew backwards hitting an end table, as the elder Larson lunged towards him. At that moment Ted's mother tried to grab her husband's arm, but was knocked back into a chair. Jonathan placed himself in front of the elder Larson and his son, as Amy's father rushed to Ted's side and her mother and Ben went to calm and assist Mrs. Larson.

It was obvious that Wilbur Larson could not tackle the football player. He stepped back as if in a daze. Ted was bleeding from the mouth and the ear and a welt was forming on his cheek. Tears flowed from his eyes. He reminded Amy of a wounded little boy, not only physically, but emotionally and spiritually.

Her father knelt beside Ted, as Amy grabbed the towel her mother had tossed onto the back of a chair when she was interrupted by the doorbell. Amy went to Ted's side. With her father's strong arm reaching up to her, she kneeled down as best as she could and used the towel to wipe the combination of tears and blood from Ted's face, ear, and mouth. He looked at her and for the first time she could see how wounded he was. Guilt came over his eyes like a curtain and softly he said the words Amy never expected to hear from his lips.

"I'm so, so very sorry Amy."

With a compassionate voice, Amy quietly spoke the words she knew was true in her heart, "I know you are Ted, and I have already forgiven you."

Wilbur Larson was not done with his tirade as he pointed at his son. "I disown you as my son! You are a miserable excuse for a son and a disgrace to your mother and me!"

Amy's father looked at Wilbur in disbelief and disgust. "Wilbur, he's your son and he needs you now more than ever!"

With a sneer on his face, Wilber took aim at Amy's father, "Luke, you beat all, you're nothing more than a self-righteous prig. Do you hate me more than my son, is that why you're defending him?"

"I'm not defending anything, but he is a hurting human being. He's your son, and if the truth be known, he is simply mirroring your attitudes and ways! It's only right that you stand by him and help him face this situation."

"Don't you lecture me Luke Lawrence! He's a disgrace and I'll have nothing to do with him. He's on his own!"

Ted's mother's firm voice cut through the electrified air. "Speak for yourself Wilbur!" She stood up from the chair to face her husband. "He's not the disgrace. Pastor Lawrence is right; he is the product of our parenting! To disown your son, means you would have to disown yourself. He is clearly a product of your arrogance, a mirror of your ruthless ways, and yes, sadly to say, neglected by a mother who has hid the fear of her husband and the despair of his indifferent, unloving, self-sufficient ways in bottles of pills and alcohol."

Glaring at her, Wilbur tried to stop his wife from revealing any more of their dirty little secrets by interrupting her, "Are you through yet?"

It was obvious that Margaret Larson had found her voice and a platform from which to speak her mind, and she was not done with her discourse. "Not by far! I have been quiet too long. As a boy he needed your approval and you lectured him about how to come out on top; and, as teenager he needed your example of what it meant to be a decent man and all he witnessed was you being a bully.

"He has sadly believed and followed your example, and now he's in big trouble and needs us more than ever. It's time to encourage him to be an honorable man by making sure he faces the consequences for his terrible behavior. And, it's clear he needs our help to walk through it; but being the big man you are, true to your questionable character, you're ready to discard him like garbage because he does not selfishly serve your purpose. I only hope he can forgive me and allow me to walk through this time with him."

It was obvious Wilbur had heard enough. "Since your choice is obvious, you'll have to live with it. I'm through with both of you!"

With bold confidence, Margaret Larson stood firm as her eyes became intense. "No you aren't because you need us to keep up your hypocritical front."

The look on Wilbur's face told onlookers that she was right, but he had to appear as if he had the last say. He threw his arms up in the air as if to fling such insignificance away as he marched through the door, slamming it behind him.

With the slamming of the door still ringing in her ears, Amy suddenly knew that it was time to get to the hospital. Her facial expression told her father something was going on.

"My water just broke," she whispered, which in the quiet room became like the shot heard around the world.

Jonathan rushed to her side to help her to her feet. He looked into her eyes for a brief moment and mouthed the words, "Well done." From that point everything became a blur to her. Jonathan volunteered to take care of Ted and his mother, while Amy's father ran to the garage to get the car. Ben took Amy's arm to help her to her waiting escort, and her mother gathered up the bag that had been prepared just for the occasion. Thanks to the well planned organization of the Lawrence family, Amy was on her way to the hospital.

***

As she explored every part of the precious bundle in her arms, and kissed soft cheeks and small, precious hands, she saw the culmination that verified what Jonathan had told her. God knows what to do with damaged goods! He had taken her broken life and cleansed and healed her. He had taken her father's life of upheaval and redefined it. He had used challenges to bring her family closer together, and He had taken the broken Larson family and penetrated it with his light to bring possible restoration. He had indeed taken a terrible experience and brought life and joy out of it. That life and joy was given an identity early on by uncle Ben, "Thomasina."

Amy's joy escalated even more when her parents, along with Ben and Jonathan, entered her hospital room to share her excitement.

Needless to say, Thomasina was the main attraction. As Thomasina was being gingerly handed to each member of the family as a type of introduction, Amy was snapping mental pictures as she observed how each of her family members looked upon her. There was an abundance of love and joy in her parents' expressions, and excitement and wonderment on Ben's face as he introduced himself to his new niece.

"Hi Thomasina. I'm your uncle and I'm the one who gave you your name, and I want you to know I'll be the best uncle ever."

The last person to hold her was Jonathan. Thomasina looked even smaller as he cradled her in his one arm and looked down at her tenderly, while he softly touched the side of her cheek with his finger.

The nurse came into the room with what turned out to be Thomasina's birth certificate. Amy recognized her as one of the nurses who had been part of the investigation that had taken place seven months ago.

"I'm sorry to bother you, but I need to fill out the rest of the birth certificate as to her name. I know Thomasina is her first name but your parents informed me I need to talk to you about her middle name and last name, as well as her father's name."

Amy was at a loss as to her middle name, but her parents agreed that the child would carry their last name.

Amy noticed that Jonathan could see her hesitation and saw an opportunity to interject his take on the matter. "I have a suggestion." Everyone looked his way in expectation, "Why not give her the same middle name as your mother first name, Lydia. And, as far as her last name," he paused before continuing, "I've been meaning to talk to you and your parents about that particular subject. It would do me a great honor if you would think about giving Thomasina my last name and putting me as her father." He paused again as if to study Amy's facial expressions, "Of course, this can only officially take place if Thomasina's mother would be willing to assume my last name as well."

Amy was trying to grapple with what Jonathan had just said.

However, Ben piped in before she could say anything. "Does this mean you want to be part of our family?"

"If your family will have me?" Jonathan's eyes were soft as he looked from Ben back to Amy. They were penetrating into her very soul as a way to make a connection. "You see Ben, I love your sister with all my heart and it would do me such honor if she would agree to be my wife and allow me to be a very big part of her life and a father to Thomasina."

Amy felt every eye riveting on her. Jonathan had said what she had been secretly waiting to hear. Even though she could sense that her exterior appeared calm, there was both a fourth of July and New Years' celebrations taking place in her emotional arena. Joy was not only exploding in her soul like fireworks, but she also had one more item to add to her growing list of how God's miraculous intervention not only turns damaged goods into new creations, but is able to create a new family out of devastation.

"You'll agree to be his wife, won't you Sis?" Ben excitedly interjected in the midst of what seemed like dead air.

Amy looked at the smiling nurse to answer her questions. "The name to put in the blank for the father is Jonathan Rudolph Davis the III," as she reached her hand out towards Jonathan, smiling, "and her full name will be Thomasina Lydia Davis."

There is therefore now
no condemnation to them
which are in Christ Jesus,
who walk not after the
flesh, but after the Spirit.
(Romans 8:1)

Damage Control

Gayle Warner felt lost and condemned. After all, she overheard a couple of women in church unknowingly confirm her condemnation. Even though the pastor talked about God's love, it didn't have the teeth to reach her and penetrate her present reality to thaw her cold heart. It couldn't push back and control the damage that had already occurred. Because of her actions, she felt unworthy to live, to even take the next breath. She was driven and tormented, and had hoped by coming to church she would find some way to escape the heavy sentence of condemnation, but instead she felt the unshakable sting of greater condemnation as the women unwittingly talked about her criminal act. The end result was clear for her: the love of God could never reach her. It may be available to everyone else, but it couldn't reach her in her deep pit of despair.

Gayle remembered how she had started out with such high hopes about life. The problem with such high hopes is that they lack reality and wisdom. As a result, she started out naive and foolish about people, which set her up to be played as a fool. As a result, her foolish hopes were no more, and all of her fantasies about having a blissful future mocked her because of one bad decision, one foolish, desperate, nightmarish act that was meant to cover up another rash deed.

She clearly had been exposed to the vanity of the world's table, and because of it she was now in her present tormented state. As a result, she had become leery of what the world was offering her. Clearly, her great crime had caused her to become lost to the only One who could give her life: God.

She remembered how she tried to forget her act through drugs and alcohol, but drugs made her sick and no matter how numb she became during her drinking binges, the numbness would inevitably wear off. She found herself coming face to face with not only the same distressing condemnation, but hangovers that occasionally caused her to have an intimate relationship with the commode in a most unbecoming manner.

Gayle also quickly discovered in her descent into despair that the world offered her a smorgasbord of alternative lifestyles to downplay the seriousness of her action in order to soothe her plunge into depression. Clearly the ways of the world cleverly tried to reason away any absolutes and justify away any sense of lasting consequences as a means to dull down the sting she felt. She struggled with the temptation to just give way to the world's ways, but inwardly, she knew that continuing down the same road would simply add to the condemnation she already felt. She could see the worldly alternatives didn't take away the desperate state that often took people, such as herself, captive.

This harsh reality was confirmed at her work place. Gayle had worked for the airport the last five years as a ticket agent, and had crossed paths with many different people. She not only worked with a variety of people, but had to interact with passengers over various issues. This required her to discern moods, make eye contact, consider one's countenance, and brace herself for the unexpected. Her encounters with people also confirmed her resolution to avoid continuing down the same road of vanity.

In her encounters with people, she quickly became a pretty good judge of character. She could differentiate when someone was trying to run away from life, from those who were flitting from one event to another to try to escape their present reality. There were also those stuck in the mud of despair, misery, and hopelessness, while others were angry and had a cruel indifference to them.

Due to her experiences and much observation of people, she had to concede that she had become a skeptic because nothing of the world appealed to her. She felt almost dead inside and resolved that any future happiness was forever lost to her.

Gayle had learned the hard way about the lies that covered the eyes and hearts of people. It was true that the world mocked moral absolutes. It advocated moral tolerance and social goodness that could be expressed in various feel-good deeds that for the most part proved to be nothing more than a self-serving veneer that hid confusion, emptiness, and desperation. Gayle had seen the emptiness many times as she looked into vacant eyes that reflected her own soul. She was aware that a seething desperation drove many who were freely partaking of the table of the world, but because their lifestyles eventually proved to have no roots or substance to hold them in place, they were left vulnerable to be taken up by the winds of false promises, endless detours of vanity, and uncertainty. In fact, these winds caused some people to become lost in a state of nothingness. In the right state, some of these individuals would fling themselves into extremes, causing them to take up their particular cause in fetish fervency. Regardless of what the cause was, it always expressed itself in an insane, angry, desperate fanaticism that had no real connection to reality.

However, regardless of the promises the world offered in each type of relationship, she had witnessed how it left people more unstable. In the end, they failed to find the promised identity, acceptance, and purpose that they were searching for. Gayle had already experienced the futility of surface relationships, knowing that they clearly left her empty, wallowing in a state that left her hitting stone walls of disillusionment and disappointment when she considered becoming involved in another relationship.

Gayle had learned that what often shores up worldly relationships are fickle, fleeting, and silly. Attractions are fickle, affections are fleeting, and emotions are unreliable. For example, if a person's undisciplined affections were not satisfied, he or she would look elsewhere. If the individual felt emptiness, his or her soul would quickly become restless to seek out that which had lasting meaning and purpose. And, in relationship to the spirit, she knew from personal experience that a fleshly euphoric high would ultimately leave a person feeling repulsed at the emptiness left in its wake. It was clear to Gayle that the alternatives the world offered in regard to happiness were a lie that had already robbed her of inner peace, killed expectations of finding something with meaning, and destroyed any hope that she would find real happiness.

It was not until she met Jay Randall that she saw a glimmer of hope for her to experience some type of life. When she met him, she had already written off all relationships as she enclosed her emotions and need for love and acceptance in a stone fortress of fear that was surrounded by shark infested waters of frustration, foul moods, anger, and utter hopelessness. To ensure that her fortress remained impenetrable, she had a "drawbridge over a moat" she could let down at any time. Her tendency was to let the drawbridge down so far, and then when the fear of being hurt, used, exposed, and discarded popped up, she would quickly pull the drawbridge up, while the infested waters of her emotions pushed back anyone who tried to pursue entrance into her fortress.

319

Jay proved to be different than most of the people who had paraded through her life. Although most of them offered something beneficial in the beginning, she quickly learned that they were out for themselves and that the only reason they showed interest in her was because they saw something in her that would serve their selfish purposes. At such times, she was quickly reminded that such a relationship is what had trapped her into the hellish world she presently found herself in. Jay on the other hand, seemed to really care about her personally and showed incredible patience when he encountered the infested waters of her emotions pushing him back with threats of rejection, while swallowing her up in frustration and despair.

Gayle's reaction towards Jay made her aware that she was in a spiral, caught up by an ominous wind that was about to fling her to the ground with devastating results. She knew her life was out of control, but she had nowhere to turn. She desperately wanted to let Jay in regardless of the risks that such a relationship presented to the raw terrain of her emotions and mind. But according to her way of thinking, she was unworthy of him. She concluded that she would defile and ruin a good man, and she cared too much for him to commit such an unacceptable act. Since she could see no future for them, she had hoped that by coming to church she would see a way out of her nightmarish reality and just maybe salvage the relationship she so badly wanted with Jay.

Going to church reminded Gayle of why she had sought it out in the first place, hoping to find a place of refuge. Even though she had grown up in a Christian home, she recognized too late that she had simply been religious, and was half-hearted in her commitment to God, leaving her wide open for defeat. She knew what was right and wrong, and foolishly perceived that she had nothing to worry about because she was a "good girl." However, she would later discover that morally, she was not a strong girl. She had strong opinions, but not moral endurance. She had religious biases, but not strong convictions. She had the appearance, but not the inner resolved. She had the language, but not heart revelation. She was a plant without roots, now withering beneath the scorching light of judgment.

She thought back to what happened seven years before. It all started out innocently. She was in her first year of college and attended a young people's Christian meeting on the college campus. There were different young people her age coming together and talking about various things including God, but it was obvious that some were there for more than fellowship. They were looking to pair off with someone else, and she was aware that she was attractive enough to catch someone's eye. Secretly, she was conscious that she hoped to meet a Christian man who she could become a twosome with. After all, it was what the world expected and by having a guy it would mark her as being normal and part of the crowd.

Someone once said, "If you're looking for something, it will surely find you." However, she conveniently forgot the rest of the statement, "But when you find whatever you think you want, it will most likely turn out to be a counterfeit, leaving you empty."

Sure enough as she looked around the room, there was that one man who definitely caught her attention. He was handsome with his dark brown hair and clear brown eyes. His smile was charismatic and he wore his mannerism with ease in light of his six foot lean frame. He would be what most women would want to see in a man.

When the man looked Gayle's way and noticed that he had caught her eye, he nodded and smiled at her. Naturally, she smiled back. After the meeting he came up to her and introduced himself. "Hi, I'm Tony Harris."

Gayle smiled back, "I'm Gayle Warner. It's nice to meet you Tony Harris."

"Likewise, Gayle Warner."

That night they exchanged phone numbers, and the next day he called Gayle and asked her out to coffee. She knew going out to coffee was usually a prelude to dating. As expected, that is what their first meeting naturally graduated to.

As expected, their time together was sweet. He courted her with such a romantic posture. He called her through the day when she had breaks between classes, and brought flowers, chocolates, and wrote sweet notes. He had a way of making her feel like she was the only woman in the world. As a result, he fit all of her notions about "Mr. Right." In her mind all of the euphoric sensations she felt around him were translated into the big "L" word: Love.

Due to the escalation of her attractions and feelings about him, within a month the momentum of her emotions grew into a wave that caused them to quickly graduate from romance into partaking of the raw lust that was manifested by intense necking in his car. That opened the door to an emotional tidal wave.

The physical attraction naturally turned into intense sexual desire that not only tempted them to explore each other in a more personal way, but it became a driving and tormenting force in their relationship that especially raged when they were alone together. Even though she fought the emotional rage within her, she sought that aloneness in his apartment to be near him. It became obvious that it was hard for him to keep his hands off of her and hard for her to not want to melt into his arms and become lost in them.

Looking back, Gayle realized she was badly bitten by the desires of the flesh. Her thoughts of Tony and her being with him consumed her during the day and through the night. She could only silence the emptiness she felt without him when she was with him once again. However, as she looked back she could see that the dangerous, destructive pattern being put into place was slowly eroding her resolve.

In spite of the warning signs that things were getting out of hand, the torment of not being with him justified her foolishly seeking the dark cover of isolation with him. Even though the Scripture's exhortation of fleeing youthful lusts would pop up in Gayle's mind like a neon sign, she ignored its warning. Since she had stopped Tony from unlawfully partaking of her fruits in the past, she concluded that she could handle it. As she evaluated their actions, she realized that each time they opened the door to the tempting world of personal exploration, seeking to somehow possess that which would satisfy the abyss, that destructive doors were being unlocked—the doors that are in place to restrain a person's deepest desires were being unlocked by the obsessive lust that was taking hold of them. Gayle found herself being pulled further and further into a seductive world that had no moral restraints or bounds, no reason or logic, no sanity or real purpose.

Gayle always made a resolution afterwards that it must not go any further until a right union of marriage could be secured between them, ensuring that any further actions would be considered lawful in God's sight. The truth was that she found herself being seduced into a surreal reality by both Tony's subtle advancements and the dark atmosphere of his apartment that was entrapping her even more so.

One night what little resolve she had left collapsed as she felt herself being caught up by feverish lusts that jerked her emotions like a bungie cord. As she found her emotions being pulled upward toward longed for ecstasy, she also found herself being pulled downward by tantalizing lust that would no longer accept being left dangled by self-denial. It was obvious the inevitable was happening and that the obsessive lusts would no longer be denied. This caused Gayle to conclude that tasting the unlawful fruit that was designated to only be tasted within the holy confines of marriage, was the right thing to do for that moment, as well as necessary if their relationship was to go further. After all, they had gone as far as they could physically and her emotions were declaring that there was nowhere else to go but through the forbidden gate. It was time to knock down the gate, ignore the "no trespassing" sign, and eat the unlawful fruit. After all, she was hungry for it, desirous of it, and had great expectation as to what it would do for her. She consoled herself by concluding that the advancement of their relationship was worth experiencing any possible consequences that might follow their action. Looking back, it was clear that reason had fled her, logic was nowhere to be found, and all remaining restraints were being cast to the wind as she gave in to the lies and appetites of her lustful flesh.

After it was over, she became keenly aware that she had given her precious fruit away and improperly partaken of his, and it left her feeling naked, empty, shameful, and confused. In her confusion she thought to herself, "Is that all there is?" She shook her head as she realized she had naively bought the propaganda of the world that was presented through TV, movies, music, romance novels, and magazines about love. It falsely presented that this one physical act would serve as the highlight and pinnacle of love and fulfillment in a relationship. However, it felt like the biggest letdown she had ever experienced. The truth was she didn't know what to expect since she never had experienced it before. Her mother never talked about it and the church she attended always presented it in light of a Scriptural "don't," but never warned about the workings and power of youthful lusts, and never explained the emotional and spiritual consequences of what happens once you betray your own moral boundaries. She found herself becoming angry towards her mother and feeling let down by her church.

She silently admitted to herself that even with such knowledge she may still have walked down the same path, but she wouldn't have any excuses. She would have walked into the situation knowing full well that the propaganda of the world was a farce. It was clear that the world's seduction wielded the tool of indoctrination in a masterful way. It produced a pinnacle of expectation in the mind that only lasted minutes in the physical realm. But in the end, it had nothing more to offer than a downside called "reality."

After the experience she had to ask herself, "Was the flesh satisfied in the end? Yes, but not necessarily in a positive way." She felt repulsed by what she did. How long would the flesh be satisfied? From the minimal experience she had, it was obvious that the flesh could easily be aroused by placing one's attractions and affections on the idea of experiencing something, but the experience fell short of the bar that had been heightened by silly expectations.

What did the experience do for her emotions? She didn't know how emotional it was for others, but it left her emotions tattered by disillusionment. Was there a spiritual aspect to the physical experience

323

called "sex"? Since God ordained marriage, there had to be a spiritual aspect to such an experience, but since their situation had started out in the flesh and its lusts had escalated the emotions, it ended in the only way it could. It was clear that whatever spiritual aspect could be applied to the experience was absent and now tainted by sin.

As she looked at Tony, he seemed pleased, but she felt betrayed and vulnerable. As she dressed, shame enfolded her like a blanket and her conscience screamed at her. Tears stung her eyes while a sick feeling in the pit of her stomach caused her to feel nauseated. What had she done?

Struggling with the turmoil in her own soul, she became repulsed as she observed Tony whistling a tune as he adjusted the collar on his shirt. Looking at her, Tony matter-of-factly stated, "Well, I better get you back to the dorm, it's getting late."

She stood stunned. It was clear that it was not a sacred time for him, but how could it be? It was not done within the sacred boundaries God had ordained. She had been told that sex was a gift God gave to marriage to ensure a legacy. It was obvious that Tony was indifferent to her inner struggle. After all, he apparently got what he wanted and was not interested in how she was being affected by their actions.

Gayle remained quiet and turned her face towards the car window as she fought back the tears of sorrow and disgrace as Tony drove to her dorm. When they reached it, Tony stopped the car but didn't make any moves to put it in gear to get out and open her door as he had done in the past. Gayle sat there to see what he would do.

He finally broke the silence as he put the car in park. "Well, I had fun."

Gayle felt all of her shame, sorrow, and despair turn into hot lava that boiled to the surface and spilled out in a flume of smoke. "FUN! Is that what our encounter tonight was to you! Just FUN? Well, whether it matters to you or not it was not FUN for me! What do you think of that?"

To Gayle's surprise, her statement didn't seem to unnerve him. A faint smirk played on his face when he looked at her, "Well, I can't imagine why it wasn't fun? After all, I did my best to ensure you had a pleasant experience."

"What does it mean that you did your best? Doesn't it bother you that what we did was morally wrong before God? As Christians we are to know better since we have been commanded to abstain from all fornication."

"Oh, now I get it. You have been struck with guilt."

Surprised, Gayle asked, "Don't you feel guilty?"

"Guilty about what? We are two normal people doing what is normal."

Gayle realized that she was so caught up with her ideas of "Mr. Right," "romance," and "love" that she had put on the rose-colored glasses of fantasy, keeping her from operating in reality. As a result, she never bothered to find out if Tony had any inner character. Waves of nausea rolled over her as she began to see Tony for the first time for who he really was and realized the implication. "Aren't you a Christian?" she asked.

Tony looked down and then up as if trying to formulate his words before he answered, "I'm a modern Christian."

"What's a modern Christian?" she asked with fervent intensity.

Tony looked at her, "A modern Christian looks at the things of God through the philosophies of the world in order to make it applicable to the times we live in. You know, we live in a time of tolerance, political correctness, where there are no absolutes, and-d-d... a time of enlightenment where we don't have to accept such old-fashioned, outdated standards anymore."

Shocked, Gayle asked, "Don't you believe in marriage?"

"I don't think it's a necessary requirement if two people want to have a sexual encounter. After all, the Bible is made up of allegories and instructions that are obsolete according to the progressive times we live in. It really doesn't have the importance it used to have. We are a much wiser and smarter generation to recognize the superstition that has been attached to it."

Still stunned, she asked, "You consider the moral boundaries attached to marriage, superstitious? What about love and honor?"

"Haven't you heard men give overtures of love to receive sex and women give sex to receive love?"

Gayle was practically speechless. "I thought we had something together that would mature into a deeper relationship."

Tony smirked, "Like marriage? My, aren't we being a bit naïve, presumptuous, and self-righteous about this situation? Hey, you gave every indication you wanted this to happen with no strings attached by coming to my apartment."

Gayle hung her head in shame. "You're right Tony. It's all my fault and you have no responsibility in it since I assumed you were a committed Christian. Just because you were attending a Christian meeting, doesn't make you or me, true, committed believers." She paused and then looked at him, "After all, I jumped before testing the water to find out how deep it was. Tonight I'm in shock to realize just how shallow the water is. And, since I'm the only one who is responsible to hold to moral standards, it's up to me to maintain them, and not expect someone of your caliber to maintain honorable intentions or actions towards me."

She paused, "But, isn't it ironic?"

Bewildered and taken back by her summary of his character, Tony looked at her, "What is ironic?"

"There are those whose union is not ordained by God, but they desire to be recognized as being married and have become almost militant and insistent in changing the laws, while labeling those who don't agree with them as being hateful. But, then you have those who could be sanctioned in an acceptable union by God, but they shun it and consider it obsolete, while flinging away all moral accountability and selling their souls so they can do as they please according to their godless philosophies. As the Bible declares, we are seeing a day where people will call good evil, and evil good to justify their wicked actions."

Tony let out a nervous laugh, "You shouldn't be so serious. You need to relax and enjoy life to the fullest. You know, you only live once."

"Yes, we only live once, Tony, but the reality is that we are only given this life to get it right, then judgment. I may be an immature, foolish Christian right now, but the one thing I know is that God above has not changed, nor has He changed His righteous standards. They apply today as they did yesterday and will tomorrow. And, those "obsolete" standards will in the end judge you and me for our sins, including those we have committed tonight."

Gayle began to open the car door, but before she exited, she turned to a somewhat frustrated Tony with one parting shot, "And, Tony, you are somewhat right. I have been naïve, but my greatest flaw in my naiveté is that it has made me utterly foolish in my ignorance, preventing me from discerning a wolf in sheep's clothing." She stepped out of the car, slammed the door as hard as she could, and then slowly walked to the dorm.

The darkness of the night wrapped itself around her as she considered the horrible incident. Torrents of regret overwhelmed her soul, causing her to curl up in the bed. Sleep fled her as she went over and over in her mind as to how could she have missed the obvious. Was she blind because she was naïve or did she choose to be deceived because it is what she wanted to see and believe? Perhaps it was both, but there was nothing more foolish than self-delusion.

Finally the first rays of the sun filtered into her room but the dark shadows of the night still clung to her. It seemed as if she was looking at the world through a dingy filter. Gayle was aware that nothing was clear or decisive. She concluded that her moral compass was off and now she was adrift in the restless ocean of life.

She tried to brace herself against whatever type of debris might wash up on the shores of her shaky life. She had survived the night and endured the initial taunting of a beginning nightmare. However, she didn't realize that not only had the nightmare begun, but it would intensify in ways she never would have imagined.

***

Gayle sat in a state of shock. How could this happen? She realized she was asking the wrong question. She knew the answer to the "how," but what she wanted to really know is "why." Why did this have to happen to her? Why would God allow it to happen? After all, it was only one indiscretion that had proved to be punishing enough by haunting her ever since that night two months ago. Was that not enough punishment?

As the truth began to sink in, she also knew the "why" of the matter. It all came down to paying the consequences for a wrong action. She recognized that in a world that refuses to operate in the absolutes, such consequences were explained away, hid away in the shadows of tolerance, or done away with in the name of rights.

Regardless of what she understood, it didn't stop fear from gripping her soul and twisting it into a pretzel. Logically, she knew she could handle the consequences according to the world, and no one would be wiser for it. Emotionally, she was not ready to take the matter to task because she was not prepared to change course in her life, and this would definitely change the whole face of her life. She had plans to pursue, dreams to experience, and life to live before she was ready to settle down into what many claim to be a "normal" life.

It was in her reasoning that Gayle realized she was vulnerable and couldn't make a sound decision. Her emotions were taking her on a bumpy ride, her logic was trying to find a way around confronting the consequences, and her wishful thinking was swinging on branches of regrets as she rocked back and forth on the "If only" she had been wise. "If only" she had been realistic! It was clear the "if only's" did not change her present reality. They only caused her to get emotionally and intellectually stuck in reverse, but the truth was she was caught in the present wave of reality. Time was marching forward regardless of the mud of confusion she was now stuck in.

Gayle was pregnant and there was no way of getting around it. In seven months the whole world would know about the shame of her indiscretion. Her life would never be the same and there was no way to reverse it. It was what it was, but in her vulnerable state she sensed she needed to avoid making any rash decisions.

There were three things she knew she had to do. She had to first inform the father of the child, Tony. Due to his character, she already suspected that he would wash his hands of the whole matter and put it back on her.

Next she needed to seek counsel. Her conscience was clear about what she needed to do, but her emotions were reeling from the possible damage that would be left in the wake of her actions. She needed to determine what was right for everyone involved in the situation.

Finally, she knew she was weak and would need the support of others. The ones she needed the greatest support from would be her parents, but she had no idea how they would react. After all, they had great plans for her life, and grandchildren at this time were not part of the equation.

Since that infamous night of comprise and indiscretion, Tony had gone on to more fertile fields, knowing that she felt a contempt towards him. It was clear at first that those who knew them had questions as to why they were no longer a couple, but because it was not unusual in the present culture to go from one romantic encounter to another, it was quickly accepted. Gayle watched Tony work his charm on his next victim and it was clear to her that he was taking captive another silly, inexperienced Christian woman who had stars in her eyes. It was then that she decided to leave the so-called "Christian" group.

Gayle will never forget the final time she attended the group. It was right after she called Tony and told him she was pregnant. Their conversation also became embedded in her memories.

Tony was surprised to hear her voice. Since there was no smooth way to move into the discussion, she was forthright. "Tony, you need to know I'm pregnant."

Even though she knew Tony's caliber, she still was shocked at his response, "Why tell me?"

Needless to say when Gayle found her tongue, anger was boiling up and over. "What do you mean, why tell you! You are the FATHER of the child I am carrying."

The dead silence on the other end only lasted for a few seconds. "How can you be sure I'm the father?"

By this time Gayle was feeling repulsed. She could tell him it was because she felt every father should be given the opportunity to have some involvement with his child, but she realized that she was casting pearls before a pig. However, she opened the door and was not about to back down until he played every one of his miserable cards. "What do you mean how can I be sure you're the father?" she cried. Even though I was stupid enough to have sex with you once, I assure you that I have never done it with anyone else. Besides, a blood test of the child will confirm it." Gayle paused, "Well it appears we aren't getting away with our one night stand. I'm now carrying the fruits of it and I want to know what you are going to do about it?"

Gayle didn't know what was happening on Tony's end, but his words clearly revealed his indifferent attitude. With a hint of cruelty and mockery he stated his intention, "I'm not going to do a thing about it. It was your responsibility to ensure you wouldn't get pregnant. And, since you didn't prevent it, it's your problem. I'll have nothing to do with it!" He hung up the phone.

She felt battered, but was not surprised at Tony's response. He had no intention of accepting any responsibility for his part. Women such as her were just notches on his belt, and could be sacrificed for the sake of his ego. It was clear that he was self-serving and had no concern about what happened to the seeds he planted. He didn't care whether they produced life, maintained a legacy, or exemplified heritage. And, in all honesty she didn't want him as a husband or a father.

However, it left a bitter taste in her soul that bruised her already weakening resolve. It was obvious he didn't care about her or the baby that was conceived in her womb. She felt alone and her situation looked hopeless. She just needed someone to care, someone to say that even though everything was collapsing around her that it would be okay in the end.

It was for this reason that she went to the Christian group at the college. There was a college student who had somewhat befriended her. Her name was Linda Jones. She was what some would consider a leader. She appeared to have everything in order. Linda talked the talk and appeared to walk the walk. Since she was in-the-know about matters, Gayle figured that she would be able to give her sound Christian advice.

At the meeting, Gayle sought Linda out and quietly asked to talk to her about a private matter. Even though she was surrounded by others who were exchanging communication in a circular setting, Linda excused herself from the activity and joined Gayle at a quiet corner table.

Although Gayle felt reluctant to admit her indiscretion and the results of it to Linda, Linda's emotionless demeanor calmed some of her nerves as Gayle confessed her sin and an unwanted pregnancy. After Gayle was finished explaining her plight, Linda sighed and shook her head before saying anything.

"Gayle, I'm sorry this happened. I should have warned you about Tony. After all, he has a reputation, but I figured it was your business and you knew what you were getting into."

Gayle was taken back, "Linda, I thought I was dating a Christian man. I had no idea he was immoral and liberal in his definition of Christianity. I was naïve and stupid and foolishly thought that what was developing between us was love, but since that night I realize the correct word for it was 'lust.'"

"I'm so sorry Gayle, I should have warned you, but would you have listened?"

In a contemplative tone, Gayle answered her, "I really don't know how I would have acted since I was never given a chance to consider the facts in the first place. As Christians, aren't we supposed to warn the vulnerable and innocent about wolves?"

"Perhaps so, Gayle. There are some women who have already experienced Tony's seductive, treacherous ways. What are you going to do about the fetus?"

Surprised, "You mean what am I going to do about this child?" Gayle firmly stated.

"Well, you know, Gayle, there is a debate about when life begins, and more knowledgeable and scientific individuals have declared that life doesn't start until it's born. There's also another professor that states life does not really start until the child is able to interact with others around it, which is around the age of two or three."

Gayle couldn't believe the insanity that Linda was spewing out of her mouth. "Linda, I thought you were a committed Christian. That's why I was seeking your advice, but what you are saying sounds like the insane thinking and teaching of our godless college professors."

Insulted by Gayle's insinuation, Linda snapped back, "Of course I'm a committed Christian! I'm just voicing the logic of the educated world. It's not up to me to set the record straight since it is accepted as scientific."

Frustrated, Gayle shot back, "It doesn't matter what the godless academic world states about a matter. What is important is what do you believe to be true as a Christian? As believers we don't stand according to the world's ideas, we stand according to what has been declared as being so according to God's Word. The Bible instructs us to choose the higher ground."

Linda's response proved that she wasn't going to allow Gayle to gain the upper hand. "If you really believe what you say Gayle, why didn't you choose the higher ground when it came to Tony?"

Gayle realized in her present situation she had no authority to take a righteous stand. Even though she thought herself noble for standing for truth, she was simply bringing a grave indictment against herself. She hung her head in shame.

Linda's next question broke the silence. "What are you going to do?"

"I gather you're asking about the baby?" Gayle then looked at Linda and asked, "What would you do?"

"Well, you know you have three options: abortion and no one is really hurt by it nor are plans interrupted; have the child and give it up for adoption and risk complications down the line of your life being disrupted if the child seeks you out; or, have the child and raise it yourself, knowing that you will have to give up future plans. You need to keep in mind that you are bringing the child into a world where it will be rejected by the father, possibly shunned by the religious world, and treated differently by those who become part of your personal world, such as a future husband."

Linda was clear about the pros and cons of the three options. Gayle looked into Linda's eyes and asked her, "What option would you choose if you were in my place?"

"I've already made that choice, not only once, but twice."

Surprised, Gayle asked, "What do you mean, you've already made that choice?"

Linda studied Gayle for a few seconds before answering, "I've had two abortions already. In fact, because of being naive and not taking preventive measures, at least half the women in this room have had one or more abortions."

Linda's answered stunned Gayle. She felt totally undone as tremors jolted her soul. Convulsive shock waves seemed to pound through her whole body. She heard herself ask weakly, "How do you know that half the women in this room have had abortions?"

"Like you, they have come and talked to me about the matter and I have given them the address of the abortion clinic that services the college girls. The clinic is backed by government funding and will do it without any questions. In fact, I carry the clinic's address with me." She then reached into her purse, found the card and handed it to a stunned, but compliant Gayle who put the card in her purse.

"Did you give them the same talk, ending with the same conclusion as you have me?" Gayle inquired.

"Yes. Abortion is a good way to control the damage that is often left in the wake of an unwanted or unexpected pregnancy."

"I don't understand—you had two abortions?"

Linda tossed her head. "The first one was because I was a naïve high school girl, but the second one was a couple of years ago, and I thought I was really in love, but the relationship became sour." She paused, "You know what's funny, I told the first man I was pregnant and received about the same response from him as you did Tony.

"But, on the second one I just went and got the abortion without telling him. Later on he found out. He was actually upset that I had not consulted him. He even told me he would have raised the child himself." A quizzical expression crossed her face. "Imagine that would you? The point is, I would have to have the child and then take all the backlash initially."

Gayle could not help but ask, "How did you come to the conclusion that abortion was the way to go and-d-d...have they affected you emotionally, such as having any regrets?"

"Well my mother helped me make the decision. She pointed out the logical aspect of it and it appeared to be a win-win situation for everyone involved from me, the absent father, and my family. It's no big deal. It's just a procedure that doesn't take long."

Gayle realized she had the information she sought, along with other facts she could have remained ignorant about. She looked at Linda, pushed back her chair, and thanked her for her time, officially ending their meeting with a good-bye.

As Gayle was walking towards the door to leave, Tony came through the door with his latest quest hanging on his arm, clearly enraptured by his charming ways. They came face to face with her. It was obvious that Tony would have preferred to avoid encountering Gayle, but she was standing right in front of him.

Gayle could see her presence was somewhat unnerving to him so she said "Hello Tony."

Nervously, he answered her, "Hi Gayle, how are you?"

"Nice of you to ask about my condition, especially since I am carrying your child."

The buzzing of voices suddenly gave way to dead silence. Tony laughed nervously, while the enraptured look on the girl's face melted into shocked horror.

Gayle directed her gaze and next statement at the girl as if to look into her soul, "I think you should be warned that you've just walked into a breeding ground of perversion and fornication, and that you are holding onto the arm of a wolf who is playing a sick game with your affections. He is after your soul so he can rob you of purity and self-respect, and then count you as one of his insignificant, silly, stupid conquests. Know that when he's done with you he'll discard you like a piece of garbage and move on to other innocent victims."

Gayle quickly glanced at a stunned Tony whose face had turned pale. His mouth hung open in horror and he seemed to be at a loss for words. She turned her head to make one last mental note of the room that had become a minefield of temptation and a cesspool that sucked innocent souls into a quagmire of destruction. There were mixed reactions from those in the room. Some were stunned, others looked to the floor in shame, and the rest looked like they had just been doused with cold water, shocking them awake. She then turned, stepped around Tony and the girl and exited through the door.

Confusion pushed aside any clarity that Gayle hoped to find. She had turned to someone whom she had respected as a Christian in order to be encouraged, but instead she was presented options. She knew then she had to go home and seek out her parents' advice.

It was hard for Gayle to describe her parents. They always took her to church, but at home they were casual about living the Christian life. They didn't really do anything wrong, but she wasn't sure if they did anything right. She realized they never stood for anything. If they moved towards a matter it was according to what seemed to be popular and acceptable to those around them. It appeared that much of the Christianity she witnessed at home left her feeling like she was in a fog. She realized that what she did understand as being true didn't come from home but from her Sunday school teachers.

As she considered her present situation, she thought to herself that surely they would take a clear stand and lead her through this maze of confusion. She wanted to do right by those who were being personally affected by this matter, and her parents clearly fit into that category. Coming to a decision to talk to her parents about her plight gave her a small measure of peace as she arranged a time to meet with them.

After Gayle sat her parents down, she nervously and tearfully confessed to her parents the error of her ways and the consequences of her actions. She was relieved that they showed no real judgment, and that they were concerned about her mental well-being. Gayle told them the three options she was already presented with, and that it was her goal to do right by everyone, including them. It was then that she asked them their advice.

She remembered her parents looking at each other. It was her mother who spoke. "Gayle, we will support whatever decision you make. You are a smart young woman and it's clear that the pros and cons of each option have already been presented to you. I'm sure your father will agree with me that our main concern is you.

"You have such a bright future and we would hate to see you have to give up your dreams in order to raise a child without any help from the father. You must keep in mind, if you have or keep this child, there will be a stigma that would naturally follow. It is hard to tell how many friends you will lose, along with respect from those at church followed by a lot of whispering and speculation. Honey, life is hard enough when everything is being done right, but a child at this time would complicate life in ways that you could never imagine."

The gratitude that Gayle felt by her parents' initial reaction was now descending into the abyss of utter depression. Perhaps she was smart, but she felt the weight of the matter was too heavy for her to carry alone. And, yet her parents had put it squarely back on her shoulders. In her present state, she didn't think of herself as being trustworthy in making a right decision. After all, there were other people who would be affected by her action.

Numbly Gayle stood up and thanked her parents for listening and went to her bedroom to make a decision. As she looked at the situation she realized that sin operated on a major lie, that a person's wrong actions are his or her business alone. However, sin is like a big net that enfolds everyone who will be affected by the action. Gayle realized that sin creates a domino effect that eventually swallows everything in its path including what is innocent and pure.

That night her tossing and turning in bed was a replica of what was happening in her soul. She struggled with each option, while determined to approach it in a mature, logical way, to avoid emotional pitfalls. She weighed each pro and con of her three choices in light of what was best for her, the future, and her parents.

When the morning arrived, Gayle had made a decision. She rose early, determined to carry out her resolution. She was wearied with thinking, tired of coming to the same conclusion that seemed right for everyone, but hollow to her soul. She knew that she couldn't think about it any longer for fear of second guessing and backing out of her decision, to only have to go through the same process again and again.

Before going back to the town where she attended college, Gayle took the clinic's card out of her purse that Linda had given her and looked at the address. It appeared that the only logical way she could do damage control was to get rid of the evidence. Except for a few, no one would be the wiser about it and everyone directly involved would be able to avoid the stigma that followed such actions.

When she arrived at the clinic, she took a breath and began to numb herself against any protest that might come from her conscience and any emotional upheaval that might cause her to turn around and flee the other way.

Linda was right that the abortion was a procedure, but she failed to explain that it took place in a sterile atmosphere of emotional indifference. In Gayle's mind there was no one or nothing present to help her walk through something that was very emotional to her. People appeared to move through the whole procedure like robots, clearly giving the appearance that it was no big deal. To get through the ordeal, Gayle took on the pose of the clinical environment as she mechanically carried out the nurses' and doctor's instructions, struggling to not think, while pushing all of her numbed emotions into a locked room.

She was totally unprepared for the tsunami of emotions that hit her as she waited for the inevitable. However, as Gayle laid there after the procedure was done. Tears began to well up in her eyes. Her conscience began to stir, her emotions started to wake up from the anesthesia her logical approach had injected into her senses, and guilt began to knock on the door. Gayle felt nauseated by the bitterness the whole ordeal had left in her soul. She sensed the presence of a lifeless vacuum that was sucking out her very life. As she walked out to the car, she felt something precious had died inside of her, and as a result she perceived herself as being part of the walking dead, those who had no real sense of life, no vital direction, and no hope.

Even though that was over six years ago, the sights, sounds, and even smells of that clinic were still vivid to her senses. In fact, at night they still haunted her in nightmares that always had the same outcome. She was left in a dark room with the stench of death threatening to strangle her. She would hear a faint cry that was quickly silenced, and there in front of her were garbage bags that were waiting to be cast into some furnace. Each time she would wake up drenched in sweat and crying out, but she was the only one in the room, the only one facing the formidable bags that once spoke of life and potential.

And, what about her dreams of college and a profession? Gayle's dreams were casualties. After the abortion, Gayle plunged into a deep depression and couldn't keep up her studies. She was forced to drop out of college. Eventually, after doing odds and ends jobs, she landed a job as a ticket agent at the airport.

Another casualty was her relationship with her parents. Instead of the abortion bringing her closer to her parents, it became a huge wedge. She felt anger towards them that she couldn't explain. She always volunteered to work on weekends and holidays, providing a reason why she was never available to come home for a visit.

Gayle was resigned to keeping up her minimal existence by enduring the tormenting nights and surviving the dreary days one at a time, until she met Jay. Jay gave her a reason to live, but her mental state was taking a toll on her energy and health. She had to do something, but she didn't know what. She had come to church only to be condemned by two women who declared that anyone who had an abortion committed the unpardonable sin.

She could not argue with them. What she did to the life in her was inexcusable. Linda had made it appear as if it was no big deal, but it had become a big deal to her, a formidable mountain that Gayle could no longer logically or emotionally get around. Even though she had nobly reminded herself that it was about damage control to ensure that she did right by others, she realized that the end product created greater damage when it came to an innocent child, her personal life and relationships.

As Gayle was leaving church the pastor's wife came up to personally greet her, introduce herself, and ask if there was anything the church could do for her. Gayle could see that she was a compassionate woman and decided to take a risk.

"Yes, I was wondering if you could recommend a good Christian counselor? I need to talk to someone about a personal matter."

The pastor's wife smiled at her. "Yes we do have a counselor that we can recommend. Wait here and I will get her card."

Within a few minutes, the pastor's wife was back and handed her the card. "I don't know what you're going through but God does, and I will be in prayer for you."

Gayle smiled and thanked her. She read the name on the card and spoke to herself while walking to the car, "Jean Graham. Well, Jean Graham, you are my last hope, my last lifeline, and if you can't help me, well then there is only one other way out of this nightmare." She shook at the prospect, but she knew that her sanity was being held intact by a thin line of hope. She had no sane place to go to find rest and no relief from her torturous conscience. It was clear something had to give soon, very soon.

***

Gayle nervously walked into the nice, but simply decorated office. She sensed that whoever Jean Graham was, she wasn't caught up with impressing others. The receptionist came from the side door and greeted her with a friendly hello.

"I gather that you are Gayle Warner."

Gayle felt some of her nervousness release as she answered her, "Guilty as charged."

The receptionist picked up the clipboard with some papers on it and handed it to her. "I hope you don't mind filling out a confidential questionnaire that would possibly give Jean insight into how to best minister to you."

Gayle noticed there was a blank sheet of paper on top of the questionnaire to ensure confidentiality even with the receptionist. She sat down to fill it out. There were a variety of questions on the questionnaire as to her Christian commitment along with any possible involvement with alcohol, drugs, cults, the occult, and the New Age. She finally came to the one question that made her heart skip a beat, "Have you ever had an abortion?"

Gayle felt her stomach tighten into a bigger knot, while she held her breath. She had been honest about her alcohol and drug use and knew she had to be honest about what had been tormenting her soul. When she marked the "x" on yes beside the ominous question, she let out her breath. Even though she hated to mark it, she felt a relief that it was not a foreign or unspeakable matter that would be avoided or ignored by the counselor.

She handed the completed questionnaire to the receptionist and the receptionist took it into the room she had exited from when Gayle had first entered the office, and once again exited a few minutes later. It seemed like Gayle waited for an eternity, but it was only five minutes when the door to the office opened and another woman walked towards Gayle.

The woman was middle height in her mid-forties, and was dressed modestly. It was clear that she wasn't interested in making a fashion statement. In Gayle's mind she was very down to earth. She smiled at Gayle as she walked towards her while reaching out her hand. "Gayle, I am Jean Graham, welcome."

Gayle took her hand and smiled back. "It's nice to meet you Ms. Graham."

"Call me Jean." Nodding towards her office, "Let's go to my office where we can get acquainted and talk."

Gayle followed her into the office. It was quaint, with two chairs that sat facing her desk, bookcases filled with a broad variety of books, and behind her chair was a computer desk with all the necessary accessories. The counselor sat down behind her desk while she invited Gayle to sit in one of the chairs facing her.

As Gayle took a seat, she noticed what she assumed was her questionnaire. "How can I help you Gayle," Jean asked.

"I really don't know if anyone can help me. I don't want to offend you, but you are my last resort."

Jean laughed, "We are known around here as the 'Last Chance Ministry.' Her laugh turned into a smile as she looked into Gayle's face. "You seem somewhat depressed and by your statement I would guess desperate right now. Why do you think you're depressed?" Jean inquired.

Gayle felt herself squirming, "If you have read my questionnaire, you might have already figured it out."

But Jean's reply told Gayle that she was not being easily let off the hook, "Gayle, it's not up to me to figure out what is depressing you; rather, it's up to you to recognize it, and then admit it so the real matter can be honestly addressed."

Gayle looked into Jean's eyes. She didn't detect any judgment, just compassion.

"I could blame it on my large alcohol assumption," Gayle responded.

Jean still wore a faint smile when she replied, "You could Gayle, but alcohol and drugs are symptoms of something else, usually an unresolved issue caused by sin, broken relationships, hurt, disappointment, or disillusionment."

Gayle hung her head as Jean paused to look into her eyes, "Gayle, you're a smart woman, and you know why you're here. You're not here to play games, because if you were going to do that you would have stayed home and not wasted your time or mine.

"It's obvious that you're here to face what has been bringing you down emotionally, mentally, and spiritually. You're here to find someone to help you walk down the path of deliverance and truth. You're looking for someone who will tell you that forgiveness and healing are not far from you and that in the end the mess in your life will count for something other than devastation left by ongoing floods of regret, shame, and condemnation that are probably constantly sweeping across your soul."

Gayle fought in vain to keep her tears from flowing. She had finally found someone who understood where she was, tormented in her soul, sick of her plight, and hopeless in her state. She had found someone who was willing to walk through the devastating terrain of her life, without being judgmental, and actually make sense out of the senseless.

Regret slammed against the door that had kept the truth at bay, overwhelming Gayle with a mocking echo as she wondered "if only" I had talked to someone like Jean at the very beginning. "If only" she had had the support, the wisdom, and the encouragement, she would have probably avoided the present gut wrenching experience. But, the "if only" never changes the harsh reality of "what is." It was true she had come to face the skeleton in the closet, the death of an innocent child, the destruction of what was pure; granted, conceived in lust, but selfishly sacrificed in the name of doing right by others. And, what about the others who were directly involved with her wrong decision? From all appearances they were self-serving, hiding behind the logic of indifference, and quick to exchange the real truth for false promises and fragile dreams to avoid what might later prove to be inconvenient and embarrassing.

Through her tears, her voice barely audible, she admitted what she had been running away from for so long, "I had an abortion." She paused as if to try to make sense out of it. "I can't tell you why I had an abortion except according to the advice of those around me, it seemed like the logical thing to do, the right thing to do for everyone involved, the way to control the damage already created by bad decisions and a wrong action."

Gayle could tell by Jean's voice that she was gently trying to challenge and expose Gayle's perception, "Gayle, there are various reasons why people get an abortion. Some do it to cover up the reality of their moral indiscretion, others because they have nowhere to turn for help, and some because they buy the lie of the world. There are those who don't want to be bothered with responsibility due to selfishness, and some for a combination of reasons to ensure, as you said, a type of 'damage control.' However, Gayle you need to be honest with yourself. Did you personally believe getting an abortion was the right thing to do, and that it was merely an act of damage control, protecting everyone else's interests?"

Jean's question penetrated the protective wall that Gayle had established. She thought she had figured it all out, but confusion slammed against any clarity she thought she had about her action, but she knew it was time for honesty to win out. "It seemed that it was alright since it appeared as if it was an acceptable solution according to some of my Christian peers and even my parents."

"Gayle, your Christian peers, as well as your parents don't serve as your inner voice nor will your tender conscience allow you to fade into the faceless masses that tout political correctness or tolerance. You are an individual and you have your own worldview as to what is right and wrong. It's clear that your worldview has been influenced by Christian teachings; therefore, what do you, according to your worldview, personally have to say about your action?"

Gayle knew that she could not protect herself by hiding behind those who gave her advice, "I guess logic silenced my conscience and my indiscretion convinced me that since I had already blown it once, it wouldn't matter if I blew it again. After all, how could I suddenly stand for what was right when it was all terribly wrong in the first place? Did I believe that those advising me were right, probably not, but I wasn't strong enough to withstand their arguments since I felt so alone. No one seemed to really want to support me, or maybe that is what I wanted to believe, that I was all alone and too weak to see it through."

It was clear to Gayle that Jean was probing through the layers of excuses to help her see her reasoning and motive, "Gayle, it's not unusual in such a circumstance to allow logic to silence one's conscience, but such silence only lasts for a short season. Eventually, the person's conscience will rise above the logic and bring them face to face with the emotional fallout of guilt, while the person's worldview rises up and condemns them. It's then that the individual begins to feel the spiritual fallout of separation from God, isolating them in a world of shame, regret, and torment."

Jean paused, "And, regardless of how the world attempts to sear everyone's conscience with lies, liberal agendas, and godless philosophies, a person with any moral sense is not wired to all of a sudden become a lifeless robot that is void of conscience with the ability to nullify their worldview.

"The Bible tells us we are what we think, and behind all of our logic lies the real conviction as to who we are, what we choose to believe, and how we have been wired as far as our cultural, family, and religious influences. When we go against those convictions, we simply betray ourselves, and then we lose our way."

Gayle knew Jean was speaking the truth and that she could not blame others for her bad decisions. She could think herself a suffering martyr, noble because she did it for the sake of others, but the truth was she knew it was the easy way out of a bad situation for her. The convenient, noble covering may have covered the obvious up front, but it created a moral crisis in her life that had caused her to become emotionally and spiritually shipwrecked. She needed to face it and own it, every bit of it, to the last drop. She felt sick to her stomach and the heaviness that she always felt griping her soul was becoming unbearable. She wanted to run but she knew she needed to see it through.

"Gayle how does your worldview define your action?" Jean asked.

Gayle hung her head. "I'm a murderer," she sobbed.

"And as a murderer, Gayle, what do you deserve according to your worldview?"

"I deserve punishment, I deserve death!" At that point Gayle found herself sobbing uncontrollably as she tried to finish her thought. "I don't deserve anything that is good. I deserve the worse judgment imaginable. It is so-o-o...very hopeless for me. I deserve hell!"

Jean's words continued to probe deep into her being, "You've been serving as the executor of your own judgment Gayle, and I want to know how have you been punishing yourself."

Through her sobs, she confessed her destructive cycle, "I have been drinking and occasionally take drugs, and I've pushed anything that is good away from me, including Jay."

"Who is Jay, and why have you pushed away the good?"

"Jay is the man I'm attracted to, but he's too good for me," she paused as she realized the inevitable, "I haven't totally pushed him away yet, but in due time I will. I don't want to but I know I will!"

Jean's voice was firm but gentle, "Gayle, just how long are you going to punish yourself by sabotaging everything that seems good to you before you feel it's enough: that you sense you have satisfied the judgment your conscience and worldview has pronounced on you?"

By this time Gayle felt a complete blanket of hopelessness wrap itself around her. Confusion rushed in as she admitted the truth. "I don't know, it all seems hopeless," she cried. "It all seems so hopeless. It all started with a moment of passion, and now I'm reaping a lifetime of sorrow and pain for it. It seems so unfair! I want to be set free from this nightmare, but I know I don't deserve to be set free!"

"Gayle, are you desperate enough to be set free?" Jean asked.

Gayle's sobbing subsided as she responded. "What do you mean am I desperate enough?"

"Being a personal executor of punishment can produce a destructive pattern that will create a morbid reality. Such a position presents a big problem mentally, emotionally, and spiritually because the conscience serves as an unmerciful referee and the worldview an indifferent judge. A dirty conscience can only call foul after it has been defiled and the worldview has no means of showing mercy when it has been affronted. As executioner you may be doing all you can to silence them, but you will never be able to. The end result is complete hopelessness and desperation.

"What you seek can only be given by the ultimate judge of all. Your conscience must be cleansed and the moral judgment of your worldview upheld before either can be silenced."

"There is only one Judge and that is God," Gayle acknowledged.

"You're right Gayle. However, the Father allotted all judgment to His Son, Jesus Christ. He alone is the only One who can forgive you, cleanse your conscience, and satisfy your worldview."

Despairingly, Gayle asked, "Why would He forgive me? I took an innocent life to cover up my sin. I know what God thought of those who offered their children to idols in the Old Testament. He perceived it as a great abomination."

Jean's words broke through Gayle indictment, "Murder is not an unpardonable sin, Gayle. If it was, King David and the Apostle Paul would be in serious, spiritual trouble. King David admitted that even though he had committed adultery with Bathsheba and had her husband killed that his sin was against God and God alone. It is true that you aborted the heritage of the Lord. Children are not only considered a spiritual heritage, but they are a gift from God. It is not up to man to play God and consider unborn children as less than human in the name of so-called "rights" or "scientific conclusions"; therefore, they can be sacrificed on the different altars of the world.

"When you consider Paul who persecuted Christians before he encountered the true light on the road to Damascus, he later stated that he was the worst of all sinners but his salvation served as a pattern for others. Paul sought the Lord's forgiveness and not only was he completely pardoned by the Lord from paying the consequences for his wicked deeds, but he was saved unto eternal life.

"Paul's life shows that sin is sin and you can seek pardon for your wicked deeds and obtain not only forgiveness but salvation. However, you have to be like David and recognize that your greatest offense was committed against God and agree with Him about your sin. If your sin is that of murder, then you must call it what it is and humble yourself and seek God's pardon which can only be obtained by receiving Christ's death on the cross as a payment for it."

The truth of Gayle's plight was being brought to the light. She had offended God and her conscience, as well as betrayed her worldview. She had become lost in a morbid reality as she strived to placate her conscience's objections with vain gestures of regret, shame, and sorrow, and silence the judgment of her worldview by executing punishment on herself through self-destruction and self-denial of what was honorable and good.

"I don't know where to begin," Gayle stated.

"Yes you do Gayle. You must start by repenting, turning from your present reality which means you have to give up the right to be your own judge, and jury, and carry out the judgment. This means also you have to quit hiding behind any fake nobility, concerning how grave and endless the judgment has become. The problem with such fake nobility is that eventually a person becomes a suffering martyr, as the judgment becomes unfair, unbearable, and unobtainable.

"It is from the point of repentance that you can confess your sins and fling yourself upon the mercy seat of God seeking His forgiveness, as you accept by faith that your sins have received the proper judgment on the cross of Jesus. Once you can accept Jesus' payment for your sins, then you can receive not only pardon from the throne of God, but Jesus' deliverance from your destructive cycle as your conscience is cleansed by the living water of His Spirit and your worldview recognizes that judgment has been paid in full for your sin; therefore, it is completely satisfied."

Gayle knew that Jean was right, but the wrestling match in her soul was intense. "I don't deserve God's forgiveness."

"You are right Gayle, you don't deserve forgiveness and it's for that reason Jesus came to be our sacrifice and now serves as a type of conduit of grace between a holy God and wretched man. Mercy means you will not receive what you deserve such as judgment, while grace points to receiving something you don't deserve such as a pardon and salvation. God holds back His judgment to give man time to repent, and once man repents and receives pardon through Jesus' work of redemption on the cross, then the Lord Jesus Christ becomes that incredible avenue in which God can pour His grace down to man in the form of eternal life and sanctification.

"Gayle, you implied on the form you filled out that you are a Christian. But because of your sins, you presently feel separated from God, unable to have and enjoy a relationship with Him, but as a Christian, you know you can come back to God because of what Jesus did, confess your sin and He is able to cleanse you from all unrighteousness.

"Right now you want to feel relief from your tormenting world by some personal effort on your part before you come to God, but no matter what you do, you don't have the position or means to obtain such a relief. You are the offender, not the judge, and only the true Judge can secure, not just relief for you, but deliverance. It is time for you to choose to believe God's Word, repent of your unbelief, and by faith turn from your present reality and receive the glorious reality of God's forgiveness and reconciliation with your Creator, receiving the restoration of your soul as a relationship is once again established with the Lord.

Suddenly Gayle completely broke in repentance and began to confess her sins of unbelief to the Lord, as well as pride, fornication, and murder. It was as if a dam had broken, allowing the list of her offenses to flow as she confessed her hatred and bitterness towards Tony, her scorn towards Linda, and her anger at her parents. As the caustic feelings bubbled up from the depths of her soul, and quickly emerged into a fast moving river, Gayle knew that they were being taken to the depth of the ocean where they would never be dredged up again by a loving God, a committed Savior, and a faithful Lord.

Gayle didn't know how long the confession or the cleansing took place. She only knew that the heaviness was gone. Her conscience was no longer calling foul and her worldview had become quiet, but sorrow remained, clinging to the outer fringes of her soul. She sensed that it could consume her at any moment.

She looked at Jean. "I feel cleansed but the sorrow is still there. Will it always be there?"

"The only way to deal with sorrow Gayle is through mourning. You must mourn the loss of your child. It's in mourning that you will be comforted."

"How can I mourn the loss of the child I murdered?"

"Gayle, how did you regard the baby when you aborted it?"

Gayle thought for a moment, "Well, the idea of being pregnant with a child was a vague notion. I never thought about it being a living baby inside of me. In fact, I avoided looking at the child as being living so that I could do what I did."

"Did your baby possess life and did God in his omniscience know who that child was and what his or her name would be if given a chance to be born?"

Gayle was trying to wrap her mind around what was being said. To her the child had no real identity, but yet she realized she aborted something, something that possessed life.

Jean's next question penetrated her thoughts. "How can you mourn something or know what to mourn if that something has no identity? How can you make peace with a life that will never be unless you acknowledged that life was important in the first place, and that life was an actual person who possessed an identity and a name?"

Gayle realized that Jean was right. How could she mourn what she did not personally know, and if she did not mourn the loss, her sorrow would remain. She had to somehow mourn the loss of her child, she had to mourn the life it would never live, and mourn the harsh reality that she would never share in seeing the child experience the joys, sorrows, and challenges of life.

In desperation, Gayle admitted her plight, "I don't know what to do. I don't know who I should mourn for. I don't know if it was a boy or a girl. I don't know anything!"

"You're right Gayle, you know nothing of the child, but God knows who that child is. He gave the names of John the Baptist and Jesus to their mothers before they were born, and likewise He knows what name would have been given to your child. It is for that reason you need to ask the Lord what the name of the child is so you can mourn for that child in order to give your intense sorrow the proper avenue in which to be addressed in a constructive way."

"Gayle figured she had nothing to lose. She needed to mourn. She started out slow, "Lord, I don't deserve to know the child's name. I don't understand everything, but I do know that I need to direct my sorrow through mourning towards a child who was offered up for no good reason. I know you have forgiven me, but I know I can't let go of the sorrow until I make peace with the child by mourning. Lord what was the name of the precious baby that I aborted?"

As soon as Gayle asked the question, a name came to her. This time she felt her heart break from sorrow, while at the same time her soul leaped with joy. It was overwhelming and confusing. Through her sobs, she shared the insight with Jean, "Her name is Faith, and the Lord is showing me at the same time that by not allowing Him to deal with my sin of fornication in the first place, and trusting Him to walk with me through my pregnancy, I also aborted my fledging faith before it could take flight and mature towards God in confidence and assurance."

It was all so overwhelming, but now Gayle could express her sorrow, "Forgive me my darling daughter, forgive me Faith for cutting your life and potential short of what God had ordained for you. Oh, please forgive me."

Jean's voice penetrated Gayle's anguish, "Gayle, you need to remember that Faith is safe in the glorious kingdom of Jesus, and that one day you will see her."

Gayle didn't understand all that was transpiring in her inner being, but she knew that she possessed the assurance that she would meet and see her daughter, and it brought her a sweet and overpowering comfort.

When Gayle left Jean's office two hours later, she was a new creation, forgiven, cleansed from within, healed, and restored. She knew only God could accomplish such a feat. She had run from His holiness because of sin, hid from His judgment because of shame, zigzagged to avoid seeking Him to absolve her wrongs, while justifying her morbid reality with attempts to right her wrongs; and, all the time the Lord Jesus had been waiting for her to turn around and seek Him. She had complicated the simplicity of Christ and had slid into an irrational reality that put the burden on her to make something so wrong, right in her own power. Granted, there was that place left in her heart by the abortion, but now it was marked by a memorial with the name "Faith" engraved on it.

Later that night she met Jay at their favorite eatery. She knew she had to admit everything to him. As she shared with him, he remained quiet and thoughtful. After she was through, he looked at her with understanding eyes, "I'm glad that you have made peace over such a tragedy. I also appreciate you sharing with me why you sometimes acted the way you did towards me. But, I realize I need to talk to this Jean. Can you give me her number?"

Gayle was a bit surprised. Jay seemed to have it together, but her admission had struck some cord with him and for some reason he needed to also talk to Jean. "It is none of my business Jay, but why would you want to talk to her?"

"I have my reasons, but I also plan to invite you to go along with me. Let's just say for now, it has to do with damage control, and leave it at that until we actually meet with her."

Jean had an appointment open in which both of them could meet with her a couple of days later. Jay seemed a bit apprehensive, but wore a determined expression on his face. When the receptionist handed him the forms, he filled it out at her desk and then came and sat by Gayle until Jean came out her office.

Jean warmly greeted both of them and after introductions the three of them went into her office. In her friendly way, Jean asked what she could do for Jay. Although Jay seemed a bit hesitant at first, the walls came down as the story spilled out.

He was a Christian who had become involved with a woman at a single Christian's club at the university. He thought he loved her and wanted to marry her. In a night of passion they got the cart before the horse and had a one-night stand. He knew it was wrong and wanted to address it, but she quickly withdrew from him.

It was later that he learned that she had become pregnant and without telling him she had an abortion. He was devastated. He was more than willing to marry her, and if she declined to marry him, he still would have personally taken care of the child, but she didn't afford him that opportunity of trying to do right by either of them.

The story sounded familiar to Gayle. She realized it could be coincidental that somebody from her past had a similar story, but there were too many facts that seemed to line up side by side. She knew she couldn't interrupt Jay's confession to confirm her suspicions one way of the other.

After he learned the terrible truth about the abortion, he became angry towards her. He fought the urge to solely blame her because he knew if he had properly honored her by fleeing youthful lust that night of temptation and passion, and personally demanded that their relationship maintain a Christian witness, he wouldn't be in the mess he was now in. However, no matter how much he tried to avoid sinking into a destructive cycle, the anger he felt towards her grew into hatred, and then bitterness. He became tormented as he quickly withdrew into a narrow pit of regret, shame, and sorrow.

He gained some semblance of hope when he met Gayle. He didn't want another failed relationship and had decided to do right by their relationship and God, but could see that both of them were carrying excess baggage. If their relationship did not sink from the baggage that was clearly weighing it down, a difficult and uncertain road still lay ahead of them.

That night when Gayle met him for dinner, and confessed everything that had transpired in her counseling session with Jean, he saw hope rising for the first time since the awful truth came out about the abortion. He realized he had been trying to deal with the fallout in his own strength and had failed to face God. He knew he needed to repent, seek forgiveness from the Lord, chose to forgive the mother of his child, receive restoration, and find healing from his deep sorrow.

As Jay finished his story, he looked at Jean. "I know what to do, but I need someone to help me until I reach the finish line. I need to confess my sin openly before the two of you to God. I need to ask Him to deliver me from my pit, heal me of the wounds left by anger and bitterness, and reveal my child's name to me so I can establish a memorial in my heart and properly mourn so I can let go of my sorrow."

Jean smiled, "Jay, you already possess the one who will help you to the finish line. He is the Spirit of the Living God who resides in you and has been quietly waiting for you to come back to the place where you left Him in anger, bitterness, and unforgiveness.

Jay shook his head yes, and through tears then proceeded to pour out his heart in repentance to the Lord, asking for forgiveness for his wayward ways. He asked the Lord to heal his broken heart and to restore the joy of his salvation, and then He asked the all-knowing God for the name of his child so that he could erect a memorial in his heart and finally mourn his great loss to silence the anguish of his soul.

After Jay's prayer, he looked at Gayle, and took her hand in his and then glanced at Jean with a smile. "I want you to know that the child that became lost to me has been identified and his name is Nathan, truly a gift from God, who now has been made alive by a memorial established in my heart. As David said of his infant son who died because of judgment on sin, that his son is unable to come to him, but one day he will go to his son. What a glorious consolation that is to my soul! Praise the holy name of God, our Creator, Redeemer, and Savior!"

There was great joy in Jean's office as the three of them rejoiced that it is God's desire to heal a broken heart, set the captive free, and heal those bruised by the sins of others. He came to preach the message that would secure healing, salvation, restoration, and liberty.

As they walked to the car from Jean's office, Gayle looked at Jay. "I hope you won't think me too nosy, but I was thinking about the woman you were involved with. How do you feel about her now?

Jay looked down for a second before answering. "No, I don't mind. I have nothing to hide. I realize that when it comes to abortion, everyone involved with it becomes a victim in some way. If she is a Christian, one day the reality of what has occurred is going to catch up with her. I hope she has someone like Jean around to help her wade through the emotional and spiritual fallout she is going to experience."

Gayle could no longer keep her curiosity at bay. "Can I ask you what her name is?"

Jay was quiet for a second, and then said in a hushed voice, "Her name is Linda Jones."

***

It seemed like a dream to Gayle. It was her wedding day and she was about to walk down the aisle to stand beside the man she would share the rest of her life with. She was humbled that the Lord would give her such a gift after she had committed such grave offenses. She was excited that even though she had taken detours the Lord was able to put her feet on the right path and lead her to a new life. She was awed that such a special time had been secured for her.

As her gaze swept over the crowd in the church, she saw Jean Graham. She quietly thanked the Lord for guiding her to Jean's office where He had met her and brought forgiveness, healing, and restoration to her tormented soul, while preparing her to receive a new beginning and a new life.

She then looked at Jay, dressed in a dark suit, smiling, waiting for her to walk down the aisle with her father by her side. Their broken lives had been put back together and now they would become one as the two of them openly committed themselves to each other and began their life together within the sanctity of marriage.

This time both had done right by the other, therefore ensuring God's blessing on their marriage. There were no dark clouds following them, no marred conscience to condemn them, and no hidden skeleton to taunt them about the past. The Lord had exposed the terrible darkness of both of their pasts with His transparent light of truth in order to address their sins and brokenness with His forgiveness and deliverance.

She occasionally mentally chided herself for not trusting the Lord with her sin and her fears and challenges. In spite of her unbelief, God in His mercy had kept her from tasting the full consequences for her actions, while in His grace He gave her a new life with meaning and purpose. Gayle realized that through the work of the Lord, she and Jay were knitted together by His very Spirit to become one in a binding unity.

They both had been damaged by the same types of sin, destined to wander in a pit of hopelessness. They had both tried unsuccessfully to control the damage that swept them into whirlpools of emotional and spiritual chaos.

In the chaos they both came to the same place of brokenness, learning that their attempts to right the wrongs of the past were foolish. From this premise they humbly sought restoration from the One who was in the ministry of reconciliation. In their plight the Lord Jesus Christ heard them, exposed and touched the damaged areas of their lives. He then did something glorious, He changed the scenario of death and despair and turned it into a sweet memorial, proving that He alone is in the business of controlling the damage left in the wake of devastating sins.

Gayle had personally learned that the world is a small place indeed and that sin creates a domino effect. Once the moral standard is let down in one area, the lies of Satan find a foundation in which to ensnare those who become confused, afraid, and shameful. Then lives and relationships begin to fall apart even more so as others become caught up and ensnared by the momentum. It is only God who can stop the momentum with His truth, control the damage with His mercy and forgiveness, and restore hope by reestablishing the promise of His abundant and eternal life.

As Gayle looked at Jay, she knew that the old life was behind her and that the new life God was giving was before them. Knowing that the old was clearly marked as being dead, it was time to leave the past behind and advance forward. She now had the assurance that the Lord would guide her steps, and she possessed the confidence that no matter how devastating the failure, God knows how to change the wrongs into living memorials, as well as blessed opportunities of healing, reconciliation, and restoration.

*If the Son therefore
shall make you free,
ye shall be free indeed.
(John 8:36)*

Freedom

Roberta Madilyn Harris Walker felt like she was in fantasy land. She was on her way to speak at Christian women's luncheon. She thought about what she was going to share with the women as various memories and past lessons paraded before her. As she collected her thoughts and the different nuggets of wisdom that were special to her, she marveled at how the Lord had led her from places of drudgery, normalcy, and failure to realize a life that operated in the freedom and heights of His Spirit.

She had discovered through the low valleys of despair and uncertainty, the plateaus of despondency, and the tough terrain of mountains, that God was faithful to lead her to pure and refreshing glacial springs, peaceful meadows, and satisfying crystal blue lakes.

As her mind retraced the path she had walked, she realized that she had spent most of her years seeking meaning and purpose. From the time she was a young girl her path had been planned out by her parents, etched in stone by traditions, and decreed so by culture. Since she was conditioned by family, put in a box by tradition, and indoctrinated by culture, she had assumed that her place in the world was already predetermined. Her whole goal was simple and her calling clear: she was to be a wife and mother. Although honorable in every way, these two positions had failed in the past to bring any resolution to her soul. When she contemplated the end of each role, she became lost and confused as she fell into a vacuum that left her feeling undone and empty.

Roberta didn't understand it at the time, but she had hit a crisis of purpose. In fact, she would discover there were three crises which often enveloped people in their lives and she would find herself being personally challenged by each one. The first crisis had to do with gender. She had to face this crisis as a teenager. Recognizing early that popularity in school, especially junior and senior high school, was based on ideas that surrounded a person's gender, she concluded that her destiny as to whether she was going to be accepted or not was already clearly outlined. The girls had to become cheerleaders and date the jocks to fit in the popular crowds, while the boys had to be good athletes to be recognized. To be intelligent wasn't always desired in such arenas. It didn't ensure positions of importance, and wasn't valued or considered the first priority by a society that appeared to always be looking for heroes in the sports field.

She was, in her mind, "passably pretty" but definitely not "beautiful." Her long dark auburn hair was naturally curly, and curly hair was not the "in thing" even though it softened her sharp features and accented her large, dark brown eyes. She was intelligent enough and had a wit about her that attracted some friends, but it was clear that she was void of the status and image to be a cheerleader. She knew that what often separated the most popular girls from the nominal and insignificant were their mannerisms, dress, and looks. As she considered the differences, she realized early that they were all surface. As different members of her family reminded her, mannerisms involved the attitude about those who maintained a certain status quo, while the type of dress pointed to money or setting the latest fashion. She realized it was all a game. To add to the game was presenting a certain outward image that had nothing to do with the inward person. A person had to be of a certain size, and for the girls their image had to be greatly enhanced by ample makeup, the right fashions, and hairstyle.

She concluded that due to her parents' honest standards she could not succumb to attitudes that simply housed arrogance driven by the fear of not fitting in and the uncertainties of ever belonging. As far as dress was concerned, her parents were not financially able to buy her the latest fashions. She dressed nice enough, but she realized dressing nice enough was not acceptable to those who touted the latest fashions. When it came to makeup, Roberta was aware that it brought out different aspects of her features, but she remembered what her uncle told her, "Any kind of paint can make an old barn look better, but it's still an old barn." It was made clear to her early in her life that the quality of a person is about inward character and not outward appearances.

As a result of her unwillingness to play games to be accepted by her peers, Roberta stood outside the popular cliques at school. She had been ignored by the in-group and forced to accept any leftovers that had been discarded by others. It became clear that she was the square peg that could never fit into the narrow round holes that had been chiseled out by the status quo.

The second crisis was the identity crisis, which happens when individuals must live up to some name, expectation, or status. Roberta had to face this crisis when she realized there were two sides of the tracks. According to the status quo, she was born on the wrong side of the tracks, and as a result, she grew up tasting prejudice and rejection at an early age. It became obvious that it didn't matter who she was, what her abilities, or hopes were—she was destined to live on the wrong side of the tracks in the minds of the society she grew up in.

Roberta's status change when she began dating the handsome Charles Walker, Jr., the only child of a well-respected business owner of the community. Charles Walker Sr. owned a successful meat-packing plant. Many in the community were employed by the plant. The Walker family represented those who ranked at the top among the socialites of the community. It was clear that everyone who wanted to be "somebody" in the community had to be part of the crowd that hung around the Walker family.

Although nothing had changed in Roberta's life, people's attitude towards her was being adjusted according to her association with Charley. It was obvious that people didn't care about who she was; rather, it was all about who she was involved with. However, she enjoyed the attention, knowing full well that it was surface and could quickly change if her status quo altered in the slightest way.

The third crisis had to do with purpose and is often associated with a mid-life crisis. This is where people pursue their idea of success, but when they obtain it, they are slammed with the harsh reality that it adds nothing of substance to their life. This leaves them with a sense that they wasted their life. They become disappointed that they bought a lie, and angry that their pursuits were nothing more than illusions that were covered by a false veneer of worldly glitter that would quickly fade when they obtained it. The personal experience of this particular crisis quickly taught her that other temptations would crop up elsewhere to lead the disappointed soul down another rabbit trail of false hope to only see the fleeing back of so-called "happiness," disappear in the distance, creating greater despair.

The third crisis proved to challenge her at different times in her life. She had become pregnant while dating Charley putting him in a position that required him to step up to the plate to maintain the family honor or end up looking like an irresponsible heel. His parents insisted his personal feelings or preferences didn't count. He made his bed and now he needed to lay in it and do what was honorable in regard to their first grandchild.

On their wedding day Charley did not appear happy about the arrangement, but Roberta was happy about her new lot and status in life. She wasn't only going to share her life with the man she loved, but in her mind she was carrying the proof of her love in her womb. Their wedding was minus much of the fanfare. It was quietly done in Charley's parent's home. Roberta's parents were there and she wore a simple cream dress, while Charley wore a nice tailored suit. The only thing that stood out to Roberta about her wedding day was that in one of his tender moments, Charley looked at her and called her "Rob," a name he had given her that in her mind had much endearment attached to it. He had assured her that everything was going to be alright.

Roberta had to admit that in spite of the precarious position Charley and her actions had put his parents in, they were gracious to her. She liked his father, Charles Sr. who was a self-made man, and was honorable in all of his dealings. His mother, Noreen, was a picture of perfection, but Roberta discovered that she was not trying to be perfect; rather, she was trying to do her best in everything she attempted. She had put high standards on herself, not to be part of the elite group, but to challenge herself to press towards that which was excellent.

It was clear that Charley's parents had tried to instill character in their son, but there was a wild streak in him that often made him belligerent and resentful towards them. Roberta had not seen his real attitude towards his parents since their relationship had been kept a secret from them. He had admitted to her that they objected to his involvement with her as far as dating, and it was only when Charley had to confess to them that she was in a "family way" that she had finally met them.

Roberta felt she had to prove herself to her new family. She had to somehow try to fit into the socialite group to make Charley and his parents proud of her. She attended some of the gatherings with her mother-in-law. It became obvious that the women, who were part of the elite socialites, barely tolerated her. They covered up their judgmental attitudes towards her with plastic smiles and a thin veneer of friendliness, but when Noreen was not present and Roberta's back was turned, the whispers and gossip inevitably started up. She knew that she was already judged and that she would never fit in. It was clear that she was a Walker in name only and would never aspire to the heights of approval because she had been born on the wrong side of the tracks.

She tried to get involved with church groups where the Walker family attended. Roberta was not raised in religion, but she had felt herself drawn to it. She saw her involvement with the church as a way to get her questions answered about God. Once introduced by Noreen to the church group, she flung herself into different projects. She learned how to make quilts for the missionaries and challenged herself to make so many in a year's time. She also participated with projects that helped the less fortunate. Sadly, she found that some of the women in the different women's church groups were not much different from the socialites.

The socialites hid their attitudes behind a veneer of phoniness, but the religious people hid theirs behind self-righteous attitudes that amounted to hypocrisy. When her back was turned, the whispers and gossip began, only it was not just because she was born on the wrong side of the tracks, but because of her moral indiscretion with Charley, along with other growing suspicions and speculations.

Secretly, she couldn't blame either group for their attitudes, but she didn't know how to reverse or change the events. She wondered who would accept her on the basis of who she was, and pondered if the socialites and self-righteous would ever give her a second chance to prove herself enough so that she could belong or be part of something that had purpose and lasting significance to it.

Thankfully, there was one person in the religious circles that became her friend. Her name was Donna Skyler. It was apparent that she loved God and immediately took an interest in Roberta when she first met her. In fact, she called Roberta, "Robbie." Roberta didn't sense that Donna had any underlying motive towards her; rather, Donna simply wanted to be friends with her.

It was due to Donna and Roberta's mother-in-law, Noreen that Roberta participated as much as she did in church activities. When she was teamed with Donna, she was allowed to be herself, laugh, and enjoy the activity. When Noreen headed a project she was involved in, she discovered a patient, motherly figure that inspired with her insights, directed according to past experiences, and instructed with wisdom. With Donna, Roberta enjoyed humor and laughter, and with Noreen, she experienced acceptance and encouragement.

Except for the projects at church that Roberta was involved with, for the most part she withdrew into her home as she decided to let her relationships as a wife and mother define her. She strived for perfection as a housewife and perceived that motherhood would probably bring her the most joy, but she eventually discovered that her personal relationships with those she loved the most exposed her weaknesses and her inabilities, while trying to make those in her environment happy and content.

She was the first to discover this harsh reality in her relationship with Charley. Even though her heart was to be a good wife, Charley, for the most part, seemed distant from her. The birth of their son, Ian brought some happiness to the couple, but Charley at best seemed to tolerate his life with her. When she got pregnant the second time, she felt that it would improve their relationship even more. Although the birth of Caroline brought some joy to the couple, Roberta sensed there was a restlessness growing in Charley. He was becoming more frustrated in his life with her and his work at his father's meat packing plant.

As the children grew, the family occasionally shared some special times, but most of Charley's activities with the family seemed as if they were points of duty or heavy burdens of responsibility. At certain functions he seemed to be ashamed to be seen with Roberta and impatient when he felt he had to do things with the children. These activities included church functions, social gatherings, and business related events.

At first Charley's despondency towards his lot in life caused Roberta to seek ways in which she could stir up former attractions, encourage an environment of romance and excitement. However, each attempt seemed to end in him displaying more frustration and occasionally a fight would ensue between them.

As a result of his foul attitude towards his marriage and occasionally his children, Charley spent a lot of time at work. He left early and came home late. She tried to adjust her schedule with a cheerful attitude but no matter what she did, her attempts proved to be futile.

It eventually became obvious to Roberta that she could never please him or make him happy. His frustration eventually turned into condescending remarks. At times he shamed her for things that didn't set right with his present mood. He mocked her when she failed to do something in an acceptable way. Sometimes she felt like a little girl being shamed by a parent, while at other times she felt uncertain and vulnerable. She never knew where she stood and felt that she had to walk on egg shells to survive his unpredictable moods.

When Ian was eleven and Caroline was nine everything that ailed Charley finally came to a head. He had come home in a foul mood and in her usual way, Roberta tried to walk the fine line between placating his mood and being pleasant regardless of how foul the environment was becoming by his presence. As she tried to present herself as a sweet, loving, submissive wife, Charley came unglued.

"Why are you placating me?" he yelled. "I wish you would quit trying to please me because no matter what you do it's nothing but a show. It's an absolute joke. I despise all of it! I wish you would leave me alone!"

Roberta was shocked. She had made a commitment to love Charley. Granted, at times she wanted to spank him for his terrible attitudes, yell at him for his indifference, and rage against him for his cruel, angry ways, but she also knew she loved him. It was also obvious that he often pushed her away, but she had made a vow to stick by him during good times and bad. It was not just a formality she went through on their wedding day; it was something she meant with all of her heart.

Still stung by his statements, Roberta calmly asked him, "What do you want from me Charley? I love you and I have been trying everything I know to make this marriage work, but it takes two to keep a marriage together and you give the impression you want nothing to do with it."

"You're right! I want nothing to do with this marriage!" he declared through clenched lips. "You don't get it Rob, do you?"

"Get what Charley?" she asked with a hurt tone.

"I never wanted to marry you in the first place. The only reason I went out with you was because my friends dared me. When I saw how it made my parents upset, I continued to date you just to get back at them.

"I figured I would have a little fun with you, but I never dreamed you would get pregnant. Since, my parents didn't want their first grandchild to be a bastard child raised by a gold-digger from the other side of the tracks, I was told that I either marry you or I would be disowned, and since I am accustomed to a certain lifestyle and status, I reluctantly agreed."

Roberta felt like she had been hit by a freight train. Her head was spinning from the impact of his statements. She felt like she was ushered into a surreal world that had all the earmarks of turning into a nightmare. She struggled to grasp the harsh reality of what she had just heard so she could actually respond in some fashion.

"I don't understand, Charley, I thought you liked-d-d-d me. You told me that you went out with me because I was witty and not a fake like the other girls. You told me you loved me. If-f-f-f I thought you didn't love me I would have never given myself to you." Roberta

359

stopped for a second to pull back the tears that stung her eyes and control the pent up anger that was seething up from the abyss of her soul.

Her voice began to rise along with her anger, "I guess our dating was nothing but a sick joke to you and our marriage a sham. You told me on our marriage day that everything would be alright...was that another one of your sick lies? And, what does our sham of a marriage make our children to you? A terrible mistake, a grave inconvenience to you, --ILLEGITIMATE?"

Roberta could tell by Charley's face that he realized he just trashed something that was sacred, stepped over a line that could not be erased, reversed, or taken back, and hurt someone who was acting in innocence. For a split second Roberta saw regret on his face.

"Rob, I didn't mean to hurt you."

"Hurt me Charley! What did you think your raw truth would do once you let it out of the bag? Just because I'm from the other side of the tracks doesn't make me less feeling than you when I am treated with such disrespect...AS IF I AM LESS THAN HUMAN OR SUBSTANDARD!"

She backed away from him. "Just because I was naïve enough to believe your lies about your intention towards me doesn't mean I deserve to drink the bitter cup of your treacherous actions! Just because I am considered unworthy of your class doesn't give you or anyone else the right to use me for some sick pleasure and then stomp on my heart and discard me like a piece of trash!"

Charley made a move towards her as if to comfort her. She jumped back from his gesture. "DON'T TOUCH ME! Who do you think you are? You transpose your treachery on me by calling me a gold-digger, as if you had something I needed. For your information, it's true my association with you gave me status that I initially became caught up with, but I recognize that in spite of the so-called 'acceptance' of the more 'elite,' it was phony, and that their arrogant attitudes towards me remained the same!

"My intentions toward you were pure and sincere. I truly loved you and that is why I did what I did. Granted, our actions were not right, and I clearly was blinded by an immature love that I felt for you, but you need to remember you're the one that lied in the first place about your real intentions!"

Clearly, Charley had opened a dam, and everything that she had been feeling erupted. "It's obvious that since I'm nothing in your mind, your deceptive actions are justifiable in your eyes! Apparently, I don't deserve respect or consideration like others from the right side of the tracks! My, Charley, you're not only a liar, you're a bon-a-fide snob of the worst type!"

By this time Charley was scrambling to maintain some type of dignity. "Come on Rob, you have to admit I saved you from an-n-n...unbecoming life and gave you name and status. You now have a beautiful home, wear the latest fashions, and drive the newest model car."

"You SAVED me from what?" she screamed. "Let me ask you what have you SAVED ME TO? A loveless marriage based on a lie? If that is real salvation, then life is a big joke and my present misery will prove to be greater than my so-called 'former misery'. As for my present name and status, it has not changed prideful attitudes. To the elite, I'm still Roberta Harris, that girl from the other side of the tracks, who now must be placated with pretend smiles that cover sneers and a forced tolerance."

"And, what about the house we live in? Granted, it is a house but is it a HOME? It's big, but empty and marked by thick darkness of indifference between us that can be cut with a knife. For the fashions I wear, well it's obvious that they can't cover what has been made cheap by selfish attitudes and wrong actions. As for the car I drive, I would prefer a clunker over the SORROW AND BITTERNESS I'm now tasting!"

Roberta narrowed her eyes at Charley as she looked into his stunned face, "You can convince yourself that you have been noble towards me. You can exalt yourself above my family roots and my former status, but there is a big difference between those who raised me and you and those of your ilk. Although my family was considered poor folks, they were always honest folks. They taught me that I must keep in mind that the greatest person I would have to ultimately face in the end is myself. Let me ask you Charley, will you be able to face yourself in the end?"

She turned around and walked away, leaving Charley speechless. Roberta realized that she had just been broadsided by a rogue wave that was so high emotionally she felt herself being taken down into the depths of a watery grave that encased her with anger, hurt, mistrust, and depression. There was nothing left of the resolve she had towards her marriage. It had been shattered into thousands of pieces, causing her hope to be aborted on the raging seas of turmoil, and her expectations to be cast on the endless waves of uncertainty.

Roberta sought the sanctuary of the guest bedroom and locked herself within its confines. She didn't want to see or talk to Charley or anyone else until she made sense out of the senseless. How could a human being be so cruel to another human being? How could a man who made a vow to her in front of others discard it and use it like a knife to rip from her common decency, whip her with the cords of cruelty, and stomp on her life as if it was a small, insignificant fire that must be put out.

She sat in the dark room and ignored the knocks and voices of Charley and the children. She became aware that around supper time Charley had taken the children out of the house, probably to dinner and had possibly instructed them not to bother her. She sought peace and quiet, but her soul was reeling from the impact of the tsunami that had emotionally sunk her. The truth is she didn't know what to do. She couldn't calm her raging feelings, nail down her tumultuous emotions, or collect her thoughts, leaving her empty as she faced the darkness that engulfed the room and her soul.

Through the night, confusion continually nipped at Roberta's raw emotions. She wrestled with who she could go to, to gain some semblance of understanding. She thought of her mother-in-law, Noreen, but Charley's statements about his parents' attitudes towards her about being a gold-digger caused uncertainty and suspicion to form a wall of mistrust against both of them. Sadly, he had managed to taint her attitude towards his parents, but she also didn't feel right about testing a parent's loyalty when it comes to his or her child.

By the time the sun arose, Roberta was exhausted from the wrestling match she endured the night before. Her eyes were red from the tears that had freely flowed down her cheeks during the dark night. Sadly, she was no closer to an answer for her plight than when the confrontation first began. In fact, she felt as if she was further away from coming to any real resolution or solution.

She looked in the mirror and realized it would take an extra measure of paint to make her swollen features presentable to the world. She knew that she had to escape the empty echo of her big house. She half-heartedly applied some makeup to avoid being accused of wearing a Halloween mask out of season by the town gossips.

She drove to her favorite coffee shop to get an espresso. As she stood staring at the different coffees and food articles on the sign, she heard the familiar voice of Donna from behind her.

"Robbie, are you alright?"

Roberta looked at her in bewilderment before she responded, "I'm a daisy."

Donna took a step back as to size her up, "What do you mean you're a 'daisy'?"

"I'm just standing here in a daze."

Donna's look of concern was interrupted by a smile that made a quick entrance, and then disappeared.

"Robbie, it's obvious we need to talk." Donna guided her over to a secluded table and sat her down in a chair with her back to the activities of the store. "Have you eaten anything?"

Roberta shook her head no. "You stay here," Donna instructed, "and I'll get us both a coffee and something to snack on while we talk."

Once Roberta had drunk most of her espresso and eaten half a bagel, she felt refreshed enough to talk.

Donna asked the obvious, "What happened Roberta? You act as if you lost your best friend."

"I did lose my best friend," Roberta looked down. "I lost my husband," she paused and looked into Donna's concerned, compassionate face. "The truth is Charley was never my friend. I kidded myself so I could live in denial about our relationship. The awful truth is he really wasn't my husband. We were married in name only and at times he simply pretended to be my husband, which means we really never had a marriage. It was all a farce!"

Roberta felt she was beginning to ramble on. However, it was from this introduction that Roberta told Donna what had transpired between Charley and her. Since Charley's words were burned on her heart, through tears of sorrow, brokenness, and rejection, she shared the complete sordid story of what had occurred the night before.

Donna quietly listened to Roberta's tale of betrayal and destruction. When Roberta was finished, Donna asked her the obvious question, "What are you going to do, Robbie?"

"I DON'T know Donna. I NEED answers, but I'm not sure I can emotionally handle them or carry them out. I hate to admit it but I'm a broken woman. I'm not sure I have anything left to give."

With great intensity, Donna responded, "Your marriage has clearly hit a crisis point, Robbie, but you need to make some decisions. And, you need to be in the right mind to make the right decisions because it's going to determine the type of person you become and the environment that will be set up as to your relationships with Charley and the children."

"DIDN'T you hear me Donna, I've nothing left to give," Roberta firmly declared.

"You're right Robbie, you have nothing left to give. You're a cracked and empty vessel right now, but I know of a Potter who can't only put you back together, but fill your life."

Roberta looked skeptically towards her friend, "And, just who is this potter?"

Donna smiled, "His name is Jesus Christ, He is the Messiah, the Son of God, and the soon and coming King. He is Creator, your Creator and He knows who you are and how He has made you. He alone knows how to put you back together."

Roberta had heard about this Jesus at church. She thought of Him as an interesting person, an honorable man, a caring leader, and was impressed that He died for sinful people. However, in Roberta's mind she was a decent person for she had come from hard-working, law-abiding, honest, and caring folks. It was true she had not been right in her relationship with Charley, but she was trying to remedy that by doing good deeds. Therefore, she didn't see that she was in need of Jesus' intervention. At the time she didn't give Jesus any real consideration because she actually thought she had it altogether and was not in need of His services.

With a firm voice, Donna penetrated Roberta's reminiscing, "Robbie, didn't you hear me? Jesus is the one who can heal you, make you whole, and fill you with His abundant, rich, eternal life."

Roberta whined, "Just how can this Jesus make things right? It is a disaster. Charley has hurt me so bad, I can't see forgiving him. I can't stand the thought of living with him, but I can't stand the idea of giving up on our marriage either." Roberta paused, "I guess I could murder him and put him out of his misery and solve the problem, but then again he isn't worth going to jail for, the... JERK."

Donna chuckled, "It's nice to see you have some sense of humor left, but don't ignore the solution that you are being offered here today."

"Donna, I've always thought myself to be a decent and reasonable person. I know Jesus came for sinners, but I'm not a liar or mean and cruel."

"So you don't think you need Jesus?" Donna asked?

"I'm not quite saying that, Donna. It's just that I'm not all that bad." She paused as anger seethed to the surface, "It's Charley who destroyed everything last night!"

"Robbie, are you telling me you do not think you're a sinner?"

"Well I'm not as bad as Charley! After all he's the one who trashed who I am and everything I tried to do. It's not fair that you have made this problem about me."

With a firm voice, Donna set the record straight, "That is where you are wrong, my friend. This is not about Charley right now, this is about you and where you are at spiritually. You're broken and hurting and Jesus came to heal those bruised by sin, the sins of others and you have been wounded and bruised by Charley."

Roberta felt the wall of stubbornness come up. She had every right to remain the victim in this situation. In her mind, it was only fair that the offender be dealt with first before she would allow herself to be healed. "Maybe I don't want to be healed, because it's only by remembering what he did to me that will keep me on guard. He'll never hurt me again…you hear me, NEVER AGAIN!"

Sternness descended over Donna's features. "Roberta, most likely he'll hurt you again in some way. It won't take much because the wounds are already there to be reopened. We are not meant to wear our wounds like badges of courage. Wounds fester and will turn into bitterness that will do greater harm in the end! You already feel as if you've been robbed of something precious, but now you're willing to give away or sacrifice what is left of your person and sanity to taste the depths of something that will poison and kill what is left, and FOR WHAT? You are waiting for Charley to get it so you feel vindicated in some way. The truth is CHARLEY MAY NEVER GET IT! You need healing right now and Jesus is the only one who can do it!

Roberta felt her wall coming down, "How can I let go of this, how can I forgive Charley?"

Donna was quick with the answer, "The same way Jesus is going to forgive you when you actually seek it from Him."

Roberta was shocked, "Why does Jesus need to forgive me?" She shook her head as if to grasp the concept she had just been presented. "In my defense, for the most part I have been pretty good. Granted, there are a few things in my life I'm not proud of, but that's true for everyone, right?"

"Let me ask you something Robbie. How many times did it take for Charley to devastate you? I mean how many times has he trashed you to bring you to this point?"

Roberta took a minute to process the question, "Well, only once, but there were a lot of comments and innuendoes that led up to it, but I don't see what this has to do with me needing forgiveness."

Donna was ready with an answer, "How many times do you need to trash Jesus, whether by an attitude of unbelief or by your actions, before you break His heart?"

Roberta was taken back by her question, "Perhaps once, but I never intended to break His heart if I have."

"Robbie, do you believe that Charley set out to break your heart?"

"Well- I-I…"

"Do you believe that Charley got up that morning and said to himself, "I'm going to literally destroy Roberta today with the intent of destroying our relationship altogether?"

Roberta had to admit that Donna was making some valid points, "No. Charley is selfish, but I don't think he intended to hurt me. In fact he looked guilty when he realized what he had done to me."

"You know what Jesus said when He was on the cross? He asked the Father to forgive those who were part of His crucifixion for they knew not what they were doing. After all, they were crucifying the very Son of God."

Roberta was beginning to get caught up with Donna's presentation, "Then why did Jesus not reveal to them who they were crucifying and avoid the cross?"

"Robbie, He told them many times who He was, but their hearts were blinded, and it had to be so for Jesus to fulfill the plan of His Father. Jesus came, Robbie, to die for me and to die for you because we have all sinned. We are all sinners because we are born with an inherent disposition that separates us from a holy God. It destroys any relationship we could have with Him. Perhaps you may have a couple of sins accredited to your account, but you cannot change what they did to God. He cannot even look at sin without judging it, so He looks away.

"However, He wants a relationship with man, and sent His Son to provide and secure a way in which man can be saved and brought back into a relationship with Him."

When Roberta heard the word "saved" she could not help but interject what Charley had said the day before, "Sorry for interrupting you, but do you know what Charley told me, that he had saved me from my lot in life, but I told him what I thought of his type of salvation!"

A knowing grin played on Donna's lips as if she could imagine the exchange but she quickly became serious again, "There's only one Savior of all people, including you, and it is not Charley. It was on the cross of Christ that mankind witnessed what sin does to God, whether it is one sin or many, but it wounds Him, and rips at Him and ultimately breaks His heart, while its grave spiritual darkness separates Him from those He loves, from those He came to die for."

Roberta was being shaken by the reality of what she was hearing, "You mean if there was only one sin that separated a person from God, Jesus would still have to die for that person?"

"Yes, Robbie, because God is that holy and sin is that bad and unacceptable to Him. Man can't do anything to change his unacceptable status before God."

Roberta was pondering the implications of sin, "You mean, Donna, that no matter what I do, I can't right my wrongs before God?"

"Let me ask you something Robbie. How offended were you by what Charley said to you?"

She still could feel the sharp wretchedness of his words upon her soul, "Beyond words. The damage was clearly done and can't be reversed."

"Is there anything Charley could do to right that offense? Can he take it away or cast it to the furthest ends of the earth?"

The light was slowing dawning for Roberta, "No he can't make it right no matter what he does, unless I somehow let go of it."

"Our sins greatly offend God, and can you or I somehow make it right?"

"I guess not."

"There's a big difference Robbie. Charley can't save you and you have no authority or power to judge Charley, but God sent His Son to save people from the consequences of eternal separation from Him, to let go of the great offenses committed against Him and cast them far away from His sight; but for those who ignore, deny, or refuse to address the offenses they have caused God, He will judge them through His Son, and they'll discover that they will have no recourse in reversing their actions or stopping God's righteous judgment. It is appointed unto man to die once, then comes judgment."

Roberta began to feel undone. She had thought herself guilty of only one bad sin that the Bible refers to as fornication, but the truth of the matter was her conscience was being pricked about sins she considered as not being so offensive. As she pondered this revelation, her offenses began to form a parade before her, bringing an overwhelming indictment against her.

Some sins were judgmental attitudes and others involved wrong thinking and unbecoming reactions towards those who offended her. There were the times she silently raged against Charley for his cruel words and thoughtless actions, as well as against those who judged her as being substandard. She began to see the pride behind her being presented as the helpless victim due to the prejudice of others— pride that had caused her to become superior in her mind. She was clearly feeling the sting of former actions that were offensive to God and no doubt hurtful to others.

However, the greatest indictment was that of unbelief towards God. She had failed to believe His Word, to see that she was a sinner in need of His forgiveness. She needed her sins taken away and cast far from the light and justice of God. She sat there wondering how she could have been so blind to the truth of her spiritual state. She was lost and didn't know it. She was standing condemned in her sins, but was clueless, and she was abiding under God's wrath and was oblivious to the way she was walking, always towards His judgment and eternal damnation.

It was then that Roberta Madilyn Harris Walker knew she was a wretched sinner, indicted by her fallen ways of rebellion and unbelief, destined to die in the misery of her sins, to taste an eternal damnation and to only know the ways of complete ruin and destruction. She was a hopeless cause, unable to reverse the wounds and offenses of her selfish actions, as well as her wretched attitudes, her wicked ways, and her evil intentions brought against God and others.

As she reeled from the awful reality of her despicable condition, she realized she was no different than Charley. Granted, Charley wounded her deeply, but she had deeply wounded the Son of God. Charley mocked her, but she showed contempt towards God's provision by casting it aside as being immaterial to her life.

Roberta could do nothing more except to cry out as she grabbed Donna's arm, "Oh, Donna, I am a TERRIBLE SINNER, lost to God, and destined for a Christ-less eternity."

She paused and took a breath before the rest of the awful realization of her plight tumbled through her quivering lips. Tears ran down her cheeks as an inner, urgent desperation grew. She felt as if she was swinging over the abyss of hell as its fires nipped at her heels, "I NEED forgiveness, I NEED mercy, I NEED my sin cast away from me, I NEED to be saved, but I don't know how to be saved. Help me Donna, I CAN'T save myself, I CAN'T change anything. I'm doomed!"

Donna grabbed Roberta's arm, "Roberta listen to me, all you feel now is the terrible weight of your sin, crushing you, but remember Jesus came to take your place on the cross to bear the terrible weight of judgment that abides upon you right now because of your sin. When He went to the grave, He took your sins so they could no longer be seen by heaven above. He rose again to prove victory over death that separates us from God. Do you believe these truths and confess them as so and receive Jesus as Savior and Lord with all of your heart, knowing that His eternal and abundant life is what will be given to you, and that He is God's unspeakable gift that the Bible talks about?"

Roberta shook her head and through sobs declared what she heard about her sin and Jesus was now true, "Yes, I believe that Jesus died for me and that He took my sins to the grave and rose again. Yes I receive Him as my Savior, confess Him as Lord, and receive His life as God's gift to me."

"Then, Robbie, believe that He has pulled you out of harm's way and set you on solid ground, the solid ground of redemption. Know your sins have been washed away and removed as far as the east is from the west, never to be recollected or remembered ever again by the just court of heaven."

As Donna's words went into Roberta's tormented soul she felt as if a stream of living water had broken forth in the depths of her being and was washing away her sins, cleansing her of all the debris of unrighteousness and healing her of the scarred terrain of her heart and soul. Her sorrowful, frightening sobs began to turn into tears of joy as she felt the presence of something new and wondrous. She did not understand it all, but she believed that it was confirming the glorious hope of her salvation.

The scene in the corner clearly took an about face. Instead of a blanket of sorrow and despair hanging over the two women, it was being parted by abounding joy as both women rejoiced in what had just occurred. Roberta couldn't fathom the change that had taken place in her but she felt different and the world no longer looked dark and formidable. She had come to the coffee shop facing the bleak reality of a marriage gone terribly wrong and a life that was being consumed by a sorrow that went so deep that at times she felt as if she could not breathe. But, now she had looked into the light of God and found hope, new life, and healing. She was no longer weighed down by the unseen weights of sin and despair, now she was almost floating as her heart leaped for joy and a new song emerged in her soul.

That day Roberta Madilyn Harris Walker was born again with the breath of heaven infusing new life into her. She had no idea what the future held for her as far as Charley was concerned, but she had the assurance that life would never be the same for her. She now had a faithful companion, who not only created the heavens and the earth, but had the power to change the terrain of her life and her relationships.

***

As Roberta walked into the building where she would be speaking at the women's luncheon, she couldn't help but recall that glorious day of salvation. She knew that day marked the beginning of her spiritual journey. She never imagined that the path specifically designed by God for her would lead her to such an event where all eyes would be focused on her and every ear open to hear what she would say.

She soon discovered after her salvation that even though her feet were on a different path, she found that Christians experience the same challenges as everyone else. The difference is that walking by faith towards God brings one through challenges, with the intent of instilling godly virtues in their inner character.

The focus of the crisis changed as well. Roberta discovered that Christians experience what many refer to as the crisis of faith. There are different crises of faith she experienced along the way. It was always amazing to her how God brought her to each point of crisis to teach her valuable lessons about faith. As the great Potter He was, and continues to be, the One who does the deep work in a person's soul. The Lord knew how to use the right instruments to forge in her Christian virtues that began to discipline her walk and define her calling and abilities.

Granted, she didn't enjoy the fires of each test, but she couldn't help but glory in the Potter's ability to bring out meekness and grace in such a beautiful way. Each crisis, each experience, and each lesson brought a refinement to her person that she would marvel at. She knew only God could accomplish such an incredible feat.

The first crisis in her faith walk that she encountered was that of the "crisis of reality." There are those who erroneously see faith as a way to move God's arm in order to change their present reality. At first it seemed like a honeymoon for Roberta and her new found love for the Lord. Some of her simple prayers were quickly answered. She clearly saw the advantages of being a Christian.

However, the honeymoon didn't last long. The truth is that her life had changed, but Charley had not changed. As a zealous Christian, Roberta had decided to forgive him and rededicate herself to their marriage. Regardless of what transpired, she realized that she needed to make a real commitment to do right towards Charley to overcome her tumultuous feelings that would come to the surface at different times. She had to overcome anger with godly love, hurt with forgiveness, feelings of vengeance with mercy, and resentment with grace.

Charley was glad to see that she was joyful in spite of their confrontation. He was tolerable towards the fact that she had found "religion" as he called it, but he was the same Charley, harboring the same attitudes and foul moods.

In the beginning of her Christian walk Roberta knew from past experiences that she could not harp at Charley about religious matters. He had a very short fuse as to tolerating any type of nagging. She realized that she had to be a quiet living example. She also asked the

Lord in a child-like way to change his heart and attitudes so that they could have a godly family. However, as time went by, she became more desperate because the more she asked the Lord to change him, the more difficult Charley became. She tried to be Christian in her attitude towards him, but found herself often running out of patience and options.

In the end she became confused, and one day in frustration she asked the Lord a simple question, "Why Lord aren't You changing him? I stuck with him and am doing the best I can, but he seems worse at times. What do you want from me?"

It was at that time that Roberta learned a very important lesson: ask the Lord but learn to listen with your heart because you could very well be on the receiving end of an answer.

In the recesses of her spirit she heard a question, "Why do you want him to change?"

Roberta looked around the living room, but she was the only one in the house and realized it was the Lord speaking to her spirit. As she examined her motive for wanting to see her husband change, she realized it had nothing to do with Charley, but with her having an easier and more pleasant time at home. She suddenly could see that although her request seemed reasonable and honorable, her motive was pure selfishness.

After the unveiling of her motive, another question was posed to her, "In what way would you expect Charley to change?"

Roberta thought about the question. Did she have lofty expectations as to the type of man Charley would be if the Lord changed him? As she honestly evaluated her expectations, she could see that they were unrealistic. The reality was that she expected the Lord to change Charley to meet her expectations, but he wouldn't end up being just a changed man, but a completely different man, a man who only existed in her imagination.

It was then that Roberta realized she was not operating in reality. She still had romantic notions about life and held to expectations that wouldn't allow for any human inconsistencies or frailties. She was shocked at her childish attitude and ideas about life. She had just read in 1 Corinthians 13 that in order to operate in God's love believers needed to put off childish ways.

Roberta realized that God was after her. He was doing a deep work in her, but He could only do it from the point of sincerity and truth. It was obvious that there were areas of deception where she operated from unrealistic expectations to wishful thinking that ended in frustration and anger. God was using her relationship with Charley to put a mirror up to reveal the character of her own soul, and she didn't like what she was seeing about herself. At the core of her motives and actions was idolatrous, wicked selfishness.

She was shocked to realize much of her willingness to do things for others was not based on doing something because it was right; rather, it was motivated by the idea of receiving approval and recognition from those who were on the receptive end of her actions. Her motive was clearly unveiled by the frustration and anger that would eventually follow when she did not receive the proper approval and acknowledgment. All she could do was repent and give the Lord permission to change her.

Roberta was to learn over a period of time that she was like an onion. God carefully peeled away layer after layer revealing something else about the attitudes and ways that were still associated with her "old man." She was forever coming face to face with those quirks that revealed how much the old Roberta was still ready to resurrect the fleshly ways and thoughts of the "old man."

There was an incident where Charley's condescending attitude came out one day while they were working together on some personal bookkeeping for tax purposes. Charley was tired of the forms and irritable with the required details to complete the task. Roberta asked a simple question and Charley's answer was short and condescending. Immediately Roberta felt offended, hurt, and angry. After all, she had done nothing against Charley, why would he always have to take it out on her? As she felt self-pity raise its head, she heard the familiar Voice in her soul, "Why are you offended?"

Roberta had an answer, "I'm offended because I don't deserve to be treated in such a manner."

Another question followed suit, "What is behind his reaction?"

Roberta had to admit since her attitude had changed in many areas, Charley was responding in a more positive way as well. In fact, he was showing himself to be friendlier towards her and they had found other common ground besides the children to talk about. There had even been moments of laughter. She knew that he was tired and agitated and that it was not personal, but she couldn't help but complain about him taking it out on her.

As she examined the situation, she realized that Charley was simply being human. She was taking offense because he didn't have patience, while at the same time claiming some right to be treated a certain way to maintain her own level of patience, while catering to her fickle pride. There was that insipid pride again, only it was hiding behind so-called "rights." However, as a servant of God her only right was to do right by God by doing right towards others.

The voice penetrated through her latest revelation, "Do you want people to give you a break when you are being human?"

Roberta remembered all of her human moments of frustration, being short when tired, venting when agitated, and flying off the handle when overwhelmed. She realized if she wanted others to give her a break during her very human moments, then she had to do likewise to them.

Each reflection of the "old man" in Roberta caused her to gain a greater understanding of just how far the Lord had to reach down in order to pull her out of the fires of hell that were inching their way upwards and towards her with each sin, delusion, and display of unbelief. As God went down each layer she realized even more just how far away from the mark she was. Gaining glimpses into the depth of her depravity produced greater compassion in her for others. The view she developed towards others in their struggles, including Charley, was that of mercy. The words "Blessed are the merciful for they shall obtain mercy," constantly came to her. She desperately needed God's mercy so she could likewise show mercy to others, while tasting the sweetness of His unmerited grace.

There was one incident where her relationship with Charley not only taught her a valuable lesson, but set her on a different course. Since her conversion, Roberta was becoming more involved with church functions. One day she was invited to the weekly lunch by a certain group of women who were attending the same Bible Study with her.

The conversation started off with surface subjects about the weather and social activities, but eventually it digressed into each woman talking about her husband. At first it seemed innocent enough. To Roberta the women were speaking of personal matters to gain perspective, and she felt she likewise needed some perspective when it came to Charley. It took over a month before Roberta realized that they each fed on the negative, irritating aspects of their husbands, but there was no counsel or instruction that followed addressing their attitudes and handling of their relationship with their husbands.

Roberta initially failed to recognize that it was a trap that would end in a feeding frenzy as each woman complained about the quirks, irritating, and what were considered "clueless" ways of their husbands. The first week Roberta walked away from the luncheon not feeling so alone in her plight with Charlie. The next week she walked away irritated at him because he didn't get it. The third week, she found herself pretty well mad at all men because it appeared as if their gender provided them with a pass when it came to showing consideration to their wives.

Within a month Roberta's attitude towards Charley was foul. In her mind, she was trying to be a perfect wife and he was not reciprocating. One day she had lunch with Donna and began to complain about Charley. Donna sat silent for about a half an hour when she finally interrupted Roberta, "Roberta where does all of this complaining come from? I thought you and Charley were doing better."

Donna's question stopped Roberta in her tracks. "Well, some of the Bible Study women get together for lunch every week after Bible Study and share their similar problems."

"Problems or irritating complaints?" Donna questioned. "I know all about those women and it's for that reason I don't even go to that particular Bible Study, as well as trying to avoid their company. These women are gossiping about their husbands. If there's a problem they should discreetly seek out wise Biblical counsel that will challenge them in their grumbling ways and not air it while their husbands are not there to confront it. Granted, some of these women may have legitimate concerns, but complaining about it will not change it; rather, it will create a foul environment that will produce worthless fruits in those who partake of it.

"Consider yourself, Roberta. When you decided the responsibility for your attitude and actions towards Charley rested with you, things started changing for you, but now you're making it all about Charley, and how is that working for you? What kind of fruits is it producing in your attitude towards your husband?"

Roberta felt the heavy hand of the Lord upon her. She knew that she was being rightfully chastised. However, Donna was not finished, "The Bible tells us evil communications corrupt good manners. As you expose yourself to these women's critical, miserable spirit, you have not only come under their wrong spirit but you are partaking of their sin."

Roberta once again saw the error of her way. She felt silly that she had fallen into their trap, and foolish that she so soon forgot that it will always come down to her personal attitude towards something that God is the most interested in.

"Robbie, the problem with looking at anyone with a critical eye, is the glass will always be half empty. As Christians we need to always look for opportunities to minister to our spouses and children. If we are constantly looking at their irritating ways, we will fail to see their potential through the eyes of God.

"The potential of every person is that they have been designated to be conformed to the image of Jesus. If we fail to keep that in mind, we will never be able to properly encourage them or address them in a constructive way. It is for this reason Christians need to learn to minister to people according to their potential in the kingdom of God. If Christians don't approach every soul in the right spirit for the right reason, they will justify away their Scriptural responsibility to do what is right by that person, bringing a reproach on Christ and their personal testimony."

Roberta realized that people are just the way the Bible describes them, sheep that can easily be taken out of the way of righteousness, and cleverly led to the slaughter. It didn't matter who the sheep were, if they lacked the moral strength to stand for righteousness on their own, they could easily be led astray by petty, non-essential matters. People clearly needed the touch of heaven's truth to operate in the right spirit.

She wondered how many times she had to go around the same mountain to learn the same lesson. She realized the scenery may look different, but it's the same mountain and the same test. She needed to always come back to center of who God is, what His Word says, and the examples that are clearly outlined in the lives of Jesus and the saints of old.

That night Roberta repented in brokenness and decided to separate herself from the small-minded company of women. However, she needed to fill her time with productive activities. It was then that she decided to attend the local college and take courses in business and bookkeeping. After all, the children attended school during the day and schedules could be easily adjusted to ensure that she would not drop the ball when it came to the mission field of her home.

Another crisis she experienced was the crisis of dependency. She always perceived that she could handle a matter by influencing the direction people were heading. However, as her children strove to find their own way in the world her perspective was greatly challenged.

Roberta recognized that Charley was set on his course and until he was thoroughly convicted by the Spirit and decided to do an about face he would remain on the same path. At first she had prayed fervently for him, but recognized that God would not step over his free will. However, she so wanted to influence her children to walk in the ways of God.

At first Ian seemed receptive towards Roberta's newfound life in God, while Caroline, even at her tender age, seemed to become quickly bored with what she referred to as the "religious scene." Roberta could see that Ian had a compliant nature to him, which made her wonder what he really believed. She wasn't sure if he was compliant because he agreed with her or if he was compliant because it was a good way for him to keep her off his back.

On the other hand, as Caroline reached her teenage years, she became more openly rebellious towards what she considered to be inferior, foolish, and beneath her. As Roberta observed her closely, she could tell that her daughter was walking in the footsteps of Charley. Granted, she might have encouraged it before she came to Christ by reminding them they were "Walkers" and had a responsibility in the community and at their local church to uphold a certain standard. She was also aware that Caroline idolized her father and wanted to be like him. After all, to her he epitomized success, business savvy, and happiness, while choosing to blatantly ignore the big gaps that were present in his character.

Roberta tried different measures to become an influential part of their world. She tried to befriend them, but often found they were embarrassed by her overtures. She tried nudging them with suggestions, but they ignored her. She tried to put some so-called "needed" pressure on them, but Ian withdrew from her more and Caroline openly defied her.

The more Roberta tried to influence her children towards God, the more their attitudes came to the forefront. When Ian was 16, he took an interest in the meat packing business, opting to work with his father and grandfather when he was not busy with school activities, while Caroline at fourteen became more caught up with the vanity of the world. As the demands of school and the business consumed Ian's time, the more complacent he became towards God, revealing the real source behind his initial compliance: it was an apparent game to keep his mother off of his back.

For Caroline she saw no need for God. She saw herself as controlling her world and destiny. The idea of God was an unnecessary distraction and would possibly confuse the issues. When she was fourteen she declared that she would have none of God or religion.

At first Roberta's prayers for her children were childlike, but as the siblings developed and leaned more and more towards the world, her prayers became desperate. She wrestled before God, and at times tried to reason with Him in regard to all of her attempts to bring them to the reality of His salvation, but as each birthday passed for them, they became more indifferent and obstinate.

All of Roberta's attempts eventually brought her to utter despair. She was weary with the wall she hit with Ian and the battles she fought with Caroline. She had tried everything she could to direct her children towards God, but they both were choosing their own paths towards the world, away from any real relationship with the Lord.

One day as she was wrestling before the Lord in prayer about her children and all of her attempts to secure their feet on the Rock, she realized her strength was all but gone. No matter what she did, it proved to be a failure. As she examined her various attempts to nudge her children a certain way, it suddenly dawned on her the crux of the problem. It rested with her trying to direct her children's life as if she was God (all-knowing), and trying to be their Holy Spirit in the area of bringing spiritual conviction, leading, vision, and purpose. In essence, she was standing in the way of God's work.

Like Abraham did with Isaac in Genesis 22, she needed to be willing to offer her children on the altar and let God have his way in their lives. It was the only way she could be assured that one day He might offer them back to her in a healthy relationship, saved, healed, and whole.

Letting go of those precious gifts and laying them on the altar created an inward struggle that proved gut-wrenching for Roberta. As she thought of Sarah's possible reaction towards Abraham offering Isaac, she felt there would have been a different story. Perhaps that is why Sarah was missing from the equation. She had no idea as to what Abraham was about to do. Roberta had to wonder if women were more emotionally attached to their children, or did Abraham's unwavering faith trump his emotions and give him the strength to offer his son?

She realized that the offering of Isaac was Abraham's test of faith and not Sarah's. And likewise, the offering of her children was her personal test. She was clearly feeling the heat from the fiery ovens that tested and refined the faith of all saints. Wading through the emotional upheaval that such an offering required, Roberta felt her heart breaking, but at the same time she knew if there was going to be any real hope for her children's spiritual well-being, she had to do it. She had to let go and let God be God in their lives and circumstances.

It took everything in Roberta to put her children on the altar and leave them in the capable hands of God. There were times she took them off the altar because God was not moving fast enough for her, but each time she did, she noticed that such attempts caused her relationship with them to go backward.

Each test of her faith, prepared her for the next testing ground of faith. Roberta did not initially realize how hot the fiery ovens of faith can become to the person's resolve. She had prepared herself in every way to stand in faith, while withstanding with truth, and when all else failed continue to stand on the hope of God's promises, but each challenge caused her to wonder if it would it be enough? She constantly assured herself that surely God is the One who gives the necessary faith for a person to stand when new challenges arise.

Roberta recognized that faith must have runways, as well as feet in order to advance forward, before it can take flight and soar in the heights of God. The runway is God's promises, the feet is that of obedience, and that which thrust a Christian into the heights of God is the expectation that comes from hope that is founded on the character of God.

She will never forget the day that she was broadsided by a formidable challenge to her faith towards God. She was preparing for two graduations, Caroline from high School and her college graduation where she would finally receive a bachelor degree in business after taking college courses off and on for six years, while juggling the affairs of her family.

She was sitting at the kitchen island studying the guest list for the party that would take place after Caroline's graduation when Charley walked in and went to the refrigerator. He was unusually quiet as he stood absent mindedly gazing into the icebox.

Roberta looked up, "Is there something I can help you find?" It seemed that when it came to the infamous fridge that unless a desired article was right in front on the shelf that neither Charley nor her children were able to locate it. She could not count the times she heard herself being paged as they declared their inability to locate a particular food in what seemed like the endless abyss of the fridge.

Charley was shaken out of his daze by her question. He looked at her, "Rob I have been meaning to talk to you about something." He closed the fridge door, walked over to the island, put his hands on the counter and slightly leaned forward.

The sound of his voice caused warning alarms to go off in her. "What about Charley?"

"Since Caroline is graduating and you now can have your own career, I feel it's time to...

In an uncertain voice Roberta encouraged him to finish his sentence, "Time to do what Charley?"

"Well-I-I, Rob, I don't know how to say it other than come out with it. I've found another woman and I want a divorce so that I can pursue a new life with her."

Roberta had sensed it was going to be unpleasant, but she had no idea that it was going to set off an atomic bomb that would devastate everything she had tried to avoid: the breakdown and death of their marriage. Utterly stunned and confused, she managed to respond in the only way she could, "I don't understand. I thought we were getting along better and that our marriage was better. I've done everything I could do to do right by you, by letting the hurts of the past go and choosing to love you. I…just don't understand!" She felt tears beginning to sting her eyes.

By this time Charley was hanging his head low. She could tell he was struggling to find the words. He must have found them because he looked at her. His words told her he was being honest, "Roberta, it's not you, but me. Since your religious experience, you have become a good wife to me and we've even become friends in a way, and I have come to value your friendship and that is why I'm being honest with you right now,…but for years I have felt I was missing out on something. I've felt that I've been a 'square peg' forced into 'round holes' that have robbed me of chances and opportunities to choose my own way and prove I can make it on my own.

"I need to be set free from what has been forced on me in the past so I can pursue my own dreams, make my own way in this world. In fact, I have secured another position in the same city that Caroline will be attending college and I'm going to resign my position from the meat-packing company and ask Dad to buy me out."

Roberta was stunned at the prospect that Charley would seek employment elsewhere, take his inheritance and run with it, "What does this woman have to do with you making your own way in this world?" Roberta inquired after hearing Charley radical plans.

Charley looked upward with a type of euphoria on his face before looking at her, "She represents something new. She makes me feel young and infallible, as if everything is possible. I realize it might be foolish on my part, but I want to ride the wave that I'm being caught up in right now and find out where it will lead me."

In a quiet voice Roberta stated, "Charley, it sounds like a midlife crisis."

Charley's voice was stern as he shot back at her, "Well if it's a midlife crisis, I have been in it most of my life!" When he saw the hurt look on her face, he took the edge out of his voice, "Rob, I never intended to hurt you again, but I have been restless most of my life, looking for something. The problem is that in the prime of my strength I felt I was deprived of finding it and making it possible. There are so many "if only's" and "what ifs" that haunt me that I live in a prison of constant regret."

He kneeled down beside her and looked into her eyes. He looked boyish and pleaded with her, "I know you probably don't understand, but please know this is something I need to do for myself. It's not that I'm trying to run away from you, Lord knows I have tried to be content; rather, I'm trying to run towards something. Rob, please set me free!"

When Charley looked at her with his boyish look, he always caused her motherly instinct to come out. At such times she either felt liked she needed to protect him or she felt sorry for him. But, at that moment she didn't know how to really feel. The whole matter was confusing and overwhelming to her. Roberta looked down, "I need time to think."

Charley stood up, "I understand." He left her alone with her thoughts. However, Roberta was in a state of shock making her emotions numb. She was grappling with what she had heard and even though it seemed unreal, she knew it was the hard reality that was going to sweep her family out into dangerous waters.

She needed to talk to someone and there was only one person who possessed the necessary wisdom to give her advice as to how to handle it. She called Donna to meet her at their favorite coffee shop. Even though Donna had other plans, the urgency in Roberta's voice caused her to drop them.

Once again Roberta poured out her pain to Donna concerning the latest development between Charley and her. She ended her story by admitting the obvious, "Donna, I don't know what to do. He's actually asking me to set him free, even though he's going to do what he's going to do. What difference would it make it if I set him free or not?"

"It makes a big difference, Robbie. He is like a caged bird. If you set him free, it will ensure an easier transition for all of you, as well as keep you from burning a bridge between you and him; keeping the door open for possible restoration between the two of you. If you don't set him free, there is going to be a ripping and tearing that may destroy everything you have established in your relationship with him."

"Maybe, I want to make it hard on him," Roberta stated, pushing back the hurt and anger she was beginning to feel. "Maybe he would come to his senses!" Roberta angrily admitted.

Donna's calm voice of wisdom penetrated through Roberta's anger. "Robbie, what is talking right now, your flesh or godly reasoning? You know better than that! It would make it worse for not only your relationship with him, but the children. There are too many marriages that end in hostility instead of in a civil way. The ones who get hurt in such situations the most are the children. Think about Ian and Caroline! This is going to be a devastating shock to the both of them."

Roberta knew she was speaking out of anger and selfishness, but she wanted to just wallow in both for a short time. After all, how much can the human heart endure? All those years of trying to be a Christian witness in front of Charley, and it was flung back in her face in a matter of seconds. It seemed as if all the investment and years were an absolute waste of time and energy.

"I've tried so hard to be a Christian wife and mother, but all my attempts seem vain. I've have always been told being a wife and mother is my lot in life. Right now both positions have been clearly shattered," Roberta admitted.

Donna intruded into her reasoning, "Robbie, your place in God's kingdom comes down to who you are in Christ. It's your position in Christ that will give you identity and purpose, as well as the discipline you need to live out the godly life in relationship to others. If you allow worldly responsibilities to define you, you'll become lost as to your real purpose for being here. Your real purpose is to glorify the Lord in whatever is at hand to do. I know that you may have a right to wallow in the mire of the present circumstances, but don't stay in there too long because you will take on the smell of it, and it might take a bit of repenting to get rid of it."

Roberta knew Donna was right. Her life was hid in Christ and not in her worldly relationships. It was from her position in Christ that all life flowed into her worldly relationships and rightly disciplined her responsibilities. It was time to crawl out of the mire and face the situation head on, but she couldn't help but voice her opinion about the mess. "It seems like all the time and energy that I have put into my marriage was a waste by having it come to this!"

"Robbie, how can you say that? If Jesus operated from the same selfish perspective, there would be no redemption. He is constantly being rejected by people. Did He think His time on earth and His death on the cross was a waste of time? Is not the Lord worthy of the consideration you have shown Him in regard to how you treated Charley in your marriage? Once again, your actions were not about you saving the marriage, but honoring the Lord in your life by manifesting the inner change He has wrought in you! I have watched you change and take on the likeness of Jesus with each right decision and action, and it has brought such edification to my own life.

"Don't be foolish by showing contempt against the personal cross that God has presently allotted you! This cross will also discipline you in your walk, and how you walk will depend on how much you love and trust the Lord to bring some good out of it."

Roberta knew Donna was rightly reproving her, but she couldn't help but add. "Is not God against divorce? How can I set Charley free knowing that God wouldn't approve of such an action?"

Donna was ready with a scriptural answer, "God hates divorce because it reveals that there is a hard heart present. However, the question is not who has a hard heart in your marriage; rather, is Charley a Christian?"

Suddenly, the Apostle Paul's instruction in 1 Corinthians 7 came to Roberta's mind. "Donna, I see what you are getting at. If Charley is not a Christian and he asks me to release him from his vow of marriage to me, I am to release him."

"Well, is he a born again Christian?" Donna asked.

Roberta looked at Donna, and with great hurt and sadness in her voice she said, "Obviously, there is only one thing I can do. I will do as he requested and set him free to go his own way."

***

The graduation ceremonies served as a cover for what needed to be done to sever the marriage, as well as a distraction from what was taking place as Roberta and Charley made moves towards sealing the coffin of their marriage. In between the graduation activities, Charley had quietly moved his possessions out of the house to an unknown location. Roberta surmised it was to his new girlfriend's place. They also both discussed how to separate their possessions and property in a fair, constructive way.

Charley volunteered to give Roberta everything in exchange for the divorce. Even though Roberta was tempted to take him up on his offer, she didn't feel it would be an honorable thing to do. Ian was planning to move to his own apartment and Caroline would be off to college, making it obvious that there was no need to keep the large house.

The children were not told about the divorce until after all the graduation ceremonies were concluded. It was agreed between Charley and Roberta that Charley would be the one who would tell them since he was the one who requested the divorce.

After they were told by their father, Ian came in and shot a glance at his mother who was sitting at the island in the kitchen looking at advertisements. He shrugged his shoulders as he went to his room, but Caroline came in crying, rushed towards her mother, and screamed, "What did you do to Dad, that he wants to leave us! You need to make him stay!"

Charley wasn't far behind her, "Caroline, I told you this is my doing and your mother has nothing to do with it! You apologize to her right now!"

"I'll never apologize to her! It's her fault, she should know how to keep you, but instead she loses you to another woman!"

Charley moved towards Caroline as if to grab her, but she bolted off to her room.

As Charley watched his daughter vanish, he apologized to Roberta, "I'm sorry Rob. I knew Caroline would be upset, but I thought she would be reasonable. She has no right to blame you. I tried to make that clear to both her and Ian that this is my decision."

"I appreciate that Charley, but right now Caroline is choosing to be inconsolable. She idolizes you and her way to keep you on the pedestal is to blame me. There is nothing we can do about it right now. Her hurt, sorrow, and disappointment will have to run its course. Perhaps, in the near future I'll be able to help her pick up the pieces and she will drop the blame game and accept the situation for what it is."

Studying Roberta's response, Charley reiterated, with a grateful tone, something that the two of them had already talked about, "You know Rob, we don't have to sell the house. It belongs to both of us and you can stay here."

"Thanks Charley, but no thank you. This house is too big and the upkeep too expensive. I prefer to sell it and divide the money between the two of us. I can buy a much smaller home and start a business with what we receive for the house. Besides, it'll give you some extra money to work with until the transition is completed in your life."

Charley looked at her with admiration, "You're being a grand sport about this Roberta, and I really appreciate it."

Inwardly, Roberta didn't feel like a "grand sport," but she knew that the grace of God was present in her, allowing her to show mercy and consideration to Charley.

"Well, I guess I better go," Charley added.

Roberta stood up to face him. "Yes I guess so." She paused and carefully considered what she was about to say, "Charley, know that I love you, but I know this is what you must do for yourself, but it's not what I want."

Charley touched her shoulder, "Rob, I love you too. I don't understand it, but I know my love is not enough for you or me." He leaned over and gently kissed her cheek and smiled at her forlornly. "Bye Rob."

As he was leaving, Roberta softly and quietly offered her benediction through tears, "Oh Charley if only, if only...but it now appears as if it will never be. Farewell my love, farewell."

As the door shut behind him, Roberta felt her heart break in pieces. She did love Charley despite his selfishness. She loved him in spite of his spoiled, demanding ways. She loved him because he was Charley, the man she gave her heart to for better or worse. She ran for the bedroom where she could silently face the emotional tsunami that was heading her way. She flung herself on the bed as the tears poured down her cheeks.

"Why, Lord, why did you heal my heart towards this man only for it to be broken again by him? Why Lord, I don't understand!"

She heard a sweet, solemn voice, "At least you have a heart that can be broken." Suddenly, she saw Jesus on the cross, His body battered, bruised, and bleeding, displaying a broken heart over the sin of mankind, broken by the rejection of those He loved, and sorrowful towards those who would spurn His love and redemption.

Then she remembered the words of Jesus in Matthew 20:23 and the Apostle Paul in Romans 8:16, 17, "Ye shall drink indeed of my cup and be baptized with the baptism that I am baptized with...the Spirit itself beareth witness with our spirit, and that we are the children of God: And if children, then heirs; heirs of God, and joint-heirs with Christ; if so be that we suffer with him, that we may be also glorified together."

***

Roberta felt herself being caught up in a whirlwind that was quickly changing the terrain of her world. The house quickly sold, but the agreement was that it would not close until Caroline was settled in college, which was a couple of months away. Meanwhile Roberta was avoiding falling into the abyss of depression by putting one foot in front of the other.

She emotionally struggled with the fallout caused by the failure of her marriage. There was a death in her life, but she was not allowed to mourn it. There were the raw emotions of anger and betrayal nipping at her heels over her loss, but she could not give them audience because it would not be considered proper to do so. She had to admit to herself that those on the outside might use the demise of her marriage to dig up old suspicions of past problems with their "judgmental shovels," while taking sides and getting caught up with the speculation and gossip. In divorce there can be no real ending and final resolution for some of the parties personally involved.

Roberta silently questioned her ability to resolve the matter of her divorce. How could a person let something with such emotional attachments go when the possibilities for life still existed? There was no grave, no headstone, and no marking that marked the finality of her marriage. There was no honor in its death, no glory in its passing, and little hope in its resurrection.

She knew she could not dwell on the bitter taste it left in her mouth. She had the tools to go forward and the circumstances required her to put them to the test. During her last semester of college, each student in her class were given an assignment to map out a plan to start a small business by first finding out what the community needed the most and providing it with a solution. Roberta had thoroughly done her homework, and was aware that many of the businesses needed a bookkeeping service. Since she did bookkeeping, she felt she was capable enough of offering her services to different businesses and build up a clientele. However, she also knew that she had to present a professional front. That meant she had to find office space that was reasonable, as well as possess a professional look.

There were not many places available that were within her price range and fit the qualifications. She struggled over the deadline that was looming ahead of her. Not only did she need to find a place for her business but she was looking for a house as well that would fit within the confines of her settlement and be a place where Caroline would have a room.

Caroline had become eerily quiet after her outburst on the day she was informed of the divorce. Her attitudes were clearly standing out and she was pouty, but she avoided talking to her mother. She spent most of her free time with her friends. It was clear to Roberta that she was either living in denial of what was happening, avoiding facing it altogether, or trying to make her mother pay for the hurt and anger she felt.

Roberta had made a decision to go to the local newspaper and advertise her forthcoming business to see if she would receive any bites, as well as put a classified in about looking for an office. As she was heading towards the newspaper, she made her requests known, "Lord, you are officially now my husband. You know my frame, that I'm a simple handmaiden. You also know what I have need of to go on with my life. I desperately need to find a house and office space. Go before me, prepare the way, and open up the right door for me to walk through. In Jesus' precious name, Amen."

She walked into the newspaper office during the noon hour. It was quiet except for a man who was typing on his keyboard. He appeared to be around her age with salt and pepper hair and nice features. He was so engrossed in what he was doing he didn't notice when Roberta walked through the door.

Roberta cleared her throat to get his attention. Startled, he immediately jumped to his feet and began to walk towards her. "Forgive me I didn't hear you come in. What can I do for you?"

"Well I'm about to start a new business, I would like to advertise it, as well as let my need for an office be known. Perhaps someone has space available that I could rent that I don't presently know about."

The man looked interested. "What kind of business are you starting?"

"A bookkeeping service," she stated. "I discovered that it's the one business that is greatly needed in this area."

The man smiled, "That's funny, I was asking this morning if there was anyone who did bookkeeping."

Roberta knew the Lord worked fast, but even this seemed a bit over the top. "Really? Well, I'm the one who can do it, that is if you don't mind the fact that I don't presently have an office location and will probably have to work from my home."

"You might be in luck. I have some office space that I've wanted to rent, but I've been waiting for the right type of business to rent it to. It seems to me a newspaper and bookkeeping service are compatible enough, don't you think, Ms-s-s...?"

Roberta could not believe her ears. The information was leaving her almost breathless. She was so caught up with the whole situation that she failed to recognize her cue to introduce herself. The man stood before her with a quizzical look on his face as a smile began to break out on his lips.

"My name is Carson Reed. I'm the owner and editor of this weekly newspaper."

The mention of his name jolted Roberta out of her stunned state. "Forgive me! My name is Roberta Walker. I would be interested in looking at the space and renting it if the price is right."

"Sounds fair to me! In fact, maybe we can do a bit of trading, since you have something I'm interested in and I own something you have need of."

Roberta smiled. "It is a possibility. Can I see the space right now?"

"I don't see why not. Follow me." He opened the swinging door attached to the front counter and led her to a door that was almost positioned in the middle of the big room that housed the workers desks, computers, and phones. He opened the door and led her into the room.

Roberta looked around to see a fair sized room. It faced the main street and had its own door and restroom. It appeared to serve as a catchall room, a type of storage where unused, discarded office furniture, as well as obsolete computer equipment was being stored.

"As you can see it is attached to the newspaper office, but it hasn't been used for a couple of years, and now serves as a catchall room. There is a lock on this side of the door that you can use to ensure there are no unwanted trespassers from the newspaper office."

"What about the furniture and computer equipment?" Roberta inquired.

"What you can't use, we plan to sell or donate."

Almost holding her breath, she asked the next question, "How much?"

"Why don't we go to my desk and work out some type of agreement?"

To Roberta's delight, Carson Reed proved to be generous in working out an arrangement she could afford, along with bookkeeping services. She was ready to walk on air except for the fact she needed to find a house as well.

"Well, Ms. Walker is there anything else I can do for you?"

"Mr. Reed, please call me Roberta. I am not much in the "Ms." category, and right now I'm in divorce proceedings and not fond of the title, 'Mrs.' either."

With a smile and nodding his head, Carson complied. "I'll call you Roberta if you call me Carson." His face then became serious, "Sorry to hear about your divorce. You don't appear to be in agreement with it."

"You're right. I'm going through with it at my husband's request. She paused, "There's one other thing I'm looking for, a house, but you probably don't know of any."

Roberta could tell Carson was refraining from getting caught up too much with her personal life. He seemed to switch gears with his next question, "What kind of house?"

"I need at least three bedrooms, two complete baths if possible, and a garage, all in a decent neighborhood."

"I know of such a house. It has good bones, has been remodeled to keep up with the changing times, and is in a decent neighborhood," Carson responded.

"Really!" Roberta exclaimed.

"Yes, it was my parents' home for close to sixty years. My father passed away a couple of years ago and my mother a couple of months ago."

Roberta's excitement took a nose dive when she heard the circumstances around the vacant house, "It's my turn to offer you my sympathy."

"Thank you, but my mother was ready to join my father. They were Christians and believed that they would be spending eternity together. There are a lot of memories associated with that home from my growing up years to the fact that my wife and two daughters spent many holidays there."

Roberta didn't understand why her heart was jolted by the latest revelation, but her voice didn't express it. "Since there are great memories attached to the house, why don't you and your wife keep it in the family?"

"My wife passed away three years ago, and my daughters are grown and have their own families. As for me, the memories in that house bring more sadness to me at this time than happiness."

Roberta realized that Carson had had his share of losses in the last three years. She could not imagine what it would be like to lose those close to you in such a short span of time. There were no words that could bring any measure of comfort, and she grappled with what to say. She decided to be honest, "I can't imagine what you have been through, and all the condolences in the world won't reach and take away the depth of your sorrow. God has his timing and it rarely makes any sense to those left behind. A person has only one recourse and that is to trust the Lord."

Carson smiled, "Thank you for being candid. Most people hide from you because they don't know what to say, and if they say something, it's usually a platitude that sounds rehearsed or comes across as being indifferent. I gather you're a Christian."

"Guilty as charged," Roberta responded with a smile.

"That's good to know," Carson replied. "You know, people say time heals and I'm sure that is true, but I recognized after my wife's passing that memories are bittersweet. They may remind you what was, but if you do not possess the sweet blessed hope of eternity, those memories can become bitter as they turn into tormentors.

"I've discovered there is nothing in the past that will bring healing to my soul, but each day is leading me to the blessed reality of the glory of Christ, and that not only stirs up my hope that I will see my loved ones again, but it serves as a healing balm to my soul."

Silence descended, causing time to stand still for Carson and Roberta as both became lost in their own personal thoughts of what was. They were both discovering the truth that the matters of the heart are often cut short by circumstances beyond people's control. Such circumstances remind people that they are not God in control of events, and that man has no power within himself to control his reality. He will not only find himself powerless, but small in the scheme of things.

It was Carson who finally broke the silence, "Are you interested in the house?"

"Yes, I am but since you're busy, can we set up an appointment for me to see it another time?"

"This is the day the paper hit the stands, allowing the hard working people of the office to have some slack time," Carson stated. "So, right now is probably the best time for me to show you the house."

"I'm free for the afternoon, let's go for it!" Roberta smiled.

Roberta fell in love with the quaint home. It had a good spirit. She sensed that if the walls could talk, they would speak of love, commitment, growth, and joy. Granted, there were trying times, and times of loss, but the commitment held those within its confines together.

Roberta looked at Carson, "Are you sure you want to sell this precious home to someone?"

"Not to someone, Roberta, but to you. I can already tell that you sense this house is more than a building. There is something sweet, real, and almost alive about it. I know you will honor the spirit, keep the integrity of the home intact, and preserve the history of it by changing and adding to it in an honorable way."

Roberta was surprised at the confidence Carson had in her. "I appreciate your vote of confidence and would do everything within my means to keep the spirit of the home intact. Now the big question is, how much are you asking for it?"

"How much are you willing to pay?" Carson asked.

"I want it to be fair. How much is the market value?"

Before their conversation was over, they had come into agreement over the amount that Roberta would pay for the house.

From that point on, Roberta felt she was in a current that was swiftly carrying her along. Everything happened so fast, and she clearly could see and sense the hand of God in all of it. In fact, she felt like she was in a bubble.

She worked hard to get the office in shape before she had to move to her new home. She was within a few days of officially opening the office when she received a surprise visit from Noreen.

The two women had not talked since Charley announced his intentions to his parents. Roberta had no idea as to what had transpired between them because Charley never confided in her, but she knew from Ian that the senior Walker agreed to buy out his son's interest in the meat packing plant and put it in Ian's name. Roberta could only surmise how Charley's decisions and actions would have affected the two of them.

Noreen looked haggard. She still flashed her sweet smile, but some of the light had gone out of her eyes.

Roberta greeted her with a hug, while Noreen apologized for interrupting her. "You aren't interrupting me," Roberta interjected. "In fact, you are giving me a reason to take a break. Would you have some tea with me?"

"That sounds nice," Noreen responded with a sigh.

They sat opposite of each other at Roberta's desk. With concern Roberta asked the obvious, "How are you doing?"

"We are doing," Noreen stated in a sad tone. "Both Charles and I are putting one foot in front of the other to avoid being swallowed by depression and despair. In fact, that's why I'm here. We are reorganizing the administration part of the business and we've been talking about hiring a full time bookkeeper to take my place. I wanted to do more church activities and work in the garden. Then I heard you were starting this business and realized you're an answer to our prayers."

Roberta was pleasantly surprised at the prospect that her in-laws would entrust her with their business' bookkeeping, "That sounds like a working deal to me, and I'm glad that I'm an answer to your prayers."

Roberta could tell there was something else on Noreen's mind. "Is there anything else I can help you with?" Roberta inquired.

"Well, I have been meaning to talk to you, Roberta--well I should say apologize to you for my son's latest decision and action. I have watched you struggle to be a good wife to Charley in every way possible, and he was foolish not to recognize who he had in you. Because of your example, Charles and I thought for a while that our son might actually change," she hung her head. "And, I guess that's why the latest revelation was such a shock to both of us."

"You don't have to apologize to me for your son's actions," Roberta stated in a compassionate tone. "He's grown up and there is nothing you could have done about it."

"I've felt like I failed him a long time ago," Noreen responded sorrowfully. "Charley always had a restless spirit and a self-centered way about him.

"Roberta, we even dedicated him to the Lord when he was first born and have prayed for him all of his life. We tried to teach him godly ways by taking him to church, and establishing moral uprightness and character in him, but he just adopted a seductive veneer that cons others, while manifesting great rebellion when no one could see it. He was simply playing a game. It was clear that he showed tendencies of having a form of righteousness but denying the power to sincerely live it.

"When we insisted that he do right and marry you, we were hoping he would grow up, but we secretly feared that he wouldn't do right by you and our grandchild," she sighed. Noreen paused.

Noreen paused long enough to allow Roberta to share something that had been on her heart for some time. "You know Charley told me that the reason you insisted on him marrying me is because you didn't want your first grandchild to be known as an illegitimate child who would be raised by a 'gold digger from the other side of the tracks.'"

Noreen turned white. "Did you believe him?"

"I was too hurt to know what to believe, but I had to admit it caused me to have some suspicion towards the two of you. But, when I came to a better understanding of what it meant to be a Christian, I realized you both lived your faith and were too honorable to harbor such attitudes."

"You're right about that!" Noreen flatly declared. "How dare he say such a cruel thing to you and misrepresent our stand and feelings about you and your marriage to him!" She shook her head before continuing, "As you will remember we never knew you during your and Charlie's courting days, but even in our ignorance, we never felt Charley was getting the short end of the stick by marrying you, but we feared that you were too young, naïve, and trusting towards him and felt that in the end you and the child would be the ones who would receive a raw deal."

Roberta began to see how hurt Noreen was. It went so deep she could sense it was like a vice-grip on her heart, squeezing the very life out of her. She wanted to somehow comfort her and was scrambling for some means of encouragement and consolation, when she thought of a subject that might bring some hope.

"Well, at least Ian is excited about working with you and his grandfather at the plant."

Noreen slightly smiled, "It does appear that Ian is stepping into the shoes of his father. I know it pleases his grandfather, but...," Noreen's voice trailed off as if she was becoming lost in other thoughts.

"But what?" Roberta asked curiously.

Noreen looked at her to size up whether she should share her observations. She must have concluded that what she was about to share with Roberta would not have any surprise element to it. She began to share her concerns. "I love Ian and Caroline, but I'm concerned for them. When it comes to Ian, I'm not sure why he's involved with the plant. He reminds me of his dad as far as playing some type of game, because he sees an opportunity. I'm not sure his whole heart is in it. I have to admit, though, he's a better worker than his father. Charley spent most of his time trying to figure out clever ways to get around work rather than just doing his job."

Roberta sighed, "You're not sharing something with me that is foreign to me. I've wondered about Ian's motives as well." She paused, I'm thankful he is learning good work habits from his grandfather and not his father."

Noreen shook her head in agreement, "As for my other grandchild, Caroline, she is like her father in a different way. She can prove to be snobbish, cruel, and self-serving. The truth is my heart has felt heavy for both of my grandchildren because they have chosen the path of their father and the world and not your path. I believe the paths they are choosing will prove to be hard for them, but if that is what it takes for God to save them, so be it."

"So be it," Roberta repeated with a knowing nod.

Noreen continued, "Children know how to break your heart, test your faith, and expose your character."

Roberta looked down for a moment before looking at Noreen, "They sure do, but we believe and serve a big God. I had to realize the Lord loves Charley, Ian, and Caroline more than I do. Granted, my love carries a lot of passion with it, but it's still selfish and greatly influenced by prideful thinking that is more concerned about how something is going to affect me or make me look than what is right for those around me.

"Trusting God with those you love is one of the hardest tests of faith. I've failed it more times than I would like to count, but when I have chosen to cling to the Rock, I've found rest and peace."

Roberta could tell that Noreen was carefully considering her words. "I know that is the place I need to come to, resting in God, trusting Him to work out the details in Charley's life and the grandchildren."

Roberta got up from the desk, walked around to Noreen and put her arms around her shoulders as Noreen grabbed her one arm. "It is time to mourn for what is so you can be healed and go on," Roberta stated. "You did your best to raise Charley, and when each of us are at the end of our best and our understanding, that is when we must chose the way of faith that leads us to the place of rest in the Lord."

Roberta felt the pressure of Noreen's sorrow break through the flood gates of her resolve. Roberta held tightly to her as Noreen let the cleansing waters free her soul from the ball and chains of utter despair.

The next month was charged with various changes. Caroline went to college without saying much to her mother. Roberta knew she was hurting and angry, and that she had focused all of her anger towards her mother, preventing Roberta from ministering to her. Caroline was cordial but cold, and only shared what she thought was necessary.

Roberta had carefully packed what she could before Caroline left, which was the day before the closing on her house, and then once the money was properly exchanged and recorded the closing for her new home would take place. She had made arrangements for the church to pick up extra furniture and accessories that wouldn't fit in her new home right after Caroline left for college. Roberta also had scheduled a moving company to put her furniture in a temporary moving storage on closing day, and hold it until the papers were done on her new house. Donna let her stay at her home until the finalization took place on Roberta's new home.

Charley showed up for the closing to sign papers and to get his share of the money. He seemed happy and almost giddy. The former couple shared casual greetings before they sat at the table to sign papers.

As Charley was walking out of the conference room where all the papers were signed, Carson was walking in to confirm some details as to the closing of his house. Both men nodded at each other. When Carson saw Roberta, he smiled and gave her a hearty greeting and Roberta responded in like manner. Out of the corner of her eye she saw Charley do a double take, and his happy look quickly gave way to a disconcerting expression. Roberta shrugged it off and thought nothing more of the incident as she happily prepared herself to say goodbye to the old, while moving forward to finalize plans to say hello to the new.

Once moved into her new home, Donna came over and helped Roberta situate the furniture. She admitted that it was a perfect house for Roberta. As they were unpacking the boxes for the kitchen, Carson dropped in to see if Roberta needed any help moving heavy boxes or furniture. That is when Donna met the infamous Mr. Reed. After all, God used him to solve two major problems for her friend and she wanted to meet this man to discern if he was genuine or had other motives.

Both ladies gladly accepted his help and used his muscles with a dolly to move heavy boxes to their perspective areas and furniture to the right places. Their conversation became a point of edifying fellowship as they talked about their different experiences with God. The fellowship caused the activities to fly swiftly by, resulting in amazing accomplishments for the day.

After Carson left, Donna shared her evaluation of him. It was simple, he was the godly man he purported to be, a man who loved God and was a natural servant at heart, and a good person to have as a friend.

Roberta's business quickly grew. Both Noreen and Carson were sending clients to her. She began to see that God was blessing her on every front, providing for all of her needs. Granted, she still struggled at night with the reality of what happened between Charley and her, but she could do nothing more than to go on towards the life God had ordained for her from the foundation of the world.

As she looked at her world, Roberta decided she wanted to enlarge it, as well as figure out how to work off stress from all the changes that were taking place. One of her clients suggested that she join a health club where people worked out on what Roberta considered to be "contraptions." It seemed like an "in-thing" to do since most everyone Roberta knew belonged to such an establishment. After all, maybe she could shed a couple of pounds while she was at it.

She visited the nearest health facility. As she entered, she immediately noticed a different type of smell. It was not an unpleasant smell, but it spoke of a different world. She walked up to the front desk and inquired about joining the facility. Before the lady at the front desk could present the information to her, she had to take a phone call, promising to answer Roberta's question after she addressed the concerns of the person on the other end of the line. Meanwhile the receptionist suggested that Roberta look around the facility.

Roberta walked into the facility that housed the formidable machines that reminded her of machines used for torture rather than exercise. She wondered who would conquer what. She even imagined herself pinned down by some of those machines and left to an unknown fate.

She walked into a partitioned area where the stationary bikes were located, and wondered how one particular part of her anatomy would fare on such small seats. She then walked into the area that had the machines that were used for stepping, walking, and running. Most of the participants were wired into headphones and watching TV. It almost looked like a hospital with people on life-support machines instead of a place to establish strong hearts and toned muscles.

She then followed music to a gym area where people were dancing, jumping up and down, and stepping up and down on some type of foot stool. Some were breathing hard; others seemed to be pacing their breathing and actions, while a few individuals came across as flying experts and appeared to be in tip top shape. All she could envision herself doing in such exercises was completely keeling over from a heart attack.

She walked into the pool area and was almost knocked over by the overwhelming smell of chorine. She saw an elderly group doing water aerobics, and surmised that was more down her alley than anything else she had observed.

Roberta meandered back to the desk and the lady that had first greeted her was free to answer her questions.

"Well what do you think of our facilities?"

Roberta somewhat rolled her eyes, "To be honest with you, it's all very formidable and overwhelming."

"Is this your first time of ever visiting such a club?" the receptionist asked.

Roberta responded with a mischievous grin, "Yes, how can you tell?"

"It always seems overwhelming to those who visit any facility such as this for the first time. But, let me assure you we teach people how to properly use our machines, assist them in building up to more strenuous activities, and eventually aid them in finding the exercise routine that would best suit them for their lifestyle or whatever goals they may have for their well-being."

"I'm sure there is a cost involved in all of this besides the membership dues," Roberta stated.

"Yes, there is a cost for a personal trainer, otherwise, the aerobics, spinning, and the use of our machines fall under your membership dues."

"What is spinning?" Roberta asked.

"Spinning is the term we use to describe the activities on the stationary bike."

Roberta could tell it was a different world from the one she was used to. It had its own language and terminology. As she looked around, she figured that she was only going to pass this way once. She might not exactly enjoy it, but it was something new to experience, and she needed new experiences to break the strangulation that the old still had on her.

Roberta signed on the dotted line for a half a year and agreed to pay a personal trainer for at least a month. The trainer would help her establish some type of program, as well as train her on those monstrous machines.

Roberta's trainer was a woman by the name of Page Miles. Page was in her late twenties, divorced and zealous about her newly acquired position as trainer. She had worked her way up to the position, and Roberta quickly surmised by their interaction that her relationship with the manager also was somewhat instrumental in her advancement.

Page started Roberta out by raising her heart rate on the treadmill. Upon surviving the treadmill, Page then took her to the weight machines. Her try on the first one proved she had no shoulder and arm muscles. Even though she started out light, she felt the machine was going to pull her shoulders out of place or end up somehow pinning her to the bench.

That night and the following day, soreness set into her muscles. It was then that Roberta began to question her own sanity. She wasn't a member of the health club to bow down to her body and then try to shape it up in order to worship the perfect image or idea of it. She just wanted to get rid of built up tension and stress in her body. Instead, she felt her body rebelling against the exercise.

As Roberta became acquainted with the machines, they became less formidable to her. She even became comfortable with the treadmill. One day as she was trying to adjust the treadmill while trying to put her feet squarely on the rubber track at the same time, the track caught her off guard. One minute she was trying to adjust the pace of the machine, and the next she was falling down in slow motion onto the track. She ended up rolling down the belt, bumping here and there as different parts of her body hit the rubber track. In her mind, she could see the byline on U-tube as she rolled down the track in her brownish sweat attire, "Have you ever wondered what a 'human potato' looks like on a conveyor belt? Here's your classic example in living color."

When she hit the end of the track it literally spit her off of it as she ended on her back on the floor. Another byline came to mind, "Ever wondered what it looked like when Jonah was spit out by the big fish?" Upon the completion of her most awkward exit from the treadmill, she looked up to see the facial reactions of the trainers and spectators. For the trainers, it was one of total abhorrence and for those around her it was complete shock.

Two trainers rushed to her side to help her up, asking if she was alright. The main bruise she was aware of was to her pride. Rolling down the track of a treadmill in such a manner certainly left her with no dignity. She was embarrassed, while those around her were concerned. After she got past the embarrassment, she almost wished she had a video of it so she could laugh at it. After all, it is something that would happen to the slapstick Three Stooges. She smiled to herself as she thought about the reason for joining the club: to add to her repertoire of experiences that she would not forget, which would now include becoming a human potato on the treadmill.

Page proved to be personable, but godless. Roberta decided to pay for another month of having her as her personal trainer. She was hoping for an opportunity to share Jesus with her. Roberta could tell that Page was searching for something satisfying and fulfilling, and knew that the world would leave her disappointed and empty.

One day they were sitting at a table together discussing Roberta's training when Page finally opened a door. "I understand you're divorced, do you have any boyfriends?"

Roberta didn't know where it would lead, but she was willing to follow the lead as far as she could. "Yes, I'm divorced but I don't have any boyfriends, probably because I'm not seeking for any."

Page looked at her in surprise as if she was weird or from another planet. "You're not looking for any boyfriend? I don't understand. Did your husband hurt you so bad that you don't want anything to do with men?"

Roberta felt that it was the right time to bring up her Christianity, "The answer to your questions is I'm a Christian, and being divorced means that if there are any possible means for reconciliation with my husband, I need to first seek it, and I'm not to seek out another husband."

Page looked at her as if she had two heads. "You're kidding aren't you?"

"No, I'm not kidding. First of all I'm still in love with my husband. He left me for another woman, but until I know there is no hope for reconciliation, I'm not free to consider another relationship. I don't allow myself to go there, whether it is watching certain shows or movies. If I'm to keep my mind under control and my body in submission, I must avoid any unnecessary temptations."

"You're like a nun," Page replied in total amazement.

"Do you mean that I am practicing celibacy during separation from my husband? Yes, I am. I believe in keeping myself pure, free from fornicating myself with that which is unacceptable to my God and His Word, as well as my conscience. If my husband and I ever got back together and I had compromised myself, I couldn't look him in the eye."

"What is fornication?" Page asked.

"Fornication is all illicit sex outside of what God has ordained as marriage between one man and one woman. God gave sex as a gift to married couples for a couple of reasons. One was for reproduction purposes, while the other reason provided a way for the couple to become one in spirit, spiritually, emotionally, and physically. People who fornicate themselves outside of the moral bounds of godly marriage open themselves up to give bits and pieces of their person, their soul away as affections are exploited and purity sacrificed. All the while such people buy into a perverted idea of love, romance, and marriage that leaves them disappointed and empty."

Page shook her head, "That's heavy and totally old-fashioned. It would seem to me if God wants us happy, He wouldn't be against what is considered a normal activity.'

"God is holy and He wants us to be holy so we can live with Him for eternity."

It was clear by Page's question that her curiosity had been aroused. "What happens to those who commit fornication? I mean it's a natural function between people, right?"

"Page, it may be natural, but it's not healthy physically, emotionally, or spiritually. According to the Bible, fornicators will end up in hell, totally separated from God."

Roberta could tell that she caused Page to become uneasy. Page's next statement revealed that she was trying to downplay the implications of hell. "Well, I won't be alone—I'll be with all of my friends."

"That's where you're wrong Page," Roberta firmly stated. "People who are in hell, are totally isolated in their own sick realities, but they will not be able to silence the torments they are in because they will have no physical body to temporary relieve the driving desires of a soul that is being consumed by unabated lusts."

It was obvious that Page was becoming irritated. "It must be nice to be such a 'religious person' in the area of morals. After all, your husband is being unfaithful to you right now."

"Two wrongs don't make a right, Page. My husband will have to answer for his own life, just as I'll have to answer for mine."

Page's irritation was diffused enough that she began to share information about herself, "Well, I can't imagine living without a man in my life. Right now I'm playing the field to find the right man for myself, and one day I just know I'll find him. I'm even corresponding with a guy on the internet from Kansas. We are getting along quite well, and plan to meet in the future to see if we are right for one another."

"Page, people are rarely what they portray themselves to be on the internet and even in dating. We all put on our best presentation and best foot forward when we first meet someone. The other problem is that because of our perverted rose tinted glasses we choose to embrace what we want to about people so we can justify what we want to believe about them in order to maintain some type of fantasy about our relationship with them. The most important aspect of a person that needs to be determined is not based on how well we get along with them and how they make us feel about ourselves, but whether they have character. True character is what gives people that sticking power to stay in a relationship, even when it does not serve their purpose or make them feel a certain way."

Roberta could tell she had Page's attention. "You need to realize Page, that romance in America is a big money-making business. It is based on propaganda that is built on fantasy and false promises and illusions presented by Hollywood. It starts from soap operas, and graduates to romance movies. They are all designed to promote unrealistic concepts of love and romance that are not only unrealistic and utterly selfish. If these individuals become entangled in the seductive lies, they soon discover that they can never be maintained. In fact, Hollywood rarely gets you past base passions that quickly evaporate into thin air once fleshly lust reaches its peak. The whole thing is a delusion that quickly dissipates into emptiness as soon as reality hits the scene.

"America's love affair with romance has caused this nation to become emotionally vulnerable and morally weak. In fact, it has been discovered that many Muslim organizations are funding their activities through the internet by selling women, such as you, the idea of having their romantic notions come true. Women correspond with these illusive individuals and give their money to them on the false pretense that they will be coming to meet them. It's a terrible scam, but American women have become weak and silly because they refuse to deal in reality about real love and the hard work that any healthy relationship will require if it is going to be forged into something satisfying and lasting.

"Take it from someone who had to learn the hard way, Page. No mere man can give you what you're looking for." Roberta paused to let the truth sink in, "Most women are looking for lasting purpose, identity, and a satisfying life. There's only one person who can give you a satisfying life and that is Jesus Christ, the Son of the Living God. He came to close the large gap between mankind's need to belong, know lasting love, and experience satisfying life by offering salvation to all who would believe and receive Him as Savior and Lord. But, you have to believe He is the only One who can help you make peace with the inward struggles and questions about life. He is the only One who can help a person make peace with the reality around them and find hope in a better future. He is the only One who can help you make peace with your restless spirit because of sins such as fornication."

Page looked at Roberta and Roberta could tell she had had enough. "I have to go for I have another appointment. I'll see you tomorrow." She excused herself and quickly walked into a side office, shutting the door behind her.

The following day, Page was nowhere to be found. Another trainer introduced himself to Roberta and told her that Page had personal affairs to attend to and that he would be taking her place for that day. However, Roberta only had one day of training left on the contract with Page. She could tell the trainer was simply going through the motions and could hardly wait for it to be over.

Roberta didn't sign up for a personal trainer for another month, and when the six months was over she didn't renew her contract with the facility. She only saw Page a couple of times from a distance, and continued to pray for her. She knew that she gave her the Gospel, and the matters of her soul were out of her hands. It would take the convicting work of the Holy Spirit to bring her into the fold.

As far as exercise went, she did find some benefit from it. However, she decided to find exercise videos she could play at home and exercise to according to her own speed and timing. She knew that she still had to discipline her time and body.

She was enjoying various blessings, which included her business growing by leaps and bounds. As a result, after nine months she was experiencing healthy "growing pains." She decided it was time to hire part-time help. She first inquired at church to see if anyone with some type of bookkeeping experience needed a part-time job. The name Carrie Iverson came up a couple of times.

Roberta sought Carrie out and was impressed with her inward beauty that manifested itself in a graceful outward beauty. She was in her early twenties, still attending college, trying to get her master degree in computer science. When Roberta approached her about working part time for her, she jumped at the opportunity to use her abilities as far as the computer and bookkeeping.

Carrie quickly became an integral working part of the office. She was always on time and ready to conquer any challenges that confronted her. In fact, she gave Roberta some breathing room to take time off for personal activities.

One day, Ian came to the office to drop off some business receipts for his grandmother, and at least say "hi" to his mother whom he rarely sought out after moving to his own apartment. When he came in, Carrie was busy working on some end of the month financial reports for the clients. Roberta could tell by Ian's reaction when he saw Carrie that he was immediately smitten by her.

From that moment on Ian dropped in after finishing his three o'clock shift, knowing that was also the time Carrie would be in the office. Although Ian pretended to come to the office for the purpose of seeing his mother, Roberta knew he had only one interest and that was Carrie.

Although Carrie was kind and gracious to him, she maintained a business air with him. She never gave him any opening to pursue anything outside of the office. Roberta began to see that Ian's impatience and frustration over Carrie's responses towards him were beginning to show in small ways, especially when he interacted with her.

Roberta hated Ian's game. He gave the impression he came to see her, when in reality he was trying to find an opening to establish some type of dating relationship with Carrie. Roberta suspected if Carrie knew what he was up to that she was not entertaining any of his overtures. She always maintained a very surface and business relationship with him.

Roberta's patience towards Ian's games hit its end on one of those infamous days where one event can set the tone for the whole day. Roberta was reading through the paper when she happened onto

401

a story about a tragic accident that ended the life of a local woman. The name of the woman stood out to her as if it was outlined with a neon sign, "Page Miles, 29 was killed in a car accident when the driver of the car she was a passenger in veered over the yellow line, overcompensated, hitting the cement median head on. The driver, from Kansas, was intoxicated at the time."

Roberta sat in disbelief. She had prayed for Page that God would have mercy on her and bring her to repentance and salvation. She was young and beautiful, and much of her life lie ahead of her, but death has no favorites. It is neither subject to the fairness of a matter as to how young or how old, or how bad or good someone might be. It continues to prove to be an equalizer regardless of money, status quo, and importance.

She wrestled with where Page was in light of eternity. She had given her the Gospel and told her people have a choice as to where they spend eternity, but Roberta had no knowledge as to what decision Page made. It was obvious she was probably with the guy she met on the internet, but Roberta had no sense or personal knowledge as to where she was spiritually. It is God who holds each person's life in His hands. Even though it appeared that Page was in the wrong place at the wrong time, God was still in control of her departure from this world.

Her heart was heavy and she was reeling from with shock when Ian made his usual appearance at the office, unaware that Carrie was off for the day doing personal errands. He casually looked around to see if Carrie was present. He started to say something, but thought better of it when he saw his mother's face.

As he sat down at her desk, he asked the obvious, "Is something wrong Mom?"

"Yes, there are a couple of things wrong, Ian. First, a young lady I knew who was only 29 years old entered eternity. The problem is I don't know if she entered into the glory of Jesus or entered into the cold, isolated darkness of hell to taste endless torment for a wasted life, lived in vanity, while pursuing foolish fantasies, and ignoring her eternal destination."

Ian was taken back by her brutal evaluation. "Aren't you being just a bit morbid, Mom?"

"Let me ask you something, if you died today, where would you end up? In heaven or hell?"

She could tell her son was scrambling for the right words, "Well, I'm pretty decent. I'm not as bad as some people, and you know I have my own religious take on things. Remember, you and Dad took me to church."

"Just what is your religious take on salvation, heaven, and hell?" Her voice was firm.

"Well, you know."

"That's the problem Ian, I don't know," she flatly stated. "You are so much like me when I thought that maybe I wasn't all that bad, but it was in relationship to the world. I later found out that before God I was a lost, wretched worm on my way to hell. And, I must state that your flimsy association with some church or with parents that took you to church is not going to save you."

Roberta was far from being done, "Neither is having some vague, feel-good, take on religion mean you are saved; rather, it means you are most likely deluded about how lost you are to God, and how far away you are from His promise of eternal life. It's people like you that are the hardest to get saved, because people like you don't realize how lost they are!"

By this time Ian was squirming. "Well, Mom, I didn't come here to get a lecture on religion."

"Why did you come here Ian?"

"Well, I dropped in to see you."

"Come on Son, you haven't gone out of your way for me since you were ten! The only time you have interacted with me is when you wanted something. So, don't try to pull the wool over my eyes and present yourself as being a loving, noble son, because you're not! Let's just be honest with each other Ian, you're here to see Carrie."

His eyes narrowed at her. "Yes, I'm here to see Carrie, what's wrong with that? You're right; I avoid you because you try to run my life! I know what I want, and right now I'm interested in Carrie."

Roberta suddenly saw her son as a type of predator, and felt a great deal of protection towards Carrie. She was pure and Roberta didn't want her purity to be defiled by her son's selfishness. "You do understand, she's a born-again believer, don't you?"

"Well, that's no big deal to me," he stated smugly. "She fits my image of what I want in a woman and I consider her worthy of me. I also see that we will get along just fine. After all, she can have her religion on the side any time she wants."

Roberta wanted to slap the smug look off of her son's face, but she knew that he still wouldn't get it. "It may not be a big deal to you, Ian, but it is everything to Carrie! Christianity is not some 'side activity' she is involved in, but it is a way of life to her. She may fit your self-serving image, but I'm sure you don't fit her idea of a godly husband.

And, in the end her Christianity will matter to you because you will find yourself coming into competition with Jesus Himself."

He looked at her with a mocking smile. "Aren't you being a bit dramatic Mom? Is this why Dad left you because he didn't fit your standard?" He smiled as if he made a slam dunk to silence her with his accusation. "It's obvious you don't have much confidence in your son. Give me time and I'll have her eating out of my hand."

"You're really arrogant aren't you," Roberta blurted out. "You know I've never pushed any religion on your father. Like you, he pretty much did what he wanted to do when it came to religion and anything else that might promote his cause."

Roberta wasn't about to let her son's smug look remain intact. "And, my, aren't you conceited about your abilities! Your conceit has blinded you so much you can't even see that Carrie is not interested in you. In your mind, she may have lots to offer you, but you're clueless to the fact you have nothing to offer her. If Carrie is interested in getting married it'll be to a committed Christian who will not be so full of himself that he can't even see what's important to her!"

Ian stood up and slammed his fist on her desk. "We'll see who's right!"

Roberta stood up to face her angry son. "I've done a lot of things wrong as a mother, Ian. One was spoiling you and your sister, which did nothing more than create self-serving, small-minded inconsiderate individuals who have no regard for others. And, the other mistake was not confronting you about your fake nobility, half-hearted commitment, and the placating games you play so you can get your way. You may think yourself wise behind your smug looks and your conceited, superior attitude, but I have two words for you, GROW UP!"

Ian was almost thrown backwards by her last two words, but Roberta was not yet finished, "You need to wise up and recognize that you're not a lone fish in some pond that will prove to be God's gift to the woman you decide is right for you. Wake up! You are on a broad path that will ultimately prove you to be a deluded fool in the end."

Ian had heard enough, he whirled around and stomped out of the office. Roberta slumped down into her chair realizing she may have destroyed whatever thread held their relationship together. She knew her interaction with Ian was not done in the most tactful way, but she was tired of seeing people lose when it came to their soul. She knew that the one thing that might have been accomplished is that Ian now knew how she viewed his complacent attitude towards God and life, and that she was privy to his insipid games. Even though there had been separation occurring between them for years, it did not prevent her heart from breaking over their relationship. She so wanted to have a right relationship with each of her children but she knew if she was to have a decent relationship with each of them, that both relationships had to be based on truth that could set them free to have honest, healthy connections.

"Lord, have mercy on my children. I know we all have choices, but I know you can save them from their foolish ways, worldly attitudes, and self-serving pursuits. You are the only One who can save them from hell. Oh, Lord save them unto yourself. Pull them out of the worldly fires of vanity and snatch them from the claims hell has on their lives."

After their confrontation, Ian quit coming in after work. Roberta didn't know what he expected to happen when he no longer showed up at the office. Perhaps, he thought Carrie might notice his absence and ask about it, or maybe she would secure his phone number either from Roberta or where he worked to find out if something was wrong. However, Carrie didn't seem to notice that Ian was missing. She never inquired as to his absence nor showed any real concern that something might have happened to him.

On the one-year anniversary of Charley and Roberta's separation, Roberta ran into a mutual friend of hers and Charley's by the name of Donald Rue in the parking lot of her bank. Since the separation and divorce, she had not seen him or his wife Leslie. Donald seemed pleased to see her.

He was the first to speak, "Hi Robbie, it's nice to see you."

"It's nice to see you too. Don. How are Leslie and the kids?"

"Doing fine. Leslie is still busy with community functions, and the kids are growing. I hear you have a thriving business."

"Yes, the Lord has been graciously blessing me in many ways," Roberta cheerfully responded.

When Roberta mentioned the Lord, Donald quickly brushed over it. "I'm glad you're doing well. I guess Charley is also doing well?"

Roberta knew that Charley's new job was in the same town where Caroline was attending college. He and his girlfriend had moved there. As a result, Caroline was seeing her father more than she had when she was growing up.

"I guess he is doing well," Roberta replied.

"Yeah in fact I heard recently that right after your divorce was final, he married that woman he was involved with."

The latest information broadsided Roberta. When she was around either of Charley's parents they never spoke of him, and when it came to Ian, he was barely speaking to her and Caroline never came to visit her and rarely talked to her on the phone. Roberta had never emotionally or intellectually braced herself for the time Charley might marry the other woman.

"Did I say something wrong?" Don asked with concern.

Roberta could only imagine the look on her face. She quickly collected her rattled thoughts enough to give a reasonable response. "No, I was just remembering something I need to do back at the office."

She turned in the direction of her office when Don cleared his throat, "Aren't you forgetting something Robbie?"

Roberta turned around to face him, "Forgetting something?"

Don nodded at the object he was standing by, "Your car?"

As she looked at her car, she had to quietly concede the latest information had completely unraveled her. She knew she should be embarrassed about her grave oversight but she was too unsettled in her emotions to even consider how stupid she might appear. She nervously let out a giggle and tried to save the day by making fun at her forgetfulness, "There are times I would lose my head if it wasn't tacked on. Thanks Don."

As she was about to get into her car, she looked at him and composed herself enough to end their meeting in a rational way, "It was nice to see you Don. Tell Leslie 'Hi' for me."

He smiled and nodded.

Roberta felt all the air had been knocked out of her. She had been holding onto the possibility of reconciliation with Charley, but now that he was married, everything had changed for her. She knew that she had to let go of him, but she didn't know how to let something go that was still unresolved for her. If Charley had died, she would be forced to accept the finality of their relationship and go on, but he was not dead and emotionally and spiritually she was still committed to him.

When she arrived at the office, she fell into her chair, trying to grab a hold of the reality of what she had just learned, trying to bring her emotions under control. What would she do now? Holding on to any possibility of reconciliation with Charley had made up a big part of her life. She had made many decisions based on the idea of getting back together with him.

As she struggled with the bombardment of uncertainty, Carson walked into the office with some receipts for bookkeeping. The minute he saw her face, he knew something was wrong.

"Is something wrong, Roberta?"

Roberta didn't want to admit that Charley was now married, but she also was not going to be rude and not answer. "I'm having problems right now adjusting to some personal issues."

"Is there any way I can help?"

"It's kind of you Carson, but I'm used to wading alone through the challenging terrain of my personal life," she let out a laugh. "If I put it all in a book, I'm sure it would be both informative and entertaining."

Carson's face lit up, "You know that's a good idea Roberta! Sometimes putting problems and challenges down on paper helps one's perspective. If you have the ability to write, then you could share valuable information in a book that could help other women."

It was as though calm came over her troubled soul, while a light of hope penetrated the dark despair that overshadowed it. She had a knack for writing. In the past it had been healing for her to write down some of her feelings and challenges. She realized she could fill the empty vacuum left by this latest challenge with something healing to her soul and constructive to her spirit, and in the end possibly help other women such as herself. She also realized it would be a daunting task. She didn't know the first thing about writing or publishing a book.

"Carson, I've written things for the school paper and the church newsletter, but I don't know anything about the process that goes into writing a book. I know that writing a book is just the beginning."

"You're right Roberta, but I know about the process. I'll make a deal with you. If you can write a good book, I'll help you through the process."

Roberta smiled, "If I manage to write a decent enough book, I'll take you up on that deal. You're right. It may never be published, but no doubt it will bring some measure of healing to my life."

Carson offered his hand to shake on it and Roberta gladly reciprocated. She had no idea as to the challenges of writing a book, but it would prove to be one of those adventures that she was excited to embark on.

***

Carrie's competence in the office gave Roberta extra time to write. She prayed about what she was to write and disciplined herself to write during every spare minute. Her biggest struggle was determining a catchy title. She finally chose "One Woman's Journey."

Another challenge was the beginning of her book. She had to immediately pull the reader into her book. After struggling with it for a couple of days, she felt she had a good beginning. From the start much of her writing seemed to become a matter of inspiration. She found the stories and incidents, some that were already recorded in her personal journals of her life, were easy to record, but as she reached into her feelings, she realized that she needed to be brutally honest about her struggles and failures as a woman, wife, mother, Christian, and person to have the freedom to write. She knew if she could properly express herself that such honesty could set other women free who struggled with similar problems.

For the most part she became a hermit. Other than Carson, Donna was the only other person who knew that Roberta was writing a book. In fact, there were times when Donna helped her to remember some of the significant occasions she was also involved in.

Roberta was only seen at the office by her clientele, and when home she was tightly shut in behind closed doors, engrossed in a world that contained both challenges and nuggets of the past. She was busy collecting memories, capturing thoughts, and nailing down feelings so she could graduate to the lessons of the present. Each time she looked backwards at her life, she could see the providential hand of God intervening on her behalf. She marveled at the gentleness of His leading, the wisdom of His intervention, the power of His ways, and His faithfulness in guiding her through the deep ravines of sorrow, the challenging valleys of despair, the plateaus of mediocrity, and up the formable mountains of disappointment and disillusionment.

At night she would write the content, and in the morning when she was fresh she would edit and rewrite what she wrote the night before. There were days that found her weary with it, but at the same time she felt revived by what she read. After two months she had a completed manuscript except for a proper ending.

She wrestled with how to end a book when the journey was not yet completed. She realized that she needed to encourage others that as long as there is breath to experience the life God has entrusted, that there are still great riches yet to be discovered. After ending it on a positive note of encouragement, she presented it to Carson to see if it was even publishable.

Carson was surprised when she first handed it to him. "So soon Roberta? I figured it would take you at the least nine months."

Roberta had an explanation, "It's easy to write when something is a matter of the heart and heavenly inspiration."

Carson read the book in three days. When he entered her office with her manuscript in hand to share his evaluation, Roberta sensed an excitement. "Roberta this is an inspirational book! You'll have no problem selling it. I've already contacted a publisher who publishes Christian books. We're going to start the process tomorrow. I will give you a list of things you need to present to him when we meet with him."

From that point Roberta became caught up in a whirlwind. As she was considering the cover, she realized that she didn't want to use her married name. In a way, she wanted to be unknown, a mysterious author, especially when it came to those who knew her. She wanted people to be influenced by the message of the book and not by any personal knowledge or familiarity with her. That is when she decided to use her middle name "Madilyn" as her first name along with her maiden name Harris.

She also decided to dedicate it to the One who proved closer than a friend to her, Jesus, and she wanted to acknowledge the support and encouragement of her two dear friends, Donna and Carson.

The publishing world proved to be another adventure. She discovered that in publishing, the bottom line is not always the content of the book but rather promotion and money. To Roberta her book was like a baby, so precious and special that everyone should agree with her evaluation about it once they opened the cover and read it. However, like a baby, there are also many other books available, and every author believes their particular book is special and that it should also be admired and desired by the public.

She quickly learned that if you don't have a famous name, it will come down to promotion. It was discussed what target group would most likely buy her book and how to reach that particular part of the population. Well thought out news releases were sent to Christian radio, TV, and organizations as bait to reel in the right person or group who would get a vision and passion for the book and then directly and indirectly promote it. There was also a push to do book signings at certain bookstores in the area.

Roberta was glad that Carson understood how it worked and would watch out for her interests. She helped pick out the cover design, and within weeks got to see what her book was going to look like. She was also given a chance to go through it once again in order to correct or rewrite parts before it was offered to the public. Once the preliminaries were out of the way, the publisher was ready to publish her book and send it out in printed and digital form. It was from there that the press releases and information about her book were sent to Christian women's groups as well as to Christian radio and TV.

Within a few weeks, Roberta received offers to be on the radio and TV to promote her book. She had never been on the other side of the inner workings of the social media. She felt nervous but at the same time she counted it as another opportunity to experience something new in her life.

She was fascinated with how sets were arranged for TV to draw viewers in and give them a certain impression, but she found radio to be the most realistic of the visual/hearing media outlets. In TV you have to beware of how you look and present yourself at all times, but in radio the only thing that connects you to the public is a microphone in a soundproof room and a disc jockey who asks you questions in order to encourage a conversation. You don't have to worry about your physical presentation because no one can see you, making it easier to sell your product without having to first sell yourself based on your looks.

One day when she was working in the office, Ian walked through the door, looking downtrodden. His wavy dark hair needed a good cut, and he hadn't shaved for a week. He had not really spoken to her since that day she confronted him about Carrie and his attitude towards God and life.

Roberta was surprised to see him. "Hello Ian, what a pleasant surprise to see you." She couldn't help but add, "Sorry, Carrie isn't here."

Ian looked at her in mild dismay. "I'm here to see you."

Joy sprung up within her. She wanted to get up from her desk, run to him and embrace him, but she knew that such an action would probably not be received. "I'm sorry, I just assumed...well anyway what can I do for you?"

Ian sat down in the chair in front of her desk, "I came to say you're right."

Stunned, Roberta nearly fell out of her chair. "Right about what?

He hung his head and quietly said, "Right about everything from Carrie to my attitude."

Roberta didn't know whether to jump up and down, yell hallelujah, or do the dance of joy, but she knew she had to rein in her emotions, keep her facial expressions in check, and mentally zip her mouth shut in order to give her son a chance to continue.

He looked at her. "I wanted to believe there could be something between Carrie and me. I even built it up in my mind. When you told me she didn't even consider me, it hurt my pride. When you told me off about my attitude and my games, it was like a slap in the face. After all, I had convinced myself I was able to fool everyone, and because of it I was superior. Ever since that day, your words have been constantly going through my mind like a ticker tape. I haven't been able to sleep well, which has affected my job performance. Even Grandpa asked me what was wrong. I told him about what happened and he advised me to come to you and make it right."

Roberta was shocked, but exuberant. She never expected to hear her son honestly admit what was going on in this present lifetime, but she remained silent because she could tell he was not yet done.

"Mom, I realized that I always assumed that you would always be there for me, while ignoring that fact that it was my attitude that was causing a separation between us. The truth is I don't want to be estranged from you. I want you always to be part of my life."

It was then Roberta felt she could interject, "I always want you to be a big part of my life, Ian."

Ian smiled. "Mom I have to be honest with you. I know you are serious about this God-thing in your life, but I'm not ready for that. I still feel there are things I want to experience in this world and if I get caught up with God like you, I'll have to change my ways and I'm afraid I will live in regret of what I have missed."

"In what way will you have to change your ways?" Roberta asked.

"If I give in to God, He will probably call me to preach or something like that, and I like working for grandpa and I like calling my own shots and choosing my own path."

She smiled, "How do you know He will call you into some type of ministry?"

Ian smiled back at her, "I don't know but I don't want to risk it. What I want is not bad, but perhaps it is not good enough and most likely it will leave me empty and dissatisfied as you have warned in the past. But, I just don't what to look back at life with regret and wonder. Do you know what I mean?"

Ian reminded her of what Charley had said before he turned his back on their life together, "I do Ian. You know I'll not stand in your way, but remember that I will be here for you."

"Thanks Mom." He stood to his feet, moved to her side and placed his hand on her shoulder. Then he leaned over and sweetly kissed her on the cheek. As he stood upright, he ended the conversation with four little words that thrilled her heart. "I love you Mom."

With tears in her eyes, she responded, "And, I love you son." She knew that there was a spiritual war going on in his soul and she was confident as to who would ultimately win the battle.

As he was walking out, Carrie was coming to work. They greeted each other casually. Carrie walked up to Roberta, "It's been awhile since I have seen Ian. He seems different."

Roberta smiled. "He is different since you last saw him, Carrie. He's actually beginning to grow up."

***

Roberta's latest adventure as an author was presenting her with various new opportunities. She did interviews that would not compromise her secret identity. When she was on the radio, she was confident those who knew her would not recognize who she was because of her name and when she was on TV, she was on stations that aired outside of the viewing area where she lived.

One day she received a surprise call from Caroline. She was in the vicinity visiting with some of her friends over the weekend and wanted to know if she could stay with her. It had been awhile since they had spent any real time together. Caroline had spent the holidays with her father and only called her mother occasionally out of duty. Their conversation was often surface and strained.

Roberta was glad to see her daughter, but she sensed her daughter was even more distant. She tried to make Caroline comfortable, but the more she tried, the more Caroline copped an attitude and excused herself to go visit with her friends.

Roberta struggled with feelings of rejection and anger. She had done nothing against her daughter to warrant such an attitude. She decided there was only one thing to do, live her life in spite of her daughter's presence.

On Sunday morning Roberta got ready for church as usual. She went down to prepare her breakfast. As she finished eating, Caroline came down the stairs in her bathrobe. She looked at her mother. "No breakfast."

"You can find all the ingredients you need to fix your own breakfast. Help yourself."

Caroline shrugged, "Are you going someplace?"

"Yes, I'm going to church," Roberta replied.

"That's a surprise, Mother! In fact, I would say it's hypocritical of you."

Caroline's statement shocked Roberta. "Just what do you mean?"

"Daddy said he met your boyfriend at the closing on the house. He figured you found someone on the side before the two of you were even legally separated."

Roberta was shocked, "What are you talking about? I have no boyfriend, and the only extra man at the signing beside the buyer for our house, was Carson Reed who owned the house I was buying!"

It was then that Roberta connected the apparent conclusion to Charley's disconcerting look that day. "I see," she declared in indignantly.

"You see what?" Caroline asked.

"It's apparent your father has transposed his perverted way of thinking onto a friendly, but innocent greeting by Mr. Reed. I have always been faithful to your father; even now I'm committed to him even though he is married to another woman"

"And, by your attitude and actions towards me, you have chosen to believe it as well. Even though it's neither of your business, Mr. Reed and I are just friends, and I refuse to let both of your perverted takes on it defile my relationship with him and make it into something that is questionable or immoral!"

Roberta's indignation began to fan into an inferno of rage. It took everything in her to maintain a firm tone without escalating two octaves higher, revealing the depth of her anger. "If you two want to cast doubt on my intentions or blame me for the breakdown of the marriage to avoid facing what is true, that will be your choice, but you are both WRONG! And, no matter how you try to make it my fault, it will not change the self-serving choices your father has made because of his own moral inconsistencies, nor will it take away or justify your snobby, unbecoming, disrespectful behavior towards me."

Roberta quickly turned, marched out the door and headed for her car, leaving Caroline standing with her mouth open. Roberta was beyond livid. She had tried to live an upright life before her family, do right by her friends, and be right before the Lord, but it took only one perverted conclusion and one judgmental suspicion to unravel everything and throw mud onto what was innocent and pure.

She suddenly was aware that she was weary with the narrow perspective selfishness creates in people. She saw how it actually develops small minds that consider everything from self-serving motives and pursuits, thereby, allowing the real culprits to transpose their sins onto the innocent. She was tired of others trashing what was pure in her life, while trying to put a face of dignity or nobility on something that was dishonorable.

Instead of going to church, she drove around and stopped at the park to walk, think, and pray. When she finally cooled down enough to return home, Caroline was gone. She left a note telling her mother that she needed to get back to finish an assignment.

Roberta loved her daughter, but she had to admit she didn't like the person she was becoming. She felt partially to blame for her daughter's spoiled, self-serving attitude. Perhaps she had given her too much of the world, stressing an outward appearance instead of inward character.

Carson was the one who interrupted Roberta's self-introspection when he knocked on her door. He had an envelope along with some other information that no doubt involved promoting her book. Even though she felt like hiding in her morbid world of introspection, she knew that it wouldn't prove to be beneficial for her.

She forced herself to open the door and smile, while trying to sound cheerful, "Carson, what a pleasant surprise. Come in."

Carson looked at her suspiciously, "Are you alright Roberta? You missed church."

Roberta dropped the smile and turned from the door, Carson following close behind her. He laid the information on the table while Roberta filled the teakettle.

"Would you like some tea, Carson?"

"I wouldn't mind some tea, but are you going to tell me what's wrong?"

"Well, I guess you might as well know. My daughter came to visit me for the first time since I moved here, but it didn't go well. She shared some slanderous information with me that originated with her father."

Curiosity washed over his face as he asked the inevitable, "What information was that?"

"That you and I were having an affair even before we signed the papers for this house."

Surprised he asked, "How could they come to such a conclusion? I only met you a little over a month before we signed the papers on the house."

"I guess we really worked fast," Roberta half smiled. "Charley saw you the day we signed papers."

Carson smiled, "He saw me? Did I see him?"

"Yes. He's the guy who nodded at you as you were coming in and he was leaving."

"That was Charley!" he exclaimed. "I thought he was one of the office workers or brokers."

"That was Charley. And, apparently, your friendly greeting towards me caught his imagination, and from there he rode the waves of perversion right up to the shores of vanity, and right on into the swamp of speculation and maliciousness. Imagine that." She looked into Carson's face, "I'm sorry you were associated to me in that way. It's not fair to you."

Carson shook his head, "It's okay. Don't worry about my reputation. People believe what they are going to believe."

"It's not fair that they defiled our relationship. You have been a good friend. You have always been there to help and encourage me. And, you have helped me with my book."

Carson cleared his throat nervously. "Roberta, I've considered you a good friend, but I have to admit I'm attracted to you. I've been trying to figure out if I'm attracted to your tender spirit, your person, or both. I've so appreciated our friendship, but I'm not sure if our relationship is not meant to be more than just a friendship."

Roberta was completely caught off guard. She never allowed herself to consider Carson in any other light but a friend. It was true that she felt a certain attraction towards him at different times, but she never gave them audience. It was disconcerting but also flattering to think that Carson could have more than feelings of friendship towards her.

"Carson, I don't know what to say. I've tried to stay true to Charley."

"Yes, Roberta I know and that is all commendable, but Charley is married to another woman. He's gone on and you need to let go so you can find the life you are meant to live."

Carson's words were definitely striking a cord in her, "You're right, but the Bible instructs a divorced person not to seek another mate."

Roberta watched Carson frown a little as he began to pace back and forth in front of her. "Come on, Roberta, neither one of us have sought the other out. Circumstances brought us together. When we met, both of us were sincere in our motives and intentions towards each other. But, it's time to consider if God is actually the One who brought us together for a greater purpose."

"Carson, you don't know what you are getting yourself into. You're a widower and have a right to remarry, but I'm divorced, a state associated with grave sin, a sin that is almost treated as the unpardonable sin by some Christians. You deserve better than that as far as your Christian testimony. You don't need to be saddled with my problems."

He stopped pacing and leaned forward to take both of her hands in his. He looked into her eyes and said, "That's my personal decision to make Roberta, not yours. Again, small-minded people are going to believe what they want to believe, but we know the truth. If Jesus wills it so, we both have some good years left to live. My wife is no longer, your marriage is over, and Charley has gone on with his life. It's time

415

for us to seek God's will as to where He is leading you and to the type of relationship He has ordained for us."

She squeezed his hands. "Carson, you could very well be right, but I've never felt the freedom to let Charley go. I don't know why, but until that door is shut once and for all, I can't consider our relationship to be anything other than a good friendship. Do you understand?"

He shook his head, "I do understand. Your commitment towards Charley is a quality that I have admired and appreciated about you. But, when you finally figure out what God intended by allowing our paths to cross, will you let me know?"

Roberta smiled, "You'll be the first to know."

After Carson left, Roberta was alone with her unbridled thoughts and emotions. As she looked at the mail and information Carson had dropped off, she noticed an envelope. She opened it to find an invitation to speak at a Christian ladies luncheon in the city where Charley lived and Caroline attended college.

As she thought about it, she figured that she didn't have to worry about Charley or Caroline finding out about it. Granted, there would be a press release, but they would use her pen name and since she never provided a picture with the press releases, she didn't have to worry about being recognized.

That night she called Irene Reynolds, the woman who sent the letter, to accept the invitation to speak. Irene Reynolds was personable and excited about Roberta's book. It had been given to her by a friend and Irene had totally related to Roberta's journey in so many ways. She knew that Roberta would also encourage many other women in their spiritual journeys.

The day came for Roberta to speak at the women's luncheon. As she walked into the hall where it was to be held, she was surprised to see how big the room was. Even with tables and chairs, it had the capacity to hold quite a few women.

She asked a lady sitting at her book table where she could find Irene. The lady smiled at her and pointed to a woman who was talking to someone about the microphone on the podium. When Roberta walked up to Irene, she introduced herself as Madilyn Harris.

Irene was excited to see her. The lady at the book table realized she had just talked to the author. She came over to personally meet Roberta and tell her how her book had blessed her. From that moment on everything became a blur. Roberta was directed to her chair and offered some tea. For the first time, she was given a front row seat where she watched excited women filling the hall.

Irene sat next to her. Roberta became engrossed in a conversation with Irene about her book. She glanced out at the crowd, only to have everything come to a standstill. Standing off to one side of the room, with another young woman, was Caroline. Her usually long blonde hair was swept up into a neat bun, causing Roberta to blink and refocus to assure herself that it was really her daughter.

About the time Roberta saw Caroline, her daughter saw her. Caroline took a double take when she realized she was seeing her mother at the front table. The young lady next to her gently nudged her, gaining her attention, motioning her to sit in one of the seats at a table in the center of the room. As Caroline sat down, Roberta could see, out of the corner of her eye, that her daughter's eyes were glued on her.

Roberta fought hard to gain her composure, trying hard to keep Irene from noticing that she felt like she was unraveling at the seams. She took a deep breath and quietly asked the Lord to help her, give her strength, and anoint her. She knew there were hurting women out there who were seeking answers, and Roberta had long ago discovered the ultimate answer to their plight.

When it was time to start, Irene got up and introduced Madilyn Harris. When Roberta stood up to take the podium, she saw complete shock on Caroline's face. She looked past Caroline at the rest of the women in the hall. They had become quiet when Irene stood up and now they were open, ready, and expecting to receive.

Roberta threw herself on the Lord and opened her mouth, not sure if anything would come out. Fortunately, the Lord has loosed her tongue. "Hello, it is an honor to be here today and I want to thank Irene Reynolds for inviting me to share with you my experience. I don't know how many of you have read my book, "One Woman's Journey," but if you have, you know that it is about my personal life. I wish I could say that wisdom and experience has guided much of my journey, but the truth is I have spent most of my time floundering, only to be caught up by circumstances orchestrated by an unseen hand of Providence that often determined the direction of the path I found myself on.

"My journey is one of self-discovery. This journey was not about discovering who I thought and hoped to be, even though I discovered various things about my character, but a journey of discovering who God intended me to be in light of His providence and plan. Only our Creator can know who we are, is able to reveal our positon in His kingdom, and unveil His intention towards us in light of His eternal plan.

"Another matter I discovered is that my womanhood was not some burdensome state but a glorious experience. There were times I wondered what was so glorious about womanhood. It often appeared as if women were an afterthought, an addition that didn't amount to too much unless we could be fitted nicely into a square-hole that was clearly not shaped with the understanding that most of us are not square. In fact, if the world hasn't noticed, we come in various sizes, forms, and shapes."

She could see some women smiling and others shaking their heads in agreement as she continued, "Even though all women have a common bond of being women, our attitudes about ourselves are often defined by religious and cultural influences that can cause diversity in how we view our roles in society. As a result, we pursue different dreams and goals, and can end up vehemently disagreeing with what it means to be a 'woman' in today's world.

"Some women think we need to be liberated, but from what? Some would answer from traditional roles; others would say prejudicial or bias classifications that cause women to be treated as second-rate slaves, or as property, or an object rather than a human being. However, are not those who are without Christ, male and female, enslaved in similar ways throughout the world, depending on their culture and religious beliefs?

"Perhaps the slavery varies as to how it manifests itself. For example, those who enslave others are even more so enslaved by their despotic philosophies that sear their conscience. Which brings us back to the question, what do people need to be liberated from, the prejudices or bias directed at their gender or the wrong attitudes and ways of thinking that have enslaved every culture throughout the world?

"I don't know about you, but it was the differences we often fight against that created a crisis in me about my own womanhood. These differences also caused me to miss the crux of the challenges that each of us as women must face. However, it was the crisis that finally brought me to the end of myself to discover the significance of being a woman.

"Some of this identity crisis happened because I became lost as a woman in a world that began to make less sense to me. I came to a place in my life that I could no longer fit as a woman in my world and survive the emotional tsunami that had left me devastated, nor could I accept what I considered to be a substandard lot that was being cast upon me as a woman.

"However, I might be getting ahead of myself. Let me begin from the very beginning. Through the years I have been known by various names. The name I use as an author is Madilyn Harris. Madilyn is my middle name and Harris my maiden name. However, my first name is Roberta and my married name is Walker. To my parents, they fondly called me Maddie due to my middle name, my former husband called me, "Rob", relatives, and friends nicknamed me Robbie, and my children called me "Ma" when they were in a hurry; "Mom" when they wanted to ask me something, and "mother" when they were irritated with me and wanted to be sure to get my attention."

Roberta paused as she let out a chuckle, while witnessing her daughter actually giggling along with other women who were also identifying with her. "I grew up on the wrong side of the tracks according to culture. I didn't fit the image of beauty according to the promotional conditioning of the world, and I was cast as an outsider in school. I was never allowed to be involved in the in-group, and was always left standing on the outside of acceptance, trying to figure out what it would take to simply belong.

"However, that all changed when I met my husband in my junior year. He was not only an upper classman, but from the other side of the tracks, and was the son of a well-respect businessman. I'll never forget the day he came to me to ask for a date. I was shocked that he even noticed a wallflower such as me. Certainly, considered beneath his class by much of society, I ignored the suspicion that arose in my being. I reasoned that since America is the land of opportunity and is beyond the caste system, why couldn't I be a Cinderella, waiting on the sidelines for my prince?

"In time I drowned out all suspicions and rode the wave of excitement as I got caught up into a world of possibilities. My status began to change as I became more identified with the man who later would become my husband. The most popular girls even showed some interest in me even though I was aware that some had their claws sticking out, ready to scratch my eyes out with envy.

"As I became caught up more and more with the possibilities of a new world, common sense and decency went out the window, resulting in inappropriate actions. At 17 I found I was pregnant. When my prince was informed, his attitude became somewhat sour. However, when his parents found out, there was only one thing to do and that was to marry.

Thus, a shaky relationship began. Up front, my husband, although initially reluctant, seemed to accept his new role as husband, but eventually he seemed to settle down into the grind of learning his father's business while attending the local college. We did have a wonderful prince, Ian, and a beautiful little princess, Caroline, to add to our small kingdom."

Roberta glanced at her daughter when she mentioned her name, and it appeared as if she was actually engrossed in what she was saying. "Although I sensed our small kingdom was fragile and unstable, I was romantic enough to believe that with the children, I could somehow make it all work as a wife. I was told if I did things a certain way, I could make my husband happy. However, the more I tried, the more he became frustrated. Eventually frustration manifested into sarcasm and anger, and the harder I tried to keep it together for the sake of the children, the further our relationship seemed to grow apart.

"I must state, at times our challenges subsided due to both of us loving our children, but I discovered we were in a negative cycle and the silent struggle that was taking place intensified to the point that the atmosphere could be cut with a knife at certain times. Each time I sought help, it seemed that all the responsibility for saving the marriage would fall on me. 'If only' I performed a certain way; 'if only' I would lose weight, dress up, make myself sexier, I would create an attraction that my husband would naturally respond too.

"All my attempts seemed futile. Our relationship became more precarious until it hit a crisis point that erupted like a volcano. When the ugly truth about our marriage spilled out, I was left devastated and quickly spiraled into a deep pit of depression. I began to see myself as a failure as a wife, and the only thing that kept me from drowning in complete sorrow and despair was the fact that I was forced to look up to recognize my real source of salvation and redemption, Jesus Christ.

"The Lord changed me, but my husband had his own will and attitude towards God. After my conversion, I renewed my commitment to love and do right by him. Granted, he appreciated the change that took place in my life because it made it easier for him to live with me. However, happiness is an inner state that is manifested when an individual accepts life for what it is and chooses to become content with what has been entrusted to him or her. Sadly, my husband could never come to a place of acceptance and contentment. For that reason he became like a restless wave on the ocean as he struggled with his rights to life on his terms. At times his inner struggles graciously subsided on the shorelines of daily responsibilities and drudgeries.

"Even though I often ignored it, I knew deep down that our marriage was in trouble. I prayed and wrestled before God about it. I sought His wisdom to know how to change the dynamics of our relationship. For the most part I stayed the course of seeing our marriage succeed; after all, I had a relationship with my Creator, and if He could speak the world into being, He could bring about an honorable resolution as to my husband's attitude about our marriage.

"However, the real crux of the matter still clearly existed; my husband had a will and mind of his own. At best he tolerated his life, but the intense struggle within his being was great. It became more apparent with each passing year that the restlessness in his inner being became tormenting and unbearable to him at times. All I could do was pray and know that God reigns and trust that He would work it out for His glory.

"In spite of a struggling marriage, I had one other card up my sleeve, that of being a mother. I decided I would be the best mother ever to define my place and purpose in the world. I did everything I could to win the affections and loyalty of my children.

"As every mother out there can relate, I didn't want my children to know the bitterness of isolation that I had because of my low position in society. As a result, I wanted the best for them, but you might say all I managed to do was spoil them. I failed to teach them that anything of value will cost them something and that without understanding the value of something, there is no gratitude in which to receive it and no need to sacrifice in order to possess or maintain it. In the end, I cheapened everything of value for them, causing them to pursue that which had no value."

As Roberta quickly sized up the reaction of the women in the meeting hall, she was surprised at how many of them were actually hanging onto every word she was speaking. She sensed an authority she never had, an authority that was making everything she said viable. In the authority, she sensed a power, a power of confidence that came from knowing that she was not only speaking from experience, but from truth, truth that could set other captive women free to discover who they were according to their Creator.

"When my children were young, instead of applying corrective discipline, I put pressure on them to live up to vague notions in order to guide their conduct. For example, since my husband's family was respected in our community, I reminded them of their high position and responsibility that their last name represented in the town as one of the means to discipline their behavior. However, they took on different poses because they were left to define what it would mean to live up to their name in the community. One became resentful, the other one a snob. What I failed to realize is that a person is not defined or shored up by some "name" but by inner character which can only be established through example, challenging wrong attitudes, and teaching and encouraging your child to choose the most excellent ways to discover his or her true gifts and potential."

Roberta glanced at Caroline to see her reaction. She could tell that what she was stating was turning on a light in Caroline's mind. She also knew Caroline recognized which of the categories she fit in.

"The other means I used was our church association. As members of a popular Protestant Church, I reminded my children that they had a responsibility to act a certain way as a Protestant. It is not that I was living the Christian example; rather, I was hiding behind the idea of religion like a mask I could put on at different times to give the impression or appearance of being 'good.' Since my children lived with me, they saw through my hypocrisy. After all, how can you lead your children in a certain way if you, yourself have never walked that way before? You can't.

"As a parent my intentions towards my children were that of a normal mother who wanted to see the best for them. I wanted to leave them with a legacy that would bring fondness to them when they thought of me and could be passed down to the next generation. I didn't realize that the only legacy that would ensure such fruits is a spiritual legacy. A legacy that helps children to know who they are in Jesus, and understand their high calling to live life above the ordinary of this present world in order to discover the extraordinary of the promised age to come.

"I also strived to become my children's friend and confidant. Since I didn't have a life per se with my husband, I wanted to become an integral part of their life to bring meaning to my own life. I failed to realize that you cannot effectively hold on to your authoritarian position as a mother and be a friend at the same time. Eventually the roles will collide. When I needed to be a mother, I was trying to be a friend, and when I needed to be a friend, I was being a mother. Children need clarity in their relationships in order to know where they stand and what to expect.

"As you probably surmised, all of my attempts to be a great mother simply resulted in me becoming an overbearing, pushy mother, causing my children to become frustrated, driving them further away from me. Needless to say, my children took different attitudes toward me and my meddling. My son would placate me to get me off his back, while my daughter began to take on a cynical attitude that ended with her becoming more embarrassed by me and resentful towards me as my desperation grew to make my life count by winning the mother of the year award."

Roberta looked at her daughter before continuing. Caroline was looking down as if she was hiding something, whether it be anger, tears, shame, or something else, Roberta could only guess.

"It was not until a series of crises rocked my life that the reality finally hit me that I had to face the futility of my personal attempts. I couldn't keep my marriage together no matter what, and I couldn't be the mother of the year no matter what I did. I was a miserable failure, facing an uncertain future that provided no place for the position I eventually found myself in, a middle-aged divorced woman who was also estranged from her children.

"The truth is I fell into a black hole. As the titles, notions, and attempts to be a perfect wife and mother were being sucked into an insatiable pit, I realized that beyond it was a type of nothingness. You may be called to accept these roles placed on you by family, religion, and society, but who establishes the script since the roles constantly change according to fickle temperaments and images of those around you, while notions change with the world's latest fads. Clearly, the demands can change in a flash. You realize that the reasons why people are dissatisfied in their relationship with you are endless, and the accusations wielded against you can prove to be cruel and indifferent.

"To make a long story short, I did fail my former husband and my children and I hope that they are able to forgive me." When Roberta mentioned forgiveness, Caroline looked up at her in surprise. Roberta looked at her daughter for a brief second as she explained why she needed to ask for their forgiveness.

"I failed them because I looked to them to give me something that they could not give: an identity. In my attempt to find purpose and life in my relationship with them, I sucked the very life out of them. I failed to come to terms with who I was and became vulnerable and needy in the end, only to discover each time a spiritual vacuum that was causing my life to spiral out of control.

"I had to face the obvious. Titles such as wife and mother do not define a woman, just her responsibilities as a woman. Her relationships with others do not define her; granted, they may serve as a mirror to her strengths and weaknesses, but they are not able to define her in a way that brings identity and lasting meaning.

"In this struggle through the years to come to terms with who I was meant to be, I found myself having to face and learn the same lesson over and over again. The only means by which I could be properly defined is from the perspective of the One who designed me in the first place, but even that knowledge initially created another type

423

of problem. As a Protestant, I was a Sunday Christian. As a religious person, I had a moral code, and as the occasional do-gooder I maintained a social gospel to the outside world. But, each of these practices were empty and also left me in despair.

"Even though I met the living Christ of the Bible, received Him as my Savior and Lord, I still had to experience the vanity of doing it my way before I finally could understand and accept why I was here, the purpose for my life, and the potential that was within my reach. But, it took much personal failure that comes from riding the different waves of worldly expectation to the shorelines of vanity and consequences for me to learn that before I can discover who I am, I must understand where I fit, my position and place in the kingdom of God. Keep in mind, position and place points to security. We women must first feel secure before we can have the freedom to accept who we are, every bit of it no matter how bad, nominal, and insignificant it may seem.

"The one consolation I had to constantly rediscover in my journey is that I knew that it was from the safety of my place in Jesus that I could discover my real person, who He intended me to be. As I grew in the knowledge of Him, I fell more in love with Him. As I grew up in my relationship with the Lord, I became more like Him, realizing my potential of being predestinated to be conformed to His very image. The more I took on Jesus' life, the greater the freedom I had to be me, to soar in victory above the devastation of my former life to discover the abundant life of Christ in me.

"So many women make the mistake of starting from the premise of being a wife or mother, but this will not keep a woman centered and clearly established on a stable foundation. The only center that will keep a person from taking detours and falling into empty pits of despair is the Lord Jesus Christ, starting with Him, learning to walk with Him, and ending with Him.

"As you can see, it has been a long process. Clearly, I didn't discover all of these truths overnight. But, it was Jesus who constantly reminded me that we must always start from our place in Him to discover the person we were designed to be and recognize that our gender does not define us; rather it becomes a point of discipline. The Bible is clear as to how men and women are to morally conduct themselves towards one another and in a marriage relationship. These disciplines are not terrible burdens; rather, they ensure order and godly harmony.

"I'd like to read a poem to you written by an Alisha Grant, entitled, "Who Is Woman?" This poem is about a Christian woman who has come to terms with her position in Christ, her person because of Christ, and the role her gender will play in her life before God.

"Who is woman?
An idea, a role, or a person,
Often defined by lifeless traditions,
Overlooked and lost in the midst of various cultures,
Taken out of the side of man,
Never meant to walk behind him as a slave,
Nor in front of him as a lord,
But beside him, knitted in oneness of spirit,
    Together in step with God's high calling.

"Who is woman?
Made by God to be a helper,
A multitasker in daily demands,
A pillar in the home,
A voice of wisdom in uncertain times,
A nurturer of souls,
A servant of the Most High,
A sweet fragrance rising from
    the inner courts of the sanctuary of the home.

"Who is woman?
Tending the countless fires of the home,
Maintaining the various altars,
Altars where tears of brokenness serve as sacrifice,
Sweat of toil becomes a form of self-denial,
Love and submission forms a cross,
A wounded heart becomes a badge of courage,
Silent prayers wield the greatest victories.

"Who is woman?
She holds many poses.
Kneeling before objects of disgrace to serve,
Silently sitting while the insignificant demands her precious time,
Standing before lifeless items to lift the burdens of others,
Accepting with grace menial tasks, while tackling giants.
Her job never done, her work never recognized,
Learning to do all for the benefit of others,
    and the glory of the One she serves.

"Who is woman?
Formed in the image of God,
Defined by her Creator, established by her ordained position,
  And disciplined by her gender.
Called to be great in His kingdom,
  Ever serving as a true servant,
Offering a perpetual sacrifice of love,
  From the enclosed garden of her heart.
Honoring the One who formed her last,
Often marked by the insignificant and menial,
Learning that the last is sometimes made first,
Ever exalted, pointing others to her Lord,
  the One who is worthy of all love and worship."

Roberta could tell that that many women were pondering what they had heard, some had tears in their eyes, while others looked down to hide the emotional upheaval that was taking place in their souls. She let a few seconds pass before she concluded her talk.

"I thought a lot about the poem I just read to you and I realized God entrusted me with my womanhood as a gift. For example, He has given me unusual altars to kneel before such as commodes and bathtubs where I can praise Him for the life He has entrusted to me," she snickered in unison with other chuckles that were coming from the audience, "tons of irritating lists and paper work to remind me to thank Him that this too shall pass, mounds of dishes where I can lift up all my cares in prayer and cast all concerns at His precious feet. Although many of the activities I must do bring irritating drudgery my way, and if faithful to such tasks at hand, eventually the giant demands will whittle down before me. And, although, much of what women do is taken for granted, I have realized that in light of Christ and all He did for me, it's my reasonable service, the least I could do; but, I also have learned that if I do all things as if I'm doing it unto Him, I can freely offer all of it as a small bouquet at the end of the day to Him as a token of my love for Him. It is in the sacrifice of the small, the offering up of all, and the consecrating of what is left that has brought me the greatest freedom to soar in the heights of who my Lord is.

"And finally, I want to leave you with this thought. As you now know, I have answered to various names and titles through my life. I have worn different hats, done various juggling acts, and even felt as if I emcee a circus at times. But, the Bible tells me there is only one name that will count in the end. It will be the name that the Lord gives me. What a glorious name that will be, because it will not speak of what I attempted to be; rather, it will speak of who I have become in light of my life and relationship with the Lord Jesus Christ.

"I want to thank you for showing such grace and kindness to me. If you have any questions or you want to buy a book or you want me to sign a book, you can find me at the book table. I'm looking forward to meeting with each of you and talking to you."

As she stepped back from the podium, the crowd erupted into applause as women began to jump to their feet to give her a standing ovation. Her daughter was one of the first ones to stand to her feet as she clapped with determined zeal.

Roberta did not hear much of the closing statement done by Irene, as she quietly made her way back to the table. She positioned herself behind the table, waiting for the women to be dismissed. Once Irene had ended the luncheon with prayer, the women flocked to the table to speak to Roberta, buy her book, and have her sign their copy. The enthusiasm and complements were freely flowing as women came to show their agreement and support as they bought her book and admitted that they related to her life.

After forty-five minutes of meeting women, talking to them, and handing them a signed book, she looked up to see Caroline patiently waiting to the side to talk to her. It was clear that she wanted to be the last one to approach her mother. As the last woman meandered out of the meeting hall, Caroline walked up to her mother, picked up a book and handed her mother some money, "Would you please sign my book?"

Roberta could tell her daughter had been on an emotional ride. She walked around the table and as Caroline faced her, she gently took her daughter's extended hand with the money, and she closed it with both hands. As she held Caroline's hand and looked into her daughter's big brown eyes she said, "Caroline, will you forgive me for emphasizing the wrong priorities, failing to challenge you to pursue what is excellent and lasting, and not ensuring that you really understood what it means to possess the most important legacy?"

Caroline couldn't contain herself any longer. She flung her arms around her mother while still holding the book and the money in her hands and began to sob. Through her sobs Roberta heard what she had been waiting so long to hear, an open door to reconciliation.

"Oh...Mom, it's I who need to ask for your forgiveness. I didn't understand. I...have been-n-n...angry with you because I was afraid that I'd lose Dad. I've been embarrassed by you...and looked down on you as my inferior because you didn't seemed to fit into the world that I was pursuing. I've...resented your meddling...I've been an ungrateful snob that has blamed you for everything that went wrong between you and Daddy...and in my life. I did it because I knew you'd never reject me...you'd never forsake me...you'd always love me no matter what."

Caroline wasn't done. "When you told me off the last time we were together, I knew you were right, and it broke my heart, but I didn't know how to change it. My friend has been talking to me about Jesus and invited me to this luncheon. I'm so glad I came."

"I'm glad you came too," Roberta responded as she held her daughter close to comfort her. Clearly, Caroline had become the victim of Charley's and her sins. She had been torn by loyalty, devastated by fear, confused by uncertainty, and robbed of her innocence as she tasted the bitterness caused by other people's selfishness.

Roberta continued to stroke her daughter's hair, "My darling Caroline there is nothing to forgive. It's time for us to make peace with the past so that we can go forward into a new, better relationship. I'll always be your mother, and I'll always love you; therefore, I'll always have a tendency to meddle, but I know I must refrain from doing so and let you become the woman God intends you to be. I must let you walk your own path, experience your own struggles, and find out who you are according to the eternal plan of your Creator."

Caroline stepped back and Roberta gently wiped tears away from her daughter's cheeks with her fingers. "Why don't we start fresh? You look at your schedule and let me know when we can have lunch and we can face the past together in order to ensure a new beginning."

Caroline smiled, "Yes let's do that!" Then she handed her mother the book, "You need to still sign this."

Roberta smiled and took the book while grabbing her pen that still lay on the table, "To my precious daughter, Caroline, We share a common bond together: we are women! May we challenge each other to excellence, allow room for personal growth, share nuggets of wisdom when needed, encourage when the challenges are great, love and forgive in times of misunderstandings, and learn to be immovable pillars when it comes to what is true and right. I'm glad you are my daughter, sharing this special experience with me. Love always, Mom."

Caroline read the inscription and hugged her mother once again. "Thanks Mom, I love you too and will cherish this always." She stepped back from her mother, "Talk to you later."

Then she left Roberta basking in the victory of it all. Roberta knew that before she went to bed that night, she would be offering a glorious, fragrant bouquet up to her Lord as a token of her love and appreciation for His sweet ministry of reconciliation.

***

Roberta couldn't believe that she was about to meet Charley at a restaurant. He had called her motel room that very afternoon, explaining that Caroline had told him she was in town. He explained he'd wanted to touch base with her for a while, but had been leery about contacting her. Roberta had no idea what he wanted to talk to her about, but down deep she sensed there needed to be some closure on her part in regard to their relationship.

For months, she had ignored the fact that she had not really emotionally let go of him. She had convinced herself that the reason was that she loved him. Roberta knew that was true to a point. There was a time that, out of love, she had opened her heart to him and entrusted it wholly to him, but when the truth came out about his affair, her heart was broken, once again wounded by his mockery and rejection. The wound had festered over and she protected it by putting up a wall. Even though Jesus had knocked on the wall, she had maintained it. Therefore, the question remained, why did she still hold onto him? Why would she not let Jesus bring down the wall and completely heal her and set her free to find her future life?

After her talk with Carson she began to reexamine her motives and realized that she had not let go because of wounded pride and insecurity. Even though much of their marriage was in a state of uncertainty and turmoil, she was secure in it because she knew her place, but now that she had found her place in Christ, she no longer needed to hold onto the false security of their marriage as if it was a pacifier.

It was time to let go, and for her that meant facing the one who had deeply wounded her to put her past to rest. She wasn't sure if her feelings for Charley were based partly on her imagination working overtime in relationship to her responsibilities and ideas of marriage. She had to see if the old was still present to put it all in perspective. She had to know if he was able to undo her with his look and make her feel small and vulnerable with his words. As she approached the hostess desk, she could see Charley sitting in a secluded booth with his hands clasped around a glass of wine, absently staring into it.

As the hostess came towards her Roberta nodded her head towards Charley and the hostess beckoned her to proceed to his table. As she approached the table she began to see a different Charley. He reminded her of a small wounded boy, yet there was also something very old about him. He looked tired, hunched over, and his "graying brown" hair was thinner. She quietly let out a sigh of relief as she realized the hurt and anger was gone, and the uncertain space where her feelings presented themselves in regard to him was quickly filling with pity and not anger.

As she approached the table she smiled. "Hello Charley."

Startled, Charley slid out of the booth, "Hi Rob." He took both of her hands and leaned over to give her a peck on the lips and she quickly turned her cheek to him.

He stepped back, and looked at her, "My you are looking good these days." In a gentlemanly way, he motioned for her to sit in the booth before sitting opposite of her.

As she sat down, she thanked him for his compliment. It was as if the "old" Charley was back, but yet she knew that it was nothing but a veneer. He had been taught manners, but there was no substance of character behind them. He was at heart a selfish man, a self-serving opportunist.

Once settled, and after ordering a cup of black coffee for her, Roberta got right to the point. "Charley, why did you ask for this meeting?"

"I'm not sure Rob. I heard you are now a famous author, congratulations! Who would have imagined?" He paused. "But, why are you using your middle and maiden name as a pen name? After all, the Walker name would give you needed clout."

If Roberta had forgotten the sting of Charley's condescending attitude towards her, she was quickly reminded of it in his nonchalant statement, but she was not about to receive his estimation of her and his attitude about the Walker name. "Yes, who would have imagined that I could be successful on my own? And, as for the 'Walker' name, it rightfully belongs to another woman. I wanted my book to strictly be identified to a person, meaning me, and not some name."

Roberta's statement apparently jolted Charley into realizing what had he said. "I'm sorry Rob. I didn't intend to put you down. I've always known you were an intelligent woman and capable of going forward without my help or any real association with my name."

Roberta stifled her disgust. "I accept your apology, but I must ask once again, why are we having this meeting?"

"I feel there is an unresolved issue with you that plagues me. I realize I haven't done right by you and I find myself confused and questioning why I ever left you in the first place."

Roberta was striving hard to assimilate what he had just said. She had waited for two years to hear him admit that he was wrong in leaving her, but when she heard it, it sounded hollow to her.

"Charley, I can tell you why you left me according to your own attitudes and words. You were bored with me and you had found someone else who made you feel alive."

Her words caused Charley to appear shriveled as he squinted and bowed his head lower. Once again she felt sorry for him and tried to take the terseness out of the air that her last statement had left. "I gather you have discovered that your new life has some snags in it."

"Snags!" He straightened and looked up at her, his eyes suddenly opening wide. "They don't describe the misery I'm now experiencing. Sure, it was exciting at first, but now it's obvious she doesn't understand me like you did. She complains about everything. She whines about the amount of money I make, and-d-d...the fact that I don't take her out as much because I am tired. And-d-d-d she even complains about how I brush my teeth. In fact, everything I do has become an irritation to her. At least you used to encourage me!"

Roberta was stunned at Charley's outburst. She had only seen Charley's new wife from a distance, but she gathered that she might prove to be a handful down the line. "Charley, what do you want me to do about your situation?"

"Maybe, we can make this mess right by getting back together. After all, you told me you still loved me and implied you would take me back."

Speechless, Roberta, struggled to find her voice. The waitress brought her coffee and after what seemed like an extended silence, she finally said, "It's true I implied that Charley, but that was before you married this woman. Your marriage has changed all of that for the both of us. We no longer have any right to explore that option. I will not become the other woman who breaks up your marriage. Besides, this is not *our* MESS, this is *your* mess, and you really need to own it."

Shaking his head, "Come on Rob, I made a mistake. Can't a man make a mistake without having to live with it the rest of his life?"

Roberta leaned back in the booth, sipping her coffee. "How many mistakes is a man allowed to make before he has to take responsibility for the reality or consequences of his decisions and actions?"

With a questioning expression, Charley asked, "What do you mean?"

"What do I mean Charley? My, what a short memory you have. It was a mistake when I got pregnant out of wedlock. It was a big mistake that you married me because I couldn't make you happy. Now it's a mistake that you married this young filly who you can't make happy. Those mistakes, Charlie, are a product of your actions and decisions, but until you take ownership for them and learn from them, you'll find yourself making the same mistakes over and over.

"Charley, you need to know that the Bible has one word for your mistakes—it's called 'sin.' Because we committed the sin of fornication, I became pregnant, but it was my fault that I allowed myself to get pregnant. You apparently had the fun, and I had to pick up the full tab because I was a silly girl and you were the poor victim of manipulation, even though you were the one who seduced me. However, when your parents insisted you do right by me and our child, you resented it and once again blamed me for putting you in that position, justifying the various bad attitudes that followed for years."

She paused to let some of her statements sink in before continuing, "The reason you blamed me is because you are one selfish, spoiled individual who doesn't know what love means. To you love is physical, self-serving, and ultimately expendable when it doesn't serve your purpose. However, God's love is the true test to the heart of Christianity and godly integrity. You called yourself a Christian, but it's simply a title you use to impress others, but you're a sinner walking according to your flesh, idolatrous in your heart, and pagan in your practices."

It was clear to Roberta that Charley didn't appreciate her blunt honesty, but it was as though he was glued to his seat by some unseen force, preventing him from escaping the truth. "Charley, it's clear that nothing has changed between us. If we got back together, we would fall into the same rotten cycle we were in before our divorce. The reason we would fall into the same cycle is because you haven't changed. You haven't realized your part in the breakdown of our marriage.

"Let's face it, you want to get back together because you aren't happy in your present situation, but this present situation is all about you and has nothing to do with whether it would be right for me. And, when you become restless again down the line, and no doubt you will, you'll be vulnerable to pursue the next 'woman' who you think will make you happy, leaving me high and dry to once again pick up the pieces." She set her half empty coffee cup on the table.

Charley went to put up his hand to quiet her but put it down when Roberta continued her exhortation. She had wanted to say these things at different times throughout their married life, but she was ignored, put down, or mocked because she was 'just the wife.' "I will not be quieted any longer by your hand gesture! I'm not a child! I'm a woman, and even though you tried to deny it, at one time I was your wife, but no longer. I had to face up to my sins in our relationship, but I won't take responsibility for your sins. I had to repent for my ways, but I can't make your self-serving ways right before God: that's your responsibility to make peace with God! I won't take blame or responsibility for your misery because of your wretched decisions.

"Charley, I've noticed that when you start becoming frustrated because life isn't bowing down to your way of thinking, or you begin to pay the consequences for your wrong decisions and actions, you become like a small boy who just got caught with his hand in the cookie jar. You begin to feel sorry for yourself, and others like myself get caught up with your 'poor me' syndrome, but I have this final advice for you. Go home, go back to your wife, and grow up by beginning to think about someone else besides yourself. Consider what it means to do right by your wife instead of thinking that she is there strictly to make you happy. Quit looking for an easy way out when the seas become rough for you in your relationships, thereby, giving you the right to abandon ship, while you consider your options as to what you think will satisfy your fleshly, insatiable lusts. But, know none of it will bring lasting happiness to you, because the problems in your life rest with you and your attitude towards God and life and not to those who happen to be around you!"

Charley sat stunned. At that moment great compassion welled up in Roberta. She leaned over and gently touched his arm and looked into his eyes. "Charley, I do care about you, and I want you to be happy. There are so many things that are endearing about you, but you are on a dead end road heading nowhere. Let me ask you have you ever received Jesus into your heart as Lord and Savior?"

The question cut through the confusion allowing Charley to find his tongue. He answered her question in an uncertain tone. "I have asked him to be my Savior. Isn't that enough?"

"Charley, there are many people who have intellectually accepted what Jesus has done for them, but the Bible tells us it must be a revelation of the heart, a revelation that changes and transforms the inner man. Have you allowed the truth of Jesus' salvation to penetrate through your pride to become a reality? You see, its pride that often stands as a wall between people's mind and heart, blinding them to their real spiritual condition and their need to be forgiven for their sins and born anew in God's kingdom."

He looked down forlornly. "Charley look at me." He once again looked at her. "It's over for both of us. We can't ever go back to what we had, and we can't really come into our new lives until we let go of the past. The truth is because the proper value was not put on our marriage in the first place, it's been squandered, exploited, and what

433

could have been has been given away for notions that will never be. All we can do is learn from our past sins and wrong decisions, accept where we are presently, and choose to advance forward in the life that's now before us."

She removed her hand from his arm and slid out of the booth. Charley followed her with wide eyes. "Charley, go home, go back to your wife where you belong. Go back and make sure you are right with God for the sake of your soul, so you also can be right before Him when it comes to your relationship with your wife. You know, He's the only one who can straighten out our messes and make sense out of them.

"Bye Charley." Without waiting for a response, she turned and made her way to the door.

At the beginning of her spiritual odyssey, she had been aware that God had gently taken the key and was beginning to unlock the shackles that had held her to the past. Now, as she began to leave behind everything she had with Charley, the shackles started falling off with each step she took. Refreshing feelings of greater liberty were giving way to a newfound joy.

She never realized how small a place she had been shackled to, and just how limited she had become in her spiritual life due to the many entanglements put on her life by the demands of the world and the standards of others. Her personal failures had confined her to a small world of accusations, despair, and conflicts, while the standards of others became shackles around her ankles, arms, and heart. Her reality had become confusing and morbid as she ate the bitterness brought on by the fruits of her decisions to hold onto things that were besetting her in her Christian walk.

It had been two long years, but the Lord had finally brought her to that large place of discovery: Discovering who He was, realizing who she was in Him, and finally seeing the path He had faithfully put her feet on that was guiding her forward to discover her potential, upward towards the eternal, and homeward to enter into the fullness of His glory.

As she walked out of the doors of the restaurant, she knew she was truly free to discover the greater heights of God as she allowed herself to be brought higher to soar on the current of His Spirit. She was free to find her place in His kingdom, and she was at liberty to be all that He had ordained her to be from the foundation of the world. She had indeed been set free by the One who redeemed her so she could go forth and shine as His reflection in this present world and at this time.

Sunshine quietly broke through vanishing rain clouds that had defined much of the day, drenched trees and shrubbery sparkled and glittered as if draped in countless diamonds, her steps slowed as she breathed deeply of the clean, fresh air, her radiant face drank in the comforting warmth of the sun. Suddenly, the second half of 1 Corinthians 7:14 once again breathed hope and future possibilities into her heart about her children. She smiled to herself and softly whispered, "Carson, I have so much to tell you."

As for this special moment in time, all that was left for her to say about her newly acquired freedom from the past was simple, true, and absolute. "Amen, so be it, for it is now so."

It was meet that we should make merry, and be glad; for this thy brother was dead, and is alive; and was lost, and is found.
(Luke 15:32)

Found

Gloria Jorgensen struggled with her attitude. Down deep she was rejoicing with her stepdaughter, Dena Eagan, but underneath she felt the stinging presence of jealousy smashing against her resolve. She also realized she was weary from the long search, the disillusionments and disappointments due to the dead ends that had plagued her for over three decades.

She knew that Dena had found her son, but as for her son, Thomas, he remained lost to her. Gloria wanted to rejoice for Dena and with her, but the reality of her own situation was enfolding her into a dark pit of despair.

Gloria didn't want to think about the past with its skeletons of unresolved issues and its tormenting ghosts of regrets, guilt, shame, and condemnation. She couldn't count the times that each of those skeletons suddenly appeared from behind a hidden door of regret that would be unlocked by a surfacing memory. Once the door was open she found herself locked in a dark, overlooked room of fear where the ghosts of yesteryear unmercifully haunted her.

As each day paraded in front of her without any resolutions to the past, Gloria knew it was only by the grace of God that she had managed to keep her sanity as she faced her present reality. Although much time had passed between that infamous day when her angry, rebellious, but precious 16-year-old son, Tom walked out the door of her living room and became lost to her, it was still fresh and painful. She wouldn't accept that he was forever lost, but each decade that passed left her older, facing her own mortality. The passing of each day taunted her, the end of every year mocked her, and the signpost of each decade tormented her that she would never see Tom again, haunting her about the events that led up to his angry departure.

She couldn't count the times she woke up crying out in the night for her lost son, or the times when a sigh unexpectedly became the channel by which his name was quietly and sadly spoken. Each time his name was spoken in such a manner, it was always followed by the same tormenting question, "Thomas, where are you, where are you?" From that point tears threatened to once again unravel her and cast her into a deep hole of depression.

Again she found she couldn't keep the memories from unlocking the door of regret and flinging her into a room of fears--unbearable fears that mocked her and spread out before her on the screen of her imagination, all played out in various possible scenarios, which ended with her son being cast from her reach to finally become what seemed forever lost to her.

Gloria had no one to blame but herself for those terrible events. It was true, the seeds of destruction began before Tom was even born, and there were others who were involved in the planting and cultivating of the devastating seeds. It all started out so innocently in the beginning, but it escalated into young zealous love that was abruptly cast down from the cliffs of expectation to be crushed on the rocks of unfulfilled love; leaving the vultures to consume and regurgitate the remains, passing the deposit on to others. What was left was the decaying residue of perversion, anger, and hatred.

Caught in the ruin and decay of the mess was Thomas, sweet in many ways and ignorant of the stigma attached to him but quickly becoming its victim. Oh! If she could only turn back time to change the outcome, she would have, but she couldn't, and the consequences of her actions came at her family like a tsunami, bringing destruction in its wake and leaving the landscape of her life devastated. She could still see the tsunami's wave of perversion corrupting everything it touched, while anger became a powerful current that swept everyone into a hateful state of suspicion, envy, frustration, and bitterness.

As the memories were once again awakened, the door opened that allowed past events to parade on the screen of her memory. She was cute back then, in her high school days, with a petite figure, long blonde hair and clear blue eyes, and the whole thing started with the sweetness of first love. Gloria had gone to the beach with her friends to start a week of celebration that would lead up to her graduation. It was at the beach that she first saw the handsome lifeguard, Kenneth Jorgensen. She had become separated from her high school classmates after going to the restroom. In her search, she had stopped in front of the lifeguard stand and stood looking for them in the crowds of people. Suddenly, she heard his deep voice, "Can I help you with something?"

Gloria looked up to see a smile that made her heart leap, and soft brown eyes that made her legs weak beneath her. Even though he was sitting at a lifeguard stand under an umbrella, she could tell he had a tall muscular frame, along with dark hair to complement his charming smile and dancing eyes.

She struggled to find her voice, and eventually managed to weakly state her dilemma, "I'm just looking for my friends. We're here to celebrate our upcoming high school graduation."

"Well, Miss…"

"It's Gloria Lancaster." Quickly recognizing a small opportunity to talk with him, she made an appropriate inquiry, "and you are?"

"Ken Jorgensen at your service." He nodded his head. "I saw what looked like a party of possibly seniors heading towards the concession stands."

Gloria timidly smiled at the lifeguard. "Thanks for the information. Have a nice day Ken."

Gloria couldn't believe how her short encounter with this stranger made her feel. She felt light-headed, giddy, and silly. She had dated a couple of her classmates since her junior year to participate in dances and proms, but none of them had swept her off her feet like Ken Jorgensen. She quietly voiced her desires, "Ken Jorgensen I hope we meet again," and since she was a romanticist at heart, she added, "and I hope this meeting was not coincidence, but a matter of fate."

Needless to say, she was thrilled when the lifeguard appeared to seek her out once he was off duty. He even asked if he could take her out for something to drink. As some of her girlfriends watched from the sidelines with giddy glee, she accepted his invitation. She quietly reminded herself that looks were not everything and that inner character was the mark of true maturity.

Ken turned out to be very engaging and respectable when it came to his attitude and actions towards Gloria. He also proved to be responsible. His father had abandoned the family when he was eight. Although his mother worked hard to provide for him and his sister, he had decided that as soon as he could get a job, he would help her to support the family. At the time of their meeting he was working at a couple of jobs to not only help his mother and sister, but he had managed to put two years of college under his belt. He had a good head on his shoulders when it came to figuring out what he wanted and what it would take to accomplish it.

Gloria had decided upon their first meeting that Ken was trustworthy, and that if the door opened to pursue any further relationship with him that she would walk through it to see where it led her. Apparently, he came to the same conclusion, because from that day on, they became an item. Even though his two jobs and schooling didn't afford them a much time together, there were special moments that they managed to capture. Such times proved to be gratifying as they learned more about each other's dreams, likes, and dislikes.

Within a month, their relationship was taking on serious tones. It was not until years later that Gloria discovered that what had been awakened and unleashed in both of them were youthful lusts. These lusts, if not put in the proper perspective, can easily escalate into raging passions that can take a couple's emotions on a high flying ride that can prove to be euphoric when together, but tormenting when separated. It takes all thoughts captive as affections are catapulted into the heights of obsession, while the will becomes putty, making the parties involved seem like marionettes, emotionally pulled between good intentions, moral piousness, and a sense that with such feelings it must be "love." Of course, love is touted as making everything right and ensuring nothing can possibly go wrong.

The sense of infallibility that comes with such fleshly passions can play havoc on tender, open hearts and immature feelings. It can confuse integrity, pervert moral discretion, and cause a person to become caught up and lost in a seductive reality.

Like other young couples, Gloria and Ken were not immune from being caught up with this overwhelming reality. They talked about their feelings and attractions, and realized that it was up to them to discipline their passions by ensuring a right environment that wouldn't allow them to explore the depths of their lust. They knew that they had to keep their lust at bay by refraining from certain activities to ensure the integrity of their relationship at all costs.

The fact that Ken wanted their relationship to be honorable caused Gloria to appreciate him even more. She inwardly struggled with the concept of real love. Her mother had been honest with her about the subject.

Since Gloria's mother, Arlene, was not a romanticist, she dealt in the reality of things. She told Gloria that when the euphoric dust settles in on "new, young love," the passions subside, and the feelings of infallibility give way to the reality of drudgery, then one can know if what he or she is experiencing is real love. It was from this perspective that Gloria had concluded that real, lasting love was more than feelings that were fickle and self-serving. Real love did not ride on some emotional wave, swing from high branches of enraptured expectation and infallibility, and flow in currents of romance and fantasy.

Real love lands on that which is solid such as real character, and grows as its roots of commitment reach down into the very being of a person. As a result, such love would stand when the realities of life's unexpected twists and turns of challenges and changes come, when testing occurs, storms of adversities rage, and the buffeting hindering currents threaten to sweep everything out into the ocean of annihilation.

Gloria wrestled with whether she and Ken possessed real love. She knew that she felt she was in a current, but when it finally brought her to the place of reality, would she find the evidence of real, lasting love. She didn't want to settle for unstable emotions or be swept away by temporary fanciful notions that would turn into disillusionment when reality set in. She wanted the love that would last no matter what came at it, a love that could be forged in the fires and come out a masterpiece.

She had no idea how soon their level of love would be tested. One night Ken came to dinner with Gloria and her parents. Her father, Thomas Lancaster, was impressed with Ken but also had some trepidation towards him. These concerns surrounded his future. As the conversation graduated from non-essential subjects such as weather, her father looked at Ken and asked what his intentions were concerning his daughter. Ken admitted that he loved her, and that his intention towards her was to do right by her in every way. That is when her father asked about his future plans.

Ken looked at Gloria and then at her father. "Well, I was going to talk to Gloria about that very subject tonight after dinner, but since you are her father, you have every right to know as well. I have been looking at what all my options are as far as college, but most seem out of my reach except for the military. In that environment, I wouldn't only have an opportunity to work at a steady job, but I can finish up college and get my bachelor's degree in engineering, while working on one for business. One of our state senators approached me about recommending me to the Naval Academy. I accepted his offer and just today received word that they have accepted me."

Gloria's heart stood still as she temporarily forgot to exhale. She could feel her face draining of all color and knew that everything was about to change, leaving her in a daze. As her father asked questions, the gravity of the matter began to set in. The military would require a commitment of anywhere from six to eight years of his life. There would be cadet school, college, and service. In the Navy, he would be out to sea from six to nine months and even more if international events dictated it.

It was her father who asked the obvious, "Ken, you told me that you want to do right by my daughter, but where will she fit into all of your plans?"

Ken looked at Gloria. "We'll have to discuss that." And, then he looked at her father again. "All I can tell you is that I don't want my life to be without her, but before I can fairly offer her something, I must make something of my life. No one ever said it would be easy."

As Ken asked to be excused, he reached for Gloria's hand. "If you don't mind, we need to talk."

Gloria's daze was turning into inner turmoil. She didn't know how to feel; therefore, she didn't know how to respond to Ken. She was not naïve enough to think that their love would endure no matter what, and she realistically knew that she selfishly wanted to talk him out of it. On the other hand, how could she properly honor him if she asked him to forsake his dreams in order to cater to her insecurities? She struggled to be strong and put on a brave front, but she felt like an emotional coward that was ready to collapse from within.

Ken led her out to the front porch. He stood still for a few moments looking up at the stars. Without looking at her he spoke, "I know this is a surprise, but what are your thoughts about it, Gloria?" He turned and looked at her.

She wanted to scream, but she heard herself say, "Ken, you have been waiting for this open door, and there's no way you should let this opportunity slip through your fingers."

"What about us?" he quietly asked.

Gloria wanted to scream, "WHAT ABOUT US? There will probably be NO us when this is over with!" But instead she heard herself softly respond, "I'm sure we can work out something. After all, there are phones and the mail. And, besides you know what they all say, absence makes the heart grow fonder." As the hollow sounding platitude came out her mouth, she had to bite her lip to keep from crying against the bitterness that was springing up in her very soul against the veneer of hypocrisy that veiled her real feelings.

As Ken looked into her eyes and took her shoulders, he said, "Know I love you and whether we are together or not, I feel I'll always love you." He lean over and gently kissed her before leaving her alone with the sweetness of his kiss and the bitterness that was ripping at her resolve. She turned and ran up to her room where she cried herself to sleep.

As Gloria once again remembered that night so long ago, she shuddered at the realization that Ken's path would take him far away from her, setting up events that put her feet on a path of sorrow and regret. Their paths would cross again, but it would leave destructive fruits in its wake.

At first his letters were constant and the calls intermittent according to the regulations of the academy. It was clear that Ken's days and activities were regimented. He hardly had time for any personal life. If he was not cramming for tests after classroom instruction, he was marching. If he was not marching he was preparing for inspections.

Meanwhile, Gloria busied herself by finding a job at a local grocery store as a cashier. She enjoyed interacting with the customers and was even acknowledged as rookie of the week by store management. She also considered her options. What did she want to become, a nurse, teacher, secretary, or maybe the most honorable vocation and calling of all, a wife and mother.

If she chose the latter, she realized that she didn't want to be totally dependent on a husband like her mother was dependent on her father. If something happened to her father, her mother would have to scramble to play catch-up. She wanted to be able to provide for herself. She realized that she liked secretarial work and office management. She decided to go to a good vocational school in her community that offered courses on what she was interested in. She signed up for the courses, while making arrangements to adjust her work schedule around her schooling.

On the third month that Ken was away, Gloria's world was shaken. Upon entering the house after working all day, she was greeted by a letter from Ken. She was living for such letters from him. She would always take them to her room with something to drink and sit in her comfortable chair, where she could read and reread them, savoring every detail of the activities of his life and the personal messages of love. They always uplifted her day. However, the letter proved to be devastating. In it Ken admitted his life was being consumed by the demands of the academy and he felt that he could not properly invest in his relationship with her and maintain the stringent schedule of the academy at the same time. He was concerned about his grades, but also feeling guilty about his inability to keep up any real significant correspondence with her; therefore, he felt it was only right to let her go so she could get on with her life.

Gloria was stunned. Hurt and anger began to seep through her shocked state. "My Ken, aren't we being noble!" She threw his letter across the room and paced back and forth, not knowing whether to cry, scream, or hit the wall. She curled up her hands into fists and hit her pillow a couple of times in passionate frustration. Tears began to flow as hurt gripped her heart, disappointment blanketed her soul, and anger took center stage as all other emotions were pushed into the background.

It wouldn't be until a few years later that she learned the real reason behind the letter. Unbeknown to her, her father had written to Ken, voicing his concerns that his relationship with his daughter was putting great limitations on Gloria, preventing her from pursuing her own life. He had advised Ken to let her go so she could find out what she really wanted from life. Since Ken was overwhelmed with a stringent schedule, he could see her father's reasoning. As he considered the reason for holding on to their relationship, it was purely selfishness on his part, while there would be few if any benefits in it for Gloria. After a couple of weeks of wrestling over it, he decided it might be wise for him to nobly let her go. With much heartbreak and despair, he wrote the letter.

Gloria had no idea if their love was strong enough to endure the lean years, but her father deprived her of facing the test, setting up events that proved to be shattering. She could see why her father did it. She was barely out of high school and didn't have time to discover her own dreams, but it was her life to do with it as she saw fit. If he had not interfered things might have been different, but the reality was, the present was what it was. Regrets couldn't change the past, and the taunting "what ifs" were based on nothing more than fanciful notions.

Ken's noble gesture was translated as unrequited love to Gloria. Her hurt turned into rebellion and the anger turned bitter in her soul while coldness settled on her heart. It was as if this whole other person took hold of her, a person who became self-serving. She was going to find her life all right and show Ken she could live without him.

One day as she was stocking shelves at the store, a man came up to her and asked her where to find a certain product. The man was slightly taller than her, with a stocky build and he had a barely discernable German ascent. She smiled at him and told him the aisle where the product could be located.

Apparently the man took some type of fancy to Gloria because every time he came to the store he sought her out in some way. Through periodically friendly conversations, she found out his name was Bernard Heinrich, and that he had come from Germany. A family member had sponsored him and together they had started a popular fish market that Gloria's mother patronized.

Eventually, Bernard got the nerve up to ask her out on a date. She wrestled with it because she wasn't sure whether she really liked him or not. She sensed something in him that was disconcerting, but she couldn't really put a finger on the problem. To avoid being judgmental and suspicious she pushed aside her concerns, and as she remembered her hurt over Ken, she became numb to the red flags, figuring that Bernard was as good as any other guy to begin to spread out her wings and explore her possibilities.

Bernard seemed nice enough. He could prove to be even a real gentleman. He began to smother her with flowers, candy, and gifts. When he met her parents, he impressed her father with his business accomplishments. Her father even mentioned that he was confident that he could financially take care of Gloria.

Even though Bernard was ten years her senior, her father had counted that as a big asset in his favor, and began to nudge his daughter towards a serious, lasting relationship with him. Granted, Gloria was impressed with all of his attention, but at the same time, she still felt uneasy. She tried to figure out what had sent some red flags initially across her bow, but any viable conclusion eluded her.

As she moved closer to a lasting relationship with Bernard, she concluded that she liked him enough, and that he appeared to have the means to not only provide for her but to be a good husband. In her mind she figured that she would be able to deal with whatever flaw he had that had initially caused her concern. After all, she could tell Bernard was quite smitten with her, and that would give her power to influence him her way. This brought her to the conclusion that if he popped the question, she would be ready with an answer.

Six months after they started dating, he did ask her to marry him. She accepted. Needless to say her father was pleased and ready to ensure that they had a great wedding, but Gloria's mother remained quiet.

When Gloria approached her mother, she asked her if she was happy for her. With a bit of hesitation, her mother spoke, "If it makes you happy, it will make me happy, but you need to make sure it's right for you and not something you are accepting because you're on the rebound."

Gloria knew her mother was talking about what happened with Ken. "Mom, you know it's over between Ken and me. He set me free so that I can continue on with my life, which I'm doing right now."

"Gloria, do you honestly love Bernard?"

"What is love, anyway Mom?" Gloria shot back at her! "In so-called 'love' I gave my heart to someone and he smashed it. I don't plan to let that happen again."

"And just what type of marriage do you think you will have with Bernard if you cannot offer your love and heart to him? Will he quietly settle for whatever small crumbs you decide to cast at him?"

By this time Gloria was being unnerved, but she couldn't back down. It was true, she couldn't explain why she was tenaciously holding the line to something that her heart wasn't in, but nevertheless she clung tightly to it. "This is something he wants Mom! He's a big boy and should know what he is getting as far as I am concerned."

"Have you told Bernard about Ken?"

Gloria refrained from outright shouting. "Mom, I told you it is over between Ken and me! So why would I have to tell Bernard about him?"

"Because Gloria, he has a right to know that he has competition. It doesn't matter whether Ken is a matter of the past. The truth is he's still a ghost that is haunting you because the whole situation hasn't been resolved in your mind. As long as it is open-ended, and the door remains open because of anger, bitterness, and hurt, it wouldn't be right to keep it from Bernard." She paused before giving her this ominous warning, "And, Gloria if you're not honest with yourself and him about this matter, it could come back to haunt you in ways you can't begin to imagine."

Gloria knew her mother was correct. "Alright, I'll tell Bernard about Ken, and you'll see that it won't matter!" she said in a fit of frustration. "He's bent on marrying me!"

In a firm voice, Gloria's mother responded, "That's fine, Gloria, but remember you'll make up half of this relationship. Just because it won't matter to him, doesn't mean it'll be right for you. In the end you could be caught up in a powerful whirlpool of regrets."

Gloria informed Bernard about Ken, and she was correct that it didn't matter to him. He simply made reference to the fact that it was over; therefore, there was nothing holding them back from marrying. However, he also made a surprising move. He wanted to forego the activities of a wedding and elope that very night.

As long as their marriage was in the future, Gloria could fantasize about their life together. Realistically she knew there would be problems, but in the scenario she had scripted and directed in her mind, they would surely work them out together and develop a strong relationship in the end.

When faced with eloping with him that very night, she was bombarded by confusion and trepidation. She struggled with the feelings that seemed to be challenging her resolve. She asked herself if a wedding was important to her, and the surprising answer was "no." It seemed almost strange to her that she didn't care if there was a public wedding. Since she decided she was going to marry him anyway, she cast all caution to the wind and agreed.

They were married that night to the dismay of her parents and friends. On the first night of the honeymoon, she felt the first twinge of regret as she questioned whether she had done the right thing. Sadly, their relationship immediately descended downward to eventually be buried by mountains of regrets.

Gloria quickly learned what had caused concern in her about Bernard. Behind his attentive veneer was a coldness that couldn't be reached or thawed. She discovered that he would substitute placating for kindness and cold calculation for reasoning. He would be condescending to her when he thought her conclusions were stupid. He played mind games to twist her into a pretzel when she was not willing to go along with what she considered in her mind to be conniving ways. It was true that he was a business man, but he was shrewd and didn't care who he used or walked over to get what he wanted.

After three months of watching him in action, Gloria was ready to leave him and seek annulment if possible and a divorce if necessary, but she discovered she was pregnant. Once again, she was being swallowed by the gravity of her decision to marry someone who she didn't really know; nor did he hold her heart.

She decided to see if a child would change the dynamics of their relationship. Bernard was excited about the news and began to once again shower attention on her. He seemed kind and gracious as he excitedly walked through the pregnancy with her. When a boy was born to them, he was elated. He wanted to call him "Warren Arnold" after his deceased father.

"Warren Arnold" it was but since Gloria wasn't too crazy about his first name, she affectionately called him Arnie for short. In the beginning it seemed Bernard relished his baby son, but he soon began to veer back into his old ways of being a cold fish in his dealings with her.

When Arnie was nine months old, their marriage hit another crisis point. She had finished her vocational training, and was looking forward to settling in as a full time mother. Bernard came home and informed her that he had sold his part of the business to his cousin and had bought a small fish market in a community located a couple hundred miles from where they presently lived. It was located right by the ocean where he could acquire fresh fish, and it provided ample opportunities for a new business to quickly grow and become successful. There was not only a market in the front of the building, but living quarters that could be enlarged and remodeled as the family grew. He also informed her that she would take care of managing the affairs of the business.

When she objected and reminded him that she wanted to be a full time mother, he informed her that since he was the man and she was the woman, his say was final. She had learned there was no arguing with him once his mind was made up. She quietly, but angrily conceded the whole matter.

It was clear that Bernard didn't feel he had to ask her advice about anything that would affect her or their son's future, nor was she supposed to have any independent opinion. It was then that she wondered why woman was given a mind to think with, the ability to form an opinion, and the audacity to have a will that might prove contrary to her husband's.

Gloria sought out Anson, Bernard's cousin to find out what happened. Anson was cut from a different cloth. He was opposite in every way from Bernard. He was truly caring and kind. Customers respected Bernard because he knew his business and how to please them, but they also sensed something about him that was a bit unnerving. As for Anson, he was friendly and was liked and often sought out by his patrons.

When Gloria approached Anson about the matter of Bernard selling his half of the business to him, he told her that Bernard's plan had always been to have his own business. He admitted that Bernard was difficult to deal with at times, but lately seemed to have become more and more contrary when it came to making business decisions together. Anson shared that Bernard's business sense had profited the business greatly, and it was not his wish for their partnership to cease, but that the environment was becoming toxic between them, threatening the welfare of the business. Anson finally agreed to buy Bernard out so he could start another business elsewhere.

When Thomas and Arlene Lancaster were told of the change of location, neither of them were pleased. They both loved their grandson, Arnie and enjoyed the times they watched him when both parents were busy at the same time with work or school.

When Gloria finally saw the business, she saw a rundown building and wondered about the business opportunities. Even though the community the business was located in was not that big, Bernard felt confident that he could build up a reputation through promotion and customer service that would draw others from outside the area to the business.

The next year proved to be a tremendous hardship for the Heinrich's. The new business struggled and Bernard became more driven to make it work. Gloria juggled many hats as she strived to take care of the office end of the business and home demands on a limited income. Since it was their business, she could take care of Arnie while doing the bookkeeping, taking orders, and waiting on customers when Bernard was off promoting the business.

No matter what Bernard tried, their business stayed in the red for the first year, causing him to become more frustrated and angry. One night he didn't come home until around two in the morning. Gloria heard him stumble into their bedroom, and collapse on the bed. When she turned over to say something to him, she not only heard him snoring, but smelled alcohol on his breath.

Gloria never knew Bernard to drink, but from that night on, he occasionally came home with alcohol on his breath, but it quickly escalated into a regular exercise. One night Gloria had had enough of his late nights of coming home intoxicated. She waited up for him and when he stumbled in he was still coherent enough to be confronted.

At the time Gloria was seething when she questioned Bernard about his drinking habits and the fact that he was using money that needed to be used for home needs or put back into the business to keep it afloat. Bernard flew into a rage and came at her with such a viciousness that she knew the outcome wasn't going to fair well for her.

He grabbed her shoulders and shook her, all the while yelling at her in German, but asking her in English just who did she think she was to question him. She was nothing more than a two-timing harlot who needed to be put in her place. After yelling at her and falsely accusing her, he raised his right hand and slapped her hard, knocking her back against the wall. He walked into their bedroom, grabbed the blanket on the end of the bed, threw it at her and then slammed the bedroom door.

Confused, Gloria gingerly got up from the floor while grabbing the blanket. She felt anger and fear at the same time. Bernard had not raised a hand towards her until that night. Perhaps it was the alcohol, or maybe it was who he really was behind his veneer and alcohol gave him the excuse. She went to the bathroom so she could examine the welt on her face and collect her thoughts.

The side of her face where he slapped her was red and beginning to swell. Bernard Heinrich may not consider her thoughts, feelings, and opinions as being nothing more than pure silliness, but she refused to be his or anyone's else's personal punching bag. She knew that she was not going to become a statistic, lost in an unpredictable world of violence. At that moment she knew she needed to get out of there. She grabbed a sleeping Arnie and packed some of his articles in a bag, collected her coat and purse and took off in the car towards the only place she knew was safe: home.

***

Gloria shook her head as she remembered how horrified her parents were at want happened to their youngest daughter. Her father took a picture of her face and told her she had to file a police report with the local sheriff as soon as possible to establish a record, and then after everyone calmed down, they would decide whether or not to take further actions.

The next day, a humbled Bernard was standing on the front steps of her parents' home. It was Gloria's father who opened the door to him. No doubt, Bernard could tell by the look on Thomas Lancaster's face that he was in trouble. It was clear that Gloria's father was not going to allow anyone to threat his daughter in such a manner.

Bernard asked to talk to Gloria. However, as Gloria later discovered, her father had some choice things to say to Bernard before a meeting could take place. The outcome of the meeting would determine if Bernard would be allowed to see Gloria again, let alone speak to her. Gloria had no idea what the two men talked about but she suspected, as she caught a glance from the upstairs window of Bernard walking to his pickup, that her father had laid down the law. She later learned that her father threatened him with every legal means and possibly some personal repercussions if he ever physically touched her again or his grandson.

Her father guaranteed Gloria that Bernard would never get away with physical abuse again as long he was alive. He also told her that she needed to think about talking to him and possibly giving him a second chance because of their marriage vow and Arnie.

Gloria did talk to Bernard and he promised he would never touch her again in such a way, and stipulated that he would only have a social drink occasionally when talking business. Their conversation only confused Gloria more. She had come to realize that she didn't like the man Bernard. He never really showed any love or honor towards her unless he wanted something, while the rest of the time he treated her as a non-essential object that was there to serve his needs. And, when she was in the way of what he wanted to do, he either ran over her with verbal putdowns or beat her down with condescending attitudes and cruel silences until there were no objections coming from her. She wondered why she ever married him, but underneath she knew why.

She had no one to blame but herself for the predicament she found herself in. In her attempt to run away from the deep hurt and anger she felt towards the situation with Ken, she jumped into the lion's den in spite of the red flags and warnings. Obviously, it would be her deserved lot in life to try to see how long it would be before she totally succumbed to the lion's attacks. She knew in time the lion would completely devour the life in her soul, the fire in her strength, the sharpness of her intelligence, and the passions of her emotions. She wondered how long it would be before she would be counted among the walking dead, those who have ceased to interact and simply react as programed, resigned to be weak and void of strength, personal opinions, and emotions.

Gloria sighed. It was her punishment and her destiny to see it through to the end with Bernard. It was her decision to walk down this road, while she rightfully began to taste the full gravity of it. "If only" Ken had fought for their relationship, stood firm for their love, and not let her go, things would be different, but it didn't happen that way. Her life with Bernard was her reality and now she had to be noble, while silently enduring her hard lot in life, and just maybe one day she would turn a corner and things would somehow be different. She shook her head at her optimism. It was wishful thinking, but it was a small thread of hope that she could hold onto.

Gloria knew what she had to do for the sake of Arnie, but she resented it. She walked out to the patio where her parents were watching Arnie playing in the sandbox her father had made for him. She sat down beside them. Her mother was the one who spoke.

"Your father and I think it would be good for you to take some time out from this mess. We can watch Arnie while you could stay at our cabin for a couple of days and get your bearings. Perhaps you'll be feeling better about what you need to do."

Gloria had almost forgotten that her parents owned a cabin at a popular lake. It was a couple of hours drive from their home and sounded inviting to her. "Perhaps you're right," she responded.

Her father piped in, "You could go upstairs and pack and leave today, just in time for the weekend."

Gloria's mother smiled. "And I will help you pack if you want me to."

Gloria nodded her head and they both went upstairs and busied themselves with packing. Before she knew it she was in the car

451

heading towards one of her favorite places. She remembered when she was young, her older sister and friends always talked about going to the ocean, while she talked about going to the lake, the opposite direction from the ocean.

When she arrived at the cabin, it seemed like a perfect refuge for her frayed nerves. Even though she had already made a decision to go back to Bernard, the time at the lake would give her some more time and space away from him. She knew she probably would end up wanting to stay and hide there, but she also knew life and its responsibilities always have a way of finding a person.

She settled in the first night and had a restful sleep. The next day, she sized up what food she needed for the next couple days. She went to a local market to get the necessary items. As she was reading a label on the back of a package, she heard someone whose deep voice sounded startled, calling her name from behind her. Her heart jumped, and before she turned around to answer, she knew who she would be coming face to face with, Ken.

Instead of feeling anger when she looked into his face, she felt weak kneed and vulnerable. Confusion overtook her because she had always imagined herself spurning him, spitting in his face, or turning her back on him altogether in total disgust, but she had no power within her to carry out any of her notions.

In the strongest voice she could muster, she heard herself say, "Ken, what are you doing here?"

His smile melted her. "I'm here to get perspective, what about you?"

She let out a nervous giggle. "I'm staying at my parents' cabin to try to get perspective."

He let out a laugh. "Since we are on the same mission, maybe we can help each other to get perspective." Suddenly, his face turned serious, "I've wanted to talk to you about what happened, but figured our paths would never cross again, and even if they did I felt I had no right to approach you."

This was Gloria's opportunity to play the spurned lover, the hurt soul, the viper ready to strike back, but curiosity took center stage. She wanted to know, to understand how he could let go of their love. She wanted to bring some type of resolution to her own soul so she could let go of the hurt and the feelings of betrayal and go on with her life. It was then that she realized that she was not even close to being over him.

He smiled, "Perhaps you would have dinner with me."

She reasoned that it was her opportunity to find out what happened. "Sure," she quickly replied.

They agreed to meet in a restaurant that had a nice outdoor patio where people could enjoy the sunshine, the lake, and the sunset. It seemed as if the afternoon drug on for an eternity before it was time for her to get ready. She arrived early, but Ken was already waiting for her. She was nervous and wondered if he was anxious about their meeting. Even though there was "water under the bridge" from the past, she still knew that she loved him. Underneath she wished she didn't because such love could do nothing more than complicate everything, but at the same time she secretly relished it.

Their talk started out casually until dinner was almost completed. It was Gloria who finally broached the issue. "Ken," she looked into his eyes, "Why did you walk away from our relationship? I really don't understand."

She could tell he was grasping for the right words. "I did my best to explain to you why it was better for us to go our separate ways."

"Don't use nobility to justify something that was devastating to me," she said with a steely coldness to her voice.

He looked into her eyes, "It was devastating to me as well."

The hurt look in his eyes confirmed his statement, defusing the anger that was building up in her. "Then, why did you drop our relationship like a hot potato?"

"Well, your father…"

"My father, what does he have to do with this?" she said tersely.

He put his hand up to quiet her. "He wrote me a letter explaining that he was concerned that our relationship would keep you from seeking out your own life and happiness. At the time I was buried in the academy demands, facing possible failure, and I didn't feel I had anything to invest in our relationship then. I have to admit, it was the lowest point in my life and I didn't have the wherewithal or the strength to disagree with him. So, I gave in, but down the line, I regretted it terribly, especially after I crawled out of my pit, but it was too late." He looked down at the table. "I heard that you were married."

Gloria felt the whole gamut of her emotions, shocked, anger at her father, and stupid for her decision to get involved with Bernard. However, one thing erupted from her lips. "How could he do this to me, my own father?"

Ken looked up at her, "Gloria, don't blame your father, he had your best interests in mind."

She looked at him. "Sure he did. I also guess he had my best interests in mind when he encouraged my relationship with Bernard."

The anger she had been ignoring was beginning to boil up and over like a geyser.

"Don't Gloria."

"Don't what Ken?" Gloria asked sharply.

"Don't transfer your hurt and anger to your father. It won't solve anything. It is what it is. You're married and I hear you have a son." He paused, "And, I'm now married and have a son, a stepson that is, and I just found out my wife is pregnant."

Gloria felt color drain from her face. She had only one question. "Are you happy?"

He looked at her, calculating his next statement, "For your sake and my sake, I probably should tell you I'm the most happiest of all men, and walk away right now. But, I have no desire to lie to you. I'm here trying to accept the fact that I'm stuck in a loveless marriage, but for the sake of Brandon, my stepson, and my unborn child I'll stay in it and make the best of it." He paused, "Are you happy, Gloria?"

Gloria was still trying to wrap her mind around the terrible joke that was now coming to fruition. They were both stuck in loveless relationships, but she was not content with speculation, she wanted to know how Ken ended up in a loveless relationship. "Was there no love between you when you married your wife?"

He let out a sarcastic laugh. "Gloria you know that my heart belongs to you." He looked at the glass of water in his hand as if trying to find an answer. "I married her mainly for Brandon. Her father is one of the officers at the academy. One night he invited some of us over to his home, where we would be recognized as being exceptional cadets in his class. That is when I met my wife, Ada and her son Brandon. Even though he was only three, Brandon and I took to each other like ducks do to water. It was from that premise that I was invited to his birthday party and somehow I found myself being pulled into what seemed like web.

"I felt sucked into Ada's reality. I knew she was spoiled, but Brandon was a gentle little boy, and I felt sorry for him because I could see how he was being ignored and left behind by his mother and used only when it served her purposes. I guess I felt like I needed to go in and save the day by marrying her, but instead I found myself entangled in a sinister game.

"Now she's pregnant, and I can't leave Brandon or a child of mine at her mercy. I think she would make that child pay for my actions. I couldn't live with myself if that happened."

Gloria felt sick and hopeless. She also knew her heart belonged to Ken. Ken's voice interrupted her thoughts as he repeated his question. "Are you happy?"

She looked at him with sorrowful eyes. "Like you, I could be noble and lie for the sake of everyone, but I'm sure you can tell by my body language and possibly the expression on my face that I'm not happy in my marriage." Then Gloria told Ken about Bernard, Arnie and the latest events. As she was sharing her story, she could tell that Ken was visibly upset and angry.

When she finished, Ken asked her the obvious, "Why did you marry him in the first place?"

Suddenly Gloria felt shame for what she had done, "I didn't marry him for noble purposes like you did Ada. I married him because I was angry with you. I convinced myself that since I couldn't have the man I loved, I would rebelliously settle for the first guy who showed any interest in me because I didn't really care. After all, if you can't have the best then you must be willing to settle for less, a lot less."

Both Ken and Gloria sat in silence after her explanation. Gloria was thinking about the web people weave for their lives. She had allowed wrong feelings to influence her decisions. Instead of ignoring her feelings and seeking first to find out who she was and what she really wanted out of life, she let an immature frame of mind determine the path she was now walking.

Ken was studying her face as if reading her thoughts. He said softly, "Would you like to take a walk?"

The sunset was beginning to paint the sky with beautiful colors that were being reflected by the water. However, it was obvious to any onlooker that Ken and Gloria didn't notice the beauty around them. They were lost in a world of emotional conflict. They were bound to the choices they had made. Although their paths had crossed, they both knew they would have to part and go their separate ways.

Gloria wanted that day, that hour, that minute, and that moment to stand still. She never wanted to move with time so their paths could be forever knitted together by some unseen providence. She wanted to grab him and never let him go, but she knew that the script was already written for both of them. They were riding on different waves and time would be the current that would usher them on their particular courses. She wanted to obtain some token to commemorate their time together, to remind her of a love that may be far away, but would always be as close as a heartbeat.

She stopped and let him take a couple of steps in front of her before he noticed that she wasn't beside him. He turned to look at her. "I don't want this to end right now, Ken."

He then opened his arms towards her and she flew into them as their hungry lips met in a torrent passion. It seemed as if there was no one else in the whole world that existed except the two lovers, once lost to each other, but now finding each other again.

Ken fought to compose himself, trying to take control of the current that was quickly carrying them towards tumultuous waters. "Gloria, we must stop now and go our separate ways."

Gloria was consumed by one reality and firmly stated it. "Ken, I won't be denied what was to be ours in the first place."

"We will live to regret this. We have no idea the type of shock waves it could later produce in our lives."

Gloria would have none of his reasoning and warnings. "Ken I'll never regret it. We were meant to be together and I won't be denied it any longer."

That night Gloria secured her token. Before rising the next morning she relived each moment and secured it in the secret place of her memory and her heart where she planned to visit it when times were hard. She also would never forget that morning.

They showered, dressed and agreed to meet for breakfast. She felt like a new bride, but Ken didn't look like a happy bridegroom.

"Is there something wrong Ken? Gloria inquired as he absent mindedly messed with his food.

"We were wrong Gloria," Ken replied.

Gloria felt hurt rising up. "What do you mean Ken? Wasn't last night special to you?"

He looked at her with soft eyes. "Yes it was Gloria, but it still was wrong. Regardless of what our mates are like, according to a vow we made to each of them, we belong to them. We had no right to give ourselves to each other."

"It's not fair." Gloria whined. "You have to admit we were cheated out of what was rightfully ours!"

"Life is not fair Gloria. And, just because it's unfair doesn't justify us in doing wrong. Besides, it was not rightfully ours to take. We gave our right to each other away when we chose the paths that we are now walking. We have no one to blame but ourselves."

Gloria was becoming more agitated, "Ken, why are you so old fashioned about this? As the woman, I should be the one to show guilt, not you. I don't feel guilty in the least, nor do I regret what happened last night. Besides, who is going to know?"

"I'll know, Gloria, every time I look in the mirror," Ken responded sadly. "And, when I have intimacy with my wife, I will be tormented not only by what I did, but that it will never mean what it should mean because now I have a forbidden night that I will always compare it to." He looked into her eyes, "And, I feel one day you're going to regret this, and I'll know that I caused the pain that will follow it, and for that I now ask your forgiveness."

Ken's statements were unnerving her. "Aren't you being dramatic Ken? Why does it bother you so? After all, how can something that feels and seems so right, be so wrong?"

"I'm not being dramatic, Ken stated. It doesn't matter if something feels right, if it's morally wrong, it still remains wrong regardless of the temporary pleasure it may bring someone. I should've been strong for both of us and fled the situation, but instead I became party to it."

Gloria was not ready to concede that their night together was wrong, "Come on Ken, it's the woman who is supposed to be morally strong, not the man. Haven't you discovered that society gives man a pass from being morally responsible? It all falls on the woman's shoulders. If it's wrong let the blame rest with me."

Almost in disbelief, Ken responded, "I'm responsible for my own actions and conduct. Perhaps, you don't understand the gravity of our actions, but I do. My mother is a deeply religious woman who taught me that morality is what maintains the purity of conscience, relationships, and societies. It ensures the character of the soul, the strength of relationships, and serves as the sustaining pillar of society. Without it the soul succumbs to complete depravity, relationships fall into ruin, and societies decay from within.

"Although I never got caught up with my mother's religious practices, I knew she was right. Without moral character there is nothing but confusion, chaos, and ruin. I knew if I didn't maintain moral integrity that my actions would betray my conscience and give cause for my worldview to unmercifully judge me. In the end, I would struggle with regret, shame, guilt, and condemnation." He paused, "I know because I'm struggling with regret right now. I defiled something that was precious to me, our relationship. I'm ashamed of what I did with you, guilty at what I did to my wife, and condemned because I know there is a just, holy God that I must answer to in the end.

"It's true, I may not know God like my mother, but her life has proved time and time again to me that He exists."

Ken stood up, "I have to go Gloria. Remember, I do and will always love you, and I hope when the regret and hurt comes, you'll find it in your heart to forgive me for failing you when you once again

457

needed me to be strong and honorable." He leaned over and kissed her on the cheek and gave her a slight smile. "Goodbye."

Gloria thought of another time she had watched Ken walk away. She silently whispered, "Goodbye." She had been so sure the night before that she needed a token of their love, but Ken's warning about regretting it was causing her to rethink her action. She thought about the thread that had just been inserted into the weaving pattern of her life, and realized that if it did go somewhere that it would somehow mar her already entangled life. In fact, she had this ominous feeling that it was already taking on some type of life.

***

Gloria's eyes were tightly shut as she remembered that night so long ago. She wished time had stood still and never advanced beyond that night. Ken's warning did come to fruition. In the end, an innocent life was sacrificed, ever causing regret, hurt, and sorrow to enfold her like a heavy wet blanket, leaving her shivering and cold inside.

Their action did take on life, and that life was given the name of Thomas Eugene. She knew when she was pregnant that it was Ken's child but it would be her secret alone to keep. There would be no rejoicing with Ken, and when Bernard found out she was pregnant, he claimed that they didn't have the finances to feed another mouth. Therefore, the entrance of Thomas into the world was considered to be a burden to him.

Since Bernard wasn't happy being straddled with another child, he didn't care when Gloria informed him that she wanted to name the next child. When Thomas was born, Gloria had already decided to give him the first name of her father and the middle name of Eugene.

In Gloria's mind, Tom was perfect in every way. She felt a special connection to him that she had to hide. Later another son was added to their family, Ronald (Ronny) Everett Heinrich.

It was clear that Bernard displayed different attitudes towards each son. Arnie was his favorite son. He was always supportive and encouraged him to excellence. Since Tom was considered the burden from the beginning, Bernard tolerated him at best and ignored him the rest of the time. When it came to Ronny, he was a plaything, someone Bernard would tease and entertain himself with. It was clear that Tom was on the outside looking in when it came to Bernard and Arnie, and as Ronny grew, the third son became frustrated that his father never took him seriously and saw him as some clown or circus entertainer who could be laughed at when he did something wrong.

As a child, Tom was sweet, loving, and affectionate, but somewhere along the line he began to withdraw and display anger. By the time he was eight years old, he didn't want to be touched by anyone, which was disconcerting to Gloria, but she figured it might just be a phase he was going through. Gloria always took comfort that she could reach his soft spots when they were alone, but she had to note that he took on a tough pose when Bernard was around. His attitudes sent up red flags, and she occasionally questioned Tom about what was going on, but he would shrug his shoulders and walk away.

Bernard hadn't displayed any outward physical aggression towards her or the boys since that day when he was threatened by her father, but he could prove to be mentally and verbally abusive. He didn't drink as much, but she was aware that he still favored the bottle, and at times wouldn't even come home after being out on the town.

Gloria knew that something was not right and that underneath the surface there was the makings of a big shift that would cause a devastating earthquake, shaking everything. Ken's warning was peeking around the various corners of her mind at different times. As the dynamics of her relationship with Bernard begin to produce unpleasant fruits in every aspect of their lives together, the secret place she had created after her night with Ken, ceased to become a place of refuge, but instead it became a place of torment, overgrown by weeds of despair and entangling bramble bushes of hopelessness. When she thought about it, it would hauntingly remind her that she had to endure her lot, while being denied of ever being with her true love.

Each time she looked in the mirror she felt greater regret and sensed shame was always knocking on some faraway door. The regret came slowly at first. It involved Tom. She cherished what Tom represented to her, but as she watched Tom become a victim to something she didn't understand, uncertainty and regret took center stage. People always think their actions hurt no one but themselves, but Gloria began to see the far reaching tentacles of consequences. Sadly, it was Tom and Ronny who were somehow being victimized by Bernard in different ways.

The only good thing that seemed to come out of it was the close relationship that Tom had with Ronny. Tom protected, encouraged, and even instructed Ronny where he could, and Ronny idolized his big brother. He followed Tom everywhere while Tom made sure that he was safe. It was as though Tom was the father and Ronny the son.

It seemed with each passing year that Tom was becoming quieter and angrier. Even though the business was prospering, the house remodeled, new landscaping added, and to any casual observer it appeared that the Heinrich family seemed like a normal American family, the environment inside the house was becoming caustic. The only one who seemed to fare well in this environment was Arnie.

Arnie became more self-centered as he strove to be Bernard's perfect son. He was condescending towards Tom and treated Ronny as a great irritation. It was clear he wanted all the world had to offer him and made moves in his high school years towards securing his place. He was valedictorian of his senior class and received a prestigious scholarship from the university.

Gloria secretly didn't like the person her oldest son was becoming, but Bernard considered him a chip off the old block. He was beaming when he learned his prized son wanted to be in politics. Arnie was selected to attend Boy's State, was elected as Student Body President, and was a page to a state senator for most of the summer. In fact, when he returned home from Washington D.C. he came across more condescending to his brothers, and even showed the same attitude towards his father. When Gloria asked Bernard if he was going to confront Arnie about his attitude, Bernard just shrugged his shoulders and stated that he was just spreading his wings.

Gloria felt her family was in crisis, but didn't know what to do. She braced herself for the shaking that she felt loomed before them.

The shaking erupted when Tom was sixteen. Instead of staying out all night in his vehicle, Bernard shocked Gloria by coming home drunk. It was about ten at night. He came in slurring his words and looked at her with a hard glaze over his eyes. He demanded his dinner even though it had been long finished and the dishes put away.

Tom and Ronny both came out of their bedrooms to see what was going on. Bernard looked at them with a sneer on his face. Gloria could tell that whatever followed would not be good. Bernard began to deride Tom and Ronny as he extoled Arnie's accomplishments. Ronny became visibly upset, while Tom stood still as a stone statue.

As Ronny began to cry, Gloria had had enough. She stood up and rebuked Bernard for his treatment of them. Bernard struggled to his feet and came at her. As she began to back away from him, Tom moved between them. Bernard cussed at him and tried to shove him aside but Tom was firmly planted. Bernard stepped back in surprise. A sinister look came over his face. He made a fist and went to punch Tom in the face. Tom blocked him with his arm and brought up his fist, upper cutting Bernard in the chin. He went flying backwards, landing on his back. He managed to get up and charged like a bull. Tom dodged to the side kicking Bernard as he flew past him. Bernard fell over a living room chair.

Bernard looked at him while clinging to the arm of the chair. He was cussing and calling Tom every foul name in German he knew, but Tom was unmoved. Bernard staggered to his feet. He came towards Tom with his hands clenched into fists. As he went to swing, Tom again blocked him with his arm, while his fist landed on Bernard's cheek, sending him flying once again backwards into the chair. His momentum was so great that when he hit the chair, the chair went backwards, taking him for a ride that ended with him hitting his head against the hardwood floor.

Gloria was in a state of shock as she watched the exchange. Ronny had his arms around her, pleading with Bernard not to hurt Tom, even though it was obvious that Bernard was the one who was receiving the brunt of the punishment.

Bernard managed to lift himself on one arm, glaring at Tom, asking who he thought he was to do this to his own father, and threatening to call the police, while having him thrown in jail for assault and attempted murder. It was then that Tom said something that sent shivers up Gloria's spine. "My, my, Mr. Heinrich. Aren't you the one, who through all those beatings I received from you for each of the family members, while claiming that you were teaching me how to be strong, preparing me to defend myself in life? You have taught me well and now I'm defending myself, you're going to call the police on me? How does it feel to be someone's punching bag?"

Gloria felt her face draining of color as she looked at Bernard. The next thing she heard was Bernard commanding Tom to get out of his home and never come back because if he did he would kill him.

Gloria felt like she had weights on her feet. She was struggling to comprehend what Tom had just said. Her middle son looked at her with a faint smile on his lips. He looked at Ronny and briefly waved goodbye to him as he turned and walked out the door. She remembered, as if it was a faraway echo, Ronny crying out to Tom to not leave him, breaking from her arms to run towards the closed door.

Bernard was lifting himself from the floor, screaming, "As they say in English, good riddance."

Ronny broke down into crying loudly. Bernard told him to shut up or he would... That is when Gloria came out of her state, "And, you'll do what?" she screamed!

Bernard had never heard Gloria raise her voice to such an octave. She once again repeated herself, "JUST WHAT WILL YOU DO?"

Bernard took a step back, declaring he didn't mean anything by what he said.

Gloria had no idea what her facial expression looked like, but she felt a fire that was burning hotly, and it wasn't about to be corralled or put out. "I want to know what Tom meant when he said he took all of your beatings for all of us."

"He's a liar!" Bernard declared. "No he's not, Mom!" wailed Ronny. "Dad used to beat him for everything that made him mad in this house. He beat him when you made him mad or I did something wrong. Tom took it so Dad wouldn't punish us."

"HE'S A LIAR TOO!" Bernard shouted. "What kind of a mother are you to raise such sons?"

"I'm not lying Mom!" Ronny cried. "I heard it and saw it more than once. He would strap Tom on his back and down his legs. Tom wouldn't tell anyone because he didn't want to cause trouble for any of us."

It all began to make sense now to Gloria. It was like a terrible light coming on to expose the darkness that had been taking place for years. It was Tom who received Bernard's physical abuse in place of her and Ronny. She felt sick as she realized that Bernard had channeled his anger by physically abusing Tom. No wonder Tom wouldn't let anyone touch him. She wanted to scream, moan, and weep for her son. In fact, she wanted blood--she wanted the head of Bernard Heinrich.

She looked at Bernard with the intensity of she-bear ready to protect her cub. Fear contorted Bernard's features. She opened her mouth, and her voice seethed with anger. "Go ahead call the police, Bernard! I want to report child abuse and I want to put a sadistic bully away for life, where he'll rot in prison! In fact, I'll going to start divorce proceedings and before it's over with I'll own everything--the house, the business, and both vehicles because the slime bag of this house, the filthy monster will finally be in prison!"

Bernard looked like a deer caught in headlights. "You wouldn't do that after all I've worked for?"

"You worked for!" she screamed. "You drank away most of our money and if it wasn't for me taking care of business, we wouldn't have anything to show for it! You get out of this house right now and find the biggest rock you can to hide under, but know before this is over with I WILL HAVE YOUR HEAD!"

Bernard backed out of the door. It never occurred to her that day she would never see Bernard walk back through that door, but neither did Tom. The truth had brought the terrible reality out about what Bernard had been doing to Tom, but it also destroyed lives.

The next day she saw Bernard again, only this time it was his lifeless body at the morgue. She was called to the morgue to identify the body of a man fitting Bernard's description that had been found on the beach by a jogger. It was hard to say what happened to him and due to events of the night before, quiet suspicion and unanswered questions ran amuck in the minds of those left behind to pick up the pieces.

Bernard often took a swim in the ocean after a night of drinking. Like the scene taking place in the Heinrich's home, the night before had been stormy. It was suspected that according to Bernard's known practice and temperament on his previous drinking binges that he had tried to defy the angry waves and plunged head first into the stormy ocean.

The pounding waves had swallowed him, pulling him into the vise grips of death, leaving others to fill in the blanks as to what he had been thinking. The sea later coughed him up on the beach for a passerby to discover. Bernard Heinrich had managed to once again avoid the consequences of his insidious actions. Gloria thought about Tom's words of being taught to be strong by taking everyone's punishment, and yet his teacher proved to be anything but strong. He had spent most of his life hiding his cowardliness behind his preferred numbing drug of alcohol.

At Bernard's funeral, Arnie was the only one who showed genuine emotion over his father's passing. Ronny set dry-eyed through the whole proceedings. Gloria shed tears, but they were not for Bernard, but for Tom. The great sorrow she felt was not because of Bernard's death, but because her son had left in the night and was nowhere to be found. Every passing day that she didn't hear from Tom caused the pain in her heart to grow.

When it came to Bernard, she didn't know how to feel about him, but she wouldn't allow herself to be pulled into the quagmire of guilt about what transpired between them. She realized she could take on tremendous guilt about their relationship, but Bernard's unforgivable actions towards Tom, caused her to steel herself against any condemnation. Bernard was an adult and made his decisions to do sadistic things to her Tom.

Ronny cried for his brother for the next couple of years. At times she caught him with a faraway look in his eyes. She would ask him what he was thinking about, and he would say the same thing, "I wonder where Tom is right now?"

The mention of Tom's name always felt like a sharp knife penetrating her heart. Sometimes the pain she felt was beyond description. It reached deep, pulling up regret, shame, and guilt. Each time she felt their sting, she had to face her own selfishness that showed no honor or regard for possible future consequences her actions might bring to others.

There were times when she didn't know how she could go on, but the current of daily living continued to carry her through each second, minute, hour, and day. The days ran together creating months, and each month seemed to pass without notice until marked by the passing of another year. She found herself mechanically walking through the demands of life.

Gloria continued to run the business. Bernard had taught other aspects of the business such as buying and processing the fish for their market. Since money wasn't being spent on alcohol, it proved to be a more successful enterprise than perceived, and provided quite nicely for their needs. Arnie was never told about what happened that terrible night. He finished college and married Clarice Ryley, a daughter of one of the prominent movers and shakers in Washington D.C. He appeared to keep his distance from her and Ronny, divorcing himself from a past where his father's death was suspicious and foolish. He also avoided laying claim to a lost brother who was a loose cannon in his mind, totally unpredictable and untrustworthy, capable of marring the image he was trying to create as the next likely candidate for some public office. It was clear that he had his life mapped out for himself.

After age 16, Ronny ceased to mention Tom's name. Gloria was not sure if it was out of hurt or the need to stop looking behind in order to continue to move forward. She encouraged him to not allow the past to define him. She was thankful to her parents because they seemed to give him the incentive to pursue his dreams by showing him they had confidence in his intelligence and capabilities. It was a tough road for him, but eventually Ronny made some good determinations about his life. He graduated from high school and went on to college. To Gloria's surprise, he wanted to run the fish market, with the intent of enlarging it. He majored in business, while working in the meat cutting department at a local store to learn the art of cutting meat as well as a means to earn extra money.

It was in his last year of college that he began to talk about a girl he had casually met at a friend's birthday party. Her name was Sandi. It was a whirlwind romance. Ronny was completely smitten with her, always talking about her special qualities. Gloria could tell he was in love and even though she was not of marrying age, she was informed by her son that he was planning to ask her to marry him right away.

She was a junior in high school, a year away from being 18. In spite of her age they had laid out their plans to marry and while he was running the business, she would finish her senior year and then take college courses on line.

One night Ronny called Gloria on the phone. He was livid. Apparently, Sandi's mother would not give her blessings to any marriage between them. She cited that her daughter was too young to know what was right for her and that Ronny had a questionable past and that he was from bad blood. Apparently, she had a private investigator do a background check on his life.

Ronny told his mother that they would make it happen and everyone would have to accept their marriage. Immediately, Gloria became concerned. "Ronny, do what is right for both you and Sandi. Don't do anything that would dishonor her or you. It you desire to marry, wait until she is the proper age and then do it regardless of her mother's blessing."

Ronny would have none of his mother's advice. He wanted to marry her and bring her back home where he was planning to help his mother run the business and bring new innovative ideas of how to enlarge it.

"What about her father?" Gloria inquired.

"I don't know Mom. He's not in the picture right now. In fact, for the last couple of years he's hardly been in the picture and seems to have a questionable character. Right now he's off pursing his own agenda, but Sandi suspects her mother is somehow responsible in part for some of his absence."

Gloria could see the possible handwriting on the wall and didn't want her son to taste the bitterness of wrong decisions and actions. She gave him a stern warning, "Ronny, Sandi's mother sounds like the type of woman that no matter what you do, she'll never bless your marriage. If you do something morally or legally wrong, she'll have you thrown in jail. You keep your cool. You need to have Sandi contact her father and tell him what's going on, and see if he will give his daughter written permission to marry you."

Ronny seemed to cool down, "You're right Mom, but I can't stand that woman! She's mean and vindictive. I'll talk to you later."

Gloria didn't hear from him the next day or the day after that. In fact, she waited, patiently at first, then with growing apprehension as she heard nothing from him. She didn't know which way to turn. She worried that Ronny would end up in jail on charges of statutory rape and fail to finish his senior year in college. She tried to get a hold of him, but the guys at his fraternity said he was in and out. She at least consoled herself that he was not yet in jail.

Two weeks later, as she was busying herself in the back of the store, trying to keep her mind occupied, she heard the front door open. When she went out to attend to business, to her pleasant surprise Ronny was standing at the counter, smiling and holding the hand of a blond headed, blue eye petite beauty.

"Hi Mom. I want you to meet the new Mrs. Ronald Heinrich."

Gloria was relieved to know her son was legally out of harm's way from the far-reaching arms of Sandi's mother. Gloria came from around the counter and embraced her new daughter-in-law. Sandi likewise returned the embrace and smiled. "I'm so glad to finally meet you Mrs. Heinrich."

"Please, don't call me Mrs. Heinrich. I'm either Gloria or Mom, but not Mrs. Heinrich. You are the official Mrs. Heinrich from now on." She paused, "And, how long have you been Mrs. Heinrich?"

"Sandi blushed. "A couple of days," She smiled and looked at Ronny, "And they have been the two happiest days of my life."

He knowingly smiled back at her. "We're here for good, Mom," Ronny added.

"What about your college graduation?" Gloria inquired.

"You know I've never been much for pomp and circumstance. I hope you don't mind but I asked them to send me my diploma. I thought we could really celebrate my graduation and my new marriage at the same time. We'll all go out and celebrate after you close up here."

"You have a deal," Gloria happily responded.

At dinner Gloria rejoiced at the excitement and sweetness of the new love that was bubbling up between her son and her new daughter-in-law. She remembered the purity and sweetness of her first love but pushed it behind her. She was robbed of experiencing the joy and excitement of discovering the magic that happens between a couple who intimately experience each other for the first time under the right circumstances.

They managed to talk about various things from the fact that Gloria was going to turn the living quarters of the store completely over to them and she would rent a duplex that was not far from the business. There were loud objections from the couple at first, but Gloria wouldn't hear of it. She reminded them that the quarters were for a family and not a single woman. She already made inquiries about renting a vacant duplex belonging to a friend that was located a couple of blocks away from the business when she first heard that Ronny wanted to get married.

It was then that Gloria received insight into Sandi's family. Her mother was a controlling woman, driving a wedge between her and her family. Her father proved to be a dichotomy to her. He seemed to always be there in the beginning but became more distant as his business grew. When she asked about him, her mother always told her that business was far more important to him than his family.

She had a brother who had to go live with her father's mother because he had gotten into trouble as a youth. Her mother wanted to put him in a detention center, but her father intervened and sent him to live with his mother. The last she heard about him is that he got religious and is now some Bible thumper.

Her older sister ended up pregnant out of wedlock and her mother sent her to a place for unwed mothers so no one would know about the disgrace she had brought upon the family, including her father. Her sister wanted to keep the child, but since she was 16 at the time her mother overruled her wishes and had the child adopted. Her sister was devastated and later confessed to Sandi that she had been viciously violated by a stranger, but still wanted to keep the baby. She was now married to an older man, Willis Eagan, who had a daughter Lisa. He tried to help her find her child, but he had already been adopted out and the records were sealed. Sadly, her sister later discovered she couldn't have any more children because of the medical complications from what had happened to her when she was violated.

Gloria began to see that her family was not the only one in crisis. Families everywhere were entangled in destructive webs because of the bad decisions and attitudes of others. She sat and marveled at how a girl of such innocence escaped the venomous ways of her mother and the despair of the happenings around her.

The next couple of days were devoted to getting the new couple settled into the living quarters of the store, and establishing Gloria in her new abode. Sandi quickly begin to fit into her new life. She proved to be a bright spot in the life of the Heinrich's. She didn't know how to cook and clean the house or do the shopping because her mother thought such activities were beneath a woman of her standing, but she was ready to pull up her sleeves and learn. New challenges didn't seem to intimidate her and learning something different seemed like a welcome adventure. She was sharp and witty and had the incredible ability to laugh at herself when she flopped at some project. Gloria realized why her son was so enthralled with his new wife.

The following day started out normal for Gloria. Sandi was excited because some of her family members were expected to visit her that day for the first time since her elopement with Ronny. Gloria had planned to gather all the necessary receipts and excuse herself when the time was right for the upcoming family reunion. The sun was shining as usual on that summer day, and she could hear the seagulls crying in the distance. No doubt the fishermen had brought in their catch for the day and the birds were excited that unwanted fish parts would be cast their way, providing a feast.

She was engrossed in looking over the receipts from the night before at the back counter when she heard the front door bell jangle, signifying someone had just entered the shop. She turned to greet the customer and suddenly froze in her steps, her mouth agape Standing there was Ken Jorgensen, a bit older, but still handsome as ever. His eyes looked weary, but still showed kindness and gentleness.

"Hi Gloria."

Gloria felt stuck in time.

"I'm sorry. I thought you might be expecting me," Ken nervously said when he saw the shocked look on her face.

Gloria was confused. How could she be expecting him? She struggled to find her voice, and after what seemed like hours she heard herself weakly ask, "Why would I expect you?"

Ken's handsome features looked genuinely shocked. "You really don't know, do you?"

Gloria felt her body tremble as her numb mind tried to come to grips with the fact that after all these years Ken Jorgensen was actually standing in her store. Somehow she managed to squeak, "Know what?"

"Sandi is my daughter and I'm here to see her and meet her new husband. In fact, I have brought her brother Brandon with me and her sister, Dena and her husband are not far behind. Brandon is out in the car waiting for me to signal him to come in."

Gloria could have been knocked over with a feather. She stood frozen in time, her brain scrambling, trying to process the information she had just heard. Her son was married to Ken's daughter! She wanted to run from the ironies of the situation, cry hysterically at the tragedy that waited to grab them and take them down into a spiral of devastation, and scream at the mockery of it, but all she could do was stand there like a mute.

She then heard Sandi's joyful voice and watched as she ran to her father and flung herself into his arms. She remembered Sandi talking about her father and siblings, but she had no idea who her father was, but to think about it, no one mentioned Sandi's maiden name in the first place. She was always just "Sandi".

A young man in his late twenties entered the shop and when Sandi saw him, she greeted him with the same excitement. Gloria surmised that it had to be Brandon. Admittedly, everything was a blur, surrealism in living color.

Ronny was not far behind Sandi. He was smiling at her excitement for him to finally meet her father and brother, but when he saw his mother's face, he became concerned. Ken also showed concern.

"Are you alright Mom?" Ronny asked. "You look like you've just seen a ghost."

Gloria knew she needed to say something to Ronny to keep him from knowing or suspecting what the real source was behind her present state. "I feel a bit lightheaded. I just need to sit down somewhere."

Ronny took one arm and Ken rushed around the counter and took the other as both of them began to lead her to a chair. By this time Sandi and her brother were alerted that something was wrong with Gloria. Once she sat down, they surrounded her. Sandi asked if she needed anything.

"Perhaps, you could get me some water."

Sandi immediately complied. A nice looking young man, with a gentle face smiled at her, "Hi, I'm Brandon, Mrs. Heinrich."

Gloria smiled and replied in a soft voice, "It's nice to meet you Brandon, but please call me Gloria."

Sandi brought a glass of water. Gloria began to sip it as she still struggled to grapple with what was going on around her. She couldn't believe that Ken was standing beside her, and she had just met the infamous Brandon who had won his heart so many years ago. She was afraid to look Ken's direction, afraid it was not him, but at the same time afraid it was him. She knew that she still loved him, but a future relationship with him was doomed, sealed by a lost son.

"Mom, are you going to be alright? You want me to call 9-1-1?"

Gloria realized it would be an easy way out. An ambulance would come and the EMT's might take her to the hospital for further tests and she would avoid facing the looming emotional storm that was on the horizon, but on the other hand, she might destroy the festivities of her son and new daughter-in-law.

The door opened again. Gloria could tell by Sandi's excitement that it must be her older sister. It appeared that Sandi's father and siblings were together in one place, except for Tom, the unknown, lost son and brother. Gloria fought back the tears that were beginning to moisten her eyes. Sandi had grabbed her sister's arm and led her to the group, first introducing Ronny and then Gloria to Dena and Willis. She explained how Gloria had had some type of spell, while Dena looked upon her with genuine concern. It was then that Sandi noticed that Gloria's eyes had tears in them. She kneeled down beside her, "Mom, are you okay, you have tears in your eyes."

Gloria couldn't let them know that it was a mixture of sorrow and joy, so she stuck with what she knew would not require any explanation. "I'm just so happy for you that you are all together." She smiled at Dena who was a beautiful woman and her husband, who was distinguished looking and his face radiated kindness. "Why don't you take your family to the living quarters and make them comfortable, and when I have my feet completely under me, I'll join you."

Protest erupted from all around her. "Alright," she conceded, "I'll let you escort me to the living room. How does that sound." Brandon took her left arm while Ronny took hold of her right arm. The two of them practically lifted her from the chair and quickly had her settled in a comfortable chair in the living room.

The two sisters busied themselves in the kitchen getting drinks for everyone. Gloria proceeded to get out of her chair to assist the two sisters, but was promptly questioned as to her intentions. Gloria explained her action, "I think I should help the girls. After all, I'm not used to being waited on."

It was Dena who put her hand on her arm. "It's okay for others to wait on you for a change." Looking towards her sister she said "Isn't that right Sandi?"

"That's right Sis!"

Sitting back in the chair, Gloria became lost in her thoughts as everyone began to chatter around her, touching on surface matters and daily demands and events. She was thinking about Tom, and the storm on the horizon that could shake and rattle the people in the room who were still trying to rebuild relationships after weathering the last tempest that had ravaged their lives. She sensed that occasionally she was being observed by those in the room, especially Ken.

After the two girls sat down, Ken was the one who cleared his throat to get people's attention. "I've something to tell all of you."

Gloria began to get up as if to excuse herself, recognizing it was a family matter. "You don't have to leave Gloria. You're part of the family and you might as well know what's going on."

A faint smile played on her lips. "I'm not really part of the family."

"You are part of Sandi and Ronny's family; therefore, you are part of the family," he replied.

She lowered herself in the chair and decided to try to become a mouse in the corner.

Ken began, "You probably suspect this but your mother and I have been separated for the last three years. I know she has put a black mark on my character and told you that business has kept me away from the family, but that was a lie to hide the truth that our marriage was over with.

"As of today, we are now officially divorced. A failed marriage is not something I wanted, nor am I proud of it, but considering the situation there were no alternatives left to consider."

"How did you get Mother to let you go," Sandi asked?

"Let's say she is a much richer woman today. In fact, that is one of the reasons I enlarged the business the last five years on a more extensive level and made some legal maneuvers so this divorce could take place."

"My question is after you gave me permission to marry Ronny, how did she handle that?" Sandi asked.

"It cost him lots more money, Sandi," Dena interjected.

"Oh, Dad, I'm so sorry," Sandi cried.

Ken waved his hand. "Don't worry Sandi, it was well worth it. What is money after all? It's wrong to stand in the way of the type of love that you and Ronny have for each other." He knowingly glanced at Gloria and then looked at Dena. "Besides your mother kept something from me that I'm still struggling to forgive her for today and it was my way of making sure she didn't mess up your life as well."

Gloria knew Ken was talking about this woman adopting out her own grandchild over the objections of her daughter who wanted to keep the child. Gloria was beginning to get a picture of this faceless woman. In her mind, she was growing horns, and had snakes for hair like the mythological character, Medusa, and also had the ability to turn those who looked upon her into cold stone. She might be beautiful but she was a monster who preyed upon her family, wielding power with cruel, vindictive calculations.

Gloria's portrait of this woman was interrupted by Brandon's voice, "Dad you must forgive Mom. She's the victim of her own bitterness and in the end she's going to be a lonely woman for it."

Brandon then looked at Ronny, "As you can see, we are far from being a perfect family, Ronny."

Ronny had quietly listened to the whole exchange. Gloria knew Ronny well enough that she could tell that the information was stirring up old memories for him. She didn't know whether to interrupt in some way or just remain quiet and let the chips fall where they may. When Ronny opened his mouth to speak, Gloria braced herself. As Ken said previously, it was what it was.

"My family isn't perfect either, Brandon," Ronny stated. "My father was a mean man and his death was suspicious because he was facing possible legal charges and ruin. My one brother, Arnie is an upcoming politician who is ashamed of his roots and family, and then there is my other brother...." Ronny's voice floated off as if becoming lost in past memories.

Gloria could feel her face turning pale. Sandi was now engrossed in what Ronny was saying, "You never mentioned you had another brother!"

Ronny looked at her. "I'm sorry Sandi, but the memories surrounding him are painful for both Mom and me." Gloria was aware that everyone looked at her. All she could do was cast her eyes downward. She was staring into nowhere, trying to find some semblance, purpose, or meaning to what had happened, lost in her own torment and sorrow.

Ronny paused as he saw Sandi looking at her. "I guess you might as well know. My brother ran away from home when he was 16. The reason is that for years my father used him as a whipping boy. In other words, if my father got mad at any of us he would look for opportunities and even set up times to take it out on my brother. He took beatings for me, my other brother at times, and my mother. He took it quietly and bravely for years."

Gloria looked up at Ronny and caught his eye. "Mom never knew because Dad whipped my brother in areas that could be covered up. I heard her a couple of times asking my brother if everything was alright because he wouldn't let anyone touch him, but he never told because Dad always told him if he did he'd destroy the whole family. In fact, he convinced him that it was a good way for him to be toughened up so he could be a man."

Ronny looked at his mother, "Mom didn't know but Arnie and I knew and that's my shame and guilt because I should've told her. I know she would have stopped it."

Gloria knew that Ronny knew what Bernard was doing to Tom, but she had no idea that Arnie also knew the terrible secret. "Arnie knew?" Gloria asked.

Ronny shook his head yes. "Yes, he said he would take care of it, but he remained silent. I should have told you but I was scared, confused, and didn't know what kind of fallout it would have created. I just hope Tom and you will forgive me." Ronny broke down and started to sob.

Sandi was crying while embracing Ronny to try and console him. Gloria stood up, went to her son, and embraced his shoulders and head. "Ronny, it wasn't your fault. You were a young frightened boy."

Through a muffled voice he reiterated his failure. "You bet I was afraid that if Tom didn't take it for me, I'd end up feeling the sting of Dad's beatings. I let him take it for me. I loved him, I idolized him, but I let him stand in my place and taste Dad's anger and hate without saying a word."

Ronny looked up into his mother's face, "I know without a doubt that if I had told you what was going on, you would've stopped it because you made that clear the night this all came out. But, I didn't give you a chance to take care of it, and now I don't know how you can even look at me."

Her heart was now breaking for Ronny. In her pain and sorrow, she had no idea of how great his pain and sorrow had become for him. "My precious, dear son, I love you and you're putting too much responsibility on shoulders too small to bear such a burden. I don't blame you at all for what happened, and somehow you need to make peace with it."

He looked at her with tears running down his cheeks. Great pain emitted from his eyes. "He went away Mom, and he hasn't come back to us. Why hasn't he come back? Dad can no longer hurt him. Why doesn't he come back to us?"

Gloria felt weariness blanket the sorrow and pain she was feeling as she looked into a distant time. "I don't know, Ronny, why he doesn't come back to us." She then let go of Ronny and went back to her chair, allowing Sandi to step into the place of sole comforter. She knew adversity is what can bring couples together as they learn to trust and lean on each other. As she sat down, she could tell everyone had been deeply affected by the hurt that the mother and son had just shared.

It was then that Brandon began to speak. "I don't know if this will help you, Ronny, but I knew of someone else who was a whipping boy on behalf of others. He was innocent of committing any real offense, but He quietly took people's beatings for them, stood in their place of judgment, and even eventually died in their place."

"How can that be, Brandon?" Ronny asked in frustration. It's so unfair! If I'm the one in the wrong, then I'm the guilty party. I was the one who rightfully deserved the punishment, not my brother."

"Like your brother, this man didn't deserve to take other's guilt and punishment, but He allowed it to happen. He could have called out

473

for assistance, but He didn't. He could have spared Himself, but instead He chose to become an offering on behalf of others."

"Why would this man allow it to happen if He could have stopped it?" Ronny inquired.

"The same reason your brother allowed it because he loved you and your mother and brother. He would rather experience the consequences of your father's wrath instead of allowing you to taste it."

It was clear that everyone in the room was being drawn into the story, especially Ronny. It was also obvious that he was asking all the right questions that would put to bed the silent heart questions that are rarely answered for those silently suffering.

"I don't think what happened to the other man was as bad as what happened to my brother," Ronny interjected. You see, it was my father that executed the terrible judgment on my brother. Talk about betrayal! I know he felt rejected by my Dad."

"There was a time in my life, I felt rejected by both parents," Brandon looked at his Dad. "I was legally adopted by my Dad. I never knew my biological father. When I was 10, my mother wanted to get back at my Dad and told me the only reason he put up with me is because he had to.

"It was a lie, but it went into my spirit and it took on the form of rebellion as I began to test the waters to see if my Dad loved me or not. However, the rebellion backfired on me. My mother wanted to send me to a detention center, but my Dad stepped in and arranged for me to live with his mother.

"It was my grandmother who told me about this Man, and helped me come to terms with my feelings of rejection. She showed me that they were based on a terrible lie. It was then that I understood that my Dad wanted to be my dad and that is why he adopted me. I also realized that before I could receive my father's love I had to be healed in order to repent and seek forgiveness for my wrong actions and be restored back to him.

"I say all of this because the one who offered up this Man in others' place was His Father. He put everything mankind had done wrong from the very beginning to now, and even in the future on His Son's shoulders so that you and I could be adopted into a heavenly family. His Son took it all, endured to the end, and then gave up His life."

In unbelief at what he was hearing, Ronny cried out, "How could this man's Father do such a thing to Him? Did He hate Him?"

"No He didn't hate Him. In fact, He loved Him with an indescribable love, but He also loved the world, each of us, and knew that only His Son could make the appallingly wrong things done by mankind right. He also knew that on the third day His Son would be raised up from the dead in wondrous glory to prove He had succeeded in making a way for each person to find his way back to forgiveness, hope, and a new life," Brandon paused, "to help man find his way back home to be part of a new family."

The rest of the room was quiet, but Gloria didn't know if their silence was out of respect or whether they had become as enthralled with the story as much as the two Heinrich's. She had heard about this Man before, but she had not given Him much thought. She had been self-sufficient, capable of working out her own problems, but now she was faced with the reality that her life lay in shambles, and what remained standing was marred and hard to bear. The greatest tragedy was that her lost son had not found his way home, and she needed hope that someday he would find it in his heart to come back to her and Ronny. This story actually was causing hope to rise out of the ashes of despair.

Brandon then focused on the real message of the story, "You know, Ronny, that Man took my place of judgment and He took your place, as well as everyone else in this room in order to bring rest to each of our souls over unresolved issues, tormenting regrets, matters of shame and guilt, to bring healing to our consciences and broken relationships."

"Isn't it enough that my brother took my place?" Ronny asked. "Why would this Man have to take my place as well?"

"Your brother had to stand in judgment for you every time you did something wrong, but this Man only had to stand in our place once to suffice all judgment. You see this Man's payment for sin was effective and perpetual because He is eternal, He is divine, deity, God in human form."

"Wow," Ronny stated. "I don't understand about deity, but I do understand what it means for someone to take my place, but I don't know what to do with all this information."

"Ronny, you admitted that you felt ashamed and guilty because your brother took your place to defuse your father's wrath against you. You let it happen because you didn't feel equipped to face it yourself. If you could talk to your brother right now, what would you say to him?"

Ronny thought for a few seconds. "I'd thank him for taking my place, ask him to forgive me because he took upon himself what I deserved, and beg him to not leave me again."

"Well, Ronny, that's what you need to do where this Man is concerned. You need to recognize He took your place to satisfy all judgment that was passed upon you for all the wrong you've done. You then need to thank Him and ask Him to forgive you for the wrong you brought upon Him, and then ask Him to come into your life forever and save you from tasting any further judgment and restore you in a right relationship with your Creator and God."

"It's that simple?"

"It's that simple Ronny."

Ronny looked lovingly at Sandi, "What do you think of this? I'm sure you don't have to have anyone stand in your place, you're innocent."

Sandi had quietly listened to the whole exchange. "Ronny, you're being sweet, but I'm not innocent. I've had bad thoughts, felt things that were not right, and done some things I'm not proud of. I need someone to stand in my place and take the punishment for my wrongs as well."

Brandon shook his head in agreement with what Sandi said. "Sandi is right Ronny. We are all in the same boat. We all stand judged and condemned and it's not just for what we have done, but who we are. We're in a bad way because our motives are selfish, our agendas self-serving, and our priorities self-centered, and in such a state, we rarely consider how we affect others and often perceive ourselves as having rights to do wrong things against others, just like your father did to your brother. We see ourselves being right or justified in our own minds regardless of how insane it may play out in reality."

Shaking his head, Ronny responded, "Wow, this Man must have been old to take on the guilt of everyone."

"He was called the Ancient of Days, but He was only 33 years young when He took our place on a cross. Your brother was also young when he took your place. How old would he be right now, Ronny?"

"He's six years older than me. I'm 22 so he would be 28."

When Sandi heard the number 28, she looked at Dena. "That's how old you are." She then turned to Ronny. "When was your brother's birthday?"

Gloria held her breath as Ronny offered the information. She knew the comparison was probably going to stir up some memories, opening a door to probabilities. The fact that Dena was a couple of months older than Tom was quickly noted. Gloria could feel her face turning red as she became aware of Ken shuffling his weight in his chair.

"Ronny, the Bible tells us if we call upon the name of this Man in humility, seeking His intervention that He'll forgive and save us. That man's name is the Lord Jesus Christ."

"I've heard the name of Jesus, but it has always been a cuss word," Ronny replied. "All I have to do is call upon His name and ask for forgiveness, and He will save me from the judgment and the guilt hanging over me?"

"Yes He will. In fact, He will save anyone who calls out to Him in need of forgiveness and salvation."

Looking up, Ronny began his simple request. "Well, Jesus, I need to be forgiven, and Brandon said all I need to do is ask in sincerity for you to forgive me of all that I've done and failed to do, and You will pardon me. Forgive me Jesus for the bad things I've done and for failing to do what I needed to do. Brandon also said you could save me, and heal me of my past so that I can go forward into a future with my precious wife without regret, shame, and despair. I need You to save me and heal me and live with me forever."

Brandon followed it with an "Amen."

Gloria was silently following her son's child-like request. She so desperately needed forgiveness and needed to be saved from the tormenting chains of regret, the heavy balls of shame, the door locks of guilt, and the prison of despair. As she followed her son's leading, she felt like she was being washed from head to toe, taking with it all that had kept her imprisoned in a world of sorrow and despair. She could tell by Ronny's voice that something wonderful was happening to him as well.

After being quiet after his request, Ronny looked at Brandon. "Brandon, do you think Jesus could find my brother and let him know that he no longer has to be the whipping boy, and maybe he would come home?"

Brandon's eyes were moist as he smiled at him. "Your brother is like a lost sheep, and the Bible tells us that Jesus looks for the one lost sheep and will bring him home. We can all ask Jesus to find your brother and bring him home."

Hope suddenly took flight in Gloria's soul. Could this Jesus bring her lost son home to her? It was clear that this wonderful Jesus was the only one who could find her son."

"What's your brother's name" asked Brandon:

Gloria once again held her breath. She was hoping that Ronny would keep the name short and to the point. "My brother's name is Tom...," Ronny paused, "Thomas Eugene."

Gloria braced herself as she let out her breath. It was Sandi who again pointed out the obvious. "Dad, he has the same middle name as you do. What a coincidence!"

Gloria knew that Ken was intelligent enough to put the small facts together. He could conclude either that Gloria named Thomas the way she did because she thought so highly of him or she secretly gave him that middle name to identify him to his real roots. If Ken asked which scenario was correct, she knew she would have to be honest with him. But, the question was what would he do with the information? Would there be other rifts created in hearts, lives, and relationships doing away with the work that had already started. It looked like a hopeless mess, but yet she now possessed a new hope that she wasn't about to let go of regardless of the fallout.

Gloria didn't dare look at Ken, but she suspected that he knew the truth. She remembered how he would not leave his unborn child at the mercy of his wife, and yet his son was the victim of a sadistic, cruel man. She hoped that he had followed Ronny's request for Jesus to come into his heart and make the difference because if he did, he would have the same hope she now possessed. She was assured that the hope would help him walk through the terrible reality of what happened to Tom.

The room suddenly lit up with excitement as each person shared how Ronny's request had affected them. She heard Ken excuse himself from the group, claiming he needed to get some fresh air. Gloria noticed that Brandon watched his father walk out and then looked at her with a knowing look.

Gloria knew she had to face Ken alone. She quietly got up and followed him out to the enclosed patio that had been one of the additions added to the living quarters. Ken was sitting at the patio table, sadly looking down in contemplation. Gloria quietly sat down in a chair facing him. Without looking at her, he reached out his hand towards her and she responded by cradling it in both of her hands.

In a low voice, overflowing with emotion, he asked the question. "Is Thomas Eugene my son?"

Gloria sadly looked at the despondent man. "Yes he is."

Still holding her hand with one of his, he put his free hand up to his head. She grew warm inside as he tightly squeezed her hand. "Now I not only have a grandson that is lost to me because of the selfishness of one woman, but now I have also a son who is lost to me because of the cruelty of one man. Is this the terrible judgment and sorrow I must bear because of my actions?"

"No it's not!" Brandon's voice suddenly interrupted.

Gloria hadn't noticed that he quietly had come upon them. "You heard everything?" Gloria asked. Ken looked towards his son.

"Yes, I have," Brandon stated.

"You probably think poorly of both of us right now," Gloria replied.

"No, Dad already told me about you and gave me a summation of the guilt and shame he has been carrying for years. In fact, it was one of the things that caused him to seek Christ's forgiveness and salvation. I didn't know who you were until today, but the interaction I witnessed through the store windows between the two of you when you turned around and saw him indicated you knew each other quite well."

Gloria was happy that Ken had received the gift of forgiveness and life, but felt sad that he had to taste the bitterness of what happened to Tom.

Brandon sat down in one of the chairs. "Dad, the loss you are feeling right now is not a judgment, it's a consequence you must face, but at least you're not alone in facing it. You can now share it with Gloria and the two of you can share it with the Lord."

Ken looked at Gloria, "How have you handled this by yourself?"

"Until tonight I couldn't bear it. It was so tormenting, especially when your warning from so many years ago kept coming back to haunt me. In the end, I became numb to it. It's the only way I could get through each day. But, tonight I was given hope through this Jesus. He took the torment out of the sorrow I had and He took away my guilt with forgiveness, and replaced my shame with hope."

Brandon's face lit up when he heard Gloria had made a heart decision for Jesus, "You see Dad, Jesus can make all things new. You both can start afresh in your relationship."

Ken looked at Gloria, "I've never quit loving you Gloria."

Gloria knew her love for Ken was still very much alive, subdued and hiding, but still there to be raised out of the ashes of hopelessness. "I still love you Ken, and I always will."

Ken looked at Brandon. "How can we start over?" Ken asked while nodding his head towards the rest who were still talking excitedly about what had transpired. "What about the rest of them?"

Brandon once again showed his wisdom, "Dad, if Gloria and you are going to start fresh, you have to come clean about the past and about Tom. I think each of those individuals have enough character to properly handle it."

"And, what happens when Tom comes back into our lives?" Ken asked.

"You need to cross that bridge when you come to it. It'll be up to both of you to discern if the truth will alienate him more or whether it will set him free."

Gloria loved hearing the word, "when" and not "if" coming from Ken's mouth. "Do you think, Ken, that our son will come back to us?" Gloria asked.

"We're going to look for him together." Ken paused, then said, "I don't know where to look for him, but we'll keep praying that the Lord will have mercy on us and bring our son home and prepare his heart for the truth so that I can ask him for his forgiveness.

"If only I knew how to find our lost son, if only...." Ken's voice floated off on the silent breezes of pain and regret.

Brandon smiled. "Dad, the Lord knows where Tom is and He's the Good Shepherd who will seek him out so he may be found and be led back home."

***

That was over twenty years ago. That very night Ken and Gloria told their families about the past, their young love, Gloria's father's interference and how through the terrible hurt, the mistakes they made including, Tom. What seemed like a bumpy road became relatively smooth, except for Arnie, who was informed later.

Arnie showed total disgust, but was not surprised. He stood there with his lips pressed into a thin line and his eyes narrowed condescendingly. "Why are you telling me this now?" he asked.

His look didn't intimidate Gloria; rather, it had the opposite effect on her. She had had enough of Arnie's judgmental, arrogant attitude. He had pretty much divorced himself from Ronny and her as he pursued his political ambitions. The only time she received any news about him was via through her parents, who kept all the newspaper articles that presented him in a favorable light, and her older sister, Helen. Due to the five-year age difference between them, Gloria had never really been close to her sister. Helen married a rich businessman. They couldn't have children and Gloria suspected that they saw Arnie as a type of son. They not only financially supported Arnie's political aspirations, but they were often by his side when it came to his different campaigns and fundraisers. She knew that behind Arnie's charming veneer he presented to people such as her parents, her sister and brother-in-law, that he possessed a similar disposition as his father.

She stood straighter to make a point. "I'm telling you this now because Ken and I will be married soon."

"Married! I'll not allow it! My mother will not play the harlot, you hear me?"

Gloria was shocked at Arnie's statement. It wasn't until later, when she had time to think about it, that she realized the shock kept her from slapping his face. However, the initial astonishment passed quickly, giving way to anger which became obvious by the look on her face and the tone of her voice. "Harlot! Why, Arnie! How can you cast such stones at me when you consider who you are playing footsie with to get politically ahead? How dare you act like my pompous judge and jury!" She paused, and then added, "And, just who is going to stop me from marrying Ken?"

Arnie must have realized he had awakened an aspect of his mother that he had rarely witnessed before, because he stepped back and approached it from a different angle. "What will people say when they learn about two people of your age and his marital status marrying?"

"I frankly don't care what people say!" Gloria flatly stated. "I'm not after the popular vote like you and I have nothing to protect or prove."

"What about my reputation? I'm trying to make a difference in this world," he retorted.

"Come on Arnie. Are you really trying to make a difference or are you just trying to make a name for yourself?"

Gloria saw anger rush into his face, "What do you know about me and my career? You've had no part in it, and it's obvious that you don't have any real concern about it."

Gloria refused to receive his accusation quietly. "Arnie who are you kidding? My lack of involvement in your political life has been your choice and not mine. You act as if Ronny and I don't exist. In fact, you give the impression to the media that my parents are the ones who raised you."

Gloria's statement clearly took the wind out of Arnie's accusation. "I want you to know, Arnie, that Ken and I plan to look for Tom."

Arnie's eyes grew wide. "Look for Tom? Isn't he old enough to come home on his own? Why don't you let sleeping dogs lie?"

Gloria was once again reminded of how self-centered Arnie was by his declaration. "I suspect, Arnie, that Tom might not feel he is welcome here. After all, he was used as a whipping boy for all of us, and that included you!"

Arnie looked shaken by Gloria's statement, "Who told you that Tom was a whipping boy for all of us."

481

"Ronny confessed the whole situation as well as indications given indirectly by Tom and your father. I also found out that you told Ronny that you would inform me as to what was going on, but for some reason you failed to tell me. The question is why didn't you inform me as to what your father was doing to Tom?"

Arnie nervously shifted his weight.   "I only witnessed Dad whipping Tom a couple of times. I figured it wasn't a regular occurrence. After all, I felt if Tom had a problem with how Dad treated him, he could always tell you."

Gloria couldn't believe the lame justification coming out of Arnie's mouth. "Now come on Arnie! You knew your father's bullying practices quite well. There were various reasons why Tom wouldn't feel at liberty to tell me. It was up to those who knew about it to tell me."

Gloria could tell by the look on Arnie's face that he was intellectually scrambling to try to come out on top of the situation. "You're right Mom. I should've told you and I have to admit I felt bad because I dropped the ball. I'll tell you what, to make amends and give you a wedding present at the same time, I'll hire the best investigator possible to locate Tom."

Gloria wanted to believe Arnie had a change of heart, but she wasn't sure he was a man of integrity. Her doubt must have registered on her face. "You look as if you don't believe me Mom." Arnie said, his voice fringed with hurt. "Tell you what, I'll give you the name of the investigator so you can check him out and all the reports he turns over to me."

Gloria agreed to talk to Ken about it. After much discussion, they both decided to give Arnie a chance to prove himself, but if there were no results, they would step in and hire their own investigator.

True to what he said, Arnie gave them the name of the investigator and any reports he gave Arnie about the investigation he delivered to Gloria and Ken. Each lead he followed ended up going cold. It was as if Tom had disappeared into thin air.

After several failed attempts on Arnie's investigator's part, Ken and Gloria hired their own investigator. However, his reports read the same as Arnie's investigator. Ken and Gloria both went in and out of despair as hope swung upward with each new lead only to end in a crash landing. Even though they made an occasional reference to Tom, they learned to quietly carry their personal sorrow, pain, shame, and guilt alone. At times the condemnation of their guilt became unbearable, and as Ken confided to her one time, they both learned the only place of solace where they could find peace and comfort was when they flung themselves on the Lord.

In the years that followed many events confronted the family. They experienced great joys as well as sorrows. Ken flourished in his business, while Ronny and Sandi enlarged their business and relocated it into a bigger building. They bought a new house that was suitable for them and the addition of three children to their family. The couple became active in their church and made every advance to make Christ the head of their family and train their children in the knowledge of Jesus Christ. As a result, they were respected in the community and their three children became blessings to them and their proud grandparents, as well as served as leaders in school and good examples to their peers.

Brandon finished his seminary studies, married, had two children, and became the pastor of a struggling church. The church grew to be a thriving Body that prepared others for ministry, supported missions, and had successful evangelistic outreaches. He continued to spiritually mentor Ronny, disciple his sisters and families, challenge his father, and encourage his stepmother.

Dena proved to be a blessing to Gloria. They became very close. Dena admitted that Gloria was the mother she never had. Her stepdaughter, Lisa, Willis' daughter from a previous marriage, was also a blessing to the Jorgensen family. She went to college, majoring in business and became part of Ken's business. She married Terrance Bellingham and they had a daughter, Leslie. But, great tragedy struck the family when Dena's husband Willis and Lisa's husband, Terrance were killed in a boating accident.

The family walked through the deep valley together, trying to console one another. They had to endure the shock waves of the unexpected; the emotional fallout of the loss, and face the empty places in their lives and homes that would mock them with silence and haunting echoes of past memories. However, they came out better for it. As a family they had weathered the storm because of God's grace and comfort. They had endured the dark night of the soul because of His faithfulness to walk each of them through it.

There was one other steady spiritual pillar in the family besides Brandon, and that was Ken's mother. She moved in with Ken and Gloria as it became harder for her to take care of herself. Gloria found Edna Jorgensen to be the spiritual giant that her son and grandson had presented her to be. When she heard about Tom, she encouraged Ken that one day God would bring him home. In times of loss, she was there to quietly console and pray for the person suffering the loss. She found a bright side to every dark side and had a sincere faith towards the Lord.

However, the light and joy was missing when it came to Gloria's family. A dark cloud overtook Gloria's parents when they found out the truth about Tom. When Gloria and Ken got back together, her parents gladly embraced the extended family but her father had to face his involvement for the mess that had occurred in the Heinrich's family. Her father fell into a deep sorrow and her mother became engulfed in great sadness as she watched her husband struggle under the tragic domino affect his interference had on everyone involved. Even though they heard about hope in Jesus, there was no indication that they really received Him as a solution. Sadly, they both passed away within a couple of months of each other without having any resolution where Tom was concerned.

Gloria realized that the tapestry of their lives had been marred by a wrong stitch and that there were dark spots that spoke of great loss, but she also realized that Jesus had changed the darkness that had covered the tapestry with such beautiful designs. Gloria could see where the tapestry was beginning to reveal the marvelous work of the Lord.

However, when she considered the tapestry, she always came back to that one wrong stitch. It seemed to remain lost in the tapestry but she knew it was there. It never went anywhere, leaving that section of the tapestry unfinished. She knew finding Tom was the only one who could bring any direction or completion to the design.

Gloria wrestled with whether she would ever see the face of her son again. At the same time she also felt trepidation over how Tom would react to the events surrounding his conception. The pull she felt between not ever seeing her son, and seeing him, only to lose him again was also gut-wrenching. Each time she was pulled into the snare of the unknown and the uncertainty about Tom, she had to choose to trust the Lord with the present and the future.

Underneath Gloria was happy for Dena that she and her son Judson Leeman who had been adopted, had located each other after many years of separation. She put down the envy and reminded herself that one more stitch was being completed on the tapestry of their lives as a family. It was clear that Judson was part of Dena's healing of the past, as well as adding sweetness to the bitterness at the loss of her husband.

Judson proved to be a wonderful young man. Gloria could tell that he had been raised in a good family. He not only showed good manners, kindness, and consideration, but he was a Christian. It was obvious that he loved, respected, and was grateful to his adopted parents. It was out of respect for his adopted mother that he never considered finding Dena until after her untimely death in a car accident.

At the time, Judson had just become engaged to a beautiful young lady by the name of Becca Addison. As the young couple talked about a family, they hit a blank about possible medical problems being passed down through family. Judson admitted that when he approached his father about the prospect of finding his birth parents he did so in trepidation. However, his adopted father encouraged him to seek them out to bring resolution to their questions. He also added that maybe they were looking for him as well.

Judson was the first one who came to meet his mother and her family. He fit like a glove. It was almost love at first sight for each member of the family. In fact, he looked a lot like Dena. He then invited his new family to his wedding. Neither Dena nor Ken were about to miss any more important events in Judson's life. The whole family agreed that they wanted to be a part of witnessing and supporting him in this important step in his life.

They made reservations at the most reputable motel. To Gloria it was another place where she could walk down the streets and pray that she would see a familiar face in the crowd—Tom's face. As she watched the activities taken place, her cell phone rang. She was surprised to see Arnie's wife's name on the caller ID.

It had been clear that Arnie and Clarice had their own life and ran in a different crowd. Their only baby had been stillborn, causing complications that prevented Clarice from having any children. In spite of the loss, Arnie cleverly maintained his "perfect front." It was clear that their lifestyle was part of the image of an upcoming politician. She had talked to Clarice about family gatherings at different times, but the invitation would ultimately be declined by Arnie.

Arnie had been clear up front that he wanted no part of her religion, while his attitudes and actions made it clear that he wanted as little interaction with her and her new extended family as possible. However, rumors began to surface that there were problems in Arnie and Clarice's marriage, such as alcoholism and infidelity. Gloria never knew which rumors were true and which ones were exaggerated or made up, but she knew that Arnie would never admit to her that there were any problems.

Gloria's greeting was cheerful. "Hello Clarice, what a pleasant surprise."

The voice on the other end was strained and nervous. "Hello Gloria. I'm sorry to bother you during this time, but I called you to let you know Arnie and I are separated."

Even though she had heard there were problems, Gloria was surprised. "Is there anything I can do for you?"

"That's very kind of you Gloria, but your son is going to need you. In fact, he should be joining you shortly. He's very upset, but I think it's because he's worried about what our separation is going to do to his political image."

Clarice paused, and then said, "I just want to set the record straight. It was never my idea to stay away from you and the rest of the family. I personally wanted to know you better, but Arnie would have none of it."

Gloria wasn't surprised, but at the same time she was confused. "I appreciate you telling me that Clarice, but why would Arnie seek me out right now, and what was his purpose in keeping you from the rest of us?" Gloria asked.

"I can only guess, but he's seeking you out because he doesn't know who else to go to. As far as his purpose for keeping us apart, I think it's because he was afraid that you would find out..." Clarice's voice faded out as if she was rethinking what she was saying.

"Find out what Clarice?" Gloria inquired. Her voice was kind, but firm.

"I don't know how else to tell you but to just come right out with it. Arnie has done everything he could to prevent you from locating Tom."

Gloria was stunned, and it was obvious that Clarice was not finished. "The investigators had leads, but he paid them off to act like the trail went cold. Tom came back to the place where you had your old business, but Arnie paid off the new owners to act ignorant about your and Ronny's whereabouts.

"I want you to know that I argued with him, especially since we lost our own child, but he always stated that Tom would tarnish his political career because there would be too many questions, and he didn't want the public to see his family the way he perceived them, as harlots, losers, and small-time business people."

Gloria was completely stunned. Shock had clearly wrapped itself around her, but at the same time she began to tremble and felt anger seething through the numbness. Even though Arnie was ashamed of his family, he didn't have to be a snake in the grass to protect his political career. She wanted to run through the motel and scream until she found something to pound on to vent all her anger. She wanted to hunt Arnie down and shake him until his teeth rattled. All these years she thought her son was lost to her, hiding from her at best or dead at worst, but it was Arnie who was pulling the strings and she wanted to know why he'd commit such an offense against Tom and her.

Clarice continued sharing information on what had been going on in their life. "I want you to know that I've been no angel. My life has been caving in since I lost the baby and our marriage has been turned upside-down. I became lost in a world of hurt, silence, and despair.

"Arnie didn't know what to do about me. He clearly forfeited my respect when he didn't do right by you and later concerning Tom, losing any credibility to reason with me. He initially ignored my state, hoping it would go away until my drinking became too excessive. He placated me when I raged at him for being incapable of helping me, and he walled himself up against hurt as I tried to make him pay with inappropriate flirtations that once resulted in infidelity.

"I know I've been a fool, Gloria. I've been unfair to Arnie. I know he still loves me, but he doesn't know how to keep me, and I don't know how not to blame him for our miserable existence. We're both drowning in a bad cycle."

Clarice then asked the question that opened the door for Gloria, causing her anger towards Arnie to flee. "How did you do it? How did you keep from going crazy over Tom? How did you and Ken let the past go so you could go on and have a good marriage? How?"

Gloria knew the answer to the question. "Clarice, it's not a matter of how, but who. There's only one person who can help people make peace with their past, cause them to walk in forgiveness towards one another, and open the door to lasting resolution and success.

"That person is Jesus Christ. He's been my hope in despair, my anchor in sorrow, and my place of refuge in the storms. Right now you and Arnie are in the midst of a terrible storm, but Jesus is the lifesaver, but you must let go of the past offenses, hurts, and bitterness in order to grab a hold of Him. You must change your course through repentance, seek healing through forgiveness, and embrace liberty by changing who and what you serve and pursue."

Gloria could tell that Clarice was softly crying. "If Jesus is the answer, I want Him. I can't live like this any longer."

It was then that Gloria led Clarice to the loving arms of Jesus Christ. The angels were rejoicing that another lost sheep had been found by the great Shepherd whose arms were never too short to embrace a lost child coming home after being swallowed in the mire of the pigpen of the world.

After the prayer, Clarice was giddy and rejoicing in the cleansing that was flowing through her being. She knew she was forgiven and put on a path where she would experience the hope of everlasting life. Gloria gave her instructions to get a Bible and find a church where she would be fashioned into a committed follower of Jesus Christ.

Gloria was excited that God had used her to point Clarice to the way, the truth, and the life. However, the joy subsided as she thought about facing Arnie. She paced back and forth in the motel room, debating whether she should tell Ken about Arnie's shenanigans. Although life went on for them, there was always that dull ache where Tom was concerned that had become a constant companion in their lives.

She heard a knock on the door. She knew it couldn't be Ken because he would use his key and she suspected that he was having some bonding time with Judson, as he and Dena were making arrangements for a family dinner where Judson's fiancé and his adoptive family, the Leeman's, had time to meet the Jorgensen side of the family before the wedding. Although some plans had already been made for the dinner by Judson's family, the final touches had to be added as to the number and a menu prepared that was conducive to any possible food allergies in the Jorgensen clan.

Gloria looked through the peephole and was startled to see Arnie standing outside her motel room. She had such mixed feelings about her son. She knew he was hurting, but at the same time he had been an inconsiderate scoundrel. She quietly asked God for wisdom to minister according to His Spirit and grace and not from fleshly feelings and emotions.

She opened the door. Arnie was staring at his shoe tops, and his body language gave her a clue that things had changed. The arrogance was gone and it looked like he was a broken man, a lost soul, a sad little boy who needed to be comforted.

He looked up at her. "Can I come in Mom?"

She stepped to the side and waved him in without saying a word. He slowly walked to one of the suite's chairs as Gloria quietly shut the door and followed him. She lowered herself into a chair facing him.

She waited for him to speak, and after an awkward pause, he looked at her. "You've probably heard that Clarice and I are separated." He paused and added, "It's not my idea but hers."

In a controlled, quiet voice, she responded, "So I've heard. What are you going to do Arnie?"

He shuffled nervously in his chair. "I don't want to lose her."

"And, why don't you want to lose her?" Gloria asked.

Arnie sat straight up in his chair and became defensive. "Because I love her! Why else wouldn't I want to lose her?"

"Arnie, she believes you don't want to lose her because of your political career."

He jumped up from the chair, waving his hands, "To blazes with my political career!" His voice began to rise as he added, "Clarice is what's important, not politics," he paused and sat down again.

"You don't have to convince me that you love her," Gloria stated. "Rather, you have to convince her. It's also good to see that you're ready to fight for her because until you are she won't believe that your relationship is more important than your political career. She'll suspect you just want her around for show."

Arnie once again got up from the chair and began to pace. "Does she consider me such a jerk? She should know who I am. We have been together over 27 years."

"Just who are you Arnie?" Gloria asked.

Arnie stopped pacing and looked at Gloria, his eyes bulging. "She told you didn't she?"

"What did Clarice tell me Arnie?"

Arnie sat down again and looked at Gloria with fear in his eyes. "She told you about Tom."

Although shaking inwardly, Gloria responded with a calm voice, "Yes she did Arnie."

He looked at the floor, "It's a wonder you even let me in the room. You probably hate me right now."

Gloria looked upon him with supernatural grace. "I don't hate you. I'm disappointed with you and confused. When I first heard it my natural tendency was to strike out at you, but what would that have accomplished?

"Arnie, I just don't understand why you did what you did. I realize today that I don't know you. You're not the same loving little boy who cried over his dead turtle. When did you change from a tender little boy to someone who comes across as cruel and indifferent to the hurts of others? Will you please explain your reasoning for such actions?"

Arnie looked at her with tears in his eyes. "I don't understand it myself. Believe it or not I have been trying to figure it out on my way here. I guess it all started over that dead turtle."

"Dead turtle?"

"Yes, that's when Dad made fun of me and told me real men don't cry. That's when I realized I had to toughen up to keep Dad from making fun of me, to make him proud of me. I had to be perfect and fearless. The problem is I was afraid of everything, but I couldn't let anyone know, especially Dad because he'd make fun of me and reject me for being weak.

"Then one day I did something to make him mad. He was about ready to hit me and Tom accidentally walked on the scene. That's when Dad got the idea to make Tom the scape goat. I'll never forget what he said to me. 'Now there's a dumb kid. Watch how I play him to serve both our purposes. After all, he's not 'one of us.'

"He called Tom over and threatened to beat me and you if he didn't take the punishment for us. I was afraid of Dad's anger, but Tom agreed to take it for me and you, and later Ronny. He quietly took it for all of us.

"There were times when my conscience was pricked by what was happening to Tom, but the shame and failure I felt about it caused me to allow Dad to convince me that I was better than Tom, and that it was only right for him to take everyone's punishment. He kept saying Tom was the source of all of his problems. He became a burden when he was born and remained so because he was not one of us."

The old haunting memories of Tom being the whipping boy were being stirred up once again in Gloria's mind. She felt the same heaviness in the pit of her stomach as she did the first time she heard it. It was a terrible nightmare, but it was one that needed to be exposed. "What did he mean that Tom was not one of us?" she asked. She knew that Bernard wouldn't have suspected that Tom wasn't really his son because she had not given him cause in their marriage.

Arnie shook his "I asked him what he meant. He shrugged his shoulders and said that there was no way a stupid kid like Tom, who quietly took his beatings could be his kid. He always bragged about how smart I was and that I was a chip off the old block.

"I began to see that each of us boys played different roles in his sick games. I was his protégé, the one who could do no wrong, the only son worth mentioning while Tom was his punching bag that he could secretly take his anger and hatred out on, and Ronny was the court jester that entertained him.

"I was glad that I was his protégé, and that I could avoid tasting his anger, but one day his anger frightened me more than other times. He was drunk and mad at everyone and wanted to punch someone out. I was trying to calm him down, but he even raised a fist at me. But, he refrained because he knew Tom would be coming home soon. Sure enough like clockwork, Tom came home and Dad was waiting for him.

"Tom was twelve at the time. Dad called him over, and I could see Tom bracing himself for the inevitable. That is the one time Tom actually said something back to Dad. He asked Dad what he was being beaten for. I'll never forget what Dad said. He told him he was being beaten for being himself. Tom asked him what was wrong with him being Tom Heinrich, and that is when Dad told him he was son of a loser by the name of Ken Jorgensen, and that he didn't deserve to breathe the same air as the rest of the Heinrich's."

Gloria's heart skipped a beat; she struggled to breathe as her breath felt practically knocked out of her as the ugly situation was being unveiled. Arnie didn't notice Gloria's reaction and continued on.

"That's when Tom stated that he was glad to know that he didn't have the Heinrich's blood running through his veins and now he didn't have to be afraid of inheriting such anger and wrath. Dad turned white and violently lunged at Tom, but Tom moved and due to being drunk, Dad fell face down on the ground, hitting a rock, dazing himself to the point he couldn't get up to carry out his wrath. Tom shrugged his shoulders and walked away.

"I asked Dad if it was true that Tom was not a Heinrich. He cussed and admitted that this Ken guy was some old boyfriend of yours that he knew about and that he was using it to toy with Tom. He added that Tom was so dumb, he'd believe it." Arnie paused, "And, then years later I found out it was true and found myself actually envying Tom."

By this time Gloria was experiencing an emotional ride. She was struggling with what she had just heard. Even though Bernard had no idea that what he was stating about Ken being Tom's father was actually true, his cruelty towards Tom was immeasurable. The fact that Tom believed it and found some comfort in it gave Gloria hope that the truth would be liberating, but she had to stay focused because Arnie was not through and she had to ask one important question.

"Did the two of you try to set the record straight with Tom about Ken?" she asked.

"No. Dad didn't want to claim Tom as a son, and I could see that it gave Tom some comfort and hope in a strange way so I let him believe it. By this time I really didn't want to be Bernard Heinrich's son either. I fed his sick ego so that I could keep his different monsters at bay but I loathed him. I loathed what he was doing to our family. I loathed the person I was becoming to keep him off my back.

"It was all so ironic."

Almost breathless Gloria asked, "What was ironic Arnie?"

Arnie let out a half laugh. "Bernard Heinrich. Here was a man who mocked cowards, was condescending towards those who showed fear, and exalted himself on the back of weakness and vulnerability. And, yet look what he did! He often took a coward's way out. Ronny did tell me what happened the night Tom left for good and your threat to bring the law down on Dad. I have no doubt that he ran like a scared rabbit from life catching up to him that night when he was confronted by you over his cruelty, and I'm not so sure he didn't chose the ocean as his executioner."

Arnie shook his head, "Recently, I realized I had become lost in Dad's sick world. Now I'm the hypocrite, envious of those I looked down on such as Ronny, who now has a good life, marriage, family, and business. I judged those with moral indiscretions such as you and Ken, only to face the harsh reality that such things now plagued my life, while your healthy marriage mocks me.

"And what was my result of becoming lost in Dad's sick world? I never discovered what it meant to be a real man. I was a coward, afraid to take my own beatings, and as an older brother stand up for Tom. What started out to be immature feelings of elitism towards Tom, turned into fear of incompetence, envy, and guilt because I knew in the end Tom would probably end up being a better man than I was. After all, cowards don't possess any substance. They become lost in other people's causes and images to maintain some sick idea of life.

"The truth is I sabotaged finding Tom because I couldn't bear facing the past about my cowardly ways and looking into the mirror to discover that my so-called 'cleverness' to avoid taking my lumps caused me to be a weak man whose life is now falling apart at the seams. I was afraid that all that Tom took on our behalf made him a much better man than me. I couldn't face the possibility that the victim became the victor, the clever one became a fool, and the abuser became the ultimate loser."

Arnie began to cry uncontrollably. It was obvious that he had become a silent victim of Bernard as well. Gloria put her arms around him and held him as he kept asking her for forgiveness and promising that he would find Tom no matter what it cost him.

"I don't know what to do, Mom!" Arnie exclaimed.

"There's only one thing you can do to be set free from your guilt, shame, and fear so you can discover who you are," Gloria softly replied.

In a muffled voice, he admitted, "I don't know how to be set free from these terrible chains in my life."

"There's only One who can set you free. He set Clarice free today, and He can set you free as well."

When Gloria mentioned Clarice's name, Arnie looked at her questioningly through tear-filled eyes. "Clarice was set free from what and how?" he asked.

Gloria stroked her son's hair. "Clarice was hurting and felt anger and guilt over various things. She needed to be healed, forgiven, and given a new lease on life. Today she received it and we talked about her working towards reconciliation with you. But, Arnie, things must change for not only her, but you if there's going to be true reconciliation."

Arnie's eyes became wide with hope. "I want that more than ever, Mom."

"There is only one way for reconciliation and that is through Jesus Christ. He's the only One who can bring hope and life to you and your marriage. But, my son, it's time to keep from hiding from your past and running from the fear of the present. It's time to turn around and face it all by looking into the glorious light of Jesus and receive His love, forgiveness, and life."

"Mom, I want to look into that light of Jesus and know that everything in my past, my present, and my future will be taken care of."

In that room another lost sheep was added to the fold of Jesus. Gloria was overwhelmed as she thought about the events that led up the Lord salvaging both Clarice and Arnie. Even though the truth was bittersweet, the sweetness of the Lord's presence in that room as Arnie humbly asked Jesus into his life was indescribable.

There was much to celebrate, not only the union of a special couple but two new souls being added to the kingdom of God.

***

Everyone was surprised to see Gloria walking arm in arm with Arnie into the restaurant's outdoor veranda. They were waiting for the last couple of stragglers to join the group before being seated for dinner.

Ken warmly welcomed Arnie and Ronny actually hugged his brother. Then the introductions began. Judson's family was warm and inviting. Gloria met his father and two sisters, all proving to be charming. She was introduced to grandparents, uncles, aunts, and cousins. She was given a seat by Judson's aunt Rachel, a woman of beauty and grace. Gloria began to interact with her, along with her adult and teenage children and grandchildren. Apparently the last people they were waiting on were Rachel's husband who was the pastor and was to officiate the couple's wedding. He was running behind because he had to pick up their youngest son from a sports activity.

In casual conversation, Gloria discovered that Rachel had five children. She was personally introduced to four of them. Three were married and two of them had a child each, while the third couple was newly married. She met their spouses and their two young children. They all seemed to take personal interest in her in spite of all the

493

activities going on around them. They all talked about various things as questions were asked followed by answers. Gloria even held one of the toddlers for a couple of minutes before she went back to her mother.

In the midst of the conversations, Gloria heard Judson jokingly say, "Well, the lost sheep have finally found their way here." Laughter followed as gaiety and expectation electrified the people on the veranda.

Since Gloria had a clear view of the entrance to the veranda, she looked up and giving a quick glance at Rachel's husband and son. As the husband walked in Gloria's quick glance became a double take as she realized there was something very familiar about him. As she focused in on him, her heart stopped as her hand flew to her mouth, muffling the name that was coming out of her mouth in disbelief. "Tom!"

Rachel's husband took several steps towards her, and then stopped within a few feet of her. He looked at her with a broad smile on his face. "Hello Mom."

Everything in the environment seemed to freeze, except Gloria. She leapt to her feet and ran to his opening arms. It was indeed Tom, thirty years older, but still touting features of his younger years. She clung to him as if she would never let him go, while looking up into his face to make sure it was not all just a dream.

"I'm not dreaming it's really you Tom?" she heard herself crying.

"Yes, it's really me, Mom. Tears streamed down his cheeks.

She became slightly aware that others were also sniffing, she looked at Ken who stood still in absolute shock. Then she looked over her shoulder to see Ronny and Arnie tears filling their eyes, mouths agape with astonishment.

When Tom looked up to see his two brothers, he said, "My arms are big enough for all of you." Then he extended his arms out to them and they both ran into them. Tears were now flowing as the three of them were encircled by his strong arms. Gloria was aware that she was surrounded by her three sons, becoming lost in unspeakable joy.

As the reality of everything was sinking in, she was reminded of some of the mothers of the Bible. She had known the bitterness of Naomi, the despair of Hannah, and the cutting sorrow of Mary. She had cried out to God, prayed silently under her breath, and admitted she did not deserve any real consideration from the Lord, but always reminding Him that He had entrusted her with a son who was now lost to her.

She had no idea that on that day, she would rejoice like Naomi, be blessed like Hannah, and see a type of resurrection of her son like Mary. In her mind, this only happened in fairy tales, but it was not a fairy tale; rather, it was the marvelous work of the Lord.

In the course of the evening, Gloria would learn how God began to connect the dots by using the prayers of a small adopted boy named Judson, who knew one of his favorite uncles missed his family but wasn't sure he would be welcome because of anger and hatred. That little boy was five years old when he began to pray about God uniting his Uncle Tom with his family and he never quit knocking on the door. He never would have guessed that almost a quarter of a century later his prayers would be answered and that the Lord would actually use him to connect vital dots.

Gloria watched as father and son met for the first time and embraced each other in the midst of tears and rejoicing. Ken was not only overwhelmed that his son knew about his real roots, but that he had legally changed his name to Jorgensen. Gloria remembered looking at her mother-in-law, seeing Edna's smile that was reminding her that God remains true to His word and promises, even if it means bringing it forth years later.

Gloria would never have imagined that she would meet Tom's wife, children, and grandchildren. She began to understand that her placement of being seated beside Rachel and her offspring at the restaurant, in direct line with the entrance of the veranda, was not by accident. Even though she had no idea who they were, they knew who she was.

The dinner at the restaurant was not only a celebration of a couple coming together in unity, but of a family being restored after three decades of separation. There were many questions to answer in order to cover many missing years, but that would not happen in one night. They could only trust that God would give them the days to rediscover what had been lost and cultivate what remained in a glorious way.

As she considered the tapestry before her, she realized that God had been working on it all the time. However, the unknown events that were happening elsewhere made the pattern invisible to her eyes. It was clear that the web that entangled the Heinrich's in despair and hopelessness had overshadowed much of the tapestry' pattern until God's penetrating light dissipated it. It became clear to Gloria that the pattern was there all along, and now it was being unveiled to her. She was amazed at its beauty.

As Gloria learned about the different highlights of Tom's life and family she realized that, as Brandon implied on that night twenty years ago when she received the gift of eternal life, that Tom was not lost, for God knew where he was. It was clear that Tom had been found by the great Shepherd over a quarter of a century ago. He was securely in the sheepfold when Brandon made the declaration.

She had always known that God's ways were not her ways and His plan embraced the whole of eternity, but it became cemented in her mind as she considered His order. As she watched the scene unfold before her, she began to recognize the omnipotent, omniscient ways of the Lord. Tom was not just used as a whipping boy to humble each member of the family, but he was also used as a tool to effectively whittle down the self-sufficiency and willful arrogance of the Heinrich's.

That is when Gloria realized she had it all wrong. In fact, she put the cart before the horse. As she followed God's pattern, she could clearly identify the wisdom and perfection of His ways. She was reminded that it's not the Lord's will that any perish, but all come to repentance, and if God had given way to her narrow focus, one son might have become lost forever. She shivered to think of how she might have overlooked the opportunity set before her as God's pattern was being made clearer to her. The missing son's location (Tom) could not be revealed until the lost son (Arnie) had finally been found by the great Shepherd and led home.

Awe came over her as part of a scripture in Revelation 15:3 burned in her soul, "Great and marvelous are thy works, Lord God Almighty; just and true are thy ways, thou King of saints."

*I press toward
the mark for the prize
of the high calling
of God in Christ Jesus.
(Philippians 3:14)*

The Calling

Rita Robertson had to turn the page of her life in order to start a new chapter. She was still struggling with turning the page, knowing she would only face a blank sheet that clearly marked the end of the latest chapter of her life. She didn't know what a new chapter would bring to her--calm waters, grave storms, or hurricane winds? However, she couldn't remain in limbo on the last page of the old chapter, while avoiding the new page of a new chapter. She had to accept that the pages of her life were being written by the ink of the Holy Spirit. It was clear that God had dipped His pen in the inkwell and was waiting for her to turn the next page so He could begin to write once again.

She was weary, and hoped that the lingering storm clouds on the horizon were ready to dissipate. She couldn't count the storms that had passed through her life, testing her character, weathering her resolve, redefining the terrain of her soul, and causing her to become desperate to seek the same refuge in each storm. It's not that she didn't know where her refuge could be found, it was the initial wrestling that took place in the buffeting winds of trials, gale waves of despair, and the outpouring of challenges that hit her from every direction before she could come to a place of refuge and peace.

She had long ago learned that the sun shines on everybody to bring blessings or purging, just as the storms of life will slam against one's resolve. She couldn't count the times that the winds had thrown her priorities up in the air to be blown away in the debris of failure, while the waves had taken her dreams and plans out into the depths to be seen no more, and her agendas were cast down in the quagmire of reality by the outpouring of consequences and judgment, only to be swallowed up in vanity and foolishness.

At times she was weary with the constant struggle of going against the current. All she ever wanted to do was serve the Lord. She had begun from the premise of small beginnings as she walked according to church protocol in light of training and preparation. As a new Christian she had started from sitting in the church pew soaking up God's Word to attending Bible Studies to grow in the knowledge of Jesus, and finally availing herself to every form of discipleship that was available. She had cleaned the church, assisted in Vacation Bible School, and eventually graduated to teaching Sunday school classes.

Although zealous and inexperienced in her initial years of salvation, her desire to become an effective servant of Christ was pure. She had recognized how Jesus had reached into the darkness of her despair and turned the light onto her stormy plight. It was the realization of her sin that caused her to seek salvation from the quagmire of hopelessness. She had cried to God for mercy and discovered His grace that freely flowed through the eternal life that came from the Lord Jesus Christ.

She vividly remembered the commencement of her spiritual journey to discover God. Like all wandering, lost sheep, she started out on the broad path of self-delusion, beginning from the premise of foolishness as a new high school graduate. She saw herself as being clever and was confident as she forged ahead on the path of self-sufficiency, while perceiving that she had the world by the tail. She calculated that she could begin as a receptionist in some legal office and receive hands-on experience while she took classes at a vocational school she enrolled in to become a legal secretary. It seemed as if life was lining up to her plans, especially after she found a job in a legal office as a file clerk.

She jumped into her new role with vigor. As things were falling into place, she perceived herself as conquering the world with her youthful strength and zeal. But, a couple of months into her job she was surprised to see that life had a way of changing directions. The change of direction came in the form of a man named Stewart Perkins.

Stewart had come into the office with his father seeking legal counsel concerning some business transaction. She happened to bump into him as she was coming out of one of the offices after delivering mail. She was immediately captivated by his mannerisms. He appeared to be a gentleman, charming, considerate, and attentive.

After their initial, encounter, she assumed they would never meet again, unless it was at her workplace. However, he pursued her by waiting for her outside of the building where he asked her out for coffee. From that point everything escalated into romance, passion, and what she later learned was fornication. Fornication led them to live together outside of marriage, a holy institution that had been sanctioned by God for the first parents in the Garden of Eden.

Although she thought it wasn't proper to live with a man unless they were married, she justified it with a familiar adage, "Everyone's doing it; therefore, it must be okay." Even though underneath she wished that marriage was in the equation, she was told by Stewart and her colleagues that such concerns were outdated and ridiculous. Stewart's excuse was that they needed this time together as a trial period to see if they were compatible. If they found they were compatible, then they could submit to the tradition of past generations and get married.

Stewart's logic resonated with her, and the idea of future marriage soothed her conscience. Their initial months together were wonderful. It seemed like they were on a perpetual honeymoon. In her mind, marriage was forthcoming. After all, it was apparent to her that they were very compatible.

When she did approach Stewart about marriage, he told her that it would take at least a year to find out if they were truly compatible. Before the first year anniversary came, problems started to raise their head in their relationship. They were not major problems, just irritations, but the romance began to wear off. Irritations disrupted harmony, which, in turn caused any assurance about a future marriage to float away with each irritation, and ended in nagging doubts about their compatibility, especially in the mind of Stewart.

In Rita's mind she figured they could work out the irritations, but as she tried to talk to Stewart about the effect these irritations had on their relationship, he become closed, and, at times, belligerent. Rita quickly surmised that it takes two to work out the kinks in relationships and that if the irritations are ignored, rather than put in proper perspective, that they'll grow into rogue waves that will eventually blindside people's relationships.

A year and a half into the relationship, Rita encountered such a rogue wave. Stewart came in and informed her he had found someone else and that it was time to part. He promptly took his clothes and left. Even though they were not married, they had purchased furniture and household items together, plus for her, there remained emotional ties that firmly tied her to him.

That night the storm raged in her soul. She was in a state of utter confusion and despair. Even though there was no marriage, a divorce of sorts was taking place for her. Perhaps it was not of a legal nature, but it was of an emotional one. There was division caused by ripping in her soul. It was not her idea to go separate ways, for she wanted to work out the relationship, but she realized an important element was missing from the equation and that was commitment on Stewart's part. Why would he care to work it out? He had all the free benefits without having to put any effort into the actual relationship that would eventually fail to live up to his expectations.

It was then that she realized that most people look through unrealistic glasses when it comes to romance and marriage. They are selfishly looking for that one right person who'll fit all of their criteria of a perfect mate. Selfishness is a lust that deals according to unrealistic expectations and becomes angry when not properly catered to, ever leaving destruction in its wake.

Rita admitted to herself that there was no way she could fit Stewart's standards any more than Stewart could fit all of her ideas, but the difference is she valued their relationship enough to work out the differences, while it became apparent if it didn't serve his purpose, he had no use for it. From this premise Rita recognized that it took something binding to force both individuals to work out a commitment. However, if there is no personal commitment present to see a relationship through regardless of the challenges, it would remain surface, preventing it from taking root in any fertile ground. Without roots, a relationship wouldn't withstand the deluge of irritations and endure the major storms of life that are bound to come when two people come together in a relationship.

Rita recognized that the majority of people could downplay marriage, make it obsolete, and logic it away, but the fruits being produced from the lack of such commitment proved they were mistaken. Marriage calls for a genuine pledge and is meant to establish boundaries that can force people to face their own level of commitment and discover whether they have inner integrity and the guts to make it work. If intimate relationships have no such boundaries, there would be no reason to ensure the relationship's integrity, and no real obligation to make it work as the road of least resistance will always be preferred and taken by those who have no moral strength or substance.

Stewart let her have all the furniture. It became clear to Rita that in his mind he was on to better things and didn't want to be bothered by such trivial matters as furniture and an old relationship. She wondered how many women he had lived with before her, always convincing them of the same lie. Whether it was all a sick game to him or whether he was looking for the right person, Rita could only guess, but she suspected that each relationship would prove to fall short of his expectations and he would end up going from woman to woman until he met a woman who played the game better than he did, or he finally became sick of settling for surface relationships.

Stewart also taught her that her gullibility about life and her abilities made her weak. Although wiser from her experience with him, she found herself to be emotionally weak. She didn't know if the emotional fallout was due to love for Stewart or whether it was because she had committed her heart to him. As she thought about their relationship, she realized that they had initially managed to sidestep the reality and drudgery found in such a relationship because they were swinging from the limbs of sensationalism.

Rita became aware of how sensationalism played a major role in their relationship. It allows people to operate in notions of fantasy about how something will make them feel. They want to always have that expectation of great romance, suspense, ecstasy, or excitement awaiting them around every bend or turn. However, Rita in her short time with Stewart realized that such notions signaled immaturity. She concluded that is why fantasies never go beyond the climax of the story because past it is the daily drudgery of simply living life and making the best out of the normalcy of everyday existence. It was clear to her that you cannot make an interesting story out of the drudgery of daily living.

As she considered the insatiable appetite of Americans for sensationalism, she could see why some easily get caught up with fantasy and sports. Through TV, books, and romanticizing different periods of history, Americans had been conditioned to become bored with normalcy and set up to seek out things that would make their fantasies come alive.

As she waded through the debris of her relationship with Stewart, she made a decision that if a man couldn't put enough value on a relationship with her by making a binding commitment to it, she needed to let go of the relationship.

It was a little over six months after her situation with Stewart that she met Michael Carr. She had gone with some friends to the bowling alley, and he was part of the group. He was a soldier who was stationed at an army base in another community located 20 miles away. The two of them began to talk and found that they had a lot in common.

Michael had also been burned in a past relationship, and as a result they both decided to start out slow. After taking what they both perceived to be slow advances, the relationship seemed to be kicked into high gear when he was informed that he would soon be given orders to South Korea. Michael and Rita began to seriously talk about marriage, but Michael wanted to wait until his first tour was over before he made such a commitment to her. They tearfully kissed each other goodbye on the day of his departure.

Michael never made it back. He was mysterious killed on the border of South Korea and North Korea. There was no real explanation for his death, leaving a door open for speculation and deep sorrow that could not be reached. Rita knew some sorrow with the breakup with Stewart, but the sorrow over losing her true love went so deep, it took her very breath away. She had memories of their relationship, but she felt she had somehow been deprived of expressing her love in the deepest way possible to him. In her mind, that meant totally giving herself to him.

She felt complete confusion as she wrestled with her erected standard not to accept crumbs from a man. Rita had wanted to do what was right in her relationship with Michael, but she felt cheated. Even though underneath she knew they had been honorable as a couple, she wondered why the way of moral uprightness left her feeling robbed.

It was at this time the loss of Michael threw her into depression. She could hardly function. She was struggling with her remaining classes and pushing herself through work to such a point that it was becoming noticeable.

It was at this time that other notions about life began to fall to the wayside. Rita found her unrealistic notions about life and her abilities were eventually slammed to the ground by disillusionment and totally overlooked and ignored by indifference from others.

She found this true and even more so at her workplace. Clearly, her bosses and co-workers were not as impressed with her abilities as she thought they would be. She also discovered that most of the people at work didn't take an interest in the personal matters of others unless you were part of the gossip that seemed to give the few friendships that existed a morsel that could be temporarily enjoyed and then spit out. For the most part, people seemed like robots that mechanically kept the rest of the office functioning as they went through their daily routines. As the harsh reality of life and people closed in on her, she noted that the world around her began to subdue her as it challenged her weak character and exposed the last abyss of her silly notions.

Initially, she had thought herself to be clever enough to manipulate people, but her relationship with Stewart, as well as some of the people she worked with, proved how her evaluation of herself was overrated by inexperience and immaturity. She quickly learned she was not as smart as she previously thought. Her attempts to secure life as she viewed it were descending into confusion and failure as she realized that she was powerless to bring about matters according to her terms. Everywhere she turned, she experienced some type of sorrow and loss. Nothing was as she thought it to be, and everything was not what it seemed to be. It all became a confusing mess to her.

Rita knew she was being consumed by her depression, but she couldn't pull herself up by her own bootstraps. She knew her attitude was bad, her thoughts chaotic and morbid, and her conclusions lacked stability and reason. However, she couldn't seem to stop her descent into darkness. The nothingness of the darkness made her feel as if she was becoming lost in a hopeless reality that had no end to it.

Rita knew that at such times, religion had become the answer for some people, but she had no real religious background. She was conditioned by her family to be suspicious of any show of kindness from a religious group. She was taught to believe that church-goers were hypocritical and possessed unsavory agendas. She was convinced by her parents' logic that these stoic people were only interested in putting notches on their belts while growing the memberships of their churches and bank accounts.

Yet in the darkness of the night she realized she had no one else to call out to. She remembered saying, "God if you are there and really care about me, show Yourself to me." For some reason she found comfort calling out in the night to this unseen entity, and even had fallen asleep.

The next day when she was in at the college in a restroom, she sat down on the couch to check her cell phone for messages and happened to see a religious tract sitting with other magazines on an end table. She picked it up and started leafing through it. She was shocked to discover that it pointed out some poignant truths about life, and described her plight. The beauty of it was that it not only pointed out the obvious about man's hopeless plight, but it offered the solution. It had to do with receiving Jesus Christ.

As she read about receiving Christ a light of hope began to dawn on the outer fringes of her mind. Rita began to understand what it said, but in another way she knew it was the beginning of something much bigger and far reaching. She realized that there were things that were not right in her life, but she didn't see such discrepancies as sins. She knew there was darkness on her soul, but she didn't realize it was because she was separated from God, left hopeless to struggle in a doomed state. As the light increasingly illuminated her plight, she realized that she was lost in her state, and separated from God because of her sin.

Rita carefully followed the prayer that was outlined in the back of the small booklet. She didn't feel any real change, but she sensed something was being awakened in her that she couldn't explain. She looked on the back of the tract and found an address of a church and decided she was going to attend the church, seeking answers to the questions that were forming in her mind.

She looked the church up on the internet for their schedule and decided she was going to make sure she was there when the doors opened. She had to know more about this Jesus and understand what it meant to be saved.

Initially Rita went to church to observe, but instead she was greeted by people who actually showed an interest in her. In fact, a woman asked if she was by herself. When Rita acknowledged that she was, the woman, Denise Lowry invited her to sit with her.

Denise helped Rita through the worship songs, which Rita enjoyed, and took a Bible out of the pew and opened it to the text of John 8 where the preacher would be speaking from. Secretly, Rita was glad for Denise. She kept her from feeling and looking foolish.

As the pastor spoke about some woman caught in adultery, Rita felt that a light was pushing away the darkness that enfolded her soul. She realized she was that woman and rightfully deserved to be stoned. Granted, the other guilty party was not standing with her, but that didn't matter. She alone would stand completely stripped by her sin before her judges and answer for her own wrongdoings.

When the pastor got to the part about Jesus, Rita really began to take note. What would Jesus do with this woman? Would He remain silent, agree with the religious people, or be the first person to pick up a stone. His action of writing in the dirt, created a curiosity in her. What was the purpose of Him writing in the dirt?

She remembered a saying that was used a few times when she was in trouble, "Your name is mud." She acknowledged that Jesus was writing in the dirt and not the mud, but how easy it would be for the dirt to become mud by adding a bit of water. She realized her imagination was getting away from her but she quickly looked at the other prospects. Whatever He was writing would either be trampled underfoot by others or wiped away by the wind. Clearly, His etchings in the dust would not remain long, but whatever He was writing meant something to the religious leaders who stood in judgment of the woman, and who were trying to test Him.

When the pastor read the words of Jesus, Rita realized what His heart was towards that woman. He didn't stand in judgment of her; rather, He wanted to give her a way out of tasting the consequences for her action by changing the focus from her to her accusers, "He that is without sin among you, let him first cast a stone at her."

Rita wouldn't forget the words of the pastor, "We are all sinners, unable to rightly judge others. These men stood condemned before Jesus just like this woman, but He didn't come to condemn them but to save all who would believe upon Him.

"According to Roman Law, these religious leaders didn't have the authority to put her to death. If Jesus had agreed with them about stoning her, He would be breaking the Roman Law, but if He didn't stand with the religious leaders, He would've been breaking His own Law given to Moses. The truth is these men didn't care about this poor woman's plight, because they were after Jesus. However, Jesus cared about this woman, for He cares for every naked soul who stands before Him in need of mercy, forgiveness, and deliverance.

"Jesus was God, and took on flesh to meet individuals like this poor woman because He came to save such poor souls from the judgment pronounced on all sin, that of eternal separation from their Creator. What Jesus was saying to these men is that since they stood in the place as her judges, it was up to them to carry out the sentencing, but first they must make sure there was no sin in their own lives that would later cause them to stand in judgment.

"We all start out like this woman, but some of us become self-righteous and take on the role of accuser, judge, and executioner of others. Such people place poor souls such as this woman in the market place of public opinion in order to exonerate themselves as authorities on spiritual and moral matters. Some of us are like Jesus, we do not want to see people taste the judgment of sin; rather, we want them to know what it means to be forgiven and restored back to a place of uprightness before God. We want them to have another chance in order to change their direction to obtain the life that God desires for them.

"Jesus will silence all such accusers in the end. That is why when her accusers left her standing before Him, He asked, 'Woman, where are thine accusers? hath no man condemned thee?'

"The woman answered, "No man, Lord.' Imagine what she was saying: That there were no men to accuse her, but she recognized that she stood before the One who could rightfully judge her when she called Jesus "Lord." Her sinful actions had made it clear that she had been unfaithful as a Jewish handmaiden and dishonorable as a servant in the household of her God. Jesus confirmed that He was the ultimate Judge when He stated that the Father entrusted Him with all judgment.

"Consider Jesus' words, 'Neither do I condemn thee: go, and sin no more.' Jesus had no desire to judge her, but she needed to cease her sinful activities by repenting and turning from her ways. From that moment on, she had to believe His Word and walk out what she knew was right and honorable to avoid the future judgment that will come upon this world.

"There is something I want you to consider. There are various places where our names can be written on legal documents, letters, plaques, and stone. We know that such places will be temporary, either destroyed in time, burned up, discarded, or broken and buried. The Bible speaks of a couple of other places our names can be written.

"The first place I want to direct your attention to is found in Jeremiah 17:13, "O LORD, the hope of Israel, all that forsake thee shall be ashamed, and they that depart from me shall be **written in the earth**, because they have forsaken the LORD, the fountain of living waters." Jesus could have been writing the names of these religious people in the dirt, signifying that they have departed from the living God and that they were subject to the winds of judgment that would come forth and erase their names for all eternity.

"Today there are those who have forsaken the Lord to go their own way. They might wear religious garb but their hearts are far away from God. They might show an outward piousness, but they are full of dead men's bones of activities that have no life to them, teachings that have no spirit, and ideas and beliefs that are void of truth. They may tout of their accomplishments and influences in this present world, but they will not be recognized by the Lord of lords in the next world as belonging to His kingdom.

"The second place our names can be written is in the Book of Life. Revelation 20:15 says, 'And whosoever was not found written in the book of life was cast into the lake of fire.' Will your name be found in the book of life? If you know Jesus because you have received Him into your life as Lord and Savior, your name will be preserved and kept visible and legible in the Book of Life. You will be spared from His wrath to come and will be identified by the seal of the Holy Spirit in your life as one who has the right to experience the fullness of redemption.

"As a servant of God I appeal to you to make sure of your standing with God. Make sure you are part of the elect, the bride of

Christ. The Bible tells us names are actually blotted out of the Book of Life. I don't know if that means before the very foundation of the world every person's name was written in the Book of Life, and at the end of his or her life if he or she fails to receive the gift of life, that person's name would then be blotted out at that time. If so, everyone here needs to make sure that your name is securely established in the Book of Life because you truly possess the Holy Spirit of life.

"Right now I want to invite anyone and everyone to come forward. If you want to make sure of your election as far as belonging to the kingdom of God, come up and stand to my right and if you want to rededicate or do business with the Lord because you have been standing on the outer fringes of a lukewarm life of half-hearted commitment, stand on my left."

Rita knew what she must do, and was thankful when Denise's voice broke through, "Would you like me to go forward with you?"

Rita shook her head yes. Denise gently took her arm and guided her to the front. As they came closer to the front Rita went to the pastor's right. She had said the prayer that was written in the small tract, but she wanted to make sure her standing before God was right and sure.

There were many people who came forward that day. There were other people who also came to help the pastor with the seeking souls who were standing in front. The pastor began to assign different people to those waiting for intervention. As the pastor passed before the group, he looked directly at Rita and Denise. He smiled at Rita, and then at Denise, "Denise, take this precious soul aside and pray with her. She is most assuredly ready to be translated into the kingdom of God's dear Son."

That day, Rita was assured of being born again with the Spirit of the Living God, infused with the everlasting life of Jesus. She felt the heavy weights of sin, sorrow, grief, and loss lift off of her soul. She felt like an eagle soaring on some incredible current, lifting her above the present world, giving her a sense of the glorious world that was yet to come.

Although she was still very much earthbound by her body, for the next couple of days she sensed the lightness of her spirit that could easily soar upward and a soul that was free to explore the heights of God. It was all so glorious, but she eventually had to land on the runway of daily living, and she wasn't sure what to do with her new experience.

Denise had given Rita her card. She could see that she was part of a ministry and decided she could advise her as to what was next in her Christian experience. She called the phone number on the card and was relieved that Denise answered the phone. She reminded Denise who she was and asked if they could get together for lunch. Denise was excited to hear from her and agreed to meet her for lunch.

The next day they met for their scheduled luncheon. Rita could hardly wait to ask her what was next in her new journey. Instead of resorting to small talk to prepare the way for serious conversation, Denise went right to the heart of the matter. "How are you doing spiritually in your new life in Christ?"

Rita sighed. "I'm so glad you asked that question, because I really don't know what to do. I was wondering if you could give me some guidelines?"

Denise studied Rita before speaking. "It depends."

Rita was puzzled, "What do you mean it depends?"

"Well, Rita it depends on how serious and committed you are to walk the Christian walk. The Christian life is not a religious practice but a disciplined walk that must be hedged in by love for God, the leading of the Spirit, and the Lordship of Jesus. Love of and for God comes only in a daily life of worship and fellowship with Him and the leading of the Spirit only can occur from the point of humility and submission. Making Jesus Lord only comes from the premise of faith towards God and obedience to His Word within the confines of what we call true discipleship."

Rita's blue eyes widened. "I thought the Christian life is free. I don't understand."

"Rita, your salvation is free because you couldn't obtain it on your own. In order for redemption to be secure for you God gave His best, His Son; and, Jesus gave His all, His life, but possessing that life for yourself is up to you. The Christian life is all about coming to what we call full age or maturity in our walk before the Lord. The more we grow in our understanding, relationship, and life in the Lord, the more we will be able to possess, or inherit, the promises of the Christian life.

"Spiritual maturity involves a process. The real goal of the Christian life is to know God in an intimate way. The cost to us to know God will include those things that have no eternal value or significance to them. It is for this reason that Jesus calls us into a life of self-denial and carrying our cross so that we can follow Him.

"Self-denial brings us to the core of the problem which is confronting our attitudes, and our personal cross is to deal with our dependency on the world. It is because of the influence of the world upon our 'old, self-life' that we have put some value on the insignificant. In order to confront these various worldly, selfish dependencies, they must first be exposed. It is then that we will come face-to-face with our heart motives, selfish agendas, silly dreams and notions, and foolish priorities."

"Christianity sounds hard," Rita responded.

"Rita, I'm not going to lie to you. The Christian life is not for the faint of heart or those who will not allow their character to be tested and refined by the various elements of life. There will be times of blessings but there will be times of testing by storms, refining pressures, fiery trials, intense temptations, and the purging heat of life. Regardless of the new life in us we are not immune from tasting the sorrow and bitterness of this present world. But, you need to know that no matter what element or challenge comes your way, God allows it for personal growth and in the end it will prove beneficial and glorious to you."

"What am I to do?" Rita asked.

"You must first learn to rest in the Lord because of His love by choosing the way of faith. Faith will help you to learn to crawl as you acquire a child-like trust towards Him. Once you start crawling in faith by being obedient to what you know is scripturally right, then you can learn to stand on His unfailing promises. Promises will strengthen you in an actual walk with the Lord. As you learn to walk by genuine faith, then you will learn to run the race to possess the glorious prize that is attached to that life."

"The prize?" Rita questioned.

"The prize is that of a greater revelation of Jesus Christ. He is referred to as the great treasure in earthen vessels in 2 Corinthians 4:7. It means putting on or applying His life in all you do, thereby, assimilating His life more and more into who you are in order to be more like Him, reflecting His glory."

"This all seems overwhelming," Rita replied.

"That is because I am presenting the whole picture to you," Denise responded. "You're the type who wants to know the game plan up front so you can honestly consider whether you are willing to give your all or not. If I gave you the impression that the Christian life was all fluff, you would not see the value in it."

Rita shook her head in agreement. She wanted to know the score. In one way she was excited about the road ahead of her, knowing that it would be a learning, growing experience, but on the other hand, sobriety was clearly present at the prospect of it being a disciplined life that must be worked in her by godly ways that could only be acquired through discipleship.

"Rita, you need to learn to first enjoy the Father's love by reading His Word and praying. You must also faithfully attend church and Bible Studies. However, your greatest growth will come when you develop an inner sanctuary where you learn to meet with the Lord daily and commune with Him in a time of intimate worship. The greatest teacher is the Holy Spirit. He will bring truth and life to the things you learn in those quiet times of seeking the Lord, meditating on His Word, and asking Him to teach you those things that will prepare you to follow and serve Him, while transforming your inner life to reflect more of the life of Jesus.

"It's vital Rita, for you to realize it's not you that will do this transforming work, it will be the Holy Spirit in you. The key is learning to humble yourself before that which is godly in example, while clearly proving to be contrary to the self-life. You must be willing to submit to the Spirit's leading when it proves uncomfortable to the old way, and do what is Scripturally right when it goes against the grain of what was natural for you in the past, while keeping in mind if the Lord does not bring about a change, then it's not a transforming change that identifies you to heaven. You must remember at all times that it's His work, His life, and His plan; therefore, it's not what you do for Him that will ultimately count; rather, it's what you allow Him to do in and through you."

Rita was beginning to see that the real key was to let God be God in her life, but it was apparent that it was not a simple process. "It seems simple enough, but yet by some of the things you say, it will prove hard, difficult, and overwhelming."

"It is, Rita, because it entails a battle between the Spirit of God and your flesh. The unusual path you are about to embark on will seem strange at first to what we call the 'old disposition,' but the new man must eventually become natural to you before you see the excellence of God's ways and experience the fullness of the Spirit's fruit in your life.

"Your flesh must be denied daily by you of its right to have life on its terms. You must then crucify it to the influence of the world before you can ensure a singleness of heart in following Jesus. The Christian life will go against everything you are used to, be contrary to everything you now know, and challenge everything that seems natural, making you become peculiar to those who belong to the world."

"What do I need to beware of?" Rita asked.

"The first trap is getting caught up with good things that become more important than the Lord and your relationship with Him."

"What kind of traps?" Rita inquired.

"Getting caught up with serving a church, rather than serving Jesus, idolizing a religious leader, rather than worshipping and following Jesus, relying on religious works instead of fruits to test the quality of your Christian life, majoring in knowing doctrine, rather than knowing Jesus. Relying on any personal strength; rather than humbling yourself before the Lord to find out what He wants you do. In Christianity, everything that is considered good can become a bad substitute in your life with the Lord, and only you can test yourself.

"I have seen three different responses from new Christians. The initial response has to do with those who intellectually respond to the Gospel. They are glad that they are now saved and see it as a type of fire insurance that is able to keep them. They have no initiative to go any further in their Christian growth. They go back into the world without giving Jesus too much consideration, and will occasionally tack Him on when it's convenient to do so.

The second response comes from new Christians who display zeal. These Christians may even have a sense as to their calling, but they have no knowledge of God's righteousness. They often become discouraged in their walk and disillusioned with God when the zeal wears off and the challenges of the Christian life start confronting them because they don't as yet have the character to stand against it nor have they been trained to stand on the correct foundation.

"The third group is made up of those who are excited about the Lord, want to serve Him, and seek the church or religious influence in which to discover or accomplish these desires. It is in such environments that people soak in important instructions and seek opportunities to learn what it means to serve, but such things can only lead a person as far as the beliefs, visions, or traditions those of the church hold to. It's not unusual to hit some unseen ceiling that keeps such individuals from discovering greater heights in the Lord. It's for this reason that church-going Christians can easily fall into three other categories.

"The first category Christians fall into is that of being an ornament that sits in the pew every Sunday. They are there to receive what they can, but have no intention of going any further because it is a tradition to them.

"The second one is the dutiful Christian. These individuals see Christianity as a duty, and part of that duty involves looking the look, talking the talk, attending church, paying tithes, and doing good-deeds to appear pious, but they deny the power that enables them to walk the walk that brings life to their religion.

"The third group is those who want to be followers of Christ and realize that sometimes He leads them away from comfortable pews, set traditions, and dutiful ways to bring them into their higher calling. Such people learn what it means to follow after the Spirit as they learn to be led by Him in order to walk in their life and high calling. You can read about such people in Hebrews 11. These are the people that will obtain a greater witness, and in some cases a witness the world is not even worthy of seeing."

Everything Denise was saying, was penetrating Rita like a sharp instrument. She knew it was true, and she wanted to be part of the third group to make sure her life counted for something. Once again she realized that the Christian life was no picnic. Clearly, it required simple submission, but wasn't easy because of the sinful ways of the old life. The new life was free but it also entailed a process that was hard, but ultimately would prove glorious.

It was then that Rita allowed Denise to see inside of her heart, "Denise, I have always felt I had a destiny, but I never understood it. I've tried to pursue this destiny according to what I thought, but all my past pursuits left me feeling empty, while my emotional quests have left me broken hearted." She paused, "And, until now I was void of any spiritual desire."

Denise smiled, "Rita, you have a glorious destiny, but to advance towards it you need to keep in mind that you'll always be walking towards your demise, the demise of the 'old man,' so the new man, Christ, can be resurrected in you, as well as the demise of the influence of the 'world' upon your soul, so that only the heavenly will be leading you. Finally, there is the demise of the right of the self-life so that Jesus can truly be Lord of your life. It's death to the old so that the great exchange with the new can completely take place. But, the 'old man' in us always refuses to go quietly.

"As you deny him his claims on you, he will try to convince you he's not so bad and that there are some good things that can be salvaged from the old way. But, you must keep in mind that there is nothing good in the old man and his very best is considered filthy rags before a holy God.

"When you apply the cross to the ways of the 'old man,' he will try to convince you that he can be reformed, made acceptable to God; therefore, you don't have to take such drastic measures. But, the truth is he's a coward, a snake in the grass, and he always will be what he always has been, an enemy of your soul. He must be mortified daily.

"When you nail his fleshly appetites to the cross to ensure that they cannot be tempted by the world, he'll declare that you are

514

depriving yourself of the one avenue where you can experience the wondrous pleasures of life. But, you must keep in mind everything the 'old man' touches he perverts and defiles in order to entrap you into lies and destruction. He is self-absorbed with his own so-called 'goodness,' selfish about his own ways, self-centered about who he thinks he is, and self-serving in what he does. He is a traitor and enemy to God and totally unfaithful in his motives, agendas, and priorities."

Rita's wondrous experience of flying high was now making a crash landing on the runway of reality. It was a sobering and abrupt landing, but one she asked for. She didn't want to flit according to unrealistic expectations, flutter in unsubstantiated ecstasy, and bounce along on the flimsy wings of fantasy, only to hit the end of such immature foolishness and fall from the heights of silliness to the hard ground of actuality.

She looked at Denise and in a flustered tone asked the obvious, "How will I know what to do?"

Denise looked at her and with a serene smile responded in a most simple way, "You can find everything you need to know in the Bible. Just make sure when you approach It, you do so in genuine faith as a seeker, who desires to know, love, and obey His truth."

***

Rita shook her head as she realized that the conversation had taken place over 20 years ago. Denise not only was her mentor through all those years, but they had become great friends. Denise had shared some good times with her, walked with her through some very bad times, and supported her through the challenging times.

Through the years Rita realized that she had fallen into every trap and taken every detour Denise had warned her of on that day so long ago. At one time the church did become her cause leaving her empty, the pastor her idol leaving her disappointed, her good works her temperature gauge leaving her judgmental, and initially she often lost various battles with the "old man" to only discover he was a liar and coward at best and an enemy of God and her soul at worst.

Every time Rita failed a test, Denise's words would replay in her mind as the Holy Spirit illuminated the passage of Scripture that dealt with the matter. Rita had wondered why she had to experience the failure of each lesson before she could learn it. She had to question whether she was smart enough or wise enough to recognize the test, but in due time she realized that for the most part she had been

515

blinded to the test by her immaturity and lack of experience, and that each failure was a humbling experience that allowed her to truly learn the lesson.

Sometimes she had to go around the same mountain more than once to learn the same lesson. She even asked Denise about it. Denise explained to her the reason a person goes around the mountain more than once is because the individual doesn't recognize the terrain. Every bend or twist in the path produces a different type of terrain. Since the terrain is different, it's natural that people don't recognize that they are being tested to see if they really have learned the previous lesson.

It was then that Denise explained to her about discernment. Every lesson the Lord presents must be properly discerned in relationship to what He is trying to show the person as far as his or her character, or enlarging the person as to his or her faith. The goal is the same. The Lord wants a person to trust Him with the details of his or her life, but he or she must pull "self" back from impulsively walking in the untested way without first coming under the leading of the Spirit.

Christians fail to recognize personal assumptions and presumptions on their part when it comes to their Christian walk. Many decide the way they will walk without first seeking the Lord, assuming He will bless them because He has been tacked on to their activities, while presuming He will be in it. Like Jesus' parents in Luke 2 during the Passover when He was twelve, this is when Christians leave Him behind, because they fail to first check to see if He was even with them.

Even though Rita finished her schooling and had secured a job as a legal secretary for a respected law firm, she was still very much a babe in Christ, wrestling with the fleshly aspects of her attitudes, ways, and practices. For the first three years of her Christianity, she found herself failing each test at every turn. Her flesh seemed to rage against denial, her pride scoffed at not giving it the proper audience, and the old man was always crying foul against being nailed to the cross. The battle was fierce at times, overwhelming at others, and despairing when she gave way to their logic and cries. Each time she failed to put them in their perspective place as a disciple of Christ, she felt hollow and restless.

In the third year of her journey, she met Len Robertson. He started to attend her church. He was seventeen years her senior, divorced, and the father of a boy, Guy and a girl, Teresa. She later learned he had custody of the children because their mother had proven abusive to all three of them.

Len was a gentle man who loved the Lord, but his life with his wife had been hard and difficult. He had married her thinking she was a Christian, but within a couple of months into their marriage her true character came to the surface. She was an angry woman. At first she controlled it, but eventually after having two children close together it became a full blown rage that would fly at him with a vengeance.

After each fit of rage she would show remorse and plead for help. In desperation, he took her to various Christian counselors and psychiatrists seeking help. There he discovered the terrible secret of her life. She had been physically abused by her father, molested by an uncle, and felt rejected by her mother. She was a hurting individual who needed healing.

She had various diagnoses, manic depression, bipolar, and schizophrenia and was put on prescription drugs, but she became addicted to some of them reducing her to a zombie. Her addiction caused a whole new set of problems as she spent days in bed and went into fits of anger when she didn't get the amount of pills she wanted to escape reality.

Christian counseling seemed to help for a season and then something would set her off into a tyrannical rage and the nightmare pattern would begin again. Eventually the nightmares ended in the same remorse, but each time the pattern started it would last longer and it seemed her heart was becoming colder and more indifferent to the hellish environment she was creating for her family.

For the most part Len took the brunt of her rage, thinking he was protecting the children. However, in one of her tirades she threatened to kill him and the children, grabbed a kitchen knife and attacked him. In the scuffle she cut his hand, but he was able to subdue her while Teresa called 911. She was taken to the hospital and put in the psych ward for evaluation and kept there for a couple of weeks.

She pleaded with Len to take her home. She promised to be better, but she could only hold it together for a couple of weeks before the same pattern started all over. One day he came home and found nine-year-old Guy black and blue where his mother had hit him and eight-year-old Teresa in complete hysterics because of what she witnessed happening to her brother. Len made a decision at that point that he needed to take his children out of that environment to protect them and salvage their own souls from the abuse of their mother.

He packed them up as their mother looked on and pleaded with him to give her another chance as she hugged Guy and asked him for forgiveness, telling him how much she loved him. Even though the children were crying to stay with their mother and give her another chance, Len braced himself against feeling sorry for her for the sake of his children. He then told her that she needed to get whatever help was necessary to resolve this problem and until then he needed to protect their children from her unpredictable, demonic tirades.

Rita admired Len for his commitment to his wife. He had stuck with her ten long years before seeking a separation from her. He had taken abuse from her, but would not stand by and allow his children to experience such abuse. Once she physically touched either child that was the signal for him to leave the situation.

For the first couple of months, Len held tightly to his wife being desperate enough to get the necessary help, but her pattern remained the same. Her initial attempts to get help were temporary. When she was forced to face the rawness and violent anger attached to her past, she clammed up and fled to her room to avoid facing the emotional pain. At that moment she would sign herself out of the program regardless of how much others tried to talk her out of it to flee to their home and call Len to complain about the program. He in turn would try to locate another program for her to participate in with the same results.

For Len it was an emotional roller coaster. He was becoming weary with it and felt for his own sanity that he had to get off of the ride. As he signed her up for one of the last programs available to her, he told her for her sake she needed to see it through because there was nothing more he could do to help her. She once again pleaded with him to be patient and promised that she would see it through. However, within a couple of weeks she followed the same pattern as usual. She was back home calling Len to complain about the program.

He told her she was on her own and it was apparent that she was not desperate enough to get help or she would have been helped a long time ago. In spite of her usual pleas Len stood his ground and maintained that when she was desperate enough to really face her demons, then she would seek out the necessary help and finally see healing through to the end.

Len admitted to her he had learned a very important lesson from her—that a person won't seek personal help for the sake of others such as family members because they are too selfish and self-centered; therefore, until they are desperate and sick enough of their plight to seek help for themselves nothing will ever change. It was clear that she wasn't ready to get help because she was content to live on the edges of insanity so she could excuse herself from being healed to deal with reality. He admitted that he didn't understand why she loved her sickness so much, but he wasn't about to let her sickness drag their children or him into her insane pit of self-destruction.

After Len's speech her pleading turned into rage. She accused him and the children of being her problem and that without them she would be just fine. Len hung up on her and that very day filed divorce papers.

It was during the divorce proceedings that Len and Rita began to develop a friendship. She taught the Sunday school class that Teresa was in. She took a personal liking to the young girl who seemed sad and uncertain. As she developed a relationship with Teresa, she also became acquainted with her brother, Guy. As her relationship grew with both of the siblings, she eventually introduced them to their need for salvation. Both were receptive and it was then that she led them through the sinner's prayer.

Guy had charming qualities but she could tell there was an anger behind him that if not confronted could prove to be destructive to him. She felt Teresa was more transparent and was tenderer towards the Lord. However, as she developed a relationship with the Robertson siblings, it became an avenue in which she also formed a friendship with Len.

The two adults found that they had the same level of commitment to the Lord and a deep desire to serve Him in some way. In spite of age differences and the fact that Len took steps to ensure he would have no more children, a romance bloomed after the divorce was final and both admitted that they were in love with one another. It was not long after the admission, that with the approval of the children, they were married in a quiet ceremony.

Since the children would be at school during the day, Rita kept her job but made sure she was home when Guy and Teresa came home from school. She also took them to their various school activities.

Len became a stable pillar to her in her Christian growth. His steadiness caused her to stay on course of a more disciplined life. Being an inexperienced mother of pre-teen children also had it challenges, but Len brought a stability there as well in the form of reason and advice.

For the most part she loved the children and they liked her. She didn't strive to take the place of their mother, but she knew she had to somehow hold a line of authority in the house. She realized that both children had raw places where their mother was concerned that caused much confusion to them as to their loyalty and attitude towards her. As a result, there were some touch-and-go moments in her relationship with them that could have proved to be destructive to the family unit, but after much prayer and submission to the Word of God on Rita's part, some destructive snares were avoided as truth and reason reigned.

As a couple, Len and Rita fit together like a hand in glove, but as a family they struggled through some major growing pains. Rita didn't know what she was getting herself into when she agreed to marry Len as far as the children were concerned, but she felt the four of them, Len, Rita, the Lord, and His Word presented a powerful tie that couldn't easily be thwarted if they were humble and submissive before the Lord.

A major crisis came to the family when Guy was 16 and Teresa 15. Their mother had supervised visitations with them. When the house was sold due to the divorce decree, she moved into an apartment. Her life seemed to straighten up and she even found a boyfriend. They were later married. Due to her conduct, it was determined by the court that Guy and Teresa could visit her at her apartment without close supervision.

Guy appeared solemn after visiting his mother and Teresa seemed confused. When questioned, they admitted that for the most part their mother acted normal and they wondered why she didn't act that way when she lived with them.

One day the police brought them home. Apparently there had been a situation in which their mother's present husband caught her doing something inappropriate with Guy. Teresa was watching TV when their mother called Guy into the bedroom to help her with something. Teresa didn't notice her mother close the door behind Guy, but within minutes her husband, who unexpectedly came home, caught her in a compromising situation with Guy.

Guy exited the bedroom embarrassed as a loud confrontation took place between their mother and her husband. It ended with her flying into a rage and attacking him, and the police were called. The whole incident was explained to the police. As a result, their mother was taken to jail in handcuffs and charged with assaulting her husband and felony molestation of her minor son.

That was the first time Len seemed to unravel. The thought of his son being compromised in an inappropriate way by his mother was hard to swallow. He tried to talk to Guy about it and found out it was not the first time that it had happened, but Guy only commented that she was lonely and needed to know someone cared, and acted as if it was no big deal. Len had known that his former wife had been capable of various things, but he never imagined that she was capable of such acts. He was literally sick to his stomach and wrestled with overwhelming feelings of anger towards his former wife.

However, the tragedy wasn't over with. While in police custody, their mother was presented with the evidence and charges. She faced at least twenty years in prison. That night she hung herself in her jail cell using a combination of her sheets and clothing. She left the world the same way she came in, naked and exposed.

It was a bitter pill for Len and the children to swallow, while Rita found herself at a loss as to how to comfort and counsel them. Len was fighting with anger, unforgiveness and regret. Guy became more withdrawn into an unknown place of introspection, while Teresa became emotionally distraught with occasional outbursts of guilt and despair.

Rita found herself on her face before the Lord. She knew that her family was facing one of its darkest times. It seemed that the heavens were silent, but Rita knew the Lord heard her prayers and that He was a breath away from her. She wrestled before Him as to the "whys" of the matter looking for some kind of answer that would bring peace to the tumultuous souls around her, but the only answer she received was, "Be still and know that I am God."

She knew it was not a platitude to be still because there was nothing she could do to change the dynamics of the situation. Only God could bring any type of order, peace, and healing to the Robertson's upside-down world.

Len eventually groped his way through the dark valley. He later admitted that the Lord had taken his hand and guided him through the long dark night of the soul. He eventually let go of his anger, forgave his former wife, and made peace with the situation by letting God replace his regret with the knowledge that if he could have changed the circumstances or foreseen the future, proper action would have been taken. He had also asked the Lord to heal Guy and Teresa.

Teresa went through various emotional upheavals. She didn't know how to feel about her mother, and whenever she came face to face with her feelings, she felt guilty, especially when she felt rage towards her instead of forgiveness. She suffered from guilt when feelings of betrayal gripped her, instead of feeling pity and compassion for her mother's state. Guilt condemned her when she felt resentment towards her mother for not being there rather than understanding the situations in lieu of her mother's past. She felt ashamed because she was blind to what her mother was doing to her brother. One type of emotion after the other clung to her like a vice grip to the point that, as she later admitted, it almost made her feel insane at times.

When she was asked about what was happening to her she didn't know where to start or how to describe her ordeal. Every time inquiry was made she would break down into tears. She couldn't talk to her father because she knew he was hurting. She felt she had let her brother down and never felt the liberty to talk to him, and she was ashamed to talk to a friend or someone in the church because it was overwhelming.

Rita could tell that Teresa needed to let go of all of her pent up feelings so she could wade through the fallout of her life and make some kind of peace with it through forgiveness. Rita feared if she didn't let it go that she would eventually have a nervous breakdown. She prayed for an opening to speak into her life so she could give her some way to release all of her feelings without fear of being judged.

One day Rita was busy in the kitchen trying to prepare some rolls and cookies for different church activities. She was up to her elbows in flour when Teresa came into the kitchen. Rita could tell that she was moping around and since she had helped her bake in the past and had enjoyed it, she decided to try to engage her into the activity. Rita asked her if she would roll out the dough to prepare some rolls for the potluck occurring the next day at church.

Teresa stepped up to the counter where the dough was waiting for attention. She took the rolling pin and slapped it on the dough, but she rolled it too thin.

Rita studied her for a couple of seconds. "Teresa, the dough is too thin. You're going to have to redo it."

Teresa slammed the rolling pin on the counter and abruptly picked up the dough and began to roughly reshape it so she could roll it out. Once she got it reshaped she took her fist and hit the dough, not just once but three times.

"Do you feel better Teresa?" Rita asked, bracing herself for a possible eruption.

"WHAT DO YOU MEAN, DO I FEEL BETTER?" she yelled as she began to pace back and forth in the kitchen.

Calmly Rita pursued it by replying, "Do you want to talk about it?"

"TALK ABOUT WHAT? My messed up family? My messed up life? How about talking about my mother who tried to destroy my Dad, my brother, and me! Boy, that would give a person something to think about, don't YA think? It would make for a 'bon-a-fide' soap opera!

"Yeah, let's just talk about how I wish I WAS NEVER BORN, but since I was born into this miserable existence, I wish you were my mother and not the wretched coward who was." Tears begin to flow from her eyes and down her cheeks. "You know, I'm not sorry she's dead and for that I feel guilty. What kind of person does that make me, cold and callused like her?

"I'm afraid that I'll be just like her--a crazy, selfish, manipulator! After all, I have her genes and I feel so much rage against her right now I could tear this room apart! I HATE her for what she did to my brother, and I don't care if she is BURNING IN HELL right now for all she has done!"

She looked at Rita. "Does that shock you? How terrible of a person does that make me?" She paused, shaking her head. Suddenly she looked up and yelled as she shook her fist in the air, "WHY DID SHE DO IT?"

"Do what, Teresa?" Rita quietly asked.

"KILL HERSELF!" she yelled. She stared at the flatted dough before continuing, "before she faced the consequences of her actions—taking her own life before I could spit at her in disgust!" It was apparent the momentum of her rage was subsiding. Under her breath she quietly added, "Before I could tell her I forgave her and that I loved her in spite of what she did, and that I wanted her to live and to be healthy, and normal."

Teresa's body began to shake as the momentum of her emotions receded, giving way to deep sobs. "I don't really want her to be in hell, but where does a person go after they abuse the innocent—after they kill themselves?" Rita went to Teresa and took her into her arms. Teresa immediately melted into them.

"I'm so terrible for what I feel about my mother!" Teresa cried.

"No Teresa, you're confused about how to feel about your mother. In your heart, you still love her, but it's the emotions that are causing such a mixture in you. You even said yourself that you forgave her and loved her in spite of her actions. However, to keep things in perspective, you need to remember your mother was a poor, lost soul who didn't know anything other than her hopeless state, and when she was cornered she wasn't prepared to make the right decision."

"Why did God let this happen? He could have prevented it," Teresa asked through her sobs.

Rita silently asked the Lord for wisdom. The matters of life can be mysterious and confusing and the only answer one has is "I don't know." However, some words of wisdom began to parade themselves across her mind that she sensed she could speak. "God desires what is good for us, but people have their own free will, such as your mother. God wants life for us, but many choose the ways of death. God didn't want your brother to experience evil, but your brother failed to tell anyone what was going on so it could be quickly confronted.

There were many bad choices that were ultimately made for different reasons. Sadly, your mother didn't know how to live because she didn't understand the real meaning of life, and it appears she chose the only way out that she could see at the time.

"Teresa, look at me." Teresa looked at Rita, "There was a man by the name of 'Jabez.' His name meant 'sorrow and trouble,' but he wouldn't allow sorrow and trouble to become his lot in life. He asked the Lord to bless him, enlarge his coast, and keep him from evil so that life would not bring grief to him, and the Lord granted his request.

"You're not your mother and you'll never be. But, you need to remind yourself that choices will determine who you become, and to never let present emotions define you. Yes, be honest about them so you can properly put them in perspective, but never let them become a gauge as to the type of person you are. Also, you must remember the day you received Jesus into your heart and that if you ask the Lord to put your feet on the right path, He will. You have what it takes to avoid the same traps your mother fell into."

"What about Guy?" Teresa quietly asked.

"Guy must decide how he's going to let this tragedy define him. You need to pray for him and encourage him in the right way." Rita gently brushed Teresa's hair back from her face. "Okay?"

Teresa smiled. "Okay."

"Now go wash your face," Rita smiled, "and then you can come back and finish the rolls."

Teresa let out a giggle as she went to the bathroom.

Rita practically collapsed against the counter as she clasped her hands together, looked upward, while offering up praise and thanksgiving to the Great Physician above.

***

Guy was another matter. Both Len and Rita could tell much was going on inside of him, but he would never openly speak about it. They asked him if he would like some kind of counseling, but he always stated he was fine. Every time they approached the subject they hit a wall. Both became frustrated and worried as to how the situation with his mother would mark and define Guy's life.

Both Guy and Teresa graduated from high school and went on to college to secure some type of profession. Guy became a sales representative for a big company and spent most of his time traveling. He only visited them occasionally. He seemed pleasant enough, but it always appeared to be nothing more than a veneer to Rita.

After her sophomore year in college at Christian camp, Teresa met the love of her life, Grant Evans. The two of them served as camp counselors. He was a Christian who felt his calling was missionary work. He had become a nurse practitioner so he could serve indigenous people who still were in spiritual darkness. He had been accepted by a missionary organization that dealt with taking the Gospel to tribal people.

Grant's calling caused Teresa to take stock of her own Christianity. She loved Jesus, but she never thought about her life in light of serving Him according to a particular calling. She became serious as she truly sought the Lord's guidance in relationship to her life. Since God apparently allowed her and Grant to cross paths and fall in love, she had to pursue the possibility that He was trying to use the circumstances in her life to cause her to recognize her true calling. After much prayer and seeking advice from those she trusted spiritually, the light began to illuminate her calling.

Teresa's calling was confirmed to her when she started to feel the stirring in her spirit towards the mission field. The stirring turned into a passion that subsided into peace. The peace signaled that she was indeed called to be in missions and she was to serve in the harvest field with Grant.

From that point on Teresa's direction changed as she prepared for a life in the mission field and a marriage to the man who held her heart. She had to play catch-up as far as training for the field and began to visit churches with Grant to seek financial support. It was a different experience for her, but one where she learned the power of prayer.

Teresa later explained to a group of church women that American Christians have romantic notions about the faith walk. As an American who instituted much of her cultural thinking into her religious notions, she assumed going to church, reading her Bible, and praying at night was all there was to Christianity. She never thought about the commission to preach the Gospel, the high calling in which to execute the commission, and the need to seek God's will in the whole matter to ensure His blessing and power in a life of service.

She also shared how God taught her the faith walk involved much prayer because if God didn't touch or bless a matter, it wouldn't multiply and produce the work that was needed to embrace His plan and purpose. She also explained that there is much opposition in the spiritual realm and if God doesn't go before you because He isn't in a matter, the enemy will gain the victory. She explained that the faith walk is about first asking God to reveal and confirm what His will is in every detail, then seeking Him in faith as one advances towards the illuminated path, knowing He is the One who brings a matter to fruition. She explained there will be times of testing that comes through adversity and challenges, but in such times one must choose to trust that the Lord will ultimately bring judgment on that which is not of Him and would hinder the way.

It was clear that Teresa was making leaps and bounds in her spiritual growth. Much of her silliness about life went to the wayside and a sobriety took root as the issues of eternity took center stage for her. The burden for the lost began to weigh heavily on her heart. She realized the cross of Jesus stood between life everlasting and eternal damnation. The cross, in a sense, served as a balance where souls were being weighed by it depending on how people responded to the Gospel message. However, how can people respond to something they have not heard, and how can they hear unless there is one who shares the message, and how can a person preach unless he or she has been sent by God?

Guy attended Teresa and Grant's wedding, but he seemed aloof from the spiritual implications that were being highlighted in the ceremony. He later mentioned to a family friend that he was concerned that Teresa was wasting her intelligence, gifts, and abilities on ignorant people who probably would never get it.

When Guy's statement got back to Len and Rita, their concern for him escalated. Guy's attitude made him come across as a judgmental snob. The man that Len and Rita knew as a boy, who once had a tender heart towards God and a caring way towards others, was becoming a stranger to them. Even though he had always appeared to be moody at times, the real changes didn't come until the incident with his mother. Len and Rita feared that they were losing him, and both were at a loss as to how to reach him before the darkness consumed him and he became completely lost to them. All they could do was pray for him.

The crisis that brought Guy's struggles to the forefront took place a couple of years later. Len and Rita were rejoicing over the birth of their first grandchild. Grant and Teresa were serving on the mission field in Mexico when they welcomed a new member into the family by the name of Josiah Grant Evans. Len was looking forward to being a grandfather and everything seemed like life was on course for the Robinsons.

However, the course took an abrupt turn when Len began to suffer some physical ailments. At first he ignored them, but eventually it became obvious that they were not going away with time, in fact they were accelerating. When the test results came back from the doctor, the word they never wanted to hear was spoken. He had lung cancer.

Len had never smoked, but he had an aggressive type of cancer that had quickly spread to other vital areas of his body. They were both stunned by the news. It took a couple of days for them to wrap their minds around the trial that slammed against their boat of life. Once they came to understand the reality of what was looming in front of them, they had to confront the waves of emotional upheaval that followed. There was great dread as they faced the challenging storms ahead. There was fear of the unknown and anxiety concerning the end results. It was clear that their boat was beginning to be tossed to and fro in the ocean of life. The one consolation was that they were anchored to the immovable Rock, and they both sought refuge in the shadow of it.

The prognosis was not good and the doctor was not giving much hope. They agreed to immediately start treatment, but the doctor wasn't sure if it was going to do much good. Both Rita and Len had been quietly trying to busy their minds as they faced the treatments that would start the next day and the uncertainty of where it would lead them.

Len was quietly sitting in his chair when he looked at Rita who was sitting on the couch trying to comprehend and retain the devotion she was reading. "You know before I get too sick I need to put my house in order. That's why I spoke to our lawyer today to make sure you're properly taken care of and all the paper work is in order."

Rita nervously laughed but his statement stuck a fearful cord in her. "Come on Len, I've never heard you dramatize a matter before. We're going to get through this together and you're going to be fine."

Len smiled at her knowing that she was trying to put on a brave, optimistic face, "Thanks Rita, but I'm not trying to dramatize this; rather, I'm trying to be realistic. Once I start the treatments, I don't know if I'll have what it takes to make sure every "i" is dotted and every "t" is crossed."

She could see that Len's eyes were watering as he expressed his concern. "Honey, I just want you to know I'm so sorry you have to walk through this with me."

Rita looked at him. Her heart was breaking because she knew this strong man's strength would be challenged and would be reduced to putty. "Len what do you mean! When we said our wedding vows it was for better or for worse. We've had some good times, some tragic times, and now we are facing some challenging times, but that's life and we'll get through it together with the Lord's strength and help."

She paused as she fought back the tears before continuing. "I know the Lord put us together and I never could have made such an exceptional choice for myself as He did when He brought you into my life. I'm so thankful for you," she paused, fighting to hold back the tears, "…and our journey together and I wouldn't trade any of it for so-called 'smooth waters.' This is the course the Lord has chosen for us and we'll take it together."

Rita knew the children had to be told. Len balked at first but when the treatments started to take their toll on him and he quickly began to go downhill, he conceded that they were part of the loose ends when it came to his household. Rita could tell Teresa was emotionally overcome by the news and stated that she and the baby would catch the first flight home; and even though Guy was quiet, she could tell that the news was difficult for him to accept.

Within the week the Robinson siblings along with the new member of the family were all under the same roof. It was a bittersweet time that entailed an overwhelming emotional ride. It was bitter for them to see how fast their father was failing and when he weakly embraced them it was with overwhelming tenderness. There was not a dry eye when the three of them witnessed Len holding, for the first time his first grandchild, and fondly looking into the face of the precious gift from God. Rita knew he longed to be a grandfather who was active in his grandson's life and growth. She knew he was cherishing the moment he had been waiting for, knowing that once his mother took him home he might not look on his sweet face again in this present life.

As the three of them sat at the dinner table to discuss Len's condition, it was obvious unless God interceded he wouldn't be long for this present world. Teresa didn't want to accept the obvious, but took consolation in remembering that their separation would not be forever, and that she would see him in the next world to come.

Guy, on the other hand remained quiet. Rita could tell there was some type of war going on within him. It was obvious that he was very sad, but at the same time he was putting on a stone front. Rita wondered how long he could hold onto the façade before it would crumble. She wouldn't have to wait long to find out the answer.

When Len became very ill, he insisted on moving into the guest room so as to not bother Rita. Rita objected but his persistence won out. They even moved a hospital bed in the room so his needs could be more effectively addressed. Rita made it a practice to go in every night and sit in a comfortable chair until she knew he was asleep before heading off to the lonely master bedroom. Occasionally, she would go to sleep in the chair and didn't wake up until early mourning.

On the night the three Robinsons had discussed Len's condition, she had fallen asleep in the chair, only to wake up around two in the morning. She didn't move from the chair until she heard Len breathing. She quietly left his room and went into the kitchen to get some water when she heard steps behind her. She turned to see Guy looking at her. Since he seemed unwilling to make the first move, she broke the silence. "Guy, what are you doing up this early?"

Guy shrugged his shoulders, "I couldn't sleep," he paused. "I can't stop thinking about Dad. I can't imagine life without him. It's so hard to process all of it."

She understood his plight because she couldn't imagine her life without Len. "I'm getting myself some water. Can I get you something Guy?" she asked in order to give him an opportunity to talk.

He shook his head yes as he sat down at the dinner table in his traditional place. She brought him a glass of water.

"I've been meaning to talk to you, and I've been waiting for the right time to tell you and Dad something. I thought I'd tell you first."

Rita felt an unseen hand of restraint on her. She didn't understand why she had the impression to move slowly forward with caution, while bracing herself, but past experiences taught her she needed to beware of such impressions and take them seriously.

"What do you want to tell me, Guy?" Rita asked.

He took a deep breath before saying anything. "I feel it's time for me to come out."

Rita knew she heard him, but everything suddenly became surreal as she struggled with whether she properly comprehended what he was saying. "What do you mean about coming out?"

"You know," Guy stated in a frustrated tone.

Rita could see why she needed to brace herself, but she wasn't about to let him off the hook. He needed to confess what he meant and make it clear. "No, I don't know for sure. You tell me," she firmly responded.

Guy shrugged his shoulders and looked down. "I'm gay, and I have been gay for a long time."

Even though Rita had braced herself for what was about to be said, she still didn't feel prepared to hear it.

Guy's voice broke through her inner turmoil. "I think I should tell Dad."

Guy's statement brought Rita back to reality. It made every alarm go off in her soul. She had to do everything she could to protect what little time Len had left.

529

"Are you serious, Guy? Do you know what that would do to your father? This cancer is robbing him of his life and dignity. What do you think this knowledge will do for him as a father? He already feels responsible for what happened to you."

"Well, what about me? I want Dad to know who I am" he whined.

"Your father knows you as his son and that's what is important to him right now. I also want to remind you that YOU'RE NOT THE ONE WHO IS DYING."

Guy spoke in a quiet tone, "I just want to clear my conscience."

"Of what?" Rita declared. "You want to clear your conscience by dumping it on your father? What purpose will that serve? In the end, will you be clearing your conscience or bringing a greater indictment against yourself for the despair you will bring him."

By this time Guy was becoming visibly frustrated. "I know you and Dad wouldn't agree with my choice of lifestyle. In fact, I knew you both would think I'm a sinner because of my preference."

"And, just how would you know that Guy?" exclaimed Rita. "Perhaps it's because you have both an inner knowing as well knowledge as to what the Bible says about such matters.

"Guy, you know as well as I do that we are all sinners because of the fallen disposition that has been passed down from Adam to all of us. We may manifest sin in different ways, but we all stand under the same death sentence. As you already know, without Christ people are all on a doomed ship like the Titanic, ready to slip into the abyss of death and eternal ruin."

"Well, I know now I was born this way! Guy retorted. "The Bible tells us God is righteous and if that is so how can a just, loving God send people to hell for being born a certain way?"

Rita was not surprised at Guy's approach, but she wasn't about to let him continue down that road, "Come on Guy, the Bible calls such practice unnatural, and those who practice it possess vile affections. You know very well that argument belongs to the world. But, since you approached it from such a premise, I'll remind you of what you know to be true. If you mean you were born with a disposition prone to sin and rebellion against God's design for life, you're right, and as you've been told various times, it's for that reason a just, holy God has provided His Son Jesus Christ as a means to give everyone a way out of tasting His wrath against all disobedience towards His authority, reign, and Word.

"But, as far as your preferences, lifestyles, and tastes, as you have already pointed out they are your choices! It's true, you may have been influenced by the spirit of the world in your preferences, indoctrinated by a godless society concerning your lifestyles, and your tastes may be greatly predisposed by a godless culture, but what you ultimately prefer and give way to will be a matter of your personal choice."

Guy's frustration was growing as Rita refused to buy his logic. He spewed out his next words. "You're wrong! I may have used the word 'choice,' but I didn't choose the way I am. I was clearly born this way!"

Rita could tell that Guy was giving way to another spirit. She knew that she was in a spiritual battle, and that she had to firmly state the truth and not be sucked into the emotional whirlpool of anger and chaos. In a firm, but calm, voice she said, "Guy, you've always chosen the way you have walked. The way you walk determines who you become, and what you come into agreement with concerning your attitudes, along with the lifestyles you adopt will ultimately determine who you allow yourself to become.

"Don't tell me you haven't chosen the wave you're now riding on. Don't tell me that you haven't determined what you believe, what you exposed yourself to, whether you were going to let your feelings define you or you were going to direct or discipline those feelings. Don't tell me you have no say over your moral conduct, where you direct your affections, how you handle and define worldly attractions, and the philosophy about life you adopt. Don't tell me that you haven't held tightly to your independence to be your own person, because you and I know according to your track record that wouldn't be true!

"You have been greatly influence by your relationship with others, I'm sure. Did you get caught up in some current that is taking you down a particular course? No doubt you have. Did you decide to buy the deceptive arguments of today's Political Correctness? I'm sure you did. However you look at it, you along the way have decided what to agree with or disagree with. You have and always will be in charge of who you are and who you become.

Rita could tell her words were unraveling Guy. His next statement revealed that he was losing control, "You're just a self-righteous, judgmental, hateful old bat. You need to get with the program which is being loving and tolerant."

Once again Rita knew that she couldn't allow his words to offend her personally. It was obvious that the Guy she had known would've never resorted to such words. She knew he was under the wrong spirit and that she had to hold the ground of truth. "Guy, why am I being self-righteous? Is it because I won't compromise and become a blatant hypocrite about what I perceive in my inner being as being right and true? Why am I judgmental? Is it because I refuse to compromise what

I believe? Why am I being hateful, Guy? Is it because I don't agree with you? Is it because I will not give up the standard of what has been outlined in God's Word, a righteous moral standard, you once agreed with?

"I'm not the one who is angry right now. I'm not denying you of your right to believe and live any old way, but you are trying to silence me with intimidation. I'm not being militant in my disagreement with your lifestyle Guy, but you are aggressive with me. I don't hate you, but you hate what I stand for.

"As for the PC worldview, it's hypocritical and insulting. It's been promoted to create hate, intimidation, and silence against any moral voice and conscience in this nation, while advocating tolerance for everything that is contrary to God, His righteousness, and His Word.

"I understand why the world hates, objects, and is always trying to throw God out of every arena in society and silence His servants, but my question is why do you hate the Christian values you once believed were true? Are you afraid I might be right in the end?"

At that point the corner of Guy's lip began to curl up in a sneer. "What do I have to be afraid of, something that's obsolete and outdated like your so-called 'morals' and your King James Version of the Bible?'

"You know there are other Bible translations that would disagree with your morals and your precious King James Version! No doubt one day this nation will outlaw your stupid version, just like it's outlawing your right to refer to your morals as being the absolute way and acceptable to your Christian, unloving God. It's all so hateful!"

Rita could now see the demonic influence all over his face. His eyes narrowed like a reptile and changed from brown to a murky green. Underneath her breath she was standing on her authority in Christ as she came against the demonic power laying claim to Guy's mind and soul. She asked the Lord to keep His hand on the demonic power so it would not wake up the rest of the household as she lifted up the sword of truth, God's Word, the one weapon that Satan had no power against.

"Guy, it wouldn't be the first time the powers of the world have outlawed the Word of God because it proves to be contrary to their wicked agendas, their insane ideology, and heretical philosophies. There may be other translations that agree with the Political Correct, Progressive, Communistic agenda, but God hasn't changed His mind about what constitutes righteousness and wickedness. He is the same today as He was yesterday when He established marriage between one man and one woman. One of the reasons He gave the gift of sex to our first parents is so they could propagate, but the lies and propaganda of Satan's world has exploited and profaned what is sacred."

It was obvious that the demonic influences wanted to scream out profanities and mock the truth, but there was a greater power present that would not allow them to claim the podium, but they still had enough of a voice to spew out their false accusations. "I'll not listen to your hateful propaganda," the voice declared. "You're insane and need to be committed to an insane asylum!"

Rita knew who to appeal to. "Guy, go ahead and stop your ears to truth and listen to the voices of lies, but it will not change what is so. You and your unclean cohorts may try to outshout people who disagree with this wicked agenda to destroy families, relationships, and purity, taking souls captive, while evil vehemently mocks moral uprightness, shuns any warnings or objections about future consequences, and ultimately kills or imprisons those who will not bow their knees to the particular "Baal" of this age. But, no one will ever do away with God's Words of truth. In the end, His Word will stand as the only truth and will rightly and justly judge everyone according to His just Law and holy ways."

Rita could tell that the truth was assaulting the claims of the demons as they made a demand. "Who do you think you are? Just shut up you hear me?"

Rita smiled and said, "I'll not be silent, nor will God's truth. I stand in the authority of Jesus Christ of Nazareth and as long as I have a voice and you're in my home, laying claims to my son, your Creator's truths will be proclaimed and upheld here, and in the end you will be silent as you submit to those truths, bow before God Almighty and then flee."

In a whiny voice, the entity brought forth another accusation. "This is not your house, it's my father's and you stole it from me. You're a thief and a witch!"

Rita could tell that the demonic influences were losing their foothold, but she couldn't let up until she reached Guy. "You're a liar," she declared, "and your master Satan, is the father of all lies, and you have no power against God's truths; therefore, I don't receive your lies or false accusations! You must be silent and let go of Guy in the name of Jesus, the Son of the Living God, and your Creator. You must allow Guy Robinson to choose who he will believe and who he will serve. You will no longer determine his reality!"

She then addressed Guy who was holding his head confused and tormented. "Guy you don't have to be a frightened little boy any longer, afraid of your feelings, hiding from confusion, and trying to be brave in the face of wickedness. Satan didn't play fair with you. He started to weave a destructive web of lies around your mind at a very young age to take not only your mind captive, but your soul and will, but you know the truth, and the truth can make you free. The Lord Jesus can set you free and bring healing to you."

Guy suddenly let out a big sigh as if some unseen force was vacating the premises. It was then that Guy started to sob. "Why? Why? Why?" he questioned through his sobs.

"Why what Guy?" Rita asked.

"Why wasn't I man enough to save my mother? Why couldn't I make her happy enough that she wouldn't have felt the need to take her life in the end? Why was I not smart enough or strong enough to keep her from being found out? I tried everything; even things that I knew were wrong to keep her from leaving us, from going away, but nothing I did helped her."

He pounded his fist in his hand. "If I couldn't be man enough to help my mother, how can I expect to be man enough to take care of a wife or children? I'm so confused and lonely. I don't know what to do. I don't know where I fit or what's true or pure anymore."

The truth about Guy's torment and despair had finally come to the light. Rita stood up and laid one hand on his hands and gently rested the other on his shoulder while praying for wisdom from above. "Listen to me Guy, you must break the lies that have taken your mind captive with the truth. Your mother was wrong to exploit you in the ways she did. She is the one with the problem and sadly she made it your problem. You were just a young innocent boy, who became a victim of someone else's warped reality, and you didn't have the experience and wisdom to discern what was going on and how to handle it.

"It's clear you tried to bravely be a man before you were allowed to become one and as a result everything became messed up for you, giving you a warped premise to view everything through from you manhood, love, and your relationship with the opposite sex, but know God can transform your mind and give you a new perspective."

"Why would He give me a new lease on life?" Guy moaned. "You're right; I chose the way I walked and what I wanted to believe to avoid facing my feelings of complete ineptness. I walked away from God into a lifestyle that temporarily satisfied my sexual appetites, but left me feeling empty and lean in my spirit. I tried hard lying to myself that I wanted that particular lifestyle, but when I saw Teresa with Josiah, I knew that it was not natural. Even though I tried to sear my conscience against it, I knew it wasn't what God designed in the beginning when He took woman out of the side of man and united them as one in a holy bond. I knew my wrong lifestyle would never provide me with the true family setting I so desired: that of a wife and children."

He paused, "When I was reminded of what God ordained in the beginning, I suddenly became confused as to what I wanted. But, my question is the same, why would God give me a new lease on life after what I did with my mother and the lifestyle I chose, knowing the truth about both?"

Before Rita could answer, a voice came from the other side of the wall, "Because God loves you Guy and His thoughts towards you are those of peace and He wants to bring about an expected end to your life."

It was Teresa's voice. Guy looked up and when he saw her, his anguished face became pale. "Did you hear everything that happened tonight?"

Teresa appeared calm, but Rita knew by the look in her eyes that she had been privy to what had transpired.

Teresa shook her head yes. "I'm sure I heard most of it."

Guy looked down, "You probably hate and despise me right now, and will never let me hold Josiah."

Teresa kneeled down by her brother's side. "I could never hate you Guy; I love you. I feel sad for you because you lost your way because of what happened to you. I understand because I lost my way for a time after our mother committed suicide. I wrestled with whether I could have done something to save her, but I had to accept the truth that there was nothing I could have done. It was our mother who set in motion her destiny by the decisions she made.

"I knew between the two of us that you received the greatest abuse, but I had no idea as to what extent. I've known that you've been hurting, and struggling with so much garbage from the past, but since you would never open up, I didn't know how to help you, except to pray for you. And, then tonight I heard voices and when I came down the stairs to investigate, I got a picture as to how wounded and lost you became. I knew all I could do was stand in the gap in prayer as Mom has." She paused and looked at Rita. "She fought for the truth to win out in your life."

Teresa once again focused on Guy. "Guy, you need to know that the Lord is waiting for you to turn around in true repentance and ask him to forgive you. He wants to restore you back on the path you started walking when Mom…," she paused to look at Rita again, "…led you to Christ so many years ago. He knows your history and He knows you now, and He has a plan for you that will prove satisfying. The Lord needs to heal you and you need to ask Him to forgive you and break the lies that hold you captive, and give you a right perspective that will enable you to pursue the life He has for you. If you do, His Spirit will empower you to be an overcomer in all matters and secure the life he has called you to."

That morning as Guy sat between the two women, he cried out to God to break the lies over his mind. He confessed his sins, poured out his heart concerning the weariness he felt about the abnormal, unscriptural way he had been living, asking the Lord to heal him and empower him to find the life He had designed for him. When his prayer was finished, all three were crying and rejoicing. Even though bitter circumstances had brought them together, it was sweetened by the fact that God had ordained it as a time to finally bring the prodigal son home.

The next couple of days before both siblings went back to their personal lives, they spent alone time with Len. Len had a simple love and faith towards his Savior and Lord. He had told Rita that there were some nuggets he wanted to share with his children. He shared one of those nuggets by telling her that he could leave them material goods, but they would last only for a season. In his mind, he wanted to impart to them an eternal inheritance, leaving a spiritual legacy behind that would ensure him that they would all spend eternity together.

After his alone time with both of them, they came out with tears in their eyes. There was a general, but unspoken consensus that they wouldn't see him alive again in this present world. Later, when Rita, Guy, and Teresa were together the siblings spoke about what Len shared with them. It was a combination of memories from the past, his love for them, and the hope of seeing them in glory. As they talked about what he had said, they both began to cry. They knew he was preparing them for the journey he would be taking without them.

It was teary-eyed Guy who turned to Rita. "Rita, you've always been a mother and friend to me and I know this has to be a very difficult time for you. I want to thank you for four things, for being a good, faithful wife to my father, for being my mother when you didn't have to, for keeping me from confessing my former lifestyle to Dad, and fighting for me so that when I faced my father, I could give him the greatest gift ever by assuring him that I would see him in heaven."

"Ditto Mom," Teresa piped in. "I couldn't have said it better."

All three started to cry as the enormity of the situation started to hit them. They all stood together to console one another with a group hug.

Before both siblings left, Len got to hold and play with his grandson as much as he could under the circumstances. Both siblings hugged and kissed their father good bye and their final greeting to him was simple. "I'll be seeing you later, Dad."

Before Guy left, he looked at Rita. "I know I've a long road ahead of me, but I know what I have to do." He grinned at her. "After all it's my choice isn't it?"

Rita smiled at him. "Yes, it's your choice and with God's help it will be accomplished."

"Rita, I want you to know," he looked up, "with God's help, I'm going to keep my promise that I'll see my Dad again."

As she hugged him, she said, "I know you will Guy."

***

Six months after his journey through the valley of the shadow of death began, Len Robinson went to sleep, only to wake up in glory. Hospice had been called in just a few days prior because it was clear that the end for him was in sight. That night Rita sat in the chair as usual, and due to exhaustion from trying to make Len as comfortable as she could in his pain-consuming state, she fell into a deep sleep.

Rita woke around 3 a.m. to Len's heavy breathing and restlessness. She slipped to his side and took his hand. She felt him lightly squeeze her hand. She knew he was weary and tired of the battle but he had struggled to hold on to the small spark of life left in him for her sake.

She also knew that it was time for her to let the love of her life go. She had to give him permission to go so that peace could come to his weary, restless soul. The Lord had given them many special gifts such as a blessed marriage, two children, and the knowledge that his time might be short for the last six months. They had taken the opportunity to say everything they could as they spoke of their life together, the love they shared for each other, the appreciation they felt for one another, the family they had become, and the possibilities in regard to the future.

Rita sensed that Len knew all along that his healing would come through the door of death. He was preparing her to let go of him at the right time. He reminded her that if he did die, it was not the end of her life, but the beginning of a new chapter.

537

As she wrestled with the end of the present chapter, she knew she was reluctant to turn the page to start a new chapter without him. She had no idea what the title of the new chapter would be or how it would start out. Rita also knew she was being selfish to hold on to the present chapter of her life. It was clear that she could determine the tone of its end. She wanted the ending to speak of selfless love and of dignity that would mark the last memories of her time with Len

Rita knew it was up to her to set the tone of the chapter's last page. She leaned over and softly whispered in his ear. "Len, it's alright to let go now and take Jesus' hand the rest of the way. Don't worry about me; the Lord will take care of me."

Her heart began to break as silent tears ran down her cheeks. She kissed him on the forehead. She whispered, "Sleep on my beloved, sleep on."

She positioned a folding chair by his bed and sat holding his hand in both of hers close to her tearful cheek, silently and prayerfully committing him into the loving hands of their Savior and Lord. Fifteen minutes later he let out what would be his last breath. It was as if his spirit had finally escaped his ravaged body, setting his soul free to be lifted up by the Spirit of God into the arms of Jesus.

She looked at his face. It was peaceful and even appeared as if there was a slight smile on his lips. Tears flowed as she rejoiced over his heavenly homecoming, but she also felt the sorrow of loss prick her heart. He was free at last, without earthly, fleshly hindrances to now praise and worship the One he so loved and adored. She would have to discover what would be written on the next chapter of her life. She put his lifeless hand gently on the bed and went to the phone to call the necessary authorities along with Guy, Teresa, their pastor, and Denise.

She felt as if she was encased in a bubble, causing the flurry of activities that followed seem surreal to her. The police came to her house, followed by those who worked with hospice. They made arrangements for a doctor to officiate and sign his death certificate. Then the hearse came to take him to the mortuary where the funeral arrangements had already been made.

She quietly sat in the chair as her pastor and church family came to offer any help or consolation. It was clear that Len was loved and respected by those of the church. However, Rita felt numb and the only time her emotions broke through was when she saw Denise.

The woman who had so long ago guided her to the front of the church to receive Christ and who had presented a clear picture of discipleship to her had not only become a good friend to her, but to the rest of the Robinson family. Her honest words of wisdom that she gave to Rita in the beginning often nudged her in the right direction.

Denise had often been called about family challenges and dark times and faithfully prayed with them and for them. Guy respected her and Teresa had sought her advice when she was trying to come to terms with her missionary calling. Through the years Len and Rita had financially supported Denise in the ministry she was involved in. The ministry entailed discipleship and training others to find their place in the kingdom of God. The ministry worked with churches, Christian organizations, and even did pioneer work in setting up places where seeking Christians could come to be discipled.

When Denise was in the area she always stayed at their home. In time, Rita's support advanced to promoting the ministry Denise was part of to other churches and Christian organizations in their area. She scheduled meetings for Denise to present the goals of the ministry to pastors and Christian outreaches.

It was during such times that Rita learned a lot about the politics that ran many of the churches and Christian organizations. She was shocked at how worldly Christian organizations were in their thinking and their procedures. Like the world, some of the organizations were caught up with appearance more than their commission, while for others the bottom line was money and not souls.

After discovering the inner workings of a number of Christian outreaches, Rita would come home disturbed and share with Len her concerns. Being the pillar that he was, he reminded her that many ministers start out with sincere hearts and motives in following Jesus, but like those who initially followed Jesus in His earthly ministry as they came closer to the cross, many departed from Him because of His hard sayings and followed Him no more. Out of the remaining twelve who made it to Jerusalem with Him, Judas Iscariot betrayed Him and Peter denied Him, while the rest scattered with the winds of fear. He explained that there are many who start out right, but because of the demands of the world, they can veer from what is important as their religious foundations are rattled, their devout notions challenged, and their understanding of God turned into a pretzel."

She still remembered the rest of his explanation. "Rita, Jesus said He brought a sword that would separate and divide even families. Well that *sword of truth* includes the cross which will test motives. If the motive isn't right, a person will not make it to Jerusalem.

"That sword includes the *Gospel*. The Gospel will try the devotion of people. If one does not have a sincere heart, devotion towards the cause of Christ, which is lost souls, he or she will lose interest in the simplicity of the Gospel and the urgency to share and preach it to others.

"The sword includes the *call to discipleship*. Discipleship will test the attitude of a person towards God and His Word. If the person's attitude is wrong, he or she will fail to see the need to follow Jesus in obedience in light of His teachings, examples, and truths.

"The sword also includes *service*. Service will test a person's vision. If people don't keep their focus on Christ, they will forget who and why they are serving Him.

"It will also reveal *character*. Either a person is faithful to Christ out of love and is resolved to please Him and bring Him glory because of who He is, or the individual will simply tack on Christ to receive recognition and blessings. Each wrong emphasis is man-centered and not Christ-centered."

Rita could see the sword coming down and causing people to make a choice. The choices they made clearly revealed the fruits of their motives, their level of devotion, along with their attitude, vision, and character when it came to the matters of God.

At times Rita had to guard her own attitude as she fought against becoming skeptical and judgmental towards what appeared to be hypocritical veneers. The inward battle would always intensify when she went with Denise to meet with different leaders to see if her type of ministry was something that could be instituted into their various church programs.

Rita was shocked at the attitudes these different leaders displayed towards Denise and the occasional exchange that took place. Some were condescending towards her, others tolerated the presentation as they occasionally looked at their watch, and there were always a few who showed interest but failed to take it any further. Most of the time Rita felt that Denise's presentation fell on deaf ears.

One day she asked Denise about the indifferent reactions from many of the religious leaders they encountered. She smiled and explained that most churches have their own programs and ministries. They don't see a need for any other work or ministry, especially from the outside. She admitted one may get past their office door to present his or her ministry, but it's only a matter of courtesy and not real interest or serious consideration.

It was then that Rita commented that spiritual matters should not be considered in light of what a church or organization may think they have; rather, it must be lifted up in prayer as to whether or not God was ordaining it. Denise admitted that she really didn't know how many religious leaders weighed a matter according to prayer and God's will.

She then shared how one minister claimed he was all his church needed and that outside ministers, such as evangelists, were not necessary. Denise sadly shook her head as she related to Rita that the doors and windows of that church were now boarded up and that the building which apparently served as a monument to the pastor's self-sufficiency was now decaying. She admitted that it's unusual for religious leaders to make the workings of the ministry revolve around them and not the Lord Jesus Christ.

Rita also began to note attitudes that religious leaders generally had towards women ministers. There was one occasion where the woman who was overseeing a ministry for women asked Denise, after finding out she had been in an abusive relationship and was divorced, if she hated men, Denise remained calm as she clarified that the reason there are problems between married couples has nothing to do with their gender, but because of the fallen disposition being passed down to each person born in the Adamic race.

After leaving the woman's office, Rita looked at Denise and asked her if that woman would have asked a divorced minister of the opposite gender the same question. Denise smiled and said, "I don't know, you need to ask her."

Later Rita had the opportunity to ask Denise whether she felt that there was an unspoken prejudice against women ministers that prevailed in the church. Rita will never forget what she said as she laughingly said, "Prejudice against women? Of course not! Then quickly added, "That is, as long as a woman stays in her proper place allotted to her by men."

Rita was appalled. "Come on, Denise," she whined. "There is a type of prejudice displayed against women in ministry. Doesn't that offend you? I mean, how many ways are you locked out, hindered, or ignored as far as being able to fulfill your ministry because of the attitudes of religious leaders? Are you not called, and if you are, why does God allow this attitude to continue on?"

"I'll do my best to try and answer your many questions," Denise commented. "First of all, the wrong attitudes others have towards women ministers is not my cause, commission, or calling. In other words, I'm not here to change people's minds about women in ministry. My cause is to lift up Christ and Him crucified. My commission is to share the Gospel where I can and disciple those who God brings to me. My calling is to avail the ministry God has entrusted to me to others. Whether they take advantage of it or not is not my concern or affair.

"Rita, ministers of Jesus Christ are mere vessels and instruments. According to His Word He doesn't consider who He uses on the basis of gender and status but on their availability to be used for His glory. Our responsibility as ministers of Jesus Christ is to be available to faithfully declare the truth; therefore, whether one receives the truth will always come down to whether the person loves it, and not the vessel God uses to deliver it. It's true, God may use a certain vessel to test and expose a person's attitude towards the truth, but if that person loves the truth, they will humble themselves to receive it in the right spirit in spite of the vessel He uses.

"I have also learned Rita, that God opens and closes doors by using people's attitudes. My responsibility is not to try to open closed doors of hearts, minds, and attitudes; rather, it's to walk through open doors regardless of how small or big the entrances may be. Even though man may close the door to me because I'm a woman and divorced, God will make another way for me. He is capable of working out all of the details without my help."

Rita was awed and impressed with Denise's attitude towards the different suspicions, accusations, and challenges that came her way. She never seemed to let things rattle her or push her into a pit of depression. She displayed a simple faith towards God that it was His work, not hers and that He was indeed working out all of the details regardless of the obstacles that stood before her. In her mind if one door closed, God would simply carve out a window of opportunity for her to enter through.

On another occasion a woman minister overseeing women's ministry in the church both Rita and Denise attended encouraged Denise to date one of the single men that served on the ministry team at church because people were voicing concerns about her being a possible lesbian. After all, the people of the church only saw her minister with other women and she showed no interest in dating men. Rita was appalled at the suggestion and disgusted at the ridiculous suspicions of Christians.

Denise looked at the woman minister and explained that she was single because after her divorce she realized that God had given her the gift of being single so she could channel all of her time and energy into serving the Lord. She then added that the reason people operated from the small premise of suspicion was because they were never properly discipled to discern such matters. She encouraged the woman minister to encourage the leadership of the church to include the discipleship and training program in the church to remedy the problem.

There was another incident where Denise was not allowed to minister because she was not under any "acceptable" covering. Rita was somewhat perplexed by the notion of covering and asked Denise what it meant. Denise explained that some Christians believe that ministers, especially women, must be under some type of covering in order to have the protection and credibility to minister.

Rita will never forget the conversation that followed. She asked Denise, "What constitutes a covering?"

"A male religious leader or organization," Denise answered. "I guess such a covering is to bring some type of accountability to the female minister."

"How can imperfect man who is limited in knowledge and flawed organizations serve as effective coverings?" Rita inquired.

Denise smiled. "That is the whole problem. The Bible is clear that we are to have wise advisors, but when it comes to a man or an organization being a spiritual covering, there are no such Scriptures to back such a notion. Clearly, such coverings are for cosmetic purposes. The truth is there are only three coverings mentioned in the Bible, an evil covering in Isaiah 25:7, the covering of the Holy Spirit in Isaiah 30:1 and a physical covering over the head." She smiled as she added the last bit of information, "And, according to 1 Corinthians 11, a woman's physical covering is her hair and the Jewish man the prayer shawl, which in the man's case was used to cover shame.

"There is only one acceptable spiritual covering and that is the Holy Spirit. That's why we must follow after, be led by, and walk in the Spirit of God. And, the only way a person can come under the correct covering of the Holy Spirit is to make Jesus his or her head."

Rita was so impressed by the example that Denise gave her that she said, "Imagine this. If man becomes a covering over other Christians, the Spirit would be quenched and Jesus' headship would be nullified. The reason for this affront against God is because the Spirit would have to run everything through man's limited, perverted understanding, and since the covering would be over the only true head of every Christian, Jesus Christ, it would make even Jesus subject to the covering of man as well!

"However, if the covering is the Holy Spirit, we know that God doesn't do things by His might or power but through His Spirit. This would make the Holy Spirit the channel in which all blessings, revelation, power, and anointing would flow down through our head, Jesus, to His Body, the Church.

"Keep in mind, the Bible is clear that no one member of Jesus' body is to be exalted over another member. The eye cannot say it's more important than the foot in order to rule over it. The truth of the matter is that each member must come into submission to one another out of the fear of God in order to grow up as one body into its head, Jesus Christ.

"It's for this reason that when I'm personally asked about a covering, I scripturally stand under the headship of Christ as to my authority and will ask people to show me in Scripture where I must seek out and come under a man's covering. Since there is no such Scripture, advocates of such beliefs will become silent or fall away because they are unable to defend it."

"Why do people have to complicate the simplicity of Christ and pervert the purity of His Word?" Rita remembered asking. "Why would people take away from the simplicity of seeking out wise advisors and changing it to the concept of having a covering?"

Denise smiled at her, "I really don't know Rita. I think the concept of 'covering' came in with a heretical teaching as a means to exert absolute control over the sheep. The problem is the package that every so-called 'new thought' or 'revelation' is presented in comes across as new, attractive, and logical. Innocent people often buy it because they are ignorant of the original intent of it. Because such false teachings seem perfectly logical, many Christians assume they are right and fail to compare their validity with Scripture.

"Rita, in most cases these teachings don't change the dynamics of these people's life in the Lord or their faith towards Him. However, the real problem with any error, regardless of how minor it is, is it can dull people down as to other dangers that are being presented in subtle forms because there's already a small weed that has found a nook in which to grow. Even a small weed can produce other weeds as a person is conditioned to buy greater error.

"It's up to Christians to scripturally compare spiritual things with spiritual truths and to discern the spirit or intent behind such matters to keep their discernment sharp. The more that we allow the weeds of error to grow in the garden of our understanding, the more our understanding of the Word will be compromised. That's why Jesus warned people to beware of how they hear something. We must never assume that just because something sounds spiritual, good, and logical that it is of God. We must make sure that we can trace its inspiration back to His Spirit and His Word."

Rita valued the lessons she learned while supporting and following Denise in her ministerial journeys. She realized through the years that Denise's friendship and spiritual sustenance were priceless. She was often the silent pillar of support that remained steady through the trying times of Rita's life. She always seemed to be close by or available when Rita needed a wise counselor, a prayer partner, or someone who would just listen.

When Denise came in, she walked through the chaos taking place, right to Rita and sat by her, taking her hand. Rita looked into her eyes and sensed that somehow she understood that there was a thin veneer covering pain and sorrow. It must have been obvious to Denise that both could break through the veneer at any moment.

Denise almost whispered, "Rita, you don't have to be strong. You must allow yourself to mourn your great loss so you can be comforted and effectively go forward."

Tears began to silently flow down Rita's face, eventually weakening the numbness that had been buffering the reality of her loss, as well as her resolve to hold it together. As the numbness gave way to the pain of loss and her resolve succumbed to the sorrow, the tears began to flow more freely, followed by sobs as she put her face into her hands. Denise embraced her as depths of mourning bubbled up from deep within the recesses of her soul. Len's departure from the present world may have been heaven's gain, but it was Rita's greatest loss.

All of the activities around Rita faded into the background as she let different waves of weariness, pain, and loss pass through the corridors of her soul. She felt a type of cleansing wash over her, enfolding her in a blanket of comfort that could only be ascribed as the tender gentleness of the Holy Spirit.

Rita realized that the reservoir had been filling up for the last six months. She had silently shed tears in the night as she watched the disease rob Len of his strength, kill his appetite, and destroy any quality of life he may have possessed. She had been at his side as much as she could and for the last couple of months took a leave of absence from her job to be at his beck and call. For the last two weeks of his life it seemed that everything she did was unsuccessful in bringing him any real lasting relief.

Her heart broke as she watched pain consume him. Towards the end, her mind was weary with trying to figure out how to help him without any success, and her body was bone tired because she never completely slept through the night. She didn't want to leave him alone. She had even prayed about it, that she wanted to be beside him when he finally entered through the blessed door of death. The Lord had answered her prayer.

Rita had let go of Len intellectually, but as the deluge of feelings emerged together, she realized she had not let go of him emotionally.

The two of them had been knitted together by the Spirit of God, making them one, and now death had brought a separation. She was missing a big part of her life. She had to face the lonely nights, accept the fact that she would never feel his physical touch again, and somehow let go so that the Lord could fill that empty place with His Spirit.

The task before her to tie up loose ends also seemed daunting. As a legal secretary, much of the paper work had been drawn up at the office where she worked and kept up to date, but there were other things that needed to be attended to. Although Len already had put various articles aside for his children and most of his clothes in a box to be given to Christian organizations, she had to face the forlorn echo of their closet and the drawers that were half empty, but would eventually demand her complete attention.

She had been confronted by the small things she had taken for granted, the smell of his cologne, his breathing in the night as he slept beside her, his laughter about something that caught his attention and his invitation to her to always share it with him. She would never see his different smiles, that mischievous grin after he had just teased her, the knowing grin that expressed a silent wisdom, his tender smile when he was trying to cheer her up, and his sweet grin when he was quietly letting her know that he loved her. How many times had his smiles spoken volumes to her through the 17 years they had known each other!

Rita braced herself to be confronted by bittersweet memories: memories that were bitter because they carried an initial sting with them. It was just the other day, when she walked outside for a breath of fresh air, that such a memory had been triggered by seeing a particular rose bush. It was one that that both Len and she had planted together. She had been pricked by its thorn, leaving her bleeding. He played the "first aid role" by carefully applying gauze and tape to it, and then ever so gently sealed it with a tender kiss as they both laughed at his performance.

Rita was a former veteran when it came to losing someone close to her heart. She knew that time would take the sting out of such memories, causing them to become markers that would crop up at different times to eventually add a bit of sweetness along the way. As she mourned her loss she was reminded that the loss of Michael had brought her to a new life in the Lord, and now the loss of Len was about to bring her to a new chapter in her life. She marveled at the thought that there first had to be some type of loss before the new could be brought forth.

Meanwhile, it was her time to mourn as Denise held her like a child. It was a time to be comforted, and a time of healing in order to be restored. It was a time to put the final touches on the old chapter so that she could face and embrace the new.

***

Len had been gone a month as Rita tied up the final loose ends of his affairs. It had been an emotional roller coaster. The Robinsons came together to share in the grief of their loss during the funeral. Grant had come with Teresa and Josiah, and Guy came the day after Len's departure to step in to take up whatever slack that might prove to be overwhelming to Rita.

Rita and Guy shared a special time, establishing a greater bond as they talked about many things. They caught each other up to the happenings since their last meeting, and both cried together as they shared in the memories of Len. Guy once again assured her that he would keep his promise to his father. It was clear that Guy had sought out avenues of accountability with those who had past experiences with his particular challenges. He had checked out possible churches he could attend throughout his assigned region. Even though the loss of his father was a point of great sadness, there was a new spring in his step, a sparkle in his eyes, and a hope resonating in his countenance.

Denise had been in and out of the various activities surrounding Rita as she juggled many of her ministry responsibilities. She always seemed to know just what to do, an encouraging word, a smile, sharing what she learned that day from her devotions, and more often than not just allowing Rita space to wade through her thoughts, feelings, and uncertainties about the unknown.

Rita was beginning to feel restlessness in her spirit she could not explain. Her life with Len had brought great satisfaction to her. Even though she had been involved with the various ministries at church, promoted the ministry Denise was a part of, witnessed at work, and prayed for her co-workers when the opportunity presented itself, she sensed the Lord had more for her to do in His kingdom. Obviously, a new season of ministry was on the horizon as she became aware that the burdens for the present mission field were lifting. She suspected that she might not be actively involved with her church or going back to work.

She had been content knowing that for the most part her true mission field had been her home for close to 16 years. However, Len was gone and the children had their own lives to live and their own paths to follow, producing the sense that there was more to do, to discover about the Lord.

In her heart she knew that for Christian servants, their work in a particular harvest field may only last a season, but their calling, although being tested and refined, lasts a lifetime. She knew she could not trust her emotions about such matters.

Rita sensed that the ending of the old chapter was clearly being written but she had to wade through confusion. In her mind, she could see how the Holy Spirit was ending it, "This particular season of Rita's life had finally come to an end, and a new season was upon her, ready to unveil God's plans, hopes, and promises for the next stage of her life."

The only one she felt she could confide in was Denise. One night she admitted her restlessness. "Denise, I feel so restless in my spirit. I realize there is nothing here for me. My work in this mission field is winding up, and I feel I have gone as far as I can go as a witness in the office. I thought about serving more in church, but if I go back to church and try to serve there, I would see it as sliding back into nominal Christianity. I sense the Lord has something else in mind for me and if I don't discover it soon, I fear I will dry up like a prune. I just don't know what to do."

"What's within your heart to do as far as the Lord is concerned?" Denise asked.

In frustration, Rita expressed her heart desires. "I just want to serve Him! I want to run the course set before me and finish the race. I want to be able to look in the Lord's face, knowing that I was as faithful as I could be to Him in my life, my worship, and my service to Him."

"You know what you are lacking right now Rita?" Denise responded.

"No I don't. What am I lacking?" Rita asked.

"Direction! You have no real focus. Ask the Lord to set your face in the right direction, and then you'll know at least which way to walk."

Rita had to silently admit to herself that she had been looking here and there for the answer. "You're right, Denise, I've had no real direction."

"The next thing you need to ask is what will be your status? In other words, you scripturally are allowed to remarry, or maybe He's calling you into a life of remaining single."

"Are you kidding Denise!" Rita exclaimed. "I have no interest in remarrying. There will never be another Len and I want to quit while

I'm ahead. I also know what Scripture states, if you want to serve the Lord, it's best to remain single."

"Rita, you need to make sure that is God's plan for your life," Denise stated. "He knows what disciplines to bring to your life to make sure you don't lose sight of Him or sway from the path He has designed for you."

Rita had to agree with her. "You're right, Denise. I need to put the confusion aside and seek the Lord before I try to establish something in stone."

That night Rita wrestled before the Lord. She felt anxious about what He might show her, but she knew that she needed to concede her life, her will, and the end results to Him. It was after she decided to accept His will for every part of her life that He began to unveil the beginning of the next chapter in her life.

Even though she felt a bit of trepidation towards what the Lord had shown her, the next morning she could hardly wait to share it with Denise. As the two settled down for their morning tea and coffee, Rita began to tell Denise that after much prayer the Lord did show her something about the direction she was to walk.

"Well, what did He show you Rita?" Denise asked, while trying to discipline her excitement.

"I'm a little uncomfortable to share it because it may seem silly or presumptuous on my part," Rita replied.

"Rita, we've known each other too long to succumb to such uncertainty now. We've always trusted each other to discern a matter. Now, what did He show you?"

"Well Denise," Rita began to slowly share the latest insight, "He showed me that I'm to quit my job and go into ministry full time by working with you until further notice." She paused, "That's why I felt somewhat reluctant to share it with you."

Denise showed no emotion one way or the other. She looked at Rita nonchalantly before responding. "I already knew that you'd be working with me."

Rita was shocked. "Why didn't you share that bit of information with me? It would've spared me some anxious, confusing moments!"

Denise smiled, "Rita, it's not up to me to reveal such a matter to you. It's God's place to do that, and my place would be to simply confirm it."

Rita shook her head in disbelief, but Denise was not finished speaking. "Rita, your life is going to completely change. You must know in your spirit what God's will is for you because once you put your hand to the plough to walk this path, you must never look back in regret as to what you left behind.

"You must know without a doubt that the path before you has been ordained by God; and, that regardless of how narrow it becomes, the obstacles that you encounter along the way, the detours of temptations that entice you, and the tough terrain that will challenge your strength and resolve, that the Lord has called you. In fact, He has gone before you to work out the details to bring about an expected end for His glory and your benefit."

Rita could see the seriousness of the matter before her. Denise had wisely remained quiet to ensure that she didn't improperly influence her one way or the other. As Rita thought about what lie before her, she was both excited and anxious. It would indeed be a new chapter in her life.

"I know, Denise, it won't be easy." She paused, But, I realize to some extent the Lord has been preparing me for this part of the journey all along. In fact, He also gave me a title to my new chapter to bring more clarity to me.

Denise interrupted. "Really? What is it?"

Rita smiled. "It is quite simple and to the point."

Denise's face lit up. "Well, don't keep me in suspense. What's the title of the new chapter of your life?"

Rita felt a little mischievous twinkle shine in her eyes as she playfully dangled the suspense for a few seconds longer. She smiled as she watched Denise waiting with great expectation. "The heading of the new chapter of my life is "The Calling."

Scriptural References

Seeking Heart

1 Thessalonians 4:3-7
1 John 4:18-19
1 Corinthians 2:11-14
Psalm 42:7; 112:5
Proverbs 2:11; 3:4-7,
    21-23; 14:12; 16:2-3
Matthew 6:12-15; 7:13-14
    10:32-33
Luke 15:4-10
John 1:29; 13:35; 14:6
Romans 5:5
Ephesians 2:6-7
Colossians 2:8
1 John 1:15-17
2 Corinthians 4:3-7
    10:3-5
Genesis 3:1-9
Romans 1:27-31; 8:6-8

Transformation

Proverbs 13:5; 16:18;
    17:17; 18:24
Isaiah 64:6
Matthew 5:13-16; 6:19-21
Luke 13:3; 23:34: 15:11-32
John 3:3, 5; 14:1-3
    15:13-16
Romans 3:10-18, 23; 5:12
    12:1-2; 9-13
1 Corinthians 6:20; 7:20-23
Ephesians 6:5-7
Hebrews 13:5
James 3:13-16

Notes:

Broken

Exodus 20:14
Isaiah 59:2
Joel 2:25-26
Matthew 5:27-32; 16:24;
    19:9
Luke 4:18; 9:56;
    15:3-7
Romans 3:23; 6:23
    10:13
1 Corinthians 3:11; 10:4
2 Corinthians 3:3-5;
    5:18-20; 6:14-16
2 Timothy 2:15; 3:15-17
1 Peter 1:15-16
1 John 1:8-10

Shattered

Psalms 7:15; 14:1; 72:14
Proverbs 5:15-19; 18:22;
    19:14: 21:8
Ecclesiastes 10:7
Matthew 6:22-23
John 3:18-21; 8:44
Romans 12:16
1 Corinthians 6:17, 20; 7:23
2 Corinthians 4:2-6; 11:2-3
Galatians 3:13; 6:7-8
Philippians 4:13
Colossians 3:2
1 Thessalonians 4:3-6
2 Thessalonians 3:11-12
1 Timothy 2:14; 4:1; 5:13
2 Timothy 2:22
Titus 2:14
Hebrews 10:22-23; 13:4
James 1:17; 4:4
1 John 2:15-17
Revelation 5:9

Notes:

Lost

Genesis 19:17-26
1 Samuel 16:7
Psalm 52:1; 86:5
Proverbs 23:23
Isaiah 11:6; 46:10
Matthew 5:19; 7:15;
   16:22-23; 18:1-6;
   19:1-9
Luke 10:3, 25-37;
   15:4-6; 16:8
John 1:12; 8:32
Romans 8:4-14, 28;
   12:1-2, 9-10, 19
1 Corinthians 7:2-15;
   13:1-8
Galatians 5:16-25
Ephesians 5:13
Philippians 4:5-9
Colossians 1:20-22; 3:2
1 Thessalonians 5:22
1 Timothy 5:19-21
Titus 1:15-16
Hebrews 3:13; 10:30-31;
   11:6
James 4:7
1 Peter 1:6-9; 4:8
1 John 1:7-10

Ruin

Genesis 25:30-34; 50:20
Psalms 7:18; 17:5; 18:2-3;
   34:18; 40:24; 51:17;
   62:7-8; 89:26; 94:18;
   116:15; 118:36; 127:5
Proverbs 15:13-17; 22:6; 17:22
Matthew 3:8; 5:16-20; 6:24;
   18:15-17; 27:29
Luke 13:3, 5
John 1:1-14; 3:18-21
Romans 6:23; 8:14-17
1 Corinthians 5:2-13; 6:15-20
2 Corinthians 5:6-8, 18-19;
   7:10; 10:3-5
Galatians 4:5-7; 5:19-21
Ephesians 1:5-7, 12-17;
   5:10-13, 21-33
Philippians 4:13
1 Thessalonians 4:14-18
1 Timothy 5:19-21
2 Timothy 1:7
Hebrews 12:14-17; 13:4
James 1:5-5, 21-25; 3:17;
   4:6-11
1 Peter 5:6-10
2 Peter 3:9
1 John 1:2

Notes:

Resurrection

Numbers 14:40-45
Psalm 119:29-30, 104;
   42:7
Proverbs 16:18; 29:23
Isaiah 9:6
Jeremiah 49:16
Matthew 1:18-25; 2:1-11
Luke 2:1-21
John 3:16; 11:25-26;
   14:27
Romans 7:5; 10:9-10
1 Corinthians 13:1-8
   15:40-56
2 Corinthians 10:5
Ephesians 4:31-32
Colossians 3:8-11
1 Thessalonians 4:5-7
Hebrews 12:15
James 1:13-15; 5:1-5

Damaged Goods

Genesis 50:20
Joshua 1:5-7
2 Samuel 13:1-16
1 King 19:18
Psalms 23:4-5; 127:1-3
   139:14-18
Proverbs 18:2-8, 24;
   26:21-29
Matthew 5:42-26; 6:12,
   14-15, 33; 7:16-20
   15:16-20
John 8:32-36; 16:33
Romans 3:10; 23; 7:18;
   8:31; 12:19; 16:18
1 Corinthians 2:4
2 Corinthians 5:17; 10:5
Ephesians 5:28-31
Colossians 2:4
1 Timothy 3:1-5
1 Peter 3:7-12
1 John 1:7; 2:9-11

Notes:

Damage Control

Genesis 3:10-13; 9:5-6
Leviticus 18:21
1 Samuel 16:7
2 Samuel 12:22-23
2 Kings 7:17-18
Psalm 14:6; 91:2; 51:4;
   127:3; 139:14-19
Proverbs 3:18; 23:7;
   28:13-14
Ecclesiastes 1:2-4
Isaiah 5:10; 25:7
Ezekiel 36:16
Malachi 3:6
Matthew 5:4; 6:22-23; 7:6;
   10:16; 13:15-17, 20-21;
   15:8-9; 18:11; 24:4
Luke 4:18-19; 15:6
John 5:22; 8:44; 10:10
   13:17
Acts 9:1-20
Romans 3:23; 6:23;
   12:9-10; 14:23
   16:17-18

1 Corinthians 3:18; 5:6-8
   6:15-20; 9:24-27
   10:12-13
2 Corinthians 5:7, 18-19
Galatians 5:19-24; 6:7-8
Ephesians 2:2-9; 4:14,
   22-23
Colossians 2:8; 3:1-2
1 Thessalonians 4:2-3
1 Timothy 1:9, 12-16;
   4:1
2 Timothy 2:22
Titus 2:11-13; 3:3
Hebrews 9:27; 10:22-24,
   30-31; 12:14-17
James 1:13-15; 4:1-5
1 Peter 2:11
2 Peter 1:3-4; 2:18-22;
   3:9
1 John 1:7-10; 3:4-9;
   4:18
Jude 16-19
Revelation 20:8

Notes:

Freedom	Found
Psalm 14:1; 103:12-15	Exodus 20:14
Proverbs 14:17; 21:9, 19; 22:6, 24; 29:22	Leviticus 20:10
	Psalms 91:2; 146:5
Micah 7:19	Isiah 53:4-5
Daniel 12:2-3	Daniel 7:9-14
Matthew 5:7; 7:1-4, 13-14, 13:22; 18:11;	Matthew 6:12-15; 7:25-28; 9:26-28; 13:38: 19:4-9
Luke 6:37-38; 19:10	27:1-54; 28:1-10
John 3:5; 5:22; 8:32; 10:10; 14:6; 16:7-11; 19:30, 34-37	Mark 15:1-39
	Luke 11:4; 15:4-6; 23:1-47
Romans 8:29, 36; 10:9-10; 12:1-3, 16	John 1:1-14, 29; 3:16-18; 8:1-12, 32-36, 44; 10:10; 14:6; 19:1-19
1 Corinthians 6:15-20; 7:8-17; 9:27; 10:13; 13:11; 15:33	Acts 4:12; 16:30-31
	Romans 3:10, 23; 6:23; 8:1, 14-17; 9:4; 10:9-10, 13
2 Corinthians 3:2-3; 10:5	12:1-2; 15-16
Ephesians 2:10; 4:26-29; 5:22-33; 6:10-13;	1 Corinthians 13
	2 Corinthians 3:5; 5:17-21
Philippians 1:6; 3:7-14; 4:8, 11-12	Galatians 4:5; 6:7-8
	Ephesians 1:7; 2:8-10
Colossians 3:1-3, 14-25	Philippians 2:6-11
2 Thessalonians 3:11	Colossians 3:1-2
1 Timothy 4:8	2 Timothy 1:7; 2:22
2 Timothy 3:5	Hebrews 12:15; 13:4-8
Hebrews 6:12; 11:1, 6; 12:1, 5-14	James 3:13-16
	2 Peter 3:9
1 Peter 1:6-9, 15-17 4:15	1 John 2:1-2
2 Peter 1:3-10	
Revelation 2:17	

Notes:

The Calling

Genesis 1:26-28; 2:24
Exodus 32:32-33
Leviticus 18:22-29
1 Chronicles 4:9-10
Psalms 46:10; 69:28;
 91:1-2; 119:89
Proverbs 14:12; 15:22;
 16:2
Isaiah 38:1; 64:6
Jeremiah 29:11
Hosea 14:2
Joel 3:14
Zechariah 4:6, 10
Malachi 3:6
Matthew 1:21; 4:14-17;
 5:45-48; 7:7-8, 13-14,
 21-23; 10:26-28, 34-38;
 13:43-48; 15:3-9;
 23:27-28; 26:41;
 28:18-20
Mark 16:15-16
Luke 6:36-38; 8:18;
 9:23-26, 62; 13:3, 5;
 18:1; 19:10
John 1:29; 3:3, 5, 18-21;
 5:22; 6:60-70; 7:6-7,
 16-20; 8:1-16, 44; 12:47;
 14:26; 15:26-27; 16:13;
 17:14

Romans 1:20-32; 3:23; 5:1-5,
 8, 12; 6:1-18, 23; 7:6, 18
 8:1, 10-14; 9:20-23; 10:2-3,
 9-10; 14-17; 13:8-10, 14
1 Corinthians 2:2, 10-14
 3:1-3, 11; 5:6; 6:18;
 7:7-10; 11:4-16; 12:12-16;
 15:31
2 Corinthians 1:3-10; 3:2-5;
 5:7; 11:2-3, 14
Galatians 2:20; 3:28; 5:16-21;
 6:14
Ephesians 1:11-14; 4:17-24;
 5:1-4, 13, 23; 6:6-7, 10-18
Philippians 1:6; 2:6-8; 3:7-14;
 4:6-8
Colossians 2:9; 3:1-3, 5-10,
 14-17, 23-25; 4:2-3
1 Thessalonians 1:4; 5:4-8,
 17
2 Thessalonians 2:10-12
2 Timothy 2:19-21; 3:5,
 15-16; 4:7-8
Hebrews 4:14-16; 6:12; 11:1,
 6: 13:4
James 4:1-4, 6-10; 5:13
1 Peter 1:2, 6-9, 21-24; 2:5-9;
 5:5-10
2 Peter 1:3-9
1 John 1:9; 2:27; 5:14
Revelation 3:5, 7-8, 14-20

Notes:

Other books by Rayola Kelley:
Hidden Manna
Battle for the Soul
Nuggets From Heaven
More Nuggets From Heaven
Heavenly Gems
More Heavenly Gems
Volume One: Establishing Our Life in Christ
My Words are Spirit and Life
The Anatomy of Sin
The Principles of the Abundant Life
The Place of Covenant
Unmasking the Cult Mentality
Volume Two: Putting on the Life of Christ
He Actually Thought it Not Robbery
Revelation of the Cross
In Search of Real Faith
Think on These Things
Follow the Pattern
Volume Three: Developing a Godly Environment
Godly Discipline
Prayer and Worship
Don't Touch That Dial
Face of Thankfulness
ABC's of Christianity
Volume Four: Issues of the Heart
Hidden Manna (Revised)
Bring Down the Sacred Cows
The Manual for the Single Christian Life
Parents are People Too
Volume Five: Challenging the Christian Life
The Issues of Life
Presentation of the Gospel
For the Purpose of Edification
Whatever Happened to the Church?
Women's Place in the Kingdom of God
Volume Six: Developing Our Christian Life
The Many Faces of Christianity
Possessing Our Souls
Experiencing the Christian Life
The Power of Our Testimonies
The Victorious Journey
Volume Seven: Discovering True Ministry
From Prisons and Dots to Christianity
So You Want to be in Ministry?

www.ingramcontent.com/pod-product-compliance
Lightning Source LLC
Chambersburg PA
CBHW061505020726
47502CB00006B/1938